THE ANNOTATED

Hans Christian Andersen

OTHER BOOKS BY MARIA TATAR

Secrets beyond the Door: The Story of Bluebeard and His Wives

The Annotated Brothers Grimm

The Annotated Classic Fairy Tales

The Classic Fairy Tales

Lustmord: Sexual Violence in Weimar Germany

Off with Their Heads! Fairy Tales and the Culture of Childhood

The Hard Facts of the Grimms' Fairy Tales

Spellbound: Studies on Mesmerism and Literature

W. W. NORTON & COMPANY

NEW YORK   LONDON

THE ANNOTATED

Hans Christian Andersen

Edited with an Introduction and Notes by

Maria Tatar

TRANSLATIONS BY
MARIA TATAR AND JULIE K. ALLEN

The Arthur Rackham pictures are reproduced with the kind permission
of his family and the Bridgeman Art Library. Illustrations by Edmund Dulac and Kay Nielsen
reproduced by permission of Hodder and Stoughton Limited. Illustrations by Charles Robinson
reproduced by permission of Pollinger Limited and the Estate of Mrs. J. C. Robinson.
Illustrations by William Heath Robinson reproduced by permission of Pollinger Limited
and the Estate of W. H. Robinson. Illustrations by Mabel Lucie Attwell © Lucie Attwell Ltd 2007.
Licensed by ©opyrights Group.

For information about permission to reproduce selections from this book,
write to Permissions, W. W. Norton & Company, Inc.,
500 Fifth Avenue, New York, NY 10110

For information about special discounts for bulk purchases, please contact
W. W. Norton Special Sales at specialsales@wwnorton.com or 800-233-4830

Manufacturing by Courier Kendallville
Book design by jamdesign
Production manager: Julia Druskin

ISBN 978-0-393-06081-2

W. W. Norton & Company, Inc.
500 Fifth Avenue, New York, N.Y. 10110
www.wwnorton.com

W. W. Norton & Company Ltd.
Castle House, 75/76 Wells Street, London W1T 3QT

1 2 3 4 5 6 7 8 9 0

FOR LAUREN AND DANIEL, AGAIN!

Hans Christian Andersen is surrounded by a group of admirers
in this photograph taken in 1863 by Henrik Tilemann.

Contents

Acknowledgments

For many years, when the time came to teach Andersen's fairy tales in my course on children's literature at Harvard University, I braced myself for a challenging week. My lecture on Andersen lingered over the cruelty of describing a child's cold corpse lying out in the streets in "The Little Match Girl," the horrors of the executioner's ax in "The Red Shoes," or the merciless torments suffered by Inger in "The Girl Who Trod on the Loaf." Every year, a phalanx of students, a few of them near tears, routinely rushed the podium after the day's lecture to report their magical childhood experiences with the fairy tales—experiences that utterly contradicted my analysis of their effects. I grounded my case in philosophical terms, using Michel Foucault's brilliant study *Discipline and Punish*; I summoned the child psychologist Alice Miller, who had denounced "black pedagogy" in *For Your Own Good*, as a witness; and I called to the stand Maurice Sendak, P. L. Travers, Angela Carter, and a host of other distinguished authors who had disapproved of Andersen. To their credit, the students in that class held their ground, rarely conceding a point.

It was, then, with some reluctance that I took up conversations with Bob Weil, at W. W. Norton, about an *Annotated Hans Christian Andersen.* Few can rival Bob's powers of persuasion, and before I knew it, I had signed on, despite my reservations about devoting years of my life to an author I did not love. For weeks, I read Andersen, working my way through the 156 tales in R. P. Keigwin's translation with the quaint, original illustrations to the tales by Vilhelm Pedersen and Lorenz Frølich. I began listening to the Danish originals on tape. I studied the work of Arthur Rackham, Edmund Dulac, Kay Nielsen, and the many other gifted illustrators who had turned to Andersen's stories to inspire their artwork. And then one day, while rereading "The Emperor's New Clothes," I experienced a sudden rush of childhood memories brought on by the description of the Emperor's clothing: "exquisite" and "light as spiderwebs." I remembered how that cloth, even though it did not exist, became an object of fascination and longing, kindling my powers of imagination to dream up something as beautiful as the words that Andersen used to describe something invisible. It was then that I began to read Andersen in a different way. And it is now that I can finally report to those students from many years ago that they have made their point.

Julia Lam and Nicole White, two students from my Freshman Seminar on Childhood, contributed in thoughtfully intelligent ways to the annotations, querying, provoking, and rephrasing. The book is much improved from their forays into Widener Library, their finds on the internet, and their enthusiastic support and collaboration, despite their demanding schedules. Annotations for "The Snow Queen" include Julia's brilliant analysis of the kiss in Andersen and its connective power. Nicole's investigative energy led to many new discoveries about films, plays, artwork, and books based on Andersen's tales.

Over the years, I have had the chance to present my thoughts about Andersen and his fairy tales to many audiences, and, each time, I returned to my desk with provocative new ideas and insights. I benefited greatly from conversations—not just about Andersen and fairy tales—with colleagues and remain especially grateful to Sanford Kreisberg, Penelope Laurans, Larry Wolff, Dorrit Cohn, Kate Bernheimer, Homi Bhabha, Susan Bloom, Sue Bottigheimer, Donald Haase, Ellen Handler-Spitz, Michael Patrick Hearn, Casie Hermansson, Perri Klass, Gregory McGuire, Stephen Mitchell, Eric Rentschler, Judith Ryan, Jan Ziolkowski, and Jack Zipes for encouraging and supporting this project.

Archival work at Houghton Library at Harvard University and at the Cotsen Library at Princeton University was always a pleasure, and I am grateful to the staff at both those extraordinary institutions.

Michael Droller generously made his books on Hans Christian Andersen available to me and shared his enthusiasm for the beauty of what he has collected. Most of the illustrations for this volume are drawn from his splendid collection.

As always, Daniel and Lauren Schuker encouraged, vetoed, applauded, and distracted in ways that made what could have been a scholarly and solitary project into a vibrant collaboration.

Bob Weil not only inspired this project but also made sure it got done. I am grateful to him for friendship, advice, and attention to detail. Tom Mayer ably kept me on course, with tactful wisdom, advice, and guidance at every turn.

It was a special pleasure to work with Julie K. Allen, whose deep knowledge of the Danish language and of Denmark's cultural life enabled a productive collaboration. Her enthusiasm and expertise kept the project alive and on course.

Hans Christian Andersen, as photographed by Henrik Tilemann in 1865.

Denmark's Perfect Wizard

THE WONDER OF WONDERS

He was a perfect wizard," August Strindberg declared in a tribute to the author whose stories had enthralled him in his childhood. "The Steadfast Tin Soldier," "The Snow Queen," "The Tinder Box," and other tales had drawn him into an enchanted world far superior to the drab realities of everyday life.[1] Charles Dickens, Henry James, Hermann Hesse, W. H. Auden, and Thomas Mann—these are just a few of the writers who either grew up with Andersen's stories, doting over them, or grew into them, admiring their imaginative force.

Today, we are rapidly losing sight of the sparkle and shimmer that Strindberg and others found in the tales of Hans Christian Andersen, the Danish writer who was born over two hundred years ago in the small town of Odense. We think of Andersen as the poet of compassion ("The Little Match Girl"), the enemy of hypocrisy ("The Emperor's New Clothes"), or the prophet of hope ("The Ugly Duckling"). While there is no reason to

---

1. August Strindberg. "H. C. Andersen. Till Andersen-jubileet 2 april 1905," in *Efterslåtter: Berättelser. Dikter. Artiklar*, ed. John Landquist, *Samlade skrifter av August Strindberg* 54, Supplementdel 1 (Stockholm: Albert Bonniers förlag, 1920), 443–45. I am grateful to my colleague Stephen Mitchell for the translation of Strindberg's remarks about Andersen.

challenge those assessments, we should not forget that Andersen does far more than parade vices and virtues before us. If his tales were only about sending messages and broadcasting morals, we would not still be reading him today.

And read him we do. UNESCO, the United Nations Educational, Scientific, and Cultural Organization, lists Andersen among the ten most widely translated authors in the world, along with Shakespeare and Karl Marx. Andersen's stories have been part of bedtime reading rituals and school curricula in Beijing, Calcutta, Beirut, and Montreal. "The Snow Queen," "The Ugly Duckling," and "The Princess and the Pea" are not just story titles but terms with a kind of global currency. How many of us have grown up admiring the child in "The Emperor's New Clothes," identifying with the newborn swan in "The Ugly Duckling," and weeping over "The Little Match Girl"?

Strindberg was exactly right to call Andersen a wizard, for there is something in his stories that transcends good and evil—something that we can, for want of a better term, call magic. That magic has nothing to do with ethics but has much to do with luck, good fortune, and chance. "The moral of every fairy tale," as Adam Gopnik tells us, "is not 'Virtue rewarded' but 'You never know' (which bean will sprout, which son will triumph)."[2] Fairy tales move in the subjunctive mode, presenting perils but also opening possibilities, telling us what could be and what might be rather than what should be. Along with what would seem to be mere randomness or serendipity also comes the reassurance that everything will, in the end, turn out all right.

We feel a catch of the breath when the Snow Queen's carriage lifts off and flies through the air. Our hearts begin to pound when an evil witch turns boys into wild swans who soar over distant seas. And we thrill to the sight of ferocious dogs, eyes the size of teacups, guarding chambers containing untold wealth. But even that magic does not fully capture what is at stake in Andersen's wizardry. Nor does it suffice to point to the mix of the wild and the weird, the charming and the brutal, the droll and the bloodcurdling in the stories, for those traits surface with predictable regularity in fairy tales from all cultures.

Hermann Hesse once hinted at what creates magic in Andersen's tales

2. Adam Gopnik, "Magic Kingdoms: What Is a Fairy Tale Anyway?" *The New Yorker*, December 9, 2002, 139.

when he recalled "the beautiful magic sparkle" of their "whole, multicolored, magnificent world." Fairy tales like Andersen's are invested above all in surfaces, in everything that glitters, dazzles, and shines. Still, they give us psychological depth, even when the characters themselves are described only in terms of appearances. Sadness is typically expressed as tears (sometimes made of crystal), and gratitude comes in the form of material objects (a miniature golden spinning wheel, a silver flute, or a dress of diamonds). As the stereotypical plots of fairy tales churn with melodramatic fervor, they also sparkle with surface beauty. The result is something I will call ignition power—the ability to inspire our powers of imagination so that we begin to see scenes described by nothing more than words on a page.[3]

Kay Nielsen: Hans Christian Andersen

Committed to color, texture, light, brilliance, and clarity, Andersen's fairy tales try to create the

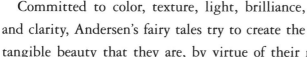

tangible beauty that they are, by virtue of their medium as mere words, powerless to capture. In "The Little Mermaid," the sun looks like a "purple flower with light streaming from its calyx"; the eleven brothers in "The Wild Swans" write on "golden tablets with pencils of diamond"; and the soldier in "The Tinderbox" enters "a huge hall where hundreds of lamps were burning." The bright wonders and vivid marvels that tumble fast and thick through the narratives go far toward explaining what drew artists like Rackham, Dulac, and Nielsen to Andersen's stories, and their illustrations, as I discovered, when read with the text, can take your breath away.

The delicate description of Thumbelina's cradle, with its mattress made of violets and its rose-petal blanket, produces something that, even if it remains invisible, is nonetheless wondrously exquisite. Andersen's "The Goblin and the Grocer" (a tale little known outside Denmark) reveals just how powerfully words on a page can transform even a dark garret into a site

3. The phrase is inspired by Elaine Scarry's concept of radiant ignition as developed and elaborated in *Dreaming by the Book* (Princeton: Princeton Univ. Press, 1999).

of aesthetic pleasure. The goblin of the tale's title peers into the room of a student, who is reading at his desk:

> How extraordinarily bright it was in the room! A dazzling ray of light rose up from the book and transformed itself into a tree trunk that spread its branches over the student. Each leaf on the tree was a fresh green color, and every flower was the face of a beautiful maiden, some with dark, sparkling eyes, others with marvelous clear blue eyes. Every fruit on the tree was a shining star, and the room was filled with music and song.

J.R.R. Tolkien recognized the power of fairy-tale discourses and the "elvish craft" that produces other worlds from mere words. Storytelling in its "primary and most potent mode" draws on the magic of language to create Elsewheres, universes that form enchanted alternatives to the real world:

> The mind that thought of *light, heavy, grey, yellow, still, swift*, also conceived of magic that would make things light and able to fly, turn grey lead into yellow gold, and the still rock into swift water. If it could do the one, it could do the other; it inevitably did both. When we can take green from grass, blue from heaven, and red from blood we have already an enchanter's power—upon one plane; and the desire to wield that power in the world external to our minds awakes.[4]

Step by step, word by word, Andersen, the "perfect magician," mapped and named the objects in his other worlds.

In his college lectures on seven great novels—all "supreme fairy tales"—Vladimir Nabokov affirmed the power of language to construct other worlds of rarefied beauty.[5] Like Andersen, Nabokov saw the supreme value of fiction in its power to create beauty through language. He considered it his duty as a writer to produce intellectual pleasure in the reader, who can observe the artist "build his castle of cards and watch the

4. J.R.R. Tolkien, "On Fairy-Stories," in *The Tolkien Reader* (New York: Ballantine, 1966), 22.

5. Vladimir Nabokov, *Lectures on Literature*, ed. Fredson Bowers (New York: Harcourt Brace Jovanovich, 1980), 2.

castle of cards become a castle of beautiful steel and glass."[6] Andersen would have understood the metaphor, for he too saw in the intersection of beauty and pleasure the supreme value of fiction. And that is why we still read him today.

We remember Andersen for the power of his images, for his castles of glass and steel. His paper cuttings, sketches, and collages remind us that he was supremely dedicated to the visual, a painter as much as a poet. C. S. Lewis once described how the *Chronicles of Narnia* were inspired by visual cues: "Everything began with images: a faun carrying an umbrella, a queen on a sledge, a magnificent lion."[7] Drawn to the fairy tale because of "its brevity, its severe restraint on description, its flexible traditionalism, its inflexible hostility to all analysis, digression, reflections and 'gas,' " Lewis instinctively recognized the importance of surface beauty and knew that he could depend on it to fuel the narrative engines of his multivolumed *Chronicles*. Like Andersen's fairy tales, his fantasy narratives depend on the evocation of breathtakingly beautiful objects, figures, and landscapes.

If Andersen's magic lies in the beauty of his tales, critics have been reluctant to call attention to it. They have, however, quite correctly described a poetics that mingles satire with sentiment, whimsy with tragedy, and passion with piety. And, above all, they have seen mirrored in the tales the maker of the tales. *Hans Christian Andersen: The Life of a Storyteller*, one of the most recent biographies of the writer, begins by declaring that its subject was a "compulsive autobiographer" and proceeds to document in superbly comprehensive ways how the art charts the stations of its author's troubled soul. In the fairy tales, we discover, the truest self-portraits are etched in generous and fulsome detail. "He is the triumphant Ugly Duckling," Jackie Wullschlager declares, "and the loyal Little Mermaid, the steadfast Tin Soldier and the king-loving Nightingale, the demonic Shadow, the depressive Fir Tree, the forlorn Little Matchgirl."[8]

Reginald Spink, an earlier biographer, summarizes the collective critical wisdom of decades in his observations about the way in which Andersen's

6. Ibid., 6.

7. C. S. Lewis, "Sometimes Fairy Stories May Say Best What's to Be Said," in *Of Other Worlds: Essays and Stories* (New York: Harcourt, 1994), 36.

8. Jackie Wullschlager, *Hans Christian Andersen: The Life of a Storyteller* (New York: Knopf, 2000), 3.

Andersen was an expert in making paper cuttings, and some of his work is astonishingly
intricate, mingling ballerinas with theater masks and death's heads.

fairy tales stage personal anxieties and desires and exorcise the demons haunting his imagination: "Andersen never stopped telling his own story. . . . Sometimes he tells it in an idealized form, sometimes with self-revelatory candor. In tale after tale—'The Tinder Box,' 'Little Claus and Big Claus,' 'The Steadfast Tin Soldier,' 'The Swineherd,' 'The Ugly Duckling'—he is the hero who triumphs over poverty, persecution, and plain stupidity, and who sometimes, in a reversal of the facts, marries the princess ('Clodpoll') or scorns her ('The Swineherd')."[9] In other words, either the stories square with the facts of Andersen's life (in which case they are purely autobiographical) or they do not at all square with those facts (in which case they are still autobiographical).

Andersen himself colluded with his critics in perpetuating the myth that the stories were all about him, but only partially. In *The Fairy Tale of My Life*, he reports that at school he told the boys "curious stories" in which he was always the "chief person."[10] In a letter of 1834 (written just before

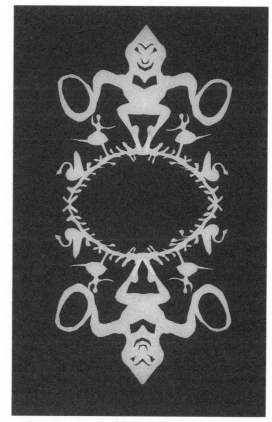

Swans and ballerinas figure frequently in Andersen's paper cuttings, and this example offers an artful mingling of the two.

he published the fairy tales for which he became renowned), he suggests, however, that the characters in his works are not just self-portraits but portraits of those he encountered in real life: "Every character is taken from life; every one of them; not one of them is invented. I know and have known them all."[11] And finally, while writing about his growing enthusiasm for the genre of the fairy tale, Andersen suggested that he was relying on *storytelling traditions*, as much as on real life: "I gained confidence and was greatly motivated to develop in this direction and to pay greater attention to the

9. Reginald Spink, *Hans Christian Andersen: The Man and His Work*, 3rd ed. (Copenhagen: Høst, 1981), 10.

10. Hans Christian Andersen, *The Fairy Tale of My Life: An Autobiography* (New York: Paddington Press, 1975), 21.

11. Wullschlager, *Hans Christian Andersen*, 3.

rich source from which I had to create."[12] Clearly, it was not all about Andersen, and the author himself tells us as much.

As tempting as it may be to map direct connections between a story and its author or to think of the tales as mirrors of their author's psyche, those moves invariably take us away from the tales themselves. The real risk of focusing too sharply on Andersen and on his anxieties and desires, his pathologies and perversities, or his aspirations and ideals is that, in the frenzy of looking for latent meanings, we lose the sense of wonder aroused by the manifest content of the tales. The Snow Queen's crystal palace, the utopian realm of poetry discovered by the Shadow, the tin soldier's dizzying voyage into the sea all lose their power to stir the senses under a barrage of biographical detail. The more we worry about the artist and his disorders, the less we care about the order of the art.

THE EMPEROR'S WONDROUS CLOTHES

Andersen's great gift was to create magic through the fairy tale in the form of arresting beauty, captivating characters, and absorbing plots. The appeal of his stories is so enduring that many operate like the oral fairy tales to which he was so attached as a child, circulating by word of mouth, creating new versions of themselves, and migrating with ease from one culture to another. Many have become part of local wisdom and lore even as they have attained a kind of global standing.[13]

Andersen's name is often mentioned in the same breath as Charles Perrault or the Brothers Grimm, the men who produced the landmark anthologies of folklore at the end of the seventeenth century in France and in the early nineteenth century in Germany. In that now renowned fairy-tale pan-

12. Hans Christian Andersen, *Das Märchen meines Lebens ohne Dichtung*, trans. Michael Birkenbihl (Frankfurt a.M.: Insel, 1979), 145–46.

13. Jackie Wullschlager refers to Andersen's double gift of adapting and inventing: "He was the first writer who was not only skilled at adapting existing stories in an original and lasting manner, he was also capable of creating new tales that entered the collective consciousness with the same mythic power as the ancient, anonymous ones. This individual achievement has never been matched. Almost two centuries after he wrote them, 'The Emperor's New Clothes' and 'The Ugly Duckling' are still bywords for elements of the human condition, while his Snow Queen, Little Mermaid, and Steadfast Tin Soldier belong with characters of folk memory" (Introduction, in *Hans Christian Andersen: Fairy Tales* [New York: Viking, 2004], xvi).

theon, Andersen, the son of a washerwoman and shoemaker, is the one who was closest to the common people and who actually grew up with the oral storytelling culture of the spinning room. Yet, ironically, he is also the one who is seen as the champion of the literary—as opposed to the traditional oral—fairy tale. Unlike the Brothers Grimm, Andersen did not reproduce what he heard from the lips of the people. Still his stories circulate just as broadly as those of Perrault and the Brothers Grimm. And the films based on them take in their share of revenue for Disney Studios. Despite their literary origins, Andersen's tales have joined those of Perrault and the Grimms to become the foundational cultural stories and formative childhood plots of Western culture. They are our folklore.

"The Emperor's New Clothes" (1837) is one of the best known of Andersen's tales, and it is repeatedly described as a classic: "charming," "beloved," and "winning." A recent illustrated retelling by a team of celebrities captures the story's iconic status: "Hans Christian Andersen's beloved tale of a king and his invisible clothes has delighted children the world over for generations. Now . . . an all-star cast of actors, celebrities, and award-winning illustrators has re-imagined the classic tale in this hilarious and sumptuously illustrated rendition. . . . *The Emperor's New Clothes* is a charming book for the whole family to enjoy."[14] The only terms overlooked in this enthusiastic declaration of family-friendly values are "timeless," "universal," and "enchanting"—attributes often ascribed to cultural stories known the world over, for example, "Cinderella" and "Sleeping Beauty."

More effectively than any of the other tales, "The Emperor's New Clothes" established Andersen's reputation as a man who created stories *for* children—not just in the sense of target audience, but also as beneficiaries of something extraordinary. The lesson embedded in it is so transparent that its title circulates in the form of proverbial wisdom about social hypocrisy. But more importantly, "The Emperor's New Clothes" romanticizes children by investing them with the courage to challenge authority and to speak truth to power.

The plucky child who declares that the Emperor has no clothes is indeed

14. Hans Christian Andersen, *The Emperor's New Clothes: An All-Star Retelling of the Classic Fairy Tale* (New York: Harcourt Brace & Co., 1998).

"beloved." A scientist working in the field of evolutionary biology borrowed the title of Andersen's tale and praised its hero: "The honesty and naïveté of the child in Hans Christian Andersen's fairy tale are sufficient to demonstrate the foolishness of the emperor and his public. The child is capable of honest observation and is willing to state the obvious."[15] "The Emperor's New Clothes" contains an underlying fantasy about our cultural desire to unmask duplicity along with self-deception and to speak the truth, no matter how painfully humiliating it may be to those in authority—or perhaps especially because it will be painfully humiliating.

D. H. Lawrence urged readers to trust the tale rather than the teller, and I want to take a closer look at this particular tale to reach, if not the truth, then at least a sharper understanding of what really matters in plots that have repeatedly been read as morality plays or as allegories of Andersen's personal sufferings and fixations. Jack Zipes, in a brilliantly irreverent biography of the Danish author as "misunderstood storyteller," has suggested that "The Emperor's New Clothes" enabled Andersen to discharge his hostility toward the aristocracy: "Andersen's anger at a pretentious and indifferent upper class that lacked sensitivity for art, especially for his particular kind of art, had to be channeled in such a way that he would not become self-destructive."[16] Zipes destabilizes that reading when he asks: "Do we need deceivers to learn the truth about decadent and deceptive emperors? Or do we need childlike honesty?"[17] If truth be told, the answers are not at all obvious. Is it possible that the two swindlers in the story are the real champions of truth, after all? Have we been deluding ourselves all along in thinking that the child is the heroic figure who exposes social hypocrisy and collective denial?

The Emperor may indeed have no clothes, but the fabrications of the swindlers—their acts of invention—are invested with a certain dramatic artfulness (they cut the air with scissors and sew with a needle that has no thread) and with a powerful degree of imaginative value (though one dia-

15. Joseph L. Graves, *The Emperor's New Clothes: Biological Theories of Race at the Millennium* (Piscataway, NJ: Rutgers Univ. Press, 2001), 1.

16. Jack Zipes, *Hans Christian Andersen: The Misunderstood Storyteller* (New York: Routledge, 2005), 127–28.

17. Ibid., 129.

metrically opposed to what is asserted by the thieves). Oddly, that "most wonderful cloth" that they produce becomes more and more substantial as it is described, and by the end of the tale the courtiers are engaging in pantomimes similar to those practiced by the swindlers while picking up the train and holding it in the air. Their art works magic, for it produces out of thin air something that is beautiful and seemingly palpable, even though it is not at all there.

Andersen's weavers, as one commentator points out, are merely insisting that "the value of their labor be recognized apart from its material embodiment."[18] The invisible cloth they weave may never manifest itself in material terms, but the description of its beauty ("as light as spiderwebs" and "exquisite") turns it into one of the many wondrous objects found in Andersen's fairy tales. It is that cloth that captivates us, making us do the imaginative work of seeing something beautiful even when it has no material reality. Deeply resonant with meaning and of rare aesthetic beauty—even if they never become real—the cloth and other wondrous objets d'art have attained a certain degree of critical invisibility. Their value has been obscured by the lesson inscribed through the embodied finger-pointing (the sure sign of a message) at the end of the tale. It is no accident that nearly every illustration of the story shows us the child gleefully calling attention to the Emperor's nakedness. When it comes to children's literature, endings count, and it is there that we habitually—sometimes mindlessly—seek meaning and morals for the child reading the story. Aesthetics rarely matters, even if it is the appearance of beauty that has engaged attention in the first place. But it is to beauty that we must look to discover why we still read Andersen today.

MATCHES AND THEIR IGNITION POWER

The wondrous objects concealed in Andersen's tales are not always easy to identify and locate, for they engage in remarkable disappearing acts, playing hide-and-seek with characters and readers alike. Take the case of the pea in the celebrated "Princess and the Pea," and it becomes evident that even

18. Hollis Robbins, "The Emperor's New Critique," *New Literary History* 34 (2004): 663.

the most ordinary objects can come to be invested with a special aura. The pea that was placed under the mattresses becomes, by the end of the story, an authentic museum piece on display in the Royal Museum. That is, if it has not yet disappeared—"if no one has stolen it," as Andersen emphasizes. The nightingale, in the story of that title, also comes and goes, singing its enchanting melodies when it pleases. The invisible cloth, the bird in the woods, and the pea have real impact on the child reading the story, for they carry an emotional charge far more powerful than the lessons that have been permanently emblazoned on the tales by well-meaning editors. William J. Bennett may insist that "The Little Match Girl" is a "simple, tragic story that stirs pity in every child's heart," but many child readers will be more moved by the girl's beautiful visions than by her abject state.

There is good reason to be cautious about enshrining beauty as the supreme value of the fairy tale. Andersen's cult of beauty is shadowed by a profound fear that the enchantments of beauty can turn demonic, evoking desires so powerful that they exceed the bounds of civilized society and turn into an indulgence that is both evil and dangerous. A deep ambivalence about beauty and pleasure becomes evident in "The Red Shoes," a story that punishes a child's quite natural curiosity and appetite for beauty. The young Karen is enamored of a princess's shoes—"There's nothing in the world like a pair of red shoes!"—and has a pair made by the local shoemaker: "They were beautiful!" But the magic of that beauty turns against Karen, taking possession of her feet, compelling her to dance endlessly, and punishing her for desires that are, on one level, innocent, natural, and benign.[19] One picture-book version of "The Red Shoes" eliminates the gory scene in which Karen's feet are chopped off and ends happily with Karen vowing to "think twice" before she makes another wish.[20]

Beneath this simple story we can hear the rustling of ancient myths. It is as if Andersen had miniaturized and domesticated the rivalry between Arachne and Athena, creating a homespun tale in which a girl vies with a

---

19. Zipes points out that the red shoes "are magical like our appetites, for they cannot be tamed on this earth, and Karen's obsessive appetite reveals the injustices and mortifying humiliation that any child from the lower classes must suffer for desiring to improve his or her lot. Though she is punished for her fetish, the harsh punishment does not fit the crime, and one must wonder why a girl's innocent longing for some beauty in her life is considered a sin" (*Hans Christian Andersen*, 88–89).

20. Barbara Bazilion, illus., *The Red Shoes* (Watertown, MA: Charlesbridge Publishing, 1997).

royal superior and is punished for daring to put beauty on display. But Andersen mingles the pious with the pagan. As a devout if not wholly orthodox Lutheran, he had good reason to feel anxious about beauty and its sensual, seductive powers. The desire it arouses can never be wholly innocent, even when, as in "The Emperor's New Clothes," it has no substance at all. Beauty can quickly turn into a force with the power to devastate, crush, and overwhelm, especially in Andersen's later tales about troubled artists and their struggles with the creative process.

But Andersen also understood that, without beauty, our lives are impoverished, and almost every story he wrote contains scenes, objects, or characters that are uplifting, stirring, and enchanting. Many begin with descriptions of landscapes that are "lovely," and it is no accident that *dejligt* (the Danish term that captures a mix of beauty, charm, and delight) turns out to be Andersen's favorite word. Andersen was dismayed that his critics took to counting the number of times the word appeared in a story.

Andersen's cult of beauty may be unwelcome news to parents and educators (especially those who seek to enlist the stories in building character), but it would have been cheering news to one writer who took up the genre of the fairy tale and reworked it in literary terms. Oscar Wilde, whose literary fairy tales celebrate compassion and good works (sometimes even at the expense of beauty), ventriloquizes through a character in *The Picture of Dorian Gray* a view that captures the aesthetics of Andersen's fairy tales: "People say sometimes that Beauty is only superficial. That may be so. But at least it is not so superficial as Thought is. To me, Beauty is the wonder of wonders. It is only shallow people who do not judge by appearances. The true mystery of the world is the visible, not the invisible."[21] Appearances always count, and Andersen's deepest commitment in the fairy tales is to the description of surface beauty.

It is not always easy to predict the "wonder of wonders" that will catch the attention of a child. For readers of *The Lion, the Witch, and the Wardrobe*, it may be the Turkish delight that Edmund is given by the witch of Narnia. Francis Spufford, whose stirring memoir about childhood reading reveals the importance of reading with the spine (rather than the brain), does not

---

21. Oscar Wilde, *The Picture of Dorian Gray* (New York: Random House/Modern Library, 1992), 25.

specifically refer to Turkish delight, but he calls attention to C. S. Lewis's ability to construct something that he calls "invented objects for my longing." In *The Child That Books Built,* he reports that the author of *The Chronicles of Narnia* "gave forms to my longing that I would never have thought of, and yet they seemed exactly right: he had anticipated what would delight me with an almost unearthly intimacy."[22]

Objects of desire appear in forms that are both obvious and subtle. For readers of Roald Dahl's *Charlie and the Chocolate Factory*, it may be the Golden Ticket itself as much as the outlandish confections at the chocolate factory that serves as the "invented object" incarnating childhood desires. In *Alice in Wonderland*, if you look closely, it is not the White Rabbit but the watch in the waistcoat pocket that makes Alice "burn with curiosity." All these invented objects produce a form of desire that serves as a reliable antidote to the boredom that can beset a child—sometimes the child in the book, sometimes the child outside the book, and sometimes both—with nothing to do.

Andersen is not often associated with beauty, in large part because Christian symbols and pious thoughts so dominate the narrative landscape of his fairy tales. "The Little Match Girl," for example, is nearly always read as a story of salvation, without reference to the visions produced by the lighting of matches. The flames lit by the girl have the power to kindle imagination, producing visions of warmth (a brass stove), whimsy (a roast goose that waddles on the floor with a fork and knife in its back), and beauty (the Christmas tree). The comparison of the match's glow to a "tiny lamp" is more than likely an allusion to the magic lamp in the story of Aladdin, a figure with whom Andersen identified when he read *The Arabian Nights* as a boy with his father. To the best of my knowledge, only Clarissa Pinkola Estés, in her compelling study of fairy tales, has understood the lighting of matches in poetic terms, and she equates the gesture with a damaging form of escapist fantasy: The little match girl loses herself in a vision "that has nothing to do with reality. It has to do with feeling nothing can be done, so one might as well sink into idle fantasy."[23]

22. Francis Spufford, *The Child That Books Built: A Life in Reading* (Holt/Metropolitan Books, 2002), 87.

23. Clarissa Pinkola Estés, *Women Who Run with the Wolves: Myths and Stories of the Wild Woman Archetype* (New York: Ballantine, 1992), 322.

For Andersen, the light of poetry was more than idle fantasy. The little match girl can be seen as possessing a power of imagination not unlike that of Andersen's "new Aladdin," who promises to renew poetry with the illuminating power of his lamp:

A bard will come, who, with a child's mind, like a new Aladdin, will enter the cavern of science—with a child's mind, we say, or else the powerful spirits of natural strength would seize him and make him their servant—while he, with the lamp of poetry, which is, and always will be, the human heart, stands as a ruler, and brings forth wonderful fruits from the gloomy passages, and has strength to build poetry's new palace, created in one night by attendant spirits.[24]

It is through beauty, poetry, and visionary power that the world will be renewed.

BEAUTY, REFLECTION, AND REPRESENTATION

Andersen revels in descriptions that evoke nature's beauty. Here is the beginning of "The Little Mermaid": "Far out at sea, the water is as blue as the petals of the prettiest cornflower and as clear as the purest glass." "The Ugly Duckling" may state in its title the antithesis of beauty, but it begins by describing the vibrant colors of country splendors: "It was so beautiful out in the country—it was summertime! The grain was golden, the oats were green, and hay was piled in tall stacks down in the green meadows." Andersen works hard to capture in words the physical beauty of earth, sea, and sky, and of the creatures that inhabit those three regions.

Beauty, as Elaine Scarry has eloquently put it, "seems to incite, even to require, the act of replication."[25] It brings "copies of itself into being," and "when the eye sees someone beautiful, the whole body wants to reproduce the person." This form of expressive desire is accomplished in its most immedi-

24. Jacob Bøggild, "Ruinous Reflections: On H. C. Andersen's Ambiguous Position between Romanticism and Modernism," in *H. C. Andersen: Old Problems and New Readings*, ed. Steven P. Sondrup (Odense: Univ. of Southern Denmark Press, 2004), 85.

25. Elaine Scarry, *On Beauty and Being Just* (Princeton: Princeton Univ. Press, 2001), 3.

ate and unmediated manner by what is probably the most famous of all Andersen's fairy-tale characters: the ugly duckling. Andersen's barnyard animal experiences the shock of beauty when he sees swans, mourns their loss, and ends by metamorphosing into the very creatures that enchanted him.

The transformation does not take place without a price, and, for Andersen, the cost for creating beauty is almost inevitably some form of suffering. The ugly duckling begins as one of the most abject of Andersen's characters, a creature that figures as the "laughingstock of the barnyard." An outcast in the animal world, he is scorned by humans as well—kicked by the maid, shot at by hunters, and struck with tongs. "It's because I'm so ugly," the duckling declares, pointing to the disruptive energy of ugliness and its capacity to elicit hatred and aggression. The ugly duckling knows beauty and has seen it in the form of "majestic birds" with "magnificent wings" and "wondrous cries." Although not driven by ambition ("How could he ever aspire to their beauty?"), he nonetheless performs as a supremely able imitator, one who comes to embody, not just replicate or duplicate, the beauty that fills him with awe and admiration.

The ugly duckling may suffer through the icy winter, but the transformation from duckling to swan requires no real effort on his part. It is, of course, part of a natural, biological process, much like the metamorphosis from caterpillar to butterfly. In the scene of transformation, the ugly duckling engages in a moment of reflection—reflection in the double sense of the term. He sees himself in the mirrored surface of the water and at the same time reflects on his condition. In this extraordinary humanizing moment—animals cannot, of course, engage in this double process—the ugly duckling transcends both ugliness and his animal condition. Reflection may not be the cause of the transformation, but it is telling that it coincides with the moment of transformation.

The process of creating beauty is not always so smooth, and, like beauty itself, it too has a dark side. "The Snow Queen" troubles the waters of "The Ugly Duckling," suggesting that the desire to strive for beauty, when it falls short of perfect imitation, can turn diabolical and destructive. Andersen's story of Kai and Gerda makes it clear that creativity can turn sinister, for it is affiliated with a disturbing form of self-division and self-deception. The magic mirror introduced in the very first paragraph of "The Snow Queen" is a tool of the devil, a surface that has the capacity to shrink what is "good and beautiful" and to enlarge what is "worthless and ugly." It may reflect reality but it also distorts it, engaging in critical disfigurement that is said to show "what people and the world were really like."

Andersen's troll/devil is a kind of artistic anti-Christ whose art consists of finding truth through satiric distortion. In the course of his arrogant, Babel-like project to take the glass up to the heavens, he creates shards that lodge in the eyes and hearts of all those down on earth, including Kai, who is seduced by the icy beauty of the Snow Queen. Kai is, in the end, redeemed by the warm, passionate tears of his beloved Gerda, but not before he almost loses himself in the frigid palace of the Snow Queen, working an ice puzzle of the mind, trying to shape frozen chunks into the word "Eternity."

In "The Ugly Duckling," we have a triumphant moment of self-reflexivity, for the transformed duckling, unlike Narcissus, does not fall in love with his image. He recognizes that what is being mirrored back to him is his own reflection. Consider Kai, however, who labors in solitude, mirror lodged in his heart, to achieve immortality. He is caught in a conflict that one critic has called the "nemesis of mimesis," the revenge of art on those who try to represent and create.[26] Striving for mathematical perfection and rarefied beauty, Kai remains trapped in narcissistic self-absorption, struggling with the Snow Queen's ice puzzle, which, when solved, will reward him, not only with the whole world and a pair of ice skates, but also with immortality. And yet "everything ends up in the trash," as we learn in "Auntie Toothache," Andersen's most astonishingly dark anti–fairy tale. Works of art may outlive their creators, but the notion of "immortality" for artists and for their creations is nothing but a cultural lie. Even works of art are doomed to decay and crumble.

ANIMATING ART

Andersen is deeply committed to art, but at the same time he recognizes the dangers of a cold, austere cult of beauty that, in its quest for immortality, endangers the artist's soul. These are grown-up matters, and the second

26. Karin Sanders, "Nemesis of Mimesis: The Problem of Representation in H. C. Andersen's *Psychen,*" *Scandinavian Studies* 64 (1992): 1–25.

installment of fairy tales in this collection was meant for adult audiences willing to follow the writer's struggle to define exactly what is at stake in artistic creation. These "high-voltage" narratives map a deeply personal poetics that complicates the straightforward aesthetics of fairy tales like "The Ugly Duckling."[27] I will turn to two tales—"The Psyche" and "The Shadow"—to deepen our understanding of questions that troubled Andersen far more profoundly than the more prominent fairy tales let on. These are stories that need to be resurrected and put in dialogue with the earlier tales if we are to understand how devotion to beauty raises a legion of devilish ethical questions.

A beautiful work of art occupies the central position of "The Psyche." Written in 1861, the story engages in its title the thematic nexus found in so many of Andersen's fairy tales: beauty, spirituality, and transformation. Psyche, the legendary beauty who marries Cupid and breaks the taboo of looking at him, bears the Greek name for "soul" and is endowed by the gods with immortality. She is only one of many mythological figures invoked by the text, which reworks the Pygmalion story and also draws on the figure of Medusa to work out its narrative terms. As in many of Andersen's tales, the pagan (Greek, Roman, and Nordic mythologies) informs the narrative in unexpected ways and bumps up against the overlay of religious themes.

The wondrous invented object in "The Psyche" takes the form of a marble statue sculpted by an unnamed perfectionist who destroys everything he creates until he achieves flawless beauty. Inspired by a young woman he sees in a garden, he molds a statue, not just of the young woman but also of an image familiar to him from his studies of art, Raphael's *Psyche*. "He had never seen such a beautiful woman before. Yes, once! He had seen one painted by Raphael, painted as Psyche, in one of Rome's palaces. Yes, her portrait was there—and here she was alive!"

When the young Roman woman sees the artist's statue and hears his passionate declaration of love for him, she turns on him. In that instant, "the face

---

27. Jack Zipes focuses on Andersen's "discourse of rage and revenge," but he too recognizes that Andersen's tales are also "theoretical speculations about the nature and beauty of art and the qualities a great artist needs to gain the recognition he deserves" (Zipes, *Hans Christian Andersen*, xv). Jackie Wullschlager describes these tales as "high-voltage," for they take up "the terror of psychological disintegration" and other existential matters. See Introduction, *Hans Christian Andersen: Fairy Tales*, trans. Tiina Nunnally (New York: Viking, 2005), p. xvii.

of beauty bore a resemblance to that petrifying face with serpent hair." Repeating the sculptor's act of turning a person into an image of stone, she transforms herself from Psyche to Medusa. Pygmalion may have brought his statue to life, but here the statue's model saps life from the artist. However much the artist's masterpiece may succeed as a work of art, it turns on him in ways so powerful that he abandons art, hoping to find salvation in monastic life.

The artist never makes a name for himself, but his work of art is unearthed long after his death and acquires immortality: "He was gone now, scattered abroad as dust is destined to be. But Psyche—the fruit of his most noble labors and the glorious work that betokened the spark of the divine in him—remained, and she would never die." The artwork effaces the artist, leaving him to molder while it gets its revenge as an admired, acclaimed, shining exemplar of beauty.

As in "The Ugly Duckling" and "The Snow Queen," an aesthetics of whiteness dominates "The Psyche." The blinding white beauty of the marble statue, "carved from snow," like Kai's letters, can be seen as what Toni Morrison, in a study that identifies the racial fault lines in black/white aesthetics, has called an "antidote for and meditation on the shadow that is companion to this whiteness."[28] Just as beauty is haunted by death even as it lays claim to immortality, white is troubled by blackness, by shadows and darkness that are a source of both fear and desire. It therefore comes as no surprise to find that Andersen had written, some fifteen years before he penned "The Psyche," a story called "The Shadow." And it is perhaps not coincidental that the Danish titles ("Psychen" and "Skyggen") come close to rhyming with each other.[29]

"The Shadow" is itself haunted by the anxiety of influence. When its protagonist, a "learned man," loses his shadow, he is less disturbed by the disappearance of the shadow than by the fact that "there was another story about a man without a shadow." "The Shadow" is mirrored by another tale: Adelbert von Chamisso's Romantic novella *Peter Schlemihl's Marvelous Story* (1814), which was quickly translated from German into many European

28. Toni Morrison, *Playing in the Dark: Whiteness and the Literary Imagination* (Cambridge, MA: Harvard Univ. Press, 1992), 33.

29. Bøggild, "Ruinous Reflections," 94.

languages, including Danish. It had established itself as a classic by the time Andersen read it. The learned man, discouraged by the notion that others will believe that he is doing nothing but imitating a literary character, decides not to tell his story at all. In a grotesque inversion of a fairy-tale ending, he is liquidated on the wedding day of his shadow, who has come to life by imitating him.

How does the shadow disengage from his proprietor to lead an independent existence? Like so many of Andersen's characters, he finds in beauty a power so seductive that it leads him to abandon his ordinary existence. One evening the learned man awakens to see "a strange glow" coming from his neighbor's balcony, where flowers gleam like flames of the loveliest colors. There he sees an "enchanting" maiden and is nearly blinded. Light quickly gives way to sound, and the learned man finds himself under the "spell" of gentle and lovely music.

The house across the way is described as some kind of magic world (*en Trolddom*). The scholar turns his back on it and retreats to his study, where he devotes himself to the good, the true, and the beautiful. The shadow, by contrast, stretches himself and crosses over into the realm of poetry, exposing himself to the transformative power of art. There, he finds the means for attaining autonomy, creating illusions, and reversing the power relations between himself and his host. The shadow's strategic alliance with beauty marks the triumph of double-dealing, duplicity, and fraud.

Andersen created in "The Shadow" a shadow of himself, a creature that feeds off his artistry but also lives on even after his creator has perished. If Andersen celebrated beauty and its transformative power in tales such as "The Ugly Duckling," he also began to explore the sinister side to beauty— its links to artifice, frigidity, and paralysis—in works ranging from "The Emperor's New Clothes" through "The Snow Queen" to "The Psyche." "The Shadow" is his supreme concession to the troubled and troubling side to beauty, a dark exploration of how beauty may not in fact engage the good, the true, and the beautiful and may instead conceal a deadly desire to destroy as it takes over life, becoming animated and, at times, even achieving immortality.

Beauty may have a beastly side, but it never loses its power to weave spells that draw us into its alluring orbit. And Andersen summons it for us again and again, as if to remind us that, through its jolts and shimmers, it still has the power to animate us. Great writers, as Nabokov reminded us, are not only storytellers and teachers but also enchanters. The storyteller produces somatic effects, speeding up our beating hearts, leaving us breathless, making us weep real tears, or prompting us to laugh. The great teachers are beyond Aesop, instructing us less in the art of problem-solving than in the art of identifying and deepening them. The enchanters—along with the effects of the spells they work—are less easy to describe, but how they work their magic becomes utterly clear when we read the fairy tales of Hans Christian Andersen.

Ordering the Tales: From the Familiar to the Strange

When we read Andersen to children today, we often rely on translations that fail to give us the full story. "The Red Shoes," newly illustrated by Barbara Bazilian in 1997, has been adapted to eliminate
the scene in which Karen's feet, with the beautiful, magical shoes
still on them, are chopped off. The little match girl, in a version of her
story published in 1944, finds "warmth and cheer and a lovely home where
she lives happily ever after." And "The Little Mermaid," under the spell of
Disney Studios, appears in countless new print editions, each ending with a
happily-ever-after wedding that contrasts sharply with the three hundred
years of good deeds assigned to the mermaid at the end of Andersen's tale.

New translations, many timed to coincide with the bicentennial of
Andersen's birth, have been more successful in capturing the letter and the
spirit of the tales. Jeffrey Frank and Diana Crone Frank's *Hans Christian
Andersen: A New Translation from the Danish* stresses the importance of working from the original language, in part because so many of Andersen's translators did not know Danish and relied on German versions of the tales. The
Franks' volume is part of a new wave of translations that shows respect both
for the broad contours of the stories as well as for their telling details. Tiina

Nunnally's *Hans Christian Andersen: Fairy Tales* seeks, in lively renditions of thirty tales, to capture the author's "unique voice" with all its stylistic quirks. Neil Philip's *Fairy Tales of Hans Christian Andersen* offers forty "enchanting masterpieces from one of the world's greatest storytellers" with the aim of providing family-friendly entertainment. Since the bicentennial of his birth, Andersen has gained much in translation.

In this volume, Julie K. Allen and I have returned to the original Danish in an effort to capture Andersen's many different voices—impassioned yet also playful, unaffected yet also complex, sweet yet also doleful, and musical yet also maudlin. We have recognized that translations can never be pitch-perfect, but we have tried to re-create Andersen's tales in English versions that lend themselves to reading out loud (a practice that Andersen himself endorsed for the stories) and to thinking out loud (a practice that we need to revive when we become aware of the full cultural force of these stories). Unlike the Grimms' tales, which circulated in hundreds of different versions as part of an oral storytelling culture, Andersen's stories are literary narratives in which every word counts and should be weighed and measured with care.

Today, we think of Andersen primarily as an author of books for children, but in his own day he was a prominent dramatist, a distinguished novelist, and a chronicler of travels that took him from London and Paris to Athens and Istanbul. To be sure, even in his own day, critics believed that his greatest accomplishment came in the form of fairy tales ("told for children," as he frequently noted in the titles to his collections). And yet many of those fairy tales took up adult themes and, with time, Andersen shifted from enchanting stories that breathe the sweet air of miniaturized fancy and whimsical beauty to carefully constructed literary tales that pulse with dark existential torment and human suffering. In between, there are stories that appear crafted for children but that enlist a pedagogy of fear that does not square with our contemporary sense of bedtime reading. The selection of stories in this volume begins in the child-centered mode of "The Emperor's New Clothes" and "The Snow Queen" and moves gradually to a darker Andersen—one not familiar to Anglo-American audiences—who is no longer thinking about the child as hero.

The first dozen tales in this volume may seem too harsh for children at times, but they constitute the Andersen canon, which has migrated successfully not only to the United States but also into 153 different literary cultures, as documented by the Hans Christian Andersen Museum in Odense. The second set of twelve tales give us a less familiar Andersen, an author who worried about art, beauty, and the creative process and who sought to produce something so luminous and large that it would serve as a bulwark against suffering and mortality. We need to know something about the less familiar Andersen in order to fully understand what is at stake in more familiar stories like "The Ugly Duckling" and "The Emperor's New Clothes." This volume gives us both sides of Hans Christian Andersen, a writer whose commitment to the transformative power of art and beauty was so deep that it altered the landscape of children's literature in profound ways, creating stories that may seem to take a moral turn but that in fact teach children that words and their art have the power to change you.

Andersen himself was aware of the fairy tale's reach, and he defined the genre in a way that makes evident its appeal for young and old: "In the whole realm of poetry no domain is so boundless as that of the fairy tale. It reaches from the blood-drenched graves of antiquity to the pious legends of a child's picture book; it takes in the poetry of the people and the poetry of the artist." Taking the poetry of the people as his point of departure, Andersen also fashioned the poetry of the artist, giving us stories that are deeply familiar, hauntingly strange, and everything in between.

PART I

Tales for Children

The Emperor's New Clothes[1]

Kejserens nye klæder

Eventyr, fortalte for Børn, 1837

ndersen's tale of the truth-speaking child has won many admirers because it pays powerful tribute to youth and innocence. "When I was a child," historian Ruth Rosen writes, "my favorite story was 'The Emperor's New Clothes.' A chorus of adults praises the Emperor's new wardrobe, but a child blurts out the truth: The Emperor is in fact stark naked. From this tale, I learned that adults could be intimidated into endorsing all kinds of flummery" (Rosen, A11).

Andersen's tale is encoded with many possible lessons, and every reader seems to take a different message from it. For the cognitive scientist Steven Pinker, the story offers a "nice parable of the subversive power of collective humor," revealing the strength that comes in numbers as well as the power of the "involuntary, disruptive, and contagious signal" sent by laughter (Pinker, 551). The child in Andersen's story, who is irreverent, fearless, and spirited, speaks truth to power even as adults—deferential, intimidated, and insecure—succumb all too easily to deception.

The voice of the child has diverted significant attention from something in the tale that is described as "beautiful," "lovely," "enchant-

1. *The Emperor's New Clothes.* The phrase "Emperor's new clothes" has become a "byword for human vanity" (Allen, 12) but also a way of describing anything that is pretentious, pompous, and ostentatious with no substance to it. Making its way into newspaper articles, literary works, congressional records, legal proceedings, and academic articles, it has established a certain authoritative descriptive power and currently appears in the titles of nearly two dozen books in print.

3

ing," "priceless," "exquisite," "extraordinary," "amazing," "mag-nifique," "splendid," "superb," and "delicate." Although "lovely" was one of Andersen's favorite words and was used by him repeatedly, it still comes as something of a surprise to find that term and its variants used so often in a story with less than two thousand words. And it is even more astonishing that those adjectives all describe something invisible, a cloth and clothing that do not exist. The Emperor's train, like his clothing, are "not there at all," as the last words of the tale tell us.

The first story in this collection speaks volumes about Andersen's art. Using nothing but words to lure objects of beauty into being, Andersen creates nightingales that sing, shoes that dance on their own, marble statues that pulse with life, underwater gardens that glitter with golden fruit—and even a cloth that is "not there at all." In the mind's eye, the nightingale, the shoes, the marble statue, the gardens, and the cloth possess a radiant energy that makes them palpably real. Invisible and "not there at all," they still remain enchanting, exquisite, and lovely. The words have a certain ignition power that allows us to imagine the world constructed by Andersen's art.

"The Emperor's New Clothes" has been translated into over a hundred languages and continues to fascinate and inspire imitation, as the recent publication The Emperor's New Clothes: An All-Star Illustrated Retelling of the Classic Fairy Tale *suggests. In that volume, Dr. Ruth Westheimer refashions the story by narrating it from the point of view of an imperial physician; Calvin Klein reports that "nothing comes between me and my Emperor!"; and Steven Spielberg makes an appearance as the "honest boy" who blows the whistle on the Emperor's birthday suit. The tale has migrated into many different media, with a Russian film of that title directed by Yuri Zhelyabuzhsky in 1919, a song by Sinéad O'Connor, a musical of 1987 with Sid Caesar as Emperor, and numerous plays, short stories, and animated films that offer enactments or send-ups of the tale.*

Many years ago there lived an Emperor who cared so much about beautiful new clothes that he spent all his money on dressing stylishly. He took no interest at all in his soldiers, nor did he care to attend the theater or go out for a drive, unless of course it gave him a chance to show off his new clothes.[2] He had a different outfit for every hour of the day and, just as you usually say that kings are sitting in coun-

2. *show off his new clothes.* For Andersen, vanity was the cardinal sin of human nature, and it often manifests itself as pride in shoes and clothing. Excessive attachment to dress appears particularly absurd and signals deep self-absorption when a monarch allows it to interfere with his royal duties. The portrait of the Emperor has been seen by some critics as an effort by Andersen to get revenge on those above him in social rank by mocking their vanity and affectations. Tall and gawky, Andersen was always self-conscious about his physical appearance and felt wounded by the frequent reminders, even after he had achieved literary fame, that he occupied a social position inferior to those with whom he mingled.

HARRY CLARKE

The bold patterns and beautiful designs reveal just how deeply both the Emperor and his courtiers value garments. Display and self-inspection obviously have real significance for this particular monarch.

3. *two swindlers appeared.* The two charlatans belong to a rich folkloric tradition of tricksters who get the better of naïve villagers or townspeople. In this case, the swindlers know exactly how to play on the insecurities and weaknesses of the upper crust. In the acknowledged Spanish literary source for the tale, a fourteenth-century cautionary tale by Infante Don Juan Manuel, a magical cloth is visible only to those who are of legitimate birth. The notion of legitimacy is transplanted from the biological sphere to the bureaucratic realm, for in Andersen's reworking of the tale, those who cannot see the clothes are "unfit for their posts."

Although this tale has not been associated with oral storytelling traditions, Andersen mines a rich folkloric vein that tells of rogues turning the tables on royalty and tricksters outwitting merchants, clergymen, and innkeepers. The swindlers succeed in taking advantage of the Emperor's vanity, but the tale also takes a moral turn and puts the spotlight on a social virtue. The final tableau does not show the clever swindlers hightailing it out of town with their ill-gotten gains but focuses instead on the child, who has the courage to speak truth to power.

The folklorist Archer Taylor has argued that tales in which swindlers fashion clothes, hats, or pictures that can be seen only by those of legitimate birth or rank failed to take root in popular oral traditions. "Possibly the tale points a moral too obviously," he added, "and the moral, that it is possible to fool all of the people some of the time, is too bitter a pill" (Taylor, 27).

4. *the clothes made from their fabrics.* The fabric "woven" by the swindlers allegedly possesses both beauty (it has impressive colors and patterns) and magical qualities (it is not visible to those "unfit for their posts" or to those who are stupid). It may

cil, it was always said of him: "The Emperor is in his dressing room right now."

In the big city where the Emperor lived, there were many distractions. Strangers came and went all the time, and one day two swindlers appeared.[3] They claimed to be weavers and said that they knew how to weave the loveliest cloth you could imagine. Not only were the colors and designs they created unusually beautiful, but the clothes made from their fabrics[4] also had the amazing ability of becoming invisible to those who were unfit for their posts or just hopelessly stupid.

"Those must be lovely clothes!" thought the Emperor. "If I wore something like that, I could tell which men in my kingdom were unfit for their posts, and I would also be able to tell the smart ones from the stupid ones. Yes, I must have some of that fabric woven for me at once." And he paid the swindlers a large sum of money so that they could get started at once.

The swindlers assembled a couple of looms and pretended to be working, but there was nothing at all on their looms. Straightaway they demanded the finest silk and the purest gold thread, which they promptly stowed away in their own bags. Then they worked far into the night on their empty looms.

"Well, now, I wonder how the weavers are getting on with their work," the Emperor thought. But he was beginning to feel some anxiety about the fact that anyone who was stupid or unfit for his post would not be able to see what was being woven. Not that he had any fears about himself—he felt quite confident on that score—but all the same it might be better to send someone else out first, to see how things were progressing. Everyone in town had heard about the cloth's mysterious power, and they were all eager to discover the incompetence or stupidity of their neighbors.

"I will send my honest old minister to the weavers," the Emperor thought. "He's the best person to inspect the cloth, for he has plenty of good sense, and no one is better qualified for his post than he is."

EDMUND DULAC

The minister tries hard to see the "exquisite" cloth being woven on the loom, although there is, of course, nothing to see. But there is plenty of loot in the trunk by the door.

be produced by charlatans, but those charlatans also set up looms and work "very busily." Andersen's weavers, Hollis Robbins points out in her superb study of the story, are merely insisting that "the value of their labor be recognized apart from its material embodiment" (Robbins, 663). The invisible cloth may never manifest itself in material terms, but the description of its beauty ("exquisite" and "as light as spiderwebs") turns it into one of the most wondrous objects found in Andersen's fairy tales. As the story unfolds, the cloth is coaxed into being with each new description of its wondrous beauty and with each new pantomime in which it is woven, cut, sewn, worn, and carried. The swindlers can be read as artists who, in an ironic twist, create beauty visible only to those who are beyond materialism.

5. *a second respected official.* The two officials experience employment anxiety that has historical roots in the administrative changes taking place in the 1820s and 1830s in Denmark. Under increasing pressure to liberalize their policies and put an end to aristocratic privilege, older bureaucrats, in an effort to retain their positions, joined forces with their younger colleagues in the reform movements sweeping Europe. In "The Nightingale," "The Bell," and "The Snow Queen," Andersen mocks the creation of grandiose titles and positions to elevate ordinary people to higher social rank. That did not stop him from feeling flattered and honored whenever he received a medal from royal hands.

So off went the good-natured old minister to the workshop where the two swindlers were laboring with all their might at the empty looms. "God save us!" thought the minister, and his eyes nearly popped out of his head. "Why, I can't see a thing!" But he was careful not to say that out loud.

The two swindlers invited him to take a closer look—didn't he find the pattern beautiful and the colors lovely? They gestured at the empty frames, but no matter how widely he opened his eyes, he couldn't see a thing, for there was nothing there. "Good Lord!" he thought. "Is it possible that I'm an idiot? I never once suspected it, and I mustn't let on that it is a possibility. Can it be that I'm unfit for my post? No, it will never do for me to admit that I can't see the cloth."

"Well, why aren't you saying anything about it?" asked one of the swindlers, who was pretending to be weaving.

"Oh, it's enchanting! Quite exquisite!" the old minister said, peering over his spectacles. "That pattern and those colors! I shall tell the Emperor right away how much I like it."

"Ah, we are so glad that you like it," the weavers replied, and they described the colors and extraordinary patterns in detail. The old minister listened attentively so that he would be able to repeat their description to the Emperor when he returned home—which he duly did.

The swindlers demanded more money, more silk, and more gold thread, which they insisted they needed to keep weaving. They stuffed it all in their own pockets—not a thread was put on the loom—while they went on weaving at the empty frames as before.

After a while, the Emperor sent a second respected official[5] to see how the weaving was progressing and to find out when the cloth would be ready. What had happened to the first minister also happened to him. He looked as hard as he could, but since there was nothing there but an empty loom, he couldn't see a thing.

"There, isn't this a beautiful piece of cloth!" the swindlers declared, as they described the lovely design that didn't exist at all.

"I'm not stupid," thought the man. "This can only mean that I'm not fit for my position. That would be ridiculous, so I'd better not let on." And so he praised the cloth he could not see and declared that he was delighted with its beautiful hues and lovely patterns. "Yes, it's quite exquisite," he said to the Emperor.

The splendid fabric soon became the talk of the town.

And now the Emperor wanted to see the cloth for himself while it was still on the loom. Accompanied by a select group of people, including the two stately old officials who had already been there, he went to visit the crafty swindlers, who were weaving for all they were worth without using a bit of yarn or thread.

"Look, isn't it *magnifique?*" the two venerable officials exclaimed. "If Your Majesty will but take a look. What a design! What colors!" And they pointed at the empty loom, feeling sure that all the others could see the cloth.

"What on earth!" thought the Emperor. "I can't see a thing! This is appalling! Am I stupid? Am I unfit to be Emperor? This is the most horrible thing I can imagine happening to me!"

"Oh, it's very beautiful!" the Emperor said. "It has our most gracious approval." And he gave a satisfied nod as he inspected the empty loom. He wasn't about to say that he couldn't see a thing. The courtiers who had come with him strained their eyes, but they couldn't see any more than the others. Still, they all said exactly what the Emperor had said: "Oh, it's very beautiful!" They advised him to wear his splendid new clothes for the first time in the grand parade that was about to take place. "It's *magnifique!*" "Exquisite!" "Superb!" —that's what you heard over and over again. Everyone was really pleased with the weaving. The Emperor knighted each of the two swindlers and gave them medals to wear in their buttonholes, along with the title Imperial Weaver.

6. *"They are all as light as spiderwebs."* The invisible cloth is described with verbal art, the one medium that can succeed in giving it substance. Elaine Scarry, in *Dreaming by the Book*, describes the principle at stake in creating the ghost-like presence of objects in the mind's eye. "Why, when the lights go out and the storytelling begins, is the most compelling tale (most convincing, most believable) a ghost story? . . . The answer is that the story instructs its hearers to create an image whose own properties are second nature to the imagination; it instructs its hearers to depict in the mind something thin, dry, filmy, two-dimensional, and without solidity. . . . What is hard is successfully to imagine an object, any object, that does *not* look like a ghost" (Scarry 1999, 24).

7. *the Emperor twisted and turned in front of the mirror.* The Emperor's vanity is further underscored by his preening before the mirror, scrutinizing his appearance and showing that he has eyes only for himself. Ironically, all his twisting and turning does not succeed in making him see what is right before his eyes. Note too that most

W. HEATH ROBINSON

A rotund Emperor examines himself in the mirror and proudly declares, "The clothes suit me well, don't they!"

On the eve of the parade, the rogues sat up all night with more than sixteen candles burning. Everyone could see how busy they were finishing the Emperor's new clothes. They pretended to remove the cloth from the loom; they cut the air with big scissors; and they sewed with needles that had no thread. Then at last they announced: "There! The Emperor's clothes are ready at last!"

The Emperor, with his most distinguished courtiers, went in person to the weavers, who each stretched out an arm as if holding something up and said: "Just look at these trousers! Here is the jacket! This is the cloak." And so on. "They are all as light as spiderwebs.[6] You can hardly tell you are wearing anything—that's the virtue of this delicate cloth."

"Yes, indeed," the courtiers declared. But they were unable to see a thing, for there was absolutely nothing there.

"Now, would it please His Imperial Majesty to remove his clothes?" asked the swindlers. "Then we can fit you with the new ones, over there in front of the long mirror."

And so the Emperor took off the clothes he was wearing, and the swindlers pretended to hand him each of the new garments they claimed to have made, and they held him at the waist as if they were attaching something . . . it was his train. And the Emperor twisted and turned in front of the mirror.[7]

"Goodness! How splendid His Majesty looks in the new clothes. What a perfect fit!" they all exclaimed. "What patterns! What colors! What priceless attire!"

The master of ceremonies came in with an announcement. "The canopy for the parade is ready and waiting for Your Majesty."

"I am quite ready," said the Emperor. "The clothes suit me well, don't they!" And he turned around one last time in front of the mirror, trying to look as if he were examining his fine new clothing.

The chamberlains who were supposed to carry the train groped around on the floor as if they were picking it up. As

HARRY CLARKE

An effete Emperor, wearing red stockings, admires himself before a mirror that is also the aperture through which we see him. The floral shape of the image, the intricate black and white patterns in the frame, and the decorative effect of the courtiers' clothing create an image of vibrant beauty even if vanity is mocked.

EDMUND DULAC

The proud Emperor struts through the streets in his underwear, putting himself on display to enact the role of vain fool. A child to the far left of the crowd is about to declare that the Emperor has no clothes.

sins are based on overinvestment in look-ing—the mirror becomes an emblem of vanity and arrogance because it perversely promotes the cult of gazing at the self.

8. *The Emperor marched in the parade under the lovely canopy.* Freud saw in the Emperor a figure living the classic night-mare of appearing in public without clothes. He viewed the two weavers as a "secondary revision" constructed to con-ceal the dreamer's exhibitionistic desire. In *The Interpretation of Dreams,* Freud explored the sense of exhibitionist glee and abject shame connected with nakedness in remarks that bear on the anxieties aroused by Andersen's tale: "Only in our childhood was there a time when we were seen by our relatives, as well as by strange nurses, ser-vants and visitors, in a state of insufficient clothing, and at that time we were not ashamed of our nakedness. In the case of many rather older children it may be

they walked, they held out their hands, not daring to let on that they couldn't see anything.

The Emperor marched in the parade under the lovely canopy,[8] and everyone in the streets and at the windows said: "Goodness! The Emperor's new clothes are the finest he has ever worn. What a lovely train on his coat! What a perfect fit!" People were not willing to let on that there was nothing at all to see, because that would have meant they were either unfit for their posts or very stupid. Never had the Emperor's clothes made such a great impression.[9]

"But he isn't wearing anything at all!" a little child declared.[10]

"Goodness gracious! Did you hear the voice of that inno-cent child!" cried the father. And the child's remark was whis-pered from one person to the next.

"Yes, he isn't wearing anything at all!" the crowd shouted at last. And the Emperor cringed, for he was beginning to

W. HEATH ROBINSON

The fleet-footed swindlers flee, one carrying a substantial bag of loot on his back. Unlike the unfortunate Emperor, they end up with more at the end of the story than they had at the beginning.

ARTHUR RACKHAM

The faces of observers register the shock of "discovering" that the Emperor is wearing no clothes.
Jaws drop, fingers point, hands cover snickers, and ears strain to listen while the child at the
center of the variegated crowd speaks truth to power.

observed that being undressed has an exciting effect upon them, instead of making them feel ashamed. They laugh, leap about, slap or thump their own bodies; the mother, or whoever is present, scolds them, saying: 'Fie, that is shameful—you mustn't do that!' Children often show a desire to display themselves. . . . In the history of the childhood of neurotics, exposure before children of the opposite sex plays a prominent part; in paranoia the delusion of being observed while dressing and undressing may be directly traced to these experiences; and among those who have remained perverse there is a class in whom the childish impulse is accentuated into a symptom: the class of *exhibitionists*" (Freud, 143). In this context, it is perhaps worth noting that the title of one biography of Andersen is "Fan Dancer," suggesting that the author fluctuated between cautious concealment and flagrant self-display.

9. *Never had the Emperor's clothes made such a great impression.* The original ending to the tale concluded with the continued self-deception of the Emperor and the collective self-deception of the townspeople: "Certainly none of the Emperor's various suits had ever made so great an impression as these invisible ones. 'I must put on the suit whenever I walk in a procession or appear before a gathering of people,' said the Emperor, and the whole town talked about his wonderful new clothes" (Bredsdorff, 312). The clothing retains a quality that preserves the effect of wonder, even if only for those who have the imaginative power to see the marvelous fabric out of which it is made, producing what one critic has called "a successful enchantment" (Robbins, 668).

10. *"But he isn't wearing anything at all!" a little child declared.* Those who ignore what is in plain sight and blindly act as if there is nothing wrong are the targets of Andersen's satire. That it takes an "innocent" child to divine a truth "His Majesty" cannot discern gives emphasis to the stultifying effects of social proprieties and conventions and underscores the duplicity and hypocrisy that the monarchy produces and perpetuates. Yet Andersen's fable also represents a collective fantasy about the efficacy of rebellious energy and irreverent behavior. In real life, we are often disinclined to pay much attention to either the voice of the child or to those who engage in cheeky, irreverent behavior.

That it takes a child to cut through the hypocrisy of the adult world is a powerful insight, one that is particularly appealing to child readers (many of whom may identify with the heroic child who is willing to declare what no adult dares to speak). Jacques Derrida emphasizes that the tale's transparency is its truth and that by staging "the truth" as something that can be unveiled and revealed, Andersen created a romantic fantasy in which anyone with courage and innocence can see and speak "the truth." But as Hollis Robbins points out, Andersen may also be critiquing the fantasy that "when there is something wrong in the world, all that is needed is a brave, insightful individual to set things right" (Robbins, 660). For Marshall McLuhan, Andersen's story illustrates the degree to which children, poets, artists, sleuths, and other socially deviant figures (as he puts it) see more clearly than others. In its celebration of the child's wisdom and candor and its revelation of adult hypocrisies, this tale has a special appeal as bedtime reading.

11. *"I must go through with it now, parade and all."* Andersen's ending deviates from the Spanish version of the tale, in which the king is forced to admit his foolishness after the truth is known. The Emperor believes that he is preserving his dignity even as he continues to lose his dignity, once the truth has been revealed.

suspect that everyone was right. But then he realized: "I must go through with it now, parade and all."[11] And he drew himself up even more proudly than before, while his chamberlains walked behind him carrying the train that was not there at all.

ARTHUR RACKHAM

A naked Emperor, protected from full revelation through the medium of the silhouette, walks through the cobblestoned street while two chamberlains carefully lift the train that is "not there at all."

The Snow Queen:
A Fairy Tale in Seven Stories

Sneedronningen: Et eventyr i syv historier

Nye Eventyr. Anden Samling, 1845

*T*he Snow Queen," one of the great quest narratives of children's literature, traces the paths of two children through wonders and marvels as they journey to the ends of the earth. Although Kai and Gerda are not biological siblings, they are bonded as brother and sister. In the course of their travels, they pass from childhood through adolescence to become adults—adults who remain children at heart. Their trialridden journey contains all the classic features of a fairy tale: a courageous heroine who maintains her wits, melodramatic contests between good and evil, helpers and donors who aid the innocent heroine in her quest, villains with seductive powers, perilous journeys that lead to breathtaking adventures, and the triumph of the innocent and pure in heart over evil. The fairy tale has also been framed as an allegory for adults, illustrating the dangerous seductions of science and reason and predicting their defeat by the life-giving forces of Christian salvation. "The Snow Queen" operates on multiple levels, its simplicity concealing depth and complexity that yield new meanings with each reading.

Much as Andersen explicitly endorses purity of soul and the faith, hope, and charity embodied in Gerda, he cannot but let slip one hint after another about the attractions of Kai's existence in the realm of the Snow Queen. If we trust the tale, we find that the realm of the Snow Queen is constructed as a world of exquisite aesthetic purity—chaste and sensual, spare yet luxurious, and disciplined but undomesticated. In the end, Gerda's pious Christian vision cannot always compete with the enchanting icy attractions available to Kai. "When we read of Kai's catastrophic predicament, the Snow Queen herself seems to preempt the author, and only a rapturous sensuality seems adequate to convey her thrilling excesses of coldness," one critic comments. "And when Kai, now on solid ground, submits without volition to little Gerda's wholesome and restorative kisses, we can't help but listen for the thrum of the returning sled, in which we once soared through the air and submitted to the dizzying, promise-filled kisses of the Snow Queen" (Eisenberg, 111). Kai may not have the power to get back on the sled, but we get back on every time we turn the pages of "The Snow Queen."

Andersen described the writing of "The Snow Queen" as "sheer joy": "It occupied my mind so fully that it came out dancing across the page." Although the story is one of the longest among his works, it took only five days to write. It has danced its way to the top of the list of Andersen's fairy tales and is seen by many as his greatest accomplishment. Andersen himself believed that many of his finest stories were written after travels to Rome, Naples, Constantinople, and Athens in 1841. He returned to Copenhagen reinvigorated by the encounter with the "Orient" and began inventing his own tales rather than relying on the folklore of his culture. Andersen believed that he had finally found his true voice, and "The Snow Queen," even if it does not mark a clean break with the earlier fairy tales, offers evidence of a more reflective style committed to forging new mythologies rather than producing lighthearted entertainments.

The earliest film adaptation of Andersen's tale was Snezhnaya Koroleva, released in the Soviet Union in 1957 and exported to America in 1959, with voices dubbed by Sandra Dee and Tommy Kirk. Since then, four other films have been made, a second in the USSR, one in Denmark, one in the United States, and one in the United Kingdom.

THE FIRST STORY, CONCERNING
A MIRROR AND ITS SHARDS

Look out! We're about to begin.[1] And when we reach the end of the story, we'll know more than we do now[2]—all because of an evil troll! He was one of the very worst—the "devil" himself![3] One day he was in a really good mood, for he had just finished making a mirror[4] that could shrink the image of whatever was good and beautiful down to almost nothing, while anything worthless and ugly was magnified and would look even worse. In this mirror, the loveliest landscapes looked like boiled spinach, and the kindest people looked hideous or seemed to be standing on their heads with their stomachs missing. Faces looked so deformed that you couldn't recognize them, and if someone had just a single freckle, you could be sure that it would spread until it covered both nose and mouth.

That was all great fun, the "devil" said. If anyone had a kind, pious thought, the mirror would begin to grin, and the troll-devil would burst out laughing at his clever invention. Everyone who attended his troll school (for he ran one) spread the news that a miracle had taken place.[5] Now for the first time, they claimed, you could see what the world and its people were really like. The students ran all over the place with the mirror until there was not a single country or person left to disfigure in it. They even wanted to fly all the way up to heaven to make fun of the angels and of God himself. The higher they flew with the mirror, the more it chuckled until finally they could barely hold on to it. They flew higher and higher, closer to God and the angels, but suddenly the mirror shook so hard with laughter that it flew out of their hands and crashed down to earth, where it shattered into a hundred million billion pieces and even more than that.

Once it broke, the mirror caused more unhappiness than ever, for some of the shards weren't even the size of a grain of

1. *Look out! We're about to begin.* Andersen does not use the impersonal, formulaic "once upon a time" of fairy tales and instead creates an embodied narrator who summons an imaginary audience to attention. His exclamatory remark also evokes a sense of physical engagement, anticipating the joy of adventure, the excitement of a journey, and the thrilling exhilaration Kai feels when hitched to the sled of the Snow Queen. Acting as a bridge between "long ago and far away" and the "here and now," Andersen's narrator also suggests that this is a tale to be read out loud, one that can build a bond between older and wiser tellers of tales and their listeners. Andersen himself, in an ingenious formulation, observed that his works were "written to be *heard*, that is how I know when they are good enough to be *read*." He conceded that his dramatic readings of the stories were not always appreciated: "I did not have enough experience to know that an author should not do this, at least not in my country" (*Travels*, 22).

2. *we'll know more than we do now.* The narrator straightaway makes the point that his story turns on the production of knowledge as well as entertainments. The introduction of the devil in the very first paragraph emphasizes a broad nexus of concerns that draws together division, sin, and the acquisition of knowledge. In some ways, readers will be repeating the experience of Kai and Gerda, who move from innocence to experience through knowledge.

3. *He was one of the very worst—the "devil" himself!* The hybrid figure of the devil/troll represents a compromise between the Christian devil and the trolls of pagan

EDMUND DULAC

The devil is represented as a figure with cloven hoofs and with the head of a learned man. He delights in the mirror he has invented, a mirror in which everything good and beautiful shrinks down almost to nothing. Oddly, the mirror held up to the devil does not reflect his own grotesque body.

HARRY CLARKE

"Those who visited the goblin school declared everywhere that a wonder had been wrought" is the caption for this image, which shows various decorative students in awe of the devil's mirror.

lore. In Scandinavian folklore, trolls live in castles and haunt surrounding areas after nightfall. When exposed to sunlight, they turn into stone or simply burst. Today, children in Anglo-American cultures know them from stories about creatures who live under bridges and make demands on those who use them—most notably the Norwegian "Three Billy Goats Gruff."

4. *he had just finished making a mirror.* Magical mirrors figure prominently in the folklore of many cultures. Mirrors can answer questions, make wishes come true, and predict the future. Moreover, they not only reflect but also transform. Whether we look at the folklore of Aztec Mexico or ancient Egypt, shadows and mirror images are generally seen as magically empowered embodiments of the soul. It comes as no surprise that bargains involving both shadows and mirrors animate the desires of devils and other fiends. Andersen weds folkloric tradition—contracts involving the soul—with literary convention, in which the mirror represents mimetic practices, capturing reality and reflecting it back to us in new ways. His mirror has magic qualities with the capacity to shrink what is "good and beautiful" and to enlarge what is "worthless and ugly." It reflects and distorts reality, and at the same time functions as a tool of the devil, who is invested in making a mockery of everything worthwhile through its surface. Andersen's contrast between the beautiful and the hideous appropriates fairy-tale aesthetics, which align the beautiful with the good and the hideous with what is morally worthless. The devil's distorting mirror can also be read as a metaphor for satiric art, which attempts not to capture reality but to engage in its disfigurement and thereby reveal what is amiss and untrue in our world.

Sabine Melchior-Bonnet, in her history of the mirror, points out that the theology of sin positioned the "mad stare" as the greatest obstacle to salvation: "All things visual, including seeing and thus knowing oneself, were linked together through sin. Most sins, pride or arrogance first and foremost, derive from sight. The mirror served as an attribute of sin because it is the emblem of the powers of sight, whose perverse effects it increases" (Melchior-Bonnet, 193). Vanity, as we know from

"The Red Shoes" and "The Girl Who Trod on the Loaf," is the cardinal sin in Andersen's fictional world. Looking and desiring to be looked at create problems for both Karen and Inger in those two stories.

5. *a miracle had taken place.* Andersen's troll-devil is a kind of artistic anti-Christ whose art consists of finding truth ("you could see what the world and its people were really like") through criticism and satiric distortion. The plan to take the mirror up to the angels and God is doomed to fail in its hubris and defiant ambition, much like the biblical effort to build a Tower of Babel that would reach to the heavens. Shattered as it approaches the heavens, the mirror produces fragments that are lodged everywhere on earth. The shattering, fragmentation, and splintering represent the opposite of love, a power that unites and overcomes oppositions and antagonism. For many theologians, the devil is seen as the being that divides and creates enmity. The devil says to Jesus: "My name is Legion, for we are many" (Mark 5:9). The transition from plenitude and wholeness to division and sin reveals the action of evil in the world. God's creation is shattered and atomizes into isolated fragments that create hell on earth.

Yet mirrors, even as they introduce the notion of self-division and self-deception, are also linked with reflection and self-knowledge. In this sense, Andersen's devil, like his biblical counterpart, can be linked with salvation as well as damnation. As the patron of multiplicity and variation, he helps to produce a world that contrasts sharply with the monotonous domain of the Snow Queen. As Roger Sale, an expert on children's literature, points out, "The Snow Queen" is long and complex, "because it must be, in order to show that the world, when it is not dominated by the Snow Queen, is not paradise but the world, multiple, varied, usually helpful to

sand, and they blew around all over the world. If a tiny particle got into your eye, it stayed there and made everything look bad or else it only let you see what was wrong with things, for every microscopic particle had the exact same power as the entire mirror. A little splinter from the mirror landed in the hearts of some people, and that was really dreadful because then their hearts became as hard as a chunk of ice. The shards were so large at times that you could use them as windowpanes, but you wouldn't want to see any of your friends through a window like that. Other pieces were turned into eyeglasses, and that caused a lot of trouble because people put them on, thinking they would see better or judge more fairly. The evil troll laughed until his sides split, and that really tickled him in a delightful way. But outside, tiny bits of glass were still flying around through the air. Now let's hear what happened next![6]

SECOND STORY: A LITTLE BOY AND A LITTLE GIRL

In the big city,[7] where there are so many houses and people that you rarely have enough room for a little garden and usually have to settle for a flowerpot, there once lived two poor children, whose garden was just a tiny bit larger than a flowerpot. They were not brother and sister, but they were as fond of each other as if they had been. Their parents lived right next to each other in the garrets of two adjoining houses. A rain gutter ran between the two houses,[8] and there was a little window on each side, right near where the two roofs met. To get from one window to the other, all you had to do was leap across the gutter.

Outside the two windows, each family had a large wooden flowerbox, with room for herbs but also for a little rosebush.[9] There was one rosebush in each of the flowerboxes, and both were flourishing. One day the parents had the idea of putting

KAY NIELSEN

A fragment from the devil's mirror lodges in a heart, turning it to ice. The crystalline forms above the heart contrast with the rounded shapes of the clouds in the sky and forms on earth. The chilling effect of the icy heart can be seen in the wilted flower.

a distressed girl if it doesn't have to go far out of its way to do so" (Sale, 71).

6. *Now let's hear what happened next!* The colloquial tone enters once again to introduce the main story and to refocus the attention of the audience, which has been distracted by the back story about the devil and his mirror. The mythological/biblical background takes advantage of comic anaphora, that is, the repeated use of parallel phrases ("A little splinter from the mirror landed in the hearts of some people," "The shards were so large at times," "Other pieces were turned into eyeglasses") that culminate in the grotesque image of the devil laughing until his sides split and thereby becoming the very embodiment of self-division. In an oral storytelling situation, the use of repetition would provide the opportunity for poetic improvisation and audience engagement, although it would also have the effect of distracting from the main contours of the plot.

7. *In the big city.* The urban landscape is introduced as a crowded, dense space, filled with houses and people, but lacking space for the organic growth found in gardens. The window boxes represent an effort to reclaim natural beauty in improbable city spaces and to create an appealing site that invites imitation by the two children, who play "happily" under the roses. The tale begins with a "cosmic prologue staging the opposition between God and the Devil," then shifts to "a small idyllic ambience created by poor bourgeois parents in order to preserve benign nature within an urban milieu" (Johansen 2002, 37). In the story "The Drop of Water," Andersen satirized the cruelties of life in the big city. No doubt he had Copenhagen in mind, a place that contrasted sharply with his native Odense, and for his entire life he had a powerful love/hate relationship with the city and its inhabitants.

8. *A rain gutter ran between the two houses.* The gutter creates a bridge and introduces the importance of connection early on in the story. As an architectural device that channels a vital natural substance coming down from the heavens, it has an important symbolic significance, particularly since the notion of fluidity and mobility will come to be opposed to rigidity and stasis.

9. *a little rosebush.* Roses were first grown about 5,000 years ago in the ancient gardens of Asia and Africa. They are among the oldest cultivated flowers and grew in the mythical gardens of Semiramis, queen of Assyria, and Midas, King of Phrygia. In every mythological system, the rose has become the emblem of beauty and love, but not without complications, for it is well known that roses do not bloom for long, that they are vulnerable to insects, blight, and wind, and that they grow on a plant that bears thorns. In Greek mythology, Aphrodite, goddess of love, is said to have created the rose by mixing her tears with the blood of her lover Adonis. Roman antiquity turned the rose into a symbol of love and beauty affiliated with Venus. For early Christians, the strong pagan associations with the rose produced resistance to exploiting its iconic power, but it was eventually declared to be a symbol of the blood of the martyrs and came to be associated with the

ARTHUR RACKHAM

Kai and Gerda enjoy their rooftop meeting place, which represents an island of greenery in an urban setting. Gerda is shown here with a book, even though it is she who will liberate Kai from the icy spell of Reason.

the boxes across the rain gutter so that they nearly reached from one window to the next. It was like having two walls of flowers, with pea-vines dangling down from the boxes and the roses sending out long tendrils that wound around the windows and then reached over toward each other, very nearly forming a triumphal arch made of greenery and flowers. The boxes were up very high, and the children knew that they were not allowed to climb out to them, but they could put their little footstools out on the roof beneath the roses, and there they played happily together.

During the winter months, though, the fun was over. The windows were often completely frosted over, but the children would heat copper pennies on the stove, press them against the frozen windowpane, and make the best peepholes you can imagine,[10] perfectly round. Behind each peephole you could see a friendly eye, one peering out from each window—the little boy and the little girl. His name was Kai and hers was Gerda.[11] In the summer they could reach each other with a single leap, but in the winter they had to run all the way downstairs, then all the way upstairs, with snow swirling outside.

"The white bees are swarming out there," Grandmother said.[12]

"Do they also have a queen bee?" asked the little boy, for he knew that real bees had one.

"Yes, they do!" Grandmother replied. "And she hovers in the thick of the swarm! She's bigger than the others, and she never lands on the ground but flies straight up into the black clouds. On many a winter night, she flies through the streets of the city and peers in through the windows. Then the glass mysteriously freezes over, as if covered with flowers."

"Yes, I've seen that!" both children said at the same time, and they knew that it was true.

"Is the Snow Queen able to come into houses?"[13] the little girl asked.

Virgin Mary (like Christ, she is the Mystic Rose that is sometimes a white rose or a rose without thorns). Because of the earlier associations with Venus, Bacchus, and other classical deities, the rose was displaced by the lily as the Virgin's floral symbol. In Dante's *Divine Comedy*, the rose becomes a symbol of Christ, who is described as "the Rose in which the Word became incarnate" (*Paradiso* 23, 73). The beauty of the rose has long been linked with the beauty of song, primarily through the association between nightingale and rose, which was said to have received its color from the blood of the nightingale.

10. *the best peepholes you can imagine.* The copper coins that create spy-holes on the frozen windowpanes are a reminder that heat and warmth have the power to defeat cold and frost. Note also the contrast that follows between summer and winter, with the one season associated with the empowering freedom of a single leap and the other marked by hurdles in the form of "lots of steps." Sight and visual pleasure are emphasized throughout the story, and the theme of vision is introduced early on through the peepholes.

11. *Gerda.* Edvard Collin, the son of Andersen's benefactor Jonas Collin, had a daughter named Gerda, who died at the age of four. In a letter to Henriette Collin, Andersen wrote: "Yesterday, when I left Kalundborg on the steamship *Gerda*, I thought about Kai and Gerda, and about the child after whom the fairy tale's Gerda was named."

12. *"The white bees are swarming out there," Grandmother said.* It is not clear whether "Grandmother" is related to Kai or to Gerda. That the parents of the two children are mentioned only in connection with the window boxes and never clearly differentiated leads to a sense of kinship

EDMUND DULAC

The diaphanous figure of the Snow Queen floats above the rooftops, barely visible, yet covering them with the ice and snow that are her element. The warm glow of the interior lights mingles with the sparkling ice scattered by her over the houses. The church in the background, with its rose window, towers behind her.

"Just let her try!" the little boy said. "I'll put her on the hot stove and melt her."

Grandmother just stroked his head and kept on telling stories.

That evening, when little Kai was back home and half undressed, he climbed up on the chair by the window and looked through the little peephole. A few snowflakes were still falling outside, and one of them—the largest of all—landed on the edge of one of the flowerboxes. The snowflake grew and grew until suddenly it turned into a woman[14] wearing a dress made of white gossamer so fine and sheer that it looked like millions of sparkling snowflakes. She was both beautiful and elegant but made of ice, dazzling, sparkling ice. And yet she was alive. Her eyes glittered like two bright stars, but there was nothing peaceful or calm about them. She nodded toward the window and beckoned with her hand. The little boy was so startled that he jumped down from the chair. Just then it seemed as if a huge bird was flying past the window.[15]

The next day was clear and cold, but then everything began to melt, and suddenly spring had arrived. The sun was shining; green shoots sprouted from the ground; swallows were building their nests; windows were opened wide; and once again the two children were sitting in their little garden high up on the roof above all the other houses.

The rose blossoms were unusually beautiful that summer. The little girl had learned a hymn with a verse about roses, and its words made her think about her own flowers. She sang it for the little boy, and he joined in:

> "Down in the valley,[16] where roses grow wild,
> There we can speak with our dear Christ child!"

The children held hands, kissed the roses, and looked up at God's clear sunshine,[17] speaking to it as if the Christ Child

between Kai and Gerda, one reinforced by the fact that the only woman present at home seems to be grandmother to both.

13. *"Is the Snow Queen able to come into houses?"* The contrasts between heat and cold, summer and winter, sun and moon, flora and frost, city and garden are expanded here to include inside and outside. The Snow Queen can thrive only out-of-doors, and for that reason, warm interior spaces provide a safe zone for humans.

14. *it turned into a woman.* In *The Fairy Tale of My Life*, Andersen describes being haunted by the image of a snow maiden who is an agent of death: "I recollected that, in the winter before, when our window-panes were frozen, my father pointed to them and showed us a figure like that of a maiden with outstretched arms. 'She is come to fetch me,' he said in jest. And now, while he was lying there on the bed, dead, my mother remembered this, and I thought about it as well" (14). Andersen's mother had also referred to the ice maiden as the figure who had carried her husband to his death. Sixteen years after writing "The Snow Queen," Andersen published a story called "The Ice Maiden," which tells of a supernatural creature who inhabits Swiss lakes and glaciers and kisses people to death. As in "The Snow Queen," death is linked with seductive beauty and erotic desire.

15. *Just then it seemed as if a huge bird was flying past the window.* It is not clear whether the presence of the bird offers a rational explanation for Kai's vision of the Snow Queen or whether the bird foreshadows Kai's flight with the Snow Queen. In Andersen's world, the boundaries between human and animal sometimes seem as porous as in the pagan world of Ovid, where humans are constantly shifting shape.

16. *Down in the valley.* The verse comes from a popular hymn, still sung in Denmark at Christmas, by H. A. Brorson, called "The Loveliest Rose."

17. *God's clear sunshine.* Sunshine, warmth, clarity, and divine powers are set in opposition to ice, chill, bewilderment, and diabolical forces.

18. *"Ouch! Something just stung my heart! And now there's something in my eye too!"* The effect of the glass splinter is felt at once and leads to a sudden metamorphosis that critics have connected with a compressed form of the physical and mental transformations of growing up. Kai can no longer tolerate childish activities, and his behavior takes a deeply cynical turn. One critic finds that Kai acts "like the typical adolescent"—a boy in crisis who must differentiate himself from women and consolidate his male identity. "The effect of the splinters," Wolfgang Lederer writes, "appears to be that they bring about the onset of a perfectly normal, if disagreeable adolescent phase. To that extent they can hardly be considered detrimental. But we do recall that the splinters are to represent sinfulness; in what manner adolescent withdrawal into intellectuality may be a sin is not at all clear" (Lederer, 27–28). In his autobiography *A Sort of Life* (1971), the novelist Graham Greene famously declared: "There is a splinter of ice in the heart of a writer." He was very likely drawing on Andersen's "Snow Queen" to explain the emotional distance writers establish to real-life sorrows and tragedies.

19. *"That rose over there has been chewed up by a worm!"* Kai cannot see the rose itself, only its flaws, which are magnified by the splinter in his eye. For him, the inorganic, mathematical beauty of the snow "flowers" becomes far more appealing than the flawed beauty of real flowers.

were right there. The summer days were glorious, and it was heavenly to be outdoors near the fragrant rosebushes, which never seemed to stop blooming.

One day Kai and Gerda were looking at a book with pictures of birds and animals when suddenly—just as the clock on the tall church tower was striking five—Kai cried out: "Ouch! Something just stung my heart! And now there's something in my eye too!"[18]

The little girl drew him close to her, and he blinked, but no, she couldn't see a thing.

"I think it's gone," he said, but it was not gone. It was one of those particles of glass from the mirror, the troll's mirror. You remember that terrible mirror, don't you, and how it could turn everything great and good into something small and hideous, while evil and wicked things were enlarged, and any flaw became instantly visible? Poor little Kai! A tiny piece had also lodged itself right in his heart, and soon his heart would turn into a lump of ice. It didn't hurt any longer, but the piece of glass was still there.

"Why are you crying?" Kai asked Gerda. "It makes you look so ugly! There's nothing the matter with me!" Then suddenly he shouted: "Ugh! That rose over there has been chewed up by a worm![19] And look, this one's just plain crooked! If you stop to think about it, these flowers all look just disgusting! They're just like the boxes they grow in!" And with that, he kicked the boxes hard with his foot and broke off two of the roses.

"Kai, what are you doing!" the little girl cried. When he saw her look of horror, he just broke off another rose and ran inside through the window, leaving dear little Gerda all alone.[20]

From then on, whenever Gerda took out her picture book, he would tell her it was only for babies. And whenever Grandmother told stories, he would interrupt with *but.* If he had the chance, he would put a pair of spectacles on his nose, follow her around, and imitate the way she talked. He did such a good job of mocking her that people would burst out laughing. Before long Kai was able to walk and talk exactly like all the people living on that street. He knew how to imitate anything odd or unappealing about a person, and people would say: "That boy must have a good head on his shoulders!" But it was the glass in his eye and the glass in his heart that made him tease even little Gerda, who adored him with all her heart.

Kai's games were now quite different from what they used to be. They had become so very clever. One winter day when snowflakes were swirling around and making drifts, he went outdoors with a large magnifying glass,[21] spread out one side of his blue coat, and let the snowflakes fall on it.

"Look through the glass, Gerda!" he shouted. The snowflakes all appeared much larger and seemed like beautiful flowers or ten-pointed stars. They were lovely to look at.

"Can't you see how fancy they are?" Kai declared. "They're far more interesting to look at than real flowers! They have no flaws at all, and they're absolutely perfect, as long as they don't melt."

A little while later, Kai showed up wearing big gloves, with a sled on his back. He shouted right into Gerda's ear: "I get to go sledding on the main square, where everyone else gets to play!" And off he went.

Over on the square, the boldest boys hitched their sleds to the farmers' wagons and rode along for a while. That was great fun. Right in the middle of the games, a huge sleigh pulled up. It was white all over, and the only person sitting inside it was wrapped in a thick white fur coat and wearing a fleecy white hat. The sleigh drove twice around the square, and Kai quickly fastened his little sled to it and took off. He rode along into the next street, going faster and faster. The driver turned around and gave Kai a friendly nod, as if they knew each other. Each time Kai wanted to unfasten his little sled, the driver

20. *leaving dear little Gerda all alone.* Kai's change in perception is followed by an effort to separate himself from Gerda, then from the grandmother, both of whom represent not just femininity but also the domestic and local. The Snow Queen, by contrast, is an exotic regal presence linked with the power of logic, reason, and calculation. Francis Spufford points out that "The Snow Queen is the inverse of Gerda; her sterility, her intellect, her icy composure, all take their force from being reversals of conventional female qualities. It is mythically apt that her roles as anti-mother and anti-wife should be vested in the lineaments of beauty, all emptied to white: white furs, white hair, white skin" (Spufford, 141). The word "alone" appears here for the first time, introducing the double notion of the solitary nature of Gerda's quest and the solitude of Kai's experience in the realm of the Snow Queen.

21. *with a large magnifying glass.* Mirrors, glass, magnifying glasses, and windowpanes form a symbolic nexus of hard, sometimes transparent substances that seem to heighten understanding and consciousness but in fact also impede it. They will, of course, be connected with the ice, snow, snowflakes, and other crystalline substances of arresting beauty but sinister power.

HARRY CLARKE

The Snow Queen dominates the image, with spikes of color that flow into the white background that is her element. Kai is connected to her visually through the golden road linking him and his sled to the enchantress. His attire is unusually formal for a sleigh ride, but Harry Clarke's compositional style is always less playful than stately.

would nod again and Kai would stay right where he was, even when they drove right through the town gates.

Snow began to fall so thickly that the little boy could not even see his hands when he held them up in front of his face as they sped on. Suddenly he dropped the rope to unhitch himself from the large sleigh, but nothing happened. His little sled was still fastened securely, and it flew along like the wind. Kai shouted as loud as he could, but no one could hear him, and the snow swirled around him, creating drifts, as the sleigh flew forward. Every now and then, it would bounce as if it were clearing ditches and fences. Kai was terrified and tried to say his prayers, but all he could remember were his multiplication tables.[22]

The snowflakes kept growing until they started to look like big white hens. Suddenly they leaped out of the way, and the big sleigh came to a halt. The driver stood up. It was a woman, and her fur coat and cap were made of pure snow. She was tall and slender, brilliantly white. It was the Snow Queen.[23]

"We've arrived safely!" she proclaimed. "But you must be freezing! Come crawl under my bearskin coat." She invited Kai to sit beside her in the sleigh and wrapped the fur coat around him. He felt as if he were sinking into a snowdrift.

"Are you still cold?" she asked and kissed him on the forehead. Brrr! That kiss was colder than ice and went straight to his heart, which was already halfway to becoming a lump of ice. Kai felt as if he were dying, but only for a moment. Then he became quite comfortable and no longer noticed the cold all around him.

"My sled! Don't forget my sled!"—that was the first thing he remembered. It was tied to one of the white chickens, which was flying behind the sleigh with the sled on its back. The Snow Queen kissed Kai again,[24] and in a flash he forgot all about little Gerda, Grandmother, and everyone else back home.

"That's the last kiss you'll get," she said, "or else I might kiss you to death!" Kai looked at her. She was so beautiful.[25]

22. *all he could remember were his multiplication tables.* Kai is drawn into an ice-cold realm of mathematical reasoning that stands in direct opposition to a domestic world of warmth in which prayer and passion perform small miracles.

23. *It was the Snow Queen.* In Norse mythology, Niflheim (Mistland) is the realm of ice and cold and constitutes the resting place for those who have died of old age or illness rather than of wounds from the battlefield. It represents the land of the dead, a frigid Nordic counterpart to the fire and brimstone hell of the church fathers. It is ruled over by Hel, Queen of Death, a figure whose kinship with Mother Holle of German folklore is unmistakable. Mother Holle may be less imposing and seductive, but she too brings the winter season when she shakes her comforter to cover the earth with snow. The Snow Queen has clear connections with these Nordic and Germanic figures of death, although she has none of their redemptive qualities.

24. *The Snow Queen kissed Kai again.* The Snow Queen secures her power over Kai through a kiss, and he begins to feel at home even as he loses the memory of his former home. Like vampires, lamiae, and other supernatural monsters, the Snow Queen uses seductive charms to trap her victims and rob them of their life substance.

25. *She was so beautiful.* The Snow Queen's beauty is connected with mathematical perfection, but her realm of deadly beauty—however exquisite, sublime, and pure—can lead only to destructive solitude and intellectual solipsism. Her connection with the harsh and cold side of what we call Mother Nature, rather than with her more benign, nurturing aspects, is captured concisely in Gilles Deleuze's formulation: "Nature herself is cold, maternal and severe. The Trinity of the masochistic dream is summed up in the words: cold—maternal—severe, icy—sentimental—cruel." Naomi Wood, who has written extensively on children's literature, points out that the Snow Queen figure can be found in the work of many British writers from Charles Kingsley to Philip Pullman: "In these fantasies, the cold mother is beautiful, frequently clad in furs, travels rapidly by flying or in a sled or some combination, and offers the child sublimity, rarefied love, and power. The child accepting her gifts understands their danger, yet that danger takes him or her to another developmental level. Under the cold mother's tutelage, the beloved child explores the far reaches of human potentiality and either dies or is translated into new levels of existence—or both" (Wood, 199).

26. *she soared away with him.* Kai not only has the chance to fly "like the wind" on land behind the Snow Queen's sleigh in his own sled, he also flies through the skies to the dark cloud that is the domain of the Snow Queen. The bleak landscape through which Kai passes contains acoustical allusions to the animals at the command of the Nordic god Odin, whose wolves are named Geri and Freki and whose two ravens, Huginn and Muninn, tellingly, represent Thought and Memory—just what Kai has lost. In this context, it is worth noting that Andersen's home town, Odense, was named after Odin, god of war and wisdom.

27. *"I don't think so!" the sunshine said.* Gerda too will leave home, but her journey takes a very different turn and occurs in the spring rather than in the winter. Instead of succumbing to the lure of the Snow Queen and taking flight to foreign regions, she first engages in dialogue with

He couldn't imagine a wiser, lovelier face. She no longer seemed made of ice, as she had when she first appeared at the window and beckoned to him. In his eyes, she seemed perfect, and he was no longer afraid of her. He told her that he could do numbers in his head—even fractions—and that he knew the square mileage for every country as well as "how many inhabitants." She just kept smiling, and he began to worry that he didn't really know enough. He looked up at the great big sky above, and she soared away with him,[26] high up into the black clouds. The storm whistled and roared, as if it were singing old ballads. They flew over forests and lakes, over sea and land. Beneath them the wind blew cold, wolves howled, and the snow glittered. Black crows screeched above them. But way up high the moon was shining brightly and clearly. Kai fixed his gaze on it all through the long winter's night, and during the day he slept at the feet of the Snow Queen.

THIRD STORY: THE FLOWER GARDEN OF THE WOMAN WHO KNOWS MAGIC

How was little Gerda managing now that Kai was gone? Where could he be? No one knew, and no one could tell her anything. The boys could only report that they had watched him hitch his little sled to a magnificent sleigh that had sped down the street and disappeared through the town gate. No one knew what had become of him. Many tears were shed, and little Gerda cried long and hard. People were sure that he was dead—he must have drowned in the river not far from town. Oh, those were long, gloomy, winter days.

And then spring came, and with it warmer sunshine.

"Kai must be dead and gone!" little Gerda said.

"I don't think so!" the sunshine said.[27]

"He is dead and gone!" she told the swallows.

EDMUND DULAC

Seated on blocks of ice that form a throne, the Snow Queen stares straight ahead with a hypnotic gaze. The perfect symmetry and frozen rigidity of her pose reveal important contrasts to what Gerda will represent in the story.

nature (sunshine and swallows), then sails down the river in search of Kai. The river can be seen as the River of Life but it also has associations with the River Styx, the stream that carried the living to the land of death in Greek and Roman mythology.

28. *"I'll put on my new red shoes."* Andersen's story "The Red Shoes" was written in the very same year that he was working on "The Snow Queen." For Gerda, the shoes are a prized object, "the most precious thing" she owns. Their color has been seen as marking an awakening to sexuality, but the shoes seem to signal vanity more than anything else. Gerda, unlike Karen, is willing to sacrifice the beautiful shoes in order to save Kai. Without shoes, she appears as a defenseless child as she makes her way in the world and the condition of being barefoot, especially in icy regions, is seen as a sign of both vulnerability and vitality. The heroine of "The Little Match Girl" is also barefoot.

29. *There was not a person in sight.* Like the children of fairy tales, Gerda will enter a realm in which nature (flowers, trees, sheep, and cows) plays a dominant role and in which she becomes a child of nature, dependent on its good offices. To be sure, she will encounter human figures, but they are generally recluses who keep company with nature rather than with other human beings. Again and again, Gerda finds herself on her own, required to make decisions without adult supervision and often required to act as an adult around creatures who behave in childish, irresponsible ways.

"We don't think so!" they replied, and soon little Gerda didn't believe it either.

"I'll put on my new red shoes,"[28] she declared one morning, "the ones that Kai has never seen. And then I'll walk down to the river to ask about him!"

Very early the next morning, Gerda kissed her old grandmother, who was still sleeping, put on her red shoes, and went all by herself out the town gate over to the river.

"Is it true that you have taken my playmate? I will give you my red shoes if you bring him back to me!"

She had a feeling that the waves were nodding to her in some odd way. And so she removed the red shoes, the most precious thing she owned, and threw them into the river. The shoes landed right near the shore, and the smaller waves washed them right back to her. It was as if the river could not possibly accept her most precious possession, for it had not taken Kai. Gerda began to worry that she had not tossed the shoes far enough out into the river, and so she climbed into a boat lying in the reeds, hidden from view. From the far end of it, she threw the shoes overboard, but, since the boat had not been moored, her movements were just strong enough to make it glide into the waters. Gerda felt the boat moving and tried to get back ashore. By the time she reached the other end, the boat was already more than two feet away and rapidly gaining speed.

Little Gerda was so terrified that she began to cry, but no one could hear her except the sparrows, and they couldn't possibly bring her back to the shore. They flew along the riverbank and tried to comfort her with their song: "Here we are! Here we are!" The boat was carried downstream by the current, and little Gerda sat quite still in her stocking feet. Her little red shoes floated along behind her, but they could not catch up with the boat, which was picking up speed.

The two sides of the river were beautiful, with lovely flowers, majestic trees, and cows and sheep grazing on steep slopes. There was not a person in sight.[29]

"Maybe the river will carry me to little Kai," Gerda thought and right away she was in better spirits. She stood up and gazed for hours at the beautiful green riverbanks. After a while, the boat drew near to a big cherry orchard, where you could see a little house with strange red and blue windows and a thatched roof. Two wooden soldiers were posted outside it, and they presented arms to everyone who sailed by.

Thinking that they were alive, Gerda shouted to them, but of course they didn't respond. She drifted quite close to them, for the current was pushing the boat right near the shore.

Gerda shouted even louder, and then a really old woman walked out of the house.[30] She was leaning on the crook of her cane and on her head she wore a huge sun hat with the loveliest flowers painted on it.

"You poor little child!" the old woman exclaimed. "How did you ever end up on this big, swift river, drifting so far out into the wide world?" The old woman waded right out into the water, caught hold of the boat with the crook of her cane, pulled it to shore, and lifted little Gerda out.

Gerda was very happy to be back on dry land, but she felt a little afraid of the strange old woman.

"Come, tell me who you are and how you found your way here!" the woman said.

Gerda told her about everything that had happened, and the old woman shook her head, saying nothing but "Hmm! Hmm!" When Gerda finished her story and asked if the old woman had seen little Kai, the woman reported that he had not yet appeared but that he probably would, sooner or later. She told Gerda to cheer up and invited her to come in and eat some cherries and take a look at her flowers, which were far more beautiful than any you can find in picture books. Each one had a story to tell. She then took Gerda's hand and walked with her into the house, locking the door once they were inside.

The windows were high up on the walls, and sunlight

30. *a really old woman walked out of the house.* The old woman, with her cane and her curious house, calls to mind the witch in "Hansel and Gretel," a story recorded by the Brothers Grimm in 1812. But it soon becomes apparent that she has a deeper mythological significance than the witch in that tale. Her garden, which contains every flower imaginable, suggests that she is, like the Greek goddess Demeter, the patron deity of agriculture and a goddess of fertility. A Mother Earth figure, her realm is not only that of vegetation and organic growth but also death and decay. As a woman who knows magic, she cultivates organic flowers, just as the Snow Queen is able to create crystalline flowers. Like the Snow Queen, the old woman also has the capacity to induce amnesia, leading Gerda to neglect her mission and dwell in a land of beauty. As she combs Gerda's golden locks, the girl begins to forget Kai and to live for the sheer pleasure of the moment. The old woman seems more interested in companionship than control, and, unlike the Snow Queen, she is more maternal than magnetic.

EDMUND DULAC

Gerda arrives in her boat (note that there are no oars) at the house of the woman who knows magic. The crone wears a hat covered with sunflowers and clothing with oval patterns. Her home is guarded by wooden soldiers, and her garden is filled with blossoms.

shone through their red, blue, and yellow panes in a strange mix of colors. On the table Gerda found a bowl with the most delicious cherries imaginable, and she ate her fill, for she was no longer afraid. While she was eating, the old woman combed her hair with a golden comb. Gerda's hair fell in shiny gold ringlets on either side of her cheerful little face, which looked like a round rose in bloom.

"I've often wished for a sweet little girl like you," the old woman told her. "Just wait and see—we're going to get along very well!" The old woman combed Gerda's hair, and the longer she combed, the less Gerda could remember about Kai, who was like a brother to her. The old woman knew magic. She wasn't a wicked witch—she just dabbled in magic to amuse herself, and she was determined to keep little Gerda around. She went down to the garden, pointed her cane at all the rosebushes, and even the ones with lovely blossoms sank down into the black earth, without leaving a trace behind them. The old woman was worried that if Gerda saw the roses, she would think about her own, remember little Kai, and run away.

The old woman showed Gerda the flower garden. How fragrant and lovely it was there! Every flower you could imagine from every season stood there in full bloom. No picture book could have been more colorful and beautiful. Gerda jumped for joy and played in the garden until the sun sank behind the tall cherry trees. Then the old woman tucked her into a lovely bed with red silk comforters filled with blue violets. There she slept, and she had dreams as lovely as those of a queen on her wedding day.

HARRY CLARKE

"How did you manage to come on the great rolling river" reads the caption, which shows Gerda arriving at the hut of the woman who knows magic. Wooden soldiers guard the modest abode with its stylized, formal gardens. Gerda is dwarfed by her surroundings and looks at the woman with some trepidation.

31. *Gerda played in the warm sunshine among the flowers.* In the realm of the woman who knows magic, Gerda lives in a place filled with aesthetic pleasures and delights: "No picture book could have been more colorful or beautiful." The old woman provides nourishment and shelter—the most delicious cherries and the loveliest bedding. Superlatives are attached to all objects and vibrant colors are seen everywhere. Yet what is "most beautiful" is missing. The flower painted on the old woman's hat—the representation of natural beauty through art—reminds Gerda of her task and she leaves with renewed determination to find Kai and to bring him back home.

32. *What did the* tiger lily *have to say?* The flowers respond to Gerda's question about Kai with stories about the all-consuming and self-immolating power of love. As symbols of self-absorption, each tells a tale that indulges in melodramatic action. The tiger lily's story about the Hindu custom of *suttee*, the burning of widows on the funeral pyres of their husbands, seems at first to illustrate the powerful sacrifices made in the name of love and the redemptive power of true passion, but in fact it turns on a variety of issues ranging from coerced marriages and infidelity to star-crossed lovers and secret ardor. The language of nature speaks in vividly expressive terms, but it does not always impart wisdom.

The next morning, and for many days after that, Gerda played in the warm sunshine among the flowers.[31] She knew the name of every single flower, but no matter how many she recognized, she was sure that one was missing, although she could not figure out which one. Then one day she was sitting and looking at the old woman's sunhat with the painted flowers. The most beautiful flower on it was a rose. The old woman had forgotten the rose on her hat when she made the real roses disappear into the earth. But that's just what happens if you don't have your wits about you!

"Why are there no roses here?" Gerda asked. She ran around all the flower beds, searching high and low, but there was not a rose in sight. Then she sat down and burst into tears. Her hot tears hit the very spot where a rosebush had disappeared, and when Gerda's warm tears moistened the earth, the rosebush suddenly shot up. It was in full bloom, just like on the day it had disappeared. Gerda put her arms around the bush, kissed the blossoms, and remembered all the lovely roses back home. That made her think about Kai.

"Oh no, I've been here far too long!" the little girl exclaimed. "I should have been looking for Kai."

"Do you know where he is?" she asked the roses. "Can it be that he is dead and gone?"

"No, he's not dead," the roses said. "We have spent time under the ground with all the dead people, and Kai was nowhere in sight!"

"Thank you so much!" Gerda said to them. She went to the other flowers, looked into their blossoms, and asked: "Can you tell me where Kai is?"

All the flowers were standing in the sunlight, dreaming up their own fairy tales and fables. Little Gerda listened to one after another, but not one of the flowers knew anything about where Kai was.

What did the *tiger lily* have to say?[32]

"Can you hear the drum? *Boom! Boom!* It has only those two

sounds, *Boom! Boom!* Listen to the mournful song of the women! Hear the cries of the priest! The Hindu woman stands in her long red robes on the funeral pyre. Flames leap up around her and the body of her husband. But the Hindu woman has thoughts only for the living man in the circle, he whose eyes burn hotter than flames and whose fiery glances have touched her heart more powerfully than the flames that will soon consume her body. Can the fire burning in the heart die in the flames of the pyre?"

"I don't understand that at all!" little Gerda said.

"It's my tale!" the tiger lily replied.

What does the *morning glory* have to say?[33]

"An ancient castle rises high above a narrow mountain path. Thick ivy grows across old red walls, leaf upon leaf, up to the balcony, where a lovely maiden is waiting. She leans over the railing to gaze down at the path. A rose still on its branch does not look as fresh as she does; an apple blossom floating in the breeze is not lighter than she is. Hear the rustling of her magnificent silken gown! 'Will he never come?' "

"Do you mean Kai?" little Gerda asked.

"I am only telling you my tale, my dream," the morning glory answered.

What does the little *daisy* have to say?[34]

"A long board is hanging from ropes between the trees—it's a swing. Two sweet little girls, wearing dresses white as snow and hats with long green silk ribbons fluttering in the breeze, are swinging back and forth. Their brother, who is older, is standing on the swing with his arm hooked around the rope to keep his balance because in one hand he has a little bowl and in the other a clay pipe. He's blowing soap bubbles. The swing goes back and forth and the bubbles, always changing color, float into the distance. The last bubble is still clinging to the bowl of his pipe, and fluttering in the air as the swing moves back and forth. A little black dog, as light

33. *What does the* morning glory *have to say?* The beautiful girl on the balcony recalls Rapunzel in the tower, waiting for the prince to arrive. Romantic longing is represented in the image of the languishing girl, whose story is told by a flower that blooms in the morning and fades by afternoon, thus representing transience. The blend of patience and edginess communicated by the girl on the balcony represents the mixed emotions stirring in Gerda as she *searches* for Kai rather than patiently waiting for his return.

34. *What does the little* daisy *have to say?* The daisy, symbol of purity, sings about the beauty of childhood innocence. The two girls, dressed like daisies with their white dresses and green silk ribbons, swing back and forth, enjoying the sheer delight of freedom and flight. The boy with his pipe produces bubbles that reflect the beauty of the scene but that periodically burst as a reminder of the evanescence of youth, beauty, innocence, and all earthly things. The image of the beautiful, colorful bubble reflecting the girls swinging highlights the importance of aesthetics in Andersen's fairy tales.

35. *"What do the* hyacinths *have to say?"* The hyacinth, said to have sprung from the blood of the beautiful youth Hyacinthus, is linked with death. The three beautiful sisters enter the woods as dancers and return from the woods in the moonlight in coffins, suggesting the perils of the journeys undertaken by Gerda and Kai. The colors of the dresses—red, blue, and white—when mixed, produce the purple of the hyacinth. As in "The Little Mermaid," color is used repeatedly to supply ignition power that will kindle the imagination of readers, inspiring them to visualize the scene.

36. *What kind of song could the* buttercup *sing?* The song of the buttercup sounds a cheerful note at last, with its description of warm, golden sunshine and the gold of kisses, hearts, eyes, and sunrises. The sunshine shimmering down the wall produces another sparkling surface, much like the mirrors, ice, glass, or the "glassy lake" of the previous song. Andersen relies on these shimmering surfaces to create dazzling aesthetic effects.

as the bubbles, gets on his hind legs and tries to climb up on the swing, which flies in the other direction. The dog loses his balance and begins barking angrily. The children laugh, and the bubble bursts. A swinging board reflected in a bursting soap bubble—that's my song."

"What you're telling me may be beautiful, but you tell it so sadly, and you haven't said a word about Kai. What do the *hyacinths* have to say?"[35]

"There once lived three lovely sisters, pale and delicate. One wore a red dress, the other a blue dress, and the third sister's dress was white. They danced hand in hand in the clear moonlight right near a glassy lake. They were not elfin folk. They were human children. The air was so sweet that the girls vanished into the forest. The scent grew stronger. Three coffins came gliding out of the woods across the lake, and the girls were lying in them. Fireflies hovered about them like small, flickering lights. Are the dancing girls asleep or are they dead? The fragrance of the flowers reveals that they are corpses and the evening bell tolls for the dead."

"You are making me feel so sad," Gerda said. "You have such a strong scent that I can't help but think of the dead girls! Is Kai really dead? The roses have looked beneath the earth, and they say no!"

"Ding, dong," sounded the hyacinth bells. "We aren't ringing for Kai—we don't even know who he is! We are just singing our song. It's the only one we know!"

Gerda went over to the buttercup, which shone brightly from among its gleaming green leaves.

"You are just like a radiant little sun," said Gerda. "Tell me, do you have any idea where I can find my playmate?"

The buttercup was shining beautifully when it looked at Gerda again. What kind of song could the *buttercup* sing?[36] It was not about Kai either.

"God's warm sun was shining onto a small courtyard on the very first day of spring. Its rays shimmered down the white wall of a house next door, near the first yellow flowers of spring gleaming like gold in the warm sunshine. Grandmother was sitting outside in her chair when her granddaughter, a poor but pretty servant girl, arrived home for a short visit. She kissed her grandmother and there was gold, a heart full of gold, in that blessed kiss. There was gold on her lips, gold in the ground where it lies, and gold in the sky when the sun rises. There—now you have my little story!" the buttercup said.

"Oh, my poor old grandmother," Gerda sighed. "I'm sure that she's missing me, and she is grieving for me just as much as she did for little Kai. But I'll be home again soon, and I'll bring Kai back with me. It's no use asking the flowers for help. They just sing their own songs, and they haven't been able to tell me anything." She gathered up her skirt so that she would be able to run faster, but the narcissus smacked her leg when she jumped over it. She stopped to look at the tall yellow flower and asked: "Do you know anything?" She bent down to listen to the *narcissus*.[37] What did it have to say?

"I can see myself! I can see myself!" the narcissus said. "And my scent is so fragrant! Up in a small attic room, a little dancer is standing up—she's half-dressed. First she gets up on one foot, then on both, and finally she kicks her heels at the whole world. But she's just an illusion. She pours water from a teapot over a piece of clothing in her hand—it's her corset. Cleanliness is a good thing! Her white dress is hanging from a hook. It was washed in her teapot and hung on the roof to dry. She puts it on and ties a scarf of saffron yellow around her neck. The dress looks more radiant than ever. Lift your leg high in the air! See how she balances on that stem! I can see myself! I can see myself!"

"I didn't like that one bit!" Gerda said. "What a story to tell me!" And she ran over to the far edge of the garden.

The gate was fastened, but she jiggled the rusty latch until

37. *She bent down to listen to the* narcissus. The narcissus, a flower linked to self-absorption, grew at the spot where Narcissus pined away looking at his mirror image in the river in Ovid's *Metamorphoses*. Listening to the vain chatter of the narcissus animates Gerda, who may also risk becoming fascinated by her own reveries and turning into a creature seduced into remaining in an earthly paradise where time stands still. The warning is sufficiently strong to propel Gerda into action as she realizes that time has flown by while she has lingered in the paradise of the woman who knows magic. Unlike Karen of "The Red Shoes" and Inger in "The Girl Who Trod on the Loaf," Gerda is not seduced by appearances or enamored of her own image.

38. *her little feet were so tender and sore.* Gerda, like the heroine of the Scandinavian tale "East of the Sun and West of the Moon," who wears out a pair of iron shoes while searching for her beloved, wears herself out in pursuit of one who has gone astray. In sacrificing her shoes to the river, she makes a profound symbolic gesture that strips her not only of vanity but also of protection from the elements. As a traveler, she has a special need for shoes, for without them her mobility is severely restricted.

39. *a big crow came hopping across the snow.* It is not by chance that Gerda meets a crow as soon as she departs from the amnesia-inducing realm of the old woman (recall that Odin's crows are named Thought and Memory). Gerda, who communicated quite easily with swallows and sparrows when she set out on her journey, is now unable to speak a language that her wise grandmother, who is attuned to the forces of nature, speaks fluently.

40. *all alone in the wide world.* Once again, the reader is reminded that Gerda remains isolated as she traverses vast expanses. And yet there is also a sense of adventure, an openness to experience that Andersen sees as the stuff of stories. In his autobiography, he writes about his decision to leave home—"just like the heroes in the many adventure stories I had read to get out—all alone—into the world" (49). Andersen's enterprising nature was fueled by the stories he read as a child: "my imagination for adventure was awakened. I thought of life itself as an adventure and looked forward to appearing in it myself as a hero" (*The Fairy Tale of My Life*, 42). As an adult, he traveled far more frequently than most of his contemporaries, and, although he declined an invitation to travel to the United States (a friend had perished crossing the Atlantic), he eagerly

it gave way, and the gate flew open. Gerda ran barefoot out into the wide world. She looked back three times, but no one was following her. Finally she could go no farther and sat down to rest on a big rock. When she looked up she realized that summer was over, and it was already late in the fall. She would never have known it inside that beautiful garden where the sun was always shining and flowers from every season were always in full bloom. "My goodness! I've wasted so much time!" said little Gerda. "It's already fall. I can't stay around here any longer!" And she got up to leave.

Oh my, her little feet were so tender and sore,[38] and everything around her was so cold and raw. The long leaves of the willow tree had turned completely yellow, and drops of mist were rolling down them as one leaf after another fell to the ground. Only the blackthorn bush still had berries on it, and they were so sour that they made your lips pucker up. How gray and dreary everything looked in the wide world.

FOURTH STORY: THE PRINCE
AND THE PRINCESS

Gerda had to stop and rest, and a big crow came hopping across the snow[39] right near where she was sitting. He stood there for a long time, watching her and cocking his head from time to time. Finally he said: "Caw! Caw! Good caw-dy day!" That was the best he could do. He wanted to be kind to the little girl and asked her what she was doing all alone in the wide world.[40] Gerda understood what he meant by "alone," and she knew the word's meaning firsthand. She told the crow the entire story of her life, and she asked if he had seen Kai.

The crow nodded thoughtfully and replied, "It's possible, entirely possible!"

"What! Have you really seen him?" the little girl cried, and she nearly smothered the crow with kisses.

"Take it easy! Take it easy!" said the crow. "It's possible that

I've seen Kai. But by now he has probably forgotten you because of the princess."

"Is he living with a princess?" Gerda asked.

"Yes, but pay attention!" the crow said. "I have a hard time with your language. If you understood crow speech, it would be much easier to explain!"

"I never learned that language!" Gerda said. "But my grandmother knows it, and she also knows P-speech. I wish I had learned it!"

"Never mind!" said the crow. "I'll tell you all about it, as best I can, but I can't promise that it will be any good." And then he told her what he knew.

"The kingdom in which we are now living is ruled by a princess so uncommonly clever that she has read all the newspapers in the world and then forgotten every word printed in them—that's how clever she is.[41] The other day, when she was sitting on her throne—and that's not nearly as amusing as people think—she started humming an old tune that went like this: 'Why, oh why, should I not marry?'

" 'There's an idea,' she said to herself, and she made up her mind to marry as soon as she could find a husband who would know how to respond when spoken to. She was not interested in someone who would just stand around looking dignified, because that would be really dull. And so she summoned her ladies-in-waiting, and, when they heard what she had in mind, they were delighted. 'Oh, we like that idea!' they said. 'We had the same idea just the other day!' "

"Believe me," the crow said, "every word I report is true. I have a tame sweetheart who has the run of the castle, and she gave me a full report." His sweetheart was, of course, also a crow, for birds of a feather flock together.

The next day's newspapers came out with a border of hearts[42] and the princess's initials right by them. Any attractive young man, it said in the paper, was welcome to visit the castle and speak with the princess. The princess was planning

accepted nearly every other invitation, traveling by carriage, boat, and even (later in the century) on a train. The sense of adventure was balanced by a recognition that travel could also produce solitude. On a trip to the Jura mountains in 1833, Andersen described feeling an overwhelming sense of loneliness as he looked at the strange darkness formed by the mountains and spruce trees. Gerda does not have the linguistic skills of her grandmother, who understands the language of birds and P-speech (academic speech).

41. *"that's how clever she is."* Andersen was a master of what is known as crosswriting, producing texts that are directed at two audiences: children and adults. The satirical barb at newspapers is embedded in a tale for children and adds spice for the adult readers. As Andersen wrote to a friend: "Now I tell stories of my own accord, seize an idea for the adults—and then tell it for the children while still keeping in mind the fact that mother and father are often listening too, and they must have a little something for thought" (Grønbech, 91–92).

42. *border of hearts.* The border of hearts provides an interesting contrast to death notices, which traditionally have black borders. The sentimental touch is not in the style of Gerda, who is less of a romantic.

EDMUND DULAC

The clever princess sits on the throne with crumpled newspapers at her feet—all the newspapers in the world that she has read and forgotten. Like the Snow Queen, she wears clothing that sparkles and glitters.

to marry the man who seemed most at home in the castle and who spoke the most eloquently.[43] "Yes, indeed," the crow said. "Believe me, it's all as true as the fact that I'm sitting here. Young men flocked to the castle, and there was a lot of pushing and shoving, but neither on the first day nor on the second was anyone chosen. No one had trouble speaking well out on the street. The moment the men entered the gates of the castle and caught sight of the royal guards wearing silver and the servants wearing gold and then reached the brightly lit halls at the top of the stairs, they were struck dumb. Facing the princess who was seated on her throne, they couldn't think of a thing to say and just repeated the last word she had uttered, which she did not particularly care to hear again. It was as if everyone in the room had swallowed snuff and dozed off. As soon as they were back outside, they had no trouble talking. People were lined up all the way from the town gates to the castle. I saw them myself!" the crow said. "They were growing hungry and thirsty, but no one from the castle brought so much as a glass of lukewarm water. Some of the more clever fellows had packed bread and cheese,[44] but they refused to share what they had with anyone. Here's what they thought: 'If that fellow looks hungry, then the princess won't choose him!' "

"But what about Kai, little Kai!" Gerda interrupted. "When did he get there? Was he there in the crowd?"

"Patience! Patience! I'm just getting to him! On the third day, a little fellow, with neither horse nor carriage, marched boldly up to the castle. His eyes sparkled like yours do, and he had lovely long hair, but his clothes were in tatters."

"That must have been Kai!" Gerda shouted, and she clapped her hands for joy. "I've found him at last!"

"He was carrying a little bundle on his back," the crow told her.

"No, that must have been his sled," Gerda said. "He had it with him when he left."

43. *the man who seemed most at home in the castle and who spoke the most eloquently.* The princess is making somewhat unusual demands (no other fairy-tale princess seeks these qualities in a man), and Andersen may have invented these traits because they matched so perfectly his own strengths. He was, of course, an expert in making himself at home in the manors and castles of aristocrats and royals, and he prided himself on his eloquence and on the fact that he had provided Denmark with a "poet."

The riddle princess is found in myths and fairy tales the world over. Turandot is perhaps the most famous of these virgins, who execute suitors unable to answer their questions or to carry out assigned tasks. Portia, in *The Merchant of Venice,* is a milder version of the type, dismissing rather than decapitating the unqualified suitors. In his essay "The Theme of the Three Caskets," Freud meditates on the motif and shows how a story about making choices for the sake of love masks an obsession with death. "The Snow Queen" might also be seen as a tale in which romance and passion are deeply enmeshed with anxieties about mortality. Andersen's princess, in the subplot to "The Snow Queen," is more whimsical and eccentric than belligerent and bloodthirsty, but the princess in his story "The Traveling Companion" has a garden in which suitors hang from trees.

44. *"some of the more clever fellows had packed bread and cheese."* Andersen creates comic effects by moving seamlessly from descriptions of courtly fashion (guards dressed in silver and servants in gold) and the protocols and players of royal life (ministers of state, various excellencies, and a princess sitting on a throne) to the buffoon-like behavior of the suitors, who parrot the princess's words and refuse to share their provisions.

45. *"Kai's boots began to creak loudly."* At his confirmation, Andersen prided himself on a new pair of boots: "My delight was extreme; my only fear was that some people would not see them, and therefore I drew them up over my trousers and marched through the church. The boots creaked, and that pleased me no end, for the congregation would know that they were brand new. My sense of piety was disturbed; I was aware of it, and I felt a terrible sense of guilt that my thoughts should be on my new boots as much as they were with God" (*Fairy Tale of My Life*, 22).

46. *"a pearl that was as big as a spinning wheel."* A precious stone with many layers, the pearl seems an odd object to serve as a throne. Its round shape and color could be seen as evoking the moon, and its use as a throne offers a humorous touch. The allusion to a spinning wheel connects the story to the instrument whose use often provided the occasion for oral storytelling and adds a humble touch to the royal throne. Here again, Andersen yokes a precious object with the homespun.

"You could be right," said the crow. "I didn't look all that closely! But I do know from my tame sweetheart that when he marched through the palace gates and saw the royal guards dressed in silver and when he climbed the stairs and saw the servants dressed in gold, he wasn't the least bit daunted. He just nodded to them and said: 'It must be terribly dull to stand on the steps all day long. I think I'd rather go inside.' The halls were brightly lit. Ministers of state and various excellencies were walking about barefoot, carrying golden trays. It was enough to make anyone nervous! Kai's boots began to creak loudly,[45] but he wasn't at all afraid!"

"Then it had to be Kai," said Gerda. "I know that he was wearing new boots. I heard them creak in Grandmother's parlor."

"Oh, they creaked all right!" said the crow, "But he was bold and walked right up to the princess, who was sitting on a pearl that was as big as a spinning wheel.[46] All of the ladies-in-waiting with their servant girls, and the servant girls with their servant girls, and all of the chamberlains, with their servants and their servants' pages, were standing at attention in the hall. The closer they were to the door, the prouder they looked. The page to the servants' servants, who never wears anything but slippers, looked so swollen with pride as he stood at the doorway that you hardly dared look at him."

"That must have been terrible," Gerda said. "And yet Kai still won the princess!"

"If I weren't a crow, I would have won her myself, even though I'm already betrothed to another. They say he spoke as well as I speak (when I use crow speech). That's what my tame sweetheart told me. He was dashing and charming. He wasn't there to court the princess but to listen to her wise words. He liked what he heard, and she took a shine to him too!"

"Then it had to be Kai," Gerda said. "He is so smart that he can do numbers in his head—even fractions! Oh, you must take me to the castle!"

"That's easier said than done," the crow replied. "How will we manage it? I'll talk it over with my tame sweetheart. She can probably give us some advice, but I'd better warn you that a little girl like you will never be allowed to walk right into the castle."

"Yes, I will!" said Gerda. "When Kai realizes that I'm here, he'll come right out to get me!"

"Wait for me over there by the fence!" the crow said, and he bobbed his head and flew away.

The crow did not return until after dark. "Caw! Caw!" he said. "My sweetheart sends you warm greetings, and here's a crust of bread for you. They have all they need in the kitchen, where she found it, and you must be hungry! They'll never let you into the castle, especially with bare feet. The guardsmen in silver and the footmen in gold will simply not allow it. But don't cry, we'll find a way to smuggle you in. My sweetheart happens to know about a little back staircase leading up to the bedroom, and she also knows where they keep the key."

Off the two went into the garden, down the tree-lined promenade where the leaves were falling, one by one. After the lights went out in the castle, one by one, the crow took Gerda around to the back door, which was standing ajar.

Gerda's heart was pounding with fear and longing![47] She felt as if she were about to do something wrong, but all she wanted to do was make sure that Kai was there. Yes, Kai had to be there, she thought, as she recalled his wise eyes and long hair. She had vivid memories of the smile on his face when

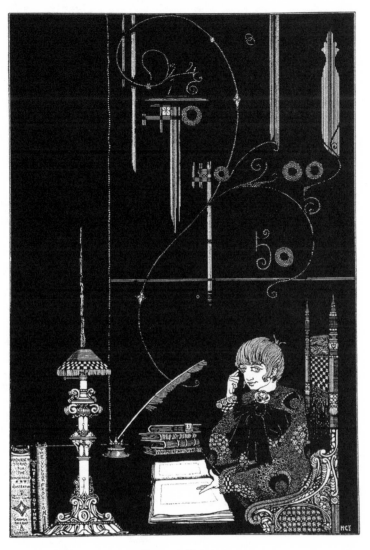

HARRY CLARKE

Kai is seated at a table that contains three volumes with the titles: "Andersen's Stories for the Household, illustrated by Harry Clarke," "The Rule of Three," and "The Vulgar Fraction." Above his head can be seen various numbers in decorative shapes.

47. *Gerda's heart was pounding with fear and longing!* Gerda, unlike her fairy-tale counterparts, possesses a transparent mind, and we learn about her thoughts and emotions throughout her adventures. Her love of Kai keeps her from despair and helps her to overcome her fear of the unknown. In the term "longing," there is one of the few

hints that her love for Kai is more than sisterly. Gerda has a psychological depth absent from fairy-tale figures like Little Red Riding Hood or Cinderella, who are revealed to us solely through their actions. As W. H. Auden put it, "In the folk tale, as in the Greek epic and tragedy, situation and character are hardly separable; a man reveals what he is in what he does, or what happens to him is a revelation of what he is" (Auden, 207).

48. *something rushed past her like shadows on a wall.* Slavic folklore often features mysterious spectral horsemen representing various times of day. The hunting parties that haunt this particular castle are described as creatures from dreams, imaginative beings that can be brought to life in fiction but that rarely inhabit fairy-tale worlds, where few characters have a dream life. Just two years after finishing "The Snow Queen," Andersen wrote "The Shadow," which offers further evidence of his deep fascination with the interplay of light and dark and the chiaroscuro effects produced.

49. *two beds that looked just like lilies.* The chaste relationship between prince and princess becomes evident from the arrangement of the beds. The riddle princess remains locked in a state of virginal purity, unable to move to a condition of mature adult sexuality. Gerda is eager to continue on her journey once she realizes her error. Both couples in "The Snow Queen" are presented as passionately drawn to each other, but without a trace of erotic desire. In real life, Andersen seemed unable to consummate a romantic relationship, and he makes sure that the couples in his fairy tales remain drawn to each other in powerful but chaste ways. Note the striking use of color in this passage and how the attributes used to kindle our imagination and to help us visualize the

they were sitting at home beneath the roses. She was sure that he would be happy to see her. And he would be glad to hear just how far she had traveled to find him and how sad everyone at home had been when he hadn't returned. Gerda was frightened but she also felt lighthearted.

Now they were on the staircase. A little lamp on a cabinet was burning brightly. There stood the tame crow, right in the middle of the room, turning her head every which way as she looked at Gerda, who curtsied just as Grandmother had taught her.

"My fiancé has spoken highly of you, my dear young lady," the tame crow said. "Your life story, your vita, as we say, is also quite moving! Please take the lamp, and I'll lead the way. We'll take the most direct route so that we won't run into anyone!"

"It feels like someone is on the stairs right behind us!" Gerda said, and something rushed past her like shadows on a wall:[48] horses with flowing manes and slender legs, gamekeepers, lords and ladies on horseback.

"Those are nothing but dreams!" the crow said. "They come and take the thoughts of their royal highnesses out hunting, which is good because then you can get a better look at them in their beds. I trust that, when you rise to a position of honor and nobility, you will show heartfelt gratitude!"

"That's no way to talk!" said the crow from the forest.

They entered the first room, which had walls covered with rose-colored satin and painted flowers. The dream shadows rushed by again, but so quickly that Gerda did not have a chance to see the lords and ladies. Each room was more magnificent than the next—almost overwhelming—and then they reached the bedroom. The ceiling in there looked like a huge palm tree, with leaves of glass, priceless glass. In the middle of the room two beds that looked just like lilies[49] were hanging from a massive stalk of gold. One was white, and the princess was sleeping in it. The other one was red, and

Gerda hoped to find Kai in it. She bent back one of the red leaves and saw the nape of a brown neck. Oh, it had to be Kai! She called out his name and held the lamp near his face, and the dreams galloped back into the room. He awoke, turned his head, and—it was not Kai after all.

The prince's neck may have looked like Kai's, but nothing else about him did. Still, he was young and handsome. The princess peeked out from the white lily bed and asked what had happened. Little Gerda started crying. She told them the entire story and described what the crows had done for her.

"You poor dear!" the prince and the princess said. They praised the crows and assured them that they were not at all angry, but that they should never do what they had done again. This time, however, they would receive a reward.

"Would you like your freedom?" the princess asked. "Or would you rather have lifetime appointments as court crows, with the right to scraps from the kitchen floor?"

Both crows bowed deeply and asked to have permanent positions, for they were thinking about the future and how important it was to have something for "our golden years," as they called them.

The prince climbed out of his bed and let Gerda sleep in it. It was all he could do for her. Gerda clasped her little hands together and thought: "How nice people and animals can be." Then she closed her eyes and slept peacefully. All the dreams came flying back in again, and they looked just like God's angels. They were pulling a little sled on which Kai was riding. He nodded in her direction, but it was just a dream, and when Gerda awoke, he had vanished.

The next day Gerda was dressed from head to toe in silk and velvet. She had been invited to stay at the castle and to live there in luxury, but instead she asked for a little carriage, a horse, and a pair of boots. That way she could go back into the wide world and look for Kai.

Gerda was given a pair of boots and also a fur muff.[50] She

scene have more to do with light and color than anything else.

50. *a pair of boots and also a fur muff.* Gerda receives a carriage—one that is linked with sunshine through its gold—but, just as importantly, she has received something to protect her hands and feet. Like the Snow Queen, she now has something made of fur and a magnificent mode of transportation. Her carriage, with its bounty of sugar pastries, fruit, and cookies, represents pure wish-fulfillment for a child. The fetishizing of feet and hands, along with boots and muffs, is intriguing, given the chaste and pious register in which the tale moves.

51. *an old robber hag.* Andersen most likely drew on the Grimms' "Robber Bridegroom," a horrific story derived from Apuleius's *Cupid and Psyche*, to construct Gerda's precarious brush with the bandits. In the Roman story from the second century, a young woman is about to be chopped into pieces by robbers when the crone who makes their supper puts her own life in jeopardy by intervening to protect her. The hag who forms part of the robber band in Andersen's story does not turn out to be an unexpectedly benign protector (like the giant's wife in "Jack and the Beanstalk") but a bloodthirsty fiend who resembles the cannibalistic witch of "Hansel and Gretel." It is never easy to predict whether the women Kai and Gerda encounter will be benefactors or villains.

was dressed exquisitely, and just as she was about to leave, a coach covered in pure gold drew up to the door. The coat of arms belonging to the prince and the princess glittered on it like a star. The driver, the footmen, and the postilions—yes, there were even postilions—were wearing crowns made of gold. The prince and princess themselves helped Gerda climb into the carriage and wished her good luck. The crow from the forest, who was now married, traveled with her for the first three miles. He sat right next to Gerda, for it would have made him ill to ride backward. The other crow stood at the gate and flapped her wings. She could not ride in the carriage because she had been suffering constant headaches from eating too much in her new position. The carriage was lined on the inside with sugar pastries, and on the seats were plates piled high with fruit and gingerbread.

"Farewell! Farewell!" the prince and the princess called out. Gerda was weeping, and the crow was shedding tears as well. The two sobbed for the first couple of miles, then the crow also had to bid her farewell, and that was the hardest separation of all. He flew up into a tree and continued flapping his black wings until the carriage, which was sparkling like bright sunshine, disappeared.

FIFTH STORY:
THE LITTLE ROBBER GIRL

They rode through a dark forest, and Gerda's carriage was like a torch. It shone so brightly that it hurt the robbers' eyes until they could stand it no longer.

"It's gold! It's gold!" they shouted, and they sped forward, seized the horses, and killed the driver, the postilions, and the footmen. They dragged Gerda from the carriage.

"How plump and tender she looks, just as if she'd been fattened up on pecans!" shouted an old robber hag,[51] who sported a long, bristly beard and brows that hung down over

EDMUND DULAC

The brightly lit carriage is an alluring target for the trio of robbers perched on the ledge, along with the two others hidden behind trees. The dark tangle of branches and the size of the menacing robbers make the coach look all the more vulnerable.

HARRY CLARKE

"She is fat—she is pretty—she is fed with nut kernels!" reads the caption to an image that shows Gerda surrounded by robbers who seem dressed more for the stage than for pillaging. Surrounded by open blades, Gerda also has birds above her and flowers at her feet. Her elaborate costume and headdress draw the viewer's attention, as does the gleam of the coach on the horizon.

her eyes. "She'll be as tasty as a fat little lamb! What a dainty dish she will make!" And then she pulled out a shiny knife, which had a dreadful glint to it.

"Ouch!" the old hag suddenly howled. She had been bitten on the ear by her own daughter, who was riding on her back and looked delightfully wild and reckless.

"You nasty little brat!" her mother said, and that kept her from chopping Gerda to pieces.

"I want her to play with me!"[52] the little robber girl said. "She will have to give me her muff and that beautiful dress she's wearing. And she's going to sleep next to me!" She bit down again so hard that the robber hag hopped up and down and spun around. The robbers all started laughing and said, "Look how she's dancing with her little brat."

"I'm going to ride in the carriage," the little robber girl said, and ride she did, because she was so headstrong and spoiled that she always got her way. She and Gerda climbed into the carriage, and the two drove over stumps and brambles, deep into the forest. The little robber girl was no taller than Gerda, but she was stronger, with broad shoulders and dark skin. Her eyes were coal-black, and they had a sad expression. She put her arms around Gerda and said, "I won't let them chop you up into pieces as long as we stay on good terms. You must be a princess."

"No," Gerda said, and she told the robber girl about everything that had happened to her and about how fond she was of Kai.

The robber girl gave her a solemn look, nodded in her direction, and said, "Even if I do get angry with you, I won't let them chop you to pieces because I'd rather do it myself!" Then she dried Gerda's eyes and put both her hands inside the beautiful muff, which was soft and warm.

When the carriage came to a stop, they found themselves in the courtyard of the robbers' castle. It had a long crack that ran from the very top to the bottom. Ravens and crows could

52. *"I want her to play with me!"* The robber girl's insistence on friendship is more terrifying than comforting. Her efforts to befriend Gerda perpetually turn into life-threatening gestures. While Gerda's relationship to Kai remains chaste, even after they mature into adults, her encounter with the robber girl is charged with passionate overtones, erotic and morbid, but also affectionate and playful.

53. *A large cauldron of soup was boiling.* From Shakespeare's *Macbeth* to Goethe's *Faust*, the cauldron functions as a sign of witchery, a vessel of plenty that would seem to nourish life but that may in fact be bubbling with toxic substances.

54. *"Kiss it!" she shouted.* The bandit girl may be the youthful progeny of the old robber woman, but, in her connection with animals, she resembles Artemis or Diana, the "Lady of the Wild Things," a virgin goddess who is also the huntress of the gods. Diana roved the hills with her maidens and hunting dogs, and any man who approached her risked being torn to bits. The little robber girl, alternately compassionate and sadistic, threatens to chop Gerda into pieces and takes some rather appalling liberties with her. Her intimacies are aggressively sensual—she heats her hands in Gerda's "beautiful muff," which is soft and warm. Her aggressive moves are charged with sexual overtones—she threatens to poke Gerda in the stomach with her knife if she does not lie still in bed.

be seen flying in and out of the holes in its walls, and bulldogs—so large that they looked as if they could devour a person in one bite—were leaping high up into the air. But the dogs did not bark at all, for that was forbidden.

A big fire was burning on the stone floor in the middle of a cavernous, soot-stained room. Smoke drifted up to the rafters and tried to find a way out. A large cauldron of soup was boiling,[53] and rabbits and hares were roasting on spits.

"Tonight you will sleep here with me and with all my little animals," the robber girl said. They ate and drank, and then went over to a corner strewn with straw and blankets. Above their heads, nearly a hundred doves were roosting on pegs and rafters. They appeared to be asleep, but they stirred just a bit when the little girls approached. "They are all mine!" the little robber girl said as she grabbed hold of the one nearest to her, holding it by the legs and shaking it until it flapped its wings. "Kiss it!" she shouted,[54] and the bird fluttered in Gerda's face.

"That's where I keep the wild pigeons," she continued, pointing to an opening high up in the wall with bars over it. "They're wood pigeons, those two, and they'd fly away in a minute if I didn't make sure to lock them up. And here is my dear old Baa," she said, tugging on the antlers of a reindeer who was tethered by a shiny copper ring around its neck. "We have to keep an eye on him too, or else he'll run away from us. Every night I tickle his neck with my knife blade. He's so terrified of it!" The robber girl pulled a long knife out of a crack in the wall and let it slide along the reindeer's throat. The poor animal kicked his legs, but the robber girl just laughed and dragged Gerda into bed.

"Are you going to keep the knife while you're sleeping?" Gerda asked, eyeing it nervously.

"I always sleep with this knife!" the little robber girl said. "You never know what might happen. But tell me again what you told me before about Kai and why you ventured out into the wide world."

Gerda told the story all over again from the beginning, and the wood doves cooed in their cage overhead, while the tame doves slept. The little robber girl clasped Gerda's neck with one arm, gripped her knife with her other hand, and fell asleep, snoring loudly. But Gerda did not dare close her eyes, since she had no idea whether she was going to live or die. The robbers sat around the fire, singing and drinking, and the old robber hag was turning somersaults. Oh, it was a terrible sight for a little girl to see.

All at once the wood doves said, "Coo, coo! We've seen little Kai. A white hen was pulling his sled, and he was seated in the Snow Queen's sleigh as it raced over the tops of the trees where we build our nests. The Snow Queen's icy breath killed all the baby pigeons except for the two of us, who managed to survive, coo, coo!"

"What's that you're talking about up there?" little Gerda asked. "Where was the Snow Queen going? Do you have any idea at all?"

"She was probably bound for Lapland,[55] where there is always snow and ice. Why don't you ask the reindeer tied up over there?"

"Yes, there is plenty of ice and snow there. It's a place of bliss and goodness!" the reindeer said. "You can prance around freely across those great glittering plains. The Snow Queen sets her summer tent up there, but her permanent residence is in a castle closer to the North Pole, on an island called Spitsbergen!"[56]

"Oh, Kai, poor Kai," Gerda sighed.

"Just lie still and be quiet," the little robber girl said, "or else I'll poke you in the stomach with my knife!"

In the morning Gerda told her everything that the wood doves had said, and the little robber girl looked thoughtful,

55. *"bound for Lapland."* Also known as Sápmi, Lapland is a region inhabited by the Sami people. It includes the northern regions of Scandinavia, Finland, and the Kola peninsula in Russia.

56. *"Spitsbergen!"* The largest island in the Svalbard archipelago, Spitsbergen is located in the Arctic Ocean and administered by Norway. The name means "jagged peaks," and the island is situated so far north that the sun disappears for four months in the winter.

57. *"my own dear, sweet goat!"* The Norse god Thor is said to have driven a chariot pulled by two powerful goats, who symbolize thunder and lightning. Goats figure prominently in Christian orthodoxy as satanic creatures who serve as familiars to witches, transporting them to the witches' Sabbath, over which a goatlike devil presides.

nodded her head, and said, "Never mind! Never mind!" Then she turned to the reindeer and asked: "Do you know where Lapland is?"

"Who would know better than I?" the reindeer replied, and his eyes sparkled. "I was born and bred there, and it was there that I played in fields of snow."

"Listen carefully!" the little robber girl said to Gerda. "You can see that all of the men are gone now, but Mother is still here, and she's not leaving. Later this morning she'll take a swig from that big bottle over there, and then she'll lie down for a little nap upstairs. That's when I'll be able to help you out." She jumped out of bed, threw her arms around her mother's neck, pulled on her beard, and said, "Good morning, my own dear, sweet goat!"[57] Her mother pinched her nose until it turned red and blue, but it was all done out of affection.

As soon as the mother had taken a swig from the bottle and was settling down for a nap, the little robber girl went over to the reindeer and said: "I'm itching to tickle you many more times with my sharp blade, because it's so much fun. But never mind, I'm going to untie your rope and take you outdoors so that you can get back to Lapland. But be quick and take this little girl to the Snow Queen's palace, where she'll be able to find her playmate. I'm sure you heard her entire story, for she was talking rather loudly and you were probably eavesdropping, as you always do."

The reindeer leaped for joy. The little robber girl lifted Gerda up on his back, took care to strap her in, and even gave her a little cushion to sit on. "And while we're at it," she said, "you can have your fur boots back, for it is going to be cold. I'll hold on to your muff, because it is just too pretty to part with, but, don't worry, you won't freeze. You can have my mother's big mittens—they'll reach all the way up to your elbows. There, put them on! Now your hands look just like my hideous mother's paws."

Gerda wept for joy.

"I don't like to see you blubbering," the little robber girl said. "You ought to be pleased! Here are two loaves of bread and a ham so that you won't go hungry." After tying both bundles to the reindeer's back, the little robber girl opened the door, called all the big dogs indoors, cut the rope with her knife, and said to the reindeer, "Run as fast as you can! But take good care of that little girl!"

Gerda stretched out her hands with those big mittens on them to the little robber girl and said good-bye. The reindeer bounded off, over bushes and brambles, through the great forest, across swamps and plains, as fast as he could run. The wolves howled, and the ravens shrieked. The sky seemed to say, "Kerchoo! Kerchoo!" as if it were sneezing red streaks of light.

"Those are my old Northern lights,"[58] the reindeer said. "See how brilliantly they are glowing!" And on he ran, faster than ever, all day and night. The loaves of bread had been eaten and the ham was gone too, but by then they were already in Lapland.

SIXTH STORY: THE LAPP WOMAN AND THE FINN WOMAN

They stopped in front of a small house. It was a wretched hovel.[59] The roof was almost touching the ground, and the doorway was so low that the family living there had to crawl on their bellies to go in or out. No one was at home except for an old Lapp woman, who was frying fish over a whale-oil lamp. The reindeer reported Gerda's entire history, but he told his own first, since he believed it was far more important. Gerda was so frozen to the bone that she couldn't even open her mouth.

"Oh, you poor creatures," the Lapp woman said. "And you still have a long way to go! It's another hundred miles at least

58. *"Northern lights."* The common name for *aurora borealis*, the Northern lights are like silent fireworks that can be seen on clear winter nights in regions near the earth's magnetic pole. The bands and streamers of colored light appear in their most spectacular form in Finnish Lapland, where the number of auroral displays can be as high as two hundred per year. The Finnish term *revontulet* for the Northern lights means "fox fires," referring to fables about arctic foxes creating the celestial spectacle by brushing their tales against the snow. As always, Andersen uses light effects to inspire the characters but also to ignite the imagination of the reader.

59. *a wretched hovel.* This new abode has been seen as a womblike dwelling. Both the Lapp woman and the Finn woman can be seen as "wise women," friendly witches who, however eccentric or macabre they may appear, provide Gerda with vital information and assistance in her travels.

60. *"Finnmark."* Finnmark forms the northernmost part of the Scandinavian peninsula. It borders on the Arctic Ocean to the north and on Finland to the south. It is the largest county of Norway, but also has the smallest population.

61. *"dried codfish."* The codfish is often dried in order to preserve it. When left to stiffen, it is as flat as a sheet of paper and can be used as a writing tablet. For a deeper understanding of the fish and its significance, particularly for Scandinavian countries, see Mark Kurlansky's *Cod: A Biography of the Fish That Changed the World.*

62. *"you can tie all the winds of the world together."* The Lapp woman, like the witches, enchantresses, and wise women of fairy tales, seems to have a special command over the forces of nature. The four winds in Andersen's story represent varying degrees of strength, but in many myths, they represent different colors. The Apache people, for example, have black, blue, yellow, and white winds. In "East of the Sun and West of the Moon," the four winds act in concert with each other as a relay team for the heroine. Gerda, like the heroine of that tale, embarks on an arduous journey to release a young man from a magical spell. Knots are often used to work magic and are seen as storing energy that can be released for a specific purpose.

to Finnmark,[60] where the Snow Queen is taking her country vacation. Every single night she sets off her blue fireworks. I don't have any paper, but I'll write a few words down on a dried codfish[61] and you can give it to the Finn woman up there. She knows more about all of this than I do!"

After Gerda warmed up and had something to eat and drink, the Lapp woman wrote a few words down on the dried codfish, gave it to Gerda for safekeeping, and strapped her back onto the reindeer. Off Baa ran, and all night long you could hear "Whoosh! Whoosh!"—and the lovely blue Northern lights were flashing overhead. At last they reached Finnmark and knocked on the chimney of the Finn woman, for she did not even have a door.

It was so hot inside that the Finn woman was walking around with practically nothing on. She was little and rather grimy. But she didn't hesitate to help Gerda unbutton and take off her mittens and boots—the heat would have wilted her otherwise—and she put a piece of ice on the reindeer's head. Then she looked at the words written on the codfish. She read the message three times until she knew it by heart and then tossed the fish into the kettle of soup, for it was still perfectly good. She never liked to waste anything.

The reindeer told his story first, then he reported what had happened to little Gerda. The Finn woman blinked her wise eyes, and spoke not a word.

"You are so wise," the reindeer said. "I know that you can tie all the winds of the world together[62] with a bit of thread. When a skipper unties just one of the knots, he has a good wind. When he unties a second, he'll get a stiff wind, and if he unties the third and fourth knots, there's a storm so fierce that it topples the trees. Can't you give this little girl a drink—one that can give her the strength of twelve men and help her overpower the Snow Queen?"

"The strength of twelve men?" said the Finn woman. "A lot of good that would do!" She walked over to some shelves, took down a large rolled-up hide, and spread it out. Strange letters[63] were written all over it, and the Finn woman pored over them until sweat began rolling down her brow.

The reindeer kept pleading with the Finn woman to help little Gerda, and the tears in Gerda's eyes implored her as well. The old woman began to blink, and she pulled the reindeer aside into a corner. While she was putting fresh ice on his head, she whispered: "It's all true. Little Kai is with the Snow Queen, and he finds everything to his liking and taste. He thinks it is the best place on earth, but that's only because he has a glass splinter in his heart and a little speck of glass in his eye. Until they are removed, he will never be human again and the Snow Queen will have him in her power."

"Can't you give Gerda something to drink that will make her more powerful than the Snow Queen?"

"I can't give her more power than she already has. Don't you see how much she possesses? Haven't you noticed how man and beast alike want to help her? Look how far she's come in the wide world on those bare feet! But we mustn't tell her about this power. Her strength lies deep in her heart, for she is a sweet, innocent child.[64] If she cannot reach the Snow Queen on her own and rid Kai of those pieces of glass, then there's nothing that we can do! The Snow Queen's garden lies two miles from here. Carry the little girl over there and put her down in the snow over by the big bush covered with red berries. But don't dawdle and be sure to hurry back!" The Finn woman lifted Gerda onto the reindeer, and he dashed off as fast as he could.

"Oh, I forgot my boots! And where are my mittens!" little Gerda shouted as she began to feel the sting of the cold wind. But the reindeer did not dare stop. He raced on until he came to the great big bush covered with red berries. Then he put Gerda down and kissed her on the lips, while big sparkling tears ran down his cheeks. Off he sped as fast as he could.

63. *Strange letters.* The Finn woman is most likely consulting runes, an ancient Germanic writing system that was thought to have sacral significance and magical qualities. Runic inscriptions were used in Iceland, the British Isles, and in Scandinavian lands for many centuries, from about the third century through 1600. The term *rune* means mystery, secret, or whisper, and each rune has special magical properties and meanings. More than 4,000 runic inscriptions and several runic manuscripts exist, with the majority from Scandinavian countries.

64. *she is a sweet, innocent child.* The importance of childhood innocence famously becomes evident in Andersen's "The Emperor's New Clothes." In "The Snow Queen," Andersen deepens the significance of that innocence, connecting it with the redemptive power of the Christ child.

65. *Gerda was standing there all alone—no shoes, no mittens.* Like the little match girl and the ugly duckling, Gerda is completely exposed to the icy elements and must fend for herself. Andersen repeatedly created solitary icons of suffering, diminutive figures set in glacial surroundings that combine the sublime and the terrible. In "The Girl Who Trod on the Loaf," he created the image of a vain child who is subjected to a humiliating display of her abject state.

66. *little angels that grew even bigger.* Gerda's warm breath serves as the perfect weapon against the "terrible snowflakes." Interiority and innocence, combined with ardent prayer, give birth to the angels that defeat the snowflakes, demolishing them as they splinter into hundreds of pieces.

Gerda was standing there all alone—no shoes, no mittens[65]—out in the middle of the icy cold Finnmark.

Gerda ran forward as fast as possible. An entire regiment of snowflakes came swirling toward her. They weren't falling from the sky, which was completely clear and ablaze with the Northern lights. The snowflakes were skimming the ground, and the closer they came, the larger they grew. Gerda recalled how enormous and strange they had seemed to her when she had looked at them through the magnifying glass, but now they were even bigger and more monstrous. They were alive, and they formed the Snow Queen's advance guard. They had the strangest shapes imaginable: some looked like ugly overgrown hedgehogs, others like clusters of snakes rearing their heads in every direction, and still others like fat little cubs with their hair standing on end. All of them were a dazzling white color. They were snowflakes that had come to life.

Gerda said her prayers. It was so cold that she could see her own breath freezing in front of her like a column of smoke. Her breath became even denser and then it began to take the shape of little angels that grew even bigger[66] when they touched the ground. All of them had helmets on their heads and were carrying spears and shields in their hands. They kept coming one after another, and by the time Gerda had finished her prayers, she was surrounded by a legion of them. When they thrust their spears at the horrid snowflakes, they shattered into a hundred pieces. Gerda kept on walking, feeling quite safe, and undaunted. The angels rubbed her hands and feet so that she wouldn't feel the cold, and she marched briskly to the Snow Queen's castle.

Now we must return to Kai and see how he is doing. He certainly wasn't thinking about little Gerda, and he never imagined that she might be waiting just outside the castle.

EDMUND DULAC

A tear rolls down the cheek of the reindeer as he kisses Gerda, who is without boots and mittens. The reindeer does everything in his power to help Gerda survive. In this scene, he has located bushes with red berries that will provide nourishment.

67. *Mirror of Reason.* As at the beginning of the tale, a mirror of powerful symbolic import appears. Unlike the devil's mirror, which produced grotesque distortions of reality, this mirror possesses geometric precision and mathematical exactitude. Its fragments do not come in all shapes and sizes, as was the case with the devil's mirror. Instead, each piece is exactly like the next, suggestive of a monstrous monotony that, as we learn, takes the form of "eternity." This mirror is even more perilous than the devil's looking glass, yet it is also an optical illusion created by the fragment of the looking glass in Kai's eye.

68. *he didn't notice anything at all.* Blue with cold, Kai begins to resemble his frigid surroundings and loses the capacity to feel, to touch, and to become aware or to be touched and moved emotionally.

69. *Chinese puzzles.* Andersen is most likely referring to the tangram, an ancient Chinese puzzle that consists of seven pieces which, when fitted together, form a square. The seven pieces include five triangles of different sizes, a square, and a parallelogram, and the object is to create specific designs with all seven pieces, which may not overlap in the new design.

70. *the designs seemed remarkable and deeply important.* The Snow Queen's element is the snowflake or crystal, which illustrates "the spontaneous creation of pattern and form" (Libbrecht, 21). Snowflakes, formed by condensation, are attractive precisely because of their patterned complexity and their symmetries even amid endless variation.

SEVENTH STORY: WHAT HAPPENED AT THE SNOW QUEEN'S CASTLE AND ELSEWHERE

The castle walls were made of snowdrifts, and the windows and doors of biting winds. There were more than a hundred rooms, all shaped by the drifting snow, and the largest stretched on for several miles. The vast, empty spaces were all lit by the bright Northern lights and looked both glacial and brilliant. There was never any real joy here, not so much as a little dance for the polar bears, for which the wind could have supplied the music as the bears walked on their hind legs to display their good breeding. Not even a little card game with paw-slapping and back-smacking, or just a cozy little coffee klatch where the white fox vixens could gossip. The Snow Queen's rooms were immense, empty, frozen expanses. The Northern lights blazed with such reliability that you could tell the time by when they were at their brightest or at their dimmest. In the middle of the vast, empty room of ice was a frozen lake. It had cracked into a thousand pieces, and each piece looked so much like every other piece that it seemed like a work of art. When she was at home, the Snow Queen would sit in the exact center, and she would call the lake the Mirror of Reason,[67] the only one of its kind and the best thing in the whole world.

Kai had grown blue from the cold—in fact he had almost turned black. But he didn't notice anything at all,[68] because the Snow Queen had kissed away his icy shivers, and by now his heart had practically turned into a lump of ice. He was racing around, moving sharp, flat pieces of ice and configuring them in all sorts of different ways—just as we arrange and rearrange pieces of wood in those little Chinese puzzles.[69] Kai was trying to work something out while he was creating ingenious patterns. It was an ice puzzle of the mind. To him the designs seemed remarkable and deeply important,[70] but

HONOR APPLETON

71. Eternity. Kai is not seeking the immortality promised by Christ: "Whoso eateth my flesh, and drinketh my blood, hath eternal life" (John 6:54). Instead he serves the master of reason and is striving to gain immortality through his intellectual labors. A. S. Byatt's meditation on the significance of the Snow Queen is intriguing. Reflecting on Yeats's dictum "The intellect of man is forced to choose / Perfection of the life, or of the work," she views "the frozen, stony women" in Andersen's work as images of "choosing the perfection of the work, rejecting . . . the imposed biological cycle, blood, kiss, roses, birth, death, and the hungry generations" (Byatt, 78).

72. *"I will give you the whole world and a pair of new skates."* The Snow Queen's offer conflates high and low registers, echoing the words of the devil: "All these things will I give thee, if thou wilt fall down and worship me" (Matthew 4:8–10). She also introduces an object of desire that, however ordinary and diminutive in contrast to the "whole world," would have a powerful appeal to children reading the tale. W. H. Auden used the reward and the scene in which Kai works on the ice puzzle to identify the difference between folklore and literature. The ice puzzle would never appear in a folktale, he insisted, "firstly because the human situation with which it is concerned is an historical one, created by Descartes, Newton and their successors, and secondly, because no folk tale would analyze its own symbol and explain that the game with the ice-splinters was the game of reason. Further, the promised reward, 'the whole world and a new pair of skates,' has not only a surprise and a subtlety of which the folk tale is incapable, but also a uniqueness by which one can identify its author" (Auden, 205).

73. *Mt. Etna and Vesuvius.* Mt. Etna lies on the east coast of Sicily and is the largest

that was only because of the speck of glass in his eye. He arranged his pieces to spell out written words, but he could never manage to put together the one word he really wanted. That word was *Eternity.*[71] The Snow Queen had told him: "If you can puzzle that out, you'll be your own master, and I will give you the whole world and a pair of new skates."[72] But Kai could not figure it out.

"Now I'm off to warmer countries," the Snow Queen declared. "I want to go take a peek at my black cauldrons!" She was referring to the volcanoes known as Mt. Etna and Vesuvius.[73] "I'm going to give them a coat of whitewash. It has to be done; it is good for the lemons and grapes!" And away she flew, leaving Kai all alone in the vast, empty room of ice that stretched on for miles. He continued to puzzle over the pieces of ice, and his head began to ache from all the thinking he had been doing. He was sitting so quietly and stiffly that he looked like someone who had frozen to death.

Just then little Gerda entered the castle through the huge portal made of piercing winds. As soon as she spoke her evening prayer, the winds began to die down, just as if they were falling asleep. The little girl entered the vast, empty, frozen room, and at once she caught sight of Kai. She recognized him immediately, threw her arms around him, held him close, and cried: "Kai! Dear Kai! I've found you at last!"

But Kai sat motionless, stiff and cold. Gerda shed hot tears,[74] and when they fell on Kai's chest, they went straight to his heart, melting the lump of ice and dissolving the little shard from the mirror. Kai looked at Gerda, and she began singing a hymn:

"Down in the valley, where roses grow wild,
There we can speak with our dear Christ child!"

Kai burst into tears. He cried so hard that the speck of glass washed right out of his eye. Suddenly he recognized Gerda and shouted, "Gerda! Sweet Gerda! Where have you been all this time? And where have I been?" He looked around and said: "It's so cold here! And it's immense and empty too!" He held Gerda tightly, and she started laughing so hard that tears of joy were rolling down her cheeks. It was all so wonderful that even the chunks of ice around them were dancing for joy. When the chunks grew tired, they collapsed on the ground to form a pattern making the exact word the Snow Queen had told Kai he must find in order to become his own master and receive the whole world and a pair of new skates.

Gerda kissed Kai's cheeks,[75] and they turned red. She kissed his eyes, and they began to shine like hers. She kissed his hands and feet, and he felt strong and healthy once again. The Snow Queen could come back whenever she wanted. The order for Kai's release was written on the floor in letters of shining ice.

Kai and Gerda strolled hand in hand out of the enormous palace. They talked about Grandmother and about the roses up on the roof. Wherever they went, the winds quieted down, and the sun broke through. When they reached the bush covered with red berries, the reindeer was waiting for them.[76] Another young reindeer had joined him, and her udder was full of warm milk for the children. She kissed them on the lips. The reindeer carried Kai and Gerda back to the Finn woman first, and they warmed themselves up in her cozy cottage and were given directions for the journey home. Then they visited the Lapp woman, who had sewn them new clothes and prepared her sleigh for them.

The reindeer, with his young companion bounding alongside, followed Kai and Gerda all the way to the border of the country, to the point where you could see the first green buds. The two children bid farewell to the reindeer and to the Lapp woman. "Good-bye," they all said. The first little birds began to chirp, and green buds could be seen everywhere in the forest. A young girl wearing a bright red cap on her head and

of Italy's three active volcanoes. In ancient times, it was thought to mark the spot of Tartarus, the Greek underworld. Vesuvius, which is located east of Naples, is famous for the destruction of Pompeii in 79 AD. Andersen made eight trips to Italy in his lifetime, the most significant of which was perhaps his first journey to Naples, in 1834. It was there that he linked the volcanic eruptions of Mt. Vesuvius with his own troubled sensual stirrings, or what he called the "Neapolitan passion." Letters to friends provide detailed accounts of the smoke, steam, and lava he witnessed, and Andersen made several pen-and-ink drawings of the "splendors" of Vesuvius and Etna. In his 1835 novel *The Improvisatore*, Andersen revealed the degree to which the smoldering volcano of Naples captured the intensity of sensual experience: "My blood was like boiling lava. . . . Everything was flames outside, as in my blood. The air currents rippled with heat, Vesuvius was aglow with fire, the eruptions lit up everything around" (Jens Andersen, 522).

74. *Gerda shed hot tears.* The tears, warm and liquid, stand in sharp contrast to the hard, frigid surfaces of the Snow Queen's realm. Gerda's animating kisses also differ markedly from the paralyzing kiss of the Snow Queen.

75. *Gerda kissed Kai's cheeks.* Described as "love's first snowdrop" (Burns), "a heartquake" (Byron), and "the shine / Of heaven ambrosial" (Keats), the kiss has long been the subject of poetic meditations. With its venerable history, from the biblical story recounting Judas's betrayal of Christ through fairy tales like "The Frog Prince" or "Sleeping Beauty" to Rodin's rendition of a lip-, limb-, and soul-locked marble couple, kisses range dramatically in meaning, signaling both seduction and betrayal as well as compassion, romance, and

KAY NIELSEN

Gerda and Kai walk hand in hand through a landscape that combines winter and spring, with a frozen tree to the left and a tree sending out shoots to the right. The glacial middle ground shows signs of a thaw both above it and below it.

holding two pistols came riding out of the forest on a magnificent horse that Gerda recognized immediately—it was the horse that had drawn the golden carriage. The little robber girl had grown tired of staying at home and wanted to head north, and, if that didn't amuse her, she was planning to go elsewhere. She recognized Gerda at once, and Gerda knew her as well. It was a happy reunion.

"You're a fine fellow, running off like that!" she said to Kai. "I wonder if you really deserve having someone go to the ends of the earth for your sake."[77]

Gerda just patted her cheek and asked about the prince and princess.

"They're traveling in foreign lands," the robber girl said.

"And the crow?" Gerda asked.

"Oh, the crow is dead,"[78] she replied. "His tame sweetheart is now a widow, and she has wrapped a bit of black woolen yarn around her leg. She complains constantly, and it's really all nonsense. But tell me now what you've been up to and how you managed to find Kai."

Gerda and Kai both told the story.

"Abracadabra, hocus-pocus, bibbety-bobbety-boo!" said the robber girl, and took them both by the hand. She promised to visit if she ever found her way to the town where they were living. And then she rode out into the wide world. Kai and Gerda walked away hand in hand, and as they walked, it turned into a beautiful spring day, with green everywhere and flowers in bloom. The church bells were ringing, and they recognized the tall towers of the town in which they had grown up. They went straight to Grandmother's door, up the staircase into the living room, where everything was just as it had been. The clock went "Tick! Tock!" and its hands spun around. As they walked through the door, they realized that they had turned into grown-ups. The roses on the roof were blooming in the open windows. The children's two chairs were still there. Kai and Gerda sat down in them and held

redemption. In Andersen's work, they are linked with both love and death. His poem "The Dying Child" ends with the child joyfully telling its mother of being kissed by an angel. "The Snow Queen" has kisses in abundance: the kisses planted on rosebushes by the young Kai and Gerda, the icy kisses of the Snow Queen, Gerda's good-bye kisses to her grandmother, the reindeer's soft kisses on Gerda's mouth, and, finally, Gerda's liberating kiss at the end of the story.

76. *the reindeer was waiting for them.* Like the Finn woman and the Lapp woman, the reindeer functions as one of a series of helpers who provide nourishment, clothing, and transportation. Each stands in contrast to the cold, boreal mother incarnated by the Snow Queen.

77. *"go to the ends of the earth for your sake."* Like the heroine in "East of the Sun and West of the Moon" (which exists in multiple variant forms in Scandinavian countries), Gerda must travel to the ends of the earth to find her beloved Kai.

78. *"the crow is dead."* The prince and princess, on the road to foreign countries, and the two crows, one in mourning and the other dead, can be seen as doublings of the couple formed by Gerda and Kai, with the prince and princess evoking adventure and voyages into the wide world, the crows representing banality and loss, and Gerda and Kai signaling a blend of what characterizes the other pairs.

79. *they were grown-ups and children at the same time.* Time has stood still, but Gerda and Kai return as adults who are still able to occupy the small chairs in which they sat as children. Retaining the beauty and innocence of childhood, they live as chaste partners in an eternal present, with the grandmother reading from the Bible in "God's clear sunshine." The concluding tableau may not be a utopia to everyone's taste, but it is decidedly a "happily ever after," with its "warm" and "wonderful" summer.

hands. They had forgotten the cold, empty splendor of the Snow Queen's castle. It was nothing more than a bad dream. Grandmother was sitting in God's bright sunshine and reading out loud from the Bible: "Unless you become as little children, you shall not enter the Kingdom of God."

Kai and Gerda looked into each other's eyes, and suddenly they understood the old hymn:

"Down in the valley, where roses grow wild,
There we can speak with our dear Christ child!"

There they sat, and they were grown-ups and children at the same time,[79] children at heart. And it was summer—warm, wonderful summer.

ON AND ON THEY SPED ...

HONOR APPLETON

The Princess and the Pea[1]

Prinsessen paa ærten

Eventyr, fortalte for Børn, 1835

1. *The Princess and the Pea.* The literal translation of the title is "the princess *on* the pea," emphasizing the test embedded in the story. I have kept the conventional English title, despite the fact that some translators insist that there is a critical difference in the formulation "on the pea."

Andersen claimed to have heard this story as a child, and it is likely that he was inspired by a version akin to the Swedish *"Princess Who Lay on Seven Peas."* The heroine of that tale is an orphaned child who sets out into the world accompanied by a pet cat or dog and who presents herself as a princess. Challenged by a suspicious queen, the girl's royal ancestry is put to the test at night, when a small object (a bean, a pea, or a straw) is slipped under her mattress. Informed by the cat or the dog about the object, the girl complains about her inability to sleep and is declared to be of royal blood. The folktale heroine uses deceit to raise her social rank, but Andersen's princess is the "real" thing and does not have to misrepresent her sensitivity.

For Andersen, a story demonstrating that "true" nobility resides in sensitivity rather than birth had a certain appeal. Constantly reminded of his lowly social origins by his many benefactors as well as by friends and critics, Andersen compensated by developing narratives demonstrating that those who are born in barnyards (the ugly duckling) or those who appear out of nowhere at the doorstep of royals (the princess) may turn out to be the real thing. As a poet, he aspired to become Denmark's representative among a European elite of *writers and thinkers. In "The Nightingale," Andersen once again took up the distinction between the real thing and sorry imitators.*

The 1959 musical Once Upon a Mattress, *starring Carol Burnett as the irrepressible princess Winnifred the Woebegone, enjoyed success on Broadway for many years and was revived in 1997 with Sarah Jessica Parker in the lead role. There have been numerous cinematic adaptations, and the story has been rewritten creatively by Jon Scieszka as "The Princess and the Bowling Ball."*

"The Princess and the Pea" remains a favorite among Andersen tales, and the princess herself has become an emblem of supremely delicate sensibilities. The casual, conversational tone and humorous touches, which operate to produce parody, redeem many features that might offend modern sensibilities. The prince's insistence on finding a "true" princess and the characterization of sensitivity as the exclusive privilege of nobility challenge our own cultural values about character and social worth. And yet the sensitivity of the princess can also be read on a metaphorical level as a measure of the depth of her feeling and compassion. Andersen also gives us a feisty heroine, one who defies the elements and shows up on the doorstep of a prince, whom she has succeeded in tracking down on her own.

2. *And he traveled all over the world in search of one.* The prince leaves home to search the world for a wife, but his quest will prove to be in vain, for what he seeks, he will find at his doorstep. Unlike his mother, he has no accurate test for measuring authenticity and simply relies on his feeling that something is "not right."

3. *One evening a terrible storm broke out.* As in "The Little Mermaid," a storm signals a life-threatening situation, but it typically produces the opportunity for a romantic alliance. Lightning and thunder, once again, produce the chiaroscuro effects that repeatedly flash through Andersen's fairy tales.

W. HEATH ROBINSON

The old king goes to the door, candle in hand and massive keys at his side, to let in the princess.

Once upon a time, there was a prince. He wanted to marry a princess, but she would have to be a *true* princess. And he traveled all over the world in search of one,[2] but something was always wrong. There were plenty of princesses around, but the prince could never be quite certain that they were *real* princesses. No matter what, something was always not exactly right. And so he would return home feeling sad, for his heart was set on marrying a real princess.

One evening a terrible storm broke out.[3] Lightning flashed, thunder roared, and rain came down in buckets—it was really dreadful! There was a sudden knock at the city gate, and the old king himself went to open it.

W. HEATH ROBINSON

The prince takes his time scrutinizing the various young women masquerading as princesses. His robe has floral designs on it but also displays a dragon. One defiant toddler seats herself on the robes of the prince, who has his back turned to us as he contemplates the surprisingly youthful candidates for marriage.

It was a princess, and she was waiting outdoors.[4] But goodness gracious! What a sight she was from all the rain and the nasty weather! Water was dripping from her hair and her clothes. It flowed in through the tips of her shoes and back out again through the heels. And she said that she was a real princess.

"Well, we shall see about that soon enough!" the old queen thought. She didn't say a word, but went straight to the bed-

4. *It was a princess, and she was waiting outdoors.* Like the French Donkeyskin and Cinderella, this princess conceals her nobility until it is put to a test. Rather than matching a foot to a shoe or a finger to a ring, she must reveal her sensitivity to a hidden object. Note that she appears out of nowhere and seems to be more of an orphan than a young woman of royal parentage.

KAY NIELSEN

A windswept princess seeks shelter in the castle and is welcomed by the king, who has the foresight to bring an umbrella when he lets in this "real" princess.

EDMUND DULAC

The canopy, the posters of the bed, the mattresses and featherbeds, and the massive timbers of the ceiling contain the tiny figure of the princess, who appears uncomfortable, despite the small mountain of cushioning protecting her from the pea. The many layers beneath the princess provide the artist with an opportunity to create several tiers of decorative touches.

KAY NIELSEN

The princess kneels atop the many mattresses in a room governed by extraordinary symmetry.
The single light in the chandelier, the mirror over one chair, and the design on the bedstead,
along with the princess herself, disrupt the symmetries.

5. *"I barely closed my eyes all night long!"* In a speech full of double entendres, the princess declares herself to have passed the test of authentic sensitivity but also creates the opportunity for risqué humor in retellings for adults.

6. *she had felt the pea.* Folklorists have noted that the pathological sensitivity, or "marvelous sensitiveness," found in Andersen's story is not common in fairy tales, but they have identified a few examples of it in fairy tales from some cultures. An Indian tale recounts the restlessness of a prince who thinks that he has slept on a wooden beam although nothing more than a hair is found in his bed. An Italian folktale called "The Most Sensitive Woman" describes how a prince's quest for a marriage partner ends when he encounters a woman whose foot is bandaged after the petal of a jasmine blossom falls on her toe.

The Grimms had included "The Princess on the Pea" in one edition of their *Children's Stories and Household Tales,* but they removed the tale once they realized that it belonged to a Danish literary tradition. Knowing that the Brothers Grimm were aware of his work, Andersen decided to pay them a surprise visit when he was in Berlin during the summer of 1844. It is not difficult to imagine his deep mortification when Jacob, the only one of the two brothers at home, was mystified by the presence of the Danish caller and declared that he had no idea who he was. A few weeks later, Jacob apologized in person to Andersen (he had read some of the tales in the interim and reported, "Now I know who you are"). The brothers remained on good terms with Andersen, and their Danish admirer spent time with them during the Christmas holidays in 1845.

Negative responses to the princess are based on what one critic calls "the cultural association between women's physical sensitivity and emotional sensitivity, specifi-

room, removed all the bedclothes, and placed a pea on the bottom of the bed. Then she took twenty mattresses and piled them on top of the pea and placed another twenty featherbeds on top of the mattresses.

The princess was going to sleep on them that night.

In the morning, everyone asked the princess how she had slept.

"Oh, just dreadfully!" the princess said. "I barely closed my eyes all night long![5] Goodness knows what was in that bed! I was lying on something so hard that I'm just black and blue all over. It's really dreadful!"

Then of course everyone knew that she really was a princess, because she had felt the pea[6] right through the twenty mattresses and twenty featherbeds. No one but a real princess would have skin that tender.

And so the prince took her as his wife, because now he knew that he had a true princess. And the pea was sent to the Royal Museum, where it is still on display,[7] unless someone has stolen it.

Now you can see, that was a real story![8]

W. HEATH ROBINSON

"I have scarcely closed my eyes the whole night through" reads the caption for this image of a distraught princess.

cally, the link between a woman reporting her physical experience of touch and negative images of women who are hypersensitive to physical conditions, who complain about trivialities, and who demand special treatment" (Esrock, 25). The princess's sensitivity is therefore often recalled by readers as a signal of bad manners rather than of her noble birth.

The feminist writer and essayist Vivian Gornick has read the princess's sensitivity as a form of dissatisfaction that will define her life in negative terms: "She's not after the prince, she's after the pea. That moment when she feels the pea beneath the twenty mattresses, that is *her* moment of definition. It is the very meaning of her journey, why she has traveled so far, what she has come to declare: the dissatisfaction that will keep her life at bay." For Gornick, the princess falls into "a petulance that mimick[s] the act of thinking. . . . Soon enough, through the painful logic of inborn grievance, the irritation becomes a wound, an infliction: a devotion and a destiny" (Gornick, 156–57).

THE PEAS WERE PRESERVED IN THE
CABINET OF CURIOSITIES

W. HEATH ROBINSON

A boy, book in hand, and a girl gaze with reverence and astonishment at the pea on the pedestal in the cabinet of curiosities.

The folklorist Christine Kawan has documented the existence of stories about boys who are subjected to a so-called bed test. These "pea seekers" or "bean kings" discover a pea or bean that appears to be an object of value. They journey to a castle, are given a bed of straw, and, after spending the night tossing and turning for fear of losing the pea or bean, are assumed to be of aristocratic lineage (they are unaccustomed to sleeping on straw) and are married to the princess (Kawan, 102).

7. *the pea was sent to the Royal Museum, where it is still on display.* For Andersen, the material objects of everyday life—needles, pincushions, and whistles—are endowed with special whimsical human qualities. Here, the pea is never endowed with human feelings, but it becomes an iconic object, signaling the princess's special sensitivity, presumably not only to a pea under the mattress but also, in an optimistic interpretive move, to the wishes of her human subjects. Once placed in the Royal Museum, the pea becomes an objet d'art, a cult object endowed with an aesthetic and material value that creates the risk of theft.

8. *that was a real story!* The last line, in declaring the story to be "real," suggests a parallel between the princess and the narrative about her. And yet, for the narrative, there is no "pea," no object that will test for its authenticity. It is the narrator who vouches for the "real," proclaiming the aristocratic lineage of his tale.

The Nightingale[1]

Nattergalen

Nye Eventyr. Første Samling, 1843

he Nightingale" reveals Andersen's deep commitment *to natural beauty over the artful and artificial. In choosing the fairy tale as his medium, Andersen hoped to align himself with the spontaneity of simple, "natural" forms and to empower his art with the same capacity as the nightingale's song to create beauty, to provide pleasure, and to animate and transform.*

Poets and singers are frequently referred to as "nightingales," and Andersen's contemporary, the singer Jenny Lind (whose repertoire included folk songs) was famously referred to as the "Swedish nightingale." "Her voice stays with me, forever, in my story 'The Nightingale,' " Andersen wrote in his travel diaries (Little, 215). Andersen's friends dubbed him the "nightingale from Fyn"—a man whose literary song had earned him adulation and fame—and Andersen referred to himself as a "male Jenny Lind." In The Fairy Tale of My Life, *he hailed her vocal powers: "Her lovely youthful voice penetrated all hearts! Here truth and nature prevailed; everything assumed significance and clarity" (208). In a memoir published by Charlotte Bournonville, daughter of the famous ballet*

1. *The Nightingale.* The nightingale ("singer of the night") is a songbird of reddish-brown plumage found in Great Britain, Asia, Africa, and on the Continent. Its celebrated song refers to the male's breeding-season calls, which are endowed with an impressive range of whistles, gurgles, and trills. Although the nightingale sings both day and night, the nocturnal refrain is considered unusual, since few other birds sing at night—hence the word "night" in its name in English and in other languages. The nightingale has enjoyed a robust literary life. It appears in Ovid's story of Procne, Philomela, and Tereus, which ends with

master who counted himself among Andersen's friends, the following story (which Andersen may well have heard) is recounted:

One of my father's dearest friends, a very musical young man, was seriously ill, and his sadness at not being able to hear Jenny Lind sing did quite a lot to make his condition even worse. When Jenny learned that news, she cried: "Dear Mr. Bournonville, allow me to sing for this man who is so ill!" Perhaps it was a dangerous experiment to expose a person who was mortally ill to such an emotional experience, but it worked. After he heard the beautiful singing . . . he was on the road to recovery.

The modesty, generosity, and passion of true art produced by those devoted to their craft contrasts sharply with the empty pleasure of an art as it is practiced by mechanical creatures, who can engage in little else but vacuous mimicry.

Igor Stravinsky's opera The Nightingale, *based on Andersen's story, premiered in Paris in 1914. Several years later, Stravinsky composed a symphonic poem, "Song of the Nightingale," for Sergei Diaghilev's Ballets Russes. The ballet was first performed in 1920, with sets by Henri Matisse and choreography by Léonide Massine.*

Jerry Pinkey's account of his decision to illustrate Andersen's "Nightingale" reveals how new images for old stories can have designs on the reader. For him, the girl in the kitchen, who is attuned to nature, becomes as important as the nightingale in restoring the Emperor's health:

The remarkable story of "The Nightingale" has always intrigued me, and in the creation of this adaptation, the plain little bird with a magnificent voice and a big heart became a symbol of the healing power of nature. The little kitchen girl, who knows where the nightingale lives, became a symbol of hope for the downtrodden. And the king, who cares for his

the transformation of Philomela into a nightingale. The thirteenth-century Middle English poem "The Owl and the Nightingale" sets down a debate between a sober owl with ascetic and unworldly views and a cheerful nightingale, who is an exponent of pleasure and beauty.

John Keats's "Ode to a Nightingale" (1819) apostrophizes the expressive power and transcendent beauty in the bird's melody. Keats's close companion, Charles Brown, describes the origins of the poem: "In the spring of 1819 a nightingale had built her nest near my house. Keats felt a tranquil and continual joy in her song; and one morning he took his chair from the breakfast table to the grass-plot under a plum-tree, where he sat for two or three hours. When he came into the house, I perceived he had some scraps of paper in his hand, and these he was quietly thrusting behind the books" (Rollins, *The Keats Circle*, II, 65). For Keats, the nightingale is a model of creative artistry, singing with a "full-throated ease" so soulful and expressive that it inspires in the poet a sense of morbid self-abandonment ("Now more than ever seems it rich to die").

In Oscar Wilde's "The Nightingale and the Rose," the bird impales itself on a thorn in order to transform a white rose into a red one. She (Wilde's nightingale is designated as female) sings of the "birth of passion" and celebrates "the Love that is perfected by Death, of the Love that dies not in the tomb." In contrast with the callous student in the tale, who dismisses love as inferior to logic and returns to the study of metaphysics, the nightingale dies with a thorn in its breast, a martyr to love and passion. Wilde's tale might have been inspired by Andersen's story, in which the nightingale is not allied with death but sings in a fashion that challenges and defies the power of death.

The Danish term *nattergal* (nightingale) contains within it the term *gal* (madman).

2. *the Emperor is Chinese.* Andersen establishes a "once upon a time" feeling by setting the tale in a distant, exotic land and in the remote past. That the Emperor of China is also a "Chinaman" (as some translations of the story have it) may not be as obvious as first appears, given the number of foreign lands controlled by colonial powers during the nineteenth century. In his almanac entry for October 11, 1843, Andersen declared that the tale, which was written in a single day, "began in Tivoli," Copenhagen's new amusement park, which featured pagodas, Chinese lanterns, and peacocks. The apparent tautology has a humorous and charming ring to it, suggesting a certain childlike levity. Andersen's travels never took him beyond Istanbul and Athens, and his contact with China was limited to European Chinoiserie, an artistic style that developed in the seventeenth century and continued to be popular through the nineteenth century.

3. *that's exactly why you should listen to it, before it's forgotten.* Andersen lived in an era when old wives' tales were in retreat. And, like the Grimms who preceded him, he felt some anxiety about oral story-

W. HEATH ROBINSON

The nightingale, framed by trees, leaves, and acorns, sings with full-throated pleasure.

people but is out of touch with them, learns what it means to feel vulnerable through his own illness. In the end the king's recovery is made possible by two of his most humble subjects, the little kitchen girl, and the nightingale.

Kara Dalkey's novel The Nightingale *(1991) situates the events in Japan and transforms the nightingale into a young woman who plays the flute.*

In China, as you may know, the Emperor is Chinese,[2] and everyone there is also Chinese. This story took place many years ago, but that's exactly why you should listen to it, before it's forgotten.[3]

The Emperor's palace was the most magnificent in the world. It was made entirely of fine porcelain, so costly and delicate that you had to be careful when you touched it. In the garden you could find the most wondrous flowers. The most splendid among the flowers were trimmed with little silver bells that jingled, and you couldn't walk by without noticing them. Yes, everything was arranged quite artfully in the Emperor's garden,[4] which stretched so far back that even the gardener could not say where it ended. If you kept on walking, you reached the loveliest forest with tall trees and deep lakes. The forest stretched all the way out to the deep, blue sea. Tall ships sailed right under the branches of the trees. In those branches lived a nightingale whose song was so enchanting that even a poor fisherman, who had many chores before him, would pause when taking his nets in at night to listen. "My God! That's really beautiful," he would say. But then he would return to his chores and forget all about the bird's song. The next evening, when the fisherman was back at work, the bird would start singing again, and he would say the same thing:[5] "My God! That's really beautiful."

EDMUND DULAC

The fisherman pauses to listen to the nightingale hidden behind the branches of the tree. Marked by poverty, he experiences a moment of sublime respite from his labors.

telling traditions, which were rapidly vanishing with the migration of certain forms of labor from the domestic to the industrial sphere. Note that Andersen connects himself to those traditions as a *teller* of tales ("you should listen") rather than to the writing practices in which he is actually engaged.

4. *Yes, everything was arranged quite artfully in the Emperor's garden.* Fragility, delicacy, and beauty: these are, as always, the characteristics of the gardens in Andersen's tales, the sites where nature meets culture. Like the undersea world in "The Little Mermaid," the Emperor's castle and gardens are places of exquisite beauty, where nature has been improved by those with refined aesthetic sensibilities.

5. *he would say the same thing.* Does beauty have a lasting effect? The fisherman's response to the nightingale's song suggests that those who habitually dwell in the vicinity of beauty remain unaffected by its transformative power and merely carry on with their daily chores. By contrast, the nightingale is a rare sight for visitors to the city, and its melody haunts them.

6. *composed the loveliest poems about the nightingale.* Here, the rich literary tradition that enshrines the nightingale as the bird of love, passion, tragedy, and beauty is invoked. The refrain of the bird inspires the song of poets—and also the work of storytellers.

7. *"Is it possible that a bird like that exists in my empire, let alone in my own garden?"* Andersen would surely have identified with a bird of song that is so famous abroad but unknown at home. He complained endlessly about how badly the Danes treated him and believed that his work was appreciated abroad far more than at home. And indeed, the critical reception of his

Travelers came from all over the world to visit the Emperor's city and to admire his palace and gardens. If they happened to hear the nightingale singing, they would all agree: "That's just the best of all."

When the travelers returned home, they would describe what they had seen, and learned men wrote many books about the city, the palace, and the garden. They never forgot the nightingale—in fact they praised the bird above all other things. Those who could write poetry composed the loveliest poems about the nightingale[6] that lived in the forest by the deep sea.

The books themselves traveled around the world, and some of them found their way to the Emperor of China. One day, he was sitting on his golden throne, reading one book after another, nodding his head in delight over the splendid descriptions of his city, palace, and garden. "The nightingale is the best of all!" the books declared.

"What on earth!" the Emperor exclaimed. "A nightingale! I don't know a thing about it! Is it possible that a bird like that exists in my empire, let alone in my own garden?[7] And to think that I had to read about it in a book."

The Emperor summoned the Chamberlain, who was so refined that when anyone of a lower rank had the audacity to address him or to ask a question, his only reply was "Puh!"[8] which really means nothing at all.

"Apparently there is a truly extraordinary bird around here called a nightingale," said the Emperor. "They say it's better than anything else in all my domains. Why hasn't anyone said a word to me about it?"

"I've never heard anyone say a word about it," the Chamberlain said. "And no one has ever presented the bird at the imperial court."

"I want it to appear here tonight to sing for me," the Emperor said. "The rest of the world knows more about what's in my kingdom than I do!"

"I've never heard anyone say a word about it," the Chamberlain said again. "But I shall look for it, and I will find it."

But where could the nightingale be? The Chamberlain sped up and down the stairs, through rooms and corridors, but nobody he met had ever heard of the nightingale. And so the Chamberlain raced back to the Emperor and told him that the bird must have been in a fable invented by those who write books. "Your Imperial Majesty should not believe what people write today. It's all made up and about what can be called black magic."

"But the book I was reading was sent to me by the mighty Emperor of Japan," the Emperor said. "So it really must be true. I am determined to hear this nightingale. It must be here by this evening. I've granted it my high imperial favor. If it doesn't show up by then, I'll have every courtier punched in the stomach right after supper."9

"Tsing-pe!"10 the Chamberlain shouted, and once again he sped up and down the stairs, through all the rooms and corridors. And half the court ran along with him, for no one wanted to be punched in the stomach. Everyone was asking questions about the mysterious nightingale, which was so famous all over the world but unknown at home.

They finally found a poor little girl in the kitchen,11 who said: "Good Lord! The nightingale? Of course I know all about it. Yes, indeed, it can really sing! Every evening they let me take home a few scraps from the table to my poor, sick mother. She lives down by the sea. When I start back, I am so tired that I have to stop to rest in the woods. That's when I hear the nightingale sing. It brings tears to my eyes. It's just as if my mother were giving me a kiss."

"Little kitchen maid," the Chamberlain said. "I'll arrange a lifetime post for you in the kitchen and give you permission to watch the Emperor dine if you can take us to the nightingale. It is supposed to give a command performance at court tonight."

work was far more positive in foreign lands than it was in Denmark. In Munich, Andersen mused about how he longed to return to Copenhagen, although he was discouraged by news about contemptuous reviews of his work: "Letters from Denmark told how my work was discarded, destroyed, how I was still the weed in the otherwise healthy garden of young Danish poets. I felt nervous about coming under attack again, being caught in the suffocating seas of criticism" (*Travels*, 72–73).

8. *his only reply was "Puh!"* In the Danish original, the reply is "P," a sound with no more significance than its English equivalent. Perhaps all that Andersen reached for here was a consonant with a brusque, dismissive sound.

9. *"I'll have every courtier punched in the stomach right after supper."* One Andersen scholar points out that "The Nightingale" presents a China "composed of all the West's shallow misconceptions of the Celestial Empire: a sort of marionette-theater China where everything is of porcelain, gold, or silk, with people nodding their heads like dolls; where conventions are so ingeniously devised as to seem actually Chinese; where the emperor can have his courtiers punched in the stomach after supper when they have displeased him; where those in authority are ridiculously impressed with their own dignity and the common people foolishly ape their masters" (Grønbech, 103). In this ritualized culture, where arrogance, sophistry, and rigid hierarchies rule supreme with brutal results, the nightingale represents a unique instance of spontaneity and pleasure. The bird's soulfulness and generosity contrast sharply with the courtiers' self-serving callousness.

10. *"Tsing-pe!"* Most likely a variation of the Chinese "ch'in p'ei," or "as you

KAY NIELSEN

The nightingale is little more than a speck in the landscape, but the kitchen maid, in a setting of rare beauty, listens to his song enthralled. She is able to renew her journey after the restorative song.

And so they all set off for the forest, to the place where the nightingale was said to sing. Half of the court followed. On the way into the forest a cow began mooing.

"Aha!" said the royal squires. "That must be it. What remarkable power for such a tiny creature. We're sure that we've heard that song once before."

"No, those are cows lowing," the little kitchen girl said. "We still have a long way to go."

Then the frogs began croaking in the marshes.

"How lovely!" the imperial Chinese chaplain declared. "It sounds just like little church bells."

"No, those are just frogs," said the little kitchen maid. "But I have a feeling we will hear the nightingale soon.

Then the nightingale began to sing.

"There it is," said the little kitchen maid. "Just listen. And now you can see it!" And she pointed to a little gray bird perched on a branch.

"Can it be?" exclaimed the Chamberlain. "That's not at all how I imagined the bird to be. How plain it looks![12] It must have lost all its color from seeing all the distinguished persons gathered around."

"Little nightingale," the kitchen maid called out in a loud voice. "Our gracious Emperor so wants you to sing for him."

"With the greatest pleasure," the nightingale replied, and it sang to everyone's delight.

"It sounds just like crystal bells," the Lord Chamberlain said. "And just look at the bird's little throat—you can tell it's singing with all its might. It's astonishing that we have never heard it before. It will be a great success at court."

"Shall I sing again for the Emperor?"[13] the nightingale asked, for it believed that the Emperor was present.

"My splendid little nightingale," the Lord Chamberlain said. "I have the great honor of inviting you to court this evening, and there you will enchant his Imperial Grace with your charming voice."

please," but the phrase could also be nonsense. Andersen's playful use of gibberish anticipates Lewis Carroll's insights into the appeal of nonsense words for children. Both authors had a clear sense of how to use words to create wonders.

11. *They finally found a poor little girl in the kitchen.* The kitchen maid is a Cinderella figure who would seem the least likely person to locate the nightingale. Unlike the courtiers and imperial rulers in the tale, she is a person of humble origins who remains unimpressed by the royal entourage. But she is quite happy to accept a promotion to "Real Kitchen Maid," a title that spoofs the 1717 Danish law that raised a person's rank with the addition of the term "real."

W. HEATH ROBINSON

The kitchen maid has a heavy load to carry as she makes her way to her mother's home. On her way, she is stopped in her tracks by the arresting sound of the nightingale's song.

W. HEATH ROBINSON

The kitchen maid has put down her bundle, and the courtly delegation stands in awe of a nightingale that combines a modest appearance with an enchanting song. Robinson's humans have a real decorative solidity that contrasts powerfully with the airy lightness of the delicate objects in the sparse landscape.

12. *"How plain it looks!"* Nicolai Bøgh kept a diary during a journey taken with Andersen in 1873. He reported Andersen's views on Jenny Lind: "They say Jenny Lind was hideous to look at, and maybe she was. The first time she walked on stage, I said the same: 'She's hideous' . . . but then she sang and became divinely beautiful. She was like an unlit lamp when she came in, and then, when you lit the lamp and she began to speak, it was as if her spirit cast a divine radiance on the stage and every seat in the theater. You weren't in the theater, you were in church" (Frank and Frank, 151).

Likewise, the nightingale itself is an

"My song sounds best outdoors," the nightingale replied, but it was glad to return with them when it learned of the Emperor's wishes.

The palace had been cleaned and polished with great care. The walls and floors, made of porcelain, were gleaming from the light of thousands of golden lamps. The loveliest flowers, trimmed with little bells, had been placed in the corridors. The commotion from all the comings and goings made the bells start ringing, and you could scarcely hear yourself think.

In the middle of the great hall in which the Emperor was seated, a golden perch had been set up, and it was for the nightingale. The entire court had assembled there. The little kitchen maid had been given permission to stand behind the door, for she now held the title of Real Kitchen Maid. People were dressed in their finery, and, when the Emperor graciously nodded, everyone fixed their eyes on the little gray bird.

The nightingale's voice was so lovely that tears began to fill the Emperor's eyes and roll down his cheeks. The bird sang even more beautifully, and the music went straight to his heart. The Emperor was so delighted that he ordered his own golden slipper to be hung around the nightingale's neck.[14] But the nightingale graciously declined it and declared that it had received reward enough.

"I have seen tears in the eyes of the Emperor," it said. "For me that is the greatest treasure. The tears of an Emperor have a wondrous power. God knows that I have received my reward." And it sang once again with a sweet, sublime voice.

"We've never seen such lovable flirtatiousness," the ladies all declared. And they put water in their mouths so they would twitter whenever they talked. They were hoping that they too could be nightingales. Even the footmen and chambermaids declared that they were satisfied, which is saying a lot, for they are the hardest to please. Yes, indeed, the nightingale was a complete success!

EDMUND DULAC

The chamberlain is appalled to discover that the nightingale is so plain and gray. Illuminated by the lamp, the nightingale is that brilliant, rare object that lights up the world with its beautiful song.

The nightingale was supposed to stay at the palace and have its own cage, as well as the freedom to go on outings twice a day, and once at nighttime. Twelve servants stood in attendance, each one holding tight to a silk ribbon attached to the bird's leg. There was no pleasure at all in outings like that.

The whole town was talking about the remarkable bird. If two people happened to meet, the first just said "Night!" and the other would respond with "Gale!" and then they would both just sigh, with no need for words. What's more, eleven grocers named their children "Nightingale," although not a single one of them was able to carry a tune.

One day a big package arrived for the Emperor. The word "Nightingale" had been written on it.

"It must be a new book about our famous bird," the Emperor said. But it was not a book. Inside the box was a work of art, a mechanical nightingale[15] that was supposed to look just like the real one except that it was covered with diamonds, rubies, and sapphires.[16] When it was wound up, the mechanical bird sang one of the melodies of the real bird, all the while beating time with its gleaming tail of gold and silver. Around its neck hung a little ribbon, and on it were the words: "The Emperor of Japan's nightingale is a paltry thing compared with the one owned by the Emperor of China."

"Isn't it lovely!" they all said, and the person who had delivered the contraption was immediately given the title Supreme Imperial Nightingale Transporter.

"Let's have them sing together. What a duet that will be!"

And so the two birds sang a duet, but it didn't work,

HARRY CLARKE

An intrigued emperor listens to the vibrant sounds of the nightingale.

unprepossessing bird, slightly larger than a robin, brown, with a broad tail and a plain appearance. Many illustrators emphasize the bird's drabness and diminutiveness, which contrast with the lavish trappings of the court.

13. *"Shall I sing again for the Emperor?"* The nightingale is not only gifted and modest but also completely obliging, willing to sing on command and to leave its home in the woods to sing at court. Moreover, unlike its mechanical counterpart,

the nightingale is able to vary and improvise.

14. *he ordered his own golden slipper to be hung around the nightingale's neck.* The European folktale "The Juniper Tree" features a bird that sings as melodiously as the nightingale of Andersen's tale. In the Grimms' recording of the tale, the bird asks for rewards while repeating its song. In one instance, it receives red slippers and picks them up with one claw, while holding a gold chain with the other.

15. *Inside the box was a work of art, a mechanical nightingale.* Yeats's "Sailing to Byzantium" contains an echo of Andersen's "Nightingale."

16. *it was covered with diamonds, rubies, and sapphires.* The nightingale is covered with precious stones in the classic fairy-tale color combination of white, red, and blue. Fairy tales, as Max Lüthi has emphasized, are concerned with surface beauty: everything that glitters, sparkles, and glows. The mechanical nightingale represents the pinnacle of artifice and human invention, and it stands in stark contrast to the "plain" nightingale, who lives in the woods and sings of nature's beauty and poetry. Artifice is set against art in the rivalry between the mechanical nightingale and the undomesticated avian creature that lives in natural surroundings. Similar themes come up in Andersen's tale "The Swineherd."

17. *"You can explain it; you can open it up and take it apart."* The superiority of the mechanical bird is based on the principle that the familiar, rational, and logical are more comforting and reassuring than the mysterious, irrational, and magical. The music master represents Enlightenment views that elevate reason over emotion and celebrate the human capacity to demystify the world.

because the real nightingale had her own style, while the mechanical bird ran on cylinders. "You can't blame it for that," the Music Master said. "It keeps perfect time, entirely in line with my theories." And so the mechanical bird sang on its own. It pleased them all just as much as the real bird, and on top of that it was far prettier to look at, for it sparkled just the way that bracelets and brooches do.

The mechanical bird sang the same tune thirty-three times without tiring out. Everyone would have been happy to hear it again, but the Emperor thought that the real nightingale should also take a turn. But where had it gone? No one had noticed that it had flown out the window, back to the green forests.

"Well, what kind of behavior is that?" the Emperor exclaimed. And the courtiers all sneered at the nightingale, declaring it to be a most ungrateful creature. "Fortunately, the best bird of all is still with us," they said. And the mechanical bird started singing the same tune, now for the thirty-fourth time. But no one knew it by heart yet, because it was a terribly difficult piece. The Imperial Music Master lavished great praise on the mechanical bird. Yes, he assured them, this contraption was far better than any real nightingale, not only because of how it looked on the outside with its many beautiful diamonds but also because of its inner qualities.

"Ladies and gentlemen—and above all Your Imperial Majesty: You never know what will happen when it comes to a real nightingale. But with a mechanical bird everything is completely under control. It will sound a certain way, and no other way. You can explain it; you can open it up and take it apart;[17] you can see how the mechanical wheels operate, how they whirl around, and how one interlocks with the other."

"My sentiments precisely," they all said. And the Music Master was given permission to put the bird on display for all to see on the following Sunday. They too should hear it sing,

HARRY CLARKE

Few illustrators choose to depict the artificial bird, but here it sings for the Emperor, who clearly values opulence and luxury.

18. *twenty-five volumes about the mechanical bird.* Once again the written word is invoked as the source of pedantic and arcane efforts to explain the obvious. Just as nature is set in opposition to artifice, so too the melodious song of the nightingale is set against the desiccated written word. Writing fails to enrich or augment, and contributes nothing to the beauty created by the nightingale, even in its mechanical form. The figure of the music master mocks the pedantry of the renowned Danish writer and critic Johan Ludvig Heiberg.

19. *"Zi-zi-zi! Click, click, click."* That the story is designed to be read out loud (and Andersen famously loved to read his fairy tales to captive audiences) becomes evident from the various amusing sounds in the text—ranging from the Chamberlain's "Puh" to noises made by the mechanical nightingale. Andersen's use of onomatopoeia becomes more pronounced over time. Beginning with the sound of the matches in "The Little Match Girl" through the chants of the robber girl in "The Snow Queen" to the sound of the fire drum in "The Golden Treasure," Andersen used language expressively and in ways that suggest how attuned he was to acoustical effects. As Jens Andersen points out, he also created the "most splendid military title in all of world literature: 'Billygoat-Leg-Field-Marshal-Brigadier-General-Commander-Sargeant'" (Andersen, 239) in "The Shepherdess and the Chimneysweep." Onomatopoetic effects and playful names and titles, as we know from the works of writers like Lewis Carroll and Roald Dahl, work magic in getting the attention of children.

the Emperor declared. And hear it they did, with so much pleasure that it was as if they had all become tipsy from drinking tea, in the Chinese fashion. Everyone said "Oh!" and held up a finger—the one you lick the pot with—and then nodded. But the poor fisherman, the one who had heard the real nightingale sing, said: "That sounds nice enough, and it's very close to the real thing. Something's missing, but I'm not sure what it is."

The real nightingale was banished from the realm.

The mechanical bird took up its place on a silk cushion near the Emperor's bed. It was surrounded by the many gifts people had given it—gold and precious stones. It had also risen in office to become Supreme Imperial Nightstand Singer. In rank it was number one to the left, for the Emperor believed the left side of the body was nobler. After all, that's where the heart is, even the Emperor's.

The Music Master wrote twenty-five volumes about the mechanical bird[18]—books so learned, long-winded, and full of obscure Chinese words that everyone claimed to have read them and understood them, because otherwise people would have said they were stupid and they would have been punched in the stomach.

A year went by in this way, and the Emperor, his court, and all the people in China knew every little twitter of the mechanical bird's song by heart, and that was exactly why they liked it so much more than anything else. They could sing its song on their own, and they did. Boys and girls in the streets sang: "Zi-zi-zi! Click, click, click,"[19] and the Emperor sang along with them. Oh, yes, it was that lovely!

But one evening, when the mechanical bird was singing with all its might and the Emperor was lying in bed listening, something inside the bird went "boing!" Something else burst and went "whirr!" Gears began spinning wildly, and then the music stopped.

The Emperor jumped right out of bed and sent for the

royal physician. But what could he do? They summoned a watchmaker,[20] who deliberated and investigated, then finally patched up the bird after a fashion. The watchmaker warned that the bird had to be kept from overdoing things, for the cogs inside it were badly worn and, if they were replaced, the music would not sound right. That was really dreadful! No one dared to let the bird sing more than once a year, and even that was almost too much. But before long the Music Master gave a little speech full of big words and claimed that the bird was just as good as new. And so it *was* just as good as new.

Five years went by, and the entire country was in deep mourning, for everyone was really fond of their ruler, and he was ill—so ill that he would probably not survive. A new Emperor had already been chosen. People were standing outside in the streets, waiting to ask the Chamberlain how the Emperor was faring.

"Puh!" he said and shook his head.

The Emperor was lying in a huge, magnificent bed, and he looked cold and pale. All the courtiers were sure that he was already gone, and they were hurrying to get out of the palace to pay homage to the new Emperor. The footmen darted around, spreading the news, and the chambermaids were holding a big party and drinking coffee. Mats had been put down in all the rooms and passageways to muffle the sound of footsteps, and that's why it was so quiet, ever so quiet. But the Emperor was not yet dead. He lay stiff and pale in his magnificent bed with its long velvet curtains and heavy golden tassels. High above him was an open window, and the moon was shining in through it on the Emperor and his mechanical bird.

The poor Emperor could barely breathe. He felt as if something was sitting on his chest.[21] When he opened his eyes, he realized that it was Death, and he was wearing the Emperor's crown on his head, holding the Emperor's golden sword in one hand, and carrying the Emperor's splendid banner in the other. Eerie-looking faces peered out between the folds of the

20. *They summoned a watchmaker.* Deism, a system of thought prominent during the seventeenth and eighteenth centuries, sometimes portrayed God as an indifferent watchmaker, who set up the universe and simply allowed it to run. Operating as precisely as the machines crafted by humans, the universe was seen to evolve in an orderly fashion.

21. *He felt as if something was sitting on his chest.* In describing the Emperor's condition, Andersen is drawing on a medical condition known as "sleep paralysis," in which an individual experiences hypnagogic hallucinations and partial muscle paralysis upon awakening. Sufferers report feeling an evil presence in the room, often in the form of a threatening incubus, hag, or monster. As in Henry Fuseli's famous painting "The Nightmare," there is the sensation that someone or something is sitting on the chest, causing suffocation. Episodes are often terminated through the perception of sounds emanating from the real world.

EDMUND DULAC

A depleted Emperor lies in bed, near death. The figure of Death is marked by emaciated boniness, but also by touches of beauty that include a helmet of gold, earrings, and peacock feathers.

great velvet curtains. Some looked perfectly dreadful, others were gentle and sweet. They were the Emperor's deeds, good and bad, and they had come back to haunt him now that Death was seated on his heart.

"Do you remember this?" they whispered one after the other. "Do you remember that?" And they told him so many things that he began to break out into a cold sweat.

"I never knew that!" the Emperor exclaimed. "Music, music! Sound the great drum of China," he cried, "so that I won't have to listen to everything they are saying."

But they would not stop, and Death nodded, like a Chinaman,[22] at every word that was uttered.

"Music, music!" the Emperor shouted. "My blessed little golden bird! Sing for me, sing! I've given you gold and precious jewels. I've even put my golden slipper around your neck. Sing for me, please sing!"

But the bird remained silent. No one was there to wind it up, and without help, it couldn't sing. Death kept on looking at the Emperor with his great hollow sockets, and everything was quiet—so dreadfully quiet.

Suddenly the loveliest song could be heard from just outside the window. It was the little nightingale—the living one—perched on a branch outdoors. It had learned of the Emperor's distress and had come from afar to sing and offer comfort and hope. While it was singing, the phantoms all around began to grow more and more pale, and the blood in the Emperor's enfeebled body began to flow more and more quickly. Death itself was listening,[23] and said, "Keep singing, little nightingale! Keep singing!"

HARRY CLARKE

Both artificial bird and nightingale appear to be singing the Emperor back to life, as demons gather around his bedside. "Music! Music!" cried the Emperor. "You little precious golden bird, sing!" The illustrator does not seem concerned about fidelity to the text in this case. He also removes the oriental element from the story through the illustration.

22. *Death nodded, like a Chinaman* The reference to the habit of nodding among the Chinese may be linked with the porcelain mandarin figures imported from China in the nineteenth century. The figures had heads attached to the body by a spring and would nod when tapped, much like today's bobbleheads. In Danish, a yes-man

is often referred to as a mandarin. The porcelain mandarin figure can be linked with the mechanical nightingale and with the notion of the automatonlike behavior that characterizes the Emperor before his transformation. In "The Shepherdess and the Chimneysweep," a porcelain mandarin figures prominently.

23. *was listening.* In ancient China, music was regarded as having transcendent power. In Andersen's story, it even has the capacity to conquer death. For nineteenth-century philosophers and other contemporaries of Andersen, like Schopenhauer, music ranked highest in the hierarchy of the arts because it does not engage in any effort to imitate, copy, or duplicate. Instead music directly captures and expresses feelings such as misery, pain, sorrow, joy, or horror.

"Yes, I will, if you give me the imperial golden sword! And if you give me the splendid banner! And if you give me the Emperor's crown!"

Death returned each of the treasures in exchange for a song. The nightingale kept on singing. It sang about silent churchyards where white roses grow, where elder trees make the air sweet, and where the grass is always green, watered by the tears of those left behind. Death began to long for his own garden and drifted out the window in a cold, gray mist.

"Thank you, thank you, you divine little bird!" the Emperor exclaimed. "Now I recognize you. I banished you once from my realm. And even then you sang until all those evil faces disappeared from around my bedside. You drove Death from my heart. How can I ever repay you?"

"You have already given me my reward," the nightingale said. "I brought tears to your eyes when I first sang for you, and I will never forget that about you. Those are the jewels that warm the hearts of singers. But go to sleep now and grow hale and hearty while I sing to you." The bird continued singing until the Emperor fell into a sweet slumber—a gentle and refreshing sleep.

The sun was shining through the windows when the Emperor awoke, restored and healthy. Not one of his servants had yet returned, for they all believed that he was dead. The nightingale was still there, singing.

"You must stay with me forever," the Emperor said. "You only have to sing when you wish, and, as for that mechanical bird, I'll smash it into a thousand pieces."

"Don't do that," the nightingale said. "It has done the very best it could—and you really should keep it. I can't live inside the palace, but let me come for a visit whenever I wish. In the evening, I'll alight on the branch by your window and bring you pleasure and wisdom with my song. I will sing about those who are happy and those who suffer. I'll sing about the good and evil that remains hidden from you. A little songbird gets around—to the poor fishermen, to the rooftops of farmers, to everyone who is far away from you and your court. I love your heart more than I love your crown, but there is something sacred about your crown.[24] I'll come to sing for you, but you must promise me one thing."

"Anything!" the Emperor replied, standing there in the imperial robes that he himself had donned and holding his heavy golden sword against his heart.

"Just one thing," the nightingale asked. "You must not let anyone know that you have a little bird that tells you everything,[25] for things will go better that way."

Then the nightingale flew away.

The servants came in to attend their dead Emperor. Yes—there they stood. And the Emperor said to them, "Good morning!"[26]

24. *something sacred about your crown.* All his life, Andersen harbored an ambivalent attitude toward monarchs and the nobility, combining contempt with reverence. However, some biographers, most notably Jack Zipes, see him as consistently "servile" and "opportunistic." For Zipes, Andersen's tales revealed a "false consciousness" and represented "literary exercises in the legitimation of a social order to which he subscribed" (Zipes 2005, 75). In "The Nightingale," Andersen mirrors his own sycophantic relationship to the aristocracy when he restores "the relationship of servitude" between bird and emperor: "Feudalism has been replaced by a free-market system; yet, the bird/artist is willing to serve loyally and keep the autocrat in power" (Zipes 2005, 67).

25. *"You must not let anyone know that you have a little bird that tells you everything."* The bird takes on a supervisory role, monitoring and reporting on the behavior of the Emperor's subjects. Note the emphasis on good deeds and bad deeds in the deathbed scene. The story ends on a moralizing note, suggesting that the nightingale does not just create beauty but also polices the ethical dimension of human actions. As in "The Little Mermaid," the moral duties assumed by the main character seem like an afterthought, and it is odd to see the nightingale, who loves the solitude of the woods, suddenly take on a social function.

26. *"Good morning!"* The Emperor's subjects are obviously receiving a shock, but the bright, sunny greeting comes as something of a surprise for the reader as well. The reversal in the Emperor's health and fortune seems to usher in a new day marked by good cheer and enlightened rule. The Emperor will, presumably, no longer threaten his subjects with punches in the stomach.

KAY NIELSEN

The nightingale sings triumphantly, perched on Death's scythe, which seems to be racing away from the Emperor's bed.

The Ugly Duckling[1]

Den grimme ælling

Nye Eventyr, Første Samling, 1843

he ugly duckling has led a charmed existence over the past century and a half, alluded to in Bram Stoker's Dracula, *celebrated in Sergei Prokofiev's music, and, less surprisingly, taken up in Walt Disney's films. The story of the abject, despised bird has taken hold in many cultures, becoming one of our most beloved—and most reassuring—childhood tales. It promises all of us, children and adults, that we have the capacity to transform ourselves for the better.*

Like many a fairy-tale character, the ugly duckling is meek and small, the youngest in the brood. A misfit out of place in the barnyard, in the wilderness, and in the domestic arena, he is unable to find a bond with other creatures. But, like Andersen himself as a youth, he is adventurous and determined, resolving to go out into "the wide world." His metamorphosis into a beautiful swan has been evoked for generations as a source of comfort to those suffering from feelings of social isolation and personal inadequacy.

Small, powerless, and often treated dismissively, children are likely to identify with Andersen's "hideous" creature, who may be unpromising but who also, in time, surpasses the promising. As Bruno Bettelheim points out in The Uses of Enchantment, *Ander-*

1. *Ugly Duckling.* Andersen conceived the story in 1842 while living at an estate named Bregentved, where he became absorbed in the beauty of the landscape. During a stay in Rome, he declared the "Book of Nature" to be his real tutor: "On my silent walks, close to the ancient manor houses, I discovered more than I could ever have derived from wisdom in books. Here, I could be independent, give myself over to and become part of Nature" (*Travels*, 230).

Andersen reports that he first contemplated the title "The Young Swans": "While I was writing I was often undecided, Duck or Swan? I ended by calling it 'The Ugly Duckling,' since I did not want to betray the element of surprise in the duckling's metamorphosis." He also emphasizes the tale's confessional nature: "This story is, of course, a reflection of my own life" (*Travels*, 232).

The term "ugly duckling" has become code for an unpromising person who ends up surprising and surpassing everyone else. In fairy tales, the despised prove their worth, the slow triumph over the swift, the stupid outsmart the clever. Jenny Lind, the "Swedish nightingale" with whom Andersen fell in love, was enraptured by "The Ugly Duckling," and she lavished praise on the story in a letter of 1844 to Andersen: "Oh, what a marvelous gift to be able to put in words your most noble thoughts. To make us see, with a mere scrap of paper but with wit, how the most outstanding people are sometimes hidden and disguised by their wretchedness and rags until the hour of transformation strikes and reveals them in a divine light."

2. *it was summertime!* For Andersen, summer was the season of hope, and he sets the scene with descriptions that capture his own sense of exhilaration at sights in the countryside. In the summer of 1842, he spent time at two Danish manors that seemed to him like "fairy caves," and his diary records landscape descriptions that anticipate what appears in "The Ugly Duckling." The pastoral scene of the beginning is set at a time when the natural beauty of the countryside is at its height.

The beautiful visual effects in this story are not at all anticipated by the term "ugly" in the title. This tale in particular led many of Andersen's contemporaries to think of him as an illustrator as well as an author, and indeed he had an artist's eye for beauty. Andersen enjoyed sketching at home and on his travels, and he left behind over three hundred drawings and well over one thousand paper cuts. He was also an enthusiastic visitor of museums and kept track of the many paintings he saw in his travel diaries.

3. *chattering away in Egyptian.* Legend has it that storks were once men and that they returned to their human state in Egypt during the winter. That storks bring babies is a familiar superstition, which seems to derive from the fact that the birds have long been perceived as har-

sen's protagonist does not have to submit to the tests, tasks, and trials usually imposed on the heroes of fairy tales. "No need to accomplish anything is expressed in 'The Ugly Duckling.' Things are simply fated and unfold accordingly, whether or not the hero takes some action" (Bettelheim, 105). Andersen suggests that the ugly duckling's innate superiority resides in the fact that he is of a different breed. Unlike the other ducks, he has been hatched from a swan's egg. This implied hierarchy in nature—majestic swans versus the barnyard rabble—seems to suggest that dignity and worth, along with aesthetic and moral superiority, are determined by nature rather than by accomplishment. Whatever the pleasures of a story that celebrates the triumph of the underdog, it is worth pondering the full range of ethical and aesthetic issues raised by that victory in a story that is read today by children the world over.

"The Ugly Duckling" was published with three other tales in a collection called New Fairy Tales. *It sold out almost immediately, and Andersen wrote with pride about its success in a letter of December 18, 1843: "The book is selling like hot cakes! All the papers are praising it, everyone is reading it! No books of mine are appreciated in the way that these fairy tales are!" (H. C. Andersen og Henriette Wulff, I, 349)*

It was so beautiful out in the country—it was summertime![2] The grain was golden, the oats were green, and hay was piled in stacks down in the green meadows. A stork with long red legs was strolling around and chattering away in Egyptian,[3] a language he had learned from his mother. All around the fields and meadows lay vast forests dotted with deep lakes. Yes, it was really lovely out there in the country! Right in the sunshine you could see an old castle[4] surrounded by a deep moat with huge burdock leaves[5] covering the stretch from the walls down to the water. The leaves were so high up that little children could stand upright beneath the

largest of them. It was just as wild in there as in the densest forest, and that's just where you could see a duck sitting on her nest. The time had come for her to hatch her little ducklings, but it was such a slow job that she was growing tired of it. There were hardly any visitors. The other ducks preferred swimming around in the moat to sitting under a burdock leaf just for the sake of a quack with her.

At last the eggs cracked open, one by one. "Cheep, cheep," they all said. The egg yolks had finally come to life and stuck their heads out.

"Quack, quack!" said the mother duck, and the little ones quacked as best they could and looked around quickly from under the green leaves all about. The mother let them feast their eyes, for greenery is good for the eyes.

"The world is so big!"[6] all the ducklings said, for they now had much more room than when they were curled up in an egg.

"Do you really think that this is all there is to the world!" their mother exclaimed. "Why, it stretches way past the other side of the garden, right into the parson's field. But I've never ventured that far out. Well, you're all hatched now, I hope." And she rose from the nest. "Wait a minute! Not everyone is out yet! The biggest egg is still lying here. How much longer

bingers of good fortune and happiness. It was believed that they picked up infants from marshes, ponds, and springs, where the souls of unborn children dwelled. Storks and birds in general (associated with freedom and hope) appear frequently in Andersen's stories, and one of the tales he wrote is entitled "The Storks."

Andersen reports that he was frequently inspired by the sight of birds—swallows and storks in particular. In 1848, he wrote: "Many of my stories are caused by a 'sighting' from outside. Anyone with the eye of a poet can look at life and nature and experience a similar revelation of beauty. It could be called 'accidental poetry' " (*Travels*, 300).

4. *an old castle*. The grounds bear a striking resemblance to Bregentved, the old manor house, complete with moats and drawbridges, where Andersen began writing the story. (Andersen had already achieved a degree of fame that allowed him to take advantage of hospitality from admirers of his work.)

5. *huge burdock leaves*. The burdock plant is a coarse, broad-leaved weed bearing prickly heads of burr. It grows wild on waste ground, by roadsides, and in wet areas and has large lower leaves on thick stalks sometimes reaching a foot in height. Its unattractiveness contrasts with the natural beauty of the area in which it grows. The plant introduces the theme of gawky unsightliness, but beyond that it also serves as a womb-like ("secret") shelter, one that connects love and birth, for the burdock's lower leaves are heart-shaped at the bottom and egg-shaped at the top.

6. *"The world is so big!"* Andersen's tales often draw a contrast between the rural and the urban or between the local delights of the village and the urban anarchy of towns and cities. (He himself had

experienced both the small-town serenity of Odense and the alluring hustle and bustle of Copenhagen.) For the newborn ducklings, as for all children, the measure of the world is taken by how far the eye can see. The "wide world" is a recurrent theme in the stories, and vast expanses are seen as both intimidating and exhilarating.

7. *looking ever so big and hideous.* The hideousness of the "duckling" contrasts with the "loveliness" of the other newborns, whose attractiveness has a moral as well as aesthetic dimension. Andersen does not use the Danish equivalent of "ugly" until the end of the tale.

is this going to take, anyway? I've just about had it!" And she sat back down in the nest.

"Well, how are you getting on?" asked an old duck who had come to pay a visit.

"One of the eggs is taking so long to hatch!" said the duck on the nest. "It just won't open. But take a look at the others—the loveliest ducklings I've ever seen. They all take after their father, the scoundrel! He never even comes to pay a visit."

"Let's have a look at the egg that won't crack open," said the old duck. "I'll wager it's a turkey's egg. That's how I was once bamboozled. The little ones gave me no end of trouble, for they were afraid of the water—imagine that! I just couldn't get them to go in. I quacked and clacked, but it didn't do any good. Let's have a look at that egg. Oh, yes, that's a turkey's egg—you can bet on it! Leave it alone and start teaching the others to swim."

"I think I'll sit on it just a little longer," said the duck. "I've been sitting so long that it can't hurt to sit a bit more."

"Suit yourself!" said the old duck, and off she waddled.

Finally the big egg began to crack. The little one said, "Cheep, cheep!" as he tumbled out, looking ever so big and hideous.[7] The duck took a look and said: "My, what a great big duckling that is! The others don't look like that. But it couldn't be a turkey chick, could it? Well, we shall soon see. Into the water he goes, even if I have to push him in myself!"

The next morning the weather was gloriously beautiful, and the sun was shining brightly on all the green burdock leaves. The mother duck came down to the water with her entire family and splash! She jumped right in. "Quack, quack," she said, and one after another the ducklings plunged in after her. The water closed over their heads, but in an instant they were back up again, floating along serenely. Their legs paddled along on their own, and now the whole group was in the water—even the hideous gray duckling was swimming right along with them.

"He's not a turkey, that's for sure," said the duck. "Look how well he uses his legs and how straight he holds himself. He's my own little one all right, and he's quite handsome, when you take a good look at him. Quack, quack! Now come along with me and let me show you the world and introduce you to everyone in the barnyard. But pay attention and stay close to me so that nobody steps on you. And make sure you watch out for that cat."

And so they made their way into the duck yard. It was terribly noisy there, because two families were fighting over an eel's head. In the end, the cat got it.

"You see, that's the way of the world," said the mother duck, and she licked her beak, because she would not have minded getting the eel's head. "Come now, use your legs and look sharp," she said. "Make a nice bow to the old duck over there. She's the most genteel of anyone here.[8] She has Spanish blood, that's why she is so plump. And can you see that crimson flag she's wearing on one leg? It's extremely lovely, and it's the highest distinction any duck can earn. It's as good as saying that no one is thinking of getting rid of her. Man and beast are to take notice! Look alive, and don't turn your toes in! A well-bred duckling turns its toes out, just like its father and mother . . . That's it. Now bend your necks and say 'quack!' "

They all obeyed. But the other ducks there looked at them and said out loud: "There! Now we have to deal with that bunch as well—as if there weren't enough of us already! Ugh! What a sight that duckling is! How can we possibly put up with him as well?" And one of the ducks immediately flew at him and bit him in the neck.

"Leave him alone," said the mother. "He's not doing any harm."

"Yes, but he's so gawky and odd-looking," said the one that had pecked him. "We can't help picking on him."

"What pretty children you have, my dear!" said the old duck

MARGARET TARRANT

The ducklings take their first plunge and have no trouble coming back to the surface. Perched on a stone, the mother duck takes note of the one anomaly in the group.

8. *"She's the most genteel of anyone here."* Note that Andersen's farmyard has its hierarchies and social rankings, and that the psychological dynamics and social organization resemble that of the human world. Andersen himself suffered perpetually under the burden of his social origins, and some critics see in the farmyard a symbolic representation of Odense, Copenhagen, Slagelse, and Elsinore, places at which Andersen documented the resistance he felt to social acceptance.

W. HEATH ROBINSON

The duckling is picked on by everyone. Even the maid who feeds the poultry threatens him, and he tries desperately to escape. Far larger than the small duckling, the maid menaces the poor creature with her pot and with the dark shadow she casts.

9. *"he's a drake, and so it doesn't matter as much."* In fairy tales, looks count less for the heroes than the heroines, who usually succeed in living happily ever after because of their perfect beauty. By contrast, even a beast can win a fair princess, although Andersen's ugly duckling does not take up that particular opportunity.

10. *pecked and jostled and was teased.* As a boy growing up in Odense, Andersen kept to himself, but he witnessed the cruelty of schoolboy taunts when his mentally unstable grandfather was chased down the street. Attending school in Slagelse, he became—as the oldest and tallest in the class—the perpetual target of teasing. Even as an adult, Andersen found himself subject to constant insults. In his travel diaries, he recalls an incident that took

with the flag on her leg. "All but that one, who didn't turn out quite right. Too bad you can't start over again with him."

"That's impossible, Your Grace," said the duckling's mother. "He may not be handsome, but he's so good-tempered and he can swim just as beautifully as the others—I dare say even a bit better. I think his looks will improve when he grows up, or maybe in time he'll shrink a little. He was in the egg for too long—that's why he isn't quite the right shape." And then she stroked his neck and smoothed out his feathers. "Anyway, he's a drake, and so it doesn't matter as much,"[9] she added. "I feel sure he'll turn out strong and be able to take care of himself."

"The other ducklings are charming," said the old duck. "Make yourselves at home, my dears, and if you should find anything that looks like an eel's head, you can bring it over to me."

And so they made themselves at home.

The poor duckling who had been the last to crawl out of his shell and who looked so hideous got pecked and jostled and was teased[10] by ducks and hens alike. "He's just enormous!" they all clucked. And the turkey, who had been born with spurs and who fancied himself an emperor, puffed himself up like a ship in full rigging and went straight at him. Then he gobble-gobbled until he was quite red in the face. The poor duckling didn't know where to turn. He was quite upset at looking so unattractive and becoming the laughingstock of the barnyard.

That's how it went the

first day, and things only got worse from there. The poor duckling was picked on by everyone. Even his own brothers and sisters were cruel to him and kept saying: "Oh, you ugly creature, if only the cat would get you." His mother said: "If only you were far away!" The ducks nipped at him,[11] the chickens pecked him, and the maid who had to feed the poultry kicked him with her foot.

At last, he ran off and flew over the hedge, making the little birds in the bushes swarm into the air with fright. "They are afraid of me because I am so hideous," he said. But he closed his eyes and kept moving until he reached some marshes[12] where wild ducks lived. He stayed there all night, feeling utterly tired and dejected.

W. HEATH ROBINSON

Alone in the world, the duckling leaves the barnyard and makes his way to marshes, where he will meet wild ducks. Like many of Andersen's characters, he must fend for himself in the "wide world."

In the morning, when the wild ducks flew up into the air, they stared at their new companion. "What kind of duck could you possibly be?" they all asked, looking him up and down. He bowed his neck in their direction and greeted them as best he could.

"You really are nasty-looking," said the wild ducks, "but we don't care as long as you don't try to marry into our families." Poor thing! He wasn't dreaming about marriage.[13] All he wanted was a chance to lie quietly among the rushes and drink a little marsh water.

place at the theater, when he intimated to an acquaintance that he might be attending a ball held by King Christian VIII. "What was your father?" the friend asked. "The blood rose to the top of my ears," Andersen recalls. " 'My father was a shoemaker!' I said. 'I am what I am, with the help of God and my own initiative, and I would hope that was something you could respect.' " Andersen adds that he never received an apology "for this slight" (*Travels*, 229–30).

11. *The ducks nipped at him.* The cumulative effect of bites, nips, and kicks drives the duckling from the "civilized" world of the barnyard to the swamp, where wild creatures live. An outcast in the animal world, the duckling is scorned by humans as well—the girl who feeds the animals represents the lack of charity in humans as well as animals toward the unsightly

appearance of the duckling. "It's because I'm so ugly," the duckling declares as he reproaches himself by pointing to the disruptive energy of ugliness and how it is seen to elicit hatred and aggression. As so often in Andersen's writing, a series of events leading to a climactic turn is captured at a breathless pace: the ducks nip, the chickens peck, and the maid kicks until the poor animal flees.

12. *until he reached some marshes.* Andersen referred to himself as a swamp plant, a form of life that had originated in murky waters. Note also that the swamp is an in-between zone, one that combines solid land with watery depths.

13. *He wasn't dreaming about marriage.* While many fairy-tale heroes rise in social station through marriage, the duckling aspires merely to social acceptance. For those who read the story in biographical terms, it is worth noting that Andersen remained a bachelor all his life.

After he had been there for two whole days, a couple of wild geese,[14] or rather two wild ganders (for they were male), came along. They had not been out of the egg for long and were very frisky.

"Look here, old pal," one of them said to the duckling. "You are so hideous that we rather like you. Why don't you join us and become a bird of passage? Not far off in another marsh there are some very nice, sweet wild geese, none of them married, and they all quack beautifully. Here's a chance for you to get lucky, as hideous as you are."

"Bang! Bang!" Shots suddenly rang out overhead, and the two wild geese fell dead into the rushes. The water turned red with their blood.[15] "Bang! Bang!" More shots—and flocks of wild geese rose up from the rushes. Then shots rang out again. It was a big hunt, and the hunters had surrounded the marsh. Some of the men were even hidden in tree branches that stretched far out over the rushes. Blue smoke from the guns rose like clouds over the dark trees and hung low over the water. Hounds came bounding through the mud—Splish, Splash! Reeds and rushes bent every which way. How they terrified the poor duckling! He was trying to hide his head under his wing when he suddenly became aware of a fearsomely large dog with lolling tongue and grim, glaring eyes. It lowered its muzzle right down to the duckling, bared its sharp teeth and—splish, splash—went off again without touching him.

"Thank goodness," the duckling sighed with relief. "I'm so hideous that even the dog can't be bothered to bite me!"

So he lay there quite still, while bullets whistled through the reeds and rushes, and shot after shot blasted through the air.

By the time the noises had died down, it was late in the day. But the poor young duckling didn't dare get up yet. He waited quietly for several hours, and then, after taking a careful look around him, he fled the marsh as fast as he could. He scrambled over meadows and fields, but the wind was so

14. *wild geese.* One critic has identified the wild geese as the young Bohemian poets with whom Andersen associated during his schooldays at Slagelse. Fritz Petit, who translated Andersen into German, and Carl Bagger, to whom the volume containing "The Ugly Duckling" is dedicated, lived loosely and encouraged Andersen—unsuccessfully—to indulge in a more reckless lifestyle. The swans that appear at the end of the story stand in stark contrast to the wild geese and have been seen as representing the great writers of Europe.

15. *The water turned red with their blood.* The soothing greens and yellows of the rustic landscape are turned red with blood and become blue with smoke from the guns. The appearance of hunters in the wilderness marks a second, even more violent, incursion by humans into settings populated by animals. Both domestic creatures and wild animals are threatened by the brutality of human agents.

W. HEATH ROBINSON

The ugly duckling is dwarfed by the cat, whose minimalist but expressive eyes suggest deep suspicion and skepticism

16. *An old woman was living in the cottage with her tomcat and hen.* The duckling has an opportunity to escape the threats from the barnyard and the dangers of the wilderness and to try out the comforts of interiority and domestic life. The old woman plays a subordinate role in the household, with the purring cat and the egg-laying hen serving as master and mistress. Unable to adjust to the two domineering figures and longing for fresh air

strong that he had trouble making any progress.

Toward evening, he reached a small run-down cottage that was in such poor repair that it remained standing only because it could not figure out which way to collapse first. The wind blew so powerfully around the duckling that he had to sit on his tail to keep from being blown over. Soon the wind grew even fiercer. The duckling noticed that the door had come off one of its hinges and was hanging at an angle that allowed him to sneak into the house through a crack, which he did.

An old woman was living in the cottage with her tomcat and hen.[16] The tomcat, whom she called Sonny, could arch his back and purr. He even gave off sparks, if you stroked his fur the wrong way. The hen had such short legs that she was called Chickabiddy Shortlegs. She was a good layer of eggs, and the old woman loved her so much that she was like a daughter.

First thing in the morning the tomcat and hen noticed the strange duckling, and the cat began to purr and the hen began to cluck.

"What's all the fuss about?" asked the old woman, looking around the room. But her eyes weren't very good, and she took the ugly duckling for a plump duck that had strayed from home. "My, what a find!" she exclaimed. "I shall be able to have some duck eggs soon, as long as it's not a drake! We'll just have to wait and see."

And so the duckling was taken on trial for three weeks, but there was no sign of an egg. Now the tomcat was master of the house, and the hen was mistress, and they always used to say: "We and the world," for they fancied that they made up half the world, and, what's more, the better half too. The duckling thought that there might be two opinions about that, but the hen wouldn't hear of it.

"Can you lay eggs?" she asked.

"No!"

"Well, then, hold your tongue, will you!"

The tomcat asked: "Can you arch your back, or purr, or give off sparks?"

"No!"

"Well, then, no one needs your opinion, especially with sensible people around to do the talking."

The duckling sat in a corner, feeling quite dejected. Then suddenly, he remembered the fresh air and the sunshine, and he began to feel such a deep longing for a swim on the water that he could not help letting the hen know.

"What are you thinking?" said the hen. "You have far too much time on your hands. That's why such foolish ideas come into your head. They would vanish if you were able to lay eggs or purr."

"But it's so lovely to glide on the water,"[17] the duckling said, "and so lovely to duck your head in and dive down to the bottom."

"Delightful, I'm sure!" said the hen. "Why, you must be crazy! Ask the cat, he is the cleverest animal I know. Ask him how he feels about swimming or diving. I won't even give my views. Ask our mistress, the old woman—there is no one in the world wiser than she is. Do you think she likes to swim or to dive down into the water?"

"You don't understand me," said the duckling.

"Well, if we don't understand you, I should like to know who does.[18] It's clear that you will never be as wise as the cat or the mistress, not to mention me. Don't be silly, child! Thank your maker for the good fortune that has come your way. Haven't you found a nice, warm room, along with a circle of friends from whom you can learn something? But

and sunshine (despite the perils of the "wide world"), the duckling returns to his natural element.

17. *"But it's so lovely to glide on the water."* The duckling, unlike the hen that can lay eggs, provides no added value in the household. Even as a swan, he will produce nothing but pleasure, gliding on the waters and diving into them to indulge himself and to evoke the admiration of observers.

18. *"I should like to know who does."* The duckling remains misunderstood, despite repeated efforts to find a place where he feels at home. Like many characters in Andersen's short stories, he is determined to seek a second home, a place where he can escape persecution.

19. *a raven perched on a fence.* Often considered birds of ill omen, ravens are also famous for their intelligence. The term "raven's knowledge" means knowledge of all things. The croaking of the raven has a venerable literary tradition suggesting doom: "The raven himself is hoarse / that croaks the fatal entrance of Duncan / under my battlements," Lady Macbeth declares (*Macbeth* I, 5). It is not by chance that common parlance refers to a "terror of ravens" or a "murder of crows." As birds who feed on carrion, ravens have come to be associated with vengeance, death, and with the doom and gloom of Poe's raven, who repeats the word "nevermore."

20. *had never seen anything so beautiful.* The story begins in an idyllic country setting marked by sunshine and summer beauty. Scenes of squalor and degradation follow, but the appearance of the swans provides a burst of beauty in a season of clouds, cold, hail, and snow. The birds are not only physically beautiful, they also have "wondrous" calls that heighten the astonishment produced by their appearance. The aesthetic effect of the birds conveys the experience of the sublime, a moment in which shock mingles with wonder, leading the duckling to let loose a cry and plunge into the waters. The "whiteness" of the swans contrasts with what is described as the "black-gray" hues of the duckling.

you're just stupid, and there's no fun in having you here. Believe me, if I say unpleasant things, it's only for your own good and a proof of real friendship. But take my advice. See to it that you start to lay eggs or learn how to purr or throw off sparks."

"I think I'll go back out into the wide world," said the duckling.

"Go ahead," said the hen.

And so the duckling departed. He dove down into the water and swam about, but no one else would have anything to do with him because he was so ugly. Autumn arrived, and the leaves in the forest turned yellow and brown. As they fell to the ground, the wind caught them and made them dance. The sky overhead had a frosty look. The clouds hung heavy with hail and snowflakes, and a raven perched on a fence,[19] crying, "Caw! Caw!" because of the bitter cold. It gave you the shivers just to think about it. Yes, the poor duckling was certainly having a hard time.

One evening, during a splendid sunset, a large flock of lovely birds suddenly emerged from the bushes. The duckling had never seen anything so beautiful;[20] the birds were dazzlingly white with long, graceful necks. They were swans. They made wondrous sounds, spread out their magnificent, broad wings, and flew away from these cold regions to warmer countries, to lakes that were not frozen. As the ugly little duckling watched them rise higher and higher up into the air, he felt a strange sensation. He spun round and round in the water like a wheel and craned his neck in their direction, letting out a cry that was so shrill and strange that he himself was frightened when he heard it. How could he ever forget those beautiful birds, those fortunate birds! As soon as he lost sight of them, he dove down to the very bottom of the waters, and when he surfaced, he was almost beside himself with excitement. He had no idea who those birds were,[21] nor did he know anything about where they were off to, but he loved them as he had never loved anyone before. He was not at all envious of them. After all, how could he ever aspire to such beauty? He would be quite satisfied if the ducks would just have let him be among them. The poor, ugly creature!

The winter was cold, so very cold. The duckling had to keep swimming about in the water to keep it from freezing solid around him. Every night the hole in which he was swimming grew smaller and smaller. The water froze so solidly that the crust of the ice crackled, and the duckling had to keep his feet moving constantly to keep the water from freezing solid. Finally, he grew faint with exhaustion and lay quite still and helpless, frozen fast in the ice.[22]

Early the next morning, a farmer walked by and saw the poor duckling. He went out on the pond, broke the ice with his wooden clog, and took the duckling home to his wife.[23] There they revived him.

The children wanted to play with him, but the duckling was afraid they would hurt him.[24] He started up in a panic, fluttering right into the milk bowl[25] so that milk splashed all over the room. When the farmer's wife let out a shriek and threw her hands up in the air, he flew into the butter tub, and from there into the flour bin and out again.

MABEL LUCIE ATTWELL

The ugly duckling's gawkiness makes him a misfit. The children react to him with astonishment and trepidation, pointing fingers and keeping their distance but also moving forward with gestures and implements that threaten the duckling's safety. The creature is clearly not in his element.

21. *He had no idea who those birds were.* Andersen takes us inside the mind of the ugly duckling. Unlike conventional fairy tales, Andersen's stories let us inhabit the minds of the central characters, feeling their pain and enjoying their pleasures. The introspective turn and perpetual self-analysis of the characters leads to a constant monitoring of their affect. The prominence of phrases such as "he felt," as in this passage, makes it clear how important it was to Andersen to have the reader establish an empathetic relationship to his characters.

22. *frozen fast in the ice.* In the pond, the ugly duckling struggles to stay alive, and, in a classic triple sequence that is a trademark of Andersen's style, he is "faint with exhaustion," "quite still and helpless," and finally, "frozen fast in the ice." The final phrase points to the duckling's glacial incarceration: he becomes a petrified ornament in the pond, dead to the world. For Andersen, a turn away from carnality (sometimes taking the extreme form of mortification of the flesh and physical paralysis) serves as the prerequisite for spiritual plenitude and salvation. This episode points up the cult of suffering embedded in Andersen's stories—physical distress and spiritual anguish are a sign of virtue. It could, alternatively, be argued that the ugly duckling undergoes a test of

his character and fortitude. Staunchly enduring taunts from others and defying the physical challenges of nature, he steadfastly paddles his legs to stay alive.

23. *took the duckling home to his wife.* In this final, failed attempt to find refuge, the ugly duckling's disruptive presence becomes evident. His "ugliness" and clumsiness become stimuli for aggression, with a farmer's wife who repeats the violence of the girl who feeds the animals in the barnyard.

24. *the duckling was afraid they would hurt him.* Andersen's surprising dislike of small children, given the audience for his stories today, is well documented. In the plan for a commemorative statue in Copenhagen, he asked that the child looking over his shoulder be removed from the design. But his hatred of one of the sketches, which reminded him of "old Socrates and young Alcibiades," may have been inspired by very different anxieties. As a child he was an avid reader, who stayed away from other children. "I never played with the other boys," he reported in a letter to his benefactor Jonas Collin, "I was always alone."

25. *fluttering right into the milk bowl.* One commentator notes that the duckling flies "into the milk (the substance of creation), butter (a source of richness and abundance), and flour (a distillation of earth energy)." Those elements are reconstituted and baked in the bread tossed by the children at the swans (Gambos, 70).

MARGARET TARRANT

The duckling flees after flying into the butter tub and overturning the flour bin. The duckling is already in a transitional stage, halfway to becoming a swan.

He was quite a sight! The woman shrieked again and chased after him with the fire tongs, and the children stumbled all over each other trying to catch him. How they laughed and shouted! It was lucky that the door was open. The duckling darted out into the bushes and sank down, dazed, in the newly fallen snow.

It would be dreary[26] to describe all the misery and hardship the duckling endured in the course of that hard winter. When the sun began to shine warmly again, he was lying in the marsh among the reeds. The lark was singing—it was a beautiful spring day once again.[27]

Then all of a sudden the duckling flapped his wings. They beat more strongly than ever and swiftly carried him away. Almost before he knew it, he found himself in a large garden,[28] where apple trees were in full blossom and fragrant lilacs bent their long green branches down on to the winding waterways. It was so lovely here, so full of the freshness of spring! Right in front of him, three beautiful white swans emerged from a nearby thicket, ruffling their feathers and floating lightly over the still waters. The duckling recognized the splendid creatures and was overcome by a strange feeling of melancholy.

"I want to fly over to those royal birds. Maybe they will peck me to death for daring to approach them, hideous as I am. But it doesn't matter. Better to be killed by them than to be nipped by the ducks, pecked by the hens, kicked by the maid who tends the henhouse, and suffer hardship in the winter."

The duckling landed on the water and swam out to the majestic swans. When they caught sight of him, they rushed to meet him with outstretched wings. "Oh please, just kill me," cried the poor bird,[29] and bowed his head down to the water, awaiting death. But what did he see reflected in the clear water? He saw his own image[30] beneath him, but he was no longer a clumsy, dark gray bird, nasty and hideous—he was a swan!

W. HEATH ROBINSON

The swan glides on the surface of the water while a girl gazes at him from the marshes with admiration.

26. *It would be dreary.* The narrator claims to suppress the desire to elaborate on the misery endured by the duckling, and yet the story of the ugly duckling provides painful details about all the hardships, physical and mental, suffered by the tormented animal.

27. *it was a beautiful spring day once again.* The return of spring signals the renewal of hope. For Andersen, every season has a different affective power, with all of the obvious cyclical associations of winter with death and spring with rebirth and renewal. Summer and spring are, as in "The Snow Queen," always a time of joy.

28. *he found himself in a large garden.* The garden represents the point at which

nature and culture meet, the place where the ugly duckling finds happiness at last. The utopian beauty of the garden, with its colors and fragrances, becomes the perfect setting to display the beauty of the swans.

29. *"Oh please just kill me," cried the poor bird.* The duckling's suffering is so intense that it moves him toward self-annihilation. It is startling that he looks on death as salvation, so long as the beautiful swans are the executioners.

30. *He saw his own image.* In this scene of transformation, the ugly duckling engages in a moment of reflection—reflection in the double sense of the term. He sees himself mirrored in the surface of the water and also analyzes his condition. In this extraordinary humanizing moment—animals cannot engage in this double process—the ugly duckling transcends both ugliness and his animal condition. Self-reflexivity may not be the cause of the transformation, but it is telling that it coincides with the transformation.

If the ugly duckling triumphs in the end and reigns supreme as the "most beautiful of all," he is also reduced to the rank of an ornament, gliding on the surface of the pond as he is admired by children who reward his preening with bits of bread. Many scholars have argued that "The Ugly Duckling" is the most deeply personal of Andersen's stories, a narrative that traces his trajectory from humble origins to a literary aristocracy with a deeply servile attitude in relation to the real aristocracy. Jack Zipes comments that it only "appears as though the swan has finally come into his own. . . . As usual, there is a hidden reference of power. The swan measures himself by the values and aesthetics set by the 'royal' swans and by the proper well-behaved children and people in the beautiful garden. The swans and beautiful garden are placed in opposition to the

HARRY CLARKE

"The new one is the most beautiful of all," exclaim the children surrounding the pond. Clarke's children are dressed in sophisticated, elegant attire that blends in with the landscape. The peacock in the foreground emphasizes the triumph of beauty in the tale's conclusion.

ducks and hen yard. In appealing to the 'noble' sentiments of a refined audience and his readers, Andersen reflected a distinct class bias if not classical racist tendencies" (Zipes 2005, 70).

Jon Scieszka and Lane Smith's "The Really Ugly Duckling" provides a postmodern revision of Andersen's tale, one in which there is no transformation, just the

move from being an ugly duckling to a "really ugly duck." As Jean Webb points out, "The convention of transformation so essential to the tradition of the fairy tale has been supplanted by the removal of the sublime experience, the achievement of the ideal. The postmodern perspective recognizes that we cannot become ideal selves, idealized forms, for there are realities which have to be accepted" (Webb, 161).

There's nothing wrong with being born in a duck yard, as long as you are hatched from a swan's egg! He now felt positively glad to have endured so much hardship and adversity. It helped him appreciate all the happiness and beauty surrounding him. The great swans swam around him and stroked his neck with their beaks.

Some little children came into the garden and threw bread and grain onto the water. The youngest cried out: "There's a new swan!"

The other children were delighted and shouted: "Yes, there's a new swan!" And they clapped their hands and danced around and ran to fetch their fathers and mothers. Bits of bread and cake were thrown on the water, and everyone said: "The new one is the most beautiful of all. He is so young and handsome." And the old swans bowed before him.

The duckling felt quite bashful and tucked his head under

31. *a good heart is never proud!* For Andersen, pride and vanity are the cardinal sins of humanity, and, despite the fact (or perhaps *because* of the fact) that he was guilty of both, he never ceased to excoriate both. Those with a humble heart are the true heroes of mankind, and they are often oppressed by the haughty, arrogant, and proud. Children from prosperous families scorned the young Andersen and mocked him with the words "Look, there's the playwright!" In his memoirs, Andersen recalls that he went home, hid in a corner, and "cried and prayed to God." Later in life, he suffered countless insults from his patron Jonas Collin and his family members, who always made him aware that he was their social inferior. Danish reviewers of Andersen's work were also less kind than critical and condescending, constantly pointing to the author's class origins and aspirations to a higher social rank. "When I was young," Andersen pointed out, "I could cry; now I can't! I can only be proud, hate, despise, give my soul to the evil powers to find a moment's comfort." As he reflected further on the vitriolic reviews of Danish critics, he warmed to his topic: "The Danes are evil, cold, satanic—a people well suited to the wet, moldy-green islands from where Tycho Brahe was exiled. . . . May I never see that place; may never a nature such as mine be born there again. I hate, I despise my home, as it hates and spits upon me!" (*Diaries*, 137–38)

MARGARET TARRANT

The swans approach the children, looking for bits of bread and cake. The red-headed girl points to the new arrival, who is also the youngest and handsomest in the quartet.

his wing—he himself hardly knew why. He was so very happy, but not at all proud, for a good heart is never proud![31] He thought about how he had been despised and scorned, and he heard everybody saying now that he was the most beautiful of all the beautiful birds. And the lilacs bowed their branches toward him, right down into the water. The sun shone so warm and so bright. Then he ruffled his feathers,

CHARLES ROBINSON.

The Big Book of Fairy Tales. London: Blackie & Son, 1911.

32. *"I never dreamed of such happiness."* In a famous essay of 1869 on Andersen, the renowned Danish literary critic George Brandes denounced the servile tone of "The Ugly Duckling" and its glorification of a tamed existence: "Let [the duckling] die if necessary, that is tragic and grand. Let it lift its wings and fly soaring through the air, jubilant at its own beauty and strength" (Bredsdorff 1993, 154). The fantasy of such sublime happiness was fulfilled in part for Andersen after the astonishing success of the fairy tales in Denmark and abroad. "The Ugly Duckling" was one of the tales that transformed him from a local writer into a celebrity of international importance.

raised his slender neck, and rejoiced from the depths of his heart. "I never dreamed of such happiness[32] when I was an ugly duckling!"

The Little Mermaid[1]

Den lille havfrue

Eventyr, fortalte for Børn, 1837

ith "The Little Mermaid," Andersen believed that he had created one of his most moving fairy tales. "I suffer with my characters," he told his friends again and again, and his readers too have endured the pain of his beautiful aquatic creature. P. L. Travers, author of the Mary Poppins books, found Hans Christian Andersen to be a master in the art of torture. "How much rather would I see wicked stepmothers boiled in oil . . . ," she declared, "than bear the protracted agony of the Little Mermaid or the girl who wore the Red Shoes." In Andersen's tales, suffering can become a badge of spiritual superiority, and his downtrodden protagonists often emerge triumphant after enduring seemingly endless humiliations.

The little mermaid has worldly ambitions that run in directions other than silent suffering. Drawn to the upper world, she is eager to sail the seas, climb mountains, and explore forbidden territory. Donning boy's clothing, she goes horseback riding with the prince, crossing gender boundaries in unprecedented ways. For all her passion for adventure and life, she is, despite her pagan nature, a creature of compassion, unwilling to sacrifice the prince's life for her own. The spirited curiosity that impels her to seek out the world of humans is

1. *The Little Mermaid.* In constructing his aquatic character, Andersen drew on varied strands of both folkloric and literary traditions about fairy creatures—selkies, nymphs, nixies, undines—who appear on earth, marry mortals, but can remain on land only under certain conditions. Stories about selkies, seals who bask seductively in the sun on outlying rocks and who have the power to turn into beautiful humans, circulate broadly on the Orkney Islands off the coast of Scotland. Nixies are akin to the Greek sirens, who lure mortals to their death, but sirens have a birdlike appearance rather than pisciform features.

It is not clear exactly when sirens evolved into mermaids, losing their ornithomorphic features to acquire fish tails (Dundes, 56). A female siren in the form of a beautiful woman with the tail of a fish famously appears in Heinrich Heine's "Loreley," a poem that recounts the death of fishermen who drown when distracted from dangerous reefs by the Loreley's enchanting song. Melusine, or Melusina, another figure of European legends and folklore, is usually represented as a woman, sometimes with wings, sometimes as a serpent or fish from the waist down.

Andersen was familiar with Friedrich de la Motte Fouqué's short story "Undine" (1811), a tale about a knight who falls in love with the daughter of the King of the Sea and betrays her. Fouqué's work inspired a host of ballets and operatic tales about the beautiful femme fatale who cannot speak about her origins: Tchaikovsky's *Swan Lake*, Dvořák's *Rusalka*, and Maeterlinck's *Pelléas et Mélisande*. Andersen did not approve of Fouqué's ending and wrote to a friend on February 11, 1837, shortly after completing his own story: "I have not . . . let the mermaid's acquisition of an immortal soul depend on an alien creature, upon the love of a human being. I'm sure that would be wrong! It would depend rather a lot on chance, wouldn't it? I won't accept that sort of thing in this world. I have permitted my mermaid to follow a more natural, a more divine path."

Andersen was also familiar with mermaid tales by the Danish writers Ingemann and Oehlenschläger, as well as Bournonville's ballet *La Sylphide*, which was performed in Copenhagen in 1836. His "Little Mermaid" in turn inspired a host of nineteenth-century tales and twentieth-century films. Oscar Wilde's "The Fisherman and His Soul" (1891) and H. G. Wells's *The Sea Lady* (1902) were both influenced by Andersen's tale. In more recent times, the mermaid has become what Susan White describes as "a pervasive cinematic symbol of the girl's difficult rite of passage to womanhood" (White, 186), with films like *I Heard the Mermaids Singing* (1987), *Mermaids* (1990), and *La Petite Sirène* (1990) taking up painful "growth" experiences. *Splash*, starring Tom Hanks and Daryl Hannah, adds many modern twists to the tale, with an

also precisely what defeats her, leading to the condition of suffering that Travers found so troubling.

The animated Disney version of "The Little Mermaid" (1989) deviates sharply from the tale that inspired it. It may end happily with a marriage, but as Marina Warner points out, "The issue of female desire dominates the film, and may account for its tremendous popularity among little girls: the verb 'want' falls from the lips of Ariel, the Little Mermaid, more often than any other—until her tongue is cut out" (Warner, 403). Still, the Disney version has in many ways kept Andersen's story alive, even if it has a heroine and an ending radically different from the story that inspired it.

Far out at sea,[2] the water is as blue as the petals of the prettiest cornflowers and as clear as the purest glass. But it's very deep out there, so deep that even the longest anchor line can't touch bottom. You would have to pile up countless church steeples, one on top of the other, to get from the bottom of the sea all the way up to the surface. The sea people live down there.[3]

Now you mustn't think for a moment[4] that there is nothing but bare, white sand down there. Oh, no! The most wondrous trees and plants grow at the bottom of the sea, with stalks and leaves so supple that they stir with life at the slightest ripple in the water. The fish everywhere, large and small, dart between the branches, just the way birds fly through the trees up here. At the very deepest spot of all stands the castle of the Sea King.[5] Its walls are coral, and the tall, arched windows are made of the clearest amber. The roof is formed of shells that open and close with the current. It's a beautiful sight, for each shell has a dazzling pearl, any one of which would make a splendid jewel in a queen's crown.

The Sea King had been a widower for many years, and his aged mother kept house for him. She was a wise lady, but also

THE LITTLE MERMAID

W. HEATH ROBINSON

ending that pays tribute to the attractions of life underwater.

The mermaid, as Dorothy Dinnerstein points out in her landmark study of human sexual arrangements, *Mermaids and Minotaurs* (1976), has traditionally been framed as a "seductive and impenetrable female representative of the dark and magic underwater world from which our life comes and in which we cannot live." Drawing voyagers into an aquatic world linked with the sinister and irrational, she "lures them to their doom" (Dinnerstein, 5). But Andersen's little mermaid is less

siren than innocent child (the prince repeatedly refers to her as a foundling and child) trying to acquire a soul. She is driven more by the desire for a soul than by love for the prince.

The great granddaughter of Jonas Collin (Andersen's benefactor in Copenhagen) danced the role of the mermaid in a ballet production of 1913. A patron of the arts gave to the city of Copenhagen a statue of a mermaid after seeing her dance. The head has been sawed off twice, once in 1964, and again in 1998. A group called the Radical Feminist Faction claimed

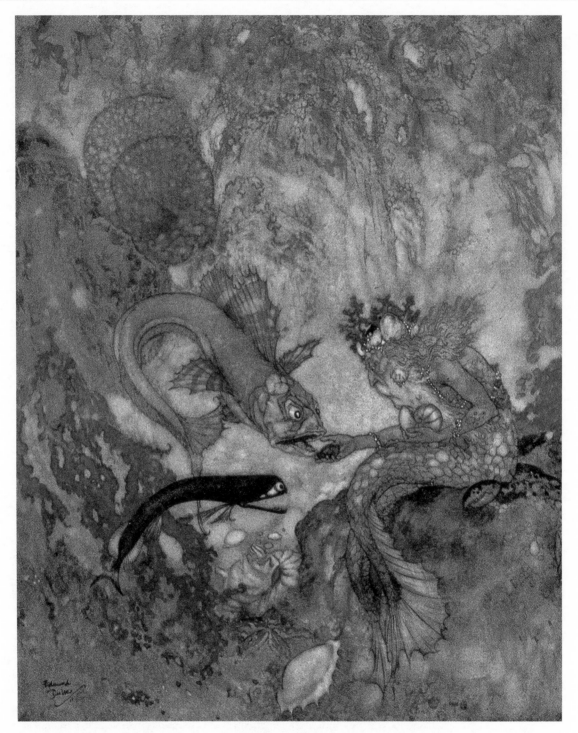

EDMUND DULAC

Holding a shell in his hand and perched on a rock with a lobster, the Sea King feeds the subjects in his aquatic domain. His crown of coral and shells and his sparkling bracelets and necklaces are the signs of his regal status.

responsibility for the act, apparently because the statue was seen as a symbol of women's abject willingness to sacrifice everything for the love of a man.

In turning an adult legend about fairies and mortals into a tale for children, Andersen also changed the story's character, placing such social values as love, duty, and the transcendent value of self-sacrifice in the foreground. In her memoir *Leaving a Doll's House*, actress Claire Bloom reminisces about the "sound of Mother's voice as she read to me from Hans Christian Andersen's 'The Little Mermaid' and 'The Snow Queen.' " Although the experience of reading produced "a pleasurable sense of warmth and comfort and safety" for Bloom, she also emphasizes that "these emotionally wrenching tales . . . instilled in me a longing to be overwhelmed by romantic passion and led me in my teens and early twenties to attempt to emulate these self-sacrificing heroines" (Bloom, 9).

Andersen scholars frequently point out that the tale was begun the day after Jonas Collin's son Edvard married, and that "The Little Mermaid" could be an expression of the writer's anguish that his friend had an attachment to a woman with whom he could never compete.

2. *Far out at sea.* Here, Andersen calls attention to the performative aspect of the story. The phrase "far out at sea" presumes that narrator and audience are on dry land and need to be plunged, through their imaginations, to the depths of the sea. The sea bottom is represented as a world completely separated from the world of humans, at a depth that makes it completely inaccessible. The proliferation of adjectives—"blue," "clear," "pretty," and "pure"—all point to an Atlantis-like beauty and grandeur, even if the sea kingdom remains a pagan site, though its distance from the human world is, ironically, measured in church steeples. (The early

introduction of church steeples is significant, for church bells, as we shall see, play a significant role in the story.)

Water appears as the source of life in nearly all creation myths, and its healing properties are celebrated in many cultures. But bodies of water are also the site of death, the source of pollution as well as cleansing, the home to beautiful creatures as well as hideous monsters, the site of drowning as well as baptism and rejuvenation. "Bodies of water," one commentator on "The Little Mermaid" points out, "are . . . emotionally charged in the human psyche, and the mythical creatures who reside in them become variously inflected with their power, with their potent blend of threat and allure" (Easterlin, 259).

3. *The sea people live down there.* The realm of the sea folk is described as a benign paradise, something of a parallel universe to the human world (with fish instead of birds, and so on) but with more natural beauty and the leisure to enjoy it. Disney's little mermaid, Ariel, inhabits a kingdom where the creatures living under the sea seem to do little more than sing and dance.

4. *Now you mustn't think for a moment.* Note the conversational tone that is taken right from the start as the narrator establishes himself as the source of authority on sea folk and vouches for their existence. The (presumably human) narrator seems to have an unbiased attitude toward merfolk. As James Massengale points out, "his narrative 'camera' . . . focuses upon the youngest of the Merking's daughters, and from that point it essentially never leaves her" ("The Miracle and A Miracle in the Life of a Mermaid," 556–57). His stance appears to be neutral and undogmatic, for he is both enchanted by the beauty of the undersea world and committed to the notion of Christian salvation. It is important to remember that he uses the term "we" to designate humans, and he reveals the spiritual shortcomings of the Sea King's world in the course of telling the story.

5. *the castle of the Sea King.* The underwater domain of the Sea King is an aesthetic paradise, a site where art (song, dance, and spectacle) meets natural beauty. Still, certain hierarchical distinctions, such as the number of oysters worn on the tail of the Sea King's mother, make it clear that this is no social utopia.

6. *But like all the others, she had no feet.* Despite the exceptional beauty of the undersea region, a clear hierarchical relationship begins to be established between humans and sea folk, in which humans are seen as superior. The "but" betrays a bias again the sea folk, who lack the feet that figure so importantly in Andersen's tales. Note also the repeated allusion to movement in the seascape. It is, however, a movement that imitates life rather than capturing it—everything moves "as if" it were alive. Sheldon Cashdan, author of *The Witch Must Die*, points out that as long as the little mermaid lacks legs, she remains unappealing to the prince: "A tail is an impediment when it comes to making love" (Cashdan, 165). But in ancient lore, the fish tail was a symbol of the mermaid's power rather than her inferiority, and the mirror she held was a symbol of the sea rather than a sign of her vanity.

very proud of her noble birth. And that's why she wore twelve oysters on her tail, while everyone else of high rank had to settle for six. In every other way she deserved great praise, for she was deeply devoted to her granddaughters, the little sea princesses. They were six beautiful children, but the youngest was the fairest of them all. Her skin was as clear and soft as a rose petal. Her eyes were as blue as the deepest sea. But like all the others, she had no feet,[6] and her body ended in a fish tail.

All day long the sea princesses played in the great halls of the castle, where real flowers were growing right out of the walls. When the large amber windows were open, fish swam right in, just as swallows fly into our homes when we open the windows. The fish glided up to the princesses, ate out of their hands, and let themselves be caressed.

Outside the castle there was an enormous garden with trees

W. HEATH ROBINSON

that were deep blue and fiery red. Their fruit glittered like gold, and their blossoms looked like flames of fire, with leaves and stalks constantly aflutter. The soil itself was the finest sand, but blue like a sulphur flame. A wondrous blue glow permeated everything in sight.[7] Standing down there, you really had no idea that you were at the bottom of the sea, and you might as well have been high up in the air with nothing but sky above you and below. When the sea was perfectly calm, you could catch sight of the sun, which looked like a purple flower with light streaming from its calyx.

Each little princess had her own plot in the garden, where she could dig and plant as she pleased. One arranged her flower bed in the shape of a whale; another thought it nicer to make hers look like a little mermaid; but the youngest made hers perfectly round like the sun,[8] and she wanted nothing but flowers that shone just as red as it was. She was a curious child,[9] quiet and thoughtful. While her sisters decorated their gardens with the wondrous objects they had gathered from sunken ships,[10] she wanted only one thing apart from the rose-red flowers that were like the sun high above: a beautiful marble statue.[11] The statue was of a handsome boy, chiseled from pure white stone, and it had landed on the bottom of the sea after a shipwreck. Next to it, the little princess had planted a crimson weeping willow[12] that grew splendidly, draping its fresh foliage over the statue and touching the blue, sandy ocean bottom. It cast a violet shadow that, like its

W. HEATH ROBINSON

W. HEATH ROBINSON

7. *A wondrous blue glow permeated everything in sight.* Blue and red are the dominant colors in the narrative, the one associated with the depths of the sea and the heights of the heavens, the other linked with sunlight, passion, suffering, and blood. Even the little mermaid is first introduced as having skin as delicate as a rose leaf and eyes as blue as the sea. Gold too makes frequent appearances and is often connected with gleaming, glittering surface beauty. It is possible that Andersen, who spent many months in Italy, may have been influenced by the blues, reds, and golds in Italian paintings of the Madonna and child.

8. *the youngest made hers perfectly round like the sun.* The little mermaid's aspirations are clear early on. She strives to transcend her aquatic nature and reach a higher stage

of existence. In the end, she does indeed become an airborne creature. Her two sisters remain wedded to marine life in choosing the shapes for their gardens (whales and mermaids), while she moves out of her own realm and her own being to represent something otherworldly (the sun). Focused on what she can perceive of the other world—the sun shining through the waters and the ships creating shadows as they pass by overhead—she exhibits desires that deviate from what is expected in the undersea realm.

9. *She was a curious child.* The little mermaid is "curious" in the double sense of the term—intellectually adventurous and also something of an oddity. She is (somewhat like Andersen himself) upwardly mobile, intent on gaining knowledge of the world above, but also destined to remain a misfit among the sea folk with her desire to inhabit land, and an anomaly among humans with her lack of a soul. As James Massengale points out: "She grows a different garden. She longs for church bells she has never heard. She saves the Prince instead of watching him drown. She pines for him instead of forgetting him as an inaccessible or inimical being. She refuses to follow her grandmother's mermaid-rules. She denies her Mermaid tendencies and her Mermaid shape, and makes a contract with the Sea Witch, which causes her to destroy her body and abandon her kingdom forever, in order to balance on the keen edge of a possibility of becoming human" (Massengale, 568).

10. *wondrous objects they had gathered from sunken ships.* The sisters' mania for collecting is transferred in the Disney film to Ariel, who hoards and fetishizes artifacts of civilization (forks, combs, and so on) as a sign of her desire to live with humans. If Andersen's little mermaid is inspired by church bells she has never heard and is driven by longing for the hustle and bustle of the big city (as was the young Andersen), Ariel—as is appropriate for a Disney character—becomes a slave to commodity fetishism.

11. *a beautiful marble statue.* If Andersen's mermaid has a fetishized object, it is the marble statue, which becomes the target of chaste feelings as well as erotic longings. Many of Andersen's stories feature inanimate figurines such as the tin soldier and ballerina in "The Steadfast Tin Soldier." The shepherdess and the chimney sweep, in the story of that title, are also both made of marble.

Stories of animated statues can be documented in folklore and literature from all over the world. The two most famous tales are of Pygmalion and Don Juan. The statue of the boy, rescued from a shipwreck, has none of the haunting qualities found in other nineteenth-century literary statues, for example, those in Prosper Mérimée's "Venus of Ile" or Henry James's "Last of the Valerii."

Andersen's "Psyche" works within a Romantic literary tradition of statues and portraits of women so disturbingly lifelike that they produce uncanny effects and (often) tragic endings. Inspired by the beauty of a real-life woman, the unnamed artist in Andersen's "Psyche" transforms a marble stone into her likeness. He falls madly in love with the statue, which is as "perfect as God's own image of the young girl." The little mermaid, by contrast, seeks the human incarnation of the marble statue that she has enshrined in her garden.

12. *a crimson weeping willow.* Note that the undersea world lacks green and that red and blue are the colors used for all living things. A traditional symbol of mourning that is refigured by Andersen in sentimental terms (the roots and the crown are always "trying to kiss each

branches, was in constant motion. The roots and crown of the tree seemed always at play with each other, as if trying to kiss.

Nothing made the princess happier than learning about the human world up above.[13] She made her grandmother tell her everything she knew about ships and towns, people and animals. She found it strangely beautiful that flowers up on the land had a fragrance—at the bottom of the sea they had none—and also that the trees in the forest were green and that the fish flying in the trees up there sang so clearly and beautifully that it was delightful to listen to them. Grandmother called the little birds *fish*, because otherwise the little sea princesses, never having seen a bird, would have no idea what she was talking about.

"When you turn fifteen,"[14] Grandmother told them, "you'll be allowed to swim up to the surface of the sea to sit on the rocks in the moonlight and watch the tall ships that pass by. You will also have the chance to see both forests and towns." In the coming year, one of the sisters was going to turn fifteen, but the others—well, they were each born a year apart, and the youngest of them had to wait five whole years before she could venture up from the depths to see how things look up here. But each promised to tell the others what she had seen and what she had liked the most on that first visit. Their grandmother had not told them nearly enough, and there was so much that they still wanted to know.

No one longed to go up more than the youngest sister,[15] the one who was so silent and thoughtful, and who also had the longest wait. Many a night she would stand at the open window and gaze up through the dark blue waters, where the fish were fluttering their fins and tails. She could see the moon and the stars, even though their light shone rather pale. Through the water they looked much bigger than they do to our eyes. If a black cloud passed beneath the stars, she knew that it was either a whale swimming overhead or a ship filled with many passengers. The people on board never imagined

other"), the presence of the tree nonetheless hints at a tragic ending. The little mermaid's garden contains elements that prefigure her future: the sun-shaped flower bed that stands for the light of the human world and for redemption, the statue that is a double of the prince, and the weeping willow that anticipates her pain and sorrow in the world above.

13. *learning about the human world up above.* It is through stories, told by one generation to the next, that the little mermaid first hears about the world of humans. The grandmother's descriptions of beauty are what attract the attention of her granddaughter. The aroma of the flowers, the green of the trees, and the song of the birds together create olfactory, visual, and acoustic pleasures. One feminist critic points out that "the sea world is rendered either invisible or mythic while the land world is endowed with cultural validity" (Sells, 178).

14. *"When you turn fifteen."* Andersen himself was just fourteen years old when he left Odense in 1819 to seek his fortune in Copenhagen. Fifteen marks the transition from childhood to adulthood, to a state of physical and emotional maturity. At that age, the mermaids are viewed as sensible enough to take a look at the upper world without being seduced by the temptation to see more. The grandmother emphasizes that they can see the world of humans only by moonlight, presumably because the sunlit upper world would be too tantalizing. It is only the "bolder" of the sisters who goes to the world of humans in daylight. Although the little mermaid is fifteen and undergoes a rite of passage from child to woman, she remains childlike even after her birthday.

15. *No one longed to go up more than the youngest sister.* Curiosity is once again emphasized as the defining feature of the little mermaid and as the trait that singles her out from others. A hybrid creature to begin with, she longs with all her being—mind as well as body (think of those outstretched arms as she watches ships sailing above her)—to attain a higher state even while she lives underwater.

16. *a pretty little mermaid was waiting below.* The term "little mermaid" is used for the first time in the story. Here, the term "little" is linked with beauty and youth. But with such phrases as "you poor little mermaid," the diminutive stature soon comes to be associated with unhappiness, longing, and suffering.

17. *You could hear the sounds of music.* The sisters, unable to communicate with humans through their song, turn into spectators and listeners who are eager to take in sights and sounds from the world above. They become "voyeurs who gleefully consume the ephemeral sights and sounds of human life as spectacles of the first rank" (Alter and Koepnick, 7). The eldest of the six sisters finds the main appeal of that domain in sound. For her, music, the sounds of everyday life, and the ringing of church bells are "wondrous things" that produce a desire to inhabit the human world.

The church bells, more than any other sound, tellingly serve as the most powerful lure to enter the world of humans for this sister. The many distractions of urban life—artificial lights, swift carriages, hectic activity—form a stark contrast to the tranquillity of the mermaid's garden and to the serenity of the churches in which the bells are ringing. The city nonetheless remains a site of fascination, with sonic and visual attractions that are a source of deep longing.

18. *she even fancied that she could hear the church bells.* Oddly, the little mermaid

that a pretty little mermaid was waiting below,[16] stretching her white arms up toward the keel of the ship.

As soon as the eldest princess turned fifteen, she was allowed to swim up to the surface.

When she returned, she had hundreds of things to report. The loveliest moment, she said, was lying on a sandbar close to the shore in the moonlight while the sea was calm. From there, you could see a city—its lights were twinkling like a hundred stars. You could hear the sounds of music[17] and the commotion of carriages and people. You could see all the church towers and spires and hear their bells ringing. And because she could not get close to all those wonderful things, she longed for them all the more.

Oh, how the youngest sister drank it all in! And later that evening, while she stood at the open window gazing up through the dark blue waters, she thought of the big city with all its hustle and bustle, and she even fancied that she could hear the church bells[18] ringing down to her.

The following year, the second sister was allowed to rise up through the water and swim wherever she liked. She reached the surface just as the sun was setting,[19] and that, she said, was the loveliest sight of all. The whole sky was covered in gold, she declared, and the clouds—well, she just couldn't describe how beautiful they were, with their crimson and violet hues, as they sailed over her head. Even more rapidly than the clouds, a flock of wild swans flew like a long white veil across the water toward the setting sun. The second sister swam off in that direction, but the sun sank, and its rosy glow was swallowed up by the sea and the clouds.

Another year passed, and the third sister swam up to the surface. She was the most daring of them all, and she swam upstream into a wide river that flowed into the sea. She could see beautiful green hills covered with grapevines[20]; castles and manors peeked out from magnificent woods; she could hear birds singing; and the sun was so hot that she often had to dive underwater to cool off her burning face. In a small cove she came upon a whole troop of human children, jumping around, quite naked, in the water. She wanted to play with them, but they were terrified and fled. Then a little black animal appeared. It was a dog, but she had never seen one before. The animal barked so ferociously at her that she became frightened and headed for the open sea. But she would never forget the magnificent woods, the green hills, and the darling children, who could swim even though they lacked tails.

The fourth sister was not nearly as daring. She stayed far out in the wild ocean and declared that it was the loveliest place of all. You could see for miles and miles around, and the sky overhead was like a big glass bell. She had seen ships, but at a distance so great that they looked like seagulls. Dolphins were sporting in the waves, and enormous whales spouted water so powerfully from their nostrils that they seemed to be surrounded by a hundred fountains.

And now it was the fifth sister's turn. Since her birthday was in the winter, she saw things the others had not seen on their first outings. The sea had turned quite green, and there were large icebergs floating in it. Each one looked like a pearl, she said, and still they were larger than the church steeples built by humans.[21] They appeared in the most fantastic shapes and glittered just like diamonds. She sat down on one of the largest, and all the ships seemed terrified, giving her a wide berth and sailing rapidly past. She stayed put, with the wind blowing through her long hair. Later that evening the sky became overcast. Thunder rolled and lightning flashed, and the dark waves lifted great chunks of ice high into the air, making them gleam when bolts of red lightning struck. The sails were taken in on all the ships, but amid the general horror and alarm, the mermaid remained serene on her drifting iceberg, watching blue lightning bolts zigzag down toward the glittering sea.

longs for the sound of the church bells, even though she has never heard them and has no understanding of their symbolic function.

19. *She reached the surface just as the sun was setting.* The powerful allure of the sun becomes evident upon the second sister's visit. She swims in the direction of the sunset, only to find that the orb has disappeared. This sister visits the earth at a time of transition from day to night, and it is no accident that she sees a flock of white swans during her expedition. For Andersen, swans are creatures that have transcended a state of gawky awkwardness to become, as in "The Ugly Duckling," incarnations of majestic splendor. Like butterflies, the romantic symbol *par excellence* for transformation, swans are able to metamorphose into a more noble physical state. The transformation of the little mermaid from sea creature to mermaid in human form to a creature of the air reflects Andersen's constant engagement with mutability and changes in identity.

20. *beautiful green hills covered with grapevines.* Andersen's landscapes are filled with vivid sights, sounds, and aromas. The third sister sees nature's beauty and also discovers how humans have entered it to cultivate it (with grapevines), build residences (castles and manors), and produce children. The mutual animosity (based on fear driven by lack of familiarity) between the two worlds becomes evident when the mermaid terrifies the children and the dog terrifies the mermaid.

21. *they were larger than the church steeples built by humans.* Again church steeples are invoked, even in the icy landscape visited by the fifth sister. The green ocean, icebergs that glitter like diamonds, black waves, and red and blue lightning create a

EDMUND DULAC

With his head only slightly above water and another wave ready to pound his body, the prince
is rescued by the mermaid as she makes her way through a spectacular ocean of blues and foam,
with a headdress of flowers that matches the element in which she lives.

When any one of the sisters reached the surface for the first time, she would be delighted by the many new and beautiful things up there. But as the princesses grew older and were allowed to go up as often as they liked, they began to lose interest. They longed to return home, and, after a month had passed, they declared that it was really much nicer down below. It was such a comfort to be at home.[22]

Many an evening, the five sisters would link arms to form a row and rise up out of the water. They had lovely voices,[23] more beautiful than the sound of any human voice. If a storm was raging and they expected a shipwreck, the sisters would swim in front of the vessels and sing seductively about the delights found in the depths of the sea. They told the sailors not to be afraid to go down there, but the sailors never understood the words they sang. They thought they were hearing the howling of the storm. Nor did they ever see the beauty promised by the mermaids, because when their ships finally sank, the sailors drowned, and, by the time they reached the palace of the Sea King, they were dead.

When the sisters floated up, arm in arm, through the water in the evening, the youngest among them would be left behind, all alone, gazing after them. She would have cried, but mermaids cannot shed tears, and so they suffer even more than we do.

"Oh, if only I were fifteen years old," she would say. "I know that I would come to love the world up there and all the people who live in it."

Finally she turned fifteen.

"Well now, soon we'll have you off our hands," said the old dowager queen, her grandmother. "Come here, and let me dress you up like your sisters," and she put a wreath of white lilies in her hair. Each flower petal was half a pearl, and the old woman clamped eight big oysters onto the princess's tail to show her high rank.

"Ow! That really hurts," said the little mermaid.

colorful spectacle of sublime delights. Here again, the conflicts between humans and merfolk are deepened, for it becomes clear that what the mermaid perceives as a source of visual pleasure is a real danger to the sailors. Humans and merfolk cannot coexist under conditions in which what is beautiful for one group is lethal for the other.

22. *It was such a comfort to be at home.* All but the little mermaid remain homebodies. Only she will find that familiarity does not breed contempt and that the world above offers more than the visual and acoustic attractions so appealing to her sisters.

23. *they had lovely voices.* The sisters have powerful vocal talents, but their "enchanting" song cannot accomplish its aim of drawing the attention of humans sailing by. No matter how beautifully the mermaids sing, the sailors cannot be seduced by them, for they hear nothing but the sounds of a storm. Andersen intensifies the divide between merfolk and humans by showing that song and storm coexist, but what is (beautiful) song to merfolk is (fatal) storm to humans.

Having a voice and the ability to display its artistry figure importantly in a tale that celebrates spectacle and sound. That the little mermaid later loses her voice reveals the drawbacks of the exchange made with the Sea Witch. While the mermaid's voice has emotive strength, it is linked above all with artistic expression. It is what makes her appealing to both merfolk and humans.

24. *"Yes, beauty has its price."* The costuming scene with grandmother and mermaid prefigures the later scene of mutilation with Sea Witch and mermaid. The grandmother, oddly, dresses the little mermaid up for a voyage that is not intended for exhibitionistic purposes—the little mermaid is rising up in order to look at others. Even in these preliminary preparations, the little mermaid learns that beauty and the power to attract exact a toll.

25. *There was music and singing on board.* The sound of music and the light of lanterns draw the little mermaid to the activity on board the ship. Like her sisters, she is attracted to the music of humans, which does not seem to have the seductive, treacherous overtones of the songs sung by the sisters. The songs and merriment on board inspire her wish to join the human throng.

26. *It was his birthday.* Note that the little mermaid and the Prince share a birthday, suggesting that they could be soul mates. The Prince is most likely either exactly her own age or a year older, since he could not have been more than sixteen years old.

"Yes, beauty has its price,"[24] the grandmother replied.

Oh, how the mermaid would have loved to shake off all that finery and remove that heavy wreath! The red flowers in her garden would have suited her so much better, but she did not dare make any changes. "Farewell," she said, as she rose up through the water as swiftly and brightly as a bubble moves up to the surface.

The sun had just set when her head rose up through the waves, but the clouds were still gleaming like roses and gold. Up in the pale pink sky the evening star was shining bright and clear. The air was mild and fresh, and the sea was perfectly calm. A tall three-masted ship was drifting in the water, with only one sail hoisted because there was not so much as a breeze. The sailors could be seen taking it easy on the rigging and in the masts. There was music and singing on board,[25] and when it grew dark, hundreds of colored lanterns were lit. They made it look like the flags of all nations were fluttering in the wind.

The little mermaid swam right up to the porthole of the cabin, and, every time a wave lifted her, she could see a throng of elegantly dressed people through the clear glass. Among them was a young prince, the handsomest person there, with big dark eyes. He could not have been more than sixteen. It was his birthday,[26] and that's why the festivities were taking place. When the young prince came out on the deck, where the sailors were dancing, more than a hundred rockets were shot into the air. They lit up the sky, making it look like daytime, and the little mermaid was so startled that she dove back down into the water. But she quickly popped her head back out again. It looked just as if all the stars up in heaven were falling down on her. Never before had she seen such fireworks. Huge suns were spinning around; magnificent fire fish went swooping through the blue air, and the entire display was reflected in the clear, calm waters below. The ship itself was so brightly illuminated that you could see even the smallest piece of rope—not to mention all the people there. How handsome the young prince looked! He shook hands with everyone, laughing and smiling as music filled the lovely night air.

It was growing late, but the little mermaid could not tear herself away from the ship or from the handsome prince. The colored lanterns had long been extinguished; the rockets were no longer being fired into the air; and the cannon volleys had stopped. Now you could hear the sea churning and groaning deep down below. Still the mermaid stayed on the surface, bobbing up and down so that she could look into the cabin.[27] The ship began gathering speed as one sail after another caught the wind. The waves rose higher; heavy clouds darkened the sky; and lightning flashed in the distance. A dreadful storm was brewing, and so the crew took in the sails, while the great ship rocked and scudded through the raging sea. The waves rose higher and higher until they were like huge black mountains, threatening to bring down the mast. The ship dove like a swan[28] between the waves and then rose again on their lofty, foaming crests. The little mermaid thought it must be fun to sail so fast, but the crew didn't think so. The vessel groaned and creaked; the stout planks burst under the heavy pounding of the sea against the ship; and the mast snapped in two as if it were a reed. The ship rolled onto its side as water came rushing into the hold.

The little mermaid suddenly realized that the ship was in real danger. She herself had to watch out for the beams and bits of wreckage drifting in the water. For an instant it was so dark that she couldn't see a thing, but then a flash of lightning lit everything up so that she could make out everyone on board. Now it was every man for himself. She was searching for the young prince and, just as the ship broke apart, she saw him disappear into the depths of the sea. At first she was overjoyed, for she believed that he would now live in her part of the world. But then she remembered that human beings

27. *bobbing up and down so that she could look into the cabin.* The little mermaid's curiosity about human beings draws her to the world of the prince. Fascinated by what is above the surface, by the unknown, and by the forbidden, she shows an investigative curiosity lacking in many fairy-tale heroines but shared with biblical figures like Eve and Lot's wife.

28. *the ship dove like a swan.* The comparison suggests that the vessel is a graceful ship, with a nobility and beauty resembling that of a creature that Andersen repeatedly frames as aristocratic. The mountains in the prince's domain are also described as having the appearance of "nestling swans." The little mermaid will perform the same graceful movements as the swanlike ship when she rescues the prince, diving into the waves and darting through the ship's wreckage. Andersen himself has been described as a "water fanatic" who loved to "throw himself into the waves so he could then rise up again—as he said—with a feeling of being reborn and see the world from a whole different perspective" (Jens Andersen, 197).

29. *Lemon and orange trees were growing in the garden.* The prince's domain is clearly in southern regions. The architecture of the buildings suggests a southern European locale, and it is likely that Andersen had Italy in mind. He had been deeply impressed by the beauty of the Italian countryside and wrote with enthusiasm about Italy's landscape and culture: "If France is the country of reason, then Italy is the country of imagination. . . . Here is all you could wish for in a landscape—the oranges hanging so yellow between the lush greenery; big, grass-green lemons greeted us with their fragrance.—Everything was like a painting. . . . When visiting the magnificent galleries, the rich churches with their monuments and magnificence, I learned to understand the beauty of form—the spirit which reveals itself in form" (*Diaries*, 48).

could not survive underwater and that only as a dead man could he come down to her father's palace. No, no, he mustn't die! And so she darted in among the drifting beams and planks, oblivious to the danger of being crushed. She dove deep down and came right back up again among the waves, and at last she found the young prince, who barely had the strength to keep afloat in the stormy waters. His limbs were failing him; his beautiful eyes were shut; and he would surely have drowned if the little mermaid had not come to his rescue. She held his head above water and let the waves carry the two of them along.

By morning the storm had died down, and there was not a trace left of the ship. The sun, red and glowing, rose up out of the water and seemed to bring color back into the prince's cheeks. But his eyes remained closed. The mermaid kissed his fine, high brow and smoothed back his wet hair. She thought that he looked just like the marble statue in her little garden. She kissed him again and made a wish that he might live.

Soon the mermaid saw land before her—lofty blue mountains topped with glittering white snow that made them look like nestling swans. Near the coast were lovely green forests, and close by was some kind of building, whether church or cloister she could not say. Lemon and orange trees were growing in the garden,[29] and you could see tall palm trees by the gate. The sea formed a small bay at this point, and the water in it was quite calm, though very deep all the way up to the dunes, where fine white sand had washed ashore. The mermaid swam over there with the handsome prince, laid him down in the warm sunshine, and made a pillow for his head with the sand.

Bells began ringing in the large white building, and a group of young girls came walking through the garden. The little mermaid swam farther out from the shore, hiding behind some large boulders that rose out of the water. She covered her hair and chest with sea foam so that no one could see her. Then she watched to see who would come to help the poor prince.

It was not long before a young girl came by. She had a frightened look on her face, but only for a moment, and she quickly ran away to get help. The mermaid watched as the prince came back to life and began to smile at everyone around him. But there was no smile for her, because of course he had no idea that she had rescued him. After he was taken into the large building, she was overcome with sorrow and dove back into the water to return to her father's palace.

The little mermaid had always been silent and thoughtful, but now she was even more so. Her sisters asked what she had seen during her first visit up above, but she did not say a word.

Many a morning and many an evening she swam up to the spot where she had left the prince. She saw the fruits in the garden ripen and watched as they were picked. She saw the snow melt on the peaks. But she never saw the prince, and so she always returned home, filled with even greater sorrow than before. Her one consolation was sitting in her little garden, with her arms wrapped around the beautiful marble statue[30] that looked so like the prince. She gave up tending her flowers, and they grew into a kind of wilderness out over the paths, winding their long stalks and leaves around the branches of the trees until everything became quite gloomy.

Finally she could bear it no longer and told one of her sisters everything. The others learned about it soon enough, but no one else knew about it, except for a few other mermaids who didn't breathe a word to anyone (apart from their closest friends). One of them knew who the prince was. She too had

HARRY CLARKE

Eels and eel-like fish serve as extensions for the Sea Witch's hair. The magical potion drifts down to the little mermaid, whose grace is admired by some of the fish below.

30. *with her arms wrapped around the beautiful marble statue.* The little mermaid clings to the statue in much the way that the flowers wind their stems and leaves around the tree, blocking its light. Drawing on the ancient marriage trope of the elm and the vine, Andersen points to the possibility that the little mermaid's feminine devotion to the prince may block light from the sun and thereby stand in the way of her salvation rather than promoting it.

EDMUND DULAC

The little mermaid, eager to win the prince's love, returns from the domain of the Sea Witch with the potion that will transform her body. The potion glows as she makes her way past sea creatures, a human skull, bones, and a gigantic octopus.

seen the festival held on board and knew where the prince came from as well as where his kingdom lay.

"Come, little sister!" the other princesses said. And with their arms on each other's shoulders, they rose in one long row to the surface, right in front of where the prince's castle stood.

The castle had been built with a gleaming, pale yellow stone, and it had grand marble staircases, one of which led straight down to the sea. Magnificent gilded domes rose above the rooftops, and between the pillars that surrounded

EDMUND DULAC

The prince, wearing oriental garments, leans up against a pillar and gazes down at the naked girl who has washed up on the marble steps to his palace. With only her long hair to cover her, the mermaid appears vulnerable in ways that she never was while at sea. In the distance appear the lights of the city that so entertained the mermaid's sisters.

31. *There was so much she would have liked to know.* The little mermaid is intent on broadening her horizons. What she sees on earth stimulates her desire for challenges. She wants, above all, to explore the world—by flying across oceans and climbing mountains—to discover what is beyond the realm of "home." Her twin longing for both the prince and the world he inhabits create two competing narrative models, one based on the male *bildungsroman,* or novel of education, the other on the female marriage plot. As Rhoda Zuk puts it, "The heroine's aspiration to progress and perfection is forwarded by the virtues appropriated from feudal romance . . . including imaginative sympathy, resourcefulness, courage, and self-discipline. Yet the tale is also predicated on the marriage quest" (Zuk, 166).

the entire building stood lifelike marble statues. Through the clear glass of the tall windows you could see grand rooms decorated with sumptuous silk curtains and tapestries. The walls were covered with huge paintings that were a pleasure to behold. In the center of the largest room was a fountain that sprayed sparkling jets high up to the glass dome of the ceiling. The sun shone through it down on the water and on the beautiful plants growing in the large pool.

Now that the little mermaid knew where the prince lived, she spent many an evening and many a night at that spot. She swam much closer to the shore than any of the others dared. She even went up the narrow channel to reach the fine marble balcony that threw its long shadow across the water. Here she would sit and gaze at the young prince, who believed that he was completely alone in the bright moonlight.

Often in the evening, the little mermaid saw him go out to sea in his splendid vessel, with flags hoisted, to the strains of music. She peeked out from among the green rushes, and, when the wind caught her long silvery-white veil and people saw it, they just fancied it was a swan, spreading its wings.

On many nights, when the fishermen were out at sea with their torches, she heard them praising the young prince, and that made her all the more happy about saving his life on the day he was drifting half dead on the waves. And she remembered how she had cradled his head on her chest and how lovingly she had kissed him. But he knew nothing about any of this and never even dreamed she existed.

The little mermaid grew more and more fond of human beings and longed deeply for their company. Their world seemed far vaster than her own. They could fly across the ocean in ships and climb the steep mountains high above the clouds. And the lands they possessed, their woods and their fields, stretched far beyond where she could see. There was so much she would have liked to know,[31] and her sisters weren't able to answer all her questions. And so she went to visit her old grandmother, who knew all about the world above, which she quite rightly called the lands above the sea.

"If human beings don't drown," asked the little mermaid, "can they go on living forever? Don't they die, as we do down here in the sea?"

"Of course they do," the old woman replied. "They too must die, and their lifetime is even shorter than ours. We sometimes live for three hundred years, but when we cease to exist, we turn into foam on the sea. We don't even have a grave down here among our loved ones. We lack an immortal soul,[32] and we shall never have another life. We're like the green rushes. Once they've been cut, they stop growing. But human beings have a soul that lives on forever, even after their bodies have turned to dust. It rises up through the pure air until it reaches the shining stars. Just as we rise up from the sea to behold the lands of humans, they rise up to beautiful, unknown regions that we shall never see."

"Why weren't we given an immortal soul?" the little mermaid asked mournfully. "I would give all three hundred years of my life in return for becoming human for just one day and having a share in that heavenly world."[33]

"You mustn't waste your time worrying about these things," the grandmother told her. "We're really much happier and also better off than the human beings who live up there."

"So then I'm doomed to die and to drift like foam on the sea, never to hear the music of the waves or see the lovely flowers and the red sun. Is there nothing I can do to gain an immortal soul?"

HARRY CLARKE

The little mermaid dances in a skirt forming an oval that contrasts with elongated leglike patterns behind her. The touch of red is reminiscent of Karen's footwear in "The Red Shoes."

32. *We lack an immortal soul.* Andersen was deeply invested in conveying Christian messages about immortal souls and eternal life, even as he and his characters clearly delight in worldly pleasures. Roger Sale finds the hierarchies set up in the tale nearly intolerable, for the prince, who is "a dense and careless man," is positioned as morally and spiritually superior to the mermaid.

33. *"having a share in that heavenly world."* It becomes clear in this passage that the little mermaid's deepest longing is not for the prince but for an immortal soul. "Why weren't we given an immortal soul?" she complains. And rather than being motivated by love for the prince, she is driven by what Gregory Nybo describes as raw terror—"an abiding fear of death." Nybo judges the mermaid harshly: "She submits to [a] horrible mutilation, which also is the symbolic and radical denial of her own identity, for reasons that now stand revealed as entirely self-serving and from a motive that is purely solipsistic and negative, that is, fear of death" (Nybo, 417).

34. *her voice was more beautiful than any other.* The beauty of the mermaid's voice makes the exchange with the Sea Witch all the more tragic. One reader of the story describes the exchange as one in which the mermaid "gives up everything magical for an unrequited and lackluster reality" (Grealy, 161). Or as Joyce Carol Oates puts it, the little mermaid must strike a bargain that requires her to "relinquish her siren's voice in return for a human shape and human love on earth—a disturbing parable of women's place in the world of men" (Oates 2004, 166).

"No," said the old woman. "Only if a human loved you so much that you meant more to him than his father and mother. If he were to love you with all his heart and soul and had the priest place his right hand in yours with the promise of remaining faithful and true here and in all eternity—then his soul would glide into your body and you too would share in human happiness. He would give you a soul and still keep his own. But that will never happen! Your fish tail, which we find so beautiful, looks hideous to people on earth. They don't know any better. To be beautiful up there, you have to have those two clumsy pillars that they call legs."

The little mermaid sighed and looked mournfully at her fish tail.

"Let's celebrate," said the old woman. "Let's dance and be joyful for the three hundred years we have to live—that's really quite time enough. After that we have plenty of time to rest in our graves. Tonight there will be a royal ball."

That event was more splendid than anything we ever see on earth. The walls and ceiling of the great ballroom were made of thick, transparent crystal. Hundreds of colossal seashells, rose-red and grass-green, were lined up on all sides, each burning with a blue flame. They lit up the entire room and, by shining through the walls, also lit up the sea. Countless fish, large and small, could be seen swimming toward the crystal walls. The scales on some of them glowed with a purple-red brilliance; others appeared to be silver and gold. Down the middle of the ballroom flowed a wide rippling current, and in it mermen and mermaids were dancing to their own sweet songs. No human beings have voices so beautiful. The little mermaid sang more sweetly than anyone else, and everyone applauded her. For a moment there was joy in her heart, because she knew that her voice was more beautiful than any other[34] on land or in the sea. But then her thoughts turned to the world above. She was unable to forget the handsome prince or her deep sorrow that she did not possess the same immortal soul humans possess. And so she slipped out of her father's palace, and, while everyone inside was singing and making merry, she sat in her own little garden, feeling sad.

Suddenly the little mermaid heard the sound of a hunting horn echoing down through the water, and she thought: "Ah, there he is, sailing up above—the one I love more than my father or my mother, the one who is always in my thoughts and in whose hands I would gladly place my happiness. I would risk anything to win him and to gain an immortal soul. While my sisters are dancing away in Father's castle, I'll go visit the Sea Witch. I've always been terrified of her, but maybe she can give me some advice and help me out."

The little mermaid left her garden and set out for the place where the Sea Witch lived, on the far side of the roaring maelstroms. She had never been over there before. There were no flowers growing there[35] and no sea grass at all. Nothing was there but the bare, gray, sandy bottom of the sea, stretching right up to the maelstroms, where the water went swirling around like roaring mill wheels and pulled everything it got hold of down into the depths. She had to pass through the middle of those churning whirlpools in order to reach the domain of the Sea Witch. For a long stretch, there was no other path than one that took her over hot, bubbling mud— the witch called it her swamp.

The witch's house lay behind the swamp in the middle of a strange forest. All the trees and bushes were sea polyps, half animal and half plant. They looked like hundred-headed serpents growing out of the ground. Their branches looked like long slimy arms, with fingers like slithering worms. Joint by joint from the root up to the very tip, they were constantly on the move, and they wound themselves tight around anything they could grab hold of from the sea, and then they would not let go.

The little mermaid was terrified and paused at the edge

35. *There were no flowers growing there.* The realm of the Sea Witch is characterized by a grotesque aesthetic very different from what is found at the palaces of the father and the prince. Colorless and without adornment, it is the site of whirlpools and bogs that threaten to engulf and swallow up intruders. Even the branches of the trees are like snakes that twist themselves around their victims; and the sea polyps too threaten to squeeze the life out of anyone who swims by. Perhaps sensing that a part of her must die in order to achieve transformation, the little mermaid seeks out the Sea Witch, whose domain is affiliated with strangulation, destruction, and death.

36. *a house, built with the bones of shipwrecked human folk.* Like the demonic Baba Yaga of Russian folklore, the Sea Witch has a house constructed of human bones. Affiliated with the grotesque and the monstrous, her realm is one of decay, death, and destruction. However, since mermaids may be the ones responsible for the shipwrecks from which the Sea Witch and the polyps benefit, the Sea Witch is not a completely alien figure.

37. *There sat the Sea Witch.* In Disney's *Little Mermaid*, the Sea Witch is given a name (Ursula) and a camp identity that enables her to steal the show. An obese octopus with black undulating tentacles, she expresses what Marina Warner terms "the shadow side of [the little mermaid's] desiring, rampant lust. . . . She is a cartoon Queen of the Night, avid and unrestrained, what the English poet Ted Hughes might call a 'uterus on the loose'" (Warner, 403). The Sea Witch and the grandmother represent antithetical maternal figures that stand in for the mermaid's absent mother.

To gain full mobility in the human world, Andersen's mermaid must sacrifice her voice to a woman who, in her connection with biological corruption and grotesque sensuality, is diametrically opposed to the promise of eternal salvation. The marsh in which she resides and the bones of the human folk supporting her house all point to a regime that vividly puts human mortality and bodily decay on display. Initially attracted to what the Sea Witch can provide by being willing to brave the dangers of a visit to her abode, the little mermaid ultimately renounces her black arts when she flings the knife meant for the prince into the sea and is rewarded with the possibility of earning salvation.

of the wood. Her heart was pounding with fear, and she came close to turning back. But then she remembered the prince and the human soul, and her courage returned. She tied her long flowing hair tightly around her head so that the polyps wouldn't be able to grab hold of it. Then she folded her arms across her chest and darted forward like a fish shooting through the water, right in among the hideous polyps that reached out to snatch her with their nimble arms and fingers. She noticed how each of the sea polyps had caught something and was holding it fast with a hundred little arms that were like hoops of iron. The white skeletons of humans who had perished at sea and sunk down into the deep waters became visible in the arms of the polyps. Ship rudders and chests were held in their grip, along with the skeletons of land animals and—most horrifying of all—a small mermaid, whom they had caught and throttled.

She finally reached a great slimy clearing in the woods, where big, fat water snakes were romping in the mire and showing off their hideous, whitish-yellow bellies. In the middle of the clearing stood a house, built with the bones of shipwrecked human folk.[36] There sat the Sea Witch,[37] letting a toad feed from her mouth, exactly the way you can feed a canary with a lump of sugar. She called the hideous water snakes her little chickadees and let them cavort all over her big spongy chest.

"I know exactly what you want," the Sea Witch said. "How stupid of you! But I'm going to grant your wish, and it will bring you misfortune, my lovely princess. You're hoping to get rid of that fish tail and replace it with two stumps to walk on like a human being. You're sure that the young prince will then fall in love with you, and then you can win him along with an immortal soul."

And with that the witch let out such a loud, repulsive laugh that the toad and the water snakes tumbled to the ground and went sprawling. "You've come here just in time," said the witch. "Tomorrow, once the sun is up, I wouldn't be able to help you for another year. I shall prepare a potion for you. You will have to swim to land with it before sunrise, sit down on the shore, and swallow it. Your tail will then split in two and shrink into what human beings call pretty legs. But it will hurt. It will feel like a sharp sword passing through you. Everyone who sees you will say that you are the loveliest human child they have ever encountered. You will keep your graceful movements—no dancer will ever glide so lightly—but every step you take will make you feel as if you were treading on a sharp knife, enough to make your feet bleed.[38] If you are willing to endure all that, I think I can help you."

"Yes," said the little mermaid, but her voice trembled. And she turned her thoughts to the prince and the prize of an immortal soul.

"Think about it carefully," said the witch. "Once you take on the form of a human, you can never again be a mermaid. You'll never be able to swim back through the water to your sisters or to your father's palace. The only way you can acquire an immortal soul is to win the prince's love and make him willing to forget his father and mother for your sake. He must cling to you always in his thoughts and let the priest join your hands to become man and wife. If the prince marries someone else, the morning after the wedding your heart will break, and you will become foam on the waves."

"I'm ready," said the little mermaid, and she turned pale as death.

"But first you will have to pay me," said the witch. "And it's not a small thing that I'm demanding. You have a voice more beautiful than anyone else's down here at the bottom of the sea. You may be planning to charm the prince with it, but you are going to have to give it to me. I want the dearest thing you possess in exchange for my precious potion. You

38. *"enough to make your feet bleed."* Feet and footwear figure prominently in fairy tales and are especially central to stories written by the son of a shoemaker. Perhaps inspired by the example of Snow White's stepmother, who dances to death in red-hot iron shoes, Andersen often located suffering in the feet of his protagonists. Like Karen in "The Red Shoes," the little mermaid must endure agonizing pain whenever she walks or dances. The renunciation of the tail for legs can be seen as a rite of passage, in which the little mermaid becomes a sexual being, as Dorothy Dinnerstein points out. But it also marks yet another moment of self-division for a heroine who is already a hybrid creature, torn between her loyalties to family, home, and the sea on the one hand, and to the prince and the possibility of earning a soul as a human on the other.

W. HEATH ROBINSON

39. *"Stick out your little tongue and let me cut it off in payment."* That the little mermaid sacrifices her voice for the promise of love has been read as the fatal bargain women make in Andersen's culture and in our own. Yet the mermaid's willingness to give up her voice is driven not only by her love for the prince but also by her desire to enter a richer and more enriching domain, one that will allow a greater range and play for her adventurous spirit. Cultural fantasies about the seductive quality of women's voices are staged in *The Odyssey,* when Odysseus orders his men to put cotton in their ears so that they will not be bewitched by the enchanting voices of the sirens.

The mermaid's bargain with the Sea Witch has been compared with Faust's pact with the devil. The mermaid wins a soul but loses her capacity to create beauty, while Faust exchanges his soul for knowledge, wealth, and power. The two themes are woven together in Thomas Mann's *Doctor Faustus,* a work in which the brilliant composer Adrian Leverkühn makes a pact with the devil and identifies powerfully with Andersen's little mermaid and her anguish through the "sword-dance of art." One critic emphasizes that Andersen's "Little Mermaid" can be read as an allegory of "the artist's painful endeavor to locate his place within a society hostile or at best indifferent to creative imagination" (Fass, 291).

The novelist Rosellen Brown writes poignantly about her childhood response to the cutting out of the tongue, how that event both terrified and fascinated her: "I think back to my attraction to this story and I truly can't reconstruct the way it made me feel. But this I can say: it was the mermaid's voicelessness that fascinated and panicked me. Or not so much her silence as her incapacity to *explain* herself. . . . Children recognize that they can't

see, I have to add my own blood to make sure that the drink will be as sharp as a double-edged sword."

"But if you take my voice away," said the little mermaid, "what will I have left?"

"Your lovely figure," said the witch, "your graceful movements, and your expressive eyes. With all that you can easily enchant a human heart. Well, where's your courage? Stick out your little tongue and let me cut it off in payment.[39] Then you shall have your powerful potion."

"So be it," said the little mermaid, and the witch placed her cauldron on the fire to brew the magic potion.

"Cleanliness above everything else," she said, as she scoured the cauldron with the water snakes, which she had tied into a large knot. Then she made a cut in her chest and let her black blood ooze out. The steam from the cauldron created strange shapes, terrifying to behold. The witch kept tossing fresh things into the cauldron, and when the brew began to boil, it sounded like a crocodile weeping. At last the magic potion was ready, and it looked just like clear water.[40]

"There you go!" said the witch as she cut out the little mermaid's tongue.[41] Now she was mute and could neither speak nor sing.

"If the polyps try to grab you on your way out through the woods," said the witch, "just throw a single drop of this potion on them,[42] and their arms and fingers will burst into a thousand pieces." But the little mermaid didn't need to do that. The polyps shrank back in terror when they caught sight of the luminous potion glowing in her hand like a glittering star. And so she passed quickly through the woods, the marsh, and the roaring whirlpools.

The little mermaid could now see her father's palace. The lights in the ballroom were out, and everyone was probably fast asleep by now. But she did not dare to go take a look, for she could not speak and was about to leave them forever. Her heart was aching with sorrow. She stole into the garden, took a flower from the beds of each of her sisters, blew a thousand kisses toward the palace, and then swam up through the dark blue waters.

The sun had not yet risen when she caught sight of the prince's palace and made her way up the beautiful marble steps. The moon was shining clear and bright. The little mermaid drank the bitter, fiery potion, and it felt to her as if a double-edged sword was passing through her delicate body. She fainted and fell down as if dead.

When the sun came shining across the sea, it woke her up. She could feel a sharp pain, but right there in front of her stood the handsome young prince. He stared at her so intently with his coal-black eyes that she cast down her own and saw that her fish tail was gone.[43] She had as charming a pair of white legs as any young girl could want. But she was quite naked, and so she wrapped herself in her long, flowing hair. The prince asked who she was and how she had found her way there, and she could only gaze back at him tenderly and sadly with her deep blue eyes, for of course she could not speak. Then he took her by the hand and escorted her into the palace. Every step she took, as the witch had predicted, made her feel as if she were treading on sharp knives and piercing needles,[44] but she willingly endured it. Hand in hand with the prince, she moved as lightly as a bubble. He and everyone else marveled at the beauty of her graceful movements.

She was given costly dresses of silk and muslin after she arrived. She was the most beautiful creature in the palace, but she was mute and could not speak or sing. Enchanting slave girls dressed in silk and gold came out and danced before the prince and his royal parents. One sang more beautifully than all the others, and the prince clapped his hands and smiled at her.[45] The little mermaid felt sad, for she knew that she herself had once sung far more beautifully. And she thought,

explain so much they would like to. I don't know that I felt particularly misunderstood but the threat is always there for children that they will be inadequate, possibly even speechless, when it's urgent that they be heard. So the idea that the mermaid, for love, would volunteer to lose her voice and thus yield up any chance to make her case—ah, this was so terrible to me I could hardly look it in the eye. And so, of course, I looked and looked" (Brown, 55).

40. *it looked just like clear water.* The purifying force of fire turns the potion into something resembling the beauty of the ocean water. Grotesque as she may appear, the Sea Witch possesses the power to transform the little mermaid into a creature who aspires to live a higher, more spiritual existence.

41. *she cut out the little mermaid's tongue.* In losing her tongue, the little mermaid sacrifices her ability to communicate. She becomes silent, mysterious, and fascinating, but also vulnerable and disempowered, bereft of the gift she had to create music and beauty. She resembles Philomela in Ovid's *Metamorphoses*, who loses the power to speak and broadcast the misdeeds of her brother-in-law. For Jack Zipes, the little mermaid becomes "voiceless and tortured, deprived physically and psychologically" and ends up serving "a prince who never fully appreciates her worth" (Zipes 1983, 84–85). Note that the little mermaid is obliged to give up an upper body part (her tongue) in order to transform a lower body part (fish tail into legs). In the Disney version, Ariel loses her voice but is not mutilated by having her tongue cut out.

42. *"just throw a single drop of this potion on them."* The instructions of the Sea Witch foreshadow the brutal act later proposed by the little mermaid's sisters. In both cases, the little mermaid abstains from violence: the first time because it is not necessary, the second time because she makes a deliberate decision to do no harm.

43. *her fish tail was gone.* The metamorphosis of the little mermaid moves her from the realm of sea creatures to that of humans. Her transformation, like that of the seal maidens and swan maidens of Scandinavian folklore, is reversible; but it occurs at some cost, as the ending to the story reveals.

44. *as if she were treading on sharp knives and piercing needles.* The little mermaid's pain has been seen by Dorothy Dinnerstein to have a double meaning: "On the one hand, it is the human pain of growth, the pain of renouncing childhood's immersion in magical fantasy life and parental care, the pain of independence and risky lonely exploit; and on the other hand—it feels like piercing knives—it is the special female pain of traditional sexual initiation" (Dinnerstein 1967, 107). There is both a "hopeful, euphoric surge of competence, movement, energy in a person on the brink of adult autonomy; and at the same moment a drastic sacrifice of intactness, a submissive preparation for invasion, an irrevocable loss of spontaneous, playful mobility."

The little mermaid's pain has also been interpreted as the agony of a woman in love: "The woman in love," Simone de Beauvoir writes, "tries to see with . . . the eyes [of the beloved]; she reads the books he reads, prefers the pictures and the music he prefers; she is interested only in the landscapes she sees with him, in the ideas that come from him" (Beauvoir, 653). Indeed, it is true that the little mermaid explores the world of the prince even as he shows no interest at all in the domain that is her home. Beauvoir saw Andersen's tale as an allegory of heterosexual romantic relations: "Every woman in love recognizes herself in Hans Andersen's little mermaid who exchanged her fishtail for feminine legs through love and then found herself walking on needles and live coals. It is not true that the loved man is absolutely necessary, above chance and circumstance, and the woman is not necessary to him; he is not really in a position to justify the feminine being who is consecrated to his worship, and he does not permit himself to be possessed by her" (Beauvoir, 654).

45. *the prince clapped his hands and smiled at her.* Andersen lived for praise and approval. He describes his buoyant feelings when his play *Love at St. Nicholas's Tower* received an ovation: "I was overpowered by joy. . . . I was bursting with happiness and rushed out of the theater, into the streets, into Collin's house, where only his wife was at home. Nearly fainting, I threw myself into a chair, sobbing and weeping hysterically. The dear woman had no idea what was going on and she began to comfort me. . . . I interrupted her, sobbing: 'They were applauding and shouting "Long Live!" ' " (*The Fairy Tale of My Life*, 64–65)

"Oh, if only he knew that I gave my voice away forever in order to be with him."

The slave girls performed a graceful, swaying dance to the most sublime music. And the little mermaid raised her beautiful white arms, lifting herself up on the tips of her toes, and floating across the floor, dancing as no one had ever danced before. She looked more and more lovely with every step, and her eyes spoke more deeply to the heart than the songs of the slave girls.

Everyone was enraptured, especially the prince, who called her his little foundling. She kept on dancing, even though it felt like she was treading on sharp knives every time her foot touched the ground. The prince insisted that she must never leave him, and she was allowed to sleep outside his door on a velvet cushion.[46]

The prince had a page's costume made for her[47] so that she could ride on horseback with him. They galloped through fragrant woods, where green boughs brushed her shoulders and little birds sang among the fresh, new leaves. She climbed with the prince to the tops of high mountains and, although her delicate feet began to bleed and everyone could see the blood, she just laughed and followed the prince until they could look down and see clouds fluttering in the air like flocks of birds on their way to distant lands.

At night, back in the prince's palace, when everyone in the household was fast asleep, the little mermaid would go over to the marble steps and cool her burning feet by standing in the icy seawater. And then she would think about those who were living down there in the deep.

One night her sisters rose up and sang mournfully as they floated arm in arm on the water. She beckoned to them, and they recognized her and told her how unhappy she had made them all. From then on, they started visiting her every night, and one night she even saw, far off in the distance, her old grandmother, who had not been up to the surface for many

46. *on a velvet cushion.* That she sleeps outside the prince's door on a cushion implies that the little mermaid is something of a waif (she is called a "foundling," after all), an exotic pet for the prince. Does he somehow suspect that she belongs to an animal species? In a study focused on representations of childhood deaths, Kimberley Reynolds includes "The Little Mermaid" as a "paradigm of *child* death" and as a story that promises "rewards for those unhappy, mistreated, or overlooked in this world" (Reynolds, 185).

47. *The prince had a page's costume made for her.* Critics who bemoan the self-effacing nature of the little mermaid often neglect to note that she is also more adventurous, spirited, and curious than most fairy-tale heroines. Cross-dressing is a sign of her willingness to cross boundaries and to take risks in order to see the world.

48. *"She is the only one in the world whom I could ever love."* Ironically, the prince labors under the delusion that the young woman who appeared in the temple was his savior. He remains unaware that he was miraculously rescued at sea by the little mermaid. The Sea Witch may have provided the little mermaid with legs, but she can do nothing to dispel the prince's conviction that his true beloved dwells in the temple. The princess functions as the earthly double of the little mermaid, just as the marble statue functioned as the oceanic double of the prince.

years, and she also saw the old Sea King, wearing his crown on his head. They both stretched their arms out toward her, but they did not dare to venture as close to the shore as her sisters.

With each passing day, the prince grew fonder of the little mermaid. He loved her as one loves a dear, sweet child, and it never even occurred to him to make her his queen. And yet she had to become his wife or else she would never receive an immortal soul. On his wedding morning, she would dissolve into foam on the sea.

"Do you care for me more than anyone else?" the little mermaid's eyes seemed to ask when he took her in his arms and kissed her lovely brow.

"Yes, you are more precious to me than anyone else," said the prince, "for you have the kindest heart of anyone I know. And you are more devoted to me than anyone else. You remind me of a young girl I once met, but shall probably never see again. I was in a shipwreck, and the waves cast me ashore near a holy temple, where several young girls were performing their duties. The youngest of them found me on the beach and saved my life. I saw her just twice. She is the only one in the world whom I could ever love.[48] But you look so much like her that you have almost driven her image out of my mind. She belongs to the holy temple, and my good fortune has sent you to me. We will never part!"

"Ah, little does he know that it was I who saved his life," thought the little mermaid. "I carried him across the sea to the temple in the woods, and I waited in the foam for someone to come and help. I saw the beautiful girl that he loves better than he loves me." And the mermaid sighed deeply, for she did not know how to shed tears. "He says the girl belongs to the holy temple and that she will therefore never return to the world. They will never again meet. I will stay by his side and can see him every day. I will take care of him and love him and devote my life to him."

Not long after that, there was talk that the prince was going to marry and that his wife would be the beautiful daughter of a neighboring king. And that's why he was rigging out a splendid ship. They said that he was going to pay a visit to the lands of a neighboring kingdom, but in fact he was going to visit the neighboring king's daughter. He was taking a large entourage with him. The little mermaid shook her head and laughed. She knew the prince's thoughts far better than anyone else.

"I shall have to go," he told her. "I must visit this beautiful princess—my parents insist. But they would never force me to bring her back here as my wife. I could never love her. She's not at all like the beautiful girl in the temple, whom you resemble. When I have to choose a bride someday, it is much more likely to be you, my quiet little orphan child with your expressive eyes." And he kissed the mermaid's red lips, played with her long hair, and laid his head on her heart so that she began to dream of human happiness and an immortal soul.

"You are not at all afraid of the sea, are you, my dear quiet child?" he asked, when they stood on board the splendid ship that was carrying them to the neighboring kingdom. He told her about powerful storms and calm waters, about the strange fish in the deep, and what divers had seen down there. She smiled at his tales, for she knew better than any one else about the wonders at the bottom of the sea.

In the moonlit night when everyone was asleep but the helmsman at his wheel, the little mermaid stood by the railing of the ship and gazed down through the clear water. She thought she could see her father's palace, and there at the top of it was her old grandmother, a silver crown on her head as she stared up through the turbulent currents at the keel of the vessel. Then her sisters rose up to the surface and looked at her with eyes filled with sorrow, wringing their white hands. She beckoned to them and smiled and would have liked to tell

49. *And he reached out and drew his blushing bride toward him.* The motif of the false bride becomes even more prominent in Disney's *Little Mermaid*, when Ursula turns herself into a beautiful rival who uses Ariel's exquisite voice to win Eric. Andersen's blushing bride may be the little mermaid's rival, but she is not marked in any way as evil.

them that she was happy and that all was going well for her. But the cabin boy came up just then, and the sisters dove back down, and the boy thought that the whiteness he had seen was nothing but foam on the water.

The next morning the ship sailed into the harbor of the neighboring king's magnificent capital. All the church bells were ringing, and trumpeters blew a fanfare from the towers. Soldiers saluted with flying colors and flashing bayonets. Every day brought a new festival. Balls and banquets followed one another, but the princess had not yet appeared. It was reported that she had been raised and educated in a holy temple, where she was learning all the royal virtues. At last she appeared.

The little mermaid was eager for a glimpse of her beauty, and she had to admit that she had never seen a more enchanting person. Her delicate skin glowed with health, and her warm blue eyes shone with deep sincerity from behind her long, dark lashes.

"It's you," said the prince. "You're the one who rescued me when I was lying half dead on the beach." And he reached out and drew his blushing bride toward him.[49] "Oh, I'm really overjoyed," he said to the little mermaid. "The best thing imaginable—more than I ever dared hope for—has been given to me. My happiness is sure to give you pleasure, for you are fonder of me than anyone else." The little mermaid kissed his hand, and she could feel her heart breaking. The day of the wedding would mean her death, and she would turn into foam on the ocean waves.

All the church bells were ringing when the heralds rode through the streets to proclaim the betrothal. Perfumed oils were burning in precious silver lamps on every altar. The priests were swinging the censers, while the bride and bridegroom joined hands to receive the blessing of the bishop. Dressed in silk and gold, the little mermaid was holding the bride's train, but her ears could not take in the festive music, and her eyes never saw the holy rites. All she could think about was her last night on earth and about everything in this world that she had lost.

That same evening, bride and bridegroom went aboard the ship. Cannons roared, flags were waving, and in the center of the ship a sumptuous tent of purple and gold had been raised. It was strewn with luxurious cushions, for the bridal couple was to sleep there during the calm, cool night. The sails swelled in the breeze, and the ship glided lightly and smoothly across the clear seas.

When it grew dark, colored lanterns were lit, and the sailors danced merrily on deck. The little mermaid could not help but think of that first time she had come up from the sea and gazed on just such a scene of splendor and joy. And now she joined in the dance, swerving and swooping as lightly as a swallow does to avoid pursuit. Cries of admiration greeted her from all sides. Never before had she danced so elegantly. It was as if sharp knives were cutting into her delicate feet, but she didn't notice, for the pain in her heart was far keener. She knew that this was the last night she would ever see the prince, the man for whom she had forsaken her family and her home, given up her beautiful voice, and suffered hours of agony without his suspecting a thing. This was the last evening that she would breathe the same air that he did or gaze into the deep sea and up at the starry sky. An eternal night, without thoughts or dreams, awaited her, since she did not have a soul and would never win one. All was joy and merriment on board until long past midnight. She laughed and danced with the others although the thought of death was in her heart. The prince kissed his lovely bride, while she played with his dark hair, and arm in arm they retired to the magnificent tent.

The ship was now hushed and quiet. Only the helmsman was standing there at his wheel. The little mermaid was leaning on the railing with her white arms and looking to the east

50. *"you must plunge it into the prince's heart."* Knives figure importantly in Andersen's work, but nowhere more so than in this story, where the implement that figuratively tortures the little mermaid's feet becomes the instrument she can turn on the prince. One critic points out how the knife reveals the mermaid to be a *femme fatale*, whose violence might erupt at any moment: "Andersen's mermaid clings winsomely to her dispossession, but her choice is a guide to a vital Victorian mythology whose lovable woman is a silent and self-disinherited mutilate, the fullness of whose extraordinary and dangerous being might at any moment return through violence. The taboos that encased the Victorian woman contained buried tributes to her disruptive power" (Auerbach, 8).

51. *she threw herself from the ship into the sea.* The little mermaid's sacrifice of her own life points to the words of Mark 8:35: "For whosoever will save his life shall lose it; but whosoever shall lose his life for my sake and the gospel's, the same shall save it." The little mermaid's death, return to the sea, and resurrection are eliminated from the Disney film, which ends with a wedding celebration. Jack Zipes suggests that Ariel's "temporary nonconformist behavior was basically a selling point in the Disney film; her rebellion was never to be taken seriously because she was destined from the beginning to wed the perfect partner and form a charming couple that would beget not only a baby, but a TV series of *The Little Mermaid* (1992–94), and a sequel, *The Little Mermaid II: The Return to the Sea* (2000)" (Zipes 2005, 114). It is hardly surprising that the spin-offs and sequels become derivative and turn into cartoon versions (as it were) of the original.

for a sign of the rosy dawn. She knew that the first ray of sunlight would mean her death. Suddenly she saw her sisters rising up from the sea. They were as pale as she, but their beautiful long hair was no longer blowing in the wind—it had been cut off.

"We gave our hair to the witch," they said, "so that she would help save you from the death that awaits you tonight. She gave us a knife—take a look! See how sharp it is? Before sunrise you must plunge it into the prince's heart.[50] Then, when his warm blood spatters on your feet, they will grow back together to form a fish tail, and you will be a mermaid again. You can come back down to us in the water and live out your three hundred years before being changed into dead, salty sea foam. Hurry up! One of you will die before the sun rises. Our old grandmother has been so grief-stricken that her white hair started falling out, just the way ours fell to the witch's scissors. Kill the prince and come back to us! Hurry— look at the red streaks in the sky. In a few minutes the sun will rise, and then you will die." And with a strange, deep sigh, they sank down beneath the waves.

The little mermaid drew back the purple curtain of the tent, and she saw the lovely bride sleeping with her head on the prince's chest. She bent down and kissed his handsome brow, then looked at the sky where the rosy dawn was growing brighter and brighter. She gazed at the sharp knife in her hand and fixed her eyes again on the prince, who was whispering the name of his bride in his dreams. She was the only one in his thoughts. The little mermaid's hand began to tremble as she took the knife—then she flung it far out over the waves. The water turned red where it fell, and it looked as if blood was oozing up, drop by drop, through the water. With one last glance at the prince from eyes half-dimmed, she threw herself from the ship into the sea[51] and felt her body dissolve into foam.

And now the sun came rising up from the sea. Its warm

and gentle rays fell on the deadly cold sea foam, but the little mermaid did not feel as if she were dying. She saw the bright sun and realized that there were hundreds of lovely transparent creatures hovering over her. Looking right through them, she could see the white sails of the ship and rosy clouds up in the sky. Their voices were melodious, but so ethereal that human ears could not hear them, just as mortal eyes could not behold them. They soared through the air on their own lightness, with no need for wings. The little mermaid realized that she had a body like theirs and that she was rising higher and higher out of the foam.

"Where am I?" she asked, and her voice sounded like that of the other beings, more ethereal than any earthly music.

"Among the daughters of the air,"[52] they replied. "Mermaids do not have an immortal soul, and they can never have one without gaining the love of a human being. Eternal life depends on a power outside them. The daughters of the air do not have immortal souls either, but through good deeds they can earn one for themselves. We can fly to the hot countries, where sultry, pestilential air takes people's lives. We bring cool breezes. We carry the fragrance of flowers through the air and send relief and healing. Once we have struggled to do all the good we can in three hundred years, immortal souls are bestowed on us, and we enjoy the eternal happiness humans find. You, my dear little mermaid, have struggled with all your heart to do what we do. You have suffered and endured and now you have been transported to the world of the spirits of the air. Through good deeds, you too can earn an immortal soul[53] in three hundred years."

The little mermaid lifted her transparent arms toward God's sun, and for the first time she could feel tears coming to her eyes.

Over by the ship, there were sounds of life, with people bustling about. The mermaid could tell that the prince and his beautiful bride were searching for her. With deep sorrow,

52. *"the daughters of the air."* Andersen had planned to call his story "The Daughters of the Air," and the airborne creatures striving for redemption are, like the mermaid and her siblings, all female. Belonging neither to the sea and to merfolk nor to land and humans, they represent a transitional phase that leads to immortality. The story emphasizes the importance of space (land, sea, and air) and how the elements (fire, water, earth, and air) have a special significance.

53. *"you too can earn an immortal soul."* The three hundred years of good deeds coincide with the life span of merfolk. The little mermaid is not in Purgatory, for she has been liberated from her aquatic state and takes on agency, bringing cool breezes and the fragrance of flowers while flying through the air. The little mermaid herself has achieved immortality in the real world, not only through her story but also through the bronze statue of her that has become Copenhagen's most popular tourist attraction.

Andersen, like the little mermaid, also wins his bid for immortality through his art but loses the chance to find "true" love. Near the end of his life, he congratulated a young man on his recent wedding: "You have got yourself a home, a loving wife, and you are happy! God bless you and her! At one time I too dreamed of such happiness, but it was not to be granted to me. Happiness came to me in another form, came as my muse that gave me a wealth of adventure and songs" (Wullschlager, 175).

EDMUND DULAC

Bearing a distinct resemblance to Ophelia, the little mermaid, now wearing splendid, regal garments, returns to her element and believes that she is about to become foam, while in the distance the sun is rising, warming the foam.

they were staring out at the pearl-colored foam, as if they knew that she had thrown herself into the waves. Unseen, the mermaid kissed the bride's forehead, smiled at the prince, and then, with the other children of the air, rose up into the pink clouds that were sailing across the skies.

"In three hundred years we will soar like this into the heavenly kingdom."

"And we may arrive there even sooner," one of her companions whispered. "Invisible to human eyes, we float into homes where there are children. For every day we find a good child who makes his parents happy and deserves their love, God shortens our time of trial. Children never know when we are going to fly into their rooms, and if we smile with joy when we see the child, then a year is taken away from the three hundred. But a mean or naughty child makes us shed tears of sorrow, and each of those tears adds another day to our time of trial."[55]

ARTHUR RACKHAM

55. *"each of those tears adds another day to our time of trial."* The contrived words at the end add a disciplinary twist to the tale, suggesting to the children outside the book that an invisible presence monitors their behavior. This lesson can be far more frightening than the descriptions of the tortures to which the little mermaid is subjected. P. M. Pickard maintains that the story ends in "a mist of mysticism utterly unsuitable for children" (Pickard, 88), and P. L. Travers forgives Andersen for much in the tale but scolds him for the ending: "It is in the last three paragraphs—so sad, so romantic, the devotees say—that Andersen, with his wanton sweetness, his too-much-rubbing of Aladdin's lamp, stands most in need of forgiveness. . . . She has given up her tail—good. She has graduated to air—better, at any rate from *her* point of view. Let her now discover patience. The soul will happen in its own time. But—a year taken off when a child behaves; a tear shed and a day added whenever a child is naughty? Andersen, this is blackmail. And the children know it, and say nothing. There's magnanimity for you" (Travers, 92–93).

The manuscript for "The Little Mermaid" contained additional lines, which were deleted before publication: "I myself shall strive to win an immortal soul . . . that in the world beyond I may be reunited with him to whom I gave my whole heart," and, as Andersen's biographer Jackie Wullschlager has pointed out, it is possible to see in this passage a reference to an 1835 letter of Andersen's to Edvard Collin, in which he imagines the two of them united "before God."

The Tinderbox[1]

Fyrtøjet

Eventyr, fortalte for Børn. Første Samling. 1835

1. *Tinderbox.* The Danish term *fyrtøjet* means, literally, "fire steel." Andersen may have been inspired by a tale from the Brothers Grimm called "The Blue Light," in which a wounded soldier is dismissed without pay from army service by an ungrateful monarch. The soldier comes into the possession of a blue light with the same magical powers as the tinderbox. But his rendezvous with a princess and revenge on the king are elaborated in slightly different fashion, with the princess forced into servitude and the king pardoned for his offenses. Gregory Frost has produced a new version of the story called "Sparks" in an anthology entitled *Black Swan, White Raven.*

Andersen's early fairy tales draw on oral storytelling traditions that revel in cruelty, violence, earthiness, and vulgarity and move in a burlesque mode very different from the pious tone of tales like "The Little Match Girl." In part because of its preposterous excesses (the soldier in "The Tinderbox" is guilty of everything from ingratitude and homicide to theft and regicide) but also its exquisitely charming moments (the three dogs filled with wonder at the wedding), the story has retained a certain appeal that allows it to stay alive despite its many violent turns.

"The Tinderbox" was the opening tale of Andersen's Eventyr, *the first installment of his fairy tales. It is based on a Danish folktale known as "The Spirit of the Candle" and has multiple allusions to other fairy tales—"Rapunzel" (the princess in the tower), "Hansel and Gretel" (the trail of grain), and "Ali Baba and the Forty Thieves" (the marking of doors). In his early stories for children, Andersen borrowed bits and pieces of tales from the oral storytelling traditions of various cultures, cobbling them together to form a complete narrative. It was only after the publication of "The Little Mer-*

maid" in 1837 that he relied fully on his own powers of imagination to construct fairy tales.

The soldier-hero of "The Tinderbox" shares many traits with war veterans found in stories by the Grimms and other European collectors. Brutal, greedy, and impetuous, he is not much of a role model for children listening to the story. Indeed, stories about soldiers returning from war were generally intended for adult audiences rather than for children, although Andersen adds enough magic and whimsy to make the tale attractive for young and old.

A soldier came marching down the road[2]—left, right! left, right! He had a knapsack on his back and a sword at his side, for he had fought in the war. But now he was returning home. On the road he met an old witch who was really hideous. Her lower lip dangled all the way down to her chest.

"Good evening, soldier," she said. "What a fine sword you have there and what a big knapsack. You're every inch a soldier! And now you shall have money too, as much as you could ever want!"

"Thanks very much, you old witch," the soldier replied.

"Do you see that tall tree over there," the witch said, pointing to a tree right near them. "It's completely hollow inside. Climb up to the top, and you'll find a hole that you can use to slip inside and then slide all the way down. I'll tie a rope around your waist, and, as soon as you call out to me, I'll hoist you back up again."

HARRY CLARKE

In a lush landscape filled with massive flowers, the soldier meets the witch and is perplexed that she would want him to climb into a hollow tree.

2. *A soldier came marching down the road.* "The Tinderbox" has been described as Andersen's version of "Aladdin," the story of a young man destined to succeed no matter how he behaves. Stith Thompson reviews the main features of the plot known to folklorists as "Aladdin and His Wonderful Lamp": the finding of the lamp in an underground chamber, the magic effects of rubbing it, the acquisition of a kingdom and a wife, the theft of the lamp and consequent loss of fortune, and the restoration of the lamp by means of another magic object. In Andersen's tale, the tinderbox is not lost through deception but is left at home by accident. Critics have seen in "The Tinderbox" a domesticated version of the Oriental tale (Oxfeldt, 53).

Andersen thought of himself as an Aladdin figure and, near the end of his life, he addressed the town of Odense, which had gathered to honor him, as follows: "I cannot help thinking about Aladdin, who with the help of his magic lamp was able to create a magic castle." Andersen added: "Then I looked out of the window, and said: 'I was once a poor boy down there, but thanks to God I was also granted a magic lamp, Poetry, and when my lamp shines out over the world, giving pleasure to people, and when they recognize that it comes from Denmark, then my heart feels ready to burst' " (*Travels*, 380).

3. *her lower lip dangled all the way down to her chest.* The witch's deformity is shared by a crone in a fairy-tale trio of old women whose physical defects serve as a powerful warning against spending too much time spinning. In the Grimms' tale "The Three Spinners," one of the women displays a foot deformed from excessive treading, a second sports a lower lip hideously enlarged from licking thread, and a third exhibits a thumb broadened out of shape from twisting thread. Witches, hags, and crones appear with some frequency in Andersen's tales, most notably in "The Little Mermaid" and "The Snow Queen."

4. *more than a hundred lamps are burning down there.* The radiant hall suggests that the underground realm is associated with celestial rather than sinister powers. The soldier, of course, has to climb *up* the tree before he slides down through it.

"Why would I ever go inside that tree?" the soldier asked.

"For the money!" the witch replied. "Listen to my words. When you touch bottom, you'll find yourself in a huge hall. It will be very bright in there because more than a hundred lamps are burning down there.[4] You'll see three doors, and you can open them up because there will be a key in each lock. If you open the first door, you'll find a large chest right in the middle of a room. A dog will be sitting on top of it. His eyes will be as big as teacups, but don't mind him at all. I'll give you a blue-checked apron, which you can spread out on the floor. Go right over, pick up the dog, and put him on the apron. Then open up the chest and take out as many coins as you like. They're all made of copper, but if silver suits you better, then go into the next room. You'll find a dog in there with eyes as big as mill wheels. But don't mind him. Just put him on the apron and take the coins. Maybe you prefer gold? Well, you can have that too. If you go into the third room, you can remove as much gold as you can carry. But there will be a dog sitting on the chest filled with money, and he has eyes the size of the Round Towers.[5] Now there's a real dog! But don't mind him either. Just put him on my apron, and he'll do you no harm. You can help yourself to as much gold as you want from the chest."

"Not bad," said the soldier. "But what's in it for you, you old witch? I'm sure you want to have a share of it too."

"No," said the witch. "I don't want a penny of it. All you have to do is bring me an old tinderbox that my grandmother left behind the last time she was down there."

"Fine with me," the soldier said. "Let's put that rope around my waist."

"There you go," the witch said. "And here's my blue-checked apron."

The soldier climbed up the tree and slid right down to the bottom until he reached—just as the witch said he would—a huge hall where hundreds of lamps were burning.

HARRY CLARKE

The dog with eyes as big as teacups guards the chest of copper coins while the soldier, in garments that are impressively variegated, contemplates the hall, with its many bright lights.

In *Kafka: Gothic and Fairytale*, Patrick Bridgwater points out that Kafka's "Parable of the Doorkeeper" was inspired in part by Andersen's "Tinderbox": "In the parable, the doorkeepers, each more formidable than the one before, are clearly based on the dogs guarding successive rooms in 'The Tinder-Box,' and the gleam of what might or might not be 'eternal radiance [light]' . . . visible through the doorway to the Law, will have been suggested, in part, by the light from the three hundred lamps in the great hall of Andersen's story" (Bridgwater, 125). Although a link between the two writers seems somewhat improbable, Kafka's tales have often been framed as modernist anti–fairy tales, driven by the same existential anxieties found in Andersen, but without the overlay of Christian sentiments.

5. *Round Tower*.   The Round Tower, located in Copenhagen, was commissioned by King Christian IV as an observatory and completed in 1642. A winding passage over 200 meters in length leads to a platform from which there is a magnificent view of the city.

6. *The dog with eyes as big as teacups was sitting right there, glaring at him.*   The terrifying creature guarding the chamber is kin to Cerberus, the multiheaded dog of Greek mythology who guards the entrance to Hades. With the tail of a dragon and a neck bristling with snakes, Cerberus is even more frightening than the third in the trio of dogs guarding the underground chambers. The giant Argus of Greek mythology, with his one hundred eyes (only two of which sleep at a time), is another watchman characterized by unusual ocular traits.

7. *as many copper coins as his pockets would hold.*   Copper, silver, and gold are known as the coinage metals, and, because they

He opened the first door he saw. Yowee! The dog with eyes as big as teacups was sitting right there, glaring at him.[6]

"You're a handsome fellow," the soldier said, and he took him and set him right down on the witch's apron. Then he took as many copper coins as his pockets would hold.[7] He closed up the chest, put the dog back on it, and went into the second room. Yikes! There was the dog with eyes as big as mill wheels.

"Don't stare at me like that," the soldier said. "You might strain your eyes." And he set the dog down on the witch's apron. When he saw all the silver coins in the chest, he threw away the copper coins and filled his pockets and knapsack with the silver ones. Then he entered the third room. What a horrible sight to see! The dog in there really did have eyes as big as the Round Tower, and they were spinning around in his head like wheels.

"Good evening," the soldier said, and he saluted, for he had never seen a dog like that in all his life. But after he had stared at him for a while, he thought, well, enough of that! And he lifted the dog up, set him down on the floor, and threw open the chest. Good Lord! What a heap of gold! Enough to buy all of Copenhagen, along with every single sugar pig[8] sold by the cake-wives, and all the tin soldiers, whips, and rocking horses in the world! Yes, that was a lot of money!

The soldier got rid of all the silver coins in his pockets and in his knapsack, and he put the gold ones in their place. Yes, sir, he packed his pockets, his knapsack, his cap, and his boots so full that he could hardly walk! Now he was made of money! He set the dog back down on the chest, slammed the door shut, and hollered up through the hollow tree: "Hoist me up now, you old witch!"

"Did you remember the tinderbox?" the witch asked.

"Confound the tinderbox," the soldier shouted back. "I forgot all about it."

He fetched the box, and the witch pulled him up. There he

was, back on the road, with pockets, boots, knapsack, and cap full of gold.

"What do you want with that tinderbox?" the soldier asked the old witch.

"None of your business," the witch replied. "You have your money now, so just hand it over."

"Stuff and nonsense," said the soldier. "Tell me on the spot why you want it, or I'll take out my sword and chop your head off!"9

"I won't," the witch shouted.

And so the soldier chopped off her head. There she lay! He took her apron, wrapped all his money up in it, slung it in a bundle over his shoulder, put the tinderbox in his pocket, and headed straight for the city.

It was a splendid city. All that money had turned him into a rich man, and so he took the best rooms at the finest inn and ordered his favorite dishes.

The servant at the inn who was supposed to polish his boots found them to be an oddly shabby pair of boots for a man of such means. The soldier had not yet had the time to buy a new pair, but by the next day he had a good pair of boots and some fine new clothes. He had turned into a distinguished gentleman, and everyone was eager to tell him about all the attractions of the city, and about the king and his charming daughter, the princess.

"How do I get a look at her?" the soldier asked.

"It's not so easy to catch a glimpse of her," they all told him. "She lives in an enormous copper palace surrounded by many walls and towers. The king is the only one allowed to visit her, for there was once a prophecy that she would marry a common soldier, and the king was not at all happy about that."

"I'd like to see her all the same," the soldier thought. But how in the world could he ever make that happen?

The soldier was having a splendid time, going to the the-

resist corrosion and do not react with other elements, they were at one time commonly used to make coins the world over. As the soldier's journey progresses, the metals become progressively more precious, leading the soldier to discard the coins he had taken from the previous room. In some fairy tales, as in "The Twelve Dancing Princesses," the sequence of metals starts with silver and gold and ends in diamonds. In *The Merchant of Venice*, Portia is famously bound to wed the man who can pick the right one of three caskets, one made of gold, another of silver, and a third of lead. Bassanio triumphs when he makes the modest choice and expresses a preference for the casket of lead.

8. *every single sugar pig.* Cakes and candy made in the shape of a pig were popular desserts in Denmark, and they make an appearance in "Ole Shut-Eye" (1850) as well. Andersen was an expert in capturing children's fantasies about what money could buy, and the sugar pigs, tin soldiers, and rocking horses are much like the toys enumerated in "The Steadfast Tin Soldier" or "the whole world and a pair of new skates" in "The Snow Queen."

9. *"chop your head off!"* With his knapsack and sword, the soldier can be seen to embody ruthless greed and violence—filling his knapsack with as much gold as possible and killing with his sword anyone who crosses him. Decapitation was a common punishment in European fairy tales, and Andersen's tales include both this scene of decapitation and one of amputation (Karen's feet are chopped off in "The Red Shoes"). Jack Zipes sees in the soldier's acts of violence a reflection of "Andersen's hatred for his own class (his mother) and the Danish nobility (king and queen)," which is "played out bluntly when the soldier kills the witch and has the king and queen eliminated by the dogs" (Zipes 1999, 94). He also sees in the tale a "formula" that leads to economic success: "Use talents to acquire money and perhaps a wife, establish a system of continual recapitalization (tinderbox and three dogs) to guarantee income and power, and employ money and power to maintain social and political hegemony" (Zipes 2005, 35).

10. *for they were all so fond of him.* Although the soldier inhabits a fairy-tale world in which the social actors are limited to those who help or harm the hero, Andersen persistently embedded biting satirical remarks into the plot. The friends seem to have no other function in the tale but to serve as reminders of shameless hypocrisy. These are the same friends who will find themselves unable to climb a flight of stairs to visit the penniless soldier.

ater and taking carriage rides in the king's gardens. He also gave a lot of money to the poor, which was to his credit, for he remembered how miserable it was not to have a penny in your pocket. Now that he was wealthy and well dressed, he had many friends who called him a fine fellow and a true gentleman. That made him feel good, but because he was spending money every day without taking anything in at all, he ended up with nothing but two pennies to his name. He had to leave the comfortable rooms in which he was living and move into a garret, where he polished his own boots and repaired them with a darning needle. None of his old friends came to see him because there were far too many stairs to climb.

One evening, while he was sitting in the dark because he could not afford even a candle, he suddenly remembered that there was the stump of one in the tinderbox that he had taken from the hollow tree which the witch had helped him climb into. He took out the tinderbox and the candle stump, and, as soon as sparks flew from the flint, the door burst open and there stood the dog he had seen before—the one with eyes as big as teacups.

"What does my master command?" the dog asked.

"What on earth!" the soldier wondered. "Is this the kind of fabulous tinderbox that will get me whatever I want?" And he gave the dog an order: "Go get me some money." The dog was gone in a flash, and in a flash he was back again, with a bag full of copper coins in his mouth.

The soldier now knew what a wonderful tinderbox he had in his possession. If you struck it once, the dog from the room with the chest of copper coins appeared. If you struck it twice, the dog with the silver coins appeared. And if you struck it three times, the dog guarding the gold coins appeared. The soldier moved back to his comfortable quarters, and he was soon wearing fashionable clothes again. It was not long before his friends began to recognize him, for they were all so fond of him.[10]

One day the soldier thought to himself: "How odd that no one is allowed to see the princess. Everyone says that she is very beautiful,[11] but what is the point if she's kept in that enormous copper castle with all those towers? Why can't I have a look at her? Now where's my tinderbox?" And then he struck fire and presto! there was the dog with eyes as big as teacups.

"I know it's the middle of the night," the soldier said. "But I would really like to see the princess, even if it's just for a moment."

The dog was out the door in a flash, and before the soldier knew it, he had returned with the princess. She was draped over the dog's back, fast asleep, and she was so beautiful that anyone could tell she was a real princess.[12] The soldier could not stop himself from kissing her—he was every inch a soldier.

The dog took the princess back home. The next day, when the king and queen were serving tea, the princess remembered a strange dream she had had that night about a dog and a soldier. She had been riding on the dog's back, and the soldier had given her a kiss.

"That's quite a story!" the queen said.

The next night one of the older ladies-in-waiting was ordered to keep watch at the princess's bedside, to find out whether she had been dreaming or if it was something else altogether.

The soldier was longing to see the beautiful princess again. That night the dog appeared and took her away again, and he ran off as fast as he could. But the lady-in-waiting pulled on her storm boots and ran right after them. When she saw them disappear into a large house, she thought to herself: "Now I know where it is." And with a piece of chalk she drew a big cross on the door. Then she returned home and went to bed, and the dog came back as well, bringing the princess with him. When the dog saw the cross marked on the door of

11. *Everyone says that she is very beautiful.* The legendary beauty of the princess becomes intensified by the fact that she is kept in a mausoleum-type domicile. The copper castle resembles the tower Rapunzel inhabits—both are structures designed to wall in the heroines and keep them out of sight. The soldier's appreciation of beauty, his desire to set eyes on the princess because of her storied beauty, makes him a true hero in Andersen's fairy-tale pantheon.

12. *anyone could tell she was a real princess.* The beauty of this princess makes superfluous a test such as the one in "The Princess and the Pea." Like the prince in "Snow White" and in "Sleeping Beauty," the soldier cannot stop himself from planting a kiss on the lips of the slumbering princess.

KAY NIELSEN

The dog with eyes as big as teacups carries the sleeping princess on his back. She seems quite comfortable on a beast whose stylized curls contrast sharply with the spare architecture in the background.

where the soldier lived, he took his own piece of chalk and marked every door in the city.[13] That was a clever thing to do, because now the old lady could not tell the right door from all the wrong doors he had marked.

The next morning, the king and queen, along with the lady-in-waiting and all the officers, wanted to find out where the princess had been.

"Here's the place," the king said when he saw the first door with a cross mark on it.

"No, it's over here, my dear," said the queen, who was looking at another door.

"But here's one, and there's another!" they all shouted. Everywhere they looked, they saw chalk marks. They quickly realized that it made no sense to continue searching.

The queen was an uncommonly wise woman who could do much more than ride around in a coach. She took a pair of big golden scissors,[14] cut a large piece of silk into pieces, and then stitched together a pretty little pouch, which she filled with finely ground buckwheat. She fastened the pouch to the princess's back and then cut a tiny little hole in it[15] so that grains of buckwheat would fall wherever the princess went.

That night the dog returned, put the princess on his back, and ran off to the soldier, who loved her so dearly. The soldier just wished that he were a prince so that he could make her his wife.

The dog never noticed how the grains of buckwheat were dropping to the ground all the way from the castle right up to the wall he ran along to reach the soldier's window. The next morning the king and queen knew exactly where their daughter had been, and they seized the soldier and threw him in prison.

There he sat. It was utterly dark and dismal, and they told him: "Tomorrow you are going to be hanged." That did not cheer him up a bit, and, as for the tinderbox, he had left it behind at the inn.

13. *marked every door in the city.* The dog knows his fairy tales, for the marking of other doors to detract attention from the right door is a form of trickery used to outwit robbers in "Ali Baba and the Forty Thieves."

14. *She took a pair of big golden scissors.* In the Hans Christian Andersen Museum in Odense can be found the large scissors that Andersen used to make nearly 1,500 paper cuttings on social occasions and while he was telling stories. Kjeld Heltoft's *Hans Christian Andersen as an Artist* has a photograph of those scissors and reproduces many of the intricate paper cuttings. Heltoft quotes Baroness Bodild Donner's description of Andersen at work: "When I was a child, I looked forward to his cutting out little dolls in white paper, all joined together, which I could place on the table and blow at so that they moved forward. . . . He always cut with an enormous pair of scissors—and I simply couldn't understand how, with his big hands and enormous scissors, he could make such pretty, dainty things" (Heltoft, 207).

15. *cut a tiny little hole in it.* The strategy is familiar from tales like "Hansel and Gretel" and "The Robber Bridegroom," in which breadcrumbs and ashes mark a path. In Andersen's story, the plan works, but, in the Grimms' "Hansel and Gretel," birds eat the breadcrumbs, obliterating the trail that was to help the two children find their way back home.

16. *rushing to the outskirts of the city where he would be hanged.* As a schoolboy, Andersen was given the day off to travel to the outskirts of Skælskør, where the wife of a farmer, his daughter, and a manservant were hanged for conspiring to murder the farmer. The event left a deep impression on the young Andersen, who later wrote about it in his autobiography: "I shall never forget seeing the criminals driven to the place of execution: the young girl, deadly pale, leaning her head on the chest of her strapping sweetheart; behind them the manservant, livid, his black hair disheveled, and nodding with a squint at a few acquaintances, who shouted 'Farewell' to him. Standing by their coffins, they sang a hymn together with the minister; you could hear the girl's voice above all the others. My legs could scarcely hold me up. These moments were more horrifying to me than the moment of death" (*The Fairy Tale of My Life*, 52). Note that the story begins with a decapitation and nearly ends with an execution.

Capital punishment was entirely eliminated as a possibility in Denmark in 1994. The last public execution was carried out in 1882, and 1892 marked the last year in which capital punishment was carried out in Denmark.

17. *now, let's hear what happened!* Mimicking the style of the folk raconteur surrounded by listeners, Andersen seems to take his cue from the soldier's query ("What's the rush?") and slows down the narrative pace by inserting a question of his own.

In the morning he looked through the iron bars of his little window and could see people rushing to the outskirts of the city where he would be hanged.[16] He heard the drums and saw the soldiers march by. Everyone was in a great rush, among them a shoemaker's apprentice wearing a leather apron and slippers. He was moving at such a fast clip that one of his shoes flew off and struck the wall, right where the soldier had his face pressed to the iron bars.

"Hey there, shoemaker's boy! What's the rush?" the soldier shouted. "Nothing's going to happen until I show up. I'll give you four pennies if you run over to my place and bring me my tinderbox. But you'll have to be quick about it."

The shoemaker's apprentice was more than happy to earn those four pennies, and he ran off to fetch the tinderbox, brought it to the soldier, and, now, let's hear what happened![17]

At the outskirts of the city a tall gallows had been erected, and soldiers were gathered around it, along with many hundreds of thousands of people. The king and queen were seated on a splendid throne, right opposite the judge and the entire council.

The soldier was already standing on the ladder, and they were about to put the rope around his neck when he pointed out that a sinner facing his punishment was always granted one last harmless request. He dearly wanted to smoke a pipe, and it was the last pipe that he would be able to have in this world.

How could the king refuse him? And so the soldier took out his tinderbox and struck fire from it—one, two, three, and presto! There stood all three dogs: the one with eyes as big as teacups, the one with eyes like mill wheels, and the one with eyes as big as the Round Tower.

"Help me now! Save me from hanging!" the soldier shouted. The dogs rushed at the judge and at the entire council, grabbing one person by the leg, another by the nose, and tossing them all so high up in the air that when they fell back down they broke into pieces.

"No, not me!" the king shouted, but the biggest dog seized him and the queen too, and tossed them up after the others. The soldiers trembled, and everyone shouted: "Little soldier, you must be our king and marry the beautiful princess!"

They carried the soldier into the royal coach. All three dogs danced in front of it, shouting "Hurrah!" while boys whistled through their fingers and soldiers presented arms. The princess emerged from the copper castle and became queen, and that suited her just fine! The wedding celebration lasted for a week, and the three dogs sat at the table, their eyes wide with wonder.[18]

18. *their eyes wide with wonder.* The dogs, who themselves aroused wonder with their eyes as large as teacups, mill wheels, and the Round Tower, now gaze with astonishment at the wedding celebration for the soldier and his beautiful princess-bride. Ending the story with the image of wide-eyed wonder points to Andersen's deep commitment to providing the old-time enchantments of oral storytellers. In many ways, Andersen's efforts to arouse wonder also anticipate Lewis Carroll's use of stories to capture the attention and imagination of children by arousing their sense of wonder. Recall the ending of *Alice in Wonderland*, with Alice's sister imagining that she might be able to "gather about her other little children, and make *their* eyes bright and eager with many a strange tale."

KAY NIELSEN

The three dogs, their eyes wide with wonder, celebrate the wedding of the soldier and princess.

The Wild Swans

De vilde svaner

Eventyr, fortalte for Børn, 1838

ndersen's source for this tale was Matthias Winther's "The Eleven Swans" (included at the end of the annotations to this tale), published in his Danish Folktales *of 1823. It is easy to imagine why Andersen would have been drawn to a tale that included majestic birds that represented for him mystery, spirituality, and sublime beauty. Andersen must also have been drawn to the mute heroine of the tale, who, like the little mermaid, suffers in silence until her moment of glory and transfiguration. Raised as an only child and always seeking "brothers" and "sisters" in his friendships, Andersen saw in this story a fantasy of sibling solidarity that he could never realize in real life.*

The Brothers Grimm had included versions of this tale type in their Children's Stories and Household Tales *published in 1812 and 1815. In "Twelve Brothers," a girl accidentally turns her brothers into ravens; in "Seven Ravens," a father curses his sons, transforming them into ravens; and in "Six Swans," a wicked queen casts the spell that enchants her stepsons. All of these tales show how curses can be undone with heroic determination and heartfelt generosity. For the cultural critic Marina Warner, these stories were childhood favorites, for they tell a tale of female heroism: "I had no brothers, but I fantasized, at night, as I waited to go to sleep, that I had, perhaps even as many tall and handsome youths as the girl in the story, and that I would do something magnificent for them that would make them realize I was one of them, as it were, their equal in courage and determination and grace"* (Warner, 392). "The Wild Swans," *like its many folkloric cousins, is the stuff of dreams, but its heroine accomplishes her task with unwavering resolve, and the bond between her and the brothers remains tender, strong, and indissoluble.*

W. HEATH ROBINSON

Elisa picks nettles in a field covered with flowers. She herself wears a dress that, with its floral designs, reveals her alliance with nature.

Far, far away, where the swallows fly when it's winter here,[1] there lived a king who had eleven sons and one daughter named Elisa.[2] The eleven brothers, princes all, went to school wearing stars on their chests and swords at their side. They did their writing on golden tablets with pencils of diamond, and they could recite their lessons just as well from memory as from a book. You could tell at once that they were princes. Their sister, Elisa, used to sit on a little stool made of mirror glass[3] and look at a picture book that cost half the kingdom.[4]

Oh, those children were truly happy, but it was not to last forever.

The children's father was king of all the land, and he married an evil queen who was not at all kind to the poor children.[5] That was obvious from the very first day. During the festivities at the palace, the children played at entertaining guests.[6] But instead of letting them have, as usual, all the cakes and baked apples that they wanted, the queen just gave

1. *where the swallows fly when it's winter here.* Although the folktale being recast has its origins in Scandinavian countries and German-speaking countries, Andersen chose to set it in southern climes, in a domain where birds settle to escape the harsh winter climate of northern countries.

2. *one daughter named Elisa.* Elisa is a shortened form for Elisabeth, from the Hebrew Elisheba, which signifies that God is "satisfaction," "perfection," or

"plenitude." Unwavering in her mission to liberate her brothers from the spell that keeps them in animal form, Elisa becomes a figure who enacts the meaning of faith and devotion.

3. *a little stool made of mirror glass.* Fairy tales famously use gold to express beauty, but glass also appears frequently—in the form of slippers, coaches, coffins, axes, and mountains—symbolizing not only beauty but also clarity and rarity. To be sure, there is something absurd about a stool made of glass, but glass, like gold, is connected with delicate radiance.

4. *look at a picture book that cost half the kingdom.* Half the kingdom is a measure frequently used as the reward for princes and young men who rescue princesses. The value attached to pictures in this context reflects the degree to which the beauty of images is—especially for children—incalculable.

5. *he married an evil queen who was not at all kind to the poor children.* Like the stepmothers of Cinderella, Snow White, and Hansel and Gretel, this second wife withholds love and tries to banish the children from the safe enclosure of family life. The ghoulish creatures that appear later in the story embody her evil character, giving it physical force.

6. *the children played at entertaining guests.* "Company's coming" was a common children's game in Andersen's time, and it is also played by the princess in "The Swineherd."

them some sand in a teacup and told them to pretend that it was something special.

The next week the queen sent little Elisa out to the country to live with peasants. And it wasn't long before she tricked the king into believing so many lies about the poor princes that his heart turned against them.

"Go out into the world and fend for yourselves," the wicked queen told the boys. "Fly away like great big birds without voices."[7] But she could not harm the princes as deeply as she intended, for they turned into eleven beautiful white swans. Uttering strange cries, they flew out the castle windows, over the park and into the woods.

It was still quite early in the morning when they reached the farmer's house, where their sister, Elisa, was sleeping. They hovered above the roof, craning their long necks and flapping their wings, but no one heard them or saw them. They had to keep flying, climbing up toward the clouds, far away into the wide world until they reached a vast, dark forest that stretched all the way down to the shores of the sea.

Inside the farmer's house, poor little Elisa was playing with a green leaf, for she didn't have any other toys. She poked a little hole in the leaf and looked at the sun through it. It was like looking at her brothers' bright eyes. Whenever the warm sunshine touched her cheek, she was reminded of their kisses.

One day was just like the next. When the wind stirred the rosebushes outside the farmhouse, it would whisper: "Who could be more beautiful than you?"[8] But the roses would shake their heads and say "Elisa is!" And when the old farmer's wife sat by the doorway on Sunday, reading her hymnal, the wind would rustle the pages asking the book: "Who could be more devout than you?" "Elisa is," the hymn book replied. And what the roses and the hymnal said was the plain truth.

When she turned fifteen, Elisa returned home. The queen saw how beautiful she had become and was filled with anger and resentment. She would have liked to turn her into a wild

7. *"Fly away like great big birds without voices."* The curses and spells in fairy tales have been seen as bearing witness "to an early and perhaps continuous belief—or at least continuous reference to—a peculiarly female ability to control, direct or affect natural powers" (Bottigheimer, 43). The evil queen is initially described as a human, but her identity as a witch is quickly revealed, first by her ability to transform humans into birds, then by the term used to designate her in the bathing scene. The transformation of the boys into birds is accompanied by a loss of voice, anticipating the vow of silence Elisa will take. Margaret Atwood recalls the special attraction to her as a child of humans transformed into birds: "Now, in real life birds were birds. They cawed, hooted, quacked and chirped, and, if they were loons, made eerie sounds at night that caused the hair to stand up on your arms. But in fairy tales, birds were either messengers that led you deeper into the forest on some quest, or brought you news or help, or warned you, like the bird at the robbers' house in 'The Robber Bridegroom,' or meted out vengeance, like the eye-pecking doves at the end of 'Cinderella'; or else they were something you could be transformed into. These last were my kind of birds" ("Of Souls as Birds," 25).

8. *"Who could be more beautiful than you?"* The rose and the hymnal, by combining beauty with piety, suggest that more is at stake than in the traditional folktale, where beauty alone is sufficient to mark the heroine's magnetic quality. Note how Andersen adds a layer of Christian morality to a tale with pagan origins. The beauty of nature (as symbolized by the rose) and the beauty of the word (as symbolized by the hymnal) pale before Elisa, who becomes "the fairest of all," but who remains unreadable because she cannot speak.

9. *three red poppies were floating on the water.* The red poppy has traditionally been a symbol of death, renewal, and resurrection. The flower has seeds that can remain dormant for years on end but will blossom when the soil is turned over. The fields of northern France and Flanders became the site of vast tracts of poppies after World War I, and their presence was commemorated in John McCrae's famous verse: "In Flanders Fields the poppies blow / Between the crosses row on row."

10. *he was horrified and insisted that she could not be his daughter.* The king's repudiation of his daughter sets the stage for a second rejection that will take place when the king who marries Elisa listens to the archbishop's denunciations of his wife. The atrocities at home are habitually repeated at the heroine's second, new home in fairytale plots.

11. *they were humble creatures and had no say in the matter.* Andersen repeatedly placed his sympathies with migratory creatures like swallows, with whom he, as an energetic traveler, identified. In a letter to Jonas Collin, he described his nomadic habits: "Now I have a home for 25 rixdollars a month, which I will probably fly away from when the first warm rays of the sun prickle me, the way they prickle the migratory birds" (Rossel 1996, 48). The watchdog may be a reference to Argos, the faithful dog who is the first to recognize Odysseus when he returns home disguised as an old beggar.

swan, along with her brothers, but she did not dare do it right away, because the king wanted to see his daughter.

Early the next morning, the queen went to the baths, which were built of marble and furnished with soft cushions and the loveliest tapestries. She took three toads, kissed them, and said to one of them: "Hop onto Elisa's head when she gets into the bath so that she will grow to become as sluggish as you are." And to the second she said: "Cling to her forehead so that she will become as ugly as you are, and her father won't recognize her." And to the third toad she whispered, "Settle on her heart and give her an evil soul so that she will suffer." Then she lowered the three toads into the clear water, which promptly turned a greenish color. She called Elisa, undressed her, and made her get into the bath. Once Elisa was in the water, one of the toads climbed into her hair, another onto her forehead, and the third against her heart. Elisa did not seem to be aware of them at all, and, when she stood up, three red poppies were floating on the water.[9] If the toads had not been poisonous and the witch had not kissed them, they would have turned into red roses, but they became flowers nonetheless, merely by touching Elisa's head and heart. She was too innocent and devout for witchcraft to have any effect on her.

When the evil queen realized this, she rubbed Elisa all over with walnut juice until she turned dark brown, smeared her beautiful face with a vile ointment, and left her lovely hair in a tangled mess. You could not recognize the beautiful Elisa. When her father set eyes on her, he was horrified and insisted that she could not be his daughter.[10] No one else would have known who she was except the watchdog and the swallows, but they were humble creatures and had no say in the matter.[11]

Poor Elisa began to weep as she thought of her eleven brothers, who were all so far away. With a heavy heart, she stole out of the palace and spent the day wandering over fields and moors until she came to a vast forest. She had no idea where to turn, but she was full of sorrow and longed to be with her brothers, who had also been driven out into the wide world. She set her heart on finding them.

Not long after Elisa entered the forest, night fell. She had wandered far away from roads and paths. She said her prayers and lay down on the soft moss, leaning her head against the stump of a tree. It was quiet, and the air was sweet. Hundreds of fireflies glittered like some kind of green fire above the grass and moss.[12] When she gently touched a branch with her hand, glittering insects darted all around her like shooting stars.

All night long she had dreams about her brothers.[13] They were children again, playing together, writing with their diamond pencils on their golden tablets and looking at her wonderful picture book that had cost half a kingdom. But they were no longer just scribbling circles and lines as they once had. No, they were writing about their bold deeds and about everything they had seen and done. What was once in the picture book had come alive.[14] Birds were singing, and people stepped out of the pages of the book and talked with Elisa and her brothers. But the moment she turned a page, they leaped back into place so that the pictures wouldn't get out of order.

When Elisa awoke, the sun was already high overhead.[15] She couldn't actually see it through the dense branches of the tall trees around her, but the sun's rays played through the tangle of branches like a golden veil aflutter. There was a fresh, green scent in the air, and the birds flew so close that they nearly perched on her shoulder. She could hear the sound of water splashing—many large springs flowed into a pond with the most beautiful sandy bottom. Thick bushes had grown all around, but in one spot deer had made a large opening, one wide enough to allow Elisa to reach the water. The pond was so clear that, if the wind had not stirred the branches and shrubs all around, you would have thought that

12. *Hundreds of fireflies glittered like some kind of green fire above the grass and moss.* Fireflies, also known as lightning bugs, and as glowworms (the term for the larvae and the wingless females), belong to the nocturnal beetles of the family Lampyridae, which have special chemicals in the abdomen that produce a flashing light. The males fly around in the evening during early summer. Andersen was fascinated with special light effects, the play of the sun's rays, the sparkling of stars, and the Northern lights. Luminescence in general works a profound aesthetic and spiritual charm in Andersen's works and, as holds true for "The Wild Swans," provides inspiration and hope.

13. *All night long she had dreams about her brothers.* Elisa, unlike Sleeping Beauty, Snow White, and other characters from oral storytelling traditions, has a lively nocturnal dream life. In her dreams—which can be seen as a slow incubation period for developing the self—she reminisces about the past, ponders the future, and discovers the means to release her brothers from their enchanted state.

14. *What was once in the picture book had come alive.* The notion of a book whose characters can step out of the pages is a literary conceit, with origins in the Romantic period that flourished when Andersen was a boy. Related to the notion that portraits and statues can come to life, the concept suggests a breaking of the boundaries between art and life. In many children's books, for example Michael Ende's *The Neverending Story*, characters can enter into the story that unfolds while they are reading. Andersen may have been influenced by *Heinrich von Ofterdingen* (1799), a novel by the German Romantic Novalis, that charted the travels of a young man on his way to becoming a poet. On his journey, Heinrich encounters a hermit who possesses an exotic volume written in a foreign language. As he leafs through the pages, he realizes that the figures in the book represent him and members of his family, all dressed in costumes from another time and place.

15. *the sun was already high overhead.* Idyllic nature scenes abound in Andersen's work, but the description of Elisa at the pond is almost unsurpassed in its beauty. The visual, aural, and olfactory elements combine to produce a utopian scene of arresting natural splendor, as the pure surface of the pond reflects and reproduces all that surrounds it.

16. *a more beautiful royal child.* The bathing scene presents a pagan baptism in which Elisa purges herself of her stepmother's evil influence. If the earlier immersion in water (at home) had a transformative effect, this second cleansing

W. HEATH ROBINSON

Elisa bathes in a pond in order to remove the stains left by the walnut oil and "vile ointment" applied by her stepmother.

they were painted on its surface. Every leaf—whether in the sun or in the shade—was reflected perfectly on the waters.

When Elisa saw her face in the water, she was frightened, for it was so stained and ugly. But when she dipped her little hand into the water and rubbed her eyes and forehead, the pale skin shone through again. She took off her clothing and stepped into the cool waters. You could not have found a more beautiful royal child[16] anywhere in the world.

After Elisa put her clothes back on and braided her long hair, she went over to the sparkling spring and drank from the hollow of her hand. Then she wandered deeper into the woods, not knowing where she was going. She thought about her brothers and about the good Lord who would surely not abandon her. He had made wild apples grow to feed those who were hungry, and he led her to a wild apple tree, its branches weighed down by fruit. Here she ate her midday meal and propped up the tree's branches. Then she entered the deepest part of the forest. It was so quiet that she could hear the sound of her own footsteps and every little dry leaf crushed under her foot. There were no birds in sight, and not a single ray of sunshine was able to penetrate the thick, dense tree branches all around. The tall trees were growing so closely next to each other that, when you looked straight ahead, it seemed as if a solid fence was surrounding you. Elisa had never before known such loneliness.[17]

The night was pitch black, and not a single firefly could be seen in the moss. Feeling sad, Elisa lay down to sleep. Suddenly the branches above her seemed to part, and the good Lord was looking down kindly upon her. Little angels peeked out from above his head and under his arms.

When Elisa woke up the next morning, she had no idea whether she had dreamed what had happened or whether it was real. She had taken no more than a few steps when she met an old woman carrying a basket of berries.[18] The old woman gave her a few, and Elisa asked whether she had ever seen eleven princes riding through the forest.

"No," the old woman said, "but yesterday I saw eleven swans with golden crowns on their heads floating down the river not far from this spot."

The old woman led Elisa some distance away to a steep slope. Down below, a stream wound its way, and trees on both banks stretched their long, leafy branches toward each other. Wherever their limbs couldn't touch, they had pulled their roots loose from the earth and leaned out over the water until their branches met.[19]

Elisa took leave of the old woman and followed the river down to where it flowed into the great open sea.

The vast, beautiful sea lay in front of the young girl, but there was not a sail in sight, and not a boat to be seen. How could she possibly continue her journey? She looked at the countless pebbles on the beach, all washed round and smooth by the water. Glass, iron, rocks, everything that had washed up had been worn down by the water, and yet the water was so much softer than her delicate hand. "It keeps on rolling and never tires, and it smoothes out whatever is hard. I want to be just as strong! Thanks for the lesson, dear waves that rise and fall. My heart tells me that someday you will carry me to my beloved brothers!"

Scattered among the seaweed washed up on shore, Elisa found eleven white swan feathers, and she gathered them up into a little bundle. There were still drops of water on them, but she could not tell whether they were drops of dew or tears. It was lonely out there by the sea, but she didn't mind,

W. HEATH ROBINSON

An old woman carrying a basket of berries emerges from the forest to help Elisa in her quest to disenchant her brothers. By contrast to the stepmother, she will offer guidance and advice.

reveals, once again, Elisa's inherent nobility.

17. *Elisa had never before known such loneliness.* After the idyllic beauty of the woodland scene comes a moment in which Elisa feels the deepest emotional despair of her entire ordeal. For the ugly duckling and other figures like Elisa, the existential crisis marks what J.R.R. Tolkien has referred to as the eucatastrophe, the dark desolation that signals a turning point that will lead to redemption.

18. *an old woman carrying a basket of berries.* Like the various old women in "The Snow Queen," the woman with the basket of berries provides physical nourishment and spiritual guidance to the solitary heroine. Although she possesses no magical powers, she serves as a counterweight to the stepmother and her evil machinations,

175

W. HEATH ROBINSON

Elisa scans the vast horizon in search of a sail, but she remains isolated on the surface of the waters.

suggesting that benevolent forces will emerge in the course of the heroine's peregrinations.

19. *leaned out over the water until their branches met.* The force of desire operates powerfully, even in nonsentient beings. The description of the trees transcending their rooted nature and reaching out to each other across the waters prefigures the strength of Elisa's desire to reunite with her brothers. The kind of contact pictured here—reaching across obstacles to meet and embrace—mirrors the poetic effect of the kiss in Andersen's works.

20. *the sea was always changing.* The notion of mutability is introduced in the descriptions of the changing landscape. The narrative begins with the transformation of the boys into swans and repeatedly takes up the theme of metamorphosis. The toads in Elisa's bath, for example, are turned into poppies. Here, the landscape participates too, albeit in more subtle ways, in the process of transformation.

21. *eleven swans with golden crowns on their heads.* The swans are presented as a wondrous sight. As in "The Ugly Duckling," their golden crowns mark them as royal beings, and their movements create the

because the sea was always changing[20]—in a matter of hours it could change more dramatically than a freshwater lake does in an entire year. When a big black cloud appeared in the sky, the sea appeared to be saying: "I can also look threatening." Then the wind would blow, and white crests would rise on the waves. But if the clouds turned crimson and the winds died down, the sea looked just like a rose petal. Sometimes it looked green, then it would turn white, but no matter how calm it might appear, there was always some kind of gentle movement at the shore. The water rose and fell softly, like the chest of a sleeping child.

Just as the sun was setting, Elisa caught sight of eleven swans with golden crowns on their heads[21] flying toward land. Like a long, white ribbon, they glided in, one after another. Elisa climbed up the slope and hid behind a bush. The swans landed near her and flapped their magnificent white wings.

When the sun had disappeared into the water, the swans shed their feathers, and there stood eleven handsome princes—Elisa's brothers. Although they had changed a great deal, she knew in her heart that she was not mistaken. She uttered a loud cry, and rushed into their arms, calling them each by name. They were overjoyed to see their little sister, who had grown so tall and lovely. They laughed and they cried, and soon they understood exactly how badly their step-mother had treated all of them.

"We brothers," said the eldest, "fly like wild swans as long as the sun remains in the sky. When it sets, we return to our human form. And so at sunset we must always try to find firm ground, because if we were still flying up in the clouds, we would come plunging down into the deep. This is not where we live. Beyond the sea there is another land as fair as this one, but it is far away. You have to cross the vast ocean to reach it and there is not a single island along the way to spend the night, just one little rock jutting up midway across. There's barely room for us to stand on it, even when we are right next to each other. If the sea is rough, the water sprays right on us. But still we thank God for that one spot where we can rest as humans during the night. Otherwise we would never be able to visit our own dear homeland. It takes two of the longest days of the year for us to complete the journey. We can visit the home of our ancestors only once a year, and we don't dare stay longer than eleven days.

"When we fly over this forest we can see the palace where Father lives and where we were born. We can see the high tower of the church where Mother lies buried. And even the trees and bushes feel like family to us. Wild horses gallop across the moors as they did when we were young, and the charcoal burner sings the same old songs to which we used to dance as children. This is our homeland. It draws us close, and here, dear sister, we have found you again. We can stay for just two more days, and then we must fly across the sea to a land which is quite beautiful, but not our own. How shall we ever manage to take you with us? We have neither a ship nor a boat."

"How will I be able to set you free?" their sister asked, and they talked for most of the night, sparing only a few hours for sleep.

The next morning Elisa awakened to the rustling of swans'

impression of an aesthetic ornament that fills the sky with beauty. Swans, as Jackie Wullschlager points out, were cherished birds in Andersen's personal mythology. They were closest to his "romantic self-image as wild, pure, lofty and loyal." They are also, as she points out, monogamous creatures who take care of their young as a pair. They appear to soar with great power in the air even as they are "elegantly resigned" on water and "uncomfortable and graceless" on land (Wullschlager, 189). And, as Boria Sax points out, their families, "at least viewed from a distance, seem close to the domestic idylls of the human imagination" (Sax, 63).

22. *who was still fast asleep.* Even as Elisa becomes savior to her brothers, she also becomes something like a child to the swan brothers. Placed in netting that resembles a cradle, she is sheltered from the sun by one of their protective wings. She is even provided with nourishment in her aerial bed.

wings overhead. Her brothers had been transformed again, and they were flying in ever widening circles until finally they were out of sight. But one of them, the youngest, stayed behind. He rested his head in Elisa's lap, and she stroked his white wings. They spent the entire day together. Toward evening the others returned, and when the sun set, they resumed their human shape.

"Tomorrow we must fly away from here," one of the brothers said, "and we will not be able to return for a whole year. But we can't leave you alone like this. Do you have the courage to come with us? My arm is strong enough to carry you through the forest, and surely the strength of our wings can be used to carry you across the sea."

"Yes, take me with you!" Elisa said.

Together they spent all night braiding a net from the softest willow bark and the toughest rushes to be found, and they made it big and strong. Elisa lay down in it. When the sun rose and the brothers had been turned back into wild swans, they lifted the net with their bills and flew high up toward the clouds with their dear sister, who was still fast asleep.[22] Since the sun's rays were shining right down on her face, one of the swans flew overhead to provide shade with his broad wings.

They were still far from land when Elisa woke up. She thought she must be dreaming, because it was so strange to be high up in the air, flying over the sea. A bunch of tasty roots and a branch covered with delicious ripe berries were at her side. They had been gathered by the youngest of the brothers and placed there for her to eat. Elisa smiled at him with gratitude in her eyes, for she could tell that he was the one flying right above her and protecting her from the sun with his wings.

They were flying so high up that the first ship they caught sight of looked like a white seagull floating on the water. A large cloud rose up behind them, the size of a mountain. Elisa

HARRY CLARKE

Lying in her net of willow bark and rushes, intertwined with decorative ribbons, Elisa flies up
to the clouds and back down again with her brothers.

23. *The clouds formed one huge, menacing wave.* During the travels of the brothers and their sister, "up," "above," and "down below" become nearly interchangeable. The clouds above take on the characteristics of the ocean, and the world becomes one vast tract without any kind of division between air and sea. Swans are, of course, at home on land, in the air, and at sea.

could see the gigantic shadows cast by herself and the eleven swans as they flew. It was the most magnificent sight she had ever seen. But as the sun rose higher and the clouds faded into the distance, the phantom shadows disappeared.

All day long the swans soared like arrows flying through the air. And yet, because they were carrying their sister, they were moving more slowly than usual. Evening was approaching, and a storm was brewing. With rising anxiety, Elisa noticed that the sun was beginning to set, and the solitary rock in the sea was still nowhere to be seen. It felt to her as if the swans were flapping their wings harder and harder. It was all her fault that they couldn't fly faster. When the sun went down, they would turn into humans, plunge into the sea, and drown. She prayed to the dear Lord with all her might, but there was still no sign of the rock. Black clouds were gathering, and strong gusts of wind warned of a storm. The clouds formed one huge, menacing wave[23] that came rushing toward them like a mass of molten lead. One lightning bolt after another flashed across the skies.

The sun was just reaching the rim of the sea. Elisa's heart was beating like mad. Suddenly the swans took a quick downward plunge. Elisa was sure it was the end, but soon they were flying straight ahead again. The sun was halfway into the water when she caught sight of the little rock below them. It looked no larger than a seal poking its head out of the water. The sun was sinking so rapidly that it was now no bigger than a star. Just as Elisa's foot touched solid ground, the sun went out like the last ember when a piece of paper finishes burning. She looked at her brothers, who were standing around her, arm in arm, and there was just enough space there for all twelve of them. The waves beat down on the rock and drenched all of them with sprays of water. The sky was lit up with fiery flashes, and thunderbolts kept crashing around them, one peal after another. Elisa and her brothers held hands and sang a hymn that gave them comfort and filled them with courage.

By dawn the air was clear and calm. As soon as the sun rose, the swans flew away with Elisa, leaving the rock behind them. The sea was still rough, and from the height at which they were soaring, the white crests of foam on the dark green waves looked like millions of swans floating on the waters.

As the sun rose higher, Elisa saw before them—almost hovering in the air—a mountain range. Its peaks were capped with glittering masses of ice, and from its midst rose a castle that seemed to be miles long, with one bold colonnade perched on another. Down below palm trees were swaying in the wind, and there were magnificent flowers as large as mill wheels[24] below. She asked whether this was the land for which they were bound, but the swans shook their heads. What she had seen was Fata Morgana's lovely castle[25] in the air, a place that was always changing. They didn't dare take anyone in there. When Elisa stared at it, the mountains, forest, and castle collapsed, and twenty splendid churches stood there, all exactly alike, with tall towers and arched windows. She thought she could hear the sound of an organ, but it was only the sea. As she drew closer to the churches, they turned into a fleet of ships sailing beneath her. She looked down again and saw nothing but sea mist drifting over the water. The scene kept changing before her eyes,[26] and then at last she saw the actual country toward which she was headed. Lovely blue mountains with cedar forests, cities, and castles rose up before her. Long before sunset, she was sitting on a mountainside, in front of a cave carpeted with fine, green vines that looked like embroidered tapestries.

"Now we'll see what you dream about tonight while you are here," her youngest brother said, showing her where she was to sleep.

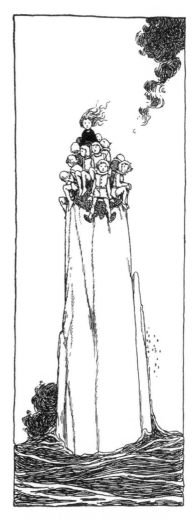

W. HEATH ROBINSON

Elisa and her brothers huddle together on a rock that has just enough room for them to stand. Black clouds, thunderbolts, and waves threaten them all around.

24. *as large as mill wheels.* In "The Tinderbox," Andersen used mill wheels to describe the size of the dog's eyes.

25. *Fata Morgana's lovely castle.* Fata Morgana, also known by the name of Morgan le Fay, is an enchantress with the ability to transform her appearance. Trained by Merlin the Magician, she is described by one source as King Arthur's shape shifting half-sister. Her name is used to describe a special type of mirage, formed by alternating warm and cold layers of air near the ground or near the water, that appears in the form of a castle half in the air and half in the sea. Fata Morgana was said to live in a castle under the sea, and the enchantress had the capacity to cause the castle to appear reflected in the air. Sailors would be lured to their deaths when they mistook her magnificent castle for a safe harbor. The term is used colloquially to denote a mirage or optical illusion.

26. *The scene kept changing before her eyes.* Mutability in the landscape creates a sense of dangerous instability. Elisa has little control over her constantly changing environment when she flies with her brothers.

27. *you may not speak.* Like the little mermaid, Elisa combines virtue with silence, epitomizing heroism as she sacrifices her own well-being for others. The yoking of virtue with silence appears frequently in earlier literature—for instance, Shakespeare's Cordelia in *King Lear* and Constance in Chaucer's "Man of Law's Tale." Marina Warner locates the origins of this fairy tale in a time when "women's capacity for love and action tragically exceeded the permitted boundaries of their lives" (Warner, 392–93). The silence in this particular tale creates a sense of powerlessness even as the heroine is developing the capacity to transform her brothers. Ruth B. Bottigheimer points out that "a historical understanding of fairy tales leads to the conclusion that insistent privation or imminent deprivation can be and have been recast into a narrative in which silence and being condemned to silence stand for the domestic, political and social experience of the poor" (Bottigheimer, 73).

"If only I could dream about how to set you free," she replied.

She was completely absorbed by this thought, and she was praying so ardently for God's help that she was still speaking in her sleep. It seemed to her that she was flying to Fata Morgana's castle in the air. The fairy who came out to meet her was dazzlingly beautiful, and she looked very much like the old woman who had given her the berries in the forest and who had told her about the swans with the golden crowns.

"You have the power to set your brothers free," she said. "But do you have the courage and perseverance? The sea may well feel softer than your delicate hands, and yet it can still change the shape of hard stones. But it does not feel the pain that your fingers will feel. It doesn't have a heart, and it doesn't have to suffer the anguish and heartache that you will have to endure. Do you see these nettles in my hand? Many of them grow around the cave where you are sleeping. Listen carefully! You can only use the ones here and the ones that grow on churchyard graves. They will burn blisters on your skin, but you have to be sure to gather only those. Then crush the nettles with your feet, and you'll get flax, which you must spin and weave into eleven shirts of mail with long sleeves. Throw those shirts over the eleven wild swans, and the spell will be broken. But remember! From the moment you start this task until it is finished, you may not speak.[27] If you utter one word, it will pierce the hearts of your brothers like a deadly dagger. Their lives depend on your silence. Don't forget what I have told you."

At that instant, the fairy touched Elisa's hand with a nettle. It burned her skin like fire and woke her up. It was broad daylight, and right near where she had been sleeping were nettles just like the ones she had seen in her dream. She fell to her knees to give thanks to God and left the cave to start her work.

With her lovely hands, Elisa picked the dreadful nettles

that burned her hands and arms like fire, raising blisters on them. She did not mind as long as it meant that she would be able to free her beloved brothers. She crushed all the nettles with her bare feet and spun them into green flax.

When the brothers returned at sunset, they were alarmed to find that Elisa was unable to speak. They thought that their wicked stepmother had cast another spell, but when they looked at her hands, it dawned on them what she was doing for them. The youngest of the brothers burst into tears. And when his tears touched Elisa, the pain was gone,[28] and the burning blisters vanished.

Elisa toiled all night long, for she did not want to rest until she had freed her beloved brothers. The next day, while the swans were away, she sat in solitude, but never had time flown by so quickly. One shirt of mail was already finished, and she set to work on the next one.

All at once, the sound of a hunting horn echoed through the mountains. She grew quite frightened. The sound came closer, and she could hear hounds baying. Terrified, she ran inside the cave, put the nettles she had gathered and woven into a small bundle, and sat down on it.

Suddenly a huge hound came bounding in from the thicket, followed by a second, and then a third. All three were barking loudly and running back and forth. Before long, a band of hunters had gathered in front of the cave. The handsomest among them was the king of the land, and he walked over to Elisa. Never before had he seen a girl so beautiful.[29]

"How did you get here, you lovely child?" he asked. Elisa could only shake her head, for she did not dare to say a word. Her brothers' lives and their freedom were at stake. She hid her hands under her apron so that the king would not see what she had to endure.

"Come with me," he said to her. "You should not stay here. If you're as good as you are beautiful,[30] I shall clothe you in silk and velvet, put a golden crown on your head, and you

28. *the pain was gone.* The power of tears to heal is evident in stories like "Rapunzel," in which the heroine's tears have the capacity to bring sight back to the prince's eyes. In "The Snow Queen," Gerda's tears break the wintry spell cast on Kai by the glass splinter in his heart.

29. *Never before had he seen a girl so beautiful.* Max Lüthi has pointed out that the actual form beauty takes in fairy tales is rarely made explicit: "The beauty is *abstract*. The listener must fall back on his own imagination." He notes further that this kind of abstract beauty does not have an erotic quality: "Beauty spellbinds and attracts, and with magic power. But there is no talk of sensual vibration, either with respect to the beautiful girl herself or with respect to those affected by her" (Lüthi, 4–5). Andersen's fairy tales, in contrast to his novels and plays, construct beautiful scenes and images that yield aesthetic rather than sensual pleasure.

30. *If you're as good as you are beautiful.* In *On Beauty and Being Just*, Elaine Scarry notes that virtue and beauty are powerfully linked: "beautiful things give rise to the notion of distribution, to a life-saving reciprocity, to fairness not just in the sense of loveliness of aspect but in the sense of 'a symmetry of everyone's relation to one another'" (Scarry 1999, 95). Elisa is fair in both senses of the term. She rights the wrongs of the stepmother and becomes an agent of justice, restoring her brothers to their human form and returning them to their natural home.

31. *even though the archbishop was shaking his head.* In most other versions of the tale, it is a mother-in-law or other evil female figure who spreads vicious rumors about the heroine, switching her newborn child with whelps or monsters and branding her a sorceress. The association of evil with an ecclesiastical figure reflects skepticism about nineteenth-century religious orthodoxies. More importantly, it is also consonant with a deeply critical attitude toward the clergy in folktales. Parsons and priests are frequently represented as freeloaders and cheats who deserve to have the tables turned on them.

shall live in my grandest palace." And the king lifted her up onto his horse. Elisa wept and began wringing her hands. The king said to her: "My only wish is to make you happy. One day you will thank me for this." Off he rode through the mountains, with Elisa seated in front of him on his horse, with the hunters galloping behind them.

By the time the sun set, the magnificent royal city with all its churches and domes lay before them. The king took Elisa into his palace, where water was splashing in grand fountains in enormous marble halls, and where both walls and ceilings were decorated with paintings. But she had no eyes for any of these things. All she could do was cry and grieve. Without resisting, she let the women dress her in royal garments, weave strings of pearls into her hair, and pull fine gloves over her blistered fingers.

She was so dazzlingly beautiful in her finery that the whole court bowed even more deeply than before. And the king chose her as his bride, even though the archbishop was shaking his head[31] and whispering that this lovely maid from the woods must be a sorceress who had bewitched the court and stolen the king's heart.

The king refused to listen. He gave commands and music was played, sumptuous dishes were served, and lovely girls began dancing. Elisa was escorted through fragrant gardens into magnificent halls, but nothing could bring a smile to her lips or make her eyes sparkle. Sorrow had set its seal upon them as if that were her eternal destiny. At length the king opened the door to a little chamber adjoining her bedroom. It was covered with splendid green tapestries and looked exactly like the cave in which she had been living. On the floor lay the bundle of flax she had spun from the nettles, and from the ceiling hung the shirt of mail she had already woven. One of the hunters had decided to bring back these curiosities.

"Here you can dream yourself back to your old home," the king told her. "This is the work that kept you occupied. Now, in the midst of all this splendor, it may amuse you to think back to that time."

When Elisa discovered all the things that were so precious to her, a smile came to her lips, and the color came back into her cheeks. Overjoyed at the thought of her brothers' salvation, she kissed the king's hand. He pressed her to his heart and ordered that all the church bells ring in honor of the wedding celebration. The beautiful mute girl from the forest was crowned queen.

The archbishop continued muttering evil things into the king's ear, but they could not reach his heart. The wedding took place,[32] and the archbishop himself had to place the crown on her head. Out of malice, he pressed the tight circlet so low down on her forehead that it began to hurt. But an even heavier band gripped her heart. The sorrow she felt for her brothers kept her from feeling any pain in her body. Her lips were sealed, for a single word would spell the death of her brothers. In her eyes shone a deep love for the kind, handsome king who was doing everything in his power to make her happy. Every day she grew fonder of him, with all her heart. Oh, if only she dared confide in him and tell him of her torment. But she had to remain mute and finish her task in silence. At night she would steal away from the king's side and retreat to her own little room, which was furnished like the cave. She finished knitting one shirt of mail after another, but just as she was about to begin the seventh shirt, she ran out of flax.

She knew that the nettles for the shirt were growing in the churchyard, and she had to pick them herself. How could she possibly get there?

"What is the pain in my fingers compared with the anguish I feel in my heart!" she thought. "I have to risk it, and I know God will not abandon me."

With fear in her heart, as if she were about to commit some kind of evil deed, she tiptoed out into the garden by the light

32. *The wedding took place.* This first wedding is a ceremony that may bring Elisa and the king together in official terms, but they remain divided because of Elisa's secret.

W. HEATH ROBINSON

Elisa steals out of the castle and makes her way to the churchyard in order to find the nettles she needs to finish the shirts.

33. *a group of hideous ghouls.* The flesh-eating witches in the churchyard are a reminder that, from the 1400s up until 1693, the Danes engaged in witch hunts (coinciding with those in Salem and elsewhere) that resulted in the deaths of hundreds of old women.

34. *the carved images of the saints shook their heads.* In "The Red Shoes," the paintings on the walls appear to fix their eyes on Karen's footwear. Certain sins are so

of the moon. She walked down avenues out into the deserted streets toward the churchyard. There she saw, seated in a circle on one of the largest tombstones, a group of hideous ghouls[33]—horrid witches. They were taking off their rags as if they were about to bathe, but then they buried their long, gaunt fingers in the new graves, snatched the bodies out of them, and began to eat their flesh. Elisa had to pass right by them, and they fixed their evil eyes on her, but she recited a prayer while she was picking the nettles that were stinging her and carried them back home to the palace.

One person had seen her—the archbishop, who had remained awake while everyone else was sleeping. He finally had proof for what he had long suspected. Something was not quite right about the queen. She must be a witch, and that was how she had managed to fool the king and all his subjects.

In the confessional, the archbishop told the king what he had seen and reported everything that he feared. As the harsh words escaped his lips, the carved images of the saints shook their heads[34] as if to say: "That's not true. Elisa is innocent!" The archbishop, however, had a different explanation. He claimed that they were bearing witness against her and that they were shaking their heads at her wickedness. Two big tears rolled down the king's cheeks. He returned home with doubt in his heart. That night he did not sleep at all, but he pretended to be asleep when Elisa got up. Night after night she arose, and each time he followed her without making any noise and saw her disappear into the little room.

Every day the king's countenance grew darker. Elisa noticed, but she had no idea what it meant. It made her worry and added to the pain she was already feeling about her brothers. Hot tears rolled down upon her royal robes of purple velvet. They glittered like diamonds, and everyone who saw this precious splendor wanted to be queen. Before long Elisa would be finished with her task. She had just one more shirt of mail to finish, but she ran out of flax again, and there was not a single nettle left. Once more, now for the last time, she would have to go to the churchyard and pick a few more handfuls. She was filled with dread at the thought of that lonely walk and of those ghastly witches, but her will was as firm as her faith in God.

Elisa went out, and both the king and archbishop followed her. They watched her disappear through the wrought-iron gates of the churchyard, and as soon as they entered, they saw the very same hideous demons sitting on a gravestone that Elisa had seen. The king turned away, for he imagined that Elisa—whose head had rested on his heart that very evening—was one of them.

"Let the people judge her," he said. And the people did judge her and condemned her to burn at the stake.

Elisa was taken from the splendid royal halls to a dark, dank dungeon, where the wind whistled through the bars of the window. Instead of silk and velvet, she was given the bundle of nettles she had gathered as a place to rest her head. The harsh, stinging shirts of mail she had woven were her comforter and coverlet. Nothing they could have given her would have been more precious. She started her work again and prayed to God. Outdoors she could hear boys in the street mocking her with their songs. Not a soul came to comfort her with a kind word.

Toward evening a swan's wing whooshed past the grating on Elisa's window. It was the youngest of the brothers. He had found his sister, who sobbed aloud with joy, even though she

brazen that even images of the dead are stirred back to life in protest. But Elisa herself, a miracle of beauty and piety, can also work wonders.

35. *Tiny mice ran across the floor.* Elisa, like many orphaned children in fairy tales, finds in nature a source of aid and support. The mice and the birds, like the birds in "Cinderella," make sure that she can complete the tasks assigned to her. Protagonists of fairy tales often become children of nature. Cut off from human help, they find in animals the help they need.

W. HEATH ROBINSON

knew that the coming night might be her last. Now her work was almost finished, and the brothers were there.

The archbishop arrived to pass the final hour with her, as he had promised the king. But Elisa shook her head, begging him with her eyes and with gestures to leave. Tonight she must finish her task or it would all be in vain—the pain, the tears, and the sleepless nights. The archbishop left, uttering cruel words about her, but poor Elisa knew that she was innocent and continued with her work.

Tiny mice ran across the floor,[35] bringing nettles right to her feet and doing everything they could to help. A thrush perched near the bars of her window and sang all night long, as cheerfully as possible, so that she would not lose her courage.

In the early hours of the dawn, an hour before sunrise, the eleven brothers arrived at the palace gate, demanding an audience with the king. That was impossible, they were told. After all, it was still nighttime. The king was fast asleep, and no one dared wake him up. They pleaded and made threats until the guards turned out and even the king came out to find out what was wrong. Then suddenly the sun rose, and the eleven brothers vanished, but eleven swans could be seen flying over the palace.

Everyone in town was streaming through the gates, for they were all eager to watch the witch burn. A decrepit old horse was pulling the cart in which Elisa was seated. She was dressed in a smock made of coarse sackcloth. Her lovely, long hair was hanging loosely around her beautiful face. Her cheeks were deathly pale, and her lips were moving while her fingers were twisting the green flax. Even on the way to her death she would not stop the work she had begun. Ten shirts of mail lay at her feet, and she was working hard on the eleventh. The mob jeered at her.

"Look at the witch! See how she's muttering under her breath. She doesn't even have a prayer book in her hands.

There she sits, with her revolting handiwork. Let's take it away from her and tear it into a thousand pieces!"

The crowds surged toward her, trying to tear her work to bits. Suddenly eleven swans appeared, flapping their wings and making a circle around her. The mob drew back in terror.

"It's a sign from heaven. She must be innocent," many whispered, but no one dared to say it out loud.

The executioner grabbed her by the arm. In haste, she threw the eleven shirts over the swans, and instantly they turned into eleven handsome princes. The youngest had a swan's wing in place of an arm, because his shirt of mail was missing a sleeve.[36] Elisa had not quite managed to finish it.

"Now I can speak," she declared. "I am innocent."

Everyone who had witnessed what had happened bowed down before her as if she were a saint. The strain, the anguish, and the pain were too much for her, and she sank lifeless into her brothers' arms.

"She is indeed innocent," the eldest brother proclaimed, and he told them everything that had happened. While he was speaking, the aroma of millions of roses began to spread,[37] for every piece of wood piled on the fire had taken root and grown branches. An enormous hedge had spread out,[38] dense with fragrant red roses. At the very top was a single blossom, gleaming white and shining like a star. The king broke it off and placed it on Elisa's chest. She woke up, feeling peace and happiness in her heart.

All the church bells began to ring of their own accord, and birds appeared in great flocks.[39] A wedding procession headed back toward the palace[40]—one grander than any king had ever seen.

36. *because his shirt of mail was missing a sleeve.* The tiny flaw that accompanies the great accomplishment provides a moment of imperfection in a genre that famously prefers perfection and utopian closure to compromise and negotiation. Falling just short of a deadline can lead to resolution, as in this tale, but more frequently it ushers in a second catastrophe.

37. *the aroma of millions of roses began to spread.* Bengt Holbek points out how innocent goodness triumphs over evil in this story. He emphasizes the difference between the virtues set forth in folktales and those celebrated in Andersen's work: "In Andersen's universe, the qualities of good and evil have become absolute. . . . We observe a number of what may be called *social* virtues like helpfulness, generosity, steadfastness in danger, faithfulness, honesty and so on" (Holbek, 157).

38. *An enormous hedge had spread out.* The dense hedge of roses is, of course, well known from "Sleeping Beauty." For Andersen, the rose bears an added redemptive layer. The white blossom signals innocence and salvation, and the red, passion and love.

39. *birds appeared in great flocks.* Birds, which can soar high into the heavens while roses remain rooted on earth, add a further dimension of spirituality to the tale. And these creatures are, of course, kindred to the boys in their avian form.

40. *A wedding procession headed back toward the palace.* This second wedding will presumably be marked by more trust than the first, for the king's willingness to listen to the archbishop and to let his wife perish by fire did not signal great confidence in Elisa.

The Eleven Swans
by Matthias Winther

Once there lived a king with eleven sons and one daughter. When they were growing up, the queen died. The king spent so much time grieving over her that he believed he would never recover. But when the twelve children were grown up, he married again, but this wife was an evil witch. She could not stand the twelve children, and she sent the daughter out to work as a servant and transformed the eleven sons so that they were swans in the daytime and humans at night. They would fly far away, and the father was left all alone with the evil woman, sighing, and thinking often of the good wife who had died. When a year had passed, the sister returned home and asked about her eleven brothers, but she was not given an answer. She wondered where they could be, and she wept all the time, for she wanted to be with her brothers. She asked her father for money, took all her brothers' clothes as well as their eleven silver spoons and went out into the wide world to find them.

She had walked for many days when she reached a great, dark forest. She wandered around for a long time until she reached a hut where an old woman was sitting and spinning. She asked whether she had seen the eleven boys, one older than the next, but the witch replied that she had only seen eleven beautiful swans floating on the river. The sister went to the river with hope in her heart and found a little straw hut. In it were eleven beds and eleven pots, with eleven wooden spoons in them. She took the wooden spoons out of the pots and put the eleven silver spoons in their place. And then she left. Towards evening, eleven snow-white swans came swimming up the river, and when they came to the hut, they turned into human beings. They were her brothers. When they went inside, they recognized their spoons, thought of their sister, and looked for her. The next day they turned again into beautiful swans and flew away over the tree-tops. But the sister had, in the meantime, made three nets, and when she finally found the eleven swans lying among the reeds, she threw nets over them and caught every single one of them. She asked how she could save them, but they could not tell her. She wept bitter tears and went with them through the woods to their hut. When thorns and bushes were in their way, she lifted the swans with care to prevent injury. She stayed with them at night, and the eleven swans put their heads on her lap and fell asleep. They turned human only in the middle of the night. During the day, the oldest brother dreamed that there was a way to save them. While remaining silent, their sister would have to go out in the morning and gather thistles in the field, then turn them into flax, spin and weave it, and sew eleven shirts from the cloth.

She went into the field to gather with her soft hands the thistles growing there. Then she turned them into flax and spun busily so that her brothers could return to their human form. One day the weather was so beautiful that she picked up the spinning wheel and took it outside into the woods. She was sitting under a tree and spinning, while the birds all around were singing to her. Her brothers were swans again and were floating far away on the river. As she sat there spinning, a king came riding past, and when he saw her, he thought that he had never seen a more beautiful woman. He took her home and married her. The old king had died just recently.

One day a message arrived for the king. He had to go to war. While he was away, the queen gave birth to two lovely children. The old queen took them away and ordered a servant to kill them. She put two motley pups in their place. Meanwhile the young queen continued spinning and weaving, thinking about her brothers and worrying about where they might be. When the king returned and heard that his wife had given birth to two pups, he became so angry that he ordered her to be murdered. By then she had finished all the shirts, except for one sleeve in the eleventh. She wept bitter tears once again, wishing that she had been able to finish her work. When the coach took her to the place of execution, eleven snow-white swans followed. They flew in circles around the queen and finally settled on the coach, fluttering their white wings. The queen threw one shirt after another on them, and, when the shirts landed on them, they turned into human beings. But the eleventh, who had the shirt with only one sleeve, kept one swan wing. The queen told the king everything that had happened. One of the servants was summoned. Out of pity, he had hidden the two princes instead of killing them. The second stepmother was put into a barrel with spikes and rolled down a hill to her death.

Thumbelina

Tommelise

Eventyr, fortalte for Børn. Første Samling, 1835

humbelina" was the first story in the second installment of Andersen's Eventyr, *published in December 1835, just in time for Christmas. Its date coincided with his first real triumph as a writer: publication of the novel* The Improvisatore, *soon reprinted and translated into German. The first volume of fairy tales had met with mixed reviews; at least one reviewer advised Andersen to stop writing them altogether. In his introduction to the third volume, Andersen conceded that such reviews "weakened the desire" to write but that he had persevered. Reviving his memory of tales heard in spinning rooms and at harvest time, he brightened up "the faded colors of the images" and used them as the point of departure for imaginative creations of his own.*

"Thumbelina," Andersen's tale of a runaway bride, has been variously interpreted as a tale teaching that "people are happy when with their own kind" (Opie, 288), as an allegory about "arranged marriages that were not uncommon in the bourgeoisie of that time" (Ingwersen 1993, 168), and as a "straightforward fable about being true to your heart" that also upholds "the traditional notion that fame and fortune aren't worth a hill of beans compared to the love of a good old-fashioned prince" (Holden, C19). Thumbelina can also

1. *an old witch.* The designation "witch" does not always signify evil in Andersen's works: The witches in "The Snow Queen" and "The Tinderbox," for example, are not particularly wicked or nasty. In "The Wild Swans" and "The Little Mermaid," however, witches have malevolent designs on the heroine. This particular witch seems to function as a midwife with magical means at her disposal to help the childless woman. In some English translations, the childless woman at the beginning of the tale is turned into a couple without children. The woman and witch both disappear quickly, but one illustrator has depicted the woman and witch as doubles, thereby suggesting that "Thumbelina's story is the imaginary projection of a childless woman longing for a child" (Nikolajeva and Scott, 48).

2. *"grain of barley."* With its countless references to a world divided between an underground realm and a domain of bright sunshine, "Thumbelina" contains a number of allusions to the myth of Demeter and her daughter Persephone. Persephone is abducted by Hades to become goddess of the underworld, and her distraught mother, goddess of agriculture, goes into deep mourning, turning the earth into a site of barren misery. Persephone is returned to her mother, but, each year, she must return to Hades for a period of several months, during which the earth yields no harvest. In this context, it is worth noting that barley seeds planted in the ground during Persephone's absence come to naught because of the goddess's anger. In Greek mythology, children of the soil (Cecrops and Erichthonius, for example), or Autochthons, were creatures born of the earth, without mother or father. Folklore contains many examples of children born in nutshells, peppercorns, hazelnuts, and groves of bamboo.

be seen as a female counterpart to the heroic Tom Thumb. Both are diminutive creatures who suffer through all manner of ordeals and survive against all odds. Thumbelina earns her good fortune and becomes a queen after an act of compassion (reviving the swallow), and Tom Thumb uses his cunning to defeat the ogre and return home to live like a king with his parents and siblings. According to Hindu belief, a thumb-sized being known as the innermost self or soul dwells in the heart of all humans and animals. Most likely the concept migrated into European folklore, surfacing in the form of Tom Thumb and Thumbelina, both of whom can be seen as figures seeking transfiguration and redemption. Note that Thumbelina is renamed Maya.

"Tommelise" is the Danish title of the tale. The first English translations of the story used the names "Little Ellie," "Little Totty," and "Little Maja." The name Thumbelina was first used by H. W. Dulcken, whose translations of Andersen's tales appeared in England in 1864 and 1866, and it is now the name used in most translations and in all films based on the tale. There have been at least five cinematic adaptations, beginning with Lotte Reiniger's in 1954 and including Barry Mahon's (1970), Shelley Duvall's (1984), Don Bluth and Gary Goldman's (1994), and Glenn Chaika's (2002). Frank Loesser's lyrics for the 1952 film Hans Christian Andersen *contain the song about Thumbelina that is still well known today: "Though you're no bigger than my thumb . . ."*

Once upon a time there lived a woman who was longing for a tiny little child, but she had no idea where to find one. Finally she decided to call on an old witch,[1] and she said her: "My heart is set on having a little child. Can't you tell me how I can get one?"

"That's easily done," the witch said. "Here's a grain of barley,[2] but it isn't the kind grown by farmers in their fields or the sort used to feed chickens. Put it in a flower pot, and you shall see what you shall see."

"Thank you so very much," the woman said, and she gave the witch twelve pennies and planted the seed as soon as she arrived back home. The seed quickly grew into a big, beautiful flower that looked just like a tulip, but its petals were folded tightly, as though it were still a bud.

"What a lovely flower!" the woman declared, and she planted a kiss on its beautiful red and yellow petals. With the kiss, the flower went pop! and opened up. It was a tulip, sure enough, but in the middle of it, on a little green cushion, sat a tiny girl. She was delicate and fair, but she was no taller than a thumb,[3] and for that reason she came to be known by the name of Thumbelina.

A brightly polished walnut shell served as Thumbelina's cradle. Her mattress was made from the blue petals of violets, and a rose petal became her coverlet. That was how she slept at night. In the daytime she spent her time playing on a table where the woman had placed a dish, filled with a wreath of flowers. The stems of the flowers reached into the water, and a big tulip petal floated on the surface. Thumbelina sat in it and sailed clear across the dish, using a pair of white horsehairs for oars. It was a charming sight! She could sing too, and no one had ever heard a voice as soft and sweet as hers.[4]

One night as she lay in her pretty bed, a hideous toad hopped in through the window[5]—one of the panes was broken. The repulsive toad, big and slimy, jumped right onto the table where Thumbelina was lying fast asleep under the red rose petal.

"She'll make a perfect wife for my son!" the toad exclaimed, and she grabbed the walnut shell in which Thumbelina was sleeping and hopped off with it, out the window and into the garden.

A wide stream wound its way through the garden, and its

3. *she was no taller than a thumb.* Diminutive figures are common in folklore, and they are often described as being the size of a thumb, hence the terms Tom Thumb, Thumbkin, Thumbling, and Thumbelina. Many tales featuring boys repeat the terms of the David and Goliath story, but Thumbelina is characterized by beauty, fragility, and vulnerability (rather like the princess in "The Princess and the Pea") as well as by her small stature. Illustrators have depicted her in a variety of ways, occasionally as an infant, sometimes as a sylphlike child, and even as a miniature grown woman.

4. *a voice as soft and sweet as hers.* Thumbelina is not only visually attractive but also possesses an enchanting voice. The many references to the chirping of birds makes it clear that Thumbelina and the swallow she rescues are linked by song.

5. *a hideous toad hopped in through the window.* In fairy tales rooted in ancient cultures, toads and frogs often function as benefactors, for they were seen as symbols of fertility, regeneration, and rebirth. Ancient Egypt, for example, associated frogs with renewal, and the water goddess Heket was represented as a woman with the head of a frog. Egyptian women often wore amulets in the form of frogs to honor the midwife goddess Hegit. In European folklore, by contrast, toads and frogs are commonly presented as hideous creatures that arouse feelings of revulsion, as in "The Little Mermaid," which describes a toad feeding from the mouth of the Sea Witch. The Grimms' "Frog King" inaugurated a tradition of repulsive frog suitors by showing a princess pursued by an amorous amphibian, who demands to dine with her, sleep with her, and be her companion. There are many European and Slavic versions of tales about benevolent

frog princesses who assist humble young bumpkins in their pursuit of wealth and power. The animal bride in all variants of that tale type is a humble, charming, and generous creature who turns into a young woman of radiant beauty once the spell is broken.

6. *"Ko-ax, ko-ax, brekke-ke-kex!" was all he could say.* The toad, unlike his mother, who has the power of human language, can utter only cacophonous noises that make him all the more frightening. Thumbelina's sweet voice and her ability to sing lullabies form a powerful contrast to the disruptive, unattractive sounds that issue from the toad's throat. The associations with mud and dirt of the earthbound and waterbound toad position him as a creature standing in opposition to the melodious birds encountered by Thumbelina during her journey.

banks were muddy and swamplike. That's where the toad lived with her son. Ugh! He was just like his mother, ugly and horrid. "Ko-ax, ko-ax, brekke-ke-kex!" was all he could say[6] when he saw the lovely little girl in the walnut shell.

"Don't raise your voice or you will wake her up," the old toad said. "She might get away from us yet, because she's as light as swan's down. We had better put her on one of those big water-lily pads out in the stream. She's so tiny and dainty that it will seem just like an island to her. That way she can't escape, and we'll have a chance to fix up the parlor down in the mud for the two of you."

There were many water lilies growing in the stream, and their big green pads looked just as if they were floating on the surface. The pad farthest away was also the largest, and the old toad swam out to it and there she left the walnut shell, with Thumbelina fast asleep in it.

The poor little thing woke up early the next morning, and when she saw where she was she began to weep bitter tears,

W. HEATH ROBINSON

Thumbelina sleeps peacefully in her walnut-shell cradle, while a toad hops off with her, hoping that she can turn the girl into her daughter-in-law.

for there was nothing but water on all sides of the big green lily pad, and she had no way to reach the shore.

The old toad was sitting in the mud, decorating the parlor with reeds and yellow water lilies, for she wanted it to look elegant for her new daughter-in-law. She and her ugly son swam out to Thumbelina's lily pad to fetch her pretty little bed, which they were hoping to set up in the bridal chamber before she arrived there herself. The old toad made a deep curtsy in the water before Thumbelina and said: "Meet my son. He is going to be your husband, and the two of you will have a delightful home down in the mud."

"Ko-ax, ko-ax, brekke-ke-kex!" was all her son could say.

Mother and son took the comfortable little bed and swam away with it. Thumbelina was left all alone on the green lily pad, weeping, for she did not want to live with the horrid toad or marry her revolting son. The little fish swimming in the water beneath her must have seen the toad and heard her words. That's why they poked their heads out of the water to take a look at the little girl. As soon as they set eyes on her, they felt very upset that anyone so lovely would have to go live with that vile toad. No! That was never going to happen! The fish gathered down below around the green stem holding up the lily pad. They gnawed the stalk in half with their teeth, and the lily pad began to float downstream,[7] taking Thumbelina far away, to a place where the toad could never reach her.

Thumbelina sailed past so many places, and little birds perched in the bushes watched her and chanted, "What a pretty little girl!" The lily pad carrying her drifted farther and farther away, and soon Thumbelina was traveling abroad.[8]

A lovely little white butterfly[9] kept circling around her and finally landed on the lily pad because he had grown fond of Thumbelina. She was so happy that the toad would not be able to find her. Everywhere she sailed it was beautiful: the

7. *the lily pad began to float downstream.* As Clarissa Pinkola Estés points out in *Women Who Run with the Wolves,* fairy-tale figures frequently encounter magic objects with "transportive and sensory abilities that are apt metaphors for the body, such as magic leaf, carpet, cloud." Cloaks, helmets, boots, and hats also often provide mobility and magical powers: "Each enables the physical body to enjoy deepened insight, hearing, flight, or protection of some sort for both psyche and soul" (Estés, 205). The ordinary comes to be invested with the extraordinary, and the magic object has the power to transport not only the body but also the senses.

In 1874, many years after writing "Thumbelina" and just a year before his death, Andersen complained about a sense of depletion and loss of motivation by referring to how the sight of a lily pad reminded him that he had already exhausted its power to inspire him: "If I see the broad leaf of a water lily, then Thumbelina has already ended her journey on it" (Rossel 1986, 119).

8. *soon Thumbelina was traveling abroad.* Thumbelina escapes her domestic prison and makes her way out into the same "wide world" that Gerda entered in "The Snow Queen." Open to adventure and eager to explore, Thumbelina has traded a sheltered existence that will drag her down into muddy foulness for an audacious journey that will expose her to risk but will also let her see the beauty of the world.

9. *A lovely little white butterfly.* As a symbol of transformation and renewal as well as of death and rebirth, the butterfly helps Thumbelina flee her muddy prison and begin a new life, one marked by a turn in her fortunes. Liberated from an earthbound existence, Thumbelina joins with the butterfly to enter airy, spiritual

domains. The butterfly, long associated with the human soul, also symbolizes the magnificence of an unworldly life. Characterized by beauty ("lovely"), daintiness ("little"), and innocence ("white"), the butterfly is almost like a double of the heroine and anticipates her elevation from an earthbound life to one characterized by regal splendor and the ability to fly.

10. *even if she didn't look at all like a beetle.* Social acceptance is always based on con-

HARRY CLARKE

The butterfly pulls Thumbelina along the water in her lily-pad boat.

sun was shining on the water and turning it into the loveliest golden color. Thumbelina undid her sash, tied one end of it to the butterfly, and fastened the other to the lily pad. The lily pad began to move much faster, and so did Thumbelina, for she was, of course, standing on it.

Just then a big beetle flew by and caught sight of Thumbelina. He grabbed her slender waist with his claws and flew up into a tree with her. The lily pad kept floating downstream, and the butterfly went with it, for he was still tied to the lily pad and could not get loose.

Goodness! How frightened little Thumbelina was when the beetle flew up into the tree with her. But she was much sadder when she thought about the beautiful white butterfly that she had tied to the lily pad. If he couldn't free himself, he would end up starving to death. But the beetle wasn't one to worry about that. He set Thumbelina down on the largest green leaf of the tree, fed her honey from the flowers, and told her how pretty she was, even if she didn't look at all like a beetle.[10] After a while, all the other beetles living in the tree came to pay a visit. They stared at Thumbelina, and all the lady-beetles shrugged their feelers and said: "Why she has only two legs—how pitiful!"

"She has no antennae!" another one shrieked. "She's pinched in at the waist—ugh!" the lady-beetles said. "Why, she looks just like a human being. How revolting!"

Yet Thumbelina was as pretty as ever. The beetle who had kidnapped her would have agreed, but all the others kept describing her as hideous. In the end the beetle went along with them and would have nothing to do with her any longer. She could now go where she pleased. The beetles brought her down from the tree and left her on a

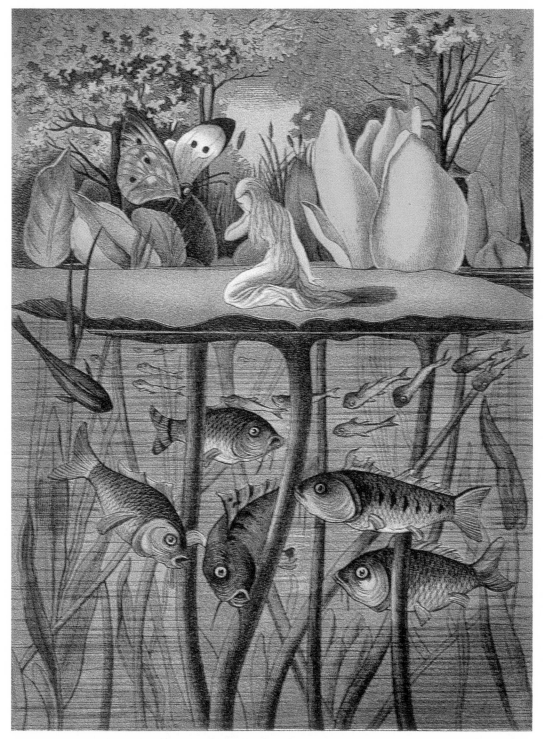

ELEANOR VERE BOYLE

Thumbelina floats on top of the water on her lily pad, which is pulled by the butterfly. The fish below seem unaware of her presence.

W. HEATH ROBINSON

Thumbelina is terrified as she flies through the air, carried by a beetle. This flight contrasts strikingly with her magically absorbing journey on the swallow's back.

formity in the worlds constructed by Andersen, and Thumbelina—for all her charm and beauty—cannot overcome differences in appearance. Andersen provides a critique of conformity in the encounter between girl and beetles by reversing and defamiliarizing the commonplace revulsion of humans for insects with a chorus of complaints from beetles about the revolting features of humans.

11. *She was terribly cold.* Like the ugly duckling and the little match girl, Thumbelina experiences not only the cruel ordeal of exile and abandonment but also the harshness of the climate. This double exposure to emotional degradation and bodily mortification is Andersen's trademark, and only the intensification of the condition leads to its reversal.

daisy, where she sat and wept because the beetles found her so ugly and would have nothing to do with her. In truth, she was the loveliest little creature you could imagine, as delicate and radiant as the most beautiful rose petal.

All summer long poor Thumbelina lived alone in the deep woods. She wove a bed for herself from blades of grass and hung it under a large burdock leaf to keep the rain away. She lived on honey from the flowers, and, every morning, she drank the dew found on the leaves. Summer and fall passed in that way, but then winter arrived, the long, cold winter. All the birds that had been singing so sweetly for her flew away, and the trees and flowers began to wither. The big burdock leaf under which she had been living curled up and soon there was nothing left of it but a dead yellow stalk. She was terribly cold,[11] for she was slender and frail, and the clothes she had were threadbare. Poor Thumbelina, she was sure to freeze to death! Snow began falling, and whenever a snowflake fell on her, it felt just the way that an entire shovel load would feel to us. We are, after all, quite tall, and she was only as high as a thumb. Thumbelina wrapped herself in a withered leaf, but it didn't keep her warm at all, and she began to shiver with cold.

At the edge of the woods was a vast field of grain, but the grain had long since been harvested, and there was nothing on the frozen ground but dry, bare stubble. For Thumbelina, it was like being lost in an immense forest, and, oh, how she was shivering with cold! She reached the door of a field mouse, right where there was a little hole amid the stubble. That's where the mouse lived, snug and cozy, with a whole storeroom of grain and a lovely kitchen and pantry. Poor Thumbelina stood at the door, just like any other beggar child, and asked for a little bit of barley corn, because she had eaten nothing for the past two days.

"You poor little thing!" the field mouse said, for she was at heart a kind old field mouse. "Come into my warm parlor and join me for dinner."

MABEL LUCIE ATTWELL

Thumbelina, shivering with cold, emerges from a vast forest to discover the home of the field mouse, who invites her to stay in her cozy abode.

W. HEATH ROBINSON

Thumbelina is seated on a dry leaf, shivering from the cold, when she is greeted by the field mouse.

The field mouse took a fancy to Thumbelina and said to her: "You are welcome to stay here with me for the winter, but you must keep my house nice and clean[12] and tell me stories, because I'm quite fond of them." Thumbelina did exactly what the old field mouse asked and settled in comfortably.

"We'll be having a visitor before long," the field mouse said. "My neighbor usually comes to see me once a week. He is even better off than I am, and his rooms are much larger. He has such a lovely black velvet fur coat.[13] If you could win him as a husband, you would be set for life. But he can't see. You'll have to tell him the most enchanting stories you know."[14]

Thumbelina was not thrilled by that idea. She did not even consider the suggestion of marrying the neighbor, for he was a mole.[15] The mole came to call, wearing his black velvet coat. All the field mouse could talk about was how wealthy and learned he was and how his lodgings were twenty times the size of hers. He had erudition as well, but he did not care at all for the sun and for flowers. He had nothing good to say about them because he had never set eyes on them. Thumbelina had to sing to him, and she sang both: "Fly, Beetle, Fly, Fly Away Home" and "The Monk Walks through the Meadows." The mole fell in love with Thumbelina when he heard her beautiful voice, but he said nothing, for he was a most discreet fellow.

The mole had just finished digging a long underground passageway from his house to theirs, and the field mouse and Thumbelina were invited to use it whenever they wanted. He told them not to be alarmed by the dead bird lying on the path. The bird still had its feathers and beak, and it must have died not long ago, just about the time when winter was settling in. Now it was buried in the very place where the mole had dug out the tunnel.

The mole picked up a piece of decaying wood, which, in the darkness, glowed like fire and worked as a torch. He

12. *"you must keep my house nice and clean."* Thumbelina's travels are followed by a period of domestic hibernation in the stillness of an underground world. Like many of her female folkloric cousins, most notably Vasilisa (the Snow White and Cinderella of Russian folklore) and the heroine of the German "Mother Holle" (a Cinderella who proves her worth by carrying out domestic chores under the tutelage of the title figure), Thumbelina finds shelter in a sphere associated with both domesticity and death. She undergoes an apprenticeship, in which she puts on display her ability to *care* for things. It is no accident that Thumbelina first makes a pact that requires her to care for things, then discovers her power to care for living beings and to heal them. The move from the domestic to the restorative is seamlessly woven into Thumbelina's underground experiences.

13. *"He has such a lovely black velvet fur coat."* Like Hades, the mole is cloaked in black and lives underground, preferring darkness and gloom to sunshine and light. The division of the earth into three regions ruled by three deities (Zeus, Poseidon, and Hades) is taken up and mapped anew in zoological terms. Moles and mice inhabit the nether world; toads and fish dominate the land and the seas; birds and butterflies soar into higher regions. Just as Hades was referred to as "the Rich One" because he possesses the treasures of the earth, so too the mole is described as a creature of great wealth (and great learning as well). Although Thumbelina finds shelter and safety with the mouse, she encounters underground a second suitor who is charged with qualities more lethal than those of the toad. Women writers from Mary Shelley to Muriel Rukeyser have used the myth of Persephone to describe the dark side of female sexual initiation, mapping the consequences of "abduction, rape, the death of the physical world, and sorrowful separation from female companions" (Gilbert and Gubar, 504).

14. *"You'll have to tell him the most enchanting stories you know."* The mole's blindness to visual beauty draws attention to his dark side and his inability to appreciate higher values—he does not care for the sun or for flowers. Still, he is enchanted by Thumbelina's voice when she sings songs to him. Although Thumbelina withholds stories from the mole, she agrees to use her voice, singing children's songs that were popular in Andersen's day.

15. *he was a mole.* Simon Meisling, the headmaster at the school Andersen attended in Slagelse, has been seen as the model for the mole. A classical scholar, Meisling treated others miserably and told Andersen he was a "stupid boy" who would never succeed in life. Cai M. Woel, in his biography of Andersen, provides the following description that hints at an identification between the mole and Meisling: "below average height with a very round head . . . his mouth thin, his nose bulbous. . . . His body was plump with a protruding stomach, big flat feet and short arms. . . . Something about the man's appearance made you think about the underworld. His hands hardly ever touched water; they were so black that a quick glance would make you think he was wearing gloves" (Frank and Frank, 76–77).

16. *you could see the dead swallow.* On a trip to Greece in 1841, Andersen's attention was drawn by a shipmate to "a little bird, who lay among the coiled ropes on the deck, so exhausted it couldn't even lift its wings. . . . I became quite irritated with the Roman cleric, because he wanted to cook it straightaway. . . . One of the Lieutenants took care of the bird, gave it

walked ahead of them, lighting the way through the long dark tunnel. When they came to where the dead bird was lying, the mole shoved his broad nose against the ceiling and made a large hole through which daylight streamed. In the middle of the floor you could see the dead swallow,[16] his beautiful wings pressed to his sides and his head and legs tucked under his feathers. The poor bird must have died from the cold. Thumbelina felt so very sorry for him. She loved all of the small birds because they had sung and chirped so beautifully for her all summer long. The mole gave the bird a kick with his stubby legs and declared: "That's the end of his chirping. Nothing could be worse than coming into the world as a little bird! Thank goodness none of my children will be birds. All they do is chirp, and then, when winter comes along, they end up starving to death."

"Yes, you're so right, sensible man that you are," the field mouse agreed. "What good does all that chirping do for birds in the wintertime? They just end up starving and freezing to death. But I suppose people imagine that to be very noble."

Thumbelina did not say a word, but when the others had turned their backs on the bird, she kneeled down, smoothed the feathers that were covering the bird's head, and kissed his closed eyes. "Maybe it was he who sang so sweetly to me in the summertime," she thought to herself. "What great pleasure you brought me, you dear, beautiful bird."

The mole closed up the hole that let in daylight and escorted the ladies back home. That night Thumbelina did not sleep a wink. She got up and wove a beautiful coverlet out of hay, took it over to the dead bird, and spread it over him, tucking him in. She placed some soft cotton she had found in the field mouse's parlor around the bird to keep him warm in the cold ground.

"Farewell, you beautiful little bird," she said. "Farewell and thank you for your lovely summer song, when the trees were still green and the sun shone so warmly on us all." Then she put her head on the bird's breast, but felt quite frightened because it seemed as if something was making a pounding noise. It turned out to be the bird's heart. He was not dead—he was only numb with cold, and now that he had been warmed up, he was returning to life.

In the autumn the swallows fly off to warmer climates, but if they linger, they can become so cold that they drop down as if dead. They end up lying wherever they happen to fall, and when the cold snow comes, it covers them up.

Thumbelina was so frightened that she began to tremble all over. The bird was so huge, just enormous compared to her own height of merely a thumb. But she gathered her courage, tucked the cotton closer around the poor bird, brought over the mint leaf that covered her own bed, and spread it over the bird's head.

The following night she tiptoed back to see the bird. He was alive now, but so weak that he could barely keep his eyes open to take a look at Thumbelina, who was standing by his side with a piece of glowing wood, all the light that she had.

"Thank you, my pretty little child," the ailing swallow said. "I feel so nice and warm again. Soon I'll be strong enough to fly back into the warm sunshine."

"Oh," she replied. "It's still cold outside—there's snow and ice on the ground. Just stay here in your nice warm bed, and I'll take good care of you."[17]

Thumbelina found a flower petal and brought the swallow some water. He drank it and told her how he had torn his wing on a thorn bush and couldn't keep up with the other swallows when they left to fly far away to the distant warm countries. He had finally landed on the ground. That was all he could remember, and he had no idea how he had ended up where he was.

The swallow stayed underground all winter long, and Thumbelina was kind to him and grew quite fond of him. She did not say a word to the mole or to the field mouse, for she knew that they would not care for the unfortunate swallow.

bread crumbs and water, and it was our guest for the whole day, indeed for the night too. It did not fly away until the next day, chirping as it went, as though in thanks for the kind reception" (*Travels*, 134).

In Danish folklore, the swallow is known as the *svale* and was said to have received its name from chirping "Svale, svale" (Cheer up, cheer up) when it flew around the suffering Christ on the cross. The swallow is part of many different folkloric traditions, but it is, above all, associated with springtime. The moribund bird can be seen, in this instance, as both a symbol of winter's petrifying and deadening effects and a reminder of Christ's entombment before his resurrection. Oscar Wilde revived the swallow as a symbol of freedom in his fairy tale "The Happy Prince," which contains multiple allusions to Andersen's tales.

17. *"I'll take good care of you."* Thumbelina cares for the swallow, bringing him back to life through her tender ministrations. When we learn that the swallow tore his wing on a thorn bush (a possible allusion to Christ's crown of thorns), it becomes evident that there are biblical undertones to Thumbelina's nurturing efforts. Notwithstanding a pagan emphasis on nature *qua* nature and allusions to mythical beings, Andersen's story also refers repeatedly to Christ's suffering and resurrection and to the Christian notion of salvation.

When spring arrived and the sun began to warm the earth, the swallow said farewell to Thumbelina, who opened up the hole that the mole had made overhead. The sunshine flooded in with splendor, and the swallow asked if Thumbelina wished to accompany him. She could climb on his back, and they would fly away into the green forest. But Thumbelina knew that the old field mouse would feel very sad if she left.

"No, I can't leave," Thumbelina said.

"Farewell, farewell, my pretty, kind child," the swallow said as he flew out into the sunlight. Thumbelina gazed at the swallow as he departed, and tears filled her eyes, because she was so fond of him.

"Tweet, tweet," the bird sang as he flew away into the green forest.

Thumbelina felt very sad. She wasn't allowed to go out into the warm sunshine. And the grain sown in the ground above the field mouse's house had grown so tall that, to a poor girl who was no bigger than a thumb, it was like a vast, dense forest.

"You must begin work this summer on your trousseau," the field mouse told Thumbelina, because her neighbor, the loathsome mole in the black velvet coat, had already proposed to her. "You'll need both woolens and linens. And you must have cushions and bedding once you become the mole's wife."

Thumbelina had to turn the spindle, and the field mouse hired four spiders to spin and weave, day and night. The mole came to call every evening, and he loved to talk about how summer would soon be over and the sun would no longer be so hot, scorching the earth and making it as hard as a rock. Yes, as soon as the summer was over, he would be marrying Thumbelina. But Thumbelina was not at all happy about it, because she did not like the dreary mole one little bit. Every morning at sunrise and every evening at sunset, she would steal out the door. When the breeze parted the ears of grain, she was able to catch glimpses of the blue sky. She would dream about how bright and beautiful it was outside, and more than anything else she wanted to see her dear swallow again. But he did not return, and he must have been flying far away into the beautiful green woods.

By the time autumn came, Thumbelina's entire trousseau was ready.

"Four weeks until the wedding!" the field mouse told her. Thumbelina began to weep and declared that she had no wish to marry the dreary mole.

"Fiddlesticks," said the field mouse. "Don't be stubborn, or I'll bite you with my white teeth. Why, you're getting a superb husband. Even the queen doesn't have a black velvet coat as fine as his. Both his kitchen and cellar are well stocked. You ought to be grateful for a fellow like that."

The wedding day arrived. The mole had already come and was planning to take Thumbelina home with him. She would have to live deep underground and would never go out into the warm sunshine again, because he disliked it so much. The poor child felt miserable, because she had to bid farewell to the sun. At the home of the field mouse, she had at least had the chance to see it through the doorway.

"Farewell, bright sun!" she said, stretching her arms toward it as she took a few steps out of the field mouse's house. By now, the grain had been harvested, and all that remained on the fields was dry stubble. "Farewell, farewell!" she said as she flung her tiny arms around a red flower that was still in bloom. "If you happen to see my dear swallow, please give him my love."

"Tweet, tweet! Tweet, tweet!" she suddenly heard overhead. She looked up and there was the little swallow, flying overhead. He was overjoyed to see Thumbelina, who told him how much she hated the idea of marrying the mole and living deep under the ground where the sun never shines. She had trouble holding back her tears.

"The cold winter is on its way," the swallow said to her.

18. *"Just tie your sash around me."* A second time Thumbelina is rescued by a winged creature, but on this occasion she is able to soar rather than skim the surface of the waters. The swallow is able to lift her into airy regions that put an end to the manifold risks on land and sea as well as underground.

19. *poked her little head out to gaze at all the wondrous sights below her.* In 1906, the Swedish author Selma Lagerlöf (the first woman to win the Nobel Prize in Literature) published part one of *The Wonderful Adventures of Nils*, a storybook commissioned by the National Teachers' Association to teach geography to schoolchildren. Lagerlöf's Nils Holgersson, alone at home and obliged by his parents to read the script of a church service he is missing, falls asleep and awakens to find that an elf is making mischief in the household. Outwitted by the creature, he is turned into an elf himself and finds that he has the ability to communicate with animals. Wild geese take him on a trip across Sweden, and, in the course of his "wonderful adventures," Nils (or Thumbietot) receives many lessons in the geography of his native land and also learns that humans do not have the world to themselves. Nils's adventures were no doubt inspired in part by Thumbelina's journeys.

20. *a dazzling white marble palace from ancient times.* Where has Thumbelina landed? Andersen was probably alluding to Italy, where he had traveled the year before. Since the swallow returns to Denmark, Thumbelina has clearly found a home in foreign regions, one that can also be seen as a kind of fairyland or even a realm of death, inhabited by angels.

"I'm going to fly far away to the warm countries. Why don't you come along? You can sit on my back. Just tie your sash around me,[18] and we'll fly far away from the hideous mole and his dark house—over the mountains to the warm countries where the sun shines so much more brightly than it does here and where it's always summer, with beautiful flowers. Fly away with me, dear little Thumbelina. You saved my life when I was frozen in that dark underground cellar."

"Why, yes, I'll come with you!" Thumbelina exclaimed, and she climbed onto the bird's back, put her feet on his outstretched wings, and tied her sash to one of the broader feathers. The swallow soared through the air, high up above forests and lakes over to the tall mountains that are always capped with snow. At first, Thumbelina shivered in the chill air, but then she crept under the bird's warm feathers and poked her little head out to gaze at all the wondrous sights below her.[19]

At last they reached the warm countries. The sun was shining more brightly there than it ever does here, and the sky seemed twice as high. Along the ditches and hedgerows grew marvelous green and blue grapes. Lemons and oranges were hanging from trees in the forest, and the air was fragrant with myrtle and mint. The most adorable children were running on the road here and there, chasing after brightly colored butterflies. The swallow flew even farther away, and everything became even more beautiful. Beneath magnificent green trees near a blue lake there stood a dazzling white marble palace from ancient times.[20] Its lofty pillars were wreathed with vines, and many swallows had made their nests on top of them. One of those nests belonged to the swallow that was carrying Thumbelina.

"Here is my home," the swallow said. "But if you want to pick out one of those magnificent flowers down below, I'll set you down on it, and you will have everything your heart desires."

W. Heath Robinson

Thumbelina sits on the swallow's back and soars through the air, gazing at the wonders below her.

ELEANOR VERE BOYLE

The swallow swoops down to deposit Thumbelina on one of the beautiful white flowers growing near his home.

"How lovely," Thumbelina cried, and she clapped her tiny hands.

One of the great white marble pillars had fallen to the ground and broken into three pieces. The most beautiful big white flowers were growing among them. The swallow flew down with Thumbelina and put her on one of the larger petals. How surprised Thumbelina was to find a tiny man sitting in the middle of the flower, as white and transparent as if he were made of glass. He was wearing the daintiest golden crown on his head, and on his shoulders were the loveliest bright wings. He was not a bit bigger than Thumbelina. He was the flower's angel. In every flower there lived a tiny man or woman just like him, but he was king of them all.

"My Lord, he's handsome," Thumbelina whispered to the swallow. The little prince was rather afraid of the swallow, for the bird was gigantic compared to him. He himself was so tiny and delicate. But he was elated when he saw Thumbelina, for she was the most beautiful girl he had ever seen. No one was surprised that he took off his golden crown and placed it on her head. He asked if he might know her name and wanted to know if she would be his wife. Then she could become queen of all the flowers. Yes, he would certainly make quite a husband—not at all like the toad's son or the mole with his black velvet coat. And so Thumbelina said yes to the handsome prince, and from every flower a tiny lady or a tiny gentleman appeared, each bearing a gift for Thumbelina. But the best gift of all was a pair of beautiful wings from a big white fly. They were fastened to Thumbelina's back so that she could also flutter from one flower to the next. Everyone rejoiced, and the little swallow sat in his nest and sang the nicest songs he could for them. But deep down in his heart he

W. HEATH ROBINSON

Thumbelina receives a pair of wings and is able to fly on her own.

HARRY CLARKE

The swallow bids farewell to Thumbelina, while she and the prince are surrounded by flowers
of dazzling beauty on a moonlit night.

was sad, for he was so fond of Thumbelina that he never wanted to be parted from her.

"Your name will no longer be Thumbelina," the flower's angel told her. "It's too ugly a name for someone as beautiful as you are. We shall call you Maya."[21]

"Farewell! Farewell!" said the little swallow as it flew away from the warm lands back to faraway Denmark, where he had a little nest above the window of the man who can tell you fairy tales.[22] To him the bird sang, "Tweet, tweet! Tweet, tweet!" and that's how we heard the whole story.

21. *"We shall call you Maya!"* The renaming signals that Thumbelina has developed a new identity, living in a world where she is no longer diminutive. The transformation takes her from adolescence to marriage and moves her from the condition of being a perpetual misfit to membership in a community of kindred spirits. In Hinduism, Maya represents the manifold appearance of the world of phenomena, a world of illusion that obscures the spiritual reality from which it emerged.

22. *the man who can tell you fairy tales.* The coda embodies the two narrators (the mellifluous bird and the Danish writer) and is reminiscent of the conventions of oral storytelling. At the end of the tale, tellers find a way of drawing attention back to themselves and to the origins or consequences of the stories they tell. The writer's association with the swallow suggests his existential kinship with Thumbelina, a creature who experiences hardship as a misfit.

W. HEATH ROBINSON

The Little Match Girl[1]

Den lille pige med svovlstikkerne

Dansk Folkekalender for 1846

1. *The Little Match Girl.* The attribute "little" before the name of a girl in a story for children often spells the character's doom. The little match girl, like Harriet Beecher Stowe's little Eva, Charles Dickens's little Nell, and Andersen's little mermaid, is destined never to become big. Children living in the streets in mid-nineteenth-century Europe and in the United States often sold matches or newspapers instead of begging outright, which was illegal. Child labor—and fourteen-hour days—were common in nineteenth-century Europe: a "multitude of children, some of them barely seven years of age, gaunt, emaciated, dressed in rags, going barefoot to the factory through rain and mud, pale, debilitated, and with misery, suffering and defeat etched on their faces" (Villermé, 46). Child labor was denounced by many novelists, among them Dickens, Hugo, and Zola. In the Communist Manifesto of 1848, Marx famously denounced modern industry's erosion of family ties and its transformation of children into "simple articles of commerce and instruments of labor."

he Little Match Girl" (written during a month-long stay with the Duke of Augustenborg) was inspired by illustrations Andersen received from the editor of an almanac, with the request that he write a story about one of them. One image, painted by the Danish artist Johan Thomas Lundbye, showed a girl selling matches. It had been popularized through its appearance in an 1843 calendar with the caption, "Do good when you give." "While I was at Glorup," Andersen later recalled in his travel diaries, "in this time of luxury and plenty, a publisher sent three woodcuts asking me to pick out one and write a little story around it. I chose a scene that depicted poverty and deprivation, a ragged little girl with a handful of matches—'The Little Match-girl'—the contrast between our life at Augustenborg and her world" (Travels, 242).

Few children's stories celebrate suffering with the kind of passion brought to the tale of the match-seller, and generations of children have admired her and wept over her death. The frail waif who freezes to death on New Year's Eve has become something of a cultural icon. She is the victim of a brutal father (far more cruel than the ogres of *fairy tales) and of a heartless social world; even nature turns its back on her, offering neither shelter nor sustenance. The fairy-tale magic is absent, and rescue comes only in the form of divine intervention.*

The narrator of the match girl's story takes us into the heroine's mental world, allowing us to feel her pain as the temperature drops and the wind howls. We also share her visions, first of warmth, then of nourishment, beauty, and finally human affection and compassion. If the final image of the story gives us a frozen corpse, the little match girl's death is still a "beautiful death," the site of radiant spirituality and transcendent meaning. Whether we read her sufferings as "tortures, disguised as pieties" (as did P. L. Travers) or consider her wretchedness as the precondition for translation into a higher sphere, the story remains one of the most memorable stories of childhood and haunts our cultural imagination.

Many will agree that the one requirement for a good children's book is the triumph of the protagonist. The death scene in "The Little Match Girl" has been adapted and rewritten many times over the last century, most notably in an American edition of 1944 that proclaimed on its dust jacket: "Children will read with delight this new version of the famous Hans Christian Andersen tale. For in it, the little match girl on that long ago Christmas Eve does not perish from the bitter cold, but finds warmth and cheer and a lovely home where she lives happily ever after." Andersen wrote this story during a decade of social unrest and political upheaval, and would no doubt have been distressed by the socially redemptive turn in a story that was intended as a powerful critique of economic inequities.

A recent self-help book reports the experience of a woman whose favorite childhood story was "The Little Match Girl": "When we asked her about it, she explained that, when the little match girl lit a match, the tiny flame became for her a roaring Christmas fire with gifts, friends and food around. This was also {her} deepest desire" (Breslin, 32).

2. *It was bitterly cold.* The story opens on a bleak note, with elaborate descriptions of intemperate weather and growing darkness, culminating in the empathetic exclamation "poor mite!" In his autobiography, Andersen described reading out loud to a clergyman's widow from a work that began with the words "It was a tempestuous night; the rain beat against the window-panes." When the woman declared her confidence that the work would turn out to be "extraordinary," the young Andersen reports, without irony, that he "regarded her insight with a kind of reverence" (*The Fairy Tale of My Life*, 17).

3. *a boy had run off with the other.* Andersen alludes often to the cruelty of children and how he himself was taunted and teased by schoolmates.

4. *bare feet.* As the son of a shoemaker, Andersen was inclined to pay special attention to what characters wear on their feet. The bare feet of the little match girl make her a particularly abject figure. But those who place a premium on their shoes run into serious moral trouble (see Andersen's "Girl Who Trod on the Loaf," with a protagonist who refuses to dirty her shoes,

It was bitterly cold.[2] Snow was falling, and before long it would be dark. It was the last day of the year: New Year's Eve. In the cold darkness, a poor little girl, with nothing on her head and with bare feet, was walking down the street. Yes, it's true, she had been wearing slippers when she left home. But what good could they do? They were great big slippers that had belonged to her mother—that's how big they were! The little girl had lost them while scurrying across the road to avoid two carriages rushing by at a terrifying speed. One slipper was nowhere to be found, and a boy had run off with the other,[3] declaring that he would use it as a cradle when he had children of his own someday.

The little girl walked along on her tiny, bare feet,[4] which were red and blue from the cold. She was carrying matches in an old apron, and she had a bundle in her hand as well. No one had bought anything from her all day long, and she had not received so much as a penny. Poor mite,[5] she was the picture of misery as she trudged along, hungry and shivering with cold. Snowflakes fell on her long, fair hair, which settled into beautiful curls at the nape of her neck. But you can be sure that she wasn't worrying about how she looked. Lights were shining in every window,[6] and the tempting aroma of roast goose drifted out into the streets. You see, it was New Year's Eve, and the little girl was thinking about that.

Over in a little nook between two houses, one of which jutted out into the street more than the other, she sat down and curled up, with her legs tucked beneath her. But even there she just grew colder and colder. She didn't dare return home,[7] for she had not sold any of her matches and had not earned a single penny. She knew that her father would beat her, and besides, it was almost as cold at home as it was here. They had only the roof to protect them, and the wind howled right through it, even though the worst cracks had been stopped up with straw and rags.

The girl's little hands were almost numb from the cold. Ah! Maybe a lighted match would do some good. If only she dared pull one from the bunch and strike it against the wall, just to warm her fingers. She pulled one out—scratch!—how it sputtered, how it flamed! Such a bright warm light—it felt just like a little lamp[8] when she cupped her hand around. Yes, what a strange light it was! The little girl imagined that she was sitting in front of a big iron stove, with shiny brass knobs and brass feet. The fire was burning so cheerfully, and it warmed her up! But—oh no! The little girl was just stretching out her toes to warm them up too, when—out went the flame. The stove vanished, and there she sat with the end of a burned match in her hand.

HONOR APPLETON

Barefoot, the little match girl sits on a snow-covered step, welcomed into the arms of her loving grandmother after lighting a match for warmth.

and "The Red Shoes," with a girl who takes pride in wearing flashy footwear unsuited for a church service).

5. *Poor mite.* Andersen often presents tableaus of suffering. The loving embellishment of the girl's wretched condition suggests a tendency to aestheticize scenes of pain, to create a verbally baroque effect while describing misery and distress.

6. *Lights were shining in every window.* The contrast between the cold and dark outdoors and the warmth and light indoors is made even more powerful by the aroma of roast goose, the traditional Scandinavian Christmas bird, drifting from the cheerful domestic interior to the cold and desolate outside.

7. *She didn't dare return home.* Andersen reported that the story was inspired in part by his own mother's experience of being sent out to beg and being told not to return until she had received some money. In his autobiography, he writes: "As a young girl, her parents chased her out to beg, and when she had no luck, she spent a whole day crying under a bridge by the river in Odense. As a child, I could imagine all of this so clearly and I wept about it" (*Fairy Tale of My Life*, 2). Later in

ARTHUR RACKHAM

The match girl lights a second flame that brings the vision of a grand tree, lit up with candles,
providing the pleasures of a feast that the girl could enjoy only as distant witness.

She struck another match. It flared up, and when the light shone on the wall,[9] it began to turn transparent, like a piece of gauze. She could see right into a dining room, where a table was covered with a snowy white cloth and fine china. The air was filled with the delicious scent of roast goose stuffed with apples and prunes. And what was even more amazing, the goose jumped right off the dish and waddled across the floor, with a carving knife and a fork still in its back. It marched right up to the poor little girl. But then the match went out, and there was nothing left to see but the cold, solid wall.

She lit another match. Now she was sitting beneath the most beautiful Christmas tree.[10] It was even taller and more splendidly decorated than the one she had seen last Christmas through the glass doors of a house belonging to a wealthy merchant. Thousands of candles were burning on the green branches, and colorful pictures, just like the ones she had seen in shop windows, looked down at her. The little girl stretched both hands up in the air—and the match went out. The Christmas candles all rose higher and higher into the air, and she saw them turn into bright stars. One of them turned into a shooting star,[11] leaving behind it a streak of sparkling fire.

"Someone is dying," the little girl thought, for her grandmother, the only person who had ever been kind to her[12] and who was no longer alive, had once said that a falling star means that a soul is rising up to God.

She struck another match against the wall. Light shone all around her,[13] and right there in the midst of it was her old grandmother, looking so bright and sparkling, so kind and blessed.

"Oh, Grandma," the little girl cried out. "Please take me with you! I know you will be gone when the match burns out—just like the warm stove, the lovely roast goose, and the big beautiful Christmas tree." And she quickly lit the entire bundle of matches, because she wanted to hold on tight to her grandmother. The matches burned with such intensity that it

life, he reported the incident from his mother's point of view: "I have never been able to ask anyone for anything. When I sat there under that bridge I was really hungry. I dipped my finger into the water and put a few drops on my tongue because I felt it would help. Finally, I fell asleep until evening came. Then I returned home and, when my mother discovered that I hadn't brought anything home, she roundly scolded me and told me I was a lazy girl." Andersen's sympathies were always with the downtrodden, and the little match girl gives us a figure who is pure victim.

8. *it felt just like a little lamp.* The matches have the power to kindle the imagination, producing visions of warmth (the brass stove), whimsy (a roast goose that waddles on the floor with a fork and knife in its back), and beauty (the Christmas tree). The comparison to a "little lamp" is likely an allusion to the magic lamp in the story of Aladdin, a character with whom Andersen identified. As a boy, he had read *The Arabian Nights* with his father. Andersen was also deeply familiar with Adam Oehlenschläger's *Aladdin or the Magical Lamp* (1805), a play that had captured the Danish popular imagination and had been set to music by Carl Nielsen.

9. *when the light shone on the wall.* The light from the match illuminates the wall to produce a screen on which desires are projected. For Andersen, brightness and illumination are signals for spirited imaginative activity.

10. *the most beautiful Christmas tree.* Andersen writes in his diaries about his own vivid sense of abandonment (as an adult) during the holidays: "Christmas Eve! Like a child I had looked forward to the Christmas tree, to celebrating with my friends—who told me later each was sure

someone else had taken care of me and that I had only to choose where I would prefer to be—but in fact I sat by myself in my room at the hotel, dreaming of home." And he adds that he opened a window "to look at the stars, they were my Christmas tree" (*Travels*, 246).

The priests of the ancient Celts saw in evergreens—which stayed alive and green when other plants appeared dead—a symbol of everlasting life. Scandinavian pagan customs included bringing evergreens indoors for festivities.

The Christmas tree tradition has been traced to sixteenth-century Germany, when Christians brought decorated trees into their homes. It is said that Martin Luther, the sixteenth-century Protestant reformer, first added candles to the Christmas tree. Returning home one winter evening, he was struck by the beauty of the stars twinkling among evergreens. To recapture the scene for his family, he adorned the branches of a tree with lighted candles. The Christmas tree makes one of its first literary appearances in Goethe's *Sorrows of Young Werther* in a scene that takes place shortly before Werther's suicide. The tree, "decorated with fruit and sweetmeats, and lighted up with wax candles," is said to be the delight of young children. In *The Battle for Christmas,* Stephen Nissenbaum points out that Christmas trees became in the nineteenth century a "timeless tradition." Their display turned into "a fashionable new ritual that was perceived . . . as an ancient and authentic folk tradition" (Nissenbaum, 197).

11. *One of them turned into a shooting star.* On the eve of Christ's birth, a star in the heavens pointed the way to his manger. It has also been said that a nova appeared on the night of his birth.

12. *her grandmother, the only person who had ever been kind to her.* In his autobiography,

Andersen recalled his maternal grandmother with great fondness: "Grandmother came every day to my parents' house, if only for a few minutes—above all to see her grandson, little Hans Christian. I was her joy and happiness. She was a quiet, much loved old woman; she had gentle blue eyes and a delicate appearance."

13. *Light shone all around her.* As Kirsten Malmkjær points out, Andersen's grandmothers and other elderly women often "shift and shimmer between the human, the spectral and the divine" (23), a trait that the Scottish writer George McDonald used to portray grandmothers in *The Princess and the Goblin* (1872) and *The Princess and Curdie* (1883).

CHARLES ROBINSON

The little match girl's light produces a table covered with a cloth and china. The roast goose jumps right off its platter and walks toward her.

14. *they flew in brightness and joy higher and higher.* As in "The Girl Who Trod on the Loaf," upward flight leads to redemption. Andersen takes advantage of the childhood fantasy of flying to capture the power of the girl's spiritual transformation.

15. *the little girl was still huddled between the two houses.* Although the frozen body of the girl presents a grotesque reprimand to passersby, her "rosy cheeks" and "smile" suggest that her death marks a joyous transition to a superior life, and that she has transcended worldly things. Bruno Bettelheim found the ending to be "deeply moving," but he also worried that children might make the mistake of identifying with the little match girl: "The child in his misery may indeed identify with this heroine, but if so, this leads only to utter pessimism and defeatism. 'The Little Match Girl' is a moralistic tale about the cruelty of the world; it arouses compassion for the downtrodden. But what the child who feels downtrodden needs is not compassion for others who are in the same predicament, but rather the conviction that he can escape this fate" (Bettelheim, 105).

Rosellen Brown has a different perspective on the tale, finding it captivating and absorbing when recalling her childhood response to its ending: "That Andersen would let his heroine die was shocking and—to some of us stories are exciting because they roil up our emotions, disturb our equilibrium even if they make us miserable—I would say *satisfying*" (Brown, 51).

was suddenly brighter than broad daylight. Grandma had never looked so tall and beautiful. She gathered up the little girl in her arms and together they flew in brightness and joy higher and higher[14] above the earth to where it is no longer cold, and there is neither hunger nor fear. They were now with God!

In the cold dawn, the little girl was still huddled between the two houses,[15] with rosy cheeks and a smile on her lips. She had frozen to death on the last night of the old year. The New Year dawned on the frozen body of the little girl, who was still holding matches in her hand, one bundle used up. "She was trying to get warm," people said. No one could imagine what beautiful things she had seen and in what glory she had gone with her old grandmother into the joy of the New Year.

The Steadfast Tin Soldier

Den standhaftige tinsoldat

Eventyr, fortalte for Børn. Ny Samling, 1838

Among the favorite paper cuttings that Andersen fashioned for his upper-class and aristocratic hosts was a row of soldiers and ballerinas. He once presented these linked figures to Crown Prince Ludwig of Bavaria, who wondered if his own collection of tin soldiers (which contained three soldiers without heads) might inspire Andersen. Just as the Danish sculptor Bertel Thorvaldsen challenged Andersen to write a story about a darning needle (and Andersen obliged), Prince Ludwig imagined that it would not be difficult for Andersen to animate his soldiers. Andersen wrote this tale at a time when he was deeply absorbed in the conflict between life and art. He published Only a Fiddler, *a novel that charted the suffering of young artists, the same year he wrote "The Steadfast Tin Soldier."*

The soldier and the ballerina in Andersen's story are incapable of movement and expression, but the soldier has, nonetheless, become a symbol of fortitude in the face of adversity. Like the ugly duckling, he endures all manner of assaults from humans and from the forces of nature, but he also has a romantic side, pining for a ballerina who fails to acknowledge his devotion. In the end, theirs is a failed romance, for they prove unable to transcend their inanimate condi-

1. *"Tin soldiers!"* Toy soldiers have served as collector's items and as war toys since antiquity. As Lois Kuznets points out, they can function as "stimuli for the reenactment of historic scenes of hostility, death, bravery, treachery, honor, and patriotism, or as nostalgic memorabilia of such violent (or gallant?) moments" (Kuznets, 76). Originally made by hand from wood, clay, stone, and metal, they were not massproduced until the end of the eighteenth century, by a Parisian firm named Mignot. Among noted collectors of the "little men" (manufactured by Mignot, Heyde, Britain's, and other companies) were Winston Churchill and H. G. Wells.

2. *he clapped his hands for joy.* Although the boy who receives the tin soldiers seems delighted by the gift, he does not appear to bond in any way with the toy, certainly not with the depth of feeling that the tin soldier has for the ballerina. In Andersen's stories about objects with inner lives, humans are often presented as callous, materialistic beings.

tion: "He looked at her, and she looked at him, but no words passed between them." They are joined, finally, in death. The tin soldier is, oddly, animated by the narrative voice that gets inside his head, and—stiff, rigid, and unresponsive throughout the story—he may be steadfast only because he has no other choice but to stand at attention. Still the substance into which the soldier is transformed in the end points to the possibility that he may embody something more than just pure matter.

"The Steadfast Tin Soldier" has inspired many dramatic and musical enactments, among them A Fairy Tale in Pictures, *choreographed by Andersen's contemporary Bournonville. Georges Bizet's* Jeux d'Enfants *contains within it "The Steadfast Tin Soldier," and the musical work was taken up by George Balanchine in 1975. Balanchine's ballet allowed the soldier and the dancer to encounter and express their love just before the ballerina is blown into the fire. "The Steadfast Tin Soldier" was also adapted for* Fantasia 2000, *and in it the tin soldier's adventures are accompanied by the music of Dmitri Shostakovich. The jack-in-the-box (or troll) ends up in the fire, and the soldier and the ballerina survive. The ballerina, who appears to be made of porcelain, gives the soldier a kiss for rescuing her. Even more recently, Kate DiCamillo's* The Miraculous Journey of Edward Tulane *(2006) takes up many of the themes enunciated in Andersen's tale.*

Once upon a time there were twenty-five tin soldiers. They were all brothers, for they had been born of the same old tin spoon. They held their rifles at their shoulders, and they looked straight ahead, splendid in their red and blue uniforms.

When the lid was lifted from the box that held them, the very first words they heard in this world were: "Tin soldiers!"[1] That's what a small boy shouted as he clapped his hands for joy.[2] The soldiers were a birthday gift, and he took

HARRY CLARKE

The tin soldier stands at attention while the troll barks at him to stop staring at the beautiful ballerina. Behind the ballerina is the design of a fan; the tin soldier is associated with the architecture of the town; and the troll has risen out of the box that normally contains him.

3. *except for one that was slightly different.* Thomas Mann, a great admirer of Andersen, wove the tale of "The Little Mermaid" into his novel *Doktor Faustus*. Mann declared in a letter to a friend that he had always identified with "The Steadfast Tin Soldier," who was "the symbol of my life." Joyce Carol Oates, in a meditation on writing, quotes Mann and asks whether the choice of story, featuring a soldier who never consummates his love, indicates that writers are "secretly in love with failure" (Oates 2004, 59–60). But Mann may have identified with the "slightly different" nature of the tin soldier and seen in him a symbol of endurance and of the writer's self-immolating commitment to his craft. Thomas Mann scholar Hans Rudolf Vaget suggests multiple possibilities for the identification, revealing the degree to which the tin soldier represents more than sheer steadfastness: "What might have prompted Thomas Mann to point to this fairy tale hero as the symbol of his life? Was it the soldierly devotion to discipline and order that he both practiced and extolled as a writer? . . . Or was it simply the combativeness of his nature . . . [or] an awareness that, as an artist and a spinner of tales, he served essentially as a kind of toy. It might even have been a secret suspicion that there was a certain tinniness to his role as the artist-soldier" (Vaget, 3).

4. *he's the one who turned out to be astonishing.* Although the tin soldier has a deficiency that is connected with mobility, he becomes a heroic wanderer resembling Odysseus or his fairy-tale counterpart Tom Thumb. The disability is emphasized at the beginning of the tale, but it quickly becomes insignificant in light of the fact that the soldier's fate would not be any different were he to possess two legs. Yet the disability remains important: "narrative embraces the opportunity that such a 'lack' provides—in fact, wills it into exis-

them out of the box right away and lined them up on the table.

All of the soldiers looked exactly alike, except for one that was slightly different,[3] for he was the last to be cast. There hadn't been enough tin for a whole soldier, and so he had only one leg. But there he stood, as steady on the one leg as any of the other soldiers on their two. And, just wait and see, he's the one who turned out to be astonishing.[4]

There were many other toys on the table with the soldiers, but the most appealing one was a charming castle made of cardboard.[5] Through little windows you could look right inside it. In front of the castle were miniature trees surrounding a little mirror that was meant to be a lake. Swans made of wax were swimming on its surface, and their reflections appeared in the mirror. All this was truly enchanting, but more enchanting than anything else was a little lady who was standing by the open entrance to the castle. She had been cut from paper, but she was wearing a dress of the finest tulle. A thin blue ribbon was draped over her shoulder as a scarf, and right in the middle of it shone a spangle that was the size of her tiny face. The little lady held both her arms outstretched, for she was a dancer, and one leg was lifted so high in the air that the tin soldier couldn't see it at all, and he imagined that she had only one leg, just as he did.[6]

"Now there's a wife for me,"[7] he thought. "But she may be too noble for me. After all, she lives in a castle. Here I am, living in a box that has to hold all twenty-five of us. That's no place for her! Still, I should try to make her acquaintance." Then he stretched out to his full length behind a snuffbox,[8] where he could admire the elegant little lady, who continued standing on one leg without losing her balance.

Later in the evening all the other tin soldiers were put back in the box, and the people living in the house went to bed. Then the toys started to play,[9] giving parties, fighting battles, and holding balls. The tin soldiers rattled about in their tence—as the impetus that calls a story into being" (Mitchell and Snyder, 55). The term "astonishing" may refer to the soldier's adventures but also to the "little tin heart" that becomes the objet d'art at the tale's conclusion.

5. *a charming castle made of cardboard.* The castle and its surroundings constitute one of the many architectural wonders and marvelous landscapes found in Andersen's works. The miniaturization makes the castle appealing, and the artful use of mirrors to create illusions reminds us that we are in the realm of creative wizardry. The swans swimming on the surface, producing reflections, are reminiscent of the ending to Andersen's "Ugly Duckling." Finally, the ballet dancer in her beautiful costume stands at the entrance, suggesting that the castle is a monument to art, beauty, and mobility.

6. *he imagined that she had only one leg, just as he did.* The tin soldier's feelings of affinity with the tiny maiden are based on an error in perception. The ballerina, although she represents grace and mobility, is made of paper and remains as incapable of movement as the tin soldier, with his single leg. Andersen's choice of soldier and ballerina is mildly ironic, in that both are associated with movement—marching and dancing. And both are figures to be admired for their display of colors and beauty.

7. *"Now there's a wife for me."* Andersen's tin soldier leads a strange in-between existence, possessing, like humans, the power to think and meditate about his future, yet also without the mobility that enables humans to act as agents. As one critic puts it: "Andersen's animated man-made objects inhabit a strange land. They are alive, so it seems; they are personified and equipped with human attributes; they are

conscious of their existence; they contemplate their experiences and become wiser for doing so; they are very sensitive creatures. On the other hand, though, they are wrong in assuming they are important to man: they are alive, but they are so much wrapped up in their narcissistic memories that they never realize that they are not free to act" (Schwarcz, 79). The soldier may have consciousness and a voice, but he remains surprisingly unappealing, even if his steadfastness is presented as admirable.

8. *behind a snuffbox.* Snuff, or powdered tobacco, was imported from North America and introduced to Europeans in the sixteenth century. The use of snuff (inhaling a pinch of tobacco, then sneezing elegantly) became fashionable in Europe, and snuff-taking was seen as a mark of aristocracy in the nineteenth century. Artisans created beautiful containers to hold the tobacco, and the presence of the snuffbox in the home is another sign of a comfortable bourgeois setting.

The novelist Kathryn Davis writes about her childhood reaction to the snuffbox in Andersen's story: "When I was seven years old I didn't have a clue what a snuffbox was, but I knew it was the right name for an object that sprang open unexpectedly to release a goblin. 'Snuffbox' dropped straight from God's mouth, where it hadn't yet acquired meaning, and into my brain. Recognizing its aptness, I *participated* in its creation" (Davis, 86).

9. *Then the toys started to play.* The animation of the toys was surely inspired by E.T.A. Hoffmann's "Nutcracker and the Mouse King" (1816), a tale in which toys come to life at midnight. In Hoffmann's Christmas Eve tale, an army of soldiers, led by the Nutcracker, defeats an army of mice. A nutcracker also appears among the toys in Andersen's story, and the troll who leaps out from the snuffbox is a diabolical figure

KAY NIELSEN

An angry troll seems intent on keeping tin soldier and ballerina apart, while on the surface below him, swans swim toward each other.

resembling Hoffmann's evil Mouse King. The uncanny effect of toys coming to life is both marvelous and magical yet also dark and sinister, suggesting a grotesque, topsy-turvy world in which the mechanical becomes real. Andersen's story, like Hoffmann's, locates romance, violence, adventure, and passion in a childhood setting.

10. *Suddenly the clock struck twelve.* Midnight is, of course, the "witching hour,"

box, for they too wanted to play but were unable to lift the lid. The nutcracker was turning somersaults, and a pencil began scribbling all over a slate. The toys were making such a ruckus that they woke up the canary, and it started chattering too, in verse, if you can imagine! The only two who didn't budge were the tin soldier and the little dancer. Without ever swerving from the tip of her toe, she held out her arms, and the soldier was just as steadfast on his one leg. Never once did he take his eyes off her.

Suddenly the clock struck twelve[10] and, Bam! the lid of the snuffbox popped open. But there wasn't a bit of snuff in it. No! out bounced a little black troll. What a tricky little move that was.

"Tin soldier," the troll shouted. "Keep your eyes to yourself!"

The tin soldier acted as if he had not heard.

"Just wait until tomorrow," the troll shouted.

When morning came and the children awoke, the soldier was put over by the window ledge. Was it the troll or was it just a gust of wind?[11] All of a sudden the window flew open and the soldier went plunging headfirst down four floors. He fell with breathtaking speed—his one leg stuck straight out in the air—landing cap first, with his bayonet thrust right between the cobblestones.

The housemaid and the little boy ran down to look for him, and, even though they nearly stepped right on the tin soldier, they couldn't see him. Had the tin soldier shouted "Here I am!" they would surely have found him, but he felt it was beneath his dignity to shout while in uniform.[12]

Before long it began to rain. One drop fell faster than the next and soon it was raining buckets. Just as the rain was letting up, two street urchins came running along.[13]

"Hey, look!" one of them said. "There's a tin soldier over here. Let's send him off to sea."

The two made a boat from a newspaper, set the tin soldier right in the middle of the boat, and away he sailed down the gutter, with the two urchins running beside him, clapping their hands. Good heavens![14] Who would have thought a gutter could have such powerful waves and strong currents! Don't forget that there had just been a downpour. The paper boat pitched from side to side, and at times it whirled around so rapidly that the tin soldier trembled and shuddered. But he remained steadfast, without changing his expression and looking straight ahead of him, standing tall with his rifle on his shoulder.

All of a sudden, the boat was washed in under a long plank used to board over the gutter. It became just as dark as it once was inside the box.[15]

"I wonder where I'll finally end up," the soldier thought. "This must be the troll's revenge. Oh, if only that little lady were sitting here in the boat with me, it could be twice as dark here for all I care."

Just then a big water rat appeared. He was living under the gutter plank.

"Do you have your passport?" asked the rat. "Let's have a look."

The tin soldier kept quiet and gripped his rifle more firmly than ever. The boat sped

the time of night when goblins, ghosts, witches, and other demons emerge to perform their pagan rituals. The black troll who pops out of the snuffbox belongs to Scandinavian folklore and is a figure who cannot tolerate the light of day—hence the fact that he remains, like vampires and other creatures of the night, in the coffin-like snuffbox.

11. *Was it the troll or was it just a gust of wind?* The rhetorical question is important, for it questions agency and proposes a natural explanation for the soldier's fall. Given the importance of the elements in the story (water, fire, and air), the question of whether the troll or nature conspires against the tin soldier is an important one.

12. *he felt it was beneath his dignity to shout while in uniform.* The tin soldier's pride is not necessarily admirable—in many instances it undermines his chances for survival. But there is an added layer of irony in the fact that the soldier does not have the power to speak, yet rationalizes his silence with the alibi of preserving his military dignity. Here, pride is affiliated with vanity (as in "The Emperor's New Clothes"), but in this case it leads to stoicism.

13. *two street urchins came running along.* As is often the case in Andersen's stories, schoolboys and street urchins can be counted on to engage in sadistic behavior. Saintly urchins like the little match girl are invariably female.

14. *Good heavens!* With this phrase, the narrator makes it evident that he is presenting an account of the events consonant with his character's point of view. The exclamation "Good heavens!" reveals the degree to which the thoughts of the narrator and his character merge, creating a narrative situation in which all sympathy is extended to the character.

15. *It became just as dark as it once was inside the box.* The soldier can be seen as undergoing a rite of passage, a three-part process defined by the renowned anthropologist Arnold van Gennep as separation, transition, and reincorporation. In the second, or "liminal," stage of transition, the soldier is neither here nor there, existing in a state of "betwixt and between." Liminality, as Gennep's disciple Victor Turner emphasized, is frequently "likened to death, to being in the womb, to invisibility, to darkness, to bisexuality, to the wilderness, and to an eclipse of the sun or the moon" (Turner, 95). The soldier himself, whether at home or in the gutter, displays the behavior of neophytes who are in that transitional phase: "passive or humble" and accepting "arbitrary punishments without complaint." The soldier, unlike the neophyte, does not undergo rebirth and transformation, although he could be said, in the end, to experience a mock reincorporation.

16. *It was even darker than under the gutter plank.* The tin soldier's lot is arduous, for he sinks from the comforts of a bourgeois home into the gutter and finally into an even darker and more dangerous site. Andersen scholar John Griffith points out that "frequently the physical ordeal Andersen's lovers must go through in pursuit of transcendent love is a descent into dark, close, filthy places—the tin soldier floats down a gutter into a sewer and is swallowed by a fish; the shepherdess and the chimney sweep have to creep up and down a chimney flue; the ball and the top meet in a garbage bin where 'all kinds of things were lying: gravel, a cabbage stalk, dirt, dust, and lots of leaves that had fallen down from the gutter' " (Griffith, 83). Andersen's tin soldier, however, seems less

along, with the rat in hot pursuit, gnashing his teeth as he shouted at the sticks and straws on the path: "Stop him! Stop him! He hasn't paid the toll! He didn't show me his passport."

The current ran stronger and stronger. The tin soldier could already see daylight ahead where the plank stopped, but he also began to hear a roaring sound that would have frightened even the boldest among us. Just imagine: right where the plank ended, the gutter led right into a huge canal. It was as dangerous for the soldier as a waterfall would be to us.

The tin soldier was so near the edge that he could not possibly stop the boat in time. It plunged forward. He stood as tall as he could, and no one could say that he so much as blinked an eye. The vessel spun around three or four times and then filled to the rim with water. It began to go under. The water was already up to the soldier's neck, and the boat started sinking deeper and deeper, with the paper dissolving faster and faster. Water began rushing in over his head. That's when the soldier thought about the pretty little dancer and how he would never see her again. In his ears, the soldier could hear an old tune:

Flee the waters, warrior brave,
Here below is thy shadowy grave.

The paper boat fell apart, and the soldier plunged right through it. And at that very moment, he was swallowed by an enormous fish.

My! How dark it was inside the fish. It was even darker than under the gutter plank,[16] and it was far more cramped. But the tin soldier remained steadfast and stretched out full length, with his rifle on his shoulder.[17]

The fish thrashed about, making the strangest movements imaginable. Finally it became perfectly still, and then something like a bolt of lightning flashed through it. The soldier

saw daylight again, and he heard a voice cry out: "The tin soldier!" The fish had been caught, taken to market, and then taken to a kitchen where the cook was cutting him open with a big knife. She picked the soldier up between her two fingers and took him into the parlor, where everyone wanted to see the remarkable traveler[18] who had taken a voyage in the belly of a fish. But the tin soldier was feeling anything but pride. They put him on a table and—lo and behold—what strange things can happen in the world. There he was, back in the same old parlor he had left. There they all were, once again: the children, the toys on the table, and the lovely castle with the pretty little dancer. She was still balancing on one leg, with the other raised high in the air. She too was steadfast.[19] The soldier felt so moved that he would have wept tears of tin, but soldiers are not supposed to cry. He looked at her, and she looked at him, but no words passed between them. Just then one of the little boys snatched up the soldier and, for no reason at all, threw him right into the stove.[20] That old troll in the snuffbox must have put him up to it.

The tin soldier just lay there, in flames. He could feel the terrible heat, but he wasn't sure whether it was coming from the fire or from love. He had lost his vibrant colors,[21] perhaps

in pursuit of "transcendent love" than aiming to display his fortitude through his upright position.

17. *stretched out full length, with his rifle on his shoulder.* The soldier is a stoic Jonah, who willingly endures life inside the belly of the fish. George Orwell once described the comforts of living within a creature: "For the fact is that being inside a whale is a very comfortable, cosy, homelike thought. The historical Jonah, if he can be so called, was glad enough to escape, but in imagination, in daydream, countless people have envied him. It is, of course, quite obvious why. The whale's belly is simply a womb big enough for an adult. There you are, in the dark, cushioned space that exactly fits you, with yards of blubber between yourself and reality, able to keep up an attitude of the completest indifference, no matter *what* happens" (Orwell, 177–78). Tom Thumb and Pinocchio undergo similar experiences in the bellies of beasts, domestic and wild.

18. *everyone wanted to see the remarkable traveler.* The soldier has undertaken the voyage of the hero, returning as a "remarkable" personage who has found his way back home again.

19. *She too was steadfast.* There is more than a touch of irony to the fact that both soldier and ballerina have no choice but to remain immobile and that the soldier is persuaded that he and the ballerina are kindred spirits because they share the quality of steadfastness.

20. *for no reason at all, threw him right into the stove.* The soldier seems to be a survivor, but in the end, he loses his life "for no reason at all"—just on a small boy's whim. The soldier attributes the boy's urge to an evil power, suggesting that the troll has engineered his death.

KAY NIELSEN

The tin soldier begins to go up in flames, consumed by the bright fire, while the ballerina seems to be leaping toward him, to her death. Surrounded by a border of hearts, the tale of the two fig-urines is framed as a love story.

from his hard journey, but perhaps also from grief, no one could say for certain.

The soldier looked at the little lady, and she looked at him, and he could feel that he was melting. But still he stood steadfast, his musket on his shoulder. Then the door flew open. A gust of wind picked up the dancer,[22] and she soared like a sylph right into the fire with the soldier, bursting into flame, and then she was gone. The tin soldier melted into a lump. The next day, when a servant girl was taking out the ashes, she discovered him in the shape of a little tin heart.[23] But all that was left of the pretty dancer was her spangle, and it had been burned black as coal.[24]

21. *He had lost his vibrant colors.* Like the ballerina, the soldier is a figure on display, with an attractive, multicolored uniform. Ole Shut-Eye, in the story of that title, also wears a suit of many colors.

22. *A gust of wind picked up the dancer.* Once again, a chance event—the opening of the door and the creation of a draft—leads to death. The ballerina, for all *her* steadfastness, cannot resist the force of the wind, just as the tin soldier succumbed to it at the beginning of the tale.

23. *in the shape of a little tin heart.* Given the importance of contingency in the tale, it seems possible that the heart-shaped mass is nothing more than an accident. It is also possible that the tin soldier's ardor was so powerful that it shaped his remains. Andersen's paper cuttings often had heart shapes in them.

24. *it had been burned black as coal.* The transformation of the brilliant spangle into a remnant black as coal contrasts with the conversion of the soldier into a little tin heart. A moral judgment in favor of the soldier is entered through the symbolic nature of the remains.

Ole Shut-Eye

Ole Lukøie

Eventyr, fortalte for Børn, 1837

le Shut-Eye is related to the figure of Jon Blund, an elf who sprinkles sand in children's eyes so that they will go to sleep. Andersen not only substitutes sweet milk for the sand but also turns Ole Shut-Eye into a storyteller, one who needs lights out and eyes shut to work his magic. Ole Shut-Eye is both an incarnation of dreams (with a brother named Death) and an unrivaled storyteller, who understands the importance of stories as a bridge between the real world and the world of imagination.

Ole Shut-Eye is related to the Sandman and Willie Winkie in Anglophone countries, and Dormette in France. Wee Willie Winkie comes from a Scottish nursery rhyme of 1841 written down by William Miller in dialect: "Wee Willie Winkie rins through the toun, / Up stairs and doon stairs in his nicht-goun, / Tirlin' at the window, cryin' at the lock, / 'Are the weans in their bed, for it's noo ten o'clock?' " Wee Willie Winkie and his kin have been used for centuries to frighten, coerce, and entice children to go to bed. Ole Shut-Eye seems the most benevolent of these spirits.

No one in the world knows as many stories as Ole Shut-Eye, and he certainly knows how to tell them!

When night falls, and the children are sitting around the table or on their little stools, behaving well, Ole Shut-Eye arrives. He comes upstairs without making noise, for he has socks on. He opens the door gently, and he flicks some sweet milk on the children's eyes—just a tiny bit, but enough to make them close their eyes so that they can't see him. He tiptoes behind them and breathes softly on their necks, making their heads feel heavy. Yes, indeed! But it doesn't hurt, for Ole Shut-Eye adores children and just wants them to quiet down, and that only happens after they've been put to bed. He wants them to be quiet so that he will be able to tell them stories.

As soon as the children have fallen asleep, Ole Shut-Eye sits down at their bedsides. He is well dressed, with a coat made of gleaming silk that changes color as he turns around, first red, then green, then blue. Under each arm he holds an umbrella. One has pictures all over it, and he opens that one up over good children. They dream the most beautiful stories all night long. The other is just a plain umbrella with nothing on it at all, and that one he opens over naughty children. They are restless and can't sleep, and when they wake up in the morning they have had no dreams at all.[1]

Now you shall hear about how Ole Shut-Eye came every day of the week to a little boy named Hjalmar and about all the things he told him. There are seven stories in all, because there are seven days in the week.

KAY NIELSEN

Hjalmar lies peacefully in bed, with his dolls at the foot of the bed. Above him Ole Shut-Eye has opened an umbrella that will enable him to have beautiful dreams.

1. *they have had no dreams at all.* Ole Shut-Eye, like Santa Claus and other benevolent figures, differentiates between naughty and nice, providing an instructive moral example in this bedtime story. Being deprived of the beautiful images in bedtime stories proves to be a powerful punishment, but not quite as bad as the one for "poor" or "mediocre" marks in school, as described at the end of the tale.

2. *until the room had become a beautiful bower.* The child's bedroom turning into a place where things grow will be familiar to readers of Maurice Sendak's *Where the Wild Things Are.* E.T.A. Hoffmann's *The Golden Flower Pot,* which also influenced Andersen's "The Goblin and the Grocer," similarly describes a writing studio turning into an outdoor landscape. From Hoffmann (one of the three writers whom Andersen acknowledged as the most important influences on his writing—the other two were Sir Walter Scott and Heinrich Heine), Andersen learned how to build the transition from the ordinary to the extraordinary, finding poetry and magic in everyday objects and in the diminutive mode.

3. *No one has ever seen anything like it!* With a few deft strokes the narrator manages to evoke a vivid new world and coax it into being. Moving from the visual ("prettier than a rose") to the olfactory ("with a fragrance so sweet") to the gustatory ("if you tasted it"), he not only "spruces things up" but creates beauty that is drenched in light ("the fruit gleamed like gold") and full of savory delights ("buns filled with currants").

4. *over in the drawer where Hjalmar kept his schoolbooks.* The imaginative and fantastic are often shadowed by the instructive and pedagogical in Andersen's stories for children. Just when Hjalmar seems to be set free for the pleasures of storytelling and dreaming, the slate and the copybook demand attention and turn the volume up so high that they cannot be ignored. Andersen saw deep conflicts between education and imagination, and he mourned how schooling banishes enchantment from the child's world: "As long as the little one has never been further than Copenhagen, and their grandmother or nurse has filled

MONDAY

"Now listen up," Ole Shut-Eye said one night after he had managed to get Hjalmar to go to bed. "First of all, I'm going to spruce things up." And before long all the flowers in their pots had grown into big trees, with their long branches arching across the ceiling and back down along the wall until the room had become a beautiful bower.[2] The branches were covered with flowers, each prettier than a rose and with a fragrance so sweet that, if you tasted it, it was sweeter than jam. The fruit gleamed like gold, and there were also buns bursting with raisins. No one has ever seen anything like it![3]

Suddenly you could hear a dreadful howling over in the drawer where Hjalmar kept his schoolbooks.[4]

"What could that be?" Ole Shut-Eye asked, as he went over to the desk and opened the drawer. The slate was throwing a fit and was about to fall apart. A sum would not come out right because an error had slipped into the calculations. The pencil was tugging and leaping at the end of its string like a little dog. It wanted to correct the sum but didn't know how.

Then Hjalmar's copybook started howling as well. It was just dreadful to hear. On each page, capital letters ran down the page, with lowercase letters right next to them, a complete column of them all the way down. They were the models, and next to them were letters that believed they looked just the same. Hjalmar had written those, and they looked as if they had tripped over the straight line, where they were supposed to be.

"Look here—this is how you are supposed to stand," the model said. "See this—sloping a bit, then with a bold stroke."

"Oh, we would be glad to," Hjalmar's letters replied. "But we can't. We're so weak."

"Then you will have to take some medicine!" Ole Shut-Eye replied.

"Oh, no," they shouted, and suddenly they stood up as straight as you would want them to be.

"No time for stories now," said Ole Shut-Eye. "I have to put them through their paces. Left, right! Left, right!" And he drilled the letters until they were just as elegant and straight as their models.[5] But after Ole Shut-Eye had left and when Hjalmar looked at them the next morning, they were just as miserable as before.

TUESDAY

As soon as Hjalmar was in bed, Ole Shut-Eye sprinkled his magic potion on all the furniture in the room, and every piece began chattering.[6] They all talked about themselves except for the spittoon, which kept quiet. It was annoyed that all the others were so self-centered and constantly talking and thinking only of themselves, without paying the least bit of attention to it, sitting so humbly in the corner and allowing others to spit in it.

A large painting in a gilt frame was hanging above the chest of drawers. It showed a landscape with tall old trees, flowers growing in a meadow, and a large lake from which a river flowed away through the woods, past many castles, far out to the open sea. Ole Shut-Eye used his magic spray on the painting,[7] and birds began to sing. The branches stirred in the trees, and clouds billowed out. You could see their shadows moving across the landscape.

Ole Shut-Eye picked little Hjalmar up and put him right at the edge of the painting so that he could step into the painting and stand in the tall grass, with the sun shining down on him through the branches of the trees. He ran down to the water and climbed into a little boat that was

their heads with enchanted princes and princesses, with mountains of gold and talking birds, the little heads will dream about this fantasy land and will look over the sea which meets the sky between the Danish and Swedish coasts. That's where it must be, they think, as they paint a picture of the lovely new world, but they grow older and go to school, and this immediately destroys the fantasy land, because they learn that beyond the water lies Prussia and all of Germany" (*Travels*, 289).

5. *until they were just as elegant and straight as their models.* Beautiful handwriting is important for Andersen, and he makes a point of emphasizing the capabilities of the artist student in "The Goblin and the Grocer." Ole Shut-Eye has the power to transform Hjalmar's handwriting, but only for the duration of his stay. The magic loses its effect with the dawning of a new day.

6. *every piece began chattering.* In "The Goblin and the Grocer," the supernatural creature in the title also has the ability to endow objects with the power to speak. He does so by placing a human tongue on pieces of furniture and other objects.

7. *Ole Shut-Eye used his magic spray on the painting.* The landscape described in the painting is one that appears frequently in Andersen's works, most notably in "The Ugly Duckling" and "The Nightingale." A forest, a lake, a castle, and flowers seem to be the primary features in many of the nature scenes, and Andersen did not hesitate to repeat those elements with little variation. Just as Hjalmar's room can transform itself into an outdoor scene, so too the painting can come to life, allowing Hjalmar to enter its domain and to travel on a boat down its river through forests

KAY NIELSEN

Hjalmar sails on a placid river, accompanied by swans. A princess extends a treat to him from
the balcony of a radiant castle on the riverbank.

right there. It was painted red and white, and its sails shone like silver. Six swans, all with golden crowns down over their necks and bright blue stars on their foreheads, towed the boat past the green woods, where the trees were telling tales about robbers and witches,[8] and the flowers were whispering about dear little elves and about what butterflies had told them.

Lovely fish with scales that seemed like gold and silver swam after the boat, leaping up now and then so that the water started to speak in splashes. Birds red and blue, large and small, flew behind the boat in two long lines. Gnats danced and May bugs went *boom, boom!* They all wanted to go with Hjalmar, and every one of them had a story to tell.

What a magnificent voyage it was! At times the woods were dark and deep, and then suddenly they turned into the loveliest garden filled with flowers and sunshine. You could see palaces of marble and glass, with princesses on their balconies. Hjalmar knew all of them well, for they were his playmates. They stretched their hands out to him, offering him the prettiest sugar pigs that any cake woman had ever sold. Hjalmar caught one end of a sugar pig as he sailed by, and the princess held on tight to the other end, so that each was left with a piece. The princess had the smaller piece, and Hjalmar had the larger one. Little princes with gold swords stood guard at the palaces and saluted. They showered Hjalmar with raisins and tin soldiers. You could tell that they were real princes!

Sometimes Hjalmar sailed through forests, sometimes through what seemed to be great halls, or even straight through towns. That's how he arrived in the town where his nanny lived, the woman who had looked after him when he was a small boy.[9] She had been very fond of him, and now she nodded and waved, singing the pretty verses she had made up on her own and sent to Hjalmar:

and towns. The painting as portal to a wonder world functions like the books and mirrors of many fantasy worlds, for example Lewis Carroll's *Alice in Wonderland*.

8. *the trees were telling tales about robbers and witches.* Hjalmar enters a world that contains many allusions to other tales by Andersen. The description of the landscape echoes that of other tales, but there are also swans with golden crowns ("The Wild Swans" and "The Ugly Duckling"), tales about robbers and witches that recall "The Snow Queen," and flowers, elves, and butterflies that indulge in activities reminiscent of what goes on in "Thumbelina."

9. *the woman who had looked after him when he was a small boy.* In meeting up with his nanny, Hjalmar seems to be regressing, moving back into the past rather than maturing and moving forward. But like Gerda and Thumbelina, he is drawn into a world of light, beauty, and poetry, thereby developing an artistic sensibility that runs counter to what he learns in school.

Hjalmar, my boy so dear,
Once I kissed your eyes so clear
And held you tight
Both day and night.
I heard your words and saw your tears,
Then good-byes after tender years.
God keep you near as you grow wise,
My joyous herald from the skies.

Birds joined in her songs, and the flowers began keeping time on their stalks. And the old trees nodded, just as if Ole Shut-Eye were telling them stories too.

WEDNESDAY

Goodness, how it was pouring outside! Hjalmar could hear the rain in his sleep, and when Ole Shut-Eye opened the window, water splashed right onto the windowsill. There was a lake right outside the window, and a fine ship right beside the house.

"Hjalmar, my boy, are you ready to go?" Ole Shut-Eye asked. "We can travel to distant lands tonight and be back by morning."

All at once Hjalmar was in his Sunday best on board the splendid ship. The weather had turned glorious as they sailed through the streets, rounded the church, and steered toward the open seas. They sailed on and on until you could no longer see land, and they met a flock of storks, who were also leaving home, bound for warmer climes. They had been flying in one long line, and had already covered a great distance. One of them was so weary that his wings could scarcely keep him in the air. He was the very last in the line, and, before long, he had been left behind by the others. He began to sink lower and lower, his wings still spread out, trying to make a few more feeble strokes, but it was no use. His feet touched the ship's rigging; he glided down the sail, and, plop! There he was on the deck.[10]

The cabin boy picked him up and put him in the chicken coop with the hens, ducks, and turkeys. The unfortunate stork looked miserable among them.

"What a funny-looking fellow," the hens declared.

And the turkey puffed himself up as big as he could and asked the stork who he was.[11] The ducks backed off and nudged each other: "Start quacking! Keep it up!"

The stork began to tell them about how hot it was in Africa, about the pyramids, and about ostriches that can run across the desert like wild horses. But the ducks could not understand what he was saying and again they nudged each other: "We all agree, don't we, that he's a fool."

"Yes, a real fool," the turkey declared with a "gobble, gobble," while the stork kept silent and turned his thoughts to his beloved Africa.

"Those are nice thin legs you have," the turkey said. "How much are they a yard?"

"Quack, quack, quack," chuckled the ducks, and the stork pretended not to hear.

"You may as well join in," the turkey told him, "for that was a really witty remark, but maybe it went over your head! No, indeed, he is not very bright, so we will have to rely on ourselves for fun."

The hens clucked away, and the ducks kept on quacking. It was dreadful to see how they made fun of him among themselves.

Hjalmar went over to the chicken coop door and called over to the stork, who hopped out on the deck. He had had a chance to recover, and it looked as if he was thanking Hjalmar by nodding in his direction.[12] Then he spread out his wings and flew away to the warm countries. The hens went on clucking, the ducks quacked, and the turkey gobbled until he was red in the face.

10. *There he was on the deck.* Like the swallow in Thumbelina, this stork is unable to keep up with the others and collapses from exhaustion. Thumbelina revives the swallow through her tender ministrations, unlike Hjalmar, who is both kind in liberating the stork from the henhouse and aggressive in threatening to use the turkey for the next day's dinner.

11. *asked the stork who he was.* The cruelty of the barnyard is well known from "The Ugly Duckling," which shows the newly hatched bird attacked as a misfit by the other animals.

12. *he was thanking Hjalmar by nodding in his direction.* The motif of the grateful animal is found in the folklore of many cultures. "The White Snake" and "The Queen Bee" in the Grimms' collection show the hero benefiting from interventions to protect the safety of animals. The hero's humility and suitability for a rise in rank are often demonstrated through his willingness to assist those who are lower in social station (beggars), less strong (old men and women), and lower on the food chain. Hjalmar's willingness to liberate the stork from the taunts of the other animals demonstrates his kindness and maturity, but at the same time it does not signify pure benevolence, for Hjalmar is not at all loath to contemplate the slaughter of the turkey for tomorrow's soup.

13. *the boy became smaller and smaller.* Magical shrinking and growth are associated most frequently with Lewis Carroll's *Alice in Wonderland*, but Andersen took advantage of miniaturization, not only here but in the tale of Thumbelina. Tom Thumb is the most famous of all diminutive fairy-tale figures, but he and Thumbelina, unlike Hjalmar, are small to begin with.

14. *"you will be able to wear the tin soldier's uniform."* Hjalmar, like the steadfast tin soldier in the story of that title, goes out into the wide world to find adventure. He is whisked off to the wedding but, as a living boy rather than as a tin soldier, retains control over his actions.

15. *touchwood.* A type of wood that readily ignites and also a form of tinder made from a species of fungus.

"Tomorrow we shall make a soup out of you," said Hjalmar, and then he woke up in his own little bed. The voyage arranged by Ole Shut-Eye had been truly astonishing.

THURSDAY

"What's next?" Ole Shut-Eye asked.

"Now don't be afraid if I show you a little mouse." And there sat the quaint little creature, right in Ole Shut-Eye's hand. "It has come," he said, "to invite you to a wedding. Two little mice are about to enter the state of holy matrimony tonight. They are living under the wooden boards in your mother's pantry in a most charming little flat."

"How will I ever be able to squeeze through that tiny mouse hole in the floor?" Hjalmar asked.

"Leave that to me," Ole Shut-Eye said. "I'll make you small enough." And as soon as he used some of the magic spray on Hjalmar, the boy became smaller and smaller[13] until he was no taller than your finger. "Now you will be able to wear the tin soldier's uniform.[14] It should fit perfectly, and uniforms are always so smart for parties."

"Rather!" Hjalmar said, and the next moment he looked like the most dashing tin soldier.

"If you'll kindly be seated in your mother's thimble," the mouse said, "I shall have the honor of pulling you."

"Are you really willing to go to all that trouble?" Hjalmar cried out. And, with that, he was whisked off to the mouse wedding.

At first they went down a long passage under the floorboards. There was just room enough for them to drive through in the thimble, and the whole passage was lit up with touchwood.[15]

"Doesn't it smell delightful here?" said the mouse. "This whole road has been greased with bacon rinds, and nothing can beat that."

Then they entered the wedding hall. To the right stood all the little lady mice, whispering and giggling as if they were making fun of each other. To the left stood all the gentlemen mice, twirling their mustaches with their forepaws. The bridegroom and bride stood in a hollow cheese rind in the center of the floor and began kissing each other like mad, in plain view of all the guests. Well, after all, they were engaged and about to be married.

Guests kept arriving, and the mice were nearly trampling each other to death. The bridal couple had posted themselves in the doorway, so that no one could come in or go out. Like the passage, this whole hall had been greased with bacon rind, and that was the complete banquet. But for dessert, a pea was carried in. A little mouse in the family had gnawed the name of the bridal couple on it—or at least the first letter of the name. That was really something out of the ordinary.

The mice all agreed that it had been a charming wedding, and all the conversations had been just perfect. Hjalmar drove back home again. He had spent time in very smart society, but he had had to put up with no end of shrinking in order to be small enough to fit in that tin soldier's uniform.

FRIDAY

"It's amazing how many grown-ups are anxious to get hold of me," Ole Shut-Eye said. "Especially the ones with bad consciences. 'Dear little Ole,' they tell me, 'we can't shut our eyes. We lie awake all night long staring at our wicked deeds sitting on the edge of the bed like ugly little goblins and making us soak in perspiration. Can't you chase them off so that we can have a good night's sleep?' And then they add with a deep sigh: 'We're only too glad to pay. Good night, Ole. The money's on the windowsill.' But I don't do anything for money," Ole Shut-Eye declared.

"Well, what should we do tonight?" little Hjalmar asked.

16. *"Shall we go to the country, or would you rather travel abroad?"* The bridegroom's innocent question provokes a deep debate about the virtues of home versus abroad. The swallow, a migratory bird that flies to warmer climes in the winter, trumpets the beauty of southern regions, while the hen insistently defends the pleasures of home. A defining paradox of Andersen's life, according to one critic, was "traveling with border- and boundary-crossing desires through a life filled with borders and boundaries" (Houe 1999, 95).

"I'm not sure if you care to go to another wedding. But it will be quite different from last night's. Your sister's big doll, the one that looks like a man and is named Herman, is supposed to marry a doll named Bertha. It's Bertha's birthday too, and that means there will be presents galore."

"Yes, I know what that means," Hjalmar said. "Whenever the dolls need new clothes, my sister lets them have a birthday or a wedding. It's happened at least a hundred times already."

"And tonight's wedding is the one hundred and first, and when this one's over, there won't be any more. That's why it's going to be so splendid. Just take a look."

Hjalmar looked over at the table. He could see a little cardboard house with lights in the window. Tin soldiers were presenting their arms outside it. The bride and bridegroom were seated on the floor, leaning up against the leg of the table and looking very thoughtful, and with good reason. Ole Shut-Eye, rigged out in Grandmother's black petticoat, conducted the ceremony. When the wedding was over, all the furniture in the room joined in to sing the following beautiful song, written for the occasion by the pencil, and sung to the tune of the soldier's tattoo:

> Our song will greet through wind and weather
> These two that love has brought together.
> Neither knows quite what's been done,
> And who's to say what has been won?
> Wood and leather blend together,
> Hurrah for them in wind and weather!

Next came the wedding presents. The pair said that they didn't need any food at all, because they were planning to live on love.

"Shall we go to the country, or would you rather travel abroad?"[16] the bridegroom asked. They consulted the swallow, who was a great traveler, as well as the old hen, who had hatched five broods of chicks. The swallow described the lovely warm countries, where grapes hang in heavy, ripe bunches, and where the air is soft. The colors on the mountains are something we never see here.

"Still, they don't have our green cabbage," the hen declared. "I once spent the summer with all my chicks in the country. There was a gravel pit there in which we could scratch all day, and then we had the use of a garden where there were cabbages. Oh, how green they were! I can't imagine anything more lovely!"

"One cabbage looks just like the next," the swallow said. "And the weather is often so bad here."

"Oh, well, we're used to that," the hen replied.

"But it's so cold here. It's often freezing."

"That's good for the cabbage," said the hen. "And besides, we have warm weather at times. Don't you remember that hot summer we had four years ago? It was so hot for five weeks that you could barely breathe. Then too, we don't have all those poisonous creatures that live abroad. And we don't have robbers.[17] Anyone who doesn't believe that ours is the most beautiful country is a scoundrel who doesn't deserve to live here!" Tears came into the hen's eyes. "I've done a bit of traveling myself. I once made a twelve-mile trip in a coop, and there was no joy in it at all."

"That hen is a sensible woman!" Bertha the doll said. "I don't fancy traveling in the mountains either, because all you do is go up and then down. No, let's move to the gravel pit and take walks in the cabbage patch."

That settled the matter.

SATURDAY

"Any stories tonight?" little Hjalmar asked, as soon as Ole Shut-Eye had got him to bed.

17. *"And we don't have robbers."* The risks associated with travel were high in Andersen's time, and the travel diaries provide a clear sense of the dangers facing tourists. On the one hand, Andersen saw travel as "invigorating, a cleansing of the soul." "I need this refreshing bath which seems to make me both younger and stronger when I return home." In his travels to Turkey and Greece, Andersen documented some of the risks he was facing. He writes about a "recent uprising in the Balkans—where it was said thousands of Christians had been murdered." Yet Andersen was undaunted: "I am not among the bravest, a fact that has often been pointed out to me. . . . However, I must explain that while lesser dangers disturb me, when an adventure presents itself I forget my fearful anticipations, and, even if I am still trembling, I meet this perhaps even more dangerous situation with equanimity" (*Travels*, 166–67). Disease (outbreaks of cholera required quarantine), bandits, political uprisings, storms at sea were just a few of the "adventures" awaiting Andersen on his travels.

18. *"We must have the whole world spruced up."* Ole Shut-Eye, for all his associations with whimsy and imagination, also tidies up and keeps order in the domestic sphere, as in celestial regions. Combining flights of fancy with good etiquette, he is a puckish pedagogue for Hjalmar.

"We haven't time this evening," Ole told him, as he opened his umbrella with the prettiest pictures on it. "Take a look at these Chinese figures." The entire umbrella looked like a large Chinese bowl, with blue trees and arched bridges, with little Chinese figures nodding their heads.

"We must have the whole world spruced up[18] by tomorrow morning," Ole Shut-Eye said. "You see, it's Sunday, a holiday. I have to go over to the church tower to make sure that the little church elves are polishing the bells so that they will sound their best. I must check the fields to make sure that the wind is blowing the dust off the leaves and grass, and then there is my hardest task, taking down all the stars and polishing them. I put them in my apron, but, before that, I have to number each one along with the place it comes from so that they can return to their proper places, otherwise they won't fit tight and we would end up with too many shooting stars, because one after another would come tumbling down."

"Oh, I say here, Mr. Shut-Eye," an old portrait hanging on the wall of Hjalmar's bedroom said. "I am Hjalmar's great-grandfather. Thank you for telling the boy your stories, but you mustn't put strange ideas in his head. The stars can't be taken down and polished. The stars are globes just like the earth. That's the beauty of them."

"Thanks very much, Great-grandfather," Ole Shut-Eye said. "I'm grateful to you. You are the head of the family, of course, the Grand Old Man, but I'm even older than you are. I'm an ancient heathen. The Greeks and Romans called me the Dream God. I visit the homes of the best families all the time. I know how to get along with all kinds of people, big and small. Now you may tell the stories on your own." Ole Shut-Eye picked up his umbrella, and off he went.

"Well! Nowadays you can't even express an opinion," the old portrait grumbled.

And just then Hjalmar woke up.

SUNDAY

"Good evening," Ole Shut-Eye said, and Hjalmar nodded, and then he turned his great-grandfather's portrait to the wall so that it wouldn't interrupt them, as it had the night before.

"Please tell me some stories," he said. "The one about the five peas living in a pod, the cock-a-doodle-doo that courted the hen-a-doodle-doo, and the darning needle who gave herself such airs[19] because she believed she was a sewing needle."

"That might be too much of a good thing," said Ole Shut-Eye. "I'd rather show you something. In fact, I'm going to introduce you to my own brother.[20] He is also named Ole Shut-Eye, but he never comes more than once to a person. When he comes, he takes you for a ride on his horse and tells you stories. He only knows two: one is more beautiful than anyone on earth can imagine, and the other is so ghastly that it's beyond description."

Ole Shut-Eye lifted Hjalmar up to the window and said: "Look, there's my brother, the other Ole Shut-Eye. He's also known as Death. You can see that he doesn't look nearly as bad as he is made out to be in pictures, where he is nothing but a skeleton. No, his coat is embroidered with silver. It's like the magnificent uniform of a hussar, with a cloak of black velvet billowing behind him over his horse. See how he gallops along!"

Hjalmar saw the other Ole Shut-Eye riding away, carrying both young and old on his horse. He placed some in front of him, others behind, but he always asked them first: "What does it say in your report card?" "Good," they all replied. Then he would say: "Let me see for myself." And then they had to show him the cards, and the ones who had "very good" or "excellent" would get to ride in front of him and hear a beautiful story.[21] But those who had "mediocre" or "poor" had to ride behind him and hear a ghastly tale. They trembled

19. *"darning needle who gave herself such airs."* Andersen's tale "The Darning Needle" begins, "There was once a darning needle, who thought herself so fine, she imagined she was a sewing needle." The proud darning needle bears a close resemblance to the steadfast tin soldier and experiences many of the same adventures, traveling and sailing, until she is run over by a wagon: "She lay there, stretched out full length, and there she may lie still."

20. *"introduce you to my own brother."* The Greek Hypnos (his Roman counterpart is Somnus) personifies sleep and was represented as a brother of Death (Thanatos) and a son of Night (Nyx). In many ancient works of art, Sleep and Death are represented as two youths slumbering or holding torches turned upside down. Andersen here evokes an association that is already powerfully present in the minds of children—the fear that falling asleep and losing consciousness is akin to dying. "If I should die before I wake" (a common nighttime prayer in the Western world) reinforces the anxiety that you might fall asleep and never wake up.

21. *hear a beautiful story.* The distinction between those with "good" cards and those with "mediocre" or "poor" cards repeats the distinction made at the beginning of the tale between good children and naughty children.

and sobbed and tried to jump off the horse, but they couldn't do that because they were stuck fast to it.

"Why, Death is a most wonderful Ole Shut-Eye," Hjalmar exclaimed. "I'm not at all afraid of him."

"No, you needn't be," Ole Shut-Eye told him. "But be sure that you always have a good report card."

"Most enlightening!" the portrait of Great-grandfather muttered. "It does some good, after all, to speak your mind." And he was quite satisfied.

There! That's the story of Ole Shut-Eye. Tonight he can tell you some more himself.

PART II

Tales for Adults

The Red Shoes

De røde Skoe

Nye Eventyr, 1845

he Red Shoes" is one of the most disturbing tales in the literary canon of childhood, and it has been read in multiple ways, but always with attention to the horrors of the chopped-off feet that dance on their own. Today, Karen's dance in Andersen's tale is read less as an act of insolent arrogance than as an expression of creativity. The tale has become for many feminist writers and critics an allegory of the violence threatening those who prefer creative fulfillment to compliance with conventional social roles. Anne Sexton's poem "The Red Shoes" expresses anxiety about how dancers in red shoes turn suicidal because they defy social norms and signal insubordination: "What they did would do them in" (Sexton, 316). The writer in Margaret Atwood's novel Lady Oracle captures the impossibility of combining artistic accomplishment with personal fulfillment and relies on Andersen's tale to capture the dilemma facing women:

The real red shoes, the feet punished for dancing. You could dance, or you could have the love of a good man. But you were afraid to dance, because you had this unnatural fear that if you

danced they'd cut your feet off so you wouldn't be able to dance. . . . Finally you overcame your fear and danced, and they cut your feet off. The good man went away too, because you wanted to dance.

(Atwood 1976, 335)

The tale of the red shoes is known to European oral storytelling cultures, where it also goes by the names "The Devil's Dancing Shoes" and "The Red-Hot Shoes of the Devil." Clarissa Pinkola Estés includes what she calls a "Magyar-Germanic" version in Women Who Run with the Wolves *(Estés, 216–19). There, the red shoes dance through the forest out of sight, and the girl remains a cripple, who "never, ever again wished for red shoes."*

1. *she had to go barefoot.* The condition of being without shoes signals abject poverty, abandonment, and exposure in Andersen's works. Gerda in "The Snow Queen" and the little match girl share Karen's fate: being deprived of protection from the cold. Note that Karen will receive two pairs of red shoes, with the first leading to her social elevation through the maternal old woman, and the second to her social degradation. Shoes have always sent strong social signals, indicating position in a hierarchy—even today we use the term "well-heeled" to mark a person of high standing. Our popular entertainments are filled with references to shoe brands. Shoes enable not just physical mobility but also social mobility.

There was once a little girl who was delicate and pretty but so poor that she had to go barefoot[1] all summer long. In the winter, she had to wear big wooden clogs that chafed against her ankles until they turned red. It was just dreadful.

Old Mother Shoemaker lived right in the middle of the village. She took some old strips of red cloth and did her best to turn them into a little pair of shoes.[2] They may have been crudely made, but she meant well, and the girl was to have them. The little girl's name was Karen.[3]

On the day that her mother was buried, Karen was given the red shoes and wore them for the very first time. It's true that they were not the proper shoes for mourning, but they were all she had, and so she put them on her bare feet, walking behind the plain coffin made of straw.[4]

Just then a grand old carriage passed by, and inside it sat a grand old woman. She looked at the little girl and took pity on her. And she said to the pastor: "How about giving the little girl to me? I will treat her kindly."

W. HEATH ROBINSON

Karen, dressed in tattered clothing, contemplates the shoes made for her by Old Mother Shoemaker, who admires her handiwork. The mirror hangs on the wall as a sign of vanity.

2. *did her best to turn them into a little pair of shoes.* This first pair of shoes remedies the disjunction between Karen's appearance ("delicate and pretty") and the poverty to which she is subjected. Karen's beauty contrasts sharply with the big ugly wooden clogs that chafe her ankles. The red shoes, linked by their color to the clogs that turn Karen's ankles red, seem to create a new social identity for Karen. But they do not entirely efface the old identity.

3. *The little girl's name was Karen.* Andersen's mother had a daughter named

W. HEATH ROBINSON

Karen has dressed up for her appearance at church.

Karen thought that all this had happened because she had been wearing the red shoes, but the old woman declared that the shoes were hideous, and she had them burned. Karen was then dressed in proper new clothing. She had to learn to read and sew, and people said that she was pretty. But the mirror told her:[5] "You are more than pretty—you're beautiful!"

One day the queen came traveling through the country with her little daughter, who was a princess. People were swarming around the castle, and Karen was there too. The little princess was dressed in fine white clothing and stood at the window for all to admire. She wasn't wearing a train, and she didn't have a golden crown on her head, but she was wearing splendid red shoes made of fine leather. Of course they were much nicer than the ones Old Mother Shoemaker had made for little Karen. There's nothing in the world like a pair of red shoes![6]

When Karen was old enough to be confirmed, she was given new clothes, and she was to have new shoes as well. A prosperous shoemaker in town measured her little feet. The shop was right in his house, and the parlor had big glass cases, with stylish shoes and shiny boots on display. Everything in them looked attractive, but since the old woman could not see well, the display gave her no pleasure. Among the many shoes was a pair of red ones that looked just like the shoes worn by the princess. They were beautiful![7] The shoemaker told Karen that he had made them for the daughter of a count, but that the fit had not been right.

"They must be made of patent leather," the old woman said. "See how they shine!"

Karen-Marie, born out of wedlock in 1799 and raised by her maternal grandmother. Andersen scrupulously avoided any mention of her in his autobiographical writings. Karen worked as a washerwoman in Copenhagen, where she lived with her husband. In 1842 Karen contacted Andersen, and he gave her a small sum of money when she paid him a visit.

4. *the plain coffin made of straw.* Coffins made of straw were widely used in Europe to bury the poor. Today the use of straw coffins has been revived as an ecologically correct form of burial.

5. *the mirror told her.* As in "The Snow Queen," a mirror figures prominently as a device promoting self-division and vanity. The voice in the mirror affirms beauty, as in the Grimms' "Snow White"; but, in Andersen's story, the reflection in the mirror has a malignant effect, turning a "delicate and pretty" child into a self-absorbed, vain creature.

6. *There's nothing in the world like a pair of red shoes!* The narrator shares Karen's delight in red shoes with an exclamation that seems to articulate a universal truth. The pleasure derived from the shoes stems from their beauty, which seems untar-nished by sin so long as the shoes are put on display in public spaces rather than at sacred sites like the church. Note that the mark of royalty has been transferred from the princess's head (the crown) to her feet (the red shoes), and that the red shoes become an emblem of nobility when they are worn by the princess. As one commentator on the story points out: "This image of the princess fixes the red shoes to a fantasy of social transcendence that would lead Karen from low to high, from rags to riches, from a little pauper in blood-stained clogs to a princess in red moroccan slippers" (Mackie, 239).

7. *They were beautiful!* The beauty of the shoes is once again emphasized; and the fact that they are exhibited twice—first as the shoes worn by the princess in greeting her subjects, then as objets d'art in the shoe-maker's display cases—affirms their status as aesthetic objects, rare and beautiful. Both the old woman and Karen call attention to the shininess of the shoes ("See how they shine!" and "Yes, they are shiny"), thereby emphasizing the luminous quality characteristic of Andersen's cult objects. The shoes turn into such powerful emblems of Karen's sinful nature that it is easy to forget that they begin as exquisite ornaments arousing wonder and admiration.

8. *She looked at her black shoes, and she looked at the red ones.* Faced with a choice between remaining a self-effacing girl raised by an old woman or becoming a princess, Karen hesitates only for a moment. Her fixation on the red shoes is driven in part by their beauty but to a great extent by their association with a princess who is acclaimed by her subjects and accompanied by her mother.

"Yes, they are shiny!" Karen said. And since the shoes fit, the old woman bought them, but she had no idea they were red. If she had known, she would never have let Karen wear them to be confirmed, but that is exactly what Karen did.

Everyone looked at Karen's feet when she walked down the aisle in the church toward the doorway for the choir. Even the old paintings on the crypts—the portraits of pastors and their wives wearing stiff collars and long black gowns—seemed to have their eyes fixed on her red shoes. That was all Karen could think about, even when the pastor placed his hand on her head and spoke of the holy baptism, the covenant with God, and the fact that she should now be a good Christian. The organ played solemnly, the children sang sweetly, and the old choir leader sang too, but, still, Karen could think only about her red shoes.

By the afternoon, the old woman had heard from everyone in the parish about the red shoes. She told Karen that wearing red shoes to church was dreadful and not the least bit proper. From that day on, whenever Karen went to church, she was to wear black shoes, even if they were worn out.

The following Sunday Karen was supposed to go to communion. She looked at her black shoes, and she looked at the red ones.[8] And then she looked at the red ones again and put them on.

It was a beautiful, sunny day. Karen and the old woman took

the path through the cornfields, where it was rather dusty.

At the church door they met an old soldier,[9] who was leaning on a crutch. He had a long, odd-looking beard that was more red than white—in fact it was red. He made a deep bow, and then he asked the old woman if he could polish her shoes. Karen stretched out her little foot as well. "Just look at those beautiful dancing shoes,"[10] the soldier said. "May they stay on tight when you dance,"[11] and he tapped the soles of the shoes.

The old woman gave the soldier a penny and then went into the church with Karen.

Everyone in the church stared at Karen's red shoes, and all the portraits stared at them too. And when Karen knelt down at the altar and put the chalice to her lips, all she could think of were her red shoes, which seemed to be floating in the chalice.[12] She forgot to sing the hymn, and she also forgot to recite the Lord's Prayer.

Everyone was leaving the church, and the old woman climbed into the carriage. As Karen was lifting her foot to follow her in, the old soldier standing nearby said: "Take a look at those beautiful dancing shoes!" Karen could not help herself—she just had to take a few dance steps. But once she started, her feet could not stop. It was as if the shoes had taken control. She danced around the corner of the church—she could not stop herself. The coachman had to chase after her, grab hold of her, and lift her into the carriage. But even

9. *At the church door they met an old soldier.* The old soldier occupies a liminal, or in-between, space at the threshold to the church. In policing entry into a sacred space, he appears to be an enforcer of socioreligious codes. His red beard points in the direction of a diabolical force linked with Karen's red shoes. That he is depicted as an invalid anticipates Karen's fate.

10. *"Just look at those beautiful dancing shoes."* The shoes are linked here for the first time with dancing. They have been seen as objects that open up the possibility of social mobility, and indeed they allow Karen to engage in activities that are both artistic and adventurous. Linking the beauty of the shoes with an expressive activity draws attention to the possibility that the moral and religious sentiments expressed in the remainder of the narrative may not necessarily be the dominant discourse of the tale. Note also how evil is associated with the act of covetous looking.

11. *"May they stay on tight when you dance."* The soldier uses a charm or curse, a *maleficium* that will lead to Karen's inability to stop dancing. He taps the soles and animates the shoes, endowing them with a life of their own. Oddly, the very figure who steps in to enforce submission to Christian values and bring Karen back to the fold is a diabolical character who uses black magic.

12. *which seemed to be floating in the chalice.* That the vision of the red shoes displaces the sacrament suggests that Karen places her faith in (and communes with) what is on her feet, not the sacrament representing the blood of Christ. She is more deeply invested in social mobility through the red shoes than in the salvation offered in church, and she will pay a price through the shedding of her own blood.

13. *Then she looked at the red shoes.* Once again, Karen is faced with a choice between duty and pleasure. Just as she turned away from the black shoes, she now leaves the old woman and elects to put on the red shoes once again. Looking and desiring lead to her downfall.

14. *Karen thought it must be the moon.* The moon, as in Andersen's "Snow Queen," is associated with diabolical forces that stand in opposition to the warmth and light generated by the sun, which is, in turn, associated with divine powers and redemption.

in there her feet kept on dancing, and she gave the kind old woman a few terrible kicks. Finally they managed to get the shoes off, and her legs began to calm down.

Once they were home, the shoes were put into a cupboard, but Karen could not help going over to look at them.

Not much later, the old woman was taken ill, and it was said that she would not live long. She needed someone to take care of her and nurse her, and who better to do it than Karen?

But in town there was to be a grand ball, and Karen had been invited. She looked at the old woman, who didn't, after all, have much longer to live. Then she looked at the red shoes,[13] for there was no harm in that. She put them on, for there was no harm in that either. Then she left for the ball and began dancing.

When Karen turned to the right, the shoes turned left. When she wanted to dance up the ballroom floor, the shoes danced down the floor. They danced down the stairs, into the street, and out through the town gate. Dance she did, and dance she must, right out into the dark forest.

Something was shining brightly above the trees, and Karen thought it must be the moon,[14] because it resembled a face, but it turned out to be the old soldier with the red beard. He nodded and said: "Take a look at those beautiful dancing shoes!"

Karen was horrified and tried to take the shoes off, but they wouldn't come off. She tore off her stockings, but the shoes had grown onto her feet. And dance she did, for dance she must, over hill and dale, rain or shine, night and day. Nighttime was the most terrible time of all.

Karen danced into the open churchyard, but the dead did not join in her dance.[15] They had better things to do than dance. She wanted to sit down on a pauper's grave, where bitter tansy weed grows,[16] but there was no rest or peace for her there. When she danced toward the open church door, she realized that it was guarded by an angel in long white robes, with wings that reached from his shoulders down to the ground. His expression was stern and solemn, and in his hand he held a broad, gleaming sword.[17]

"Dance you shall!" he said to her. "Dance in your red shoes until you turn pale and cold, and your skin shrivels up like a mummy. Dance you shall from door to door, and wherever you find children who are proud and vain, you will knock on the door so that they will hear you and fear you![18] Dance you shall! Dance!"

"Have mercy!" Karen shouted. But she did not hear the angel's reply, for the shoes were already carrying her through the gate, along highways and byways, and she had to keep on dancing.[19]

One morning, she danced past a door she

15. *the dead did not join in her dance.* Karen may be wearing beautiful shoes and her dancing may free her from the constraints of village life, but that dancing is also linked more emphatically to death than to life. She is presented as a solitary figure performing what was known in medieval times as the dance of death, or *danse macabre* and "skeleton dance." The concept originated in the late thirteenth and early fourteenth centuries and gained greater prominence during the outbreak of the plague in European countries. The *danse macabre* overturns social hierarchies by presenting a row of figures, sometimes led by the personified figure of Death, in descending order of social rank, beginning with the pope and ending with a peasant—all are equal before death. The dance of death could also be performed by the dead, who rose from their graves and danced in the cemetery before going out to fetch the living.

16. *where bitter tansy weed grows.* Tansy ragwort (*Senecio jacobaea*) is a noxious Eurasian weed that causes liver damage in cattle and horses.

17. *he held a broad, gleaming sword.* When Adam and Eve were expelled from the Garden of Eden, two angelic beings were placed at the gate, with "a flaming sword which turned every way, to keep the way of the tree of life" (Genesis 3:24). Dazzling in his whiteness, the angel contrasts sharply with the soldier, whose most prominent feature is a red beard.

18. *"they will hear you and fear you!"* Karen becomes a figure of warning, reminding children that pride (her desire for social mobility) and vanity (the wish to put herself on display) must be avoided. Her story becomes a cautionary tale about making the effort to aspire to the nobility of the princess waving to the crowds.

19. *she had to keep on dancing.* Karen's compulsive dancing became the inspiration for the 1948 film *The Red Shoes,* directed by Michael Powell and starring Moira Shearer. Victoria Page, the ballerina in the film, is deeply committed to her professional life as a dancer and makes her name in the ballet *The Red Shoes*. She is torn between her desire to dance and her love for her husband. The film and novel that inspired it end when Victoria Page leaps to her death just before the performance of *The Red Shoes*. With her last dying breath, she bequeaths the shoes to her husband, shoes that are "alas, more red than ever before," as noted in the novel (Powell and Pressburger, 279). By removing the shoes, she signals to her husband the decision to abandon her career.

Ivor Guest, in a history of the romantic ballet, captures the way in which ballerinas are continually driven to dance: "Rest! Does a dancer ever rest? We were just poor wandering Jews at whom M. Barrez incessantly shouted, 'Dance! Dance!' . . . And do not imagine that such brutal fatigues only last for a short time. They must continue forever and be continually renewed" (Guest, 25). Andersen understood the rigors of the ballet, for he sang and danced on stage before returning to his studies in the town of Slagelse.

20. *"go to church and let everyone see me."* Karen makes the fatal mistake of going to church in order to put herself on display, this time as a wounded creature who has liberated herself from the torments inflicted by beautiful shoes.

knew well. Inside you could hear a hymn, and then a coffin covered with flowers was carried out. Karen knew that the old woman must have died. Now she was all alone in the world and cursed by the angel of God.

Dance she did and dance she must, dance through the dark night. Her shoes took her through thickets with briars that scratched her until she bled. She danced across the heath until she reached a lonely little house. She knew that this was the home of the executioner, and she tapped on the window with her finger and said: "Come outside! Come outside! I can't come in because I'm dancing!"

The executioner said: "You don't know who I am, do you? I chop off the heads of evil people, and I can feel that my ax is getting impatient."

"Don't chop my head off!" Karen cried. "If you do, I won't be able to repent. But go ahead and chop the red shoes off my feet."

Karen confessed her sins, and the executioner chopped off the feet in those red shoes. And the shoes danced across the fields and into the deep forest, with the feet still in them.

The executioner made wooden feet and crutches for her. He taught her a hymn that was sung by sinners. Then she kissed the hand that had wielded the ax, and off she went across the heath.

"I have suffered long enough because of those red shoes," she said. "It's time to go to church and let everyone see me."[20] She hobbled over as fast as she could to the church door, and, when she got there, the red shoes were dancing in front of her. Horrified, she turned back.

All week long she was miserable and wept many bitter

tears. When Sunday came, she said: "I have suffered and struggled long enough. I have a feeling that I am just as good as many of the people sitting in church and holding their heads high." She set out confidently, but when she reached the gate she saw the red shoes dancing in front of her.[21] She turned away horrified and, this time, repented her sins with all her heart.

Karen went over to the parsonage and asked if she might be taken into service there. She promised to work hard and to do everything asked of her. Wages were of no interest to her. All she needed was a roof over her head and the chance to stay with good people. The parson's wife took pity on her and hired her. Karen was thoughtful and hardworking. In the evening, she would sit quietly and listen to the parson as he read from the Bible. The children were all fond of her, but whenever they talked about dressing up in frills and finery and looking as beautiful as a queen,[22] she would shake her head.

The next Sunday they all went to church and asked if she wanted to join them. Tears came to her eyes as she looked with sorrow over at her crutches. The others went to hear the word of God while she retreated to her lonely little room, just big enough to hold a bed and a chair. She sat down with her hymnal and was reading it devoutly when the wind carried the sounds of the organ from the church to her. She raised her tear-stained face upward and said: "Help me, O Lord!"

The sun began to shine brightly, and an angel in white robes—the one that she

21. *the red shoes dancing in front of her.* The shoes, with bloody feet inside them, are charged with a powerful spirit of resistance and dance off on their own. They return to haunt and mock Karen as a talisman of her earlier desires.

22. *looking as beautiful as a queen.* Karen recognizes in the make-believe activities of the children her own desire to imitate the princess. Discrediting the attractions of beauty, she accepts the codes of her community and dedicates herself to a life of hard work and piety.

23. *no one there asked her about the red shoes.* The red shoes presumably continue their manic dance on earth, achieving a kind of immortality through a magic blend of beauty and horror.

had seen at night in the church door-way—appeared before her. Where he had once held a sword with a sharp blade he now had a beautiful green branch covered with roses. He touched the ceiling with the branch, and it rose high up into the air. A golden star was shining on the spot he had touched. Then he touched the walls, and they moved outward and away. Karen looked at the organ and heard it playing. She saw the portraits of the pastors and their wives. The congregation was seated in carved pews and singing from hymnals.

The church itself had come to the poor girl in her tiny crowded room, or perhaps she had gone to the church. She was sitting in a pew with others from the parsonage. When they finished the hymn, they looked up, nodded in her direction, and said: "It was right for you to come, Karen."

"I'm here by the grace of God," she replied.

The organ swelled, and the children in the choir lifted their voices in soft and beautiful sounds. Bright, warm sunshine flooded through the window into the church pew where Karen was seated. Her heart was so filled with sunshine, and with peace and joy, that it burst. Her soul flew on the rays of the sun up to God, and no one there asked her about the red shoes.[23]

The Shadow[1]

Skyggen

Nye Eventyr. Andet Bind, Første Samling. 1847

ndersen wrote much of "The Shadow" in 1846 when he was in Naples. In a diary entry of June 8, he complained: "The heat is pouring down. I hardly dare go outside." The following day, he announced: "In the evening, began writing the story of my shadow." Note the use of the possessive pronoun, with Andersen cast as the "learned man" from "cold lands" so that "The Shadow" becomes a reflection—or shadow—of its author.

The tale marks a real turning point in Andersen's literary production, for it establishes him as an author whose work is animated by the theme of artistic and existential crisis. Like his British, European, and American contemporaries, he became fascinated with doubles, shadows, portraits, and statues, finding in them metaphors for exploring the divided self.

The autonomous shadow has appeared in many nineteenth-century literary works, most notably Adelbert Chamisso's The Marvelous Story of Peter Schlemihl *(1814), which was translated into many languages shortly after its publication. Andersen met Chamisso when he traveled to Berlin in 1831 and noted in his autobiography that he had found in the Prussian poet of French descent a "life-long"*

1. *Shadow.* Edgar Allan Poe's "Shadow: A Parable" (1850), Oscar Wilde's "The Fisherman and His Soul" (1891), J. M. Barrie's *Peter Pan* (1904), and Hugo von Hofmannsthal's *The Woman without a Shadow* (1919) are all about what it means to lose a shadow. Often seen in symbolic terms as a manifestation of the soul ("the shadow of the body is the body of the Soul," Wilde tells us in his story), the shadow can also function as an uncanny double that detaches itself from the body to haunt others. The shadow becomes a spectral presence that generally incarnates the darker desires and longings of the self. The Danish term for shadow, *skygge*, can mean both shade (in the sense of a ghost or a spirit) and shadow.

2. *the sun can really scorch you.* The opening sentences, in Andersen's signature casual, conversational tone, make light of what will become a weighty matter. The scholar has entered a domain in which your skin color can change (note that the implied reader has white skin) to brown or black. Instead of risking that particular metamorphosis, in which he could be "baked black," the scholar takes up residence in a "moderately hot" country and avoids heat and light, retreating into his study to investigate the good, the true, and the beautiful (thereby remaining "white"). Ironically, his "black" side nonetheless emerges in the form of a shadow that achieves dominance.

The menacing shadow has dark habits. In his first appearance as a man, he is "dressed in black, with clothes made from the finest cloth," with a black hat. But his transformation is achieved through exposure to the "brightness" of the apartment that is described as the dwelling place of Poetry. And he begins to sport accessories that are generally associated with the sparkle and shimmer of art. The sharp distinctions between black and white established at the beginning of the story through skin color begin to break down in both moral and aesthetic terms.

3. *Along with all other sensible souls, he had to stay indoors.* The use of the term "sensible," along with the description of the learned man as a scholar dedicated to the life of the mind, suggests that the warmer countries lack the intellectual power found in northern regions. Yet the term "sensible" may also be used ironically, as it is when the narrator notes that the learned man decides not to write about himself, "which was very sensible of him."

4. *It was really unbearable!* The living conditions are unbearable in part because of the heat and in part because of the claus-

friend. Andersen deepens Chamisso's story by turning the shadow into the sinister force of the tale, suggesting that truly menacing forces emerge from within.

In the hot countries the sun can really scorch you![2] People can turn as brown as mahogany, and in the hottest countries they can be baked black. One day, a learned man traveled from the cold countries to one of the moderately hot countries. He was sure that he would be able to go about his business just as he had back home, but he soon discovered otherwise. Along with all other sensible souls, he had to stay indoors.[3] All day long, the shutters were drawn and the doors were kept closed. It looked just as if everyone was still sleeping or not at home. The narrow street on which the man lived was lined with tall buildings and was laid out so that it was flooded with sunshine from morning until evening. It was really unbearable![4] The learned man from the cold countries—he was a young man, a clever man—felt just as if he were sitting inside a blazing hot oven. It wore him out. He grew quite thin, and even his

VILHELM PEDERSEN

The learned man is already overshadowed by his shadow as he reads at his desk. The illustration captures the drama that will unfold between the man and his shadow in a closed, claustrophobic space.

shadow began to shrink until it was much smaller than it had been at home. The sun took its toll on it as well. Not until the evening, after sundown, did the man and his shadow come back to life.[5]

It was a real pleasure to watch that happen! As soon as a candle was brought into the room, the shadow would stretch itself out all the way up the wall and would even reach the ceiling, it made itself so long. It had to stretch out like that to get its strength back. The learned man went out on the balcony to stretch, and, as soon as stars appeared in the lovely, clear sky, he also seemed to come back to life.

People appeared on all the balconies up and down the street —and in the warm countries every window has a balcony— because you have to breathe fresh air, even if you are used to being mahogany colored. Things grew quite lively, upstairs and down. Cobblers and tailors and everyone else moved out into the street. Tables appeared, then chairs, and candles were lit—there were over a thousand candles burning. One person would be talking, while another sang. People strolled down the street, carriages drove by, and donkeys trotted along, with their bells sounding *ding-a-ling-ling*. Hymns were sung as the dead were buried; urchins set off firecrackers; and church bells were ringing. Oh yes, it was very lively down in that street.[6]

Only one house stayed quiet[7]—the one directly across from where the learned man was living. Someone must have been living there, because there were flowers growing on the balcony. They were thriving, even under a hot sun, and how could they unless there was a person there to water them? Someone had to be watering them, and so there must be people living in the house. As it turns out, the door across the way was left ajar every evening, but it was completely dark inside, at least in the front room. From somewhere farther back in the house you could hear the sound of music. The learned stranger thought the music was quite fabulous, but it

trophobic living conditions. Shutters and doors close the learned man off from the world, and his contact with the outside world seems limited to the nocturnal outings on the balcony, where he appears as an observer rather than as a participant, looking onto a narrow street with tall buildings. It is precisely by shutting himself off from the world and retreating from life that the learned man creates the conditions for the separation of shadow from self. On his own trips to Italy, Andersen rarely closeted himself in and spent much of his time visiting sights, meeting literary worthies, and socializing with his fellow travelers. In his diaries, he describes the effects of the sun during a stay in Naples: "The heat from the sun followed us, becoming more and more oppressive as the sirocco blew hot and dry air; I thought as a Northerner that the heat would do me good. I should have noticed that the Neapolitans stayed at home, or crept along in the shadow of the houses, as Paar and I dashed from one museum to the next or down to the pier. Then, one day, my breathing started to fail, the sun burnt into my eyes, the rays going through my head and back, and I fainted dead away" (*Travels*, 257).

5. *did the man and his shadow come back to life.* Even at this early point in the story, the shadow has been anthropomorphized with its own identity and agency. It seems to shrink, stretch, and become animated on its own.

6. *it was very lively down in that street.* The effervescent quality of everyday life forms a sharp contrast to the quiet, hermetic existence in which scholar and shadow dwell and to the silence of the building in which Poetry dwells. The scholar, while aware of the life below, finds himself attracted more powerfully to the mysterious, silent abode. Andersen, like many

writers, found himself divided between the lively attractions of the real world and the beauty of an imaginative, inner world. The learned man, however, seems to reside in a limbo, not daring to engage with one or the other.

7. *Only one house stayed quiet.* The beauty of the flowers is the most compelling attraction of the building across from the scholar. The "fabulous" music breaks the silence of the front rooms and deepens the aura of mysterious beauty in the architectural wonder situated in the urban landscape.

8. *a strange, shimmering light on his neighbor's balcony.* It is not clear whether the enchanting maiden is dream or reality. The stranger thinks he sees a peculiar glow and is then persuaded that the flowers *are* indeed gleaming like flames, but when he opens his eyes and rouses himself "from sleep," the vision of flowers in flames and of the maiden vanishes. The vision produces uncertainty in the mind of the character and the reader. That uncertainty is symptomatic of an effect that the literary critic Tzvetan Todorov has called "the fantastic," as opposed to "the marvelous," which is truly supernatural, or "the uncanny," which is strange but not contrary to natural laws. The fantastic is the hallmark of the poetic fairy tales written by E.T.A. Hoffmann, Friedrich de la Motte Fouqué, Adelbert von Chamisso, and the other German Romantics who inspired this particular story.

is possible that he was just imagining all this, for he thought that everything in the warm countries was really marvelous, except for the sun. The stranger's landlord said that he had no idea who was renting the house across the street. No one seemed to be living there, and, as for the music, he found it terribly dreary: "It sounds as if someone is practicing a piece that is beyond him—always the exact same piece. 'I'll get it right one of these days,' he probably tells himself, but he just never does, no matter how hard he tries."

The stranger woke up once in the middle of the night. He was sleeping right near the open balcony door, and when a breeze lifted the curtain, he thought he saw a strange, shimmering light on his neighbor's balcony.[8] The flowers were glowing like flames in the most beautiful colors. Right in the middle of the flowers stood a slender, enchanting maiden, and she seemed to be glowing too. The brightness hurt his eyes, but that was because he had just woken up and opened them too wide after rousing himself so suddenly. Then he jumped out of bed and, without making a sound, peered through the curtains, but the maiden had vanished and so had the light. The flowers were no longer in flames and looked just fine, as they always did. The door was ajar, and from far inside came the sound of music so lovely and soothing that you could lose yourself in sweet thoughts. It was enchanting. But who was living there? Where was the real entrance? The entire ground floor was nothing but shops, and people couldn't constantly be walking through them.

One evening the stranger was sitting out on his balcony. In the room behind him a candle was burning, and so it was quite natural that his shadow appeared over on the wall across the way. Yes, it appeared right there with the flowers on the balcony. And whenever the stranger moved, the shadow moved too, for that is what shadows do.

"I think my shadow is the only living thing you can see over there," the learned man thought to himself. "Look how much at home it is among the flowers. The door is wide open. If only my shadow were clever enough to step inside,[9] have a look around, and come back to tell me what it had seen."

"Yes, you would be doing me a real service," he said jokingly. "Kindly step inside. Aren't you going in?" He nodded to the shadow, and the shadow nodded back at him. "Run along now, but don't get lost!"

The stranger rose, and his shadow on the opposite balcony got up with him. The stranger turned, and his shadow turned as well. If anyone had been paying attention, they would have seen the shadow enter the half-open balcony door in the house across the street at the very instant when the stranger returned to his room, letting the drapes fall behind him.

The next morning the learned man went out to drink his coffee and read the newspapers. "What's this?" he said, as he stepped out into the sunlight. "My shadow is gone! So it actually did leave me last night, and it hasn't come back. That's really irritating."

What annoyed him most was not so much the loss of his shadow as the fact that there was already a story about a man without a shadow.[10] Everyone back home in the cold countries knew that story. If he returned home and told them his own story, they would just say that he was copying the other one and shouldn't bother going on. So he decided to say nothing at all about it, and that was certainly the sensible thing to do.

That evening he went back out on the balcony. He put a candle directly behind him, because he knew that shadows always like to use their masters as a screen, but he could not entice it to come back. He made himself short, and he made himself tall, but there was just no shadow. It refused to show up. "Ahem, ahem!" he repeated, but it was no use.

This was all very annoying, but in the hot countries everything grows quite rapidly, and in a week or so he noticed to his great satisfaction that a new shadow had started grow-

9. *"If only my shadow were clever enough to step inside."* "No sooner said than done" takes on a new depth of meaning here. The learned man speaks words that work magic, for his wish is quickly—and subtly—translated into reality. He has, in a sense, willed his shadow to detach itself from him, commanding it to do what he is afraid to do. At first the shadow's moves are in concert with its owner ("the shadow moved too"), then the shadow appears to have an independent existence ("Look how much at home it is among the flowers"), and finally it actually walks in the opposite direction, entering the building across the way. Note the absence of witnesses ("If anyone had been paying attention"), a fact that emphasizes the possibility that the learned man is hallucinating.

10. *a story about a man without a shadow.* The story that everyone in the "cold countries" knows about is most likely Adelbert von Chamisso's *The Marvelous Story of Peter Schlemihl.* Chamisso's story of a man who sells his shadow to the devil became so well known that it was cited in works by E.T.A. Hoffmann ("Adventures on a New Year's Eve," written in the year *Peter Schlemihl* was published) and Nathaniel Hawthorne ("The Intelligence Office" of 1844). Note the anxiety of influence expressed in the scholar's fear that others will believe that he is simply copying another author and creating a shadow of another story. That shadow of the story of Peter Schlemihl does exactly what the shadow of the learned man does: disappear only to reappear in an unexpected new form. In Andersen's tale, the shadow detaches itself from the scholar to lead a successful, independent life.

11. *a new shadow had started growing.* The growth of a new shadow points to the possibility that the learned man is simply hallucinating, but it may also function as an event that reinforces the supernatural turn to the story once the shadow detaches itself.

12. *"I can't get over it!"* The literal meaning of the learned man's words are "I can't come to my self!" It is at this point that the text, as Clayton Koelb points out, acts out a literal meaning that is ordinarily impossible. "That 'I' should meet 'myself' is a simple matter for language," he observes, "but we do not expect that grammatical possibility to be thus transformed into practice" (Koelb, 207).

13. *"I've been following in your footsteps since childhood."* The playful rhetoric in the midst of existential crisis is characteristic of the tale's style, and here the shadow plays on the figurative and literal dimensions of language, revealing how he has, for most of his life, taken after the scholar.

ing[11] at his feet whenever he went out into the sunlight. The root must have been left behind. Within three weeks he had a decent enough shadow, which, when he set out to go back north, grew longer and longer until it became so long and broad that half of it would have been quite enough.

The learned man returned home. He wrote books about what was true in the world and what was good and what was beautiful. Days turned into years, and many years went by. Then one evening he was sitting in his parlor and heard a faint knock at the door.

"Come in," he said, but no one did. He opened the door and there before him stood a man so extraordinarily thin that it gave him an eerie sensation. The caller was, by the way, dressed faultlessly and was no doubt a distinguished fellow.

"With whom do I have the honor of speaking?" the learned man asked.

"Oh," the distinguished visitor said. "I had a feeling you wouldn't recognize me now that I've put some flesh on my body and have some clothes on. You probably never expected to see me in such fine shape. Can't you tell that I'm your former shadow? You probably didn't think I would ever show up again. Everything has gone exceptionally well for me since I last saw you. I've become a wealthy man in every way, and, if I have to buy my freedom, I can." With that, he rattled a bunch of valuable seals hanging from his watch and began to stroke a massive gold chain around his neck. His fingers seemed to glitter from all the diamond rings on them. And the jewelry was all real.

"I can't get over it!"[12] the learned man said. "What can this all mean?"

"It's definitely not something you see every day," the shadow said. "But then you're also no ordinary man, and, as you know, I've been following in your footsteps since childhood.[13] As soon as you thought I was mature enough to go out into the world on my own, I went my way. And now I find myself in splendid circumstances, but a strange longing to see you one last time before you die overcame me. You are going to die, you know! I always wanted to return to this region, because we all love our homeland. I know that you have a new shadow. Do I owe you—or it—anything?[14] Please let me know if I do."

"Is it really you?" asked the learned man. "This is highly unusual. I would never have imagined a shadow could return as a human being."

"Just let me know what I owe," the shadow said, "because I don't want to be in anyone's debt."

"How can you talk like that?" the learned man said. "What kind of debt are we talking about? You're as free as anyone else. I'm just delighted to learn of your good fortune. Sit down, old friend, and tell me how all this came about and what you saw in the house across the street in the hot country."

"I'll tell you all about it," the shadow said, sitting down. "But you must promise me that if we run into each other in town, you won't tell a soul that I was once your shadow. I'm considering getting engaged, and I'm wealthy enough to support more than one family."

"Don't worry," the learned man said. "I won't tell anyone who you really are. Let's shake on it. I promise, and a man is as good as his word."[15]

"And a word is as good as its—shadow," the shadow replied, for that was the only thing it could say.

It was really quite remarkable how human the shadow had become. It was dressed in

14. *"Do I owe you—or it—anything?"* Note how the shadow here, in acknowledging the new shadow as "it," also validates the division of self and shadow even as he sets up a hierarchy that privileges the learned man ("you") over his shadow ("it"). The shadow seems to have the success in commerce that the learned man himself never achieved.

KAY NIELSEN

The shadow appears at the home of the learned man. He is dressed in black and carries in one hand the flat top hat and wears diamond rings, along with a watch on a chain. Confident and debonair, he cuts a dashing figure on the moonlit evening.

15. *"a man is as good as his word."* In this key dialogue between the man and his shadow, the learned man asserts that a man is his word and his shadow declares that a word is his shadow. Both man and shadow have the word in common, and, in this rhetorical sleight-of-hand, it becomes evident that, through language, man and shadow can reverse their positions, as they do in Andersen's narrative. As soon as shadow and learned man take these oaths, the shadow begins to take over the life of the man.

16. *It was dressed in black.* The shadow, appropriately, wears clothing that reflects his true identity, including a hat that can be closed so that only the crown and brim (for which the Danish word is "shadow") remain. At the same time, he wears brilliant, costly jewelry—gold and diamonds that point to his wealth and to the fact that he has, at least in part, transcended his dark existence and affiliated himself with the bright light of art, even if in its vulgar, material manifestation.

17. *didn't move or make a sound.* The second shadow, which has grown as a replacement for the first, seems also to have human qualities. Note that the first shadow contemplates the possibility of obtaining the scholar's second shadow, perhaps to facilitate his full transformation into a man. Unlike the learned man, the shadow has "a root" and can continue to grow new copies of itself.

18. *"Poetry!"* The learned man had perceived the building across the way as an enchanted world (*en Trolddom*), and he discovers, retrospectively, that the maiden he saw was Poetry, a figure who appears at nighttime, but with a brightness rivaling that of the sun, "as radiant as the Northern lights." Like the sun, the maiden creates a lethal abundance of light, enough to

black,[16] with clothes made from the finest cloth, and it was wearing patent-leather shoes along with a top hat that could be pressed perfectly flat until only brim and top remained, not to mention what we have already seen—those seals, the gold chain, and the diamond rings. Yes, indeed, the shadow was exceptionally well dressed, and that's just why it appeared to be so human.

"Well, let me tell you!" the shadow said, stepping down as hard as it could with those new patent-leather shoes on the sleeve of the learned man's new shadow, which lay like a poodle at his feet. Maybe this was arrogance, but maybe it was just trying to make the new shadow stick to his own feet. The shadow on the floor didn't move or make a sound.[17] It was no doubt listening carefully so that it could learn how to win its freedom and someday become its own master.

"Do you know who was living in the house across the street?" the shadow said. "She was the most beautiful of all creatures—Poetry herself. I was there for three weeks, and I might as well have been there for three thousand years, reading everything that has ever been written. That's what I'm telling you, and it's the truth. I've seen everything, and I know everything."

"Poetry!"[18] the learned man cried. "Oh, yes, yes—she often keeps to herself in the big cities. Poetry! Yes, I saw her myself, for one brief moment, but my eyes were heavy with sleep. She was standing on the balcony, as radiant as the Northern lights. Tell me more! Tell me more! You were up on the balcony. You went through the door, and then—"

"And then I was standing in the antechamber," the shadow said. "You used to stare into that room all the time from across the street. There were no candles in there, and the room was in a kind of twilight. But one door after another stood open in a long row of brilliantly lit halls and rooms. The blaze of lights would have killed me if I had gone all the way into the room where the maiden was. I was level-headed and took my time—that's what you have to do under those circumstances."

"And what did you see?" the learned man asked.

"I saw everything, and I'll tell you all about it. But—and I'm not saying this to be arrogant—if you take into account that I'm a free man with considerable talents, not to mention my social position and my considerable fortune, it makes sense for you to address me in a more formal manner,[19] and I would be grateful for the courtesy."

"I beg your pardon, Sir!" the learned man said. "I'm just falling back into an old habit that is hard to change. You're perfectly right, and I'll be more careful now. But now, sir, tell me about everything that you saw."

"Everything!" the shadow said. "You realize, then, that I saw everything and that I know everything."

"What did it look like all the way back?" the learned man asked. "Was it like a green forest?[20] Was it like a holy temple? Was it like the starry skies when you stand high up on a mountain?"

"Everything was there," the shadow said. "I didn't go all the way inside, as you know. I stayed in that antechamber in the twilight, but that was the perfect place to be. I saw everything, and I know everything. I have been in the antechamber of Poetry's court."

"But what did you see? Did the ancient gods march through the halls? Were the heroes of times past fighting there? Were sweet children playing there and talking about their dreams?"

"I'm telling you, I was there, and you have to realize that I saw everything there was to see. Had you come over there, it would not have made a man of you, but it did make a man of me. I learned to understand my innermost nature, what I was born with, and my connection with Poetry.[21] Yes, back when I was living with you, I never thought at all about such matters. But you must remember how astonishingly large I

have "killed" the shadow, who cannot tolerate too much brightness, given his dark nature (shades of the mole in "Thumbelina"). The encounter between the dark shadow and the bright spirit of Poetry allegedly leads to knowledge ("I've seen everything, and I know everything") and also gives flesh to the shadow, but, ironically, it appears to have turned him into a cynical, sinister figure who uses his shadowy abilities to intimidate others, betray the learned man, and dupe the princess.

19. *"address me in a more formal manner."* In Danish, as in French and many other languages, a distinction is made between the formal "you" (*De*) and the familiar "you" (*Du*). During their first encounter, the man uses the familiar *Du*, and the shadow speaks with the man using *De* until finally insisting on also being addressed with *De*. Andersen himself had been deeply humiliated when his offer to Edvard Collin (the son of his benefactor) to shift to the *Du* form of address was rejected. On May 28, 1831, Collin wrote to him: "There is something that I simply can't explain in my reaction. . . . When someone I've known for a long time—a person I admire and like—invites me to use *Du*, I develop a mysteriously unpleasant reaction."

20. *"Was it like a green forest?"* The learned man assumes that either verdant nature or powerful spiritual beings will occupy the halls of Poetry. His reference to the "starry sky" could be alluding to Kant's declaration, from the *Critique of Practical Reason* (1788), that he was moved to awe and wonder by "the starry sky above me and the quiet law within me." Those words were chosen by Kant's friends for his tombstone and became a commonplace expression.

21. *"connection with Poetry."* As an entity affiliated with darkness and shady matters,

the shadow claims to be completely at home in the sphere of poetry. Dwelling there, he manages to discover his innermost being and to develop depth despite the fact that he is a two-dimensional being. Poetry here fulfills its mission of cultivating profundity, but it does not succeed in achieving moral improvement of any kind.

22. *"because I know you won't put it in a book."* The learned man has not only liberated his shadow by declaring it to be free, he has also abdicated the power to tell his story because he fears being perceived as an imitator. This double disavowal, first of his shadow, then of his narrative voice, deepens the identity crisis he faces even as it is symptomatic of an attempt to achieve singularity. "The Shadow" is, of course, told by a third-person omniscient narrator, not by the learned man.

23. *"I ran up and down the streets."* The shadow, despite the fact that he has become a man, still resembles a shadow. That he stays at home when it rains (a time when shadows disappear) is further evidence that he has not completely evolved into a human being.

24. *"I saw what no one else could, or should, see."* The shadow asserts his kinship with poetry and describes himself as a creature who can pry, eavesdrop, and snoop, gaining access to the secret life of the soul. And yet he does not translate this knowledge into any kind of poetic insight, using his observations for nothing other than venal purposes. Dickens, to whom Andersen had paid a visit in 1857 when he traveled to London, writes about a proposed commentator for a periodical he was planning and sketches a character much like Andersen's spectral figure: "a certain SHADOW, which may go into any place, by sunlight, moonlight, starlight, fire-

became at sunrise and sunset. And the moonlight made me almost more visible than you. I didn't understand myself at the time, but in that antechamber, I came to know my true nature. I became a man and returned completely transformed. But you were no longer in the hot regions. Being a man, I was ashamed to be seen as I was. I needed boots, clothing, and all the surface polish that makes a person recognizable.

"I went into hiding—and I'm going to tell you this because I know you won't put it in a book[22]—under the skirts of the woman who sells cakes. That woman had no idea how much she was concealing. I didn't venture out until evening, and then I ran through the streets in the moonlight and stretched myself tall against the walls. It really tickled my back. I ran up and down the streets,[23] taking peeks into the highest windows, into parlors and into garrets. I looked in where no one else could look. I saw what no one else could, or should, see.[24] If truth be told, it's a nasty world. I wouldn't even want to be human except that everyone seems to think that it's so grand. I saw the most unthinkable things going on between men and women, and between parents and their perfectly darling children."

"I saw," the shadow continued, "what nobody knows but what everyone would like to know, the scandalous behavior next door. If I had written a newspaper, everyone would have been reading it! Instead I just wrote to the people directly involved, and everywhere I went there was a huge uproar. They were terrified of me, but they also became terribly fond of me. The professors appointed me a professor, and the tailors made me new clothes—in fact, my wardrobe is almost complete. The master of the mint coined new money for me, and women told me that I was quite handsome. And so I became the man I am now. For now I must bid you farewell. Here's my card. I live on the sunny side of the street, and I am always at home when it rains." And off he went.

"That was really strange," the learned man said.

Days and years passed, and the shadow called again. "How are you doing?" he asked.

"Not so well, I'm afraid," the learned man said. "I'm still writing about the good, the true, and the beautiful,[25] but no one wants to hear about such things. I'm in utter despair, because I take it all personally."

"Well, I don't," said the shadow. "I'm putting on weight, and that's what we all should try to do. You don't understand the ways of the world, and that's why your health is suffering. You really have to get away. I'm taking a trip this summer. Would you like to join me? I'd enjoy having a traveling companion. Will you come along as my shadow? It would be such a pleasure to have you accompany me, and I'll even pay all the expenses."

"That's going too far," the learned man said.

"It all depends on how you look at it," said the shadow. "It would do you a world of good to travel. If you promise to be my shadow, the trip won't cost you a thing."

"This has gone far enough!" the learned man declared.

"But that's how the world is," the shadow told him. "And that's how it will always be." And off he went.

Things were not going well at all for the learned man. Misfortune and all kinds of trouble plagued him, and what he had to say about the good, the true, and the beautiful was as appealing to most people as roses are to a cow. In the end, he became quite ill.

"You look like a shadow of yourself," people said to him, and the learned man would tremble because it made him stop to think.

"You really have to spend some time at a spa," the shadow told him when he came for a return visit. "It isn't really a matter of choice. I'll take you with me for old times' sake. I'll pay for the trip, and you can write up an account and do your best to amuse me along the way. I need some time at a spa as well, for my whiskers are just not growing out the way they

light, candlelight, and be in all homes, and all nooks and corners, and be supposed to be cognizant of everything, and go everywhere, without the least difficulty. . . . a kind of semi-omniscient, omnipresent, intangible creature" (Forster, II 419–20). Like the nightingale in the tale of that title and the daughters of the air who appear at the end of "The Little Mermaid," the shadow has the capacity to supervise and surreptitiously monitor behavior.

25. *"the good, the true, and the beautiful."* The learned man is committed to a Platonic vision in which reality is nothing but a refraction of the world of ideas in which the good, the true, and the beautiful are one. His search for the good, the true, and the beautiful reveals an inability to engage with reality, and that inability has real consequences, for the shadow emerges to claim all the materialistic, venal, sinister traits that the learned man has worked so hard to purge from his life.

26. *The shadow was now the master, and the master was the shadow.* Despite the fact that the shadow does not become fully human, he begins the process of overshadowing his host. The learned man has become nothing more than a shadow of himself. The interplay between shadow and self continues in a verbally playful manner but in a situation charged with malice. The learned man may be kind and gentle, but his shadow operates with calculation and ruthlessness, aiming for a complete reversal of positions.

27. *"to call you by yours."* The shadow claims to meet the learned man halfway, but he is, of course, gaining the upper hand by offering to use the informal form of address. The reversal in forms of address marks the point at which subjection becomes complete. The shadow has now become "the real master."

28. *the disease of being able to see too well.* The princess suffers from a malady that the shadow may well understand, since he has "seen everything." That she immediately perceives the shadow's lack of a shadow and understands that the failure to grown a beard is simply a cover for deeper problems suggests that she may have some redeeming virtues, but in fact she is easily taken in by the shadow and proves less insightful than she initially appears. She may see too much, but she cannot see through the shadow and his machinations.

should be. That's a trial as well, because you can't get along without a beard. Come now, be reasonable and accept my proposal. We'll travel together, just like friends!"

And off they went. The shadow was now the master, and the master was the shadow.[26] They drove together; they rode together; they walked together, side by side, in front or in back, depending on where the sun stood in the sky. The shadow made sure that it always took the lead, and the learned man himself didn't spend much time thinking about it, for he was a kindhearted person, exceedingly amiable and gentle. One day he said to the shadow: "Now that we have become traveling companions and because we have been together since childhood, shouldn't we call each other by our first names? That would be much more agreeable."

"You have a point there," said the shadow, who was now the true master. "What you say is very candid and tactful, and so I will be equally candid and tactful with you. As a learned man, you are perfectly well aware of how strange human nature can be. Some people cannot bear to touch gray paper—it makes them feel queasy. Others recoil when they hear the sound of a nail scraping against a windowpane. As for me, I have a queasy sensation when I imagine you calling me by my first name. I feel pressed down to the ground just as I was in my former position with you. As you can see, it's just a feeling—it has nothing at all to do with arrogance. I just can't let you call me by my first name. But I'm entirely happy to meet you halfway and to call you by yours."[27] And from then on, the shadow called his former master by his first name.

"This has really gone too far," the learned man thought. "Now I'm calling him by his last name and he is using my first name." But he had to put up with it.

They arrived at last at the spa, where there were many people from foreign lands, among them a beautiful princess. She was suffering from the disease of being able to see too well,[28] and that can be highly distressing. She noticed right away that the newcomer was a very different sort of person from all the rest. "They say he is spending time here so that his beard will grow. But the real reason is obvious to me. He can't cast a shadow."

Once her curiosity was aroused, the princess went out for a stroll and struck up a conversation with the stranger. As the daughter of a king, she could come right to the point, and so she said, "Your problem is that you can't cast a shadow."

"Your Royal Highness must have improved considerably!" the shadow replied. "I know that you suffer from seeing things far too clearly. But you are getting over it, and I see that you are just about cured. As a matter of fact, I have a most unusual shadow. Do you see that fellow who is always by my side? Other people have ordinary shadows, but I'm not fond of the ordinary. Some people give their servants finer livery than they themselves wear. In that spirit, I've dressed up my shadow as a man. As you can see, I've even outfitted him with a shadow of his own. Yes, it's very expensive, but it's worth it to have something unique."

"What?" the Princess thought to herself. "Can it be true that I've recovered? This is the best spa anywhere, and these days the waters are said to have wonderful medicinal powers. But I'm not planning on leaving now, because this place is just starting to become interesting. I've taken a liking to that stranger. I just hope that his beard doesn't start to grow, because then he'll leave."

That evening, the princess and the shadow danced in the grand ballroom. She was light on her feet, but he was even lighter.[29] She had never danced with a partner like that. She told him the name of the country she was from, and he knew it well. He had spent some time there, but while she had been away. He had peeked in every window, high and low. He had seen this, and he had seen that. And so he found it easy to talk with the princess and to make references that astonished her. She was convinced that he had to be the wisest man on earth.

29. *She was light on her feet, but he was even lighter.* The narrator continues to engage in word play, with the shadow, despite his darkness, being "light," if only in the sense of insubstantial and without weight.

30. *"What a man he must be to have such a wise shadow!"* It is telling that the learned man retains the quality that has been his chief attribute all along, as signaled in the adjective "learned." In the end, however, even his intellect is appropriated through the clever ruse of the shadow, who understands how to get the upper hand on every count.

His knowledge impressed her deeply, and, when they started dancing again, she fell in love with him. The shadow was aware of this, for she was practically looking right through him. Then they danced again, and she came very close to telling him, but she hesitated. She really had to consider her country and her throne, as well as all the people she would rule in her kingdom.

"He's a wise man," she said to herself. "And that's all to the good. He's a superb dancer, and that's also good. But I wonder if he has a deep knowledge of things—that's just as important. I'll have to test him." She began asking more difficult questions, questions she herself could never have answered. The shadow gave her a strange look.

"You can't answer my questions?" asked the king's daughter.

"They are mere child's play," said the shadow. "Even my shadow over there by the door could answer those questions."

"Your shadow!" said the princess. "That would be quite remarkable."

"I'm not saying for certain," the shadow said. "But I believe he can, because he has been following me around all these years and paying attention. Yes, I'm inclined to think he can. But if Your Royal Highness will permit, I must explain that he is so proud of being able to pass for human that, if you want to put him in a good mood—and he will have to be in a good mood in order to answer properly—you will have to treat him as if he were a regular human being."

"That's fine with me!" the princess replied.

And so she walked over to the learned man, who was standing in the doorway. She talked with him about the sun and the moon, and about people, what they are like on the inside as well as on the outside. He answered her wisely and well.

"What a man he must be to have such a wise shadow!"[30] she thought. "What a blessing it would be for my people and for my kingdom if I were to marry him. And that's just what I'm going to do."

The princess and the shadow soon came to an understanding, but no one was to know anything until after she had returned to her kingdom.

"No one. Not even my shadow!" the shadow said. And he had his reasons for saying that.

They arrived at last in the country where the princess ruled when she was at home.

"Listen, my good friend," the shadow said to the learned man. "Now that I am as happy and powerful as anyone can be, I'd like to do something special for you. You can live with me in the castle, drive around with me in the royal carriage, and make a hundred thousand a year. But in return you will have to let everyone call you a shadow, and you can never claim that you were once a human being. Once a year, when I'm sitting on the balcony in the sunshine, you must lie at my feet as shadows do. I am planning on marrying the king's daughter, and the wedding is to take place tonight."

"No! That's going too far," said the learned man. "I refuse. I refuse to do it! That would mean betraying the entire country and the princess as well. I'm going to tell everyone the whole story[31]—that I'm the man and that you are just a shadow dressed up like a man."

"No one will believe you," the shadow said. "Be reasonable, or I'll call the guards."

"I'm going straight to the princess," the learned man said.

"But I'll get there before you," said the shadow. "And you are going to jail." And that's exactly where he went, because the guards decided to obey the man who was going to marry the princess.

"You're trembling," the princess said, when the shadow came into her room. "Has something happened? You mustn't get ill on the night that we are going to be married."

31. *"I'm going to tell everyone the whole story."* The scholar decides to tell his story at last, but too late to ensure his own survival. Ironically, he fails to write about himself for fear of being perceived as an imitator, and ends up, not just as a shadow of himself, but as a shadow of his shadow, doomed to mime his every move. Storytelling has been linked with survival ever since the time of Scheherazade, who told her thousand and one tales to delay her execution by King Shariyar. For the scholar, the impulse to tell his story and thereby save his life comes too late, for the shadow has already secured the power he needs to engineer an execution.

"I have just been through the most dreadful experience you can imagine!" said the shadow. "Just think! Well, I suppose a poor shadow's brain can't take very much. But imagine! My shadow has gone mad. He thinks that he is a human, and—picture this—he takes me for his shadow."

"That's horrifying!" said the princess. "He's locked up, isn't he?"

"Oh, of course. But I doubt he will ever recover."

"Poor shadow," said the princess. "He must be terribly unhappy. It would be an act of compassion to liberate him from the little bit of life left in him. If I stop to think about it, there's no choice but to do away with him—very quietly."

"How painful that is," the shadow said. "He was such a loyal servant." And he managed to let out what sounded like a sigh.

"What a noble character you have," the princess declared.

VILHELM PEDERSEN

The shadow and the princess appear on the balcony to acknowledge the cheering crowds at their wedding ceremony.

That evening the entire city was brightly lit. The cannons boomed, and the soldiers presented their arms. It was quite a wedding![32] The princess and the shadow appeared on the balcony to be admired by all, and they received another round of cheers.

The learned man didn't hear any of that, for by then they had taken his life.[33]

KAY NIELSEN

The shadow itself (or the shadow of the shadow), in silhouette against the prison, gazes down at the cross marking what is presumably the gravesite of the learned man.

32. *It was quite a wedding!* Ending like a fairy tale, with a wedding between the title character and a princess and the execution of a "villain," the story also violates the conventions of the fairy tale in perverse ways, punishing the figure who seeks the good, the true, and the beautiful while rewarding the sinister character who uses deception to win the hand of a princess. "The Shadow" is a kind of anti–fairy tale, reversing the terms of the genre. Only a few of Andersen's fairy tales end happily with marriages, and tales like "The Tinderbox" and "Thumbelina," for example, are closer to anomalies than representative tales.

33. *they had taken his life.* The final sentence can be read as having a double meaning, for the shadow and the princess kill the scholar but also take their life from him—that is, they exist because of him. "The Shadow" can be read as a fable about how characters take their life from their authors and then, once they become "immortal," also outlast their authors, putting them in the shade. Andersen had originally planned to have the learned man beheaded, but friends urged him to tone down the violence. Koelb notes that the conclusion takes us into morally troubled waters but also points to an artistic triumph: "Although the shadow has succeeded in wiping his master from the page, 'The Shadow' has effectively displaced another progenitor, Chamisso's *Peter Schlemihl*. The defeat of the author, his absolute destruction in terms of the plot, is his great victory" (Koelb, 220). "The Shadow" is not at all about a "once-upon-a-time" existence in which a character emerges from a position of subordination to defeat villains and live happily ever after. It stages the struggles of a self divided against itself and reveals that we ourselves sometimes produce our worst enemies.

The Psyche[1]

Psychen

Nye Eventyr og Historier. Anden Samling, 1862

1. *Psyche.* In Apuleius's story "Cupid and Psyche" from the second century A.D., Psyche, whose name is the Greek word for "soul," disobeys her husband Cupid and lights a lamp in order to see him. When Cupid flees, Psyche pursues him, undertaking a series of tasks, which, although not successfully completed, lead to a reunion with the beloved and bestow on Psyche immortality. The deep irony of the artist's quest in Andersen's story becomes apparent with the realization that, in the ancient story, Psyche acquires immortality through her marriage to a figure who embodies Eros. The two give birth to a child named Pleasure. The soul is represented in many cultures as a butterfly (symbol of metamorphosis) that leaves the body at the moment of death.

Andersen reported that this story was inspired by an incident that took place in Rome: a beautiful statue of Bacchus was unearthed when a grave was being dug for a young nun. The blend of allusions to the myths of classical antiquity and the biblical stories of sin and redemption also connect Andersen's story to the German Romantics, particularly E.T.A. Hoffmann and Josef von Eichendorff, who were enamored of Italy and used it as the setting for their novellas. Albert Küchler, a Danish artist who became a monk, may have been the model for the sculptor in "The Psyche."

"The Psyche" was published the same year as Andersen's "The Ice Maiden," a terrifying tale about an icy kiss of death from a Nordic femme fatale. In Stravinsky's musical adaptation of that tale for the ballet Le baiser de la fée (1928), the fairy in the title is a muse who captures the hero for the world of art. From the start, with his first novel The Improvisatore, Andersen was troubled by the nature of art, which aspires to the divine but often descends into the demonic. In "The Psyche," as in "The Shadow" and other works written in the last decade of his life, he was committed to exploring the complications of a life devoted to creativity and to a cult of beauty.

At dawn, a large star, the bright morning star, shines through the red clouds. Its beams tremble on the white wall,[2] as if it were planning to write a story there about everything it has seen here and there over the thousands of years it has looked down on our earth as it rotates.

Let's listen to one of its tales.

A short time ago—although the star's short time ago is centuries in human time—my beams shone down on a young artist.[3] He was living in the city of the popes, in Rome, one of the world's greatest capitals. Many things have changed there since that time,[4] but they have not changed as quickly as humans alter in the course of moving from childhood to old age. The imperial fortress was then, as now, a site of ruins. Fig trees and laurels were growing among the upturned columns, and, in the baths, the walls were still gleaming with gold even though they had been destroyed. The Coliseum stood in ruins. Church bells were ringing, and the fragrance of incense filled the air as processions with lighted candles and magnificent canopies passed through the streets. A holy event was

LORENZ FRØLICH

2. *Its beams tremble on the white wall.* The star is identified as the story's first narrator and makes an attempt to write the story down with its rays as pen. But that act of writing remains in the realm of "as if," and the star ends up *telling* the first part of the story. Although the morning star seems to witness much of what happens, the narrator occasionally has access to events that are not seen by the star ("the bright star did not report it"). The artist in the story may be haunted by anxieties about usurping God's power to create life, but the narrator remains supremely untroubled by any possible rivalry between him and the star, who witnesses the events and tries unsuccessfully to write them down. The two seem to work in partnership, with the star as the oral teller of the tale, and the narrator as scribe, a figure who engages in the very same activity as the artist by trying to create the semblance of reality through his art.

3. *a young artist.* Ironically, the artist, who is intent on making a name for himself, is never given a name in the story. Unlike Raphael and Leonardo, who inspire him, he remains unknown. He may have been modeled in part on the Danish sculptor Bertel Thorvaldsen, who moved to Rome in 1797 and did not return to Copenhagen until 1838. While visiting Thorvaldsen in Rome, Andersen mentioned that the sculptor's statue of Pontius Pilate was dressed more like an Egyptian than a Roman. Thorvaldsen destroyed the figure and Andersen was scolded for having forced the artist "to destroy an immortal work" (*Travels*, 234–35).

4. *Many things have changed there since that time.* The notion of metamorphosis is introduced right away in a story that sets up oppositions between permanence and change, death and immortality, the fleeting and the durable. It is no accident that

the events take place in Rome, a site known as "the eternal city" even as it stands in ruins. The city had been Andersen's travel destination on more than one occasion. Teeming with life, with lights, sounds, and scents, Rome is also seen as a place of decay and bears everywhere the signs of destruction. Ruins can be particularly attractive because they show nature reclaiming culture even as they display the remnants of that culture.

5. *Raphael.* In a diary entry of 1833, Andersen describes seeing Raphael's representation of Psyche: "Went to the Palazzo Farazina, where Raphael and his pupils had painted the story of Psyche in a fresco on the ceiling." Raphael died in 1520, and Michaelangelo lived until 1564. "The Psyche" is therefore set in sixteenth-century Renaissance Italy. In 1833, Andersen visited Raphael's villa and drew a sketch of it. He was impressed by the violets growing in the garden and sent a pressed violet from the garden to a friend.

6. *Art was supported, revered, and rewarded.* The high status of art and the deference paid to it by the Pope stand in apparent contrast to modern times. The nostalgic view of a golden age in which art and religion were in harmony rather than in competition reflects Romantic views that originated in Germany and England and migrated to Scandinavian countries.

taking place, and art too was hallowed and considered sacred. The world's greatest painter, Raphael,[5] and the greatest sculptor of his time, Michelangelo, were living in Rome at the time. The Pope himself held both in high esteem and honored them with his visits. Art was supported, revered, and rewarded.[6] Nonetheless, not all talents and abilities were seen and acknowledged, even back then.

Down a little, narrow street, there was an old house that had once been a temple. In it lived a young artist, poor and unknown but with many young friends—artists all, young in spirit, mind, and thought. They told the artist that he was blessed with talent and skill but that he was a fool for lacking confidence in those abilities. He was always destroying what he had sculpted from clay. Never satisfied with what he made, he could not finish anything, and of course you had to be able to do that if you wanted to be known, celebrated, and make a living.

"You're a dreamer!" his friends told him. "And that is your misfortune! Your problem is that you haven't yet lived and enjoyed life in the way that it should be savored, in great big healthy doses. It is precisely when you are young that you can and should become one with life! Look at the great master Raphael, whom the Pope honors. He is not beyond enjoying bread and wine."

"I'll say. And he's likely to gobble up the girl at the bakery too, the charming Fornarina," said Angelo, one of the rowdiest of the artist's young friends.

Yes, indeed, the friends all weighed in on the matter, each according to his age and attitude. They were intent on drawing the young artist into a life of merriment, wildness, what could also be called madness. And sometimes, for a moment, he would feel the desire to succumb. His blood was hot, and he had a lively imagination. Occasionally he would join in the spirited banter and laugh noisily with the others. But the thought of what they called "Raphael's carefree way of living" disappeared like the morning mists when he saw the divine brilliance of the master's great paintings or when he stood in the Vatican before the beautiful statues that great artists had shaped from blocks of marble so long ago. His chest would heave deeply with longing, and he could feel a power—noble, holy, uplifting, great and good—inspiring him to create the same kinds of figures, to carve them from marble. He was determined to create an image of what made his heart soar up to the firmament. But how and in what shape? His hands molded soft clay effortlessly into beautiful shapes, but the very next day, as always, he would destroy what he had created.

One day, he happened to pass by an opulent palace, one of many in Rome, and he paused before a wide entrance with open gates and saw inside colonnades adorned with statues, surrounding a little garden filled with the most beautiful roses. Enormous white calla lilies with lush green leaves were growing in the basin of a marble fountain, where clear water was splashing. The contours of a delicate, graceful, marvelously beautiful young woman could be seen gliding through the garden and past the fountain—the daughter of the noble family living there. He had never before seen such a beautiful woman. Wait! Once before he had seen a beauty like that, painted by Raphael, painted as Psyche, in a Roman palace. Yes, her portrait had been there, and here she had come to life and was walking around.[7]

The artist carried her image in his heart and thoughts. When he returned to his humble quarters, he began to mold a Psyche in clay. The figure was the wealthy, young daughter of Rome, a noble maiden, and, for the first time ever, he was satisfied with his work. It meant something to him: it was she. When his friends saw the statue, they were overjoyed. Here was the work of true genius that they had always known to be there and that the world would now also appreciate.

7. *here she had come to life and was walking around.* Like photographs, shadows, and mirrors, paintings have been seen as producing doubles that both capture the soul and can take on a life of their own. The animated portrait has a venerable history, reaching back to folktales from China, India, and Persia that depict subjects stepping out of their framed representations. Andersen, like Poe, Hawthorne, Wilde, and other nineteenth-century writers, draws on the theme to illuminate the complex relationship between an artist and his work and to reflect on the power of artists, who ceaselessly violate the biblical taboo against making images and who fashion lifelike figures that rival God's creation. ("Thou shalt not make unto thee a graven image, nor any manner of likeness of any thing that is in Heaven above or that is in the earth beneath or that is in the water under the earth," Exodus 20:4–5.)

8. *This Psyche had to come to life in marble.* Among the many mythological references embedded in the tale, the story of Pygmalion is the most pertinent. Ovid's *Metamorphoses* contains one story about a sculptor who has no interest in the women of Cyprus and, inspired by an image of Aphrodite, carves a woman out of ivory. He falls in love with the statue, and Aphrodite, taking pity on him, brings the statue to life. Andersen's artist, like Pygmalion, creates a statue from an already-existing work of art—an image of an image—even if he claims to be creating the image of the Roman maiden.

9. *soiling its purity.* In Andersen's work, the sublime can coexist with the impure, polluted, or grotesque, often undermining the transcendent values attributed to a person or thing. Gutters, garbage heaps, and refuse serve as reminders of mortality, decay, and transience.

10. *but it also crushed him!* Much as the artist appears to be enamored of the young Roman girl, he feels mortified when he realizes that he cannot duplicate the enchanting smile of the living woman.

Clay is supple and lifelike, but it does not possess the whiteness and permanence of marble. This Psyche had to come to life in marble,[8] and the artist already owned a precious slab of marble. For years, it had taken up space in his parents' courtyard, with broken glass, stalks of cabbage, and artichoke leaves collecting around it and soiling its purity.[9] But on the inside, the slab was as white as shining mountaintops covered with snow. Psyche would emerge from this piece of marble.

Now, it happened one day (the morning star did not report this because it never knew about it, even though we do) that a party of Romans stopped in the narrow, uninviting street. The carriage in which they were traveling was parked at the top of the street, and the visitors walked down to the house in order to see the young artist's work, which they had learned about only by chance. Who were these distinguished visitors? Poor young man! Or should we call him a young man who will become happy, perhaps too happy? The young maiden herself was right there in his dwelling, and what a smile broke out on her face when her father declared: "Why, it's your image, as you live and breathe!" That smile, that gaze—what a wondrous look she gave the young artist! It cannot be carved, and it cannot be created. It was a look that inspired him and ennobled him—but it also crushed him![10]

"Psyche must be realized in marble," the rich gentleman proclaimed. And those were words of life for the dead clay and for the heavy marble block, just as they animated the young man, who was deeply moved. "When you have completed the work, I shall buy it," the noble gentleman added.

It was as if the humble studio had suddenly come to life. It was lit up by joy and good cheer, and accompanied by a buzz of activity. The bright morning star watched as the work progressed. The clay itself had come to life since *she* had been there. It molded itself into the familiar features with heightened beauty.

"Finally I know what life is!" the artist rejoiced. "It is love! It is sacred devotion to the ecstatic rapture of losing yourself in beauty! What my friends called life and pleasure is as unreal and as fleeting as the bubbles made by yeast in dough. It has nothing to do with the pure, divine altar wine that consecrates life."[11]

The marble block was hoisted into place, and the chisel began to cut away large chunks. Measurements were taken; points and lines were drawn on the stone; the work of the craftsman was done. Before long, the stone began to transform itself into Psyche, a figure of beauty as graceful and perfect as God's own image of the maiden.[12] The weighty stone was turned into a hovering, graceful, sprightly Psyche with the smile of divine innocence that had been captured in the mirror of the young sculptor's heart.

The star of the rosy-colored dawn saw it and knew right away what was stirring the young man's soul. It understood why his cheeks kept changing color and why his eyes were flashing while he was representing what God had created.

"You are like one of the masters from ancient Greek times," his friends told him. "Soon the entire world will be admiring your Psyche!"

"My Psyche," he repeated. "Mine! Yes, she must be mine! I am like one of the artists of old who are no longer with us! God has given me this divine gift and raised me to be the equal of nobles!"[13]

He fell to his knees and wept tears of gratitude to God. But he soon forgot about God and thought only of her and of her image in marble—*his* Psyche who was standing there as if she had been formed of snow,[14] blushing in the morning sunlight.

He was supposed to go see her—the living, breathing Psyche, whose words were like music. Finally he could announce the news in the stately palace that the marble Psyche was finished. He entered the gates, crossed the open courtyard,

11. *"divine altar wine that consecrates life."* This allusion to the yeast used to make bread and also to altar wine is one of many references to bread and wine, and wine's sustaining influence. Unlike Raphael, who appreciated the value of both bread and wine, the artist makes a distinction between the two. The symbolic power of the sacrament figures importantly in a story about art's power to represent the soul.

12. *as graceful and perfect as God's own image of the maiden.* The artist's creation is repeatedly set in opposition to God's creation of man. Adam was made from what has variously been translated as dust, earth, and clay, and God breathed life into him. The artist too begins with clay, then translates his clay image into the refined purity of marble. The sacred breath may never enter his creation, but the statue endures long after God's own image in the maiden is gone.

13. *"the equal of nobles!"* The aspirations of the artist go beyond sculpture. His success, he believes, will lead to social mobility as well as to fame, a connection that was not trivial in Andersen's mind.

14. *as if she had been formed of snow.* The white of the statue is compared repeatedly to snow, to icy mountaintops, and to other natural marvels. The artist's art consists precisely of creating something that does not appear to be artifice but rather is completely natural. Through snow, the statue comes to be linked with Andersen's other women in white: the Snow Queen and the Ice Maiden, both deadly to men.

15. *Is a volcano aware that its eruptions produce fiery lava?* In *The Improvisatore*, Andersen describes an amorous encounter using the same terms, but literally in this case, rather than figuratively, since the protagonist, Antonio, lives in Naples: "When I reached the street, everything was in flames, just like my blood! A current of air blew the heat toward me. Vesuvius was glowing with flames—eruptions followed one another rapidly, illuminating everything around. . . . The sea was shining like the fire of the red lava, which was rolling down the mountain. Wherever I looked, I could see her standing there, as if painted with flames."

16. *"Go away! Get out of my sight!"* The young woman's words anticipate what the artist will say first to himself after the night of revelry, then to the statue of Psyche when he lowers it into the well, and finally to his friend Angelo who tries to persuade him to return to life. In this last instance, the artist uses the term "Apage Satanas," emphasizing a need to exorcise the devil. On two other occasions the phrase is repeated by the artist, who seems to labor under the compulsion to appropriate the words of the woman whose image he created. Ironically, the artist's efforts to remove the statue from sight, to lower her into a grave, and to bury her in darkness lead to the return of the repressed.

where water was splashing from the mouths of dolphins into marble basins and where calla lilies and fresh roses were blooming in abundance. He walked into a long, lofty entryway, with walls and ceilings painted in beautiful colors and covered with coats of arms and works of art. Uniformed servants, haughty and pretentious, swaggering like sleigh horses decked out with bells, strutted up and down. A few of them even stretched out lazily and boldly on the carved wooden benches, as if they were the masters of the house.

The artist explained his errand and was escorted up polished marble steps covered with thick carpets. Marble statues lined both sides of the staircase. He walked through magnificent rooms with paintings and floors of mosaic. The sight of so much brilliance and finery was overwhelming, but he quickly regained his composure. The noble master of the house received him kindly, even warmly. When the artist was taking his leave, he was told to visit the young *signorina*, who wished to see him again. A servant took him through more magnificent rooms, until he was ushered into a room where she was the most brilliant ornament.

The young woman spoke to him, and even a prayer of mercy or church song would not have had the same great power to melt his heart and lift his soul. He took her hand and pressed it to his lips. Even rose petals were not as soft as that hand, but flames—flames of some kind—leaped from it. He felt grand sentiments coursing through him. Words flowed from his lips, but he had no idea what he was saying. Is a volcano aware that its eruptions produce fiery lava?[15] He confessed his love to her. She drew herself up before him, astonished, offended, and proud, with a look of contempt on her features, as if she had just touched a cold, wet frog. Her cheeks turned red; her lips grew pale; and her eyes flashed pitch-black, as dark as the night.

"You madman," she cried. "Go away! Get out of my sight!"[16] And when she turned her back on him, the face of

LORENZ FRØLICH

beauty bore a resemblance to that petrifying face with serpent hair.[17]

The artist descended the stairs in a stupor and found his way back to the street. He managed to reach his lodgings, moving like a sleepwalker, but came to in a fit of rage and pain. Taking his hammer in hand, he raised it high in the air and was about to smash the beautiful marble image. He was so beside himself that he did not even realize that his friend Angelo was standing right next to him. With a strong grip, Angelo held his arm back.

"Are you mad? What's the matter?"

The two struggled, but Angelo was stronger and prevailed. Exhausted and breathing heavily, the young artist flung himself into a chair.

"What happened?" Angelo asked. "Pull yourself together. Tell me what happened!"

But what could he say! And since Angelo could not understand his ravings, he gave up.

"You'll get into trouble with your eternal dreaming! Be a man, like your friends, and stop living in a fantasy world.

17. *bore a resemblance to that petrifying face with serpent hair.* The artist transforms *his* Psyche into a Medusa figure, who returns his petrifying gaze with her own stony look. In October 1833, after seeing Leonardo da Vinci's *Medusa*, Andersen wrote to his friend Henriette Wulff: "The head has something magical about it that attracted me—the foam of the abyss in its most beautiful shape. It is a hell that has created the head of a Madonna with warm poison streaming out of her mouth. The serpent's hair is moving as the person beholding it becomes petrified."

Andersen expressed his horror at how the animating power of imagination can devolve into the petrifying power of a Medusa in those who are mad. Visiting an asylum, he observed: "Imagination, this life's best cherub, that conjures up an Eden for us in the sandy desert—is here a frightful chimera, whose Medusa-head petrifies reason and thoughts, and breathes a magic circle around the unfortunate victim, who is then lost to the world" (Bøggild, 79).

18. *"The girls from the campagna."* "Campagna" is the Italian term for countryside, and the Roman campagna is the region around Rome. For Andersen, Rome and its surroundings were "like a book of fairy tales . . . where new wonders are constantly being uncovered so one can immerse oneself in a world of fantasy" (*Travels*, 256).

19. *"They are all daughters of Eve."* That a painter named Angelo who is dismissed with the phrase "Apage Satanas" tries to convince the artist that women are all tainted by sin shows how deeply the story is invested in staging a religious debate about sin and innocence and about death and immortality in gendered terms.

20. *a lamp was burning before the image of the Madonna.* The untroubled juxtaposition of sacred and profane in the tavern reveals the degree to which the artist suffers from self-division in a unique way, with his art preventing him from partaking of the pleasures of life and the consolations of religion. Note too that the tale features both the Madonna and the Medusa.

21. *saltarello.* The *saltarello* was a lively dance whose origins can be traced to thirteenth-century Naples. It is in triple meter and is named after its characteristic leaping step, from the Italian verb *saltare* ("to jump"). The dance became part of the popular traditions of the Roman Carnival and appears in Felix Mendelssohn's *Italian Symphony,* which was written after the composer had attended the Roman festivities in 1831. In his travel diaries, Andersen describes seeing girls in Rome dancing the *saltarello.* The Italian dance made a strong impression on him, and during his second visit to Rome he bemoaned the fact that he no longer heard "tambourines ringing in the streets" and that the "young girls dancing the *saltarello*" had disappeared (*Travels*, 256).

You'll go crazy. Get a little tipsy, and you'll sleep it off! A beautiful girl can be your healer. The girls from the campagna[18] are as beautiful as your princess in the marble castle. They are all daughters of Eve,[19] and when you're in paradise, you won't be able to tell them apart. Take the advice of your Angelo. I'm your angel now, your angel of life! The time will come when you will be old, and your body will fall apart. Then, on a beautiful, sunny day, when everyone else is laughing and having a good time, you'll lie there, like limp straw with no life left in it. I don't have much faith in what the priests tell us about life beyond the grave. That's a nice fantasy, a fairy tale for children—quite pleasant if you can persuade yourself that it's true. As for me, I deal in reality. Come along with me! Start acting like a man!"

The artist was able to drag himself along, at least for the moment. He felt fire in his blood. A change had taken place in his soul, and he sensed a deep desire to move away from the familiar and to tear himself loose from his old self. And so he followed Angelo.

On the outskirts of Rome, there was a tavern frequented by artists. It had been built into the ruins of ancient baths. Large yellow lemons could be seen among dark, shining leaves and covered part of the old reddish-yellow walls. The tavern consisted of a vaulted chamber, almost like a cavern located in the ruins. Inside it, a lamp was burning before the image of the Madonna.[20] A fire was blazing in the hearth, and there was much cooking and roasting. Outdoors, beneath the lemon and laurel trees, there were tables covered with food.

The two young men were greeted with shouts of joy by their friends. They didn't eat much, but they drank a lot, and that raised everybody's spirits. There was singing, and someone was playing the guitar. Then the *saltarello*[21] was played, and everyone began dancing merrily. Two young Roman girls who were working as artists' models joined in the dance and festivities—two charming Bacchantes,[22] not as lovely as Psy-

LORENZ FRØLICH

22. *two charming Bacchantes.* The allusion to Bacchus is a reminder of the inspiration for the story—a statue of Bacchus rather than Psyche. Andersen develops in this story a distinction that Nietzsche famously made between the Apollonian and Dionysian—the serene world of Apollonian appearances, beauty, and light versus the fluid, sensual, orgiastic union of opposites in the cult of Dionysus. Angelo's encouragement to "Let yourself go with the flow all around you" is a reminder that the artist is turning from the pleasures of the Apollonian to the delights of the Dionysian.

23. *On the floor there were many sketches.* The sketches of the girls from the campagna are not part of a cult of art but come to be connected, through their position on the floor, with refuse.

che, to be sure, not delicate, beautiful roses, but fresh, sturdy, vibrant carnations.

How hot it was that day! There was fire in the blood, fire in the air, fire in everyone's eyes. Gold and roses were glowing in the air; life was gold and roses.

"At last you have joined us. Let yourself go with the flow all around you and in your soul."

"I've never felt so healthy, so full of joy," the young artist said. "You're right, you were all right. I've been a fool and a dreamer. We should live in reality and not in fantasy."

Singing and playing their guitars, the young artists left the tavern and strolled through the narrow streets under the clear, starlit skies. The daughters of the campagna, those colorful carnations, accompanied them.

They returned to Angelo's room, where colored sketches, folios, and sensuous, lustrous images were scattered all around, and their voices became quieter but were no less animated. On the floor there were many sketches[23] that resembled the daughters of the campagna, showing their robust beauty from many different angles. And yet the women were far more attractive than the images. Every candle on the six-armed candelabra had been lit, and it was blazing and glow-

24. *resounded within and were spoken by his own lips.* If the artist first imitated the living Psyche by creating a sculpture of her, he now mimics her words, internalizing her reproaches to him and repeating them to himself.

ing. And from deep within the artist's soul, something divine was also blazing and glowing.

"Apollo! Jupiter! I'm carried aloft to your heavens and into your glory. The flower of life in my heart has blossomed for the first time."

Yes, it blossomed, and then it bent, broke, and a nauseating vapor arose from it, blinding his eyes, numbing his thoughts, and extinguishing the fireworks of the senses. Everything turned black.

He was back in his room again, and there he sat on his bed, collecting his thoughts. "Shame on me!"—those words came out of his own mouth, from the depths of his heart. "Get out of my sight, be gone, you wretched man." He heaved a deep, painful sigh.

"Go away! Get out of my sight!" Those words, the words of the living Psyche, resounded within and were spoken by his own lips.[24] He buried his head in the pillow, and, with confused thoughts in his head, he fell asleep.

He awoke the following day at dawn with a start and tried to collect his thoughts again. What had happened? Had it all been a dream? Had he just dreamed about going to see her, about the trip to the tavern, and the evening spent with those two purple carnations from the campagna? No, it was all reality, a reality that he had not known up until now.

The bright morning star shone through the purple-tinted air. Its rays fell on him and onto the marble Psyche. He began to tremble when he looked at the image of immortality. His gaze seemed to taint the work. He threw a sheet over the statue, and then he touched it one more time to uncover the figure, but he was no longer able to look on his own work.

The artist sat alone all day long, quiet, gloomy, and absorbed in his thoughts. He did not hear a bit of what was going on outdoors. No one knew what was stirring in that human soul.

Days passed and weeks went by. The nights seemed endless. The twinkling star saw him rise from his bed one morning, pale and feverish. He walked over to the marble statue, pulled back the sheet covering it, and gazed one last time, with pain and longing, at his work. And then, staggering under its weight, he took the statue down into the garden, where there was a dried-up well that was now nothing more than a hole in the ground. He lowered Psyche down into it,[25] threw dirt over her and then scattered dry sticks and nettles over the spot.

"Go away! Get out of my sight"—that's all there was to the burial service.

The morning star witnessed everything in the rosy-red air, and its beams illuminated big tears on the deadly pale cheeks of the young man. Feverish and mortally ill, he was said to be on his deathbed.

Brother Ignatius came to see him often, as both friend and physician. He brought the consolations of religion to the ailing artist and told him about the peace and happiness that comes from the church, and he spoke of man's sin and about grace and the peace found through God. His words were like warm sunshine landing on tilled soil that sends forth clouds

25. *He lowered Psyche down into it.* Just as the block of marble was covered by refuse, so the statue returns to the earth, covered with leaves and dirt. In lowering the statue into the ground, the sculptor buries it (as if it were a living thing), represses it (trying to bury the painful conflict it produces in him), and returns it to the earth (giving it back to Mother Nature).

LORENZ FRØLICH

291

26. *"Taste and you shall become like God."* These are the words from Genesis 3:5, used by the serpent to tempt Eve: "You shall be as gods, knowing good and evil."

of mist, fantastic thoughts, and images that were also reality. The ailing artist reviewed human life from these floating islands. It was nothing more than error and deception, for him as for everyone else. Art was nothing but a sorceress that fuels vanity and earthly desires. We betray ourselves, our friends, and God. The serpent within keeps telling us: "Taste and you shall become like God."[26]

It seemed to him that for the first time he understood himself and had finally found the road to truth and to freedom. In church you could find God's light and wisdom, and, in the monk's cell, you could find the peace needed by the human tree to strike roots and grow through all eternity.

Brother Ignatius strengthened his resolve, and his mind was made up. A worldly creature was about to become a servant of the church. The young artist renounced the world and entered the monastery.

The brothers received him warmly, and it was a festive day when he took his vows. It seemed as if God was standing right there in the sunlight of the church, radiating his presence from the sacred images and the shining cross. When he was in his little cell that evening at sunset, he

LORENZ FRØLICH

looked out from his window across old Rome with its desolate and its great, if dead, Coliseum and saw the city
adorned in its springtime garb, with its acacias in bloom, its
fresh evergreens, its abundance of roses, its glistening
lemons and oranges, its waving palms. Then he felt moved
and fulfilled as never before. The wide, open campagna
stretched out as far as the bluish, snow-capped mountains,
which seemed as if painted in the sky.[27] Everything melted
together, breathing peace and beauty, floating, dreaming—
it was all a dream!

Yes, the world here was like a dream, and dreams can last
for hours and can return for hours, but life in the monastery
is a matter of years, many long years.

Much of what taints humans comes from within—that
much was confirmed for the artist. What flames burned in
him at times! Why did the evil that he wanted so much to
defy refuse to go away? He chastised his body, but the evil was
coming from within. A small part of his mind wrapped itself
as lithely as a snake around him and crawled with his con-
science under the mantle of universal love and comforted him
with these words: "The saints pray for us, the Madonna prays
for us, and Jesus himself gave his blood for us." Was it childlike innocence or the flippancy of youth that partook of grace
and felt elevated by it, elevated over many others now that he
had rejected the vanity of the world? After all, *he* was a son of
the church.

One day, after many years had passed, he met Angelo, who
recognized him at once.

"My boy!" Angelo cried out. "It's you! Are you happy now?
You sinned against God by throwing away the gifts that he
gave you. You forfeited your mission in this world. Have you
ever read the parable about the talents?[28] The wise man who
told that story spoke the truth. What have you earned and
what have you found? Don't you think that you are living a
dream, a religion that is simply in your head, the way it is for

27. *which seemed as if painted in the sky.*
The artist has obviously not been completely converted, for God's presence
seems to radiate from images and symbols
in the church, and he looks at God's creation, not as nature, but as if it were a
beautiful work of art.

28. *"Have you ever read the parable about the
talents?"* Matthew 25:14–30 tells the
parable about the talents, which are not
talents in the sense of abilities or aptitudes
but units of weight or currency: "Again, it
will be like a man going on a journey, who
called his servants and entrusted his prop-
erty to them. To one he gave five talents of
money, to another two talents, and to
another one talent, each according to his
ability. Then he went on his journey. The
man who had received the five talents
went at once and put his money to work
and gained five more. So also, the one with
the two talents gained two more. But the
man who had received the one talent went
off, dug a hole in the ground and hid his
master's money." The master returns and
rewards the first two servants, who have
used their talents wisely: "For everyone
who has will be given more, and he will
have in abundance. Whoever does not
have, even what he has will be taken from
him."

When Andersen's compatriot the Danish artist Albert Küchler proposed that
Andersen join an order to which he had
converted in Rome and "live in peace with
God," Andersen replied quickly: "I could
stay here for a few days, and then I would
have to leave, go out in the world again
. . . live in it, be in it" (*Travels*, 339).

29. *Eternity.* Eternity is the word that Kai is trying to form from blocks of ice in "The Snow Queen." The search for immortality in "The Psyche" is also connected with whiteness, purity, and cold, hard surfaces.

others? What if everything were just a dream, a fantasy, and beautiful thoughts!"

"Get thee behind me, Satan," the monk shouted and walked away from Angelo.

"The devil exists, and he is made of flesh and blood! I saw him today," the monk muttered. "Once I gave him my little finger, and he grabbed my whole hand! But no," he sighed, "the evil is in me and in him too, but it doesn't weigh him down. He walks around free as a bird and lives comfortably while I struggle to find comfort in the consolations of religion. If only it were a consolation! If only everything here were just beautiful thoughts, like the world that I left behind—illusions, like the beauty of the rose-colored evening clouds, like the drifting blues of the distant mountains. Up close they look quite different. Eternity[29]: you are like the vast, boundless, silent seas that beckon and call and fill us with hopes. But as soon as we wade in, we start to sink, vanish, and die. We cease to exist. Deception! Go Away! Fall down!"

Without shedding any tears and completely absorbed in his thoughts, he sat down at his place of prayer, bowed down, but before whom? Before the stone cross in the wall? No, it was sheer habit that led him to assume this position.

The deeper he looked into himself, the blacker the darkness seemed. "Nothing within, nothing without! My entire life squandered." And these thoughts grew like a snowball that became larger as it rolled along until finally it crushed him—wiping him out.

"I can't confide in anyone or tell anyone about the worm that is gnawing away at my insides! My secret is my prisoner, and if I let him escape, I'm his."

And the divine power within him suffered and struggled.

"God, my heavenly God," he called out in his anguish. "Have pity on me! Give me faith! I left my mission unfulfilled. I squandered the talent you gave me. I lacked the strength, for it was not given to me. Immortality, the Psyche in my breast—go away, down with you! It must be buried like that Psyche which was the finest ray of hope in my life. She will never rise from her grave."

The star in the rosy-red skies was shining, the very star that will some day fade and disappear even as the soul lives and shines. Its trembling beam landed on the white wall, but it wrote nothing at all about God's glory, about his blessings, about his love, about all those things that resound in the hearts of those who have faith.

"The Psyche within me will never die! To live in consciousness? Can the unfathomable happen? Yes, yes, my being is unfathomable, and you, oh Lord, are unfathomable! Your entire creation is a wondrous work of power, glory, and love!"

His eyes were glowing, and then they dimmed. The sound of the church bells was the last thing he heard before he died. His body was lowered into soil that had come from Jerusalem and that had been mixed with dust from the corpses of pious souls.

Many years later his bones were disinterred, as had also happened with monks who had died before him. His skeleton was clothed in a brown monk's robe and a rosary was put in his hand. It was placed in the ranks with others in the cloisters of the monastery. And while the sun was shining outdoors, incense was burned indoors and the mass was read.

Many years went by, and the bones of the skeletons had crumbled. The skulls had been gathered together to make a wall around the church. There they all were—his among them—in the burning sunlight. There were many there, and no one knew their names. Nobody knew his name either. But look! Something was moving in the sockets of his skull, and it was alive! What could it be? A spotted lizard was darting around in the hollow skull, leaping in and out of the empty eye sockets.[30] The lizard was now the only form of life in that skull that had once entertained bold thoughts, bright dreams,

30. *leaping in and out of the empty eye sockets.* The story turns in many ways on the visual, on beautiful images and their seductive power. The gaze, sight, vision, light, and blinding are further emphasized in the repeated invocation of the morning star, which beams down and witnesses the events taking place. The image of the white skull with its dark sockets not only negates the beauty of the "immortal" marble sculpture but also reveals that the power of vision itself is only fleeting.

31. *dust returned to dust.* In Genesis 3:19 God tells Adam and Eve: "By the sweat of your brow you will eat your food until you return to the ground, since from it you were taken; for dust you are and to dust you will return."

32. *butterfly wings appeared.* Ironically, the butterfly appears only when the statue is unearthed, not when the artist's bones are disinterred. As noted, Psyche means both soul and butterfly in Greek. Andersen habitually connected swans, butterflies, and ballerinas in the many whimsical paper cuttings he created over the years at social events. Butterflies, related through flight to the many avian creatures in Andersen's stories, appear frequently in the fairy tales, most notably in "Thumbelina" and in a story about a winged bachelor called "The Butterfly."

and a love of art and splendor—it had shed hot tears and aspired to immortality. The lizard jumped and then disappeared. The skull crumbled, and dust returned to dust.[31]

Centuries later the bright morning star could be found continuing to shine, large and radiant, as it had for thousands of years. The skies were aglow in hues of red, fresh as roses, red as blood.

A monastery now occupied the site of the temple that had been on that narrow street and had lain in ruins. A grave was being dug in the convent's garden. A young nun had died and was to be buried at dawn. The spade hit a stone, and a dazzling ray of whiteness gleamed through the dirt. The perfect form of a shoulder made from marble emerged from the ground. The spade was guided with greater care, and the head of a woman was uncovered, and then suddenly butterfly wings appeared.[32] The gravediggers lifted the marvelous figure of Psyche—chiseled from white marble and resplendent in the rose-red hues of the dawn—from the grave where the nun was to be buried. "How beautiful, how perfect she is! A work of art by one of the great masters!" people were saying. Who could that master have been? No one knew, no one had known him but the bright, shining star that had sent its beams down for thousands of years. It was familiar with the course of his life on earth, his sufferings and weaknesses, and also knew that he was a man, nothing more! But he was gone now, scattered abroad as dust is destined to be. But Psyche, the fruit of his most noble labors and the glorious work that revealed the spark of the divine in him, remained, and she would never die. She had transcended fame and fortune, and her glory would remain here on earth. She would be seen, appreciated, admired, and idealized.

The bright morning star in the rose-tinted air sent its sparkling beams down on Psyche and on the lips and eyes of her admirers, who were smiling with delight as they beheld the soul carved from a block of marble.

Everything that is of the earth will crumble and be forgotten. Only the star in the vast firmament will remember. What is heavenly will shine through the ages, and when that too has passed, Psyche will live on.[33]

LORENZ FRØLICH

33. *Psyche will live on.* Andersen develops a strong link to Ovid's *Metamorphoses*, a work that establishes a firm bond between poetic artistry and immortality. If Ovid ends his work about the metamorphic nature of creativity by confidently declaring "Vivam" ("I shall live"—meaning both the book and its creator), Andersen concludes by emphasizing that the work of art will triumph over its creator and attain the immortality for which he longed. Despite the artist's efforts to plunge the statue into darkness, to lower it into the nether regions, and to bury it and return it to the earth, the statue emerges in all its pure, gleaming, transcendent glory, even as the monk's white skeletal remains (the skull through which the lizard darts) turn to dust.

The Most Astonishing Thing

Det utroligste

Det Utroligste. Et Eventyr, 1870

irst published in the United States in The Riverside Magazine for Young People, *"The Most Astonishing Thing" was considered by Andersen to be one of his best stories. A tale written near the end of his life, it is an unlikely candidate for a children's magazine, for in it Andersen summed up the essence of art. The clock that serves as "the most astonishing thing" represents both temporality and transcendence. It keeps time, but it is also an objet d'art that resists destruction, coming back to life even after it has been smashed to bits. It houses the biblical and the mythical, the seasons and the senses, the visual and the acoustical, the carnal and the spiritual. Everything that Andersen wanted in art is housed in that extraordinary clock that astonishes everyone.*

The art of astonishment was no small matter to Andersen. It is telling that the winner of the contest staged in this story is a man who creates an object that shocks precisely because it provides the semblance of life. The modest craftsman makes a clock that is more than a mechanical thing—it pulses with life and captures the imagination of all who see it. The work he produces mingles the secular with the sacred and the pagan with the Christian: it brings together prophets and wise men, monks and muses. Above all, it becomes a second creation, a work with a life of its own and even a degree of immortality. The clock and the figures in it, like the statue of Psyche in Andersen's story of that name, defy destruction and live on in a way that humans cannot. Here, as in other tales, beauty transcends decay and destruction.

Whoever could do the most astonishing thing was to earn the king's daughter and half the kingdom.

Young men, and, yes, old ones too, strained every thought, muscle, and sinew to win. Two ate themselves to death[1] and one of them ate so much that he exploded. But that was not how it was meant to be.[2] Street urchins practiced spitting on their own backs; that's what they thought would be the most astonishing thing imaginable.

On the appointed day, there was to be a display of the most astonishing things, and everyone was to show his best possible work. Judges had been appointed, ranging from three-year-old children to people in their nineties. There was an exhibition of astonishing things, but everyone agreed without hesitation that the most astonishing thing of all was a huge clock in a case,[3] an extraordinary contraption, both inside and out. At the stroke of each hour, lifelike figures appeared to tell the time. There were twelve performances in all, each with moving figures that could sing or speak.

LORENZ FRØLICH

1. *Two ate themselves to death.* Andersen borrows from folklore the motif of excessive eating and drinking as part of a contest to reveal strength. Gluttony also figures as one of the seven deadly sins that march out of the clock.

2. *But that was not how it was meant to be.* Feats accomplished by the body will not win this particular contest. The narrator alerts us to the fact that real astonishment will be produced by something very different from displays of excess.

3. *a huge clock in a case.* The most astonishing thing is a work of art with "lifelike" figures. But it is also a mechanism that marks the passage of time on an hourly basis and memorializes ephemerality.

4. *writing the first commandment on the tablets.* It is deeply ironic that the first figure to emerge is Moses, who, in the Bible, enunciates the commandment forbidding representation. Words about images follow the warning about having no other gods: "You shall not make for yourself an idol, whether in the form of anything that is in heaven above, or that is on the earth beneath, or that is in the water under the earth" (Exodus 20:3).

5. *the sun had baked him.* Similar ideas about skin color are presented at the beginning of "The Shadow," and they become more significant in that text. Andersen's notions of race remain quite naïve, and he habitually works in terms of the binary black/white, with black representing a "baked" quality (as he puts it). It is a hue associated with Italy rather than Africa, while white is generally the color of innocence and purity, though, when applied as an attribute to skin, it can take on a demonic quality.

6. *a procession of the five senses.* Synesthesia, the engagement of all the senses, plays an important role in Andersen's aesthetics. It is therefore no accident that the work of art contains within it a group of allegorical figures representing all five senses.

Everyone agreed: "That clock is the most astonishing thing ever seen."

The clock struck one, and Moses appeared on the mountain, writing the first commandment on the tablets[4]: "Thou shalt have no other gods before me."

The clock struck two, and there was the Garden of Eden, the place where Adam and Eve met, both quite happy even though they did not have a clothes closet, nor did they need one.

At the stroke of three, the Three Wise Men appeared. One of them was black as coal, but he couldn't help it, the sun had baked him.[5] The kings brought incense and precious gifts.

At the stroke of four, the seasons advanced in their order. Spring carried the green branch of a beech tree, with a cuckoo perched on it. Summer appeared with a grasshopper on a ripe ear of corn. Autumn had only an empty stork's nest, and Winter emerged with an old crow that could tell tales in a corner behind the oven, tales of times past.

At the stroke of five, there was a procession of the five senses.[6] Sight was a man who made spectacles. Hearing was a coppersmith. Smell was accompanied by violets and sweet woodruff. Taste was a chef. And Feeling was a mourner in black crepe that reached all the way down to the heels.

The clock struck six, and a gambler cast a die, with six on top.

Then came the seven days of the week or the seven deadly sins—no one could agree on that and they could not be told apart easily.

Next came a choir of monks to sing the eight o'clock evening song.

The stroke of nine brought the nine muses. One was an astronomer; one was a historian working in an archive; the others were connected with the theater.

When ten o'clock struck, Moses reappeared with his tablets. All the commandments were written on them, and there were ten in all.

The clock struck again, and boys and girls leaped in the air, playing and singing:

> Heigh, Ho, heaven,
> The clock has struck eleven.

7. *The whole thing had been destroyed.* The act of destruction came to have representative importance. "The Most Astonishing Thing" was reprinted in 1942 in a volume of stories edited by a group of scholars who were to become leaders of the Danish Resistance Movement. As Jackie Wullschlager points out: "Radical new illustrations were used to smuggle past the censors a message of hope and resistance to a wide readership. In the final picture, the night watchman who strikes down the destroyer is a Jewish rabbi with hat and beard, standing in condemnation of a brawny, semi-naked Aryan pinned to the floor by the tablets of Moses inscribed in Hebrew letters, watched by a crowd of 'ordinary' Danes in contemporary 1940s dress. . . . 'Andersen would have been pleased to know that some of his works became a useful tool against the oppressors at a time when Denmark was not master in her own house' " (Nunnally and Wullschlager, 437).

And the clock struck eleven.

Then came the stroke of twelve, and out marched a night watchman, wearing a cape and carrying a spiked nightstick called the morning star. He was singing a song you often heard from night watchmen:

> 'Twas in the midnight hour,
> That our Savior was born.

While he was singing, roses began to unfold and turned into the heads of angels with rainbow-colored wings on their backs.

The clock was charming to look at and lovely to hear. It was a thing of beauty superior to any other work of art. It was a most astonishing thing, as everyone agreed.

The artist who had made it was a young man, kindhearted, happy as a child, a faithful friend and also a great help to his parents, who were poor. He really deserved the princess and half the kingdom.

On the day that the winner was to be proclaimed, the entire town had been decked out, and the princess was sitting on her throne, which had been newly stuffed for the occasion but was no more snug or comfortable than it had been before. The judges winked knowingly at the apparent winner, who was beaming happily, for he had, after all, done the most astonishing thing.

"No," a tall, bony, powerful fellow roared at the last moment. "I'm the one who will do the most astonishing thing," and, with that, he lifted his ax to strike the work of art.

Bam, crack, crush! The whole thing was lying on the ground. Wheels and springs went flying in every direction. The whole thing had been destroyed.[7]

"I did that," the lout said. "My work beat his and amazed everyone here. I have done the most astonishing thing."

8. *dressed in her costly garments.* Like many of the royal female personages in Andersen's tales (most notably the princess in "The Swineherd"), this young woman focuses on material wealth and remains perfectly happy as long as she has a comfortable throne and fine dresses to wear.

"To destroy a work of art like that!" the judges gasped. "Why, that's the most astonishing thing imaginable!" And since everyone agreed, he was to have the princess and half the kingdom, because a promise is a promise, even if it is astonishing.

Trumpets sounded from the ramparts and towers in the city. "The wedding is about to begin!" The princess was not particularly happy about the turn of events, but she looked charming nonetheless, dressed in her costly garments.[8] The church looked beautiful at night with all the candles glowing in it. The ladies of the court sang as they escorted the bride. The knights also sang and escorted the groom, who strutted and swaggered as if no one could ever get in his way. Then the music stopped. It became so quiet that you could hear a pin drop and then, suddenly, the great church doors flew open with a crash and a bang. Right, left, left, right, everything that had been part of the clockwork came marching down the aisle and slipped between the bride and groom. Dead people can't get back on their feet—we know that—but a work of art can run again. Its body may have been shattered, but not its spirit. The spirit of art was on the prowl, and that was no joke.

The work of art stood there intact, as if it had never been

touched. The hours struck, one after another, up to twelve o'clock, and then all the figures swarmed forth, first Moses, whose forehead had a bright flame on it. He hurled the heavy stone tablets at the bridegroom's feet and then tied his feet to the floor of the church.

"I can't lift the tablets back up again," Moses said, "for you broke my arm. Stay right where you are."

Then Adam and Eve came forward, as did the Three Wise Men as well as the four seasons. They all told him unpleasant truths. "Shame on you!" But he was not at all ashamed.

All of the figures that appeared at every stroke marched out of the clock, and they began to grow to a surprising size. There was scarcely any room left for real people. And when, at the stroke of twelve, the watchman strode out in his cape and with his nightstick, there was an odd commotion. The watchman went right up to the bridegroom and hit him over the head with his morning-star club.

"Just lie there," the watchman said. "An eye for an eye. We are getting our revenge and our master's too. And now we will vanish."

And the work of art disappeared without a trace, but the candles all around the church turned into flowers of light, and the gilded stars in the dome cast down rays of light. The organ began to play on its own.[9] Everyone said that that was the most astonishing thing they had ever seen.

"Should we summon the right man now?" asked the princess. "The one who made that work of art will be my husband and my lord."

In a flash he was right in the church, accompanied by everyone in town. They were overjoyed and gave him their blessing. Not a soul there felt envy[10]—and, yes, that was really the most astonishing thing.

9. *The organ began to play on its own.* The work of art is miraculously reconstituted. In the sacred setting of the church, miracles continue to happen, first when the figures come to life, then when the organ produces sounds on its own.

10. *Not a soul there felt envy.* Once the villain is vanquished, the envy that initially invaded the town during the contest disappears, and the story ends on a utopian note.

The Story of a Mother

Historien om en moder

Nye Eventyr. Anden Samling, 1848

ndersen's moving story about mother and child was first published in English as a "Christmas book" in London in 1847. It was intended by Andersen as a tribute to his British audience, and he entitled the volume (which included four other tales) A Christmas Greeting to My English Friends. *Dedicated to Charles Dickens, whom Andersen had met in the summer of 1847 ("I musch see Andersen," Dickens is reported to have said about the Dane whose English was notoriously difficult to understand), the collection was warmly received. Andersen's British fans, a group that included publishers, journalists, bankers, ministers, along with dukes and duchesses, swarmed his lodgings at Leicester Square. Andersen had reached what he believed to be the "pinnacle of success," but he complained bitterly about how the British appreciated him in ways that his fellow Danes never could.*

Andersen wrote to Dickens on December 6, 1847, about the stories dedicated to him:

I am back again in my quiet Danish room, but my thoughts are still with you in England. While occupying myself with a longer work, five stories sprang from my head, as flowers sprout up in the woods. I feel moved to bring you these fresh flowers from the garden of my poetry. I admire all of your books, and since we met, you yourself have become a fixture in my heart. Dear, noble Charles Dickens, you were the last to say good-by to me on the shores of England, so it is natural that I should want you to be the first to receive my greeting from Denmark, which only an affectionate heart can send.

(*Travels*, 287)

On his seventieth birthday, Andersen's publishers presented him with a special volume entitled The Story of a Mother: In Fifteen Languages. *"The Story of a Mother" may have been inspired by the mid-nineteenth-century pictorial tradition of representing the dying and deceased child. In July 1846, a year before the story was published, Andersen had visited the poet Jean Reboul in Nîmes and described in his diary the portraits on display in his home: "On the wall were two pictures illustrating his poem. One showed a dying child, a serious angel, and the mother who has fallen asleep while keeping a painful vigil. The other was an oil-painting. In it, the angel soared off with the child while the mother remained draped over the cradle." Andersen said that the plot of the story came to him out of the blue, one day while he was taking a walk.*

KAY NIELSEN

Time has stopped, with a clock that has neither numbers nor hands, in the simple room where the cradle stands that was rocked by the mother. The moonlit landscape reveals a bare tree that is a portent of what is to come.

A mother was sitting at her child's bedside.[1] She was full of sorrow, so afraid that he might die. The child was very pale, and his little eyes were shut. His breath was faint, but every now and then he would sigh deeply and struggle for

1. *A mother was sitting at her child's bedside.* The tableau that begins the story depicts a scene that was not uncommon in nineteenth-century life and literature. Given the high mortality rate for children in an earlier age, parents faced bleak odds and could prepare themselves for the worst with tales that offered some kind of solace. The folklore of many cultures has stories like this one, meant to comfort mothers grieving the loss of an infant. It is possible that Andersen was inspired by Danish tales that he had heard in the spinning rooms of Odense as a child.

2. *Everything outdoors was covered in ice and snow.* Winter is the season of death in Andersen's poetic lexicon, and the figure of Death in this story has an icy breath that blights whatever it contacts.

3. *The clock stopped.* The stopping of the clock coincides with the end to the child's heartbeat. Death is marked by the end of time, and, with the end of time, the mother undertakes a journey into Death's territory to retrieve her child. The journey has a decidedly fairy-tale quality (resembling the heroine's travels to "the end of the world" in the Scandinavian folktale "East of the Sun and West of the Moon"), but the mother has a mission far different from that of fairy-tale characters, who are generally in search of a prince or a princess.

air. Then the mother would gaze with even greater sorrow at the little soul.

There was a knock at the door, and in walked a gloomy old man, wrapped in what looked like a big horse blanket. It kept him warm, and that's what he needed to protect him from the chilly winter air. Everything outdoors was covered in ice and snow,[2] and the wind was blowing so hard that it would sting your face.

The old man was shivering from the cold. The child was sleeping quietly for the moment, and so the mother put a little pot of beer on the stove to warm it up for the old man. The old man began to rock the cradle, and the mother sat down on a chair nearby. She watched over her ailing child, who was laboring with each breath, and she lifted his little hand.

"I'll be able to keep him, won't I? Surely the good Lord won't take him from me!"

The old man, who was Death himself, nodded his head in a strange way that could mean yes but could also mean no. The mother bowed her head, and tears ran down her cheeks. Her head began to grow heavy.

For three days and three nights, she had not closed her eyes, and now she was dozing off, but only for a moment. She gave a start and awoke, shuddering from a chill in the air.

"What was that?" she asked, looking all around her. The old man had vanished, and her little child was gone as well. Death had taken the child away. The old clock in the corner was spinning and whirring. Its heavy lead weight dropped to the floor with a thud. Bam! The clock stopped.[3]

The poor mother rushed out of the house, calling for her child.

Out there in the snow she saw a woman, dressed in long black robes. "Death was in your house," she said. "I just saw him rush off with your child in his arms. He moves faster than the wind, and he never returns what he takes with him."

KAY NIELSEN

Death heads in a direction that is filled with clouds and flowers and illuminated by a heavenly
body. The mother, whose hair has turned white, is in mourning, while Death, with a scythe in
his pocket, has his back turned as he walks away with the child.

4. *"I am Night, and I love lullabies."* The mother encounters four different figures before meeting up with Death. With each, she engages in some kind of barter or transaction that will improve her chances of finding her child. The allegorical figure of Night is enamored of the mother's songs, which are associated with tears and grief.

5. *A hawthorn bush was growing at the cross-roads.* The hawthorn, like the oak and hazel, has been seen as sacred, having protective powers. It is small and characterized by fruit known as "haws" and thorny branches. Native to northern Europe, in Celtic lore it was famous for healing broken hearts. Hawthorn was sometimes put into the cradles of infants to protect them from harm.

6. *The mother pressed the hawthorn bush to her breast to warm it up.* Andersen was haunted by a recurring nightmare about a child lying on his breast. Over two decades after writing this story, he recorded the following in his diary: "Slept fitfully and had a hideous dream about a child lying on my breast and how it turned into a wet rag" (June 1, 1868). On August 29, 1874, he wrote, "The horrible dream I often have about a child who is wasting away at my breast and becomes nothing but a wet rag troubled me again." One critic points out that the tale can be read in biographical terms: "The mother's sacrifices for her child may represent the poet's sacrifices for his art: when the mother sings for the night, it is the poet's song; when her blood flows for the thorn bush, it is the artist offering his heart to the public" (Stecher-Hansen, 103). The thorns of the hawthorn conjure associations with Christ's crown of thorns, and the mother's love becomes transformative, turning the icy branch into one that blooms. Oscar Wilde, who was deeply

"Tell me which way he went," the mother pleaded. "Only tell me which way, and I will find him."

"I know the way," said the woman wearing black. "But before I tell you, you must sing all the songs you once sang to your child. I am Night, and I love lullabies.[4] I hear them often. When you sang them, I saw your tears."

"I shall sing them again. You shall hear every one of them," said the mother. "But don't slow me down and keep me from finding my child. I'm in a hurry and have to catch up with them."

Night remained silent and still. The mother sang and wept, wringing her hands all the while. She sang many songs, but she shed even more tears. At last, Night said to her: "Take the path to the right into the dark pine forest. That's where Death was headed with your child."

Deep in the forest, the mother reached a crossroads and had no idea which path to take. A hawthorn bush was growing at the crossroads.[5] It had neither leaves nor flowers, since it was wintertime, and its branches were covered with frost.

"Did you see Death pass by here with my child?"

"Yes, I did," the hawthorn bush replied. "But I won't tell you where he went unless you warm me up against your heart. I'm freezing to death. I'm turning into ice."

The mother pressed the hawthorn bush to her breast to warm it up.[6] Its thorns dug so deeply into her flesh that big drops of red blood began to flow. The hawthorn bush felt such warmth at the heart of a sorrowful mother that it put forth fresh green leaves and blossomed on that cold winter night. And the hawthorn bush told her where she should go.

Soon the mother reached a great lake, where there were neither ships nor boats. The ice on the lake was too thin to hold her weight, and the waters were not open enough or shallow enough to let her wade across. But she had to figure out a way to cross if she wanted to find her child. She stooped down and was planning to drink the lake dry, even though she knew that it was not humanly possible. The unfortunate woman was hoping for a miracle.

"That will never work," the lake told her. "Why don't the two of us make a deal instead? I collect pearls, and your eyes are the clearest I have ever seen. If you promise to cry them out for me, then I will carry you over to the great greenhouse where Death dwells and tends his trees and flowers. Each one is a human life."

"Oh, I would give anything to find my child," the mother said in tears, and she began to cry even harder. Her eyes sank to the bottom of the lake[7] and turned into two precious pearls. The lake lifted her up as if she were on a swing, and she flew in one great swoop to the other side of the lake where there was the strangest house you could imagine. It rambled on for many a mile, and it was impossible to tell whether it was a cavernous mountain covered with forests or whether it had just been hammered together. The unfortunate mother was not able to see it, for she had cried her eyes out.

"Where can I find Death, who took my little child from me?" she asked.

"He has not yet returned," said the old woman who was taking care of the graves and was in charge of Death's great greenhouse. How did you find your way here, and who helped you out?"

"The good Lord helped me," she said. "He is so merciful, and you must be as well. "How can I find my little child?"

"I can't tell which one is your child," the woman said. "And you can't see! Many flowers and trees have withered overnight, and Death will soon be here to transplant them. As you know, all humans have a tree or flower of life, depending on what kind of person they are. The ones here look just like other plants, but they have a heart that beats. A child's heart beats too. You know the sound of your child's heartbeat. Listen for it, and maybe you will recognize it. If I tell you what else you have to do, what will you give me?"

influenced by Andersen's fairy tales, writes of the sacrificial love of a bird for a flower in "The Nightingale and the Rose."

7. *Her eyes sank to the bottom of the lake.* In bartering her eyes, the mother relies on her wisdom and inner vision to guide her. Andersen took advantage of the popular Romantic trope pairing blindness with insight.

8. *And she gave her beautiful black tresses away.* In this last of four bargains, the woman trades her youth and beauty for information about her child. Like the sisters in "The Little Mermaid," she is willing to sacrifice her beautiful hair for the sake of another person.

"I have nothing left to give," the unfortunate mother said. "But I will go to the ends of the earth for you."

"There's nothing there that I need," said the woman. "But you can give me your long black hair. You must know how beautiful it is, and I really like it. I will give you my white hair in return. That's better than nothing."

"Is that all you want?" the mother asked. "I'm happy to give it to you." And she gave her beautiful black tresses away[8] in exchange for the old woman's white hair.

They both went into Death's great greenhouse, where flowers and trees were growing with astonishing abundance. There were delicate hyacinths kept under glass bells, and around them big, hardy peonies. Water plants were growing there as well, some thriving, others ailing. Water snakes were resting on them, and black crabs had attached themselves to their stalks. You could see tall palm trees, plane trees, and oaks. Parsley was growing there with fragrant thyme. Each tree and flower had its own name, for each was the life of someone still living in China, in Greenland, or in some other part of the world. There were some big trees whose roots were about to burst the small pots confining them. There were also some wretched little flowers that had failed to thrive in spite of the attention lavished on them and the rich soil, with its mossy surroundings, in which they were planted. The sorrowful mother bent over the smallest plants and listened to their heartbeats, and among the millions she recognized her child's.

"This is the one!" she cried, reaching toward a little blue crocus that had wilted and was drooping sadly to one side.

"Don't touch that flower," the old woman said. "Stay here. Death will be along any minute now, and you can try to keep him from pulling it up. Threaten to pull up other plants. That will frighten him, because he has to account to our Lord for each one. They can't be uprooted without his permission."

Suddenly a chilling wind blew through the room, and the blind mother knew that Death had arrived.

"How did you find your way here?" he asked her. "How did you get here before me?"

"I am a mother," she said.

Then Death stretched his long hand out to the little wilted flower, but she cupped her hands around it, afraid that she might touch one of the petals. Death blew on her hands, and his breath was chillier than the coldest wind. Her hands fell limply to her sides.

"You have no power over me," Death said to her.

"But the Lord does," she said.

"I merely carry out his will," Death said. "I am his gardener. I take his flowers and trees and transplant them to the great Garden of Paradise in the unknown country.[9] But I can tell you nothing about how they fare there or what their life is like."

"Give my child back to me," the mother pleaded, weeping. Suddenly she seized hold of two beautiful flowers, and, clutching one in each hand, she shouted at Death: "I'm desperate enough to start tearing your flowers out by the roots."

"Don't touch them!" Death said. "You talk about how miserable you are, and yet you are willing to make another mother just as miserable."

"Another mother!" the woman said, and she let go of the flowers.

"You can have your eyes back," Death said. "They were shining so brightly that I fished them out of the lake. I had no idea they were yours. They are even clearer than they were before. Take them and look down into the deep well over here. I'll give you the names of the flowers that you were about to uproot, and you'll be able to see their future—the lives that you were planning to disturb and destroy."

The woman looked down into the well, and it was sheer delight to see how one of the lives turned into a blessing for the world, spreading joy and happiness all around. Then she looked at the other life and saw nothing but sorrow and misery, fear and suffering.

9. *"the great Garden of Paradise in the unknown country."* Andersen had originally written "the flowering garden" for "the unknown country," a phrase that may have its origins in Hamlet's famous reference to death as "The undiscovered country, from whose bourn / No traveler returns." Death becomes a source of mystery, the destination of a second journey, one that promises regeneration through the transplantation from greenhouse to garden.

10. *"Which one is condemned to misery and which one is blessed?"* Andersen may have been familiar with the Grimms' tale "The Little Old Mother," which was included in their "Legends about Children" at the end of *Children's Stories and Household Tales,* published in 1815. In that tale, a little old lady grieves over her losses, including the death of her husband and two children. She attends a religious service and realizes that she is the only living soul in the church. There she discovers that her two sons, both of whom died young, would have lived to become criminals, with one dying on the gallows and the other tortured on the wheel. She falls to her knees and declares her gratitude to God.

11. *And Death went with her child to the unknown land.* The first draft of the tale ends with the awakening of the mother from a nightmare about the death of her child. It concluded in the following way: "He lay there in a sweet, healthy sleep, and the sun shone on his cheeks so that they seemed red, and when the mother looked around, she found herself sitting in her little room. . . . Death was not in the room. The mother folded her hands, thought of the house of the dead, of the child's future and said again 'God's will be done!'" (Stecher-Hansen, 97). That Andersen elected to use the tragic ending may have had something to do with the fact that the tale was a Christmas gift—drawing attention to Christ's death at the time of his birth—for the British, who were schooled in melodrama through Dickens.

"Both are God's will," Death said.

"Which one is condemned to misery and which one is blessed?"[10] the mother asked.

"I can't tell you," Death replied. "But I can tell you this much: One of those two flowers represents your own child. You saw your own child's fate, your own child's future."

The mother shrieked with terror. "Which of the two was my child? Tell me! Save the innocent one! Spare him such wretchedness. Better to take him from me. Deliver him to God's kingdom. Ignore my tears. Ignore my pleas and everything I've said and done."

"I don't understand what you're saying," Death said. "Do you want your child back, or should I take him inside, to the land unknown to you?"

The mother began wringing her hands, and she fell to her knees, praying to God: "Do not listen to me when I defy your will, for you know better. Don't listen to me! Don't listen to me!"

She bowed her head deeply.

And Death went with her child to the unknown land.[11]

KAY NIELSEN

The Girl Who Trod on the Loaf

Pigen, som traadte paa brødet

Nye Eventyr og Historier. Tredie Samling, 1857

he Girl Who Trod on the Loaf' is without doubt the least child-friendly of Andersen's narratives, with a chilling display of punishment beyond the disciplinary excesses found in nineteenth-century Anglo-American and European children's literature. Even the notorious Struwwelpeter *of 1845 by the Frankfurt physician Heinrich Hoffmann, with its images of children going up in flames after lighting matches or losing their thumbs after sucking them, looks tame by comparison.*

Andersen's title refers to the folksong "The Girl Who Trod on the Loaf," which inspired his retelling of the girl's story. Kathryn Davis, in her novel named after the folksong, gives an account of the plot's origins:

Originally a folksong, "Pigen, der trådte på brødet," it chronicles the horrible fate of a vain young woman from the town of Sibbo, in Pomerania, whose punishment for loving a pair of shoes more than a loaf of bread is to be "frozen like a boulder" before she's swallowed up in a mud puddle. Toward the end of the eighteenth century the song was published as a broadside and despite its heavyhanded morality and plodding rhymes ("O human soul keep this in mind, /

1. *The story has been written down and put into print as well.* While many versions of the ballad exist, Andersen seems to be the only writer to turn Inger's misfortunes into a prose narrative. "The Girl Who Trod on the Loaf" is one of a small number of stories based, like the Grimms' fairy tales, on oral sources. Andersen briefly summarizes the events in the ballad, then turns to what really interests him: the story of Inger's salvation.

2. *she enjoyed catching flies, pulling off their wings.* Inger is one of many nineteenth-century brats in British and European children's literature who manifest their "evil" by torturing animals. Inger's sadistic streak has been seen by some readers as an appealing trait. One reader reminisces about reading the story as a child: "I was immediately smitten by Inger's macabre sense of humor. Her wicked mirth cast a spell on me and I wished she would go even further. In her portrait, I recognized myself. Hadn't I stranded tadpoles on sunny boulders just to watch them struggle to hop back in the water on their half-formed haunches?" (Flook, 120).

3. *"some desperate remedies to cure your stubborn ways."* The mother's lament rephrases a well-known Danish proverb that small children tread on a mother's apron, while grown ones tread on her heart. Note that stubbornness is added to pride, vanity, and cruelty. In nineteenth-century Anglo-American and European cultures, it was the duty of parents to tame the strong will of the child. The Grimms began one of their fairy tales ("Mother Trude") in a fashion typical for children's stories of the time: "Once upon a time there was a girl who was stubborn and curious, and whenever her parents told her to do something, she would not obey them. Well, how could things possibly go well for her?"

Abandon pride's temptations, / And leave all other sins behind, / They were her ruination . . .") it's remembered for having inspired Hans Christian Andersen's story of the same name.

(The Girl Who Trod on the Loaf, 14)

The name "Inger" was Andersen's invention, and he may have been inspired by Inger Meisling, the wife of the detested schoolmaster in Slagelse. Andersen freely admitted the role of revenge in his construction of narratives: "Many times when people have behaved in an irritating way and I have been unable to hit back, I have written a story and put them into it" (Travels, 91).

You have probably heard about the tribulations of the girl who trod on a loaf of bread to keep from soiling her shoes. The story has been written down and put into print as well.[1]

She was a poor child, but proud and vain. And people said that she had a bad streak. As a very small child, she enjoyed catching flies, pulling off their wings,[2] and turning them into creeping things. She would take a May bug and a beetle, stick each of them on a pin, then place a green leaf or bit of paper up against their feet. The poor creatures would cling to it, twisting and turning, trying to get off the pin.

"Now the May bug is reading," little Inger would say. "Look how it's turning over the leaves!"

As she grew older, she became worse rather than better. But she was very pretty, and that was probably her misfortune, for otherwise she would have been punished more often than she was.

"It'll take some desperate remedies to cure your stubborn ways,"[3] her mother told her. "When you were little, you used to stomp all over my aprons. Now that you're older, I'm worried that you will stomp all over my heart."

And, sure enough, that's what she did.

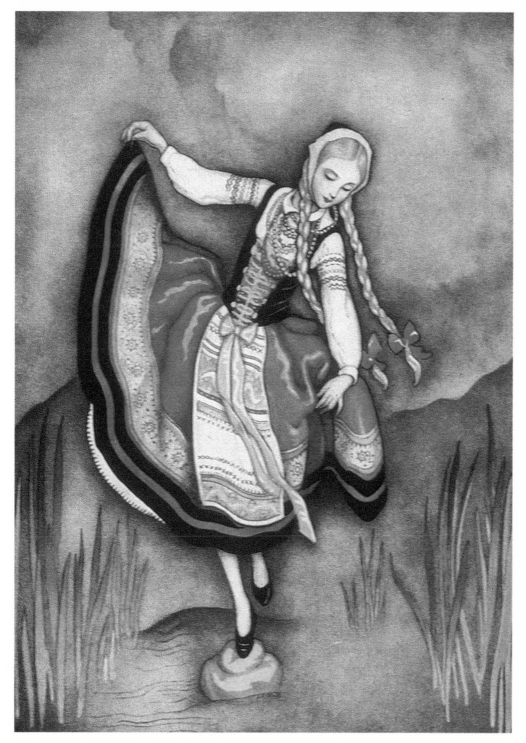

JENNIE HARBOUR

Dressed in beautiful clothes, Inger looks completely carefree, unaware of the grave consequences that will attend stepping on a loaf of bread to keep her shoes from getting dirty.

4. *Inger was ashamed.* Although Andersen wrote fondly about both his parents—his father had a "truly poetical mind" and his mother had "a heart full of love"—he was haunted all his life by skeletons in the family closet: an aunt who ran a brothel in Copenhagen, a half-sister named Karen-Marie (whose name the protagonist of "The Red Shoes" shares), and a grandfather who wandered the streets singing wild tunes and being chased by schoolboys.

One day she went out to work for gentry living in the countryside. They treated her as kindly as if she were their own child and dressed her in the same way. She looked very beautiful now and became more vain than ever.

After she had been with the family for about a year, her mistress said to her: "Isn't it time to go back and visit your parents, Inger dear?"

So she did, but she only went because she wanted to show off and let them see how refined she had become. When she reached the village, she caught sight of a group of girls gossiping with some young fellows near a pond. Her mother was there too, pausing to rest on a rock, with a bundle of firewood she had gathered in the forest. Inger was ashamed[4] that she, who was dressed so smartly, should have a mother who went about in rags collecting sticks. She wasn't in the least sorry to turn back. But she was annoyed.

Another six months went by.

"You really should go home sometime soon to visit your old parents, Inger dear," her mistress said. "Here, you can take this big loaf of white bread to them. They'll be happy to see you again."

Inger put on her best clothes and wore a pair of fine new shoes. She picked up the hem of her skirt and walked very carefully so that her shoes would stay nice and clean. No one can blame her for that! But when she reached the place where her path crossed over marshy ground, with a stretch of pud-

LORENZ FRØLICH

dles and mud before her, she flung the loaf down on the ground as a stepping-stone so that she could make her way across with dry shoes. Just as she put one foot down on the bread and lifted the other, the loaf began to sink, carrying her

LORENZ FRØLICH

down deeper and deeper until she disappeared altogether and there was nothing to see but a black, bubbling swamp![5]

That's the story.

What became of her?[6] She went down to the Marsh Woman, who brews underground. The Marsh Woman is aunt to the elf maidens,[7] who are known everywhere, for people sing songs about them and paint pictures of them. But nobody knows much about the Marsh Woman, except that when the meadows begin steaming in the summer, it means that the old woman is brewing things below. Inger sank down into her brewery, and that's not a place you can stay for very long. A cesspool is a place of luxury compared with the Marsh Woman's brewery. Every vat reeks so horribly that you would faint,[8] and they are all packed closely together. Even if you

5. *there was nothing to see but a black, bubbling swamp.* In the *Inferno*, Dante travels to the fifth circle of hell, descending "grayish slopes" into "the marsh whose name is Styx." There he sees unfortunate souls "within that bog, all naked and muddy—with looks / Of fury." They are "lodged in slime" and remain sullen in "black mire" (*The Inferno of Dante*, pp. 71–73). In Andersen's *The Improvisatore,* the main character, Antonio, is passionately interested in the works of the Italian poet. It is not surprising that Andersen, who hoped to become Denmark's most celebrated writer, dedicated himself to the study of Dante, Shakespeare, Goethe, and the other great figures who became the representative writers of their culture.

6. *What became of her?* In his commentary on the story, Andersen explained that he had set himself the goal of showing how Inger converts from a life of sin and moves to a state of atonement, creating the opportunity for her salvation. Picking up where the ballad leaves off, Andersen's narrative remains deeply committed to the story of Inger's salvation but also lavishes attention on the details of her punishment, perhaps to intensify the cathartic effects of Inger's release and transformation.

7. *aunt to the elf maidens.* Elf maidens, or *Ellefruwen,* make frequent appearances in Scandinavian folklore. They are related to *Skogsnuva,* creatures who look appealing from the front but turn out to be rotting when seen from behind. In Andersen's late novel *Lykke Peer* (1870), the eponymous protagonist dreams of being tempted by the elf maidens to abandon his mortal existence but staunchly resists their lure. In that same work, Andersen refers to the Swedish ballad of Sir Olaf, who rode out to greet his wedding guests and became entranced by elf maidens who forced him to perform a dance of death.

8. *Every vat reeks so horribly that you would faint.* An overwhelming stench has been seen to symbolize moral and sexual corruption. Oddly, Inger's effort to keep her shoes *clean* results in her immersion into a polluted and contaminated space.

9. *just as amber attracts bits of straw.* *Kahroba,* a word for amber derived from Persian, means "that which attracts straw," in reference to the power of amber to acquire an electric charge by friction.

10. *the brewery was being visited that day by the devil and his great-grandmother.* The underground space seems dominated by women (the Marsh Woman and the devil's great-grandmother) rather than by the devil himself. Andersen viewed the role of the devil in much the same way that Goethe presented Mephistopheles in *Faust,* as a necessary and, in his own way, admirable opponent to mankind. "Everyone speaks badly of Satan," Andersen wrote. "They never recognize that he is merely fulfilling his duty. It is his job, after all, to seduce the children of humanity. He is the touchstone in this world; it is through him that we will be purified for the better; he is this struggle and flame, this *aspera* moving *ad astram,* and so he has here an important, meritorious role in the great drama of life" (Jens Andersen, 541). The devil's grandmother makes an appearance in a Grimm tale ("The Devil and His Grandmother") and functions as a benefactor to the hero, much like the giant's wife who protects and assists the protagonist in "Jack and the Beanstalk."

11. *How cleverly that old great-granny could sew, embroider, and weave!* The devil's grandmother seems to serve as a folkloric version of the Norns from Norse mythology, creatures who live beneath the roots of Yggdrasil at the center of the world. There they weave the fate of humans, with

could find a space wide enough to squeeze through, you wouldn't be able to get by because of all the slimy toads and the fat snakes tangled up in there. That's where Inger landed. The whole nasty, creepy mess was so icy cold that her every limb began to shiver, and she grew stiffer and stiffer. The loaf was still sticking to her feet, dragging her down, just as amber attracts bits of straw.[9]

LORENZ FRØLICH

The Marsh Woman was at home, for the brewery was being visited that day by the devil and his great-grandmother,[10] an extremely venomous old creature whose hands are never idle. She always has some needlework with her, and she had it with her this time too. Her pincushion was with her that day so that she could give people pins and needles in their legs and make them get up and run around. And she was busy embroidering lies and crocheting rash words that might have fallen harmlessly to the ground had she not woven them into mischief and slander. How cleverly that old great-granny could sew, embroider, and weave![11]

When the devil's great-grandmother saw Inger, she put on her spectacles and took a good look at her. "That girl has talent," she declared. "I'd like to take her back with me as a souvenir. She'd make a perfect statue for my great-grandson's entrance hall." And she got her!

That's how little Inger ended up in hell. People can't always go straight down there, but if they have a little talent, they can get there in a roundabout way.

The antechamber there seemed endless. It made you dizzy to look straight ahead and dizzy to look back. A crowd of anxious, miserable souls were waiting for the gates of mercy to be flung open. They would have to wait for a long time! Huge, hideous,

each string in their loom representing a life. The Norns are related to the Greek Moirae, whose spinning activities determine fates: Clotho spins the thread at birth, Lachesis weaves it, and Atropos cuts it at the end of life. Three in number as well, the Norns (Urth or Wyrd, Verthandi, and Skuld—representing the past, present, and future, respectively) appear in Shakespeare's *Macbeth* as the three weird sisters.

LORENZ FRØLICH

12. *a snake had wound itself into her hair and was dangling down her neck.* The snake in Inger's hair links her with the figure of Medusa, one of the three Gorgons. Like her monstrous sisters Stheno and Euryale, Medusa has brass hands, sharp fangs, and poisonous snakes in place of locks of hair. Athena turned Medusa's hair into snakes that coiled around her head when Medusa tried to vie in beauty with her. Anyone who dared behold Medusa was turned into stone. Inger may share Medusa's vanity and pride, along with her serpentine tresses, but it is she who is turned into stone by the gaze of others ("they were all staring at her").

During Andersen's trips to Italy and Greece, he immersed himself in Roman and Greek mythology, educating himself in sculpture and in painting and spending time with Danish artists who were living in Italy. Andersen characterized himself as a traveler who was driven by curiosity—"always in motion, trying to use every minute to see everything."

fat spiders were spinning webs that would last a thousand years around the feet of those waiting, and the webs were like foot screws or manacles that clamped down as strongly as copper chains on the feet. On top of all that, there was a deep sense of despair in every soul, a feeling of anxiety that was itself a torment. Among the crowd was a miser who had lost the key to his money box and now remembered that he had left it in the lock. But wait—it would take far too long to describe all the pain and torment suffered in that place. Inger began to feel the torture of standing still, just like a statue. It was as if she were riveted to the ground by the loaf of bread.

"This is what comes from trying to keep your shoes clean," she said to herself. "Look at how they're all staring at me." Yes, it's true, they were all staring at her, with evil passions gleaming in their eyes. They spoke without a sound coming from their mouths, and it was horrifying to look at them!

"It must be a pleasure to look at me," Inger thought. "I have a pretty face and nice clothes." And then she turned her eyes, for her neck was too stiff to move. Goodness, how dirty she had become in the Marsh Woman's brewery! She hadn't thought of that. Her dress was covered with one great streak of slime; a snake had wound itself into her hair and was dangling down her neck[12]; and from each fold in her dress an ugly toad was peeping out, making a croaking noise that sounded like the bark of a wheezy lapdog. It was most disagreeable. "Still," she consoled herself, "the others down here look no less dreadful."

Worst of all was the terrible hunger Inger felt. If she could just stoop down and break off a bit of the loaf on which she was standing! Impossible—for her back had stiffened, her arms and hands had stiffened, and her entire body was like a statue made of stone. All she could do was roll her eyes, roll them right around so that she could see what was behind her, and that was truly a ghastly sight. Flies began to land on her, and they crawled back and forth across her eyes. She blinked, but the flies wouldn't go away. They couldn't fly away because their wings had been pulled off, and they had become creeping insects. That made Inger's torment even worse, and, as for the pangs of hunger, it began to feel to her as if her innards were eating themselves up. She began to feel so empty inside, so terribly empty.[13]

"If this goes on much longer, I won't be able to bear it," she said, but she had to bear it, and everything just became worse than ever.

Suddenly a hot tear fell on her forehead.[14] It trickled down her face and chest, right down to the loaf of bread. Then another tear fell, and many more followed. Who could be weeping for little Inger? Didn't she have a mother up there on earth? The tears of grief shed by a mother for her wayward child can always reach her, but they only burn and make the torture all the greater. And now this unbearable hunger—and the impossibility of getting even a mouthful from the loaf she had trod underfoot! She was beginning to have the feeling that everything inside her must have eaten itself up. She was like a thin, hollow reed that absorbs every sound it hears. She could hear everything said about her on earth above, and what she heard was harsh and spiteful. Her mother may have been weeping and feeling deep sorrow, but still she said: "Pride goes before a fall.[15] That's what led to your ruin, Inger. You have created so much sorrow for your mother!"

Inger's mother and everyone else up above were all aware of her sin and how she had trod upon the loaf, sunk down, and disappeared. They had learned about it from the cowherd, who had seen it for himself from the crest of a hill.

"You have brought me so much grief, Inger," her mother said. "Yes, I always knew it would happen."

"I wish I had never been born!"[16] Inger thought. "I would have been so much better off. Mother's tears can do me no good now."

Inger heard her master and mistress speaking, those good

13. *She began to feel so empty inside, so terribly empty.* Inger's emphasis on appearances leads to a kind of spiritual hollowness and emptiness that is literalized when her insides begin to consume themselves down in hell. Like the mythical Tantalus who is doomed to eternal hunger even when fruit and water seem within reach, Inger stands on the loaf yet cannot use it for sustenance.

14. *Suddenly a hot tear fell on her forehead.* The heat of the tear contrasts with the chilling cold of hell. A symbol of warmth, kindness, and empathy, the tear contrasts with the cold rigidity of the netherworld where Inger is held captive and immobilized.

15. *"Pride goes before a fall."* The phrase derives from Proverbs 16:18: "Pride goes before destruction, and a haughty spirit before a fall."

16. *"I wish I had never been born!"* Inger's words echo Mark 14:21, which alludes to a far more momentous sin, the betrayal of Christ: "But woe to that man by whom the Son of man is betrayed. It would have been better for that man if he had not been born."

17. *Inger heard that a ballad had been written about her.* The production of the ballad during Inger's lifetime solidifies the chain of communication between earth and the nether regions. Despite the fact that the two realms are segregated, those above are aware of the misery of those in hell, and those below are aware of the judgments being passed on earth.

18. *"such a little thing?"* The one small step that leads to seemingly eternal punishment is of course not an isolated instance. Inger's pride and vanity are to blame, yet it becomes clear that the misstep is what counts when it comes to her damnation.

19. *Inger's heart became even harder than her shell-like form.* Impermeable, hard, rigid, stony, icy surfaces embody for Andersen the quintessence of sin. The hollowness of her body and the hardness of her heart turn Inger into an emblem of human degradation. Much like Kai in "The Snow Queen," Inger becomes completely isolated in a region that is affiliated with petrifaction and loss of feeling.

20. *Her story was being told to an innocent child.* This child, unlike the others, manages to feel empathy. She becomes a model for Inger in her humility and embodies the wisdom of Matthew 18:3–4: "Truly I say unto you, unless you turn and become like children, you will never enter the kingdom of heaven. Whoever humbles himself like this child, he is the greatest in the kingdom of heaven." (The ending of "The Snow Queen" also takes up the theme of becoming like children in order to enter the kingdom of heaven.)

people who had been like parents to her. "She was always a sinful child," they said. "She had no respect for the gifts of our Lord, but trampled them underfoot. It will be hard for her to squeeze through the gates of mercy."

"They should have done a better job raising me," Inger thought. "They should have cured me of my bad ways, if I had any."

Inger heard that a ballad had been written about her[17]— "The proud young girl who stepped on a loaf to keep her shoes clean." It was being sung from one end of the country to the other.

"Why should I have to suffer and be punished so severely for such a little thing?"[18] Inger thought. "Why aren't others punished for their sins as well? There would be so many people to punish. Oh, I am in such pain!"

Inger's heart became even harder than her shell-like form.[19] "Nothing will ever improve while I'm in this company! And I don't want to get better. Look at them all glaring at me!"

Her heart grew even harder and was filled with hatred for all humans.

"I dare say that they will have something to talk about now. Oh, I am in such pain!"

And she could hear people telling her story to children as a warning, and the little ones called her Wicked Inger. "She was so horrid," they said, "so nasty that she deserved to be punished."

The children had nothing but harsh words for her.

One day, when hunger and resentment were gnawing deeply away in her hollow body, she heard her name spoken. Her story was being told to an innocent child,[20] a small girl who burst into tears when she heard about proud Inger and her love of finery.

"Won't she ever come back up again?" the girl asked. And she was told: "She will never return."

LORENZ FRØLICH

"What if she asks for forgiveness and promises never to do it again?"

"But she won't ask to be forgiven," they replied.

"Oh, how I wish that she would!" the little girl said in great distress. "I'll give up my doll's house if they let her return. It's so horrible for poor Inger!"

These words went straight to Inger's heart and seemed to do her good. It was the first time anyone had said "Poor Inger" without adding anything about her faults. An innocent little child had wept and prayed for her. She was so moved that she would have liked to weep as well, but the tears would not flow, and that too was torture.

The years passed by up there, but down below nothing changed. Inger heard fewer words from above and there was less talk about her. Then one day she heard a deep sigh: "Inger, Inger, what sorrow you have brought me! I always said you would!" Those were her mother's dying words.

Sometimes she heard her name mentioned by her former mistress, who always spoke in the mildest way: "I wonder if I

21. *"Do not forsake me in this final hour!"*
Note the allusion to Psalms 71:9: "Do not cast me away when I am old; / Do not forsake me when my strength is gone"; and to Psalms 38:21: "Do not forsake me, oh Lord / Oh my God, be not far from me"; and finally to Psalms 27:10, which is relevant to Inger's plight: "When my father and mother forsake me, the Lord will take me up."

shall ever see you again, Inger. There's no knowing where I'll end up." But Inger knew well enough that her honest mistress would never end up in the place where she was.

A long time passed, slowly and bitterly. Then Inger heard her name spoken once again, and she saw above her what looked like two bright stars shining down on her. They were two gentle eyes that were about to close on earth. So many years had passed since the time when a small girl had cried inconsolably for "Poor Inger" that the child was by now an old woman, and the good Lord was about to call her to himself. In that final hour, when all the thoughts and deeds of a lifetime pass before you, the woman recalled clearly how, as a small child, she had wept bitter tears when hearing the sad story of Inger. That moment and the sense of sorrow following it were so vivid in the old woman's mind at the hour of her death that she cried out these heartfelt words: "Dear Lord, have I not too, like poor Inger, sometimes thoughtlessly trampled underfoot your blessings and counted them without value? Have I not also been guilty of pride and vanity in my inmost heart? And yet you, in your mercy, did not let me sink but held me up. Do not forsake me in this final hour!"[21]

The old woman's eyes closed, and the eyes of her soul were opened to what had been hidden. And because Inger had been so profoundly present in her final thoughts, the old woman was actually able to see her and to understand how deeply she had sunk. At the dreadful sight of her, the saintly soul burst into tears. She stood like a child in the kingdom of heaven and wept for poor Inger. Her tears and prayers rang like an echo down into the hollow, empty shell that held an imprisoned, tormented soul. Inger was overwhelmed by all the unexpected love from above. To think that one of God's angels would be weeping for her! How did she deserve this act of kindness? The tormented soul thought back on every deed she had performed during her life on earth and was convulsed with sobs, weeping in ways that the old Inger could never have wept. Inger was filled with sorrow for herself, and she felt certain the gates of mercy would never open for her. She was beginning to realize this with the deepest humility, when, suddenly, a brilliant ray flashed down into the bottomless pit, one more powerful than the sunbeams that melt the snowmen that boys build outdoors.[22] And at the touch of this ray—faster than a snowflake turns into water when it lands on a child's warm lips—Inger's stiffened, stony figure vanished. A tiny bird soared like forked lightning up toward the world of humans.[23]

The bird seemed timid and afraid of everything around it, as if ashamed and wanting to avoid the sight of all living creatures. It hastened to find shelter and discovered it in the dark hole of a crumbling wall. It cowered there, and trembled all over, without uttering a sound, for it had no voice.[24] It stayed there for a long time before it dared to peer out and take in the beauty all around. And, yes indeed, it was beautiful. The air was so fresh, the breeze gentle, and the moon was shining brightly. Among the fragrant trees and flowers, the bird was perched in a cozy spot, its feathers clean and dainty. How much love and splendor there was in all created things![25] The bird was eager to express in song the thoughts bursting from its heart, but it could not. It wanted to sing like the nightingale or the cuckoo in the springtime. Our Lord, who can hear even the voiceless hymn of the worm, understood the hymn of praise that swelled up in chords of thought, like the psalms that resonated in David's heart before they took shape in words and music.[26]

For days and weeks, these mute songs grew stronger. Someday they would surely find a voice, perhaps with the first stroke of a wing performing a good deed. Was the time not ripe?

The holy feast of Christmas was nigh.[27] A farmer had put a pole up near the wall and had tied an unthreshed bundle of oats to it, so that creatures of the air might also have a merry Christmas and a cheerful meal in this season of the Savior.

22. *more powerful than the sunbeams that melt the snowmen that boys build outdoors.* Sunbeams, rays of light, and flashes of lightning are all contrasted to stone, ice, and snow. In this story, as in "The Snow Queen," light, warmth, and fluidity are associated with salvation while gloom, cold, and petrifaction become the attributes of damnation.

23. *A tiny bird soared like forked lightning up toward the world of humans.* The mute bird, like the ugly duckling, must wait patiently for its transfiguration. But for salvation it must also perform good deeds—it cannot simply suffer silently as the ugly duckling does.

24. *it had no voice.* The bird's voice returns with the performance of good deeds and adds to the beauty of nature. Like the little mermaid and Elisa in "The Wild Swans," the bird is unable to express its true feelings and must suffer in silence.

25. *How much love and splendor there was in all created things!* Andersen's description of sights, sounds, and aromas is a reminder of the degree to which he valued natural beauty and the splendors of earthly life.

26. *like the psalms that resonated in David's heart before they took shape in words and music.* Inger's story contains many allusions to the Psalms, and it is not surprising that David is invoked at last to emphasize language's capacity to capture the richness of emotional life.

27. *The holy feast of Christmas was nigh.* It is in the season of Christ's birth that Inger finds salvation. Note that the farmer's good deed plays a role in lifting the burden of muteness from the bird, and that Inger in her avian form is enabled to perform good deeds by the farmer's generosity.

28. *The idea of a good deed had awakened.* For Lutherans, it is by faith alone (*sola fide*) and by grace alone (*sola gratia*) that salvation is possible. In Luther's doctrine of redemption, good works and merit are important, but they are no guarantee for redemption and are undertaken simply for their moral value.

29. *so many crumbs that they equaled in weight the loaf.* The requirement to reconstitute the loaf seems almost perverse in its fetishizing of "our daily bread." Inger's failure to value her daily bread, along with her obligation to recreate it by assembling crumbs, suggests that the loaf is charged with deep symbolic significance as God's gift to man.

30. *the bird's gray wings turned white and spread out.* The transformation from gray to white repeats what happened to the ugly duckling, who turns from a black-gray hue to white.

The sun rose that Christmas morning and shone down brightly upon the sheaf of oats and all the twittering birds gathered around it. A faint "tweet, tweet" sounded from the wall. The swelling thoughts had finally turned into sound, and the feeble chirp turned into a hymn of joy. The idea of a good deed had awakened,[28] and the bird flew out from its hiding place. In heaven they knew exactly what kind of bird it was.

Winter began in earnest; the ponds were frozen over with thick ice; and the birds and wild creatures were short of food. The tiny bird flew along country roads, and, there, in the tracks of sledges, it managed to find a grain of corn here and there, or in the best places, a few crumbs of bread. It would eat but a single grain of corn and then alert the other famished birds so that they too could find food. It also flew into the towns, inspecting the ground, and wherever a kindly hand had scattered breadcrumbs from the window for birds, it would take just a single crumb and give the rest away.

By the end of the winter the bird had collected and given away so many crumbs that they equaled in weight the loaf[29] upon which little Inger had trod to keep her fine shoes from being soiled. And when it had found and given away the last crumb, the bird's gray wings turned white and spread out.[30]

"Look, there's a tern flying across the lake," the children

cried out when they saw the white bird.[31] First it dipped down into the water, then it rose into the bright sunshine. The bird's wings glittered so brightly in the air that it was impossible to see where it was flying. They say that it flew straight into the sun.[32]

31. *the children cried out when they saw the white bird.* As in "The Ugly Duckling," children are the first to take note of an avian creature that is striking because of its whiteness. "The Emperor's New Clothes" also ends with a child calling the attention of adults to another shock effect, this time of nakedness rather than of beauty.

32. *They say that it flew straight into the sun.* The sun, invariably associated with warmth and with salvation, signals Inger's redemption.

The Phoenix

Fugl Phønix

Digterens danske Værker, 1850

he Phoenix" is the most lyrical of Andersen's tales. Eulogizing the bird of paradise, it combines biblical narratives with Scandinavian lore and ancient mythologies to construct an aesthetic in which beauty constantly renews itself in bursts of cataclysmic destruction. Nature becomes the model for an art that pulses with organic vitality and the promise of metamorphosis and rebirth. Ducks, swans, sparrows, storks, butterflies, and other ordinary winged creatures perpetually find their way into Andersen's narratives. Sometimes they enact fables about human behavior, sometimes they encounter humans to offer wisdom, direction, or assistance, and frequently they incarnate the human soul in flight. The phoenix, with its glorious color and song, rises above the ordinary to serve as the model for an art that will never perish, even as it repeatedly goes up in flames. That winged creature has inspired one critic to refer to Andersen's art as governed by "the phoenix principle," a profound faith in the power of art to endure beyond its material existence.

Beneath the tree of knowledge in the Garden of Eden,[1] a rosebush was growing. From its first blossom, a bird was born, with beautiful plumage, glorious colors, and an enchanting song.

When Eve plucked fruit from the tree of knowledge, she and Adam were driven from Eden, and a spark flew from the flaming sword of the angel into the bird's nest and set it on fire. The bird perished in the flames, but a new bird arose from the egg glowing in the nest, the only one of its kind, the peerless phoenix. Legend tells us that it comes from Arabia[2] and that it sets itself on fire every hundred years. But almost at once a new phoenix, the only one in the entire world, flies out from the egg glowing in the nest.

The bird darts around us as swiftly as light. Its colors are glorious, and its wondrous song captivates us. When a mother sits by a cradle, it flits around the pillow, creating a halo around the infant's head. It flies through a shabby parlor, spreading sunshine, and suddenly a humble cupboard smells of violets.

The phoenix is not native to Arabia alone. In the glimmer of the Northern lights, it soars over the icy plains of Lapland

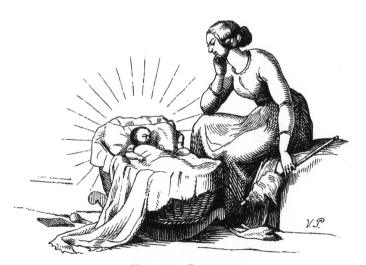

VILHELM PEDERSON

1. *Beneath the tree of knowledge in the Garden of Eden.* The rosebush growing in Eden is Andersen's invention, but he remains otherwise faithful to the biblical story. The angel with the flaming sword is described in Genesis 3:24: "After he drove the man out, he placed on the east side of the Garden of Eden cherubim and a flaming sword flashing back and forth to guard the way to the tree of life."

2. *Legend tells us that it comes from Arabia.* The phoenix is associated in many cultures with death, resurrection, and immortality. In ancient Egyptian myths, the phoenix was a male bird with gold and red plumage. At the end of its life span (the exact number of centuries varies), it was said to build a nest of sweet-smelling wood, to which it set fire. From the ashes of the phoenix arose a young new bird. The new phoenix took the ashes of the old and made of them an egg of myrrh, which was deposited in Heliopolis ("city of the sun" in Greek) on the altar of Ra, the Sun God. In the Egyptian myth, the bird was known as Bennu and was sometimes represented on sarcophagi as a heron. Russian folklore has its counterpart to the phoenix in the firebird.

In Andersen's story "Garden of Eden," the South Wind reports the following about the phoenix: "I saw the phoenix set fire to its nest, and I just sat there while it burned like a Hindu's widow. The dry branches made a crackling sound, and there was smoke and perfume! Finally, everything went up in flames, and the old phoenix burned to ashes. But its glowing red-hot egg was lying in the fire, and then burst with a loud noise, and the young one flew out. Now it rules over all birds and is the only phoenix in the world."

3. *beneath the copper mountains of Falun.*
Located in the central part of Sweden, the
great copper mines of Falun were put into
operation as early as the twelfth century.
Andersen traveled to Sweden (where there
were no "roaring cannon") in 1849, when
fighting erupted between Denmark and
Prussia. He published a travel memoir,
Pictures of Sweden, in 1851, documenting
his appreciation of the Swedish landscape.
The copper mines in Sweden also served as
the setting for *The Mines of Falun,* a short
story by E.T.A. Hoffmann. Andersen's
inventory of geographical sites, including
Falun, is intended to underscore that the
myth shows no signs of cultural fatigue.

4. *seated in the carriage of Thespis.*
Renowned as the inventor of tragedy,
Thespis was born in Attica in the sixth
century B.C. He is said to have introduced
the notion of an actor (as opposed to the
chorus), as well as costumes, masks, and
make-up, which he carried through
Athens in a cart for his street performances. The term *thespian,* denoting actors
and actresses, comes from his name.

5. *looking like Odin's raven.* Odin, the
chief god of Norse mythology, has two
ravens, Huginn and Muninn, and they fly
all over the world to bring news back to
him. (The melodious bird in Andersen's
"Nightingale" takes on a similar role for
the Emperor in China at the end of that
story.)

6. *it fluttered through the halls of the Wartburg.* Wartburg Castle, built early in the
eleventh century, overlooks the town of
Eisenach, in Thuringia, Germany. It
became the site of courtly culture, in particular the so-called Sängerkrieg, or Contest of Minstrels, at the beginning of the
thirteenth century. Participants included
the renowned poets Walter von der Vogel-
weide and Wolfram von Eschenbach. The

and hops about amid the yellow flowers in Greenland's brief
summer. It can be seen beneath the copper mountains of
Falun[3] as well as in England's coal mines. It hovers like a
powdery moth above the hymnal resting in the hands of a
pious miner. It floats down the sacred waters of the Ganges on
a lotus leaf, and the eyes of Hindu maidens brighten when
they behold it.

The phoenix! I'm sure you know it. It is the bird of Eden,
the blessed swan of song. It was seated in the carriage of Thespis[4] and sat back there like a chattering raven, flapping its
gutter-stained black wings. The swan's red beak, resounding
with song, swept over the harps of Iceland's bards. It sat on
Shakespeare's shoulders, looking like Odin's raven,[5] and
whispered the word "immortality" in his ear. At the minstrels' contest, it fluttered through the halls of the
Wartburg.[6]

The phoenix! I'm sure you know it. It sang the "Marseillaise" to you,[7] and you kissed the feather that dropped from
its wing. It landed in all the glory of paradise, but perhaps
you turned away to look at the sparrow perched before you
with gold-tipped wings.

Oh bird of paradise, renewed with each new century, you

are born in flames and die in flames. Framed in gold, your portrait adorns the halls of the wealthy, yet you yourself soar through the air and off course, nothing but a myth. The phoenix of Arabia!

When you were born beneath the tree of knowledge as the first rose in the Garden of Eden, God kissed you and gave you your proper name: Poetry.

Sängerkrieg is at the center of Richard Wagner's opera *Tannhäuser*.

7. *It sang the "Marseillaise" to you.* The "Marseillaise," now France's national anthem, was written and composed in 1792. It was sung during the French Revolution by troops from Marseille upon their arrival in Paris. By Andersen's time, it had already become the international revolutionary anthem.

The Goblin and the Grocer

Nissen hos spækhøkeren

Historier. Anden Samling, 1853

Despite the fact that both goblin and grocer appear in the title, the goblin is the real hero of the tale. Oddly, Andersen has a cast of three but does not include the student/poet in the title. The goblin, a creature of fantasy, bridges the student's world of poetic visions and the grocer's world of commerce and commodities. He lives out the dream of receiving material sustenance from the grocer (housing and a bowl of porridge) and spiritual nourishment from the poet (the visions that emerge from the pages of books).

"The Goblin and the Grocer" was included in Andrew Lang's famous fairy-tale series of books for children published at the end of the nineteenth century and still in print today. And yet it has not attained the canonical status of other tales by Andersen, in part because it is less a fairy tale for children than an allegory of reading for adults. The story, written in 1849, around the time that Andersen's short stories were becoming increasingly occupied with art, celebrates the power of words on a page to transform themselves into shimmering visions of beauty and also extols the pleasures of witnessing the act of reading. While the student is reading from a "tattered book," his tiny attic room transforms itself into a luminous paradise, filled with sights, sounds, and aromas. The goblin, solely by observ-

ing the student, is able to experience for himself the visionary power of the book. Drawn to the material and to the spiritual, the goblin finds a way to have his porridge and eat it too.

There was once a student who was living in a garret.[1] He owned absolutely nothing. There was once also a grocer, who was living on the ground floor of that very house, and he owned the whole place. The household goblin[2] was devoted to the grocer, for every Christmas Eve he was given a bowl of porridge with a big pat of butter right in the middle of it. The grocer had the goods, and so the goblin stayed in his shop, and that is all very instructive.

One evening the student came in through the back door to buy some candles and cheese. He had no one to run his errands, and that's why he was there in person. He found what he was looking for, paid up, and the grocer and his wife nodded "Good evening." The wife was a woman who could do more than just nod, for she had the gift of gab. The student nodded in return, but he stopped in his tracks when he started reading what was on the piece of paper wrapped around his cheese. It was a page torn out of an old book that ought never to have been torn up, for it was a book of poetry.[3]

"There's more of it over here!" the grocer said. "I gave an old woman some coffee beans for it. If you're willing to pay me a couple of pennies, the rest of it is yours."

"If I may," said the student. "I'll take the book instead of the cheese. I don't mind eating my bread without any cheese on it. It would be a sin to tear the book completely apart. You're a splendid fellow, a practical man, but you know about as much about poetry as that tub over there."

Now that was a rude way to speak, especially with the tub there, but the grocer laughed and the student laughed too. After all, it was all in jest. But the goblin was offended that

1. *There was once a student who was living in a garret.* Impoverished students appear frequently in Andersen's work, and they are often associated with poetry, as is the case with this story and with "Auntie Toothache." It is no accident that the "poetic" student lives in aerial regions, while the more materialistic grocer (grocers are always slightly vulgar for Andersen in their preoccupation with sustenance for the body) inhabits the ground floor.

2. *household goblin.* In Scandinavian countries, the *nisse*, or household goblin, figures importantly in Christmas traditions. Often sporting a white beard and wearing a red cap, he is a benevolent local spirit who guards the security and prosperity of the family with whom he lives—not at all like the gremlins and imps we associate with goblins in Anglo-American cultures. His annual reward at Christmas is a big bowl of porridge with a pat of butter floating in it.

3. *it was a book of poetry.* The mingling of the sacred and the profane—a page of poetry used to wrap cheese—introduces the story's major theme, for the goblin finds himself divided between his allegiances to the grocer, who provides porridge, and the student, who provides beauty and poetry. One sustains the body; the other warms the soul.

4. *suddenly had a voice.* Speaking objects play an important role in Andersen's works: a jack-in-the-box uses menacing words with other toys, a tub talks to a pot, and a collar proposes to a pair of scissors. When it was said of Andersen that he could create a story in which a darning needle came to life, Andersen obliged with a talking darning needle that aspires to become a sewing needle. The gift of gab that is said to belong to the grocer's wife is circulated among the items in the shop. The glib linguistic fluency found downstairs takes the form of emotional outbursts and sentimental effusions. The different voices at one point form "the opinion of the majority," and they could represent a satirical thrust at the many Danish critics who disparaged Andersen's works in the popular press. In contrast, the poetry that radiates from the book purchased by the student has a quite different effect.

5. *the goblin peeped through the keyhole.* The goblin lives a vicarious existence, staying behind the scenes and finding pleasure in witnessing and listening rather than acting. He becomes a charming connoisseur and gourmand.

6. *A dazzling ray of light rose up from the book.* The visionary tableau in the student's garret resembles a utopian moment in "The Golden Pot: A Modern Fairy Tale" by E.T.A. Hoffmann. Anselmus, the student-poet in that tale, takes a job working as a scribe, and, when he begins to study the exotic characters he must copy, the room in which he is writing begins to transform itself: "He heard strange music coming from the garden, and he was surrounded by sweet and lovely fragrances. . . . At times it also seemed to him that the emerald leaves of the palm trees were rustling and that the clear crystal tones which Anselmus had heard under the

anyone would dare say such things to the grocer, to a man who not only owned the house but also sold the very best butter around.

That night, after the shop had closed and everyone was in bed but the student, the goblin stole into the grocer's bedroom and borrowed the tongue of the grocer's wife, who had no use for it while she was sleeping. Any object on which he placed the tongue suddenly had a voice[4] and could pour out its thoughts and feelings as fluently as the grocer's wife herself. But only one object at a time could use the tongue, and that was a blessing, for otherwise they would have spoken at the same time.

First the goblin placed the tongue on the tub in which old newspapers were kept. "Is it really true," asked the goblin, "that you know nothing about poetry?"

"Of course I know about poetry," the tub replied. "It's the stuff that they put near the bottom of the page in the newspapers, and sometimes it gets cut out! I dare say I have more poetry in me than that student, and I'm a mere tub by comparison to the grocer."

Next, the goblin put the tongue on the coffee grinder, and did it ever chatter away! He placed it on the butter vat and on the cash box. Everyone agreed with the tub, and you really have to respect the opinion of the majority.

"I'll give that student a piece of my mind!" and with those words he tiptoed up the stairs to the garret where the student was living. A candle was still burning, and the goblin peeped through the keyhole[5] and could see that the student was reading from the tattered book that he had brought upstairs from the shop.

How extraordinarily bright it was in the room! A dazzling ray of light rose up from the book[6] and transformed itself into a tree trunk that spread its branches over the student. Each leaf on the tree was a fresh green color, and every flower was the face of a beautiful maiden, some with dark, sparkling

ARTHUR RACKHAM

The goblin peers through the keyhole of the door to the student's garret. The book he is reading illuminates the dark attic space and creates greenery. Down in the cellar the various kitchen utensils are gossiping, and on the ground floor, the grocer, who is considerably more prosperous than the student, blows out the candle, creating darkness instead of light.

elder tree . . . were dancing and flitting through the room. . . . He discovered that he was looking at a lovely and glorious maiden who was coming towards him from the tree, looking at him with ineffable longing with those dark blue eyes which lived in his heart. The leaves appeared to reach down and to expand" (Kent and Knight, 63). Beauty, in the form of sights, sounds, and aromas, emanates here too from the words on the page.

eyes, others with marvelous clear blue eyes. Every fruit on the tree was a shining star, and the room was filled with music and song.

The little goblin had never dreamed that such splendor could exist, let alone that he would ever have the chance to see it and listen to it. He stood there on tiptoe, gazing for all he was worth until the light in the garret finally went out. The student must have blown out the candle and gone to bed, but the little goblin stayed right where he was, for the music continued softly and splendidly as a lovely lullaby to put the student to sleep.

"There's no other place on earth like this one," the goblin exclaimed. "I would never have dreamed this was possible. That's it! I'm going to live here with the student." He stopped to think—for he was a creature of reason—and then he sighed deeply: "Of course the student doesn't have any porridge at all." And so he went back down the stairs to the grocer, and it was a good thing too, for the tub had nearly worn out the tongue of the grocer's wife. It had first turned to the left and blurted out all the things it had been holding in. Then, just as it was about to turn around to do the honors from the right side, the goblin walked in and returned the tongue to the grocer's wife. From that moment on, the entire shop, from the cash box on right down to the kindling wood, formed all their ideas based on what the tub had to say. Their respect for it was so great and their confidence ran so high that when the grocer read the art and theater reviews in the evening paper, they were all convinced that the opinions in it had come straight from the tub.

But the little goblin was no longer satisfied with the wisdom and knowledge that he had picked up from eavesdropping downstairs. As soon as light shone down from the garret, he felt as if the rays were great anchor ropes drawing him upward and that he had to take a look through the keyhole. He was overwhelmed by the same sense of the sublime we experience when we are on the endlessly churning ocean and God passes over it in the form of a storm. Tears came to his eyes, and, although he did not know why he was crying, he was overcome by strange sensations that warmed his heart. How fabulous it would be to sit with the student beneath that tree of light! He realized that that was impossible, and he was therefore perfectly content to peer through the keyhole. When the autumn wind began to send wintry blasts through the trapdoor leading up to the attic, the goblin was still there every evening on the cold landing. It was dreadfully cold, but the little fellow didn't notice until the light went out in the garret and the music dissipated in the wind. Ouf! then he began to shiver and would crawl down to his own little cozy corner, where it was pleasant and comfortable. And when Christmas came around, along with the bowl of porridge and big pat of butter in it, why, then the grocer was king.

In the middle of the night, the goblin was awakened by a hullabaloo. People were banging on the windows, and the watchman was blasting away on his horn. A house was on fire,[7] and the entire city seemed to be ablaze. Was it the grocer's house or was it next door? Where could it be? Everybody was terrified! The grocer's wife was in such a panic that she took off her golden earrings and put them in her pocket so that she could at least rescue something. The grocer ran to get his documents and permits, and the servant ran for the black silk mantilla that she had managed to buy from her savings. Everyone wanted to rescue what they treasured the most, and that was true of the little goblin as well. With a leap and a bound he made it upstairs and landed in the room of the student, who was standing calmly at the open window, watching the fire that was raging in the house across the street. The goblin snatched the book lying on the table, tucked it in his red cap, and clutched it in his arms. The treasure of the house had been saved. And then he raced out, first up to the roof, and then right up onto the chimney. There he sat, lit up by

7. *A house was on fire.* Here once again, as in "The Steadfast Tin Soldier," is evidence of the phoenix principle at work in Andersen's stories. The conflagration produces the same light and heat as the book, yet is seen as destructive rather than creative— hence the goblin's race to rescue the book. And yet, like the phoenix which rises from the ashes, the book that is consumed by fire might turn the student from a reader and consumer of words to a writer and creator of words. As one critic puts it, "Loss of identity as the first step to renewal of identity, failure as success, defeat as necessary condition for a triumphant victory of poetry" (Detering, 56).

the flames of the house across the street, clutching with both his hands the cap holding the treasure.

Suddenly he realized what he truly desired and to whom his heart belonged. But once the fire had been put out, and the goblin had a chance to think long and hard about it—well!

"I'll simply have to divide myself between them," he declared. "That way, each one will have a little something. How can I give up the grocer? He's the one with the porridge."

And that was spoken in truly human terms! If we're really honest about it, then we have to admit that the world is like that. The rest of us would end up at the grocer's too. We need the porridge.

Auntie Toothache

Tante Tandpine

Nye Eventyr og Historier. Anden Samling, 1872

story about the failures of poetry, "Auntie Toothache" ends by validating the power of poetry. "Everything ends up in the trash," the story famously ends, and the trash is precisely the place where the story "Auntie Toothache" is found, but then revived, circulated, retold, and put into print in a way that assures its power to endure. One critic has classified "Auntie Toothache" as a "euphoric" text, for in it, "the poetical dimension more and more wins over, permeates and sees through the terrible phenomenal and psychological mess" (Barlby, 516). To be sure, poetry and pain are secret accomplices, both signs of absence and decay, but in this story poetry wins the day by representing the life and writings of the student-poet and assuring that imagination will triumph over pain. "Auntie Toothache" was written in 1872, the year Andersen had his last remaining tooth extracted. He joins a pantheon of writers ranging from Dostoevsky and Poe to Thomas Mann and Martin Amis who have written about the poetry of dental pain, yoking suffering and art and also taking advantage of what has been called the nexus of "potency, beauty, and pain" associated with teeth (Theodore Ziolkowski 1976, 11). As Leonato puts it in Much Ado about

1. *Where did we get this story?* The narrator raises the question of origins at the start, beginning with an authorial "we," as in "Heartache," but shifting quickly to "I." His question implies an audience interrogating him about the source of the story. He claims to provide nothing more than the frame for the story that bears the title "Auntie Toothache." He nonetheless becomes a double of that story's author, for both are writers and both have produced stories with the title "Auntie Toothache," even if one story is embedded in the other. The framed tale was not uncommon in nineteenth-century European novellas, but Andersen used it sparingly.

2. *They are needed as wrapping paper for starch and coffee beans.* Books, the narrator observes, are constantly recycled, circulated, and disseminated, even if in odd ways that do not conform to the author's aspirations. The narrator receives mere pages or fragments of the student's narrative, and he sends those pages out into the world, reconstituting them to form a new narrative that will also circulate in various forms, sometimes as trash, but sometimes as the inspiration for new stories.

3. *I know a grocery boy.* The narrator names his source, revealing a connection between nourishment for the body and the nourishing of the soul. The grocery boy, who begins life in the basement and is dedicated to commodities, stands in sharp contrast to the poet who occupies a garret and has lofty aspirations. Carl Spitzweg popularized and sentimentalized the image of the starving poet in his 1839 painting *The Poor Poet*, which shows an (aging) poet in a garret, books at his side, nightcap on his head, and umbrella perched above him to protect him from leaks in the roof.

Nothing, *"For there was never yet philosopher / that could endure the toothache patiently"* (5, 1).

"Auntie Toothache" is more in the mode of the uncanny short story than the fairy tale. It represents the writing of a mature poet who is struggling to find meaning in a life dedicated to creating "immortal" works of art even as he is experiencing the pains of mortality. Andersen began to feel the first symptoms of the liver cancer from which he died shortly after finishing this story, which is his last tale. "Auntie Toothache" represents one of his greatest achievements, yet it is rarely included in anthologies of his work, in large part because it takes up existential questions in a savagely nihilistic manner. Auntie Toothache gives voice to morbid anxieties that haunted the poet in the final year of his life but that also trouble our faith in the power of art to create effects that rival (or compensate for) the force of a simple toothache.

Where did we get this story?[1]

Would you like to know?

We took it out of the basket, the one in which you throw wastepaper.

Lots of good rare books end up at the delicatessen or at the grocer's, not to be read but for more basic purposes. They are needed as wrapping paper for starch and coffee beans,[2] as well as for salt herring, butter, and cheese. Used writing paper also comes in handy.

Things are sometimes tossed in the trash when they don't really belong there.

I know a grocery boy,[3] the son of a butcher. He worked his way up from the cellar to the street-level shop. He is a well-read person, who has seen a lot of printed and handwritten material on the paper used for wrapping. He has an interesting collection, consisting of important official documents from the wastepaper baskets of busy, absentminded officials, a few confidential letters from one lady friend to another, and scandalous news that was to go no further, not to be mentioned by a soul. He is a living rescue operation for more than a significant portion of our literature, and his collection covers a range of topics. He has the run of his parents' shop as well as the shop of his employer. In both places he has saved many a book or pages from books that are well worth reading more than once.

He showed me his collection of printed and handwritten materials from the trash, the most valued items coming from the delicatessen. There were several pages in it from a large composition book. The unusually clear and beautiful handwriting caught my eye at once.[4]

"A student wrote that," he said. "The student who lived just across the street and who died about a month ago. He was suffering from a terrible toothache, as you will learn. It is rather amusing to read. There is not much left of what he

4. *The unusually clear and beautiful handwriting caught my eye at once.* Clarity and beauty are characteristics valued by Andersen the author, and the handwriting of the student signals something positive about the quality of his writings.

LORENZ FRØLICH

The grocer's boy shows the author his collection of papers that come from the trash can.

5. *half a pound of green soap.* In Danish, something too slippery to handle is as slippery as "green soap."

6. *AUNTIE TOOTHACHE.* The title of the student's narrative is the same as the title of Andersen's story. As Jacob Bøggild points out, we cannot trust the student's claim that the manuscript was not meant for publication. "Why provide it with a title, then" (Bøggild, 33)? The student also constantly makes appeals to the reader or addresses the concerns of an implied reader: "Who was Auntie Millie and who was Brewer Rasmussen?"

7. *There's something of the poet in me.* The touch of poetry, the student narrator insists, exists in every human being as a beam of sunshine, the aroma of a flower, or a haunting melody. Appreciation of nature's beauty suffices to ignite the divine spark. Note that poetic consciousness is developed through sensual experiences from the real world—light, smell, and sound.

8. *I feel as if I am walking through a vast library.* The narrator turns the world into an opportunity for reading. The transformation of the city into a text designed for his consumption reveals the distance he keeps to the world, yet it also demonstrates the fertility of his imagination, which uses the outside world as a stimulus for fantasy and philosophy.

9. *Just then a leaf, fresh and green, fell down from a linden tree.* The leaf carried in through the window can be seen as both a leaf from a tree and a page from a book. The student "reads" the leaf, just as he reads everything in the world around him and uses those readings as a point of departure for fantasy and philosophy. Indeed, the student begins to philosophize about how the leaf demonstrates our limited

wrote. Once there was a whole book and more on top of that. My parents gave the student's landlady half a pound of green soap[5] in exchange for it. Here's what I managed to save of it."

I borrowed it, I read it, and now I'll tell you what it said.

The title was: AUNTIE TOOTHACHE[6]

I

Auntie gave me sweets when I was little. My teeth could stand it then, and they weren't ruined. Now I've grown up and become a student, and she still spoils me with sweets and tells me that I am a poet.

There's something of the poet in me,[7] but not enough. Often when I go walking through the streets of the city, I feel as if I am walking through a vast library.[8] The houses are bookcases, and each floor is a shelf lined with books. Over there you'll find a story of everyday life; next to it is a good old-fashioned comedy; and there are scholarly books from every field. Over here you'll find trash and some good reading. I can fantasize and philosophize about all those books.

I have something of the poet in me, but not enough. Many people have just as much of it in them as I do, but they don't carry a sign or wear a collar with the word "Poet" on it.

We've all been given a divine gift, a blessing large enough for ourselves, but much too small to be portioned out to others. It appears like a ray of sunshine and fills your soul and your mind. It comes like the scent of a flower, like a melody you know but can't remember from where.

The other evening I was sitting in my room, and I felt the urge to read but didn't have a book, not even a page. Just then a leaf, fresh and green, fell down from a linden tree.[9] The breeze carried it to me through the window.

I examined the veins that branched out on it. A little bug

was crawling across them, as if it were planning to make a thorough study of the leaf. That made me think about human wisdom. We also crawl around on a leaf, and that's all we know. And yet we immediately start lecturing about the whole big tree, its roots, trunk, and crown. The big tree: God, the world, and immortality, and all we know of that is one little leaf!

While I was sitting there, Auntie Millie came to visit.

I showed her the leaf with the insect and told her about my thoughts. Her eyes lit up.

"You're a poet!" she declared. "Perhaps the greatest we have! If I live to see it happen, I will go to my grave with joy. Ever since Brewer Rasmussen's funeral, you have never ceased to astonish me with your powerful imagination."

That's what Auntie Millie said, and then she kissed me.

Who was Auntie Millie, and who was Brewer Rasmussen?

LORENZ FRØLICH

Auntie Millie declares that the author is a poet and that he has extraordinary powers of imagination.

II

As children, we always called my mother's aunt "Auntie"—we had no other name for her.

She would give us jam and sweets, even though it was very bad for our teeth.[10] But she claimed to have a weakness for sweet children. It was cruel to deny them a few sweets when they were so fond of them.

That's why we loved Auntie so much.

She had been a spinster for as far back as I remember, and she had always been old. Her age never seemed to change.[11]

She had once suffered a good deal from toothaches[12] and

knowledge of the whole: We are doomed to know only fragments (leaves) but are forever in search of knowledge about "the whole big tree." The narrative before the reader also represents nothing more than single leaves, providing only partial knowledge of its author(s). "Auntie Toothache" repeatedly mourns fragmentation even as it attempts to achieve it through a life-narrative that comes to us as single leaves or fragments.

10. *even though it was very bad for our teeth.* Much as the narrator's aunt is presented as benevolent, her indulgence of the children with sweets affiliates her with the misery of the toothaches brought on by the second aunt in the story, a double of the real-life Auntie Millie.

11. *Her age never seemed to change.* That the aunt is well-preserved may be to her

credit, but it also underscores the fact that there is something about her that is *unnatural*, rather like her artificial teeth.

12. *She had once suffered a good deal from toothaches.* That Auntie "once" suffered from toothaches suggests that her white teeth are in fact artificial, and Brewer Rasmussen knows the secret to her "beautiful white teeth."

13. *He had no teeth at all, just a few black stumps.* Brewer Rasmussen's lack of teeth is invoked just before we learn about Auntie's "beautiful white teeth." The "whiteness" of her teeth—which may be the result of a cosmetic intervention—is matched against "black" stumps, creating a strong contrast between beautiful gleaming surfaces and a grotesque darkness and lack. The plenitude, wholeness, and immediate presence of Auntie's teeth—whether artificial or real—are juxtaposed to the hollow, decaying, fragmented absence in Rasmussen's mouth. The teeth are more than they appear to be, for they come to be implicated in the deeply problematic relationship between wholeness and fragmentation in the poetics set forth by the author.

Andersen suffered all his life from bad teeth, and in a diary entry of January 19, 1873, he describes losing his last tooth: "Dr. Voss arrived around three o'clock and extracted my last tooth. He gave me an anaesthetic, but I could still feel the wrenching pain. . . . I was lighthearted at the thought that I no longer had any teeth left, but not quite as ecstatic as the other day when he extracted the first of the four loose ones. Well, now I am completely toothless."

14. *As a child he had eaten too much sugar.* Ever the educator but also the tempter, Andersen cannot let the opportunity slip

was always talking about them. And so it happened that her friend, Brewer Rasmussen, who was a great wit, started to call her Auntie Toothache.

He had not done any brewing for the last few years and was living on the interest from his money. He frequently visited Auntie, and he was older than she. He had no teeth at all, just a few black stumps.[13]

As a child he had eaten too much sugar,[14] he told us children, and that's how he came to look as he did.

Auntie couldn't possibly have eaten sugar as a child, for she had the most beautiful white teeth.

She also used them sparingly. In fact, she didn't even sleep with them at night,[15] Brewer Rasmussen told us.

We children felt that this was a nasty thing to say, but Auntie told us that he didn't mean anything by it.

One day at lunch she told us about a terrible dream she had had during the night. A tooth had fallen out.

"That means that I'm going to lose a true friend soon," she said.

"Was it a false tooth?" the brewer asked with a chuckle. "If it was, that means that you will just lose a false friend."

"You are a rude old man!" Auntie said, angrier than I've ever seen her before or since then.

She later told us that her old friend had only been teasing and that he was the noblest soul on earth. The day that he died he would become one of God's little angels in heaven.

I wondered a good deal about this transformation and whether I would be able to recognize him in his new state.

When Auntie was young, and he was young too, he had proposed to her. She decided to think it over and didn't do anything, then thought for too long. She became a spinster but always remained his true friend.

Then Brewer Rasmussen died.

He was carried to his grave in a very expensive hearse and

was followed by a procession of mourners, some in uniform wearing medals.

Dressed in mourning, Auntie stood at the window, together with all of us children, except our little brother, whom the stork had brought just a week ago.

When the hearse and the procession had passed and the street was empty, Auntie was preparing to leave, but I didn't want to. I was waiting for the angel named Brewer Rasmussen. Surely he had now become a child of God with wings and would make an appearance.

"Auntie," I asked. "Don't you think he'll be here in a moment? Or maybe the next time the stork brings us a baby brother, he'll also bring us Angel Rasmussen?"

Auntie was quite overwhelmed by my imagination, and said: "That child is going to become a great poet!"[16] She repeated those words during all the years I went to school, even after my confirmation and right into my university days.

She was, and still is, my most devoted friend, when I have toothaches and poet-pains.[17] I get attacks of both.

"Just write down all your thoughts,"[18] she said, "and put them in your desk drawer. That's what Jean Paul[19] did, and he became a great poet, although I'm not a great fan of his. He just doesn't inspire me. You have to be inspiring. And, yes, you will be inspiring!"

The night after that speech, I lay awake in agony, longing with the desire to become the great poet that Auntie saw in me and sensed I was. I was suffering from poet-pains, but there is an even worse pain: a toothache. It was grinding and crushing me. I became a writhing worm, with an herb compress and a mustard plaster.

"I know just what that's like," Auntie said.

She had a sorrowful smile on her lips, and her white teeth gleamed.

to warn children about the hazards of eating sweets in excess.

15. *In fact, she didn't even sleep with them at night.* As Nathaniel Kramer points out, "the revelation that Auntie Millie has dentures appears harmless enough, but the fact that this presumption of health and wholeness is shown to be false has significant consequences for what Auntie Millie represents. That Auntie Millie's teeth are in fact false points toward a corruption in the concept of wholeness and totality that she embodies. Such a full and complete presence that has escaped fragmentation is shown to be a counterfeit and a fake. The hopes and aspirations with which she plies the student can also be shown to be equally false" (Kramer, 20–21).

16. *"That child is going to become a great poet!"* Andersen's mother had consulted a fortune-teller when he was a child and learned from her that he would one day attain fame as a poet.

17. *When I have toothaches and poet-pains.* The connection between Auntie Millie and Auntie Toothache is made explicit here, suggesting that the physical pain associated with decay parallels the activity of writing, which also serves as a compensation for corruption and loss.

18. *"Just write down all your thoughts."* Auntie's naïve attitude toward writing suggests that she embraces an unproblematic notion of poetry, one that associates it with a spontaneous outpouring of feeling that will serve the purpose of diversion and create popular entertainments. Rather than seeing it as craft that has to be perfected and practiced (consider the poet's different drafts of the experiences in his house later in the story), she sees writing as effortless.

19. *"Jean Paul."* Johann Paul Friedrich Richter (1763–1825) was a well-known German writer famous for his sprightly erudition and humorous, digressive style.

20. *"it's a very noisy house."* The rant that follows may be a conscious imitation of Jean Paul's sprawling, associative style. The student's interior space cannot be insulated from the outside world, which is constantly invading his domestic space (carriages outside, for example, make the pictures inside rattle). The noise and commotion take on the character of a barrage of aggressive assaults on the narrator's desire for tranquillity. The litany of complaints culminates in the deeply ironic declaration "Otherwise, it's a perfectly nice house, and I'm living with a quiet family."

Andersen himself grumbled about acoustical assaults from the outdoors. In Rome, he complained constantly about the heat and noise: "It is oppressively hot. . . . There is a frightful din in the streets, an eternal ringing of cowbells, goats with smaller bells, a screaming and screeching; and then I live right across from someone who practices figured bass or tunes piano for the whole town. It's a grabbing, roaring, screaming, rending maelstrom for the ears; blacksmiths hammer, wagons roll, boys scream and people who are talking quietly about household affairs seem to be having a fight" (*Diaries*, 159–60).

But I must now begin a new chapter in this story about me and my aunt.

III

I moved into new lodgings and had been living there for about a month. I told Auntie all about it.

"I'm living with a quiet family. They don't pay any attention to me, even if I ring the bell three times. And, by the way, it's a very noisy house[20] full of commotion and disturbances from whatever or whoever blows through. I live right above the entryway. Every carriage driving in or out makes the pictures on the wall rattle. When the gate slams, it's just like an earthquake hitting the house. When I'm lying in bed, I can feel the shock going right through my body, but they say that's good for the nerves. When the wind blows, and it always blows in this country, the long window latches outside swing to and fro, hitting the wall. The bell on the neighbor's gate clangs whenever there's a gust of wind.

"The lodgers come trickling in at all hours, from late in the evening until deep into the night. The one right above me, the one who gives trombone lessons in the daytime, is the last one home and does not go to bed until after he has taken a little midnight stroll, with heavy footsteps and hobnail boots.

"There are no double windows, but there is a broken pane in my room. The landlady has pasted some paper over it, but the wind still blows through the crack and makes a sound like a buzzing fly. It's the kind of music that puts you right to sleep. When I fall asleep at last, I'm soon awakened by the sound of the rooster crowing. The rooster and hens in the chicken coop kept by the basement tenant announce that it's morning. The little ponies don't have a stable, but they are tied up in the storeroom under the staircase, and they constantly kick against the door and the paneling for exercise.

"The day dawns. The porter, who lives with his family in

the attic, comes barreling down the stairs. His wooden clogs clatter, the gate bangs, and the house shakes. Then, when that's over, the lodger living above me starts his exercises, lifting heavy iron balls that he somehow can't keep in his hands so that they end up falling on the floor. At just about that time the children living in the house are getting ready for school and rush out, screaming, with all their might. I go over to the window and open it up for some fresh air, and it is such a relief—when I can get it—as long as the young woman in the back building isn't cleaning gloves with a stain remover, which is how she makes a living. Otherwise, it's a perfectly nice house, and I'm living with a quiet family."

That's the report I gave Auntie about the flat. It was livelier at the time, for spoken words have greater vibrancy than written words.[21]

"You're a poet!" Auntie exclaimed. "Just write down everything you told me, and you'll be as good as Dickens.[22] To my mind, you are far more interesting. You paint when you speak.[23] You describe the house in a way that lets me see it. It sends chills up my spine. Keep writing! Enliven it with some people—charming people, but also be sure you have some unhappy ones."

I actually did write down my description of the house, with all its noises and nuisances. But I was the only one in the story[24]—there was no plot. That came later.

IV

One evening during the wintertime, late at night, after the theaters had closed, a dreadful snowstorm blew in that made it almost impossible to get anywhere.

Auntie had gone to the theater,[25] and I was there to escort her home. It was hard enough for me to walk on my own, let alone look out for someone else. The hansom cabs were all engaged. Auntie lived on the outskirts of town, but my flat

21. *spoken words have greater vibrancy than written words.* Andersen placed great stock in the oral, not only through the conversational tone he maintained in many of his narratives but also through his practice of reading the stories out loud to adult audiences (he always insisted on complete silence). The student-poet, although devoted to the written word, finds oral expression a more congenial mode of communication.

22. *"you'll be as good as Dickens."* Andersen had met Charles Dickens in 1847 and was ecstatic that his admiration for the writer was returned, as he reported in a letter of July 22, 1847, to Henriette Wulff: "We seized each other by the hand, gazed in each other's eyes, laughed and were overjoyed. We knew each other so well, even though we were meeting for the first time—it was Charles Dickens. He is very much like the best image I had formed of him." What began as a promising friendship ended in 1857 when Andersen overstayed his welcome by several weeks at Dickens's country home in Gad's Hill, Kent. After Andersen's departure, Dickens pinned a note to the door of the room in which the Danish author had slept: "Hans Andersen slept in this room for five weeks—which seemed to the family *ages*!" Dickens is held up here by the aunt as a model of popular success.

23. *"You paint when you speak."* Auntie Millie unknowingly alludes to Horace's famous dictum in the *Ars Poetica*: *ut pictura poesis* (as is painting so is poetry), a phrase that has served as the point of departure for many treatises on the relationship between painting and writing. The lengthy description of the home in which the student lives could be seen as a poetic genre painting, enlivened by its attention to detail. Just as poets may strive to attain the power of painters to represent reality,

so too painters can make an effort to endow their images with meaning and action.

24. *I was the only one in the story.* Thus far the student's descriptive powers have been limited to effects rather than actions and interactions. In the next narrative, he will move from the mode of mere representation to psychological analysis and emotional depth.

25. *Auntie had gone to the theater.* Auntie is repeatedly associated with the arts, primarily in her ability to reminisce and shape memories, but also in her role as a supporter of the arts, encouraging her nephew to become a poet and attending theatrical events. She embodies in some ways the seductions of popular culture, representing the voices of approval that greet those who provide mindless confections for the public.

26. *And it happened.* The odd description of the walk home (trudging, lifting, falling softly) and of undressing, preparing beds, and locking doors adds a weirdly erotic quality to this episode. Capped by the phrase *og det skete* (and it happened), the events take on a confusing quality, in part because of the use of double entendre where it seems entirely out of place.

27. *although not as cozy as Auntie's parlor in the wintertime.* Unlike Auntie, the poet is unable to insulate himself from the outside world and its acoustical assaults. He is not only tormented by the noises that surround his flat but also subject to invasions from icy blasts. And it is in his porous abode that Auntie Toothache can materialize.

was not far from the theater. If it had not been for that, we would have had to seek shelter for a while in the sentry box.

We trudged through the deep snow, with snowflakes swirling like mad around us. I picked her up, held her, and pushed her along. We fell only twice, both times landing softly.

We reached my gate, where we shook off some of the snow. On the stairs we shook off more, and yet there was so much snow that it almost covered the floor of the entrance hall.

We took off our overcoats and undercoats and everything else that was wet. The landlady gave Auntie dry stockings and a dressing gown. She would need them, the landlady said, and added that it would be impossible for my aunt to return home that night, which was true enough. She invited Auntie to settle in the parlor, where she would make up the sofa that was in front of the door to my room, a door that was always kept locked.

And it happened.[26]

A fire was burning in my stove, and a tea urn was placed on the table. The little room began to grow quite cozy, although not as cozy as Auntie's parlor in the wintertime,[27] with its thick drapes covering the door, heavy curtains over the windows, and double layer of carpets over three layers of thick paper. You would sit there feeling as if you were in a tightly corked bottle, filled with warm air. Still, as I said, it was quite cozy in my place. Outside the wind was whistling.

Auntie began to reminisce and tell stories about her youth and about the brewer—old memories were revived.

She could remember when I got my first tooth and how excited the family was.

The first tooth! The tooth of innocence, gleaming like a little white drop of milk, my baby tooth.

After one came, more followed, a whole row of them, side by side, above and below—the finest baby teeth, although these were only the advance troops, not the real ones that would last for a lifetime.

They also appeared, and the wisdom teeth as well, the flank guards in the row, born in pain and great tribulation.

They disappeared too, every single one of them. They leave before their tour of duty is over. When the very last one goes, that is not a day for celebration but a day of mourning.

That's when you're old, even if you feel young.

That kind of chatter and thoughts like that are not very pleasant, yet we talked about all those things. We returned to the childhood years, talking on and on. It was midnight before Auntie retired to the parlor next door.

"Good night, my sweet child," she called out. "I shall sleep as snugly as if I were in my own bed."

And she slept peacefully, but there was no peace inside the house or outdoors. The wind rattled against the windows, banging the long, dangling iron latches on the house and making the neighbor's back-yard bell ring. The lodger upstairs returned home. He was taking his little nightly stroll up and down the room. He kicked off his boots and finally got into bed to sleep, but his snoring was so loud that anyone who wasn't deaf could hear it right through the ceiling.

I could not sleep nor could I calm down. The weather didn't calm down either. It remained animated. The wind howled and sang in its own way. My teeth also began to act up, humming and singing in their own way. An awful toothache was on its way.

A draft came in through the window. The moon was shining onto the floor. Its beams came and went as storm clouds come and go. Light and shadow alternated restlessly, but all at once a shadow on the floor began to take shape.[28] I stared at the moving form and felt an icy blast.

A tall, thin figure was seated on the floor, the kind of figure children draw with a pencil on their slates and that is sup-

28. *a shadow on the floor began to take shape.* With the onset of the toothache comes the visit from Auntie Millie's double—it is no coincidence that she makes her appearance on the night that the real aunt is sleeping in the flat. "Madame Toothache" serves as a reminder of decay, absence, and the futility of trying to create something that is of lasting value. Her spectral shape—first as a shadow, then as a line drawing, and finally as a three-dimensional figure draped in a cloth—emerges only gradually, after the narrator has rehearsed one more time the origins of the various noises in the house. Note also that the play of shadow and light (those chiaroscuro effects) lead to her materialization.

29. *Her Horrible Highness.* Auntie Toothache invites comparison to other regal female figures in Andersen's work, most notably the Snow Queen, who also appears when it is snowing, but who emerges from whiteness rather than from the interplay of light and dark. Both Auntie Toothache and the Snow Queen, like the allegorical figure of Death in "The Story of a Mother," have a chilling effect, like the icy winds of winter.

LORENZ FRØLICH

Auntie Toothache appears as an accusatory wraith who will get her revenge on the author for aspiring to be a poet.

posed to look like a person. Its body was a single thin line, with two more lines making the arms, another two the legs, and the head as a polygon.

The figure quickly grew more distinct. A very thin, fine cloth was draped around it, showing the figure of a woman.

I heard a buzzing. Was it she or was it the wind droning like a hornet through the crack in the windowpane?

No, it was she, Madame Toothache herself! Her Horrible Highness,[29] *Satania infernalis.* God save us from her visits.

"How pleasant it is here," she buzzed. "These are nice quarters—marshy ground, filled with bogs! Mosquitoes have been buzzing around here with poison in their stingers. And now here I am with my sting. I have to sharpen it on human teeth, and that fellow over there on the bed has such nice white shiny ones. They have stood up to sweet and sour things, heat and cold, nutshells and plum pits. But I'll make them wiggle and waggle, feed them with a drafty gust and give them a chill right down to their roots!"

What a terrifying speech! What a terrifying visitor!

"So you are a poet!" she said. "I'll make sure you're well versed in the meters of pain. I'll thrust iron and steel into your body and seize all the fibers of your nerves."

It felt as if a red-hot awl was being driven through my cheekbone. I began to writhe and twist.

"What an excellent set of teeth," she said. "What an organ to play on! A splendid mouth-organ concert—with kettle-drums and trumpets, piccolos, and a trombone in the wisdom tooth. Grand poet, grand music!"

And then she began to play.[30] She looked horrible, even though I couldn't see much more of her than her hand, that shadowy, gray, ice-cold hand with its long fingers, thin as awls. Each of them was an instrument of torture; the thumb and index finger were pincers and a screw. The middle finger ended in a sharp awl. The ring finger was a drill, and the little finger squirted mosquito poison.

"I'll teach you how to write in meters!" she said. "A great poet must have a great toothache. Little poets have only little toothaches."

"Oh, let me be a little one!" I begged. "Let me be nothing at all. I'm not a poet at all. I just have fits of poetry, like these fits of pain. Go away! Go away!"

"Will you finally admit that I'm more powerful than poetry,[31] philosophy, mathematics, and even music?" she asked. "Mightier than all those feelings painted on canvasses and carved in marble? I am older than every one of them. I was born near the Garden of Eden, just outside it, where the wind was blowing and toadstools were growing in the damp earth. It was I who made Eve wear clothes in the cold weather, and Adam too. Believe me, there was power in that first toothache!"

"I believe everything you're telling me," I cried. "Just go away! Go away!"

"Well then, if you promise to give up being a poet and

30. *And then she began to play.* Auntie Toothache, despite her hostility to the student, is something of an artist, although she aims to produce pain rather than pleasure through her music. As early as 1831, on a journey to Berlin, Andersen complained bitterly about an "unbearable toothache": "My teeth are monstrously painful. The nerves are in fact delicate tangents that imperceptible movements of air play upon, and that's why those teeth are playing the devil with me—first piano, then crescendo, all the melodies of pain at every shift in the weather" (*Diaries*, 25). And from Rome he complained about an "excruciating toothache" and how his teeth played a "nervous orchestra." The depth of his pain becomes evident in his elaborate descriptions of dental agony: "A solid Danish toothache cannot be measured against an Italian one. The pain here was focused on the tangents of the teeth, as if Liszt were playing them, sometimes in front, sometimes at the back, while my left canine sang the Diva's part with embellishments, roulades, and crescendos. There was a unity, a power in the whole, and soon I did not feel like a person at all" (*Travels*, 117–18).

31. *"Will you finally admit that I'm more powerful than poetry?"* Auntie Toothache is the apostle of bodily pain, which, as Elaine Scarry has pointed out, shuts down language and has the power to undo the world. Scarry cites Virginia Woolf's shrewd observation about headaches and their applicability to more severe forms of pain: "English, which can express the thoughts of Hamlet and the tragedy of Lear, has no words for the shiver or the headache. . . . The merest schoolgirl when she falls in love has Shakespeare and Keats to speak her mind for her, but let a sufferer try to describe a pain in his head to a doctor and language at once runs dry" (Scarry 1987, 4). Auntie Toothache stands in stark opposition to the arts and disciplines that include poetry, philosophy, mathematics, and music in large part because she is completely spectral, a figment of the imagination that, like pain, cannot be described and put into words. And yet, much as pain is positioned as the obverse of creativity, it is also conflated with creativity in the student's life (as in Andersen's), becoming its unwilling accomplice.

32. *"You dear sweet child."* Auntie Toothache repeats Auntie Millie's words to the student, making a mockery of her tender feelings for her nephew.

33. *"Die, melt away like the snow!"* Andersen often captures the transitory nature of life in the melting snow and in clouds that dissipate with the wind. At the end of "The Snow Queen," the ice is melted by Gerda's kisses and Kai returns to the world of mortals, and in "The Snowman," the figure of the title, predictably, melts with the arrival of spring. Inger in "The Girl Who Trod on the Loaf" is released from her torment by a ray that operates faster than the "sunbeams that melt the snowmen that boys build outdoors."

never again put verse on paper, slate, or any kind of writing material, then I'll leave you alone. But if you start to write again, I'll be back."

"I swear," I said. "As long as I never have to see or feel you again!"

"See me again you shall," she said. "But in more substantial shape, one that is dearer to you than I am. You shall see me as Auntie Millie, and I shall say to you: 'Write, my sweet boy! You are a great poet, perhaps the greatest we have!' And believe me, if you start writing poetry, then I will set your verses to music and play them on your mouth organ. You dear sweet child.[32] Remember me when you see Auntie Millie!"

Then she vanished.

Her parting shot was a jab in the jawbone with what felt like a glowing awl. But the pain soon subsided, and then I felt as if I were floating on gentle waters. I saw white water lilies, with their large green leaves, give way and sink beneath me. They withered and dissolved, and I sank along with them and slipped into a peaceful slumber.

"Die, melt away like the snow!"[33] the waters sang. "Fade away into the clouds and drift away like the clouds!"

Grand names and inscriptions glowed and shone down to me through the waters—fluttering banners of victory, proclaiming immortality but written on the wings of a mayfly.

My slumber was deep and without dreams. I did not hear the whistling wind, the slamming gate, the clanging neighbor's bell, or the lodger's vigorous gymnastics.

What bliss!

A sudden blast of wind blew open the locked door to Auntie's room. Auntie leaped to her feet, put on her shoes, pulled on her clothes, and came into my room.

I was sleeping like one of God's angels, she said, and she didn't have the heart to wake me up.

I woke up on my own and opened my eyes. I had completely forgotten that Auntie was in the house. But as soon as

I remembered, I also remembered the toothache apparition. Dream and reality merged.

"I suppose you didn't do any writing last night after we said good night to each other?" she asked. "I hope you did. You're my poet, and you always will be."

It seemed to me that she was smiling ever so slyly. I couldn't tell whether it was the kind Auntie Millie, who loved me so dearly, or the horrible one, to whom I had made a promise the night before.

"Have you written any poetry, my sweet child?"

"No, no!" I shouted. "You are Auntie Millie, aren't you?"

"Who else could I be?" she asked. And it was Auntie Millie.

She kissed me, climbed into a hansom cab, and rode home.

I wrote all this down. It is not in verse, and it will never be published . . . [34]

The manuscript ends here.

My young friend, the grocer's apprentice, could not find the missing pages. They had gone out into the world as wrapping paper for salted herring, butter, and green soap. They had fulfilled their mission.

The brewer is dead; Auntie is dead; and the student is dead, the one whose sparks of genius ended up in the trash.

Everything ends up in the trash.[35]

And that's the end of the story, the story about Auntie Toothache.

34. *It is not in verse, and it will never be published.* Ironically, the student's "poetry," even if not in verse, ends up making it into print through Andersen's publication of the story "Auntie Toothache." The student remains unnamed and may not achieve "immortality," but his story circulates, first as handwriting on sheets that become wrapping paper for groceries, then in the oral narrative that is embedded in the text, and finally in print form with Hans Christian Andersen as author.

35. *Everything ends up in the trash.* One critic shrewdly comments that "Auntie Toothache" challenges our expectations about endings. Citing Henry James, who declared that endings are places where there is "a distribution . . . of prizes, pensions, husbands, wives, babies, millions, appended paragraphs, and cheerful remarks," he points out that Andersen "inverts the wealth bestowed by the end into a poverty that claims only a few scraps of paper as its legacy and turns on art itself, the very thing to which it aspires" (Kramer, 7). Of course, the fact that we, as readers, continue to take in the story of the student suggests that there is, contrary to the assertion about everything ending up in the trash, the possibility of constant renewal and revival through art. The poet lives on, or, if not the poet, then at least the story he has written, even if some copies of it may end up in the trash.

The Flying Trunk

Den flyvende kuffert

Eventyr, fortalte for Børn, Ny Samling, 1839

A fairy tale with an embedded fable, "The Flying Trunk" offers both exotic romance and social satire. Even with a setting in Turkish lands and motifs from The Thousand and One Nights, *the tale is distinctively Danish, with characteristic Andersen touches. The haughty matches that flare up and quickly extinguish were evidently meant to mock contemporary Danish critics. The section with speaking objects was originally intended to be a separate story called "The Matches," with the pots, tinderbox, and quill pen each representing a different social acquaintance. The caged nightingale might be a reference to Andersen himself, who can also be seen as the nomadic merchant's son, forever destined to tell tales rather than to settle down and marry a princess.*

"The Flying Trunk" stages Andersen's ambivalence about home and abroad in dramatic terms, and, for that reason, I have included it in the section of tales for adult audiences. On the one hand, the author of fairy tales seems to delight in the trivial chitchat of the domestic objects, orchestrating their conversations to reveal their shallow, narrow-minded views. Yet he also sends his hero into exotic lands and delights in grotesque caricatures of its inhabitants. Just as Chinese Emperors punch their subjects in the stomach, the Turks are

presented in stereotypical terms, wearing gowns and slippers and toss-ing their slippers up to their ears when they witness something aston-ishing. In the end, the merchant's son elects to travel around the world, settling down nowhere. A nomadic existence seems to suit him best, as he turns from the world of commerce, then magic, to storytelling.

There was once a merchant so wealthy that he could pave an entire street and maybe a little alley as well with sil-ver coins, but he didn't. He had other ways to use his money. When he spent a penny, he received a dollar in return. That's the kind of merchant he was. And then he died.

His son inherited his entire fortune and lived extrava-gantly. He attended costume balls every night, made origami dragons out of bank notes, and skipped stones on the lake using gold coins instead. With a life like that, money can van-ish quickly, and it did, until finally he was left with no more than four pennies. He had nothing to wear but a pair of slip-pers and an old dressing gown. His friends no longer cared about him,[1] since they couldn't go out on the town together, but one of them, who was nice, sent him an old trunk and said, "Pack up!" That was very nice of him, but he had noth-ing to pack, so he just sat down in the trunk.

It was an odd trunk. As soon as you pressed on the lock, the contraption would fly through the air, which is what hap-pened to him. Swoosh, up the trunk went with him over the chimneys, high above the clouds, farther and farther away. Its bottom began creaking and he was terrified that it would fall to pieces, for he would have had quite a spill! God help us!

He arrived in the land of the Turks[2] and hid the trunk in the forest under dry leaves. Then he went into town. He could do that without problems, because the Turks all walk around wearing just what he was wearing: a dressing gown and slip-

1. *His friends no longer cared about him.* The merchant's son resembles in many ways the soldier in "The Tinderbox." Both fellows lose their friends as soon as the money runs out. Both court princesses whose parents are opposed to a marriage.

2. *in the land of the Turks.* The South and the Orient were Andersen's destinations as a tourist, and he avoided traveling in northern regions. As he wrote to Henriette Hanck in 1835: "I do not belong here in the Northern countries and regard it as one of my earthly accidents that I was born and brought up on the corner of Green-land and Novaja Sembla" (Kleivan 289). Andersen traveled to the Orient, as he called it, over a period of nine months in 1840 and 1841. After seeing Athens, he sailed through the Dardanelles and the Sea of Marmara to Constantinople. According to Jens Andersen, no Dane before Ander-sen had made that journey.

KAY NIELSEN

The merchant's son arrives in Turkish lands with a burst of light and energy. The crescent, which is on the Turkish flag today, appears in each one of Nielsen's illustrations for "The Flying Trunk."

pers. First he encountered a nanny with a little child. "Hello, Turkish nanny," he said. "Tell me about that large castle over there near the city, with the windows set up so high."

"The king's daughter lives there," she said. "Since it has been foretold that some man will make her very unhappy,[3] no one is allowed to see her unless the king and queen are present!"

"Thank you," said the merchant's son, and he went into the forest, sat down in his trunk, flew up to the roof, and climbed in through the princess's window.

She was lying on the sofa, fast asleep. She was so beautiful that the merchant's son had to kiss her.[4] The princess awoke and was dreadfully frightened, but he told her that he was the god of the Turks and that he had come down to her from the sky. She was quite happy about that.

The two sat next to each other, and the merchant's son told the princess tales about her eyes. They were the loveliest dark pools, with thoughts swimming in them like mermaids. He described her forehead, which was like a snow-covered mountain with the most magnificent chambers and images. And he told her about the stork, who brings adorable babies.

He told lovely stories, and then he proposed to the princess, and she accepted right away.

"But you must come here on Saturday," she said, "The king and queen will be here for tea[5] then! They will be very proud that I am going to marry the god of the Turks, but be sure that you have a really lovely fairy tale to tell, because my parents are especially fond of fairy tales. My mother likes them to be serious and have morals, but my father likes them to be funny, so he can laugh!"

"Then I will bring a fairy tale as my bridal gift," he said. And then they parted. The princess had given him a sword covered in gold coins that he really needed.

Off the merchant's son flew. He bought a new dressing gown, then he settled down on a spot in the forest and made

3. *"some man will make her very unhappy."* The same prophecy appears in "The Tinderbox," and the princess in that story is also kept isolated from the rest of the world.

4. *She was so beautiful that the merchant's son had to kiss her.* A sleeping princess (again, as in "The Tinderbox") is irresistible, and the merchant's son awakens his sleeping beauty with a kiss. The attractions of beauty are so powerful that they lead to an irrepressible desire for erotic contact.

5. *"will be here for tea."* The mix of the bourgeois and the banal with the regal and the poetic is more pronounced here than in many other works by Andersen. The mingling of high and low, aristocratic and ordinary, foreign and familiar imparts a certain charm, as it does in "The Nightingale."

6. *"one that will also make us laugh."* The requirement that stories be both instructive and entertaining goes back to Horace's dictum that poets can strive to delight or instruct (*aut prodesse volunt aut delectare poetae*). The merchant's son must combine the two in order to satisfy both the sultan and his wife.

up a fairy tale. It had to be finished by Saturday, and that's not as easy as you might think.

At last he was finished, and by then it was Saturday.

The king, the queen, and the entire court came to tea in the princess's rooms. He was welcomed in such a charming way!

"Could you please tell us a fairy tale?" the queen asked. "One that is profound and instructive."

"But one that will also make us laugh,"[6] said the king.

"Absolutely," he said, and began telling his own story. But we must listen carefully to it.

There was once a bundle of matches, and they were extraordinarily proud of their noble heritage. Their ancestral tree—that is to say, the large pine tree from which they were splinters—had been a great old tree in the forest. The matches were now lying on a shelf between a tinderbox and an old iron pot, and they told the two of them about their youth.

"Yes, that was the life back then," the matches said. "We were really living in the lap of luxury! Every morning and every evening we drank diamond tea that came from the dew; we soaked up rays of sunshine all day long while the sun was out; and we heard stories from the little birds. We knew that we were rich, because the hardwood trees were only dressed up in the summer, while our family could afford to wear green in the summer and winter. When the woodcutters came, there was a huge upheaval, and our family was scattered. The main trunk became the mast of a magnificent ship that could sail around the world if it wanted to. The other branches went other places, and we now have the job of bringing light to the down-trodden masses. That is how aristocrats of our kind ended up down here in the kitchen."

"My story is entirely different," said the iron pot, the one right next to the matches. "Ever since I came into the world, I've been scoured and boiled many times! I take care of substantial things and I am, when it comes right down to it, the finest object in the house. My only joy—after dinner, that is—is lying on the shelf all clean and shiny and having a good chat with my friends. But, with the exception of the water bucket that sometimes goes down into the courtyard, all of us spend our lives indoors. Our only source of news is the market basket, but she talks in such a distressing way about the government and the people that just the other day an old ceramic pot got so upset that he fell over and broke into pieces! The market basket is surely liberal-minded, I can tell you!"

"Now you've talked too much," said the tinderbox, and the steel struck the flint so it sent out sparks. "Couldn't we just have a pleasant evening?"

"Oh yes," said the matches. "Let's talk about who among us is the finest!"

"No, I don't like talking about myself," said the clay pot. "Let's have some evening entertainment. I'll start by telling about something that everyone has experienced. We can all relate to that kind of thing so well,[7] and that's a nice feeling: On the shore of the Baltic Sea among the Danish birches—!"

"That's a lovely start," said all of the plates. "That is definitely going to be a story that we can enjoy."

"Yes, that is where I spent my youth, with a quiet family; the furniture was polished, the floors were washed, and the curtains were changed every two weeks."

"You really know how to tell an interesting story," said the feather duster. "You can tell right away when a woman is telling a story. There's such a clean streak in it!"

"Yes, you can feel that," said the water bucket, who, out of delight, made a little hop and then clattered on the ground.

The pot continued telling its story, and the ending was as good as the beginning.

All of the plates clattered with joy. The feather duster took some green parsley out of the storage room and crowned the pot, knowing that this would annoy the others, and thought, "If I crown her today, she'll crown me tomorrow."

7. *"We can all relate to that kind of thing so well."* The clay pot's notion of "safe" narratives that merely evoke the familiar and remain in the register of the idyllic is a jab at Danish critics, who veered away, in Andersen's view, from anything that was exotic, edgy, and controversial.

8. *"we won't say anything mean about that tonight."* Andersen mocks his critics by representing one of them as a quill pen who believes that birds need to study music before they sing rather than creating song spontaneously. "The Flying Trunk" contains Andersen's most sustained critique of the Danish critics who disparaged him for his lack of education, and he delighted in reading the story out loud.

9. *"if I had wanted to."* Like many of the inanimate objects in Andersen's stories, most notably the tin soldier, the objects claim voices and agency yet are unable to speak or move when humans enter the room. Note how the maid's entrance produces stillness and silence.

"Now I want to dance," said the poker, and danced. God save us, how it could raise its single leg! The old chair cover over in the corner ripped just from watching it! "May I please be crowned?" asked the poker, and she was.

"They are just commoners," thought the matches.

Now it was the teapot's turn to sing, but it had a cold, and said it couldn't sing unless it was boiling. But that was just snobbery: it didn't want to sing unless it could stand on the table in front of the master and mistress.

Over in the window sat an old quill pen that the maid used for writing. There was nothing unusual about it, except that it had been dipped far too deeply into the inkwell, and it was quite proud of that. "If the teapot doesn't want to sing," the quill said, "then leave it alone. There's a cage right outside with a nightingale in it that can sing. It hasn't studied music, of course, but we won't say anything mean about that tonight."[8]

"I find it quite inappropriate," said the tea kettle, who was the kitchen singer as well as half-sister to the teapot, "that we should listen to a foreign bird like that. Is that patriotic? I'll let the market basket decide."

"I am just annoyed," said the market basket. "I am more deeply annoyed than you can imagine! Is this an appropriate way to spend the evening? Wouldn't it be much better to put the house to rights? Everything would be in its proper place and I would direct the whole show. That would be something!"

"Yes, let's put on a show!" they all said together. At that very moment, the door opened. It was the maid, and so they all fell quiet. No one let out a peep. But there was not a pot among them that did not know what it was capable of and how fine it was. "Yes, if I had wanted to,"[9] they thought, "it would have been quite a lively evening!"

The maid took the matches and struck them—God almighty, how they spluttered and burst into flame.

"Now everyone can see that we are the finest," they thought. "How we gleam! What light!"[10]—and then they burned out.

"That was a lovely fairy tale," said the queen. "I felt just as if I was in the kitchen with the matches. Yes, you shall have our daughter now."

"Certainly," said the king. "You shall have our daughter on Monday." They now addressed him informally, since he was going to be part of the family.

The wedding was arranged and the night before the ceremony, the whole town was illuminated. There were rolls and pastries for the masses; street urchins stood on their toes, crying "Hurrah!" and whistling through their fingers. It was really magnificent.

"Well, I had better do something as well,"[11] thought the merchant's son. He bought rockets, noisemakers, and as many kinds of fireworks as you can imagine, put them into his trunk, and flew up into the air with it.

Boom, how the fireworks crackled! How they sparkled!

All the Turks jumped in the air when they saw the fireworks, and their slippers flew up to their ears. They had never before seen such a sight in the heavens. Now they knew that it was indeed the god of the Turks who was going to marry their princess.

As soon as the merchant's son landed back down in the forest on his trunk, he thought: "I've got to go into town to hear what people have to say about it!" And it was completely clear why he wanted to do that.

Well, people surely were talking! All the people he asked had seen it in their own way, but it had been lovely for all of them.

"I saw the god of the Turks himself," one of them said. "He had eyes like shining stars and a beard like foaming waters!"

"He flew in a cape of flames," said another. "The loveliest angel children peeked out of the folds of it."

10. *"What light!"* In "The Little Match Girl," the light from the matches supplies only a brief moment of illumination, but one that is incandescently poetic. Here the matches claim to offer the same kind of luminosity, but in fact they seem to sputter and fizzle quickly, providing none of the sparklingly brilliant effects found in the visionary experiences of the match girl. Andersen intended them to represent his critics.

11. *"I had better do something as well."* Up until this point in the narrative, the merchant's son has relied on words alone to impress first the princess, then her parents. Inspired by the lighting up of the city, he decides to use sound and light to impress its inhabitants. But note that these brilliant effects consume themselves, turning into nothing but ashes. The matches too can only flare up and then expire, leaving nothing behind but burnt flint or ashes.

12. *traveling all around the world, telling fairy tales.* Just as Andersen represents himself at the end of "The Nightingale" as the poet at whose window the nightingale has made a nest, he provides a self-portrait here by presenting the merchant's son as a traveler famous for telling fairy tales that combine wit and humor with moral instruction.

He heard lovely things, and he was going to be married the next day.

The merchant's son returned to the forest to get back in the trunk—but where was it? The trunk had burned up. A spark from the fireworks had been smoldering and caught fire, and the trunk had turned into a pile of ashes. He could no longer fly, and he could not go back to his bride.

All day she stood on the roof, waiting for him. And she is still waiting while he is traveling all around the world, telling fairy tales.[12] But they are not as funny as the one he told about the matches.

KAY NIELSEN

The patient princess, with a crescent on her head, waits serenely for the merchant's son.

Heartache

Hjertesorg

Historier, Anden Samling, 1853

This gem of a story encapsulates many of the major themes in Andersen's works, taking us from death and existential anxiety to suffering and social grief. It can be seen as a poetics in a nutshell. Its origins lie in a diary entry of May 26, 1847, in which Andersen described the incidents of "part one," then turned to the description of a beggar, an abject figure who arouses both empathy and fear: "There was somebody knocking at the door. A dreadful tramp had managed to find my room. I gave him 24 pennies. 'Were you not born in the neighborhood of Odense?' he asked. I got him out but feared he might hide and return in the dead of night to steal" (Thomas Bredsdorff, 7). In contrast to the beggar, the girl in "Heartache" arouses empathy. Seen from above and at a distance, she elicits aesthetic pleasure by combining beauty, youth, poverty, and suffering.

Despite the narrator's insistence that the prelude is unnecessary, the story in fact needs both parts, with one introducing the narrator as a "heartless" figure who is unable to connect with the widow's deeper reason for coming to sell her shares and the other presenting the narrator as equally "heartless" in his inability to act to relieve the girl's "heartache." The author sees in these encounters nothing more than an *opportunity for telling tales, for positioning himself as an agent of art, relentlessly keeping himself spatially above and emotionally beyond the heartaches of the real.*

The story we have for you is really in two parts. The first part could be left out,[1] but it provides some background information that will be useful!

We were staying at a manor house in the country, and it happened that the owner was away for a day or two. In the meantime, a lady arrived from a neighboring town, bringing her little dog with her. She explained that she had come to sell her shares in the tannery. She had her certificates with her, and we advised her to put them in an envelope and to write on it the address of the proprietor of the estate, "General War Commissary, Knight, etc."

She listened to us carefully, picked up a pen, hesitated, and then asked us to repeat the address, this time saying it slowly. We did that, and she started writing, but as soon as she got to "General War," she stopped, took a deep breath, and said: "I'm only a woman!" Her little pug was down on the floor while she was writing, and he was growling, for the dog had come with her for pleasure and for his health, and he shouldn't have been obliged to stay on the floor. He could be recognized by his snub nose and fleshy back.

"He won't bite," the lady said. "He doesn't have any teeth. He's really like one of the family, devoted but grumpy, but my grandchildren are to blame for that. They put on weddings and want him to play the bridesmaid, but that's just too much for the poor old fellow."

She left the certificates and picked her little dog up. That's the first part of the story, which I could have left out!

Moppsie died![2] That's part two.

About a week later we went back to town and stayed at an

1. *The first part could be left out.* The bridge between the two parts seems indeed to be quite slight. The first part of the story offers background on the owner of the tannery and on the dog for whom the funeral is staged by the children in part two. Death is introduced early on in the form of the status of the old lady as widow who is liquidating her assets in a business that traffics in death.

2. Moppsie died! The hinge between the two parts of the story is provided by the death of the dog, whose owner appears in part one and whose grave is prepared by the children in part two. The sentence is italicized and given an exclamation mark to make it more momentous, and it forms an odd contrast to the fact that the tanner's death is never mentioned and is signaled only by his wife's status as a widow and in her selling of the shares in the tannery.

3. *Our windows looked out into a courtyard.* The narrator, whose identity is concealed behind a "we," is looking *down* on a scene that involves children. The courtyard, like the story, is divided in two, but half of it remains invisible—only the area with the tannery is described. The narrator's "other half" also remains concealed, and it is odd to find Andersen the bachelor presenting himself here as part of a couple.

4. *skins and hides, raw and tanned.* A tannery is the site of death for animals, and there is an important contrast between the pampered dog (who resents being on the floor) and the animals who have been slaughtered and skinned.

5. *it belonged to the widow.* The widow, and not just her deceased husband, is implicated in the business of death.

6. *a little girl dressed in rags.* Like the little match girl, this waif is alone, isolated from the others through her poverty and, despite her beauty, unable to elicit sympathy from the other children.

7. *She alone had not seen Moppsie's grave.* It is not at all clear that the girl is grieving for Moppsie. She seems instead to be disconsolate because she is excluded from the childhood ritual and from seeing the artful gravesite created by the other children. But this is, of course, the narrator's reading of her grief.

inn. Our windows looked out into a courtyard,[3] which was divided in two by a wooden fence. One section had skins and hides, raw and tanned,[4] hung up to dry. You could see all the equipment needed to run a tanning business, and it belonged to the widow.[5] Moppsie had died that morning and was supposed to be buried in that part of the yard. The widow's grandchildren, that is, the tanner's widow's—for Moppsie had never married—had filled in the grave, which was so beautiful that it must have been a real pleasure to lie in it.

The grave had a border of broken flowerpots with sand strewn all over it. At its head, someone had put a bottle of beer, with the neck turned upward, and that wasn't at all symbolic.

The children performed a dance around the grave, and the oldest of the boys, a practical lad of seven, proposed charging admission of one trouser button to give everyone on the street the chance to see Moppsie's grave. Any boy could afford that, and boys could also pay for girls. The proposal was adopted by acclamation.

All the children living on the street, and even those living on the little lane behind it, came marching in, and each one paid one button. Many of them could be seen that afternoon with just one suspender, but then again they had seen Moppsie's grave, and the sight of that was worth far more than a button.

Outside near the entrance to the tannery you could see a little girl dressed in rags.[6] She was beautiful, with the prettiest curls and with eyes so clear and blue that it was a pleasure to look into them. She didn't say a word, and she wasn't crying, but every time the gate opened, she gazed into the yard for as long as she could. She didn't have a button, as she knew very well, and so she had to stand sorrowfully outside until all the others had seen the grave and everyone was gone. Then she sat down, put her little brown hands up to her eyes and burst into tears. She alone had not seen Moppsie's grave.[7] It was the kind of heartache that usually is experienced only by grown-ups.

We witnessed all this from above—and from above you can always smile[8] at this incident as well as at many of our own heartaches and those of others! That's the story, and whoever doesn't understand it should go buy a share in the widow's tannery.[9]

8. *from above you can always smile.* The view from above makes the entire incident poignant rather than wrenching. But it also suggests that distance—whether seen in terms of space, class, or generation—promotes empathy even as it produces an ironic gap, allowing the narrator to derive pleasure ("smile") at the sight of suffering.

9. *should go buy a share in the widow's tannery.* In this, one of his most impenetrable stories, Andersen adds a provocative statement directing readers who fail to understand his meaning to turn to commerce rather than poetry. And yet the narrator himself could be accused of lacking "understanding" and of failing to engage with the characters he presents in any meaningful way. He dismisses the widow's state of mourning, smiles at the girl's grief, and becomes emphatic only when it comes to the death of the dog. He presents scenes that require his reader to understand more than he does.

The Bell

Klokken

Maanedsskrift for Børn, 1845

The motif of the bell is a favorite one among German and Danish Romantic poets, evoking reverence through its religious associations and awe through its acoustical wonders. The renowned "Song of the Bell" (1799) by the German poet Friedrich Schiller was familiar to Andersen, and he wrote a story about its composition called "The Old Church Bell" (1862), in which he clearly identifies with Schiller, who grew up in poverty but rose to artistic distinction. Schiller's poem takes a political, ideological turn rather than moving in an aesthetic, religious direction. Twelve years after writing "The Bell," Andersen published "The Bell Deep" (1857), a story capturing the main features of a legend about a river ghost in Odense and about a mysterious bell that rings from the river. "The Bell" is a deeper, broader staging of Andersen's poetics, enacting an allegory that unites poetry with nature and broadcasting a democratic ideal in which a prince joins hands with a pauper.

The tale provides a crowning utopian moment in Andersen's literary work, and the scenes describing the beauties of the forest remind us that visual delights were as important to Andersen as the arresting acoustical enchantments of the bell. As in "The Emperor's New

Clothes," the child is more knowing than adults, and Andersen's moving portrait of prince and pauper joining hands reminds us that deep cynicism about human nature is not inconsistent with a bedrock of faith in our capacity for transformation.

Toward evening in the narrow streets of a big town, when the sun was about to set and clouds were shimmering like gold up above the chimneys,[1] you could often hear a strange sound, like the ringing of a church bell, but only for a moment, for it was soon lost in the racket of rumbling carriages and loud voices. "The evening bell is ringing," people would say. "Now the sun will be going down!"

The people who lived outside the town, where the houses are farther apart with gardens and small fields in between them, could see the magnificent sky more clearly and hear the sound of the bell more distinctly. It was like the sound of a church buried deep inside the silent, fragrant forest. When people looked in that direction, they turned quite solemn.

Many years went by, and people began to talk with each other about the sound: "I wonder if there really is a church out there in the forest. That bell does have an unusual mysteriously enchanting sound. Shouldn't we go out there and see what it looks like?"

The rich took carriages, and the poor went on foot, but the road seemed terribly long to all of them. When they reached a grove of willow trees growing right at the edge of the forest, they sat down, looked up into the branches, and imagined that they were right in the heart of the forest. The town baker went out there and set up a tent, and then another baker came, and he hung up a bell right above his tent. It was a leather bell, tarred to withstand the rain, and it did not have a clapper.

When everyone returned home, they said that it had all

1. *clouds were shimmering like gold up above the chimneys.* The appearance of radiant light marks a moment of arresting beauty that evokes the sound of celestial music that, in turn, stops people in their tracks. The hustle and bustle of the city conceals the transcendent beauty of nature (the "silent, fragrant forest") and the heavenly sounds of man-made art in the service of religion (the ringing of the bell).

2. *more amusing than a tea party.* The aside about tea parties is intended to deride the fashionable literary tea salons of the day, where new literary works or unpublished manuscripts were read aloud. The trivialization of authentic art was a source of constant irritation for Andersen.

3. *Bell-Ringer of the World.* In "The Nightingale" and in other tales, Andersen ridicules the invention of absurd honorific titles and rituals that have no substance.

4. *Confirmation Day.* Confirmation is a rite in many Christian churches, and it is usually marked by the taking of the sacrament at a time when a child is believed to have attained the age of reason, and also of faith. The children of the story, even though they have been confirmed, remain in a state between childhood and adulthood. Like Kai and Gerda in "The Snow Queen," they possess the innocence of the child and the wisdom of the adult.

been so romantic, and more amusing than a tea party.[2] Three people claimed to have walked all the way to the far side of the forest, and they kept hearing the mysterious bell over there, but at a certain point it sounded to them as if it were coming from the direction of town. One of them wrote an entire ballad about it and said that the bell sounded like a mother's voice speaking to a beloved child. No melody was sweeter than the sound of that bell.

The emperor of the land learned about the bell and issued a proclamation declaring that whoever discovered the source of the sound would be given the title Bell-Ringer of the World,[3] even if the bell was not the source of the sound.

Many people began to go to the forest for the sake of acquiring that fine title, but there was only one person who returned with any kind of explanation. No one had traveled deep enough into the forest—and neither had he, for that matter. But just the same he said that the sound came from a very large owl inside a hollow tree, a wise owl that was constantly beating its head against the trunk of the tree. He could not say with certainty whether the sound was made by the owl's head or whether it came from the hollow tree trunk. And so he was appointed "Bell-Ringer of the World," and every year he wrote a little tract about the owl. But no one was the wiser for it.

Confirmation Day[4] arrived. The minister delivered a sermon that was splendidly moving. The candidates for confirmation had been deeply touched by it. It was an important day in their lives, for on that day they would be transformed from children into adults, and their childlike souls would migrate into the bodies of grown-ups. It was a gloriously sunny day, and, just as the newly confirmed children were walking out of the town, the great unknown bell began to peal with mysterious clarity from the forest.

All at once the children felt a powerful desire to find it, except for three. One needed to go home and try on her ball gown—it was only for the sake of that gown and that ball that she had been confirmed this time, otherwise she would have had to wait a year! The second was a poor boy who had borrowed his confirmation clothes and boots from his landlord's son, and he had to return them on time. The third said that he never went anywhere strange without his parents and that he had always been an obedient child and wanted to stay that way, even after his confirmation. No one should make fun of that! But everyone did.

The three of them did not go along, but the others skipped off into the woods. The sun was shining, and the birds were singing. The children sang too, walking hand in hand. They had not yet received any offices or responsibilities and were all newly confirmed in the sight of our Lord.[5]

Two of the youngest children grew tired and returned to town. Two other little girls sat down and began to weave garlands, and so they did not go any farther. The others continued until they reached the willow trees, where the baker had set up his tent. "Just look," they said. "Now that we've arrived out here, it's clear that the bell doesn't really exist. It's just something people imagined."

At that very moment, deep within the forest, the bell rang so sweetly and solemnly that four or five of them decided to go a little deeper into the forest after all. The underbrush was so thick and so full of leaves that it was difficult to make any progress. Woodruff and anemone were growing almost too high, and the branches of blooming bindweeds and blackberry bushes were draped in the trees, where nightingales sang and sunbeams were playing in the leaves. Oh, it was enchanting, but there was no path for the girls to follow. They would have ripped their dresses to shreds.

Giant boulders stood everywhere, overgrown with moss of every color. Fresh spring water gurgled and made a "glug, glug" sound.

"Could that be the bell?" one of the boys wondered, and he

5. *newly confirmed in the sight of our Lord.* The phrase alludes to the pronouncement "We are all sinners in the eyes of the Lord."

6. *wearing wooden shoes.* Wooden shoes are a sign of poverty—as opposed to the boots borrowed for Confirmation Day. The pairing of prince and pauper famously became the subject of Mark Twain's novel of that name, although in that work, the two trade places. It is in the woods that the two boys become equals, joined in their humility before the splendors of nature suffused with divine meaning through the art of the bell's song.

lay down to listen to it. "I had better listen carefully." He remained behind and let the others go on.

The other children reached a hut made of bark and branches. A large tree with apples hung over the roof covered with rose blossoms. It seemed to be showering blessings on the house. The long branches clung to one of the gables, where a little bell was hanging. Could that be what they were hearing? They all agreed that it must be, except for one boy, who said that the bell was too small and fine to be heard from so far away and that its tones did not move the heart in the same mysterious way. The boy who spoke was a prince, and so the others said, "Someone like that always thinks he's right."

They let the prince go on alone, and the farther he went, the more his heart was filled with the solitude of the forest. He could still hear the little bell that the others were playing, and, occasionally, when the wind came from the direction of the bakery, he could also hear voices singing at the tea table.

The deep tones of the mysterious bell swelled up above everything else, almost as if an organ were accompanying it. The sounds came from the left, from the side where the heart is located.

Suddenly there was a rustling in the bushes, and a little boy stood before the prince, wearing wooden shoes[6] and a shirt so tight that the sleeves did not come down to his wrists. The two knew each other, for the boy was one of the newly confirmed, the one who couldn't come along since he had to go home and return his clothes and boots to the landlord's son. Once he had done that, he had set out on his own, wearing his wooden shoes and shabby clothes, for the bell had sounded so powerfully and so deeply that he had to follow its call.

"Let's go together," said the prince. But the poor boy in the wooden shoes was very shy. He tugged on his sleeves, which were too short, and said that he was afraid that he wouldn't be able to keep up. Besides, he thought they should search for the bell to the right side, where everything looked more grand and beautiful.

"Then I'm afraid we won't be able to go together," said the prince, and he nodded to the poor boy, who went into the darkest, deepest part of the forest, where thorns tore his shabby clothes to shreds and drew blood from his face, hands, and feet.

The prince received some scratches too, but at least the sun was shining on his path. He is the one we will follow, for he was a lively lad.

"I must find the bell and I will!" he said. "Even if I have to go to the ends of the earth!"

High up in the trees nasty monkeys sat and grinned, gnashing their teeth at him. "Shall we pelt him with something?" they chattered. "Let's pelt him! After all, he's a prince!"

He continued on his way unharmed, going deeper and deeper into the woods, where the most wondrous flowers were growing. White star-lilies with blood-red stamens were growing there; sky-blue tulips gleamed in the breeze; and apple trees bore fruit that looked every bit like shining soap bubbles. You can imagine how the trees must have sparkled in the sunlight! All around, on the loveliest green meadows, where stags and does played in the grass, massive oaks and beeches were growing. If there was a crack in their bark, mosses and long tendrils grew out of them. There were large stretches of forest with quiet lakes, where beautiful white swans floated and flapped their wings. The prince often stopped to listen, for it seemed as if the tones of the bell were rising from the depths of one of the lakes. But, then again, he was sure that the sounds were coming from a place even deeper in the forest.

As the sun went down, the clouds began to turn a fiery red. Everything became quiet, so very quiet in the forest. The

7. *What a magnificent sight!* Andersen strains his verbal resources to paint a picture of nature that is suffused with beauty and sacred meaning. This description will usher in the allegorical union of nature and poetry in the final paragraph. Anticipating turn-of-the-century aesthetics, Andersen presents nature as a place of plenitude, rich in sensation and laden with meaning.

8. *they ran toward each other and joined hands.* The reunion of the prince and the pauper takes place when land, sky, and ocean melt into each other to produce a scene of arresting beauty, in which sights, sounds, colors, and aromas melt into each other. As the two join hands, they stage a fantasy that preoccupied Andersen his entire life: acceptance as a man equal in rank to a prince. The poor boy with "short sleeves" and "wooden shoes" has had a rough ascent, but unobtrusively he has made it to the summit and witnesses with the prince the triumph of beauty.

prince fell to his knees and sang his evening hymn. "I will never find what I am looking for," he said. "The sun is setting, and night is coming, the dark night. And yet perhaps I can catch one more glimpse of the round, red sun before it sinks below the horizon. I'll climb up the cliffs over there, for they are as high as the tallest trees!"

Grabbing hold of vines and roots, he made his way up the slippery rocks, where water snakes were curled up and toads and frogs seemed to be croaking at him. He managed to reach the summit before the sun had gone down completely. What a magnificent sight![7]

The ocean, the great, glorious ocean that rolled its long waves against the coast, stretched out before him, and the sun stood like a great, shining altar out there where the sea and sky meet. The whole world seemed to melt together in glowing colors. The forest was singing; the ocean was singing; and the boy's heart was singing too. Nature was a vast, sacred temple, with the trees and floating clouds as columns, flowers and grass as the woven altar cloth, and the sky itself as the great dome. Up above, the red colors vanished as the sun disappeared, but millions of stars lit up, like millions of diamond lamps, and the prince spread out his arms in joy to the skies, the sun, and the forest.

Just then, from the right-hand path, the poor boy with the short sleeves and the wooden shoes appeared. He had arrived there just as quickly by his own path. Overjoyed, they ran toward each other and joined hands[8] in the great temple of nature and poetry, while above them sounded the invisible, holy bell. Blessed spirits floated around them and lifted their voices in a joyful Hallelujah!

PART III

Biographies

A Fairy-Tale Life?

HANS CHRISTIAN ANDERSEN

ndersen constructed myriad fictional doubles, shadows, and reflections, but he also did not resist the temptation to represent himself in more prosaic terms. In fact, he gave in to that temptation multiple times, writing no fewer than three full-length autobiographies, each an effort to shape a life in ways that would enable him to live on like his fictional characters.[1] Making a name for himself, pursuing fame and fortune, achieving immortality: these were the motives behind many of the autobiographical writings, as Andersen himself conceded. "Every day I get a better sense of how much I am recognized," he declared with undisguised glee. "In Germany it seems as if my name will soon be as well known as it is here at home. Yesterday I completed my biographical sketch, which will be placed at the beginning of *Only a Fiddler*."[2]

It is no accident that two of the three versions of his life contained the term "fairy tale" in their titles and that even the third is entitled *The Book*

---

1. Andersen's first autobiography was entitled *Levnedsbogen* (*The Book of My Life*) and was written in 1832. Not meant for publication during his lifetime, it was first published in 1926. Andersen wrote a second autobiography for a German edition of his works called *Das Märchen meines Lebens ohne Dichtung*. It was published in London in 1847 as *The True Story of My Life*. The German autobiography was expanded and published in Danish in 1855 as *Mit Livs Eventyr* (*The Fairy Tale of My Life*).

2. "H. C. Andersens brevveksling med Henriette Hanck," *Anderseniana*, 1943, 238.

of My Life. The True Fairy Tale of My Life was commissioned by a publisher to introduce a German edition of Andersen's works and was written in 1846. It was later published in English as *The True Story of My Life*. It is to that life that I will now turn, for, even if it does not take us more deeply into the fairy tales, it provides background and context for them, bringing to life the author and the culture in which he wrote the tales. For that reason, I have also not hesitated to include annotations that reveal something about Andersen the man, for the fairy tale of his life is as absorbing, improbable, and captivating as many of the tales he produced.

All three of Andersen's autobiographies were, despite a commitment to getting out the facts, exercises in making fiction, in creating the illusion of an untroubled life and indulging in cheerful self-promotion. Consider the opening paragraphs of *The Fairy Tale of My Life*, published in 1855 as the definitive autobiography:

> My life is a lovely story, happy and full of adventures. If, at the time when I was still a boy and going out into the world poor and without friends, a good fairy had come along and said, "Choose your course in life and the goal of your efforts. . . . I will guide and protect you until you attain it," my destiny could not, even at that time, have been guided more happily, more prudently, or more fortunately. The history of my life will reveal to the world what it tells me—there is a loving God who directs all things for the best.[3]

Andersen continues with a description of his parents (who, according to him, doted on each other), and he draws on all his verbal resources to describe the two as loving, compassionate, hardworking, and thoughtful. He paints the picture of a childhood in which he is the adored center of attention. The household becomes the site of art (with pictures, books, songs), and even domestic objects sparkle with beauty (the plates as well as the pots shine).

> In the year 1805 there lived in Odense, in a small, humble room, a young married couple, who were extremely attached to each other. He was a shoe-maker, scarcely twenty-two years old, a man with a richly gifted and truly

3. Hans Christian Andersen, *The Fairy Tale of My Life: An Autobiography* (New York: Paddington, 1975), 1. I have edited the language of the translation for the sake of accuracy and readability.

poetical mind. His wife, a few years older, did not know much about life and the world, but she possessed a heart full of love. . . . During the first day of my existence, my father is said to have sat by the bed and read Holberg out loud, but I ended up crying all the time. . . . Our little room, which was packed with the shoemaker's bench, the bed, and my crib, was the abode of my childhood. The walls were covered with pictures, and over the workbench was a cupboard containing books and songs. The little kitchen was full of shining plates and metal pans.[4]

Reality was quite different from the childhood paradise described by Andersen. It also diverged sharply from the Hollywood fantasy of Andersen as portrayed by Danny Kaye singing "wonderful, wonderful Copenhagen." As the Swedish novelist Per Olov Enquist puts it: "He did not grow up in a Danish idyll. He was born into the ragged proletariat, in among dirt, decay, promiscuity, and prostitution—and into a family where there was a great deal of mental sickness. . . . His maternal grandmother was a prostitute with three illegitimate children, one of whom was Hans Christian's mother. In her turn, she appears to have spent time as a prostitute; she became an alcoholic at an early age and died of delirium tremens in the workhouse in Odense."[5] Andersen's life story may have ended with "happily ever after," and, somewhat ironically, it reads exactly like a real fairy tale. Its beginnings are marked by classic dysfunctional family behavior and by all the horrors of what emerges right after "once upon a time" and before "happily ever after."

In the last years of her life, Andersen's mother, the woman with a "heart full of love," sent a steady stream of letters to her son, asking for financial help. The promising young writer ignored most of those pleas while he was on the road, traveling on a royal stipend to Rome, where he worried about his teeth, and to Naples, where he took careful notes about items in the Secret Room (a private collection once known as the Cabinet of Obscene Objects). Andersen was, to be sure, worried that any money he sent might be wasted on spirits, but it is clear that he was never as attentive to his

4. Ibid., 2.

5. Per Olov Enquist, "The Hans Christian Andersen Saga," trans. Joan Tate, *Scandinavian Review* 74 (1986): 64–65.

mother as might be expected from the testimony in his autobiography. "All my childhood memories, every spot seems dark to me," Andersen later confessed in a letter to his friend Edvard Collin, written from Odense a year before his mother's death. On hearing news of his mother's death, he mourned her loss with characteristic narcissistic grief: "Her situation was a harsh one, and there was almost nothing I could do for her. . . . I am truly alone—no one is bound by nature to love me." Twenty years later, he repeats the sentiment while reminiscing about his "endlessly bitter anguish": "I wept but could not accustom myself to the idea that now I have not a single person in the world who, by blood and nature, must love me. . . . I cried my heart out and had a feeling that the best had happened for her. I would never have been able to make her last days bright and free of sorrow. She died with a joyous faith in my happiness, that I *was somebody*."[6]

Creating a "somebody" was of paramount importance to Andersen. As noted earlier, when he was a boy, his mother consulted a fortune-teller, who prophesied a grand future for the gawky youngster: "He will have better luck than he deserves. He will be a wild bird, flying high up and being grand. One day the town of Odense will be illuminated in his honor."[7] Becoming that "somebody" meant, if not denying his humble origins, then at least taking some of the tarnish off the reputation of his relatives. Andersen fashioned for himself a new identity, one that elevated him from the provincial shabbiness of Odense and the hardscrabble circumstances of his family life to a more genteel rank. He was fond of referring to his birthday not as April 2, 1805, but September 6, 1819, the day that, at the age of fourteen, he arrived in Copenhagen to turn himself into a somebody and to enact the fairy-tale plots that he had heard as a child and was to refashion as an adult.

The town of Odense, located on the island of Fyn and separated from

6. Jens Andersen has harsh words for Andersen's behavior toward his mother: "While Anne Marie Andersdatter was dragging out her life in the poorhouse in Odense, her son was performing Holberg in the Hofmansgave garden, learning waltz steps at Bramstrup, and being luxuriously conveyed from one estate to the other in a coach-and-four, accompanied by the landed gentry." Letter of July 3, 1832, in *H. C. Andersens Brevveksling med Edvard og Henriette Collin* (Copenhagen: Levin and Munksgaard, 1933), I, 104. Letter of December 16, 1833, in *H. C. Andersen og Henriette Wulff. En Brevveksling* (Odense: Flensteds Forlag, 1959), I, 151. Hans Christian Andersen, *Mit Livs Eventyr*, in *Samlede Skrifter* (Copenhagen: C. A. Reitzel, 1855), XXI, 163.

7. Bo Grønbech, *Hans Christian Andersen* (Boston: Twayne, G. K. Hall, 1980), 20. Andersen refers to this incident in *The Fairy Tale of My Life*, 22.

Copenhagen by the Baltic Sea, was the fourth largest town in Denmark, with a population of about 7,000. Here the young Andersen was exposed to storytelling, superstition, and colorful local customs. More importantly, Odense had a theater. Traveling players from the Royal Theater in Copenhagen performed there, turning Andersen's interest in thespian culture into a lifelong passion. The provincial "Clumsy Hans" sang, danced, declaimed, and wrote plays. He was able to take his passion and throw himself—young, virtually penniless, and uneducated—into a new urban and urbane environment, absurdly confident that he would be able to make contacts with the right people and eventually make a name for himself in Copenhagen.

"THE GREAT POET YOU THINK YOU'LL BE"

Andersen's journey to Copenhagen in 1819 required a boat ride to the small port of Korsør and a thirty-six-hour ride by mail coach to the city's outskirts, where unofficial passengers were dropped off. Carrying a small bundle of clothes, the fourteen-year-old Andersen walked to the city gates and made his way to his lodgings, at 18 Vertergade. He had 10 *rigsdaler* in his pocket (his "savings" from bit parts as a page and a shepherd in Odense) and began knocking on doors. One evening he turned up at the home of Giuseppe Siboni, the choirmaster and conductor of the Royal Theater, where he was offered, in keeping with the city's charitable custom, something to eat. In the kitchen he recited the fairy tale of his life to the housekeeper. She whispered the story to Siboni, who decided to entertain his guests with the aspiring actor. The boy's repertoire in Siboni's parlor was evidently "a quaint blend of the high and the low: an aria from a ballad opera, which he had learned back home in Odense from a visiting Frøken Hammer; a couple of ample scenes from plays by Ludvig Holberg; as well as some home-brewed poems that no doubt sounded both provincial and pathetic."[8] Siboni's dinner guests included many of Denmark's leading literary lights, among them the poet Jens Baggesen, who declared to those assembled: "I predict that he's going to make something of himself one day!"[9]

8. Andersen, *Hans Christian Andersen*, 22.

9. Ibid., 23.

Siboni's offer of free singing lessons, along with leftovers from the dinner table, enabled Andersen to take the first real step toward creating a new identity along the lines of the fairy-tale narrative that he had constructed. But only a few months later, Andersen's fine soprano voice broke (he blamed himself for wearing bad shoes in the winter), and Siboni advised him to return to Odense. Andersen was distraught: "I who had described to my mother in the rich colors of the imagination the happiness which I actually felt, now had to return home and become an object of scorn! Filled with agony at this thought, I felt as if crushed to pieces. Yet just in the midst of this apparently great unhappiness lay the stepping-stones to a better future."[10]

One of those stepping-stones led in the direction of writing for the theater rather than performing on stage. In 1822, at the age of seventeen, Andersen submitted three different plays to the Royal Theater, each more bombastic and derivative than the next, but not wholly without merit, as one of the theater managers imagined. "When one takes into consideration the fact that this play is the product of a person who can barely manage decent penmanship, who knows nothing of orthography or Danish grammar . . . and furthermore possesses in his brain a hodgepodge of good and bad all jumbled together . . . one can still find in his work individual glimpses."[11] Given what Andersen had been able to confect with no education at all, he was recommended for a stipend to attend a grammar school. Jonas Collin, a senior government official who was to become Andersen's patron and mentor, worked with the directors of the Royal Theater to secure the funds that would enable the hopeful young dramatist to make up for his educational gaps by attending a school in Slagelse, a provincial backwater that would have none of Copenhagen's distractions.

Andersen's five years in Slagelse and later in Helsingør (Elsinor) under the tutelage of Simon Meisling cannot have been easy. Placed into classrooms with younger, smaller boys, he felt physically awkward and intellectually inferior: "I was just like a wild bird confined to a cage. I had the greatest desire to learn, but for the moment I floundered about, as if I had been thrown into the sea. One wave followed another: grammar, geography,

10. Andersen, *The Fairy Tale of My Life*, 31.

11. Andersen, *Hans Christian Andersen*, 49.

mathematics. I felt myself overpowered by them. . . . The Rector, who took a peculiar delight in turning everything to ridicule, did not, of course, make an exception in my case. . . . One day, when I replied incorrectly to his question . . . he said that I was stupid."[12] Andersen endured humiliation and torment, living under what he termed the "most horrible strains." Meisling was a tyrant who haunted his dreams years after his education was complete. Elias Bredsdorff, Denmark's greatest expert on Andersen, records how, over a period of forty years, Meisling ceaselessly troubled his pupil's sleep: "Nasty dreams with Meisling in them"; "Slept restlessly, dreamt about Meisling"; "Dreamt I had to be examined by Meisling"; "a painful dream about Meisling, in front of whom I stood miserable and awkward."[13]

Andersen applied himself to his studies, but not without complaint. Letters to his patrons openly expressed his frustrations and were so laden with self-pity that one of his benefactors wrote back: "You certainly do your best to tire your friends, and I can't believe that it can bring you any amusement—and all because of your constant concern with YOURSELF—YOUR OWN SELF—THE GREAT POET YOU THINK YOU WILL BE. My dear Andersen! Don't you realize that you are not going to succeed with all these ideas and that you are on the wrong track?"[14]

Andersen was on his own, navigating waters troubled by Meisling's humiliating pedagogical style, by Inger Meisling's seductive behavior toward the bewildered young man, and by the taunts of younger students mystified by the presence of a seventeen-year-old who towered over them physically but who could not find Copenhagen on a map. Forbidden to read "frivolous" literature or to indulge his equally frivolous desire to write, he nonetheless took the risk of expressing himself through poetry, writing, among other things, "The Dying Child," a poem published in 1827 on the front page of *Kjøbenhavnsposten*. Unusual in its expression of the child's point of view, it also reveals the profound emotional burden carried by Andersen during the years at Slagelse and Elsinor:

12. Andersen, *The Fairy Tale of My Life*, 45.

13. Elias Bredsdorff, *Hans Christian Andersen: The Story of His Life and Work, 1805–75* (New York: Scribner, 1975), 67–68.

14. *Breve til Hans Christian Andersen,* ed. C.S.A. Bille and N. Bøgh (Copenhagen, 1877), I, 580, March 8, 1827.

Mother, I am weary and want to sleep,

Let me fall asleep on your heart;

But do not cry, promise me you won't,

For I feel hot tears running down my cheek. . . .

You must put an end to those sighs,

If you cry, I will weep with you.

Oh, I am so weary and must close my eyes—

Mother—look! There's an angel kissing me.[15]

By 1827 Andersen, despite the many temptations to succumb to failure, passed his *examen artium*, and the rigors of his formal education were finally behind him.

Publication of "The Dying Child" was followed by an outpouring of verse—ballads, nature poems, portraits, romances, sketches, fantasies—collected in multiple volumes over a period of two years. Andersen remained throughout his life a prolific writer, with thirty-six theatrical works, six travel books, six novels, and nearly two hundred fairy tales and stories flowing from his pen, not to mention constant diary entries and letters to friends (sometimes as many as fourteen a day). The productivity sometimes worked against him. A letter from Edvard Collin is almost perversely cruel in chiding Andersen for being so productive:

You write too much! While one work is being printed, you are halfway through the manuscript of the next. This mad, deplorable productivity depreciates the value of your works so much that no bookseller wants them, even to give away. . . . It is extraordinarily selfish of you to assume such interest in your work, and the fault is no doubt yours, for the reading public has certainly not given you any reason to think so, and the critics least of all.[16]

Curiously, Andersen seemed to thrive on degrading comments of this type, responding to the stinging humiliations with predictable "shock" and

15. The translation is mine.

16. Diana Crone Frank and Jeffrey Frank, "Introduction: The Real H. C. Andersen," in *The Stories of H. C. Andersen*, trans. Diana Crone Frank and Jeffrey Frank (Boston: Houghton Mifflin, 2003), 8–9. The letter from Collin is dated December 18, 1833.

"despair," then cheerfully bouncing back to apply himself to his writing with more determination than ever. Outwardly he expressed a sense of shame and humility; inwardly he seems to have redoubled his efforts to make the grade as a writer, drawing on his social failures for the material that would shape his literary success. Andersen practiced time and again what one critic calls the "phoenix principle"—the notion that a new identity can be established only once the old one has been crushed. Defeat and failure are the necessary, if not always sufficient, conditions for the triumph of poetry.[17] Andersen's story about the phoenix, included in this volume, invests the beautiful bird with the power of poetry and ends by apostrophizing its regenerative power: "Oh bird of paradise, renewed with each new century, you are born in flames and die in flames."

THE GREAT, WIDE WORLD

The Improvisatore (1835), Andersen's first novel, offered clear evidence that writing well was the best revenge. Dedicated to the entire Collin family, the volume can be seen as tribute and reprimand. In a garret facing a cluster of lime trees, Andersen completed a novel that many Danish readers could easily recognize as a roman à clef. Antonio, an Italian version of Andersen, is born in the slums of Rome and has a talent for singing that attracts the attention of the Borghese family. Sent to a Jesuit college with a tyrannical director, he gradually wins acceptance into a new social class through his success as an artist. His happiness is clouded by the unfortunate tendency of well-meaning friends to lecture him endlessly, offering "helpful" criticism in an effort to "educate" him.

With the publication of this bildungsroman, Andersen joined the ranks of the great British and European novelists, and his name came to be mentioned in the same breath as Dickens, Balzac, and Goethe, even if he did not share their stature. He began riding what he himself described as the crest of a wave: "Never before has a work of mine absorbed people so intensely. Hertz came to see me . . . telling me, in quite a beautiful way, that many

17. Heinrich Detering, "The Phoenix Principle: Some Remarks on H. C. Andersen's Poetological Writings," in *Hans Christian Andersen: A Poet in Time*, ed. Johan de Mylius et al. (Odense: Odense Univ. Press, 1999), 50–65.

people here who no longer cared about me, are now devoted to me."[18] The work was translated almost immediately into German, English, Swedish, Russian, Dutch, and French and marked the true launching of his literary career.

Just after completing the manuscript for *The Improvisatore*, Andersen, almost as an afterthought, began to write some tales for children. To be sure, the focus on childhood in *The Improvisatore* and its fairy-tale ending can be seen as building a sturdy literary bridge to the new enterprise that courted the attention of children rather than adults. But Andersen had something different in mind. In 1835, on New Year's Day, he wrote to a friend: "Now I am beginning to write some 'Fairy Tales for Children.' I want to win the next generations, you see." "People will say this is my immortal work!" he added. "But that is something I shall not experience in this world." Others had greater confidence in a rapid ascent to literary fame. In 1835, Andersen wrote that his friend H. C. Ørsted (the Danish physicist known for his study of the magnetic fields produced by electric currents) had declared that the tales would make him "immortal." "I myself do not think so," he added, with uncharacteristic modesty.[19]

The first review of *Eventyr, fortalte for Børn* (Fairy tales, told for children) was disappointing. The anonymous critic failed to find any "edifying effect" and expressed hope that "the talented author, with a higher mission to follow, will not waste any more of his time in writing fairy tales for children."[20] Other reviewers were not particularly generous, complaining about the "disorderly" language. Like the Grimms before him, Andersen was accused of writing in a roughhewn, conversational style that was not sufficiently literary. This first volume of the fairy tales, which included "The Tinderbox," "Little Claus and Big Claus," "The Princess and the Pea," and "Little Ida's Flowers," was in many ways the Danish answer to the Brothers Grimm. The first three tales reworked stories Andersen had heard as a boy in the spinning room of an asylum in Odense known as Greyfriars Hospital

18. Hans Christian Andersen, letter to Henriette Wulff, April 29, 1835, *H.C. Andersen og Henriette Wulff. En Brevveksling* (Odense: Flensteds Forlag, 1959), I, 151.

19. Hans Christian Andersen, letter to Henriette Hanck, January 1, 1835, in "H. C. Andersens Brevveksling med Henriette Hanck," *Anderseniana* (1942), 104.

20. Ibid., 124.

(his grandmother worked there and let him wander the enclosed grounds and public spaces). Only the fourth was his own invention.

All four fairy tales hiss and crackle with narrative energy. Brisk and breezy, they were meant for reading out loud, with numerous nods in the direction of oral storytelling conventions ("A soldier came marching down the road—left! right! left! right!") and also to Andersen's own animated, exclamatory style ("That was a real story!"). Although scholars have made us aware that Denmark's most famous author of children's tales had a well-known aversion to being around children (he was outraged that a statue in his honor was designed to include children hovering around him), there is also evidence that Andersen spent plenty of time with the children of various wealthy families that offered him hospitality. He often went out of his way to entertain them with stories and with his famous paper cuttings. Edvard Collin reports that Andersen told stories

> which he partly made up on the spur of the moment, partly borrowed from well-known fairy tales; but whether the tale was his own or a retelling, the manner of telling it was entirely his own, and so full of life that the children were delighted. . . . He didn't say, "The children got into the carriage and then drove away," but "So they got into the carriage, good-bye Daddy, good-bye Mummy, the whip cracked, snick, snack, and away they went, giddy up!"[21]

Like Lewis Carroll, who rehearsed *Alice in Wonderland* by telling stories out loud on "golden afternoons," Andersen tested and developed his style with the children who would become the audience.

Many commentators have pointed to the explosive fantasies of social revenge embedded in the early tales: Little Claus outwits Big Claus, and the soldier in "The Tinderbox" dethrones the king and queen. These stories, Jackie Wullschlager astutely observes, provided an outlet for Andersen's "rage against the bourgeois society that tried to make him conform."[22] But it is important to keep in mind that the tenor of Ander-

---

21. Grønbech, 89.

22. Jackie Wullschlager, *Hans Christian Andersen: The Life of a Storyteller* (New York: Knopf, 2000), 153. Jack Zipes writes that, when Andersen took pen in hand, "it was to shield himself from his fears and to vent his anger" (*Hans Christian Andersen: The Misunderstood Storyteller* [New York: Routledge, 2005], 1).

sen's tales does not deviate sharply from the standard of many other European collections of fairy tales, where revenge figures importantly as part of the happy ending. Still the deep sense of resentment that wells up in Andersen's writing was emphasized again and again by contemporaries, including one of Andersen's fiercest critics: Søren Kierkegaard, the other great Dane of the nineteenth century. A philosopher and theologian best known for his monumental *Fear and Trembling* (1843), Kierkegaard was the founding father of existentialism and a man whose patrician upbringing, academic earnestness, and austere confidence stood in direct opposition to everything that Andersen was.

The years following the publication of *The Improvisatore* and the first installment of the fairy tales were good ones for Andersen. "My name is gradually starting to shine," he wrote in 1837, "and that is the only thing I live for."[23] In the next decade, he would write nearly all the fairy tales for which he is known, with one volume appearing on an annual basis between 1835 and 1845. *Nye Eventyr* (New fairy tales), which contained both "The Ugly Duckling" and "The Nightingale," appeared in 1845, showing Andersen at the height of his narrative powers. His melodramatic plays and rambling novels—*The Improvisatore* was followed by *O.T.* and *Only a Fiddler*—are not often read today, but they were moderately successful, even if they did not turn Andersen into "Denmark's foremost novelist," as he had hoped. *Only a Fiddler* is remembered today primarily because it was the subject of Kierkegaard's eccentric first book, *From the Papers of One Still Living, Published against His Will,* which contained a long essay entitled "On Andersen as a Novelist: With Constant Reference to His Latest Work, *Only a Fiddler.*" With consummate sophistication and erudition, Kierkegaard offers a penetrating critique of Andersen's novel, shedding light on its weaknesses, but more importantly laying bare the strategies of a narrator who is constantly defending his characters against social slights. If Kierkegaard makes the error of using Andersen's fiction to draw conclusions about his character, moving the focus from the work itself to its author, his critique nonetheless offers some insight into the cult of suffering that shadows the cult of beauty in Andersen's works.

23. Ibid., 179.

ONLY A VICTIM

Andersen reports that he ran into Kierkegaard on the streets of Copenhagen shortly after *Only a Fiddler* appeared. Kierkegaard commiserated with him about the stupidity of critics and promised a favorable review of the book. Yet what the philosopher put into print turned out to be a heavy-handed Hegelian rant, one that even Andersen realized might end up with no more than two readers: the reviewer and the author of the book. The two made amends later in life, and Andersen sent Kierkegaard a copy of his *Nye Eventyr* (1848) with a witty dedication: "*Either* you approve of my things, *or* you do not approve of them, yet you come without *fear or trembling*, and that at least is something." Kierkegaard, in return, sent Andersen a copy of *Either/Or*. Andersen's acknowledgment suggests that the wounds had healed: "You have given me great pleasure by sending me *Either/Or*! I was really surprised, as I'm sure you can imagine; I had no idea that you would look kindly on me, and yet here I see that you do! God bless you for that!"[24]

Kierkegaard takes Andersen to task for his failings as both artist and man. What particularly irritates the philosopher about *Only a Fiddler* is Andersen's habit of expressing his "livid indignation against the world" through his characters, even when that sentiment is irrelevant to the narrated events. Andersen could not resist the temptation to turn his heroes into "clients," whose interests he is constantly defending and whose dignity he is constantly seeking to protect. "Lack . . . of dutiful attentiveness, even in the case where attentiveness is so far from being dutiful that it would even be unreasonable, does not go unpunished."[25] Kierkegaard cites as an example the description of the hero's appearance at a dance hall in *Only a Fiddler*: "With hat in hand he bowed politely in all directions. No one noticed it." An attentive and doting narrator, Andersen hovers over his main characters, tirelessly polishing their haloes. At the same time, he makes it a habit to scold and chastise those who fail to acknowledge the virtues of the figures he favors.

24. Andersen, *Hans Christian Andersen*, 257.

25. Søren Kierkegaard, "Andersen as a Novelist: With Continual Reference to His Latest Work, *Only a Fiddler*," in *Early Polemical Writings*, ed. Julia Watkin (Princeton: Princeton Univ. Press, 1990), 91.

For Kierkegaard, Andersen makes the grave error of constructing a hero who passively succumbs to his fate rather than challenging it. As author, he then "sits and cries over his unfortunate heroes who must go under, and why?—because Andersen is the man he is. The same joyless battle Andersen himself fights in life now repeats itself in his poetry."[26] Kierkegaard further refines the frontal-attack by pointing out that two paths are open for Andersen's hero: a "broken manliness," stemming from a failed attempt to work against fate, or a "consistent womanliness," based on a failure to put up any resistance at all. Kierkegaard had, as one of Andersen's biographers puts it, "uncovered the female soul in Andersen's character."[27]

In his attack on the central character and narrator of Andersen's novel, Kierkegaard believed that he had laid bare more than Andersen's "female soul." He demonstrated how sharply the author's narcissism and masochism etched itself on his literary portraits, creating a cult of passive suffering that was particularly repellent to a philosopher who endorsed defiantly robust genius. "Genius is not a rush candle that goes out in a puff of air but a conflagration that the storm only incites," Kierkegaard insisted.[28] Despite the contempt he held for individual characters, he still admired the deep personal stake Andersen had in his characters and plots.

If Kierkegaard can be credited with some shrewd insights in his critique of Andersen's novel, he seems somewhat off the mark when it comes to the novel's author, whose resilience in the face of disparagement and disapproval was nothing short of astonishing. The censorious review, like all the cutting remarks made by patrons, friends, and journalists, may have wounded, but it also satisfied Andersen's *amour propre* perfectly and, far from producing disaffection and defeat, only renewed his desire for self-display, now with an added dose of self-effacing humor. "I remained an object of derision," Andersen declared with undisguised pride. "There is, in the Dane, a fondness for mockery, or, to put it more kindly, we have a sense of the absurd."[29] Ander-

26. Ibid., 75.

27. Andersen, *Hans Christian Andersen*, 253.

28. Kierkegaard, "Andersen as Novelist," 88.

29. Hans Christian Andersen, *Travels,* trans. Anastazia Little (Los Angeles: Green Integer, 1999), 22.

sen struck back with the weapons that had been used against him, deploying irony, humor, satire, and pastiche—what he referred to as "salt"—to enliven plots that might otherwise have been mired down in histrionics and melodrama.

In 1838, Andersen turned a financial corner and also received a substantial boost in self-confidence. That year King Frederik VI of Denmark awarded him an annual stipend of 400 rigsdaler, enough money to allow him to write, travel, and take up permanent residence in Copenhagen's fashionable Hotel du Nord. If there is any need of further evidence that Kierkegaard was at least half right in his assessment of Andersen's personality disorders, it is readily available in a letter to Count Conrad Rantzau-Breitenburg, whom Andersen recruited to plead his cause with Frederik VI:

> The happiness of my entire life and all my future endeavors I place in your hands. Just tell the king what I know you have said with such affection to others about me! Do not refuse my plea! If you believe that there is anything moving inside me, then speak for me. I am begging your indulgence just this one time. *You will earn distinction through me!* [my emphasis] . . . My happiness in life is at stake. Deliver my application to the king, and with God's help, you will not find reason to be ashamed![30]

When Andersen received news of the stipend, he was filled with "gratitude and joy," in no small part because the stipend had, at one time or another, been awarded to nearly all of Denmark's literary worthies. He was thrilled that he was no longer "*forced* to write in order to live" and believed that he would now be "less dependent" upon his friends and patrons, with whom he had regular dining arrangements nearly every day of the week: "Mondays at Mrs. Bügel's . . . Tuesdays at the Collins' . . . Wednesdays at the Ørsteds' . . . Thursday again at Mrs. Bügel's . . . Fridays at the Wulffs' . . . Saturday is my day off, then I dine wherever I happen to be invited . . . Sundays at Mrs. Læssøe's, or in the Students' Union if I do not feel well

30. C. St. A. Bille and N. Bøgh, *Breve fra Hans Christian Andersen* (Copenhagen, 1878), I, 397–98.

enough to make the long walk." "A new chapter of my life began," he proudly reported.[31]

"I'M IN FASHION"

The liberation from financial anxieties was accompanied by an expansion of geographical and intellectual ambitions. Andersen's journey to the "Orient" in 1841 is well documented in *The Poet's Bazaar*, a travelogue that charts his travels through Germany to Rome and Naples, and finally on to Athens and Constantinople.[32] For a man who was deathly afraid of fire (he carried a nine-meter-long rope ladder with him when he traveled), suffered bouts of agoraphobia (he needed a guide to cross a square), and constantly worried about robbers and murderers ("Oh how good I am at tormenting myself!"), Andersen was eager and adventurous, traveling fearlessly through storms at sea and enduring—as we learn from the diaries—everything from quarantines and threats of robbery to mosquitoes and undrinkable coffee.[33] Even Edvard Collin, habitually stingy with praise, declared: "You are a damn good traveler."[34] Andersen's travels eastward had less of an impact on his writings than on his general outlook and health:

> It was as if a new life were about to open for me, and that was exactly what happened. If this can't be seen in my later writings, it animates my views about life and my entire inner development. I no longer felt as if I were ailing. As I observed my European home, if I can call it that, vanish behind me,

31. Elias Bredsdorff cites the schedule as reported by Andersen in a letter to Henriette Hanck (Bredsdorff, *Hans Christian Andersen*, 132). As Rossel points out, "Andersen's daily life was extremely comfortable during his later life. He continued to see his old friends at least once a week as their dinner guest, a tradition that stemmed from his early years in Copenhagen. He saw in this way Edvard and Henriette Collin on Mondays, Adolph and Ingeborg Drewson on Tuesdays, Brigitte Ørsted, the widow of Hans Christian Ørsted, and her daughter Mathilde on Wednesdays, Moritz and Dorothea Melchior on Thursdays, Ida Koch, the widowed sister of Henriette Wulff, on Fridays, and Martin and Therese Henriques on Sundays" (Rossel 1996, 73).

32. Hans Christian Andersen, *A Poet's Bazaar: A Picturesque Tour in Germany, Italy, Greece, and the Orient* (New York: Minerva, 2004).

33. Wolfgang Lederer, *The Kiss of the Snow Queen: Hans Christian Andersen and Man's Redemption by Women* (Berkeley: Univ. of California Press, 1986), 83.

34. Bredsdorff, 150.

it was as if a current of amnesia passed over all bitter and unhealthy memories. I felt health rush into my blood, into my mind. With courage and strength, I raised my head high once again.[35]

After completing his thirteenth trip abroad, Andersen reveled in the power of travel to cleanse the soul: "Travel to me is invigorating. . . . I feel the need, not just to acquire new material—there is enough of that inside me already, and life is indeed too short to plumb the depths of that spring—but in order to put my impressions on paper I need this refreshing bath which seems to make me both younger and stronger when I return home"[36]

In the 1840s, Andersen made a number of victory tours through European countries, delighting in the earnest attention paid to him and the outpourings of affection. In Denmark, he remarked, he was a stranger, "a stranger like nowhere abroad." "I wish I had never seen that place! . . . I hate home, just as it hates and spits on me," he complained shortly after one of his plays was booed on its premiere in Copenhagen.[37] In Paris he was received by royalty as well as by the great poets and writers of the century: Victor Hugo, Heinrich Heine, Alexandre Dumas, Alfred de Vigny, and Honoré de Balzac. In Germany he consorted with dukes and hobnobbed with royalty. In England, he became the darling of the aristocracy and sat for a famous sculptor. When he was abroad, Andersen was sought after and celebrated, treated like a genius and a celebrity, much to his satisfaction. It is at this point that his autobiography becomes tedious reading, deteriorating into detailed lists of medals and decorations and the names and titles of those who had bestowed them.

Yet even as one part of the fairy-tale fantasy—prosperity and fame—was fulfilled, another part continued to elude him: love and marriage. To a friend he affirmed that he did not yet have the means to marry: "I must have 1000 a year before I dare fall in love, and 1500 before I dare marry, and before even half of this happens, the young girl will be gone, captured by someone else, and I'll be an old, wizened bachelor. Those are sorry prospects. . . . No I will

35. Hans Christian Andersen, *Mit eget Eventyr uden Digtning* (Copenhagen: C. A. Reitzel, 1959), 107.

36. Andersen, *Travels,* 166.

37. Hans Christian Andersen, letter to Henriette Wulff, April 1843, in Bille and Bøgh, II, 82.

never be rich, never satisfied and never—fall in love!"[38] Andersen did not marry, but he fell in love many times, although as a rule only when marriage could be completely ruled out as a possibility.

Riborg Voigt, the sister of a fellow student, was engaged when Andersen met her in 1830, and he could bemoan the fact that she would never be his: "I see that I will never be happy," he wrote sullenly. "All my soul and all my thoughts cling to this one creature, a clever, *childlike* creature such as I have never met before. . . . Next month she becomes a *wife,* then she will, then she must forget me. Oh, it is a deadly thought! . . . If only I were dead, dead, even if death were total annihilation."[39] To Riborg, he wrote despondent letters, declaring his love but also acknowledging that she belonged to another.

The "childlike" continued to appeal, and when Andersen famously fell in love with Jenny Lind, he again used that term to describe the object of his affections. Andersen was thirty-five, and Jenny Lind was twenty when they met for the first time. The brilliant Swedish nightingale, who began singing for the stage at age ten and who created a sensation on tours to Europe and the United States, was "courteous" but "distant" and "cold," although she came to love Andersen "as a brother." "No book and no person has had such an ennobling influence on me as Jenny Lind, which is why I dwell on these memories . . . because she can never be mine."[40] Andersen saw in Jenny Lind his female double, a woman to whose talent and success he aspired: "She sings German the way I no doubt read my fairy tales; something familiar shines through, but, as they say of me, that's exactly what makes it interesting." And when he discovered that his fame was great in the city of Berlin, he wrote to the Collins: "I'm a lion, I'm a Berlin lion, I've become a male Jenny Lind. I'm in fashion."[41]

Andersen's sexual desires and practices have become the subject of detailed speculation in the several biographies that have appeared since the bicentenary of his birth. His disastrous visits to brothels (always ending in panicked flight), his homoerotic desires, and his physiological complaints

38. Hans Christian Andersen, letter to Henriette Wulff, May 3, 1843, in Bille and Bøgh, II, 405.

39. Wolfgang Lederer, *The Kiss of the Snow Queen,* 79.

40. Andersen, *Travels,* 215.

41. Andersen, *Hans Christian Andersen,* 310, 312.

have all been subjected to careful documentation and analysis.[42] What many of these accounts miss is the degree to which Andersen's narcissism conspired with his cult of suffering to ensure that he would have an unending love affair with himself. There are good reasons why he remained a bachelor, and that was the role in which he was happiest, for it allowed him to remain the object of fussy attention from many well-off female admirers and to travel for extended periods. It seems almost prophetic that as a child, while other boys played on the banks, he sat by the lake, weaving a crown of reeds and sending small ships into the waters.

The fortune-teller who had predicted that Odense would one day be illuminated in Andersen's honor was proved right on December 6, 1867, when officials awarded Andersen the so-called freedom of the town. Speeches and a banquet were followed by a torchlight procession that Andersen observed from the town hall. "How happy I was," he reports.

> . . . I was overcome in my soul, and also physically overcome. . . . My toothache was intolerable; the icy air which rushed in at the window made it blaze up into a terrible pain, and so instead of fully enjoying the happiness of these minutes which would never recur, I looked at the printed song to see how many stanzas were left before I could slip away from the torture which the cold air sent through my teeth.[43]

Who can fail to be surprised that the promise of what Andersen described as "heavenly bliss" was tainted by pain and sorrow?

The last years of Andersen's life were marked by infirmity, depression, and a range of cruel ailments including rheumatism and jaundice. "I have spent endlessly long days recently," he wrote. "I am not looking forward to anything, have no future any more, the days are washing over me, and I am really only waiting for the curtain to fall."[44] Even writing had lost its appeal, and Andersen found himself lacking in "new, fresh impulses." Walking through his garden, looking at the roses, snails, and water lilies, he felt

---

42. Jackie Wullschlager's biography provides extensive documentation and full elaboration of fantasies, anxieties, and encounters.

43. Ibid., 252–53.

44. Bredsdorff, *Hans Christian Andersen,* 266.

as if they had already whispered their secrets to him: "No fairy tales occur to me anymore."[45]

In his last years, Andersen was cared for by the Melchior family, and the writer spent his last days at Rolighed, a manor with the kind of natural beauty described in many of his fairy tales. Attended to by Dorothea Melchior, who brought him a fresh flower from the garden each morning, he knew that the end was near. He died on a summer morning in 1875. On his travels, he had made it a custom to place a sign with the words "I only appear to be dead" by his bedside. Andersen was familiar with stories about people who were put in coffins, then discovered to be still alive. This time, the card was unnecessary, but it would have had a certain truth if it had been placed by his death bed.

"Will the beauty of the world die when you die?" the fly asks the oak tree in Andersen's tale "The Old Oak Tree's Last Dream." The oak tree reassures the fly in ways that ring true for the beauty of Andersen's stories: "It will last longer, infinitely longer than I can imagine!"

45. Ibid., 269.

Andersen's Illustrators

HONOR APPLETON (1879-1951)

Born in Brighton, England, Honor Charlotte Appleton studied at the South Kensington Schools, Frank Calderon's School of Animal Painting, and the Royal Academy Schools. She published her first book, *The Bad Mrs. Ginger*, in 1902 and joined the ranks of professional book illustrators with Blake's *Songs of Innocence* (1910). Influenced by Kate Greenaway and Mabel Lucie Attwell, she illustrated over one hundred and fifty books in her lifetime but is best known for her collaboration with Mrs. H. C. Cradock on a series about a little girl named Josephine and her beloved toys. In the 1930s and 1940s, she worked for George G. Harrap publishers and illustrated literary classics for children, among them *Alice's Adventures in Wonderland*, *Ali Baba*, and *Black Beauty*. Her 1919 illustrations for an adapted version of Andersen's "Snow Queen" were followed by beautifully muted pastel watercolors for a volume of the fairy tales.

MABEL LUCIE ATTWELL (1879-1964)

Born in Mile End, London, Mabel Lucie Attwell was the ninth of ten children in a family of extraordinary musical and artistic talent. At age fifteen, she submitted her art work to a publisher and received what she described with pride as "a cheque for two guineas." The proceeds from her drawings enabled her to attend art schools, and soon she was taking commissions from book publishers and magazine editors.

In 1908, Attwell married Harold Earnshaw, a successful artist who worked in pen, ink, and watercolor. Peggy, the first of their three children, was born in 1909 and served as the inspiration for the innocent wide-eyed wonderment in Attwell's portraits of children. Commercial firms were quick to discover the appeal of Attwell's chubby, rosy-cheeked toddlers, placing them in advertisements for Jaeger Footwear ("For Tiny Toes"), Swan Fountain Pens ("A Present for Daddy"), and Velvet Skin Soap ("Baby Chooses"). Valentine and Sons enlisted her to design postcards, calendars, greeting cards, and plaques. Her artwork decorated not only the walls of homes but also, according to at least one report, World War I dugouts.

Attwell began illustrating fairy tales and children's books in 1910 with *Grimms' Fairy Tales* and *Mother Goose,* followed by *Alice in Wonderland* (1910), *Andersen's Fairy Tales* (1914), and *The Water-Babies* (1915). At the request of J. M. Barrie, she created illustrations for a gift-book edition of *Peter Pan and Wendy*, which appeared in 1921 and became a best-seller. It remains the most successful of all her books. Unlike Rackham, Dulac, and the Robinsons, she aimed to please the child rather than the adult.

Never short of work, Attwell even found a patron for her art in Marie, Queen of Romania. In the 1930s and 1940s she worked with manufacturers to produce china figures and rubber dolls while continuing to produce illustrations, plaques, postcards, and posters. She moved to Fowey in Cornwall in 1945 and stayed there until her death in 1964.

Further Reading:
Beetles, Chris. *Mabel Lucie Attwell*. London: Pavilion, 1988.

ELEANOR VERE BOYLE (1825-1916)

Eleanor Vere Boyle, born Eleanor Gordon, illustrated a small number of children's books, including Andersen's *Fairy Tales* (1872) and the gift book *Beauty and the Beast: An Old Tale New-Told* (1875). Her lavish color plates included figures with Italianate costumes and stylized depictions of nature.

Andersen himself was unimpressed by Boyle's illustrations, finding them lacking in aesthetic quality despite the lavish images. He remarked that royalties for the English-language edition would be far more interesting to him than the images created by Boyle. Toward the end of her life, EVB (as she signed herself) illustrated books on gardening.

HARRY CLARKE (1889–1931)

Harry Clarke has been hailed as Ireland's major Symbolist artist, an illustrator and craftsman whose commitment to fin-de-siècle aestheticism and mysticism led to the creation of images both beautiful and macabre. The son of a glass worker, he attended a Catholic boys' school (Belvedere College) as well as the Metropolitan School of Art in Dublin and the South Kensington School of Design in London.

In 1913 Laurence Waldron, a governor of Belvedere College, commissioned Clarke to produce a set of illustrations for Pope's *Rape of the Lock.* The six images, heavily influenced by Aubrey Beardsley, used pen and ink to evoke rococo decorative effects. Shortly thereafter George Harrap turned to Clarke with plans to issue an illustrated edition of Hans Christian Andersen's fairy tales. "But for me," the publisher reported, "he would probably have abandoned the idea of illustrating books" (Bowe, 30). Harrap's *Fairy Tales by Hans Christian Andersen* came in the wake of Hodder and Stoughton's *Stories from Hans Andersen,* illustrated by Edmund Dulac, and *In Powder and Crinoline: Old Fairy Tales,* illustrated by Kay Nielsen. In the early part of the twentieth century, new technologies for reproducing images enabled book illustration to flourish.

Clarke dedicated several months to illustrations for Andersen's fairy tales, combining that project with artwork for several stories by Edgar Allan Poe, including "The Fall of the House of Usher" and "The Tell-Tale Heart." Illustrated volumes of Keats's *La Belle Dame sans Merci,* Goethe's *Faust,* and Coleridge's *The Ancient Mariner* (the plates for the latter were destroyed during an armed uprising in Dublin) followed in quick succession. Clarke alternated between commissions for illustrating literary works and designs for stained glass windows to be installed in the Honan Chapel in Cork, a building that displays the vibrant qualities of the Irish Arts and Crafts movement. The beauty of these windows is widely acknowledged. Here, Clarke was able to display his mastery of color, design, and craft.

The publication of *Fairy Tales by Hans Christian Andersen* in 1916 saw praise from *The Bookman*, which lauded Clarke as "a craftsman who devotes to each drawing an infinity of pains which is little less than marvelous, and it is difficult to know which to admire most, his fresh conceptions or his delicate and intricate details." Other reviews were less generous, criticizing the derivative nature of the illustrations, which would have been "more agreeable if his admiration for Beardsley had been less pronounced."

Harry Clarke maintained a sense of reverence toward the stories he illustrated. "I feel I do not do a book as it should be done. I see my drawings and there is only a hazy background of Book, whereas the drawings should, as you have *so* many times said, be subordinate to the whole," he wrote to one publisher. "I did my best to convey what I felt," he wrote about Goethe's *Faust*, when booksellers criticized what Clarke called the "lewd and stinking" illustrations, which left a "nasty taste in the mouth."

In 1929 Clarke left Dublin to spend time at a sanatorium in Davos, Switzerland. Although he was to return to Ireland for a few months the following year, he never recovered his health and died in his sleep in a small Swiss village at the age of forty-one.

Further Reading:

Bowe, Nicola Gordon. *The Life and Work of Harry Clarke.* Dublin: Irish Academic Press, 1989.

Frazier, Adrian. "Harry Clarke and the Material Culture of Modern Ireland." *Textual Practice* 16 (2002): 303–21.

EDMUND DULAC (1882–1953)

A passion for pattern, texture, and pigment marks the illustrations produced by Edmund Dulac. Although Dulac was remarkably versatile as an artist—designing everything from postage stamps and paper money to theater costumes and furniture—he is best known today as one of the eminent illustrators of a period known as the golden age of children's book illustration. During the decade preceding World War I, Arthur Rackham, Kay

Nielsen, Charles Robinson, and W. Heath Robinson adorned children's books with stunning color plates. While Rackham remained faithful to his British roots and turned to Nordic mythology for his inspiration, Dulac, born in France in 1882, became a passionate Anglophile who also looked to Asia to enrich the manner and matter of his art. Rackham, it has been said, painted with his pencil, while Dulac, master of sensuous designs and exotic settings, drew with his brush.

A native of Toulouse, Dulac studied art while attending law classes at the university. After receiving a prize for his painting, he abandoned his legal studies to devote himself fully to art school. An ardent admirer of William Morris, Walter Crane, and Aubrey Beardsley, Dulac changed the spelling of his first name from "Edmond" to the more British "Edmund," whereupon his friends began referring to him as "l'Anglais."

It was in London that Dulac got his start in the art of book illustration. The publishing house of J. M. Dent commissioned sixty watercolors for a complete set of the Brontë sisters' novels. Encouraged by the offer, Dulac decided to stay in London, working as a contributing illustrator to the *Pall Mall Gazette*, a monthly magazine. The publishing house of Hodder & Stoughton, competing against William Heinemann, who had just signed on Rackham, hired Dulac to illustrate *The Arabian Nights*, a perfect match for the artist. Using varied shades of blue—indigo, cobalt, cerulean, lilac, lavender, and mauve—Dulac produced starry backgrounds with a magical quality so powerful that they dominated the composition. Dulac effaced differences between background and foreground, producing a visual plane that required the viewer to scan the entire surface. Increasingly, Dulac liberated his art from Western artistic conventions, eliminating the conventional use of perspective and investing his energy in decorative surfaces with rich hues and designs. "The end result of objective imitative art," he wrote, "is nothing less than colored photography."

Dulac's illustrations for "Beauty and the Beast," "Cinderella," "Bluebeard," and "Sleeping Beauty" were produced to accompany Sir Arthur Quiller-Couch's *Sleeping Beauty and Other Tales from the Old French* (1910). *Stories from Hans Andersen* appeared just two years later. During World War I, when business was slack, Dulac was commissioned to prepare illustrations for a book of fairy tales that became known as *Edmund Dulac's Fairy Book—*

Fairy Tales of the Allied Nations. The volume, published in 1916, revealed Dulac's adaptability, for he was able to produce illustrations that captured the artistic styles of the different nations represented in the volume. While Dulac's interest in fairy-tale illustration waned as the years passed, he remained artistically active until his death, composing music, designing banknotes, and developing an interest in spiritualism.

Further Reading:

Larkin, David. *Edmund Dulac.* Toronto: Peacock/Bantam, 1975.

White, Colin. *Edmund Dulac.* New York: Scribners, 1976.

KAY NIELSEN (1886-1957)

The art historian Sir Kenneth Clark once confessed that Arthur Rackham's fairy-tale illustrations had stamped "images of terror" on his imagination. How much more troubled might he have been by the illustrations of Kay Nielsen, the Danish Aubrey Beardsley whose heroes and heroines, bent with sinewy determination, make their way through powerfully eerie landscapes. Nielsen arrests our attention with his flattened perspectives and graceful linework in vast, arctic terrains.

Born in 1886 in Copenhagen, Nielsen was the son of parents who were part of a robust theatrical culture. His mother was a leading lady and popular singer, while his father worked as managing director of the Royal Theater. "They brought me up in a tense atmosphere of art," the artist reported of his parents. As a child, Nielsen was accustomed to meeting such notables as Henrik Ibsen and Edvard Grieg on a regular basis. The young Nielsen was determined to become a physician, but by age seventeen his plans changed, and he moved to Paris, where he studied art for nearly a decade.

Nielsen was fascinated not only by the work of the British artist Aubrey Beardsley but also by the Art Nouveau style in general and by Japanese woodcuts. In Paris, he was commissioned to illustrate volumes of poems by Heinrich Heine and Paul Verlaine. In 1913 he produced twenty-four watercolors for a book of fairy tales retold by Sir Arthur Quiller-Couch. *In Powder and Crinoline* was subsequently published in the United States under the title *Twelve Dancing Princesses.* The volume secured Nielsen's reputation as an illustrator and led to additional commissioned works, the most important of which was *East of the Sun and West of the Moon,* a collection of Norwegian fairy tales that proved a congenial match for the Danish artist, whose works pulse with eerie decorative energy.

Nielsen's career lost its momentum with the onset of the war years, and he returned to Copenhagen, where set design occupied his attention. For the Danish State Theater, he produced sets for a theatrical version of *Aladdin,* as well as Shakespeare's *The Tempest* and *A Midsummer Night's Dream.* During the interwar years, Nielsen illustrated two additional volumes of fairy tales, a collection of Andersen's fairy tales (1924), and an anthology of tales by the Brothers Grimm (1925).

Nielsen spent the last two decades of his life in the United States. Los Angeles proved attractive to him and his wife and, despite straitened economic circumstances, he enjoyed his short spell at Disney Studios, where he designed the "Bald Mountain" sequence for *Fantasia.* He was unwilling to compromise his artistic standards for commercial success, however, and was reduced to raising chickens for a time. Painting a mural at the local high school helped him eke out a living (the $34' \times 19'$ image was stripped from the wall a year later to make way for charts of school districts).

Nielsen died in 1957 and left to family friends seemingly worthless paintings illustrating *The Thousand and One Nights.* They remain among the most stunning of Nielsen's artworks, although they have never been incorporated into an edition of the tales.

Further Reading:

Britton, Jasmine. "Kay Nielsen—Danish Artist." *The Horn Book* (May 1945): 168–73.

Larkin, David. *Kay Nielsen.* Toronto: Peacock/Bantam, 1975.

Poltarnees, Welleran. *Kay Nielsen: An Appreciation.* La Jolla, CA: Green Tiger Press, 1976.

VILHELM PEDERSEN (1820–1859) AND LORENZ FRØLICH (1820–1908)

When Andersen's fairy tales first appeared, they were not illustrated. Pedersen, an officer in the navy, was asked to provide images for a complete set of the stories. Engraved on wood at the Leipzig firm of Kretschmar, the pencil drawings (of which there were over a hundred) first appeared in a German translation of 1848.

After Pedersen's death, Lorenz Frølich took over work on the fairy tales, with the first drawings appearing in 1870.

ARTHUR RACKHAM (1867–1939)

During the golden age of children's books launched by Lewis Carroll's *Alice in Wonderland*, the British illustrator Arthur Rackham fashioned images both sprightly and haunting for fairy tales and fantasy literature. Known for his "wide and elfish grin," Rackham used himself as a model for many of the whimsical creatures that inhabit his illustrated books. The uncanny resemblance between him and his creations was often noted. "I thought he was one of the goblins out of Grimms' Fairy Tales," his nephew recalled.

Rackham grew up in a respected, middle-class Victorian family. As a child, he showed a talent for drawing and often smuggled paper and pencil with him into bed. On the recommendation of a physician, the sixteen-year-old Rackham left school to take a six-month sea voyage, journeying to Australia in 1893 with family friends and returning in improved health. Convinced that his real calling was at the easel, he entered the Lambeth School of Art but was obliged to spend the years 1885 to 1892 working in an insurance office. He left the insurance business to become a full-time graphic journalist at the *Westminster Budget*, where his "Sketches from Life" received critical and popular acclaim.

In 1900 Rackham was invited to illustrate *The Fairy Tales of the Brothers Grimm.* The success of that volume launched him as an illustrator, and in 1902 he created the images for J. M. Barrie's *A Little White Bird.* His publication of an edition of *Rip Van Winkle* in 1905 secured his reputation as the Edwardian era's most prominent illustrator. In constant demand as an artist, he was commissioned to illustrate Barrie's *Peter Pan in Kensington Garden* (Rackham had "shed glory" on the work, Barrie believed) and Lewis Carroll's *Alice in Wonderland.*

For Rackham, illustrations conveyed the pleasures of the text and communicated the "sense of delight or emotion aroused by the accompanying passage of literature." He endorsed the importance of fantasy in books for children and affirmed the "educative power of imaginative, fantastic, and playful pictures and writings for children in their most impressionable years."

Rackham's projects included illustrations for adult readers as well. Wagner's *Ring of the Nibelung* and Shakespeare's *Midsummer Night's Dream* ranked among his greatest critical and commercial successes. In 1927, he sailed to New York, where his works were on exhibit and where he personally met with an enthusiastic reception. In his last years, he completed the illustrations for Kenneth Grahame's *Wind in the Willows*, a work to which he maintained a powerful sentimental attachment.

In total, Rackham illustrated nearly 90 volumes. Influenced by Albrecht Dürer, George Cruikshank, John Tenniel, and Aubrey Beardsley, he is best known for his sure sense of line, his muted hues, and the creation of a mysterious world filled with gnomes, nymphs, giants, elves, sea serpents, and fairies amid intricate landscapes of gnarled branches, foaming waves, sinuous vines, and anthropomorphized trees. A firm believer in the partnership between author and illustrator, he endorsed the notion that illustrations take an interpretive turn, giving an "independent view of the author's subject." Rackham exercised a strong influence on future generations of illustrators, most notably Disney Studios, whose feature film of *Snow White* contains scenes clearly inspired by his style. Rackham died of cancer in 1939, just a few weeks after he had put the final touches on *The Wind in the Willows.* His last drawing shows Mole and Rat loading the rowboat for a picnic.

Further Reading:

Gettings, Fred. *Arthur Rackham.* New York: Macmillan, 1975.

Hamilton, James. *Arthur Rackham: A Life with Illustration.* London: Pavilion, 1990.

Hudson, Derek. *Arthur Rackham: His Life and Work.* London: Heinemann, 1960.

Larkin, David, ed. *Arthur Rackham*. 2nd ed. Toronto: Peacock Press, 1975.

Riall, Richard. *A New Bibliography of Arthur Rackham*. Bath, England: Ross, 1994.

W. HEATH ROBINSON (1872–1944)

Storyteller, artist, and cartoonist, William Heath Robinson was the youngest of three brothers, all of whom became renowned illustrators. He is best known today for *Hans Andersen's Fairy Tales* (1913) and for his drawings of humorous contraptions that are the precursors of Rube Goldberg machines. Heath Robinson worked on three illustrated editions of Andersen in total, one of which was a collaboration with his brothers. A reviewer of the first Andersen volume noted that "the demand for Hans Andersen's fairy stories seems to be endless. . . . A new one—and a very good one—is illustrated by the clever brothers, Thomas, Charles, and William Robinson."

Born in London into a family of artists and craftsmen, Heath Robinson left school at age fifteen to study at the Royal Academy Schools. "Frankly, there was no limit to my ambition," he later recalled. " . . . To me, as yet, anything seemed possible" (Lewis, 18). Robinson hoped to become a painter of landscapes, but quickly shifted to line drawing and watercolor when he realized the commercial potential of illustration. His drawings for Edgar Allan Poe's poems, which (as he himself acknowledged) reveal the influence of Aubrey Beardsley, Walter Crane, and of his own brother Charles Robinson, established him as the equal of his older brothers in the art of book illustration.

In 1897, Robinson produced images for four volumes: *The Giant Crab and Other Tales from Old India*, *Danish Fairy Tales and Legends of Hans Andersen*, *Don Quixote*, and *Pilgrim's Progress*. Throughout his career, he focused his efforts on high culture and popular culture, producing illustrations for works by Homer, Rabelais, and Shakespeare but also for fairy tales and children's stories. In 1914, he published his vibrantly accomplished illustrations for *A Midsummer Night's Dream*. A year later, he drew a delightful set of images for Charles Kingsley's *Water Babies*. He published two children's books: *The Adventures of Uncle Lubin* (1902), a whimsical tale of an eccentric uncle in search of his nephew, and *Bill the Minder* (1912), a series of tales about the King of Troy and a boot-cleaner named Bill. In 1938, he completed his autobiography, *My Line of Life.*

Of the three Robinson brothers, W. Heath was known as the one with a sense of humor. He produced hundreds of "absurdities" (the title of a collection designed to bring together his humorous drawings) that included a chair for removing warts from the top of the head, an "ice-hole clamspearer for use in the Frozen North," a "magnetic apparatus for putting square pegs into round holes," and a "multimovement Tabby Silencer," which threw water on wailing cats. His machines were generally run by bald, bespectacled gentlemen and were powered by kettles or candles. The name "Heath Robinson" is still in use today as a term for overly complex machines made of knotted string, old ironwork, and recycled parts kept in service through constant tinkering. A machine built to assist in decrypting German messages was named "Heath Robinson."

After the outbreak of World War I, paper shortages led to the gradual disappearance of the gift books that had flourished in the early part of the century. Robinson expanded the advertising side of his work and continued to produce comic art through the 1920s and 1930s. The last fifteen years of his life were marked by a heart condition that led to deteriorating health. Scheduled to undergo surgery in 1944, he removed the tubes, drips, and catheters (painfully reminiscent of his "absurdities") when left alone and died shortly thereafter.

Further Reading:

Beare, Geoffrey. *The Art of William Heath Robinson.* London: Dulwich Picture Gallery, 2003.

Day, G. Langston. *The Life and Art of W. Heath Robinson.* London: Herbert Joseph, 1947.

Hamilton, James. *William Heath Robinson.* London: Pavilion, 1992.

Jordan, R., ed. *The Penguin Heath Robinson.* Middlesex: Penguin, 1966.

Lewis, John. *Heath Robinson: Artist and Comic Genius.* London: Constable, 1973.

Robinson, W. Heath. *My Line of Life.* London: Blackie & Sons, 1938.

MARGARET TARRANT (1888–1959)

Born in London, Margaret Winifred Tarrant trained as an art teacher but shifted to book illustration because she lacked confidence in her teaching abilities. Charles Kingsley's *Water Babies* was her first subject, and she published her illustrated version of it in 1908. Her collaboration with the Medici Society publishers provided her with the opportunity to produce books, posters, postcards, greeting cards, and calendars that met with great popular success in the 1920s and 1930s. Famed for her light and airy portraits of children, fairies, and animals, she collaborated with Marion St. John Webb on a highly successful series of Flower Fairy books. She is also known for her illustrations of Andersen's fairy tales (1910), Perrault's fairy tales, and *Alice in Wonderland* (1916). In 1936, shortly after the death of her parents, the Medici Society funded her travels to Palestine, and her work thereafter took a religious turn. She died in Cornwall.

PART IV

Andersen's Readers

How did Andersen affect his readers? That is a challenging question, for readers move like travelers through the landscapes of his stories, leaving few traces behind and only occasionally providing glimpses of their experiences through memoirs. I have assembled here some of those souvenirs of reading, including reminiscences of writers, artists, historians, and others whose insights into Andersen's tales often capture their power in remarkable ways. They remind us that the stories throb with beauty and charm, but also pulse with horror and dread.

AUGUST STRINDBERG

In Sweden, we don't say H. C., we just say Andersen, for we only know of one Andersen, and that is Andersen. He belongs to us and our parents, our childhood and adulthood and old age.

When, as a child, I was given a Christmas calendar, I always skipped over the poetry, because it seemed so artificial and prosaic to me. So, when I got my hands on Andersen's Fairy Tales, I asked an older expert if this wasn't poetry. "No, it is prose!" the wise man answered.

"Is this prose?"

I can remember the little book with the Gothic type, I remember the woodcuts, the willow tree that belonged in "The Tinder Box," "The Ball and the Top," "The Tin Soldier," "Ole Shut-Eye", "The Snow Queen," and all the others. And when I read and had finished reading, life seemed so difficult to me. This terrible everyday life with its peevishness and unfairness, this dreary, monotonous life in a nursery became unbearable to me. Like little plants, we were right up next to each other and felt crowded, quarreling over food and favors. Through Andersen's fairy tale world, I became certain that there was another world, a golden age, where righteousness and mercy existed, in which parents truly caressed their children and did not just pull their hair, in which something completely unknown to me cast a rosy glow even over poverty and humiliation, the glow that is called by a word that cannot be used anymore today: love.

He also reminded me of Orpheus, the bard who sang in prose, so that not just the animals, plants, and stones listened to him and were touched, but toys also came to life, elves and trolls became real; schoolbooks, those terrors, became poetic; he covered all of Danish geography in four pages! He was truly a wizard!

And so we parted! But one day, at the age of twenty-five, I had to translate "Andersen's last fairy tales" for a publisher. I could tell that Time had passed for both him and me; it was the time of utilitarianism and the national economy, and there was nothing evil in that, but Pegasus pulled a plow. These fairy tales were a little prosaic, but one of them was amusing; it was called "The Great Sea-Serpent" and dealt with the telegraph cable in the Atlantic Ocean and the fishes' confusion about this new fish "that had no end." It was a brilliant idea and I still remember it.

When I was thirty, my friend Carl Larsson was to illustrate Andersen and so I renewed my acquaintance with him, but this time I had the joy of sharing the book with my children. Since they were children of their time, they asked me "if all of that was true." I don't remember what I answered! It was about 1880, when all of the old truths had come under discussion.

I turned forty and discovered Andersen's novels, in German. I was amazed at the clumsiness with which Andersen's novels had been treated. *Only a Fiddler* is, after all, a great fairy tale and one of the best, and it can no longer be considered a mistake for a novel to be poetic!

I turned fifty and spent time on the Danish coast. Cavling remembers that I stayed in a little cottage with grapevines running along the walls, I wandered through the beech forest and swam in the sound, and borrowed Andersen's fairy tales from the lending library. Now we shall see if they have kept their value!

They had! The Tinder Box still made sparks, the Willow Tree bloomed with growth, the Tin Soldier shouldered his rifle, although he had had contact with the gutter, and the year 1900, after utilitarianism and the national economy passed over with their steamrollers. He was a hardy youth!

On Saturday, my youngest daughter will be four years old, and she shall receive Andersen's fairy tales in Danish, so she can at least look at the pictures. Perhaps she can also read the stories, even if I don't know of it; for she is a child prodigy, and her grandmother was Danish, from Odense. Andersen keeps, and Andersen follows me!

Politiken has asked what I owe to Andersen. My answer is: Read my "Simple Things" from 1903 and see for yourself where I have gone to school!

I have had many teachers: Schiller and Goethe, Victor Hugo and Dickens, Zola and Peladan, but, all the same, I will sign this interview as

August Strindberg

Student of H. C. Andersen

From: August Strindberg, "H. C. Andersen. Till Andersen-jubileet 2 april 1905," in *Efterslåtter: Berättelser. Dikter. Artiklar*, ed. John Landquist, *Samlade skrifter av August Strindberg* 54, Supplementdel 1 (Stockholm: Albert Bonniers förlag, 1920), 443–45

CHARLES DICKENS

It has been given to *Hans Andersen* to fashion beings, it may almost be said, of a new kind, to breathe life into the toys of childhood and the forms of antique superstition. The tin soldier, the ugly duckling, the mermaid, the little match girl, are no less real and living in their way than *Othello*, or *Mr. Pickwick*, or *Helen of Troy.* It seems a very humble field in which to work, this of nursery legend and childish fancy. Yet the Danish poet alone, of all who have laboured in it, has succeeded in recovering, and reproducing, the kind of imagination which constructed the old fairy tales.

From: *London Daily News*, April 5, 1875

HERMANN HESSE

When we were little children, who had only just learnt to read, we owned, like all children, a beautiful, favorite book. It was called *Andersen's Fairy Tales,* and every time, once we had read it, we would pick it up again. It was our faithful companion until the end of our boyhood years, our dear childhood, with its treasures and fairies, kings and rich merchants, poor beggar children and bold fortune seekers. . . . In my memory there were no sentences and words, only the things themselves, the whole, multicolored, magnificent world of old Andersen, and it was so well preserved in my remembrance and was so beautiful that I took great care in later years not to open this book again (which seemed in any case lost). For I had unfortunately already, at an early age, made that painful discovery: the books which in earliest childhood and youth were the source of all our bliss, should never be read again; otherwise their old shine and sparkle will be no more and they will appear changed, sad and foolish.

But the story which I read was good. It was not at all as fabulous and effusive and artificial as I had secretly been almost dreading. On the contrary, it looked with fully alert eyes at the real world and sent forth its fairy enchantment not out of vanity and foolish high spirits, but from experience and compassionate resignation. The enchantment was genuine, and as I read again and attended once more to many of the old stories, there reappeared the same beautiful magic sparkle as before. From the furrowed disappointment arose a joy and exuberance, and wherever it lacked something and failed to resound with its old completeness, the fault lay with me and not with old Andersen.

From: "Andersen's Fairy Tales," in *A Literary History in Reviews and Essays* (Frankfurt a.M.: Suhrkamp, 1970)

W. H. AUDEN

Much . . . can be said against middle-class family life in the nineteenth century, but in the midst of its heavy moral discipline, its horsehair sofas and stodgy meals, the average child was permitted and even encouraged to lead an exciting life in its imagination. There are more Gradgrinds now that there were then, and the twentieth century has yet to produce books for children equal to Hans Andersen's *Tales*, Edward Lear's *Book of Nonsense*, the two *Alices, Struwwelpeter*, or even Jules Verne.

Houses are smaller, servants are fewer, mothers have less time, or think they have, to read to their children, and neither the comic strip nor the radio has succeeded so far in providing a real substitute for the personally told tale which permits of interruptions and repeats. . . .

It is to be hoped that the publication of the tales of Grimm and Andersen in one inexpensive volume will be a step in the campaign to restore to parents the right and the duty to educate their children, which, partly through their own fault, and partly through extraneous circumstances, they are in danger of losing for good.

From: "Grimm and Andersen," in *Forewords and Afterwords*, ed. Edward Mendelson (New York: Modern Library, 1952), 198–99

LOUISA MAY ALCOTT

"Now we shall try a new way. You and I will read these pleasant little Märchen together, and dig nor more in that dry book, that goes in the corner for making us trouble."

He spoke so kindly, and opened Hans Andersen's fairy tales so invitingly before me, that I was more ashamed than ever, and went at my lesson in a neck-or-nothing style that seemed to amuse him immensely. I forgot my bashfulness, and pegged away (no other word will express it) with all my might, tumbling over long words, pronouncing according to the inspiration of the minute, and doing my very best. When I finished reading my first page, and stopped for breath, he clapped his hands and cried out, in his hearty way, "Das ist gut! Now we go well! My turn. I do him in German;

gif me your ear." And away he went, rumbling out the words with his strong voice, and a relish which was good to see as well as hear. Fortunately the story was "The Constant Tin Soldier," which is droll, you know, so I could laugh, and I did—though I didn't understand half he read, for I couldn't help it, he was so earnest, I so excited, and the whole thing so comical.

From: *Little Women* (New York: Simon & Schuster, 2000), 526–27

HENRY JAMES

The small people with whom he played enjoyed, under his spell, the luxury of believing that he kept and treasured—in every case as a rule—the old tin soldiers and broken toys received by him, in acknowledgement of favors, from impulsive infant hands. Beautiful the queer image of the great bene-factor moving about Europe with his accumulations of these relics. Wonder-ful too our echo of a certain occasion—that of a children's party, later on, when, after he had read out to his young friends "The Ugly Duckling," Browning struck up with the "Pied Piper"; which led to the formation of a grand march through the spacious Barberini apartment with Story doing his best on a flute in default of bagpipes.

From: *William Wetmore Story and His Friends: From Letters, Diaries, and Rec-ollections* (Edinburgh: Blackwood and Sons, 1903), 285–86

ELIZABETH BARRETT BROWNING

Andersen (the Dane) came to see me yesterday, kissed my hand, and seemed in a general *verve* for embracing. He is very earnest, very simple, very child-like. I like him. Pen [Elizabeth Barrett Browning's twelve-year-old son] says of him, "He is not really pretty. He is rather like his own ugly duck, but his mind has developed into a swan"—That wasn't bad of Pen, was it?

From: *The Letters of Elizabeth Barrett Browning*, ed. F. G. Kenyon (London: Smith, Elder, 1897), II, 448

VLADIMIR NABOKOV

A bewildering sequence of English nurses and governesses, some of them wringing their hands, others smiling at me enigmatically, come out to meet me as I re-enter my past. . . . There was lovely, black-haired, aquamarine-eyed Miss Norcott, who lost a white kid glove at Nice or Beaulieu, where I vainly looked for it on the shingly beach among the colored pebbles and the glaucous lumps of sea-changed bottle glass. Lovely Miss Norcott was asked to leave at once, one night at Abbazia. She embraced me in the morning twilight of the nursery, pale-mackintoshed and weeping like a Babylonian willow, and that day I remained inconsolable, despite the hot chocolate that the Petersons' old Nanny had made especially for me and the special bread and butter, on the smooth surface of which my aunt Nata, adroitly capturing my attention, drew a daisy, then a cat, and then the little mermaid whom I had just been reading about with Miss Norcott and crying over, too, so I started to cry again.

From: *Speak, Memory: An Autobiography Revisited* (New York: Vintage, 1989), 81

VINCENT VAN GOGH

This morning I visited the place where the dustmen deposit the rubbish. My heavens, it was beautiful! Tomorrow I shall have some interesting things brought to me from this dump, including some broken street lamps to delight my eye or—with your permission—to use as models. It would be a splendid subject for a fairy tale by Andersen, all the rubbish cans, kettles, tin bowls, chamber pots, metal jugs, pieces of rusty barbed wire and stove pipes which people have thrown away. I am sure I shall dream about it tonight.

Don't you think Andersen's fairy tales are very beautiful? I am sure he must draw illustrations as well.

From: *Letters to Anton G. A. Ridder van Rappard*, 1882, 1883. Cited by Kjeld Heltoft, *Hans Christian Andersen as an Artist*, trans. David Hohen (Copenhagen: Christian Ejlers' Forlag, 2005), 11–12

URSULA K. LE GUIN

Part of Andersen's cruelty is the cruelty of reason—and of psychological realism, radical honesty, the willingness to see and accept the consequences of an act or a failure to act. There is a sadistic, depressive streak in Andersen also, which is his own shadow; it's there, it's part of him, but not all of him, nor is he ruled by it. His strength, his subtlety, his creative genius, come precisely from his acceptance of and cooperation with the dark side of his own soul. That's why Andersen the fabulist is one of the great realists of literature.

Now I stand here, like the princess herself, and tell you what the story of the shadow means to me at age forty-five. But what did it mean to me when I first read it, at age ten or eleven? What does it mean to children? Do they "understand" it? Is it "good" for them—this bitter, complex study of a moral failure?

I don't know. I hated it when I was a kid. I hated all the Andersen stories with unhappy endings. That didn't stop me from reading them, and rereading them. Or from remembering them . . . so that after a gap of over thirty years, when I was pondering this talk, a little voice suddenly said inside my left ear, "You'd better dig out that Andersen story, you know, about the shadow."

From: "The Child and the Shadow," in Ursula K. Le Guin, *The Language of the Night: Essays on Fantasy and Science Fiction*, ed. Susan Wood (London: The Women's Press, 1989), 51

P. L. TRAVERS

There are no rabbits in Hans Andersen. But, for all that, unlike the Grimms, he has never been in eclipse. His tales were among my early grims and I loved, and still love, his retellings of what he was told in childhood—tough, shrewd, ironic, witty—and his own folksy, miniscule fables, "Five Peas in the Same Pod," "The Darning Needle," "Soup on a Sausage Pin," "Auntie Toothache," as well as that subtle story, "The Shadow," wherein he showed himself, for once, to be wiser than he knew. But the great reverberant set-pieces, so admired, wept over, doted upon—"Mermaid," "Snow Queen," "Red Shoes," etc., filled me, in childhood, with unease and a feeling that I was being got at. Oh, I wept and, I suppose, doted—but felt no better for it. Grimms' belonged to the sunlight, asked nothing, never apologized, curdled the blood with delight and horror, dispensed justice, fortified the spirit. Andersen, moon-man, asked for mercy, was always sorry, curdled the feelings with bane-and-honey and undermined the vitality by his endless appeal for pity. When the millstone was dropped on the wicked stepmother, I did not miss a breath. That was how it should be. But for Karen who had her feet cut off because she preferred red shoes to God, I had to break my heart; suffer for Kay and his monstrous word—"the artifice of Eternity," as Yeats put it—when Now, as it seemed to me then, and does still, would have been a better, if more demanding word; and try, ever failing, to be a good child in order to shorten, by three hundred years, the term of the Mermaid's waiting time.

From: "The Primary World," *Parabola* 4 (1979): 92

MAXIM GORKY

I took with me to school the *Stories from the Bible* and two tattered little volumes of Andersen's *Fairy Tales*, three pounds of white bread and a pound of sausage. In a dim, tiny bookshop near St. Vladimir's Church I found *Robinson Crusoe*, a thick book bound in yellow, with a picture of a bearded man in a fur cap and a wild animal's skin on his shoulders in the front. This I didn't like at all, but the fairy tales appealed to me at once, in spite of their tattered binding.

In the dinner-break I shared out the bread and sausage and we began reading that marvelous story "The Nightingale," which had us all enthralled from the first page.

"In China all the people are Chinese, and the Emperor himself is a Chinaman." I remember how that phrase enchanted me not only by its simple, laughing music but by something which was wonderful and good besides.

There was no time to finish "The Nightingale" in school-time and when I got home I found Mother frying eggs over the stove.

In a strange, faded voice she asked:

"Did you take that rouble?"

"Yes, I did. Look at these books."

She gave me a thorough hammering with the frying pan, took away the volumes of Andersen and hid them away for good, which I found a lot more painful than the beating.

From: *My Childhood*, trans. Ronald Wilks (New York: Penguin, 1991), 214

LAFCADIO HEARN

Consider the stories of Hans Andersen. He conceived the notion that moral truths and social philosophy could be better taught through little fairy-tales and child stories than in almost any other way; and with the help of hundreds of old-fashioned tales, he made a new series of wonderful stories that have become a part of every library and are read in all countries by grown-up people much more than by children. There is, in this astonishing collection of stories, a story about a mermaid which I suppose you have all read. Of course there can be no such thing as a mermaid; from one point of view the story is quite absurd. But the emotions of unselfishness and love and loyalty which the story expresses are immortal, and so beautiful that we forget about all the unreality of the framework; we see only the eternal truth behind the fable.

From: "On Reading," in *Life and Literature* (New York: Kessinger, 2005), 18

ALISON LURIE

Though some of his stories are brilliant and moving, most are sad, distressing, or even terrifying. As a child I was frightened and upset by many of them, especially those in which a little girl misbehaves and is horribly punished. The crime that seemed to cause the most awful result was vanity, and it was always little girls who met this fate, never boys. In "The Red Shoes," for instance, Karen thinks of her new morocco-leather shoes even when she is in church, and as a result she is condemned to dance in them to exhaustion; she is only saved from death when she asks the local executioner to chop off her feet with his axe. Even worse in some ways was "The Girl Who Trod on a Loaf." In this tale a "proud and arrogant" child called Inger also comes to grief because of love of her new shoes. . . .

I was also deeply disturbed by one of Andersen's most famous tales, "The Little Mermaid," in which the heroine gives up her voice and agrees that every step she takes will feel like walking on knives, so as to have the chance of attracting the love of a prince whom she first saw at his birthday party on board a ship. . . . I took her story as a warning against self-sacrificial and hopeless love. I did not realize that in this tale Andersen had foretold his own future. He would be rejected again and again by those he loved most, but unlike the Little Mermaid he never gave up his voice, and the best of the stories he told would survive for hundreds of years, "wherever there are children."

From: "The Underduckling: Hans Christian Andersen," in *Boys and Girls Forever: Children's Classics from Cinderella to Harry Potter* (New York: Penguin, 2003), 9–11

FAY WELDON

"Does it hurt?" he asked at last.

"Of course it hurts," she said. "It's meant to hurt. Anything that's worth achieving has its price. And, by corollary, if you are prepared to pay that price you can achieve almost anything. In this particular case I am paying with physical pain. Hans Andersen's little mermaid wanted legs instead of a tail, so that she could be properly loved by her Prince. She was given legs, and by inference the gap where they join at the top, and after that every step she took was like stepping on knives. Well, what did she expect? That was the penalty. And, like her, I welcome it. I don't complain."

"Did he love her," asked the judge, "in return?"

"Temporarily," said Polly Patch.

From: *The Life and Loves of a She-Devil* (New York: Ballantine, 1983), 172–73

HAROLD BLOOM

Andersen was a visionary tale-teller, but his fairy-realm was malign. Of his aesthetic eminence, I entertain no doubts, but I believe that we still have not learned how to read him.

From: Introduction to *Hans Christian Andersen* (New York: Chelsea House, 2004), xv

ARTHUR M. SCHLESINGER JR.

I particularly remember my mother sitting in her chair reading aloud to her children. She was a splendid reader, spirited and expressive, and Tom and I insisted that she keep on reading to us long after we were able to read to ourselves. . . . My mother began with fairy tales, the Brothers Grimm and Hans Christian Andersen; with Greek and Roman mythology, especially as marvelously rendered by Hawthorne in *The Wonder Book* and *Tanglewood Tales*; and with the wondrous *Arabian Nights*.

From: Arthur M. Schlesinger Jr., *A Life in the Twentieth Century: Innocent Beginnings, 1917–1950* (New York: Houghton Mifflin, 2000), 62

ROSELLEN BROWN

And what of "The Little Mermaid"? . . . I know that in the mermaid's voicelessness Andersen captured one of our—I mean humans'—primal terrors, that much I can vouch for. He gave us an implicit judgment of the limitations of mere beauty, beauty unendowed with self. He held forth an ideal of love and loyalty to the point of death and made us, while we're admiring it, wonder if the game is worth the candle. He suggested that too much wanting can change the one who desires (whatever her object) to the point of deformity. He reminded us of how difficult, perhaps even how impossible, it is to try to leap certain barriers and successfully become something we are not.

Which of these, at age eight or nine, did I grasp? Which of them helped to form my storytelling soul and which did I respond to because I was already partway to who I was to become? I could write a convenient fiction here that would connect all these dots, Andersen's and mine, but I want to end where I began, invoking the modest truth and admitting how little of it I possess where my own childhood is concerned. How mysterious these stories were, that's all I know I felt, and how wonderfully dangerous and disorienting, coming at me out of nowhere. How amazing to break the silence, like the Ancient Mariner to lay a firm hand on the listener's arm and begin anywhere, anywhere at all.

From: "It Is You the Fable Is About," in *Mirror, Mirror on the Wall: Women Writers Explore Their Favorite Fairy Tales*, ed. Kate Bernheimer (New York: Random House/ Anchor, 2002), 58

KATHRYN DAVIS

The point is ownership. The point is, I believed these were my stories. Mine. I didn't think they'd been written for me, Andersen having "had me in mind," or that they conveyed my view of things with unusual precision— no, when I heard these stories I was infused with that shiver of ecstasy that is an unmistakable symptom of the creative act. I felt as if I'd created the stories, as if they had their origin in my imagination, as if they were by definition my *original* work, having "belonged at the beginning to the person in question"—that person being me.

From: "Why I Don't Like Reading Fairy Tales," in Bernheimer, *Mirror, Mirror on the Wall*, 85–86

PETER RUSHFORTH

In the fairy-tales collected by the Brothers Grimm, the innocent and pure in heart always seemed to triumph, even after much fear and suffering: Hansel and Gretel outwitted the witch and escaped; the seven little kids and their mother destroyed the wolf; the three sisters in "Fitcher's Bird" overpowered even death itself to defeat the murdering magician. But he could still remember the mounting desolation with which he read some of the Hans Christian Andersen fairy-tales when he was little. He had read them over and over again, hoping that this time the ending would be a happy ending, but the endings never changed: the little match-girl died entirely alone, frozen to death on New Year's Eve, surrounded by burned-out matches; the little mermaid melted into foam after bearing her suffering bravely; and the steadfast tin soldier and the ballerina perished in the flames of the stove, leaving only a little tin heart and a metal sequin behind. He had been unable to put them away and forget about them. He had been drawn, compulsively, to read them with engrossed attention, and had wept as he found himself realizing what the inevitable and unchanged end of the story would be.

From: *Kindergarten* (New York: Avon Books, 1979), 112

BARBARA SJOHOL

Not all of Andersen's tales appeal to me anymore, and many make me shudder. I believe Gerda is the reason I can still reread "The Snow Queen" without gagging on the saccharine Christian symbolism that spoils some of his other works. Though there's a bit of the sentimental in the ending of the story when Gerda and Kai return by foot (Gerda presumably still without shoes) to the garden of their childhood, the effect is deeply satisfying. If our hearts are open, we can return to the Edens of our youth, even if we are, like Gerda and Kai, now fully grown.

From: "The Ice Palace" in *Rereadings,* ed. Anne Fadiman (New York: Farrar, Straus and Giroux, 2005), 193

LOIS LOWRY

"Tell me a story, Annemarie," begged Kirsti as she snuggled beside her sister in the big bed they shared. "Tell me a fairy tale."

Annemarie smiled and wrapped her arms around her little sister in the dark. All Danish children grew up familiar with fairy tales. Hans Christian Andersen, the most famous of the tale tellers, had been Danish himself.

"Do you want the one about the little mermaid?" That one had always been Annemarie's own favorite.

From: *Number the Stars* (New York: Laurel Leaf, 1998), 11

ROBERT K. GREENLEAF AND PETER B. VAILL

A friend of mine in Madison, Wisconsin, tells a story about Frank Lloyd Wright many years ago when his studio, Taliesen, was at nearby Spring Green. Mr. Wright had been invited by a women's club in Madison to come and talk on the subject "What is Art?" He accepted and appeared at the appointed hour and was introduced to speak on this subject.

In his prime, he was a large, impressive man, with good stage presence and a fine voice. He acknowledged the introduction and produced from his pocket a little book. He then proceeded to read one of Hans Christian Andersen's fairy tales, the one about the little mermaid. He read it beautifully, and it took about 15 minutes. When he finished, he closed the book, looked intently at his audience and said, "That, my friends, is art," and sat down.

From: *The Power of Servant Leadership* (San Francisco: Berrett-Koehler, 1998), 61–62

LYNNE SHARON SCHWARTZ

I read whatever I found in the house. It was an age of sets, and several were stored in the bedroom I inherited when I was ten and my sister left to get married. Dickens in brown leather with a black horizontal stripe was cozy looking, but the Harvard Classics in black leather and gold trim were forbidding—especially Plutarch's *Lives* and Marcus Aurelius and the *Confessions* of Saint Augustine. I did manage to find one, though, volume 17, containing all the Grimm and Andersen fairy tales, which I practically licked off the page. They tasted bitter and pungent, like curries. The most bittersweet story, exotic yet familiar, was "The Little Mermaid," and rereading it today, I can easily see why. Like me, the "silent and thoughtful" mermaid lusted after the world. No matter how ravishing and secure the undersea realm she shared with her five loving sisters, the world way above lured her from her earliest years. She craved light, the great ball of the sun that beneath the water's surface was translated into a purple glow.

From: *Ruined by Reading: A Life in Books* (Boston: Beacon Press, 1996), 24–25

HUGH WALPOLE

Hans Andersen was not, I would say, exactly a charming person. He was ugly, conceited, sensitive, quick-tempered, and elusive. As the hero of a novel he would annoy many readers. He would seem feckless and ungrateful, and a bit of a muff. And yet he is part of all of us. If you feel the pathetic and humorous and lonely uniqueness of human beings, you must know that only the very unperceptive and heavy-minded are irritated by him; and out of that strange personality he produced these wonderful fairy stories, wonderful because they are filled through and through with that sense of oddity and loneliness that gives human beings so much beauty.

From: Foreword to *It's Perfectly True and Other Stories by Hans Christian Andersen*, trans. Paul Leyssac (New York: Harcourt, Brace & World, 1938), vi

PHYLLIS M. PICKARD

Children have always gained immensely from listening to adult communications. What caused many of the children to suffer nightmares were the occasions when Andersen's own unresolved problems came through in inartistic form. For instance, there are some lurid accounts of death beckoning, of the gallows, of murderous treatment of grandmothers. It is all understandable when facts about Andersen are known, but it is not artistry for children. He loved his blue-eyed grandmother, but it was she who took him to the asylum and the prison through which he suffered so much. His resentment comes out, for instance, in a tale in which a robber hits his grandmother on the head, uses her corpse for climbing on to reach the money, and even finds a second grandmother to slay.

From: *I Could a Tale Unfold: Violence, Horror and Sensationalism in Stories for Children* (London: Tavistock, 1961), 89–90

BETTY ADCOCK

Most of Andersen's stories have sad endings, and that may have been one of their attractions for me. At seven, I had already seen my mother vanish, her sudden death the new defining point in my life. I had lost a place as well, having been moved to another house. I had seen my father fold into himself, quit his job, become a wanderer in the forests, a hunter spellbound by grief, his tamped spirit somehow comforted by the rough riverbanks, the difficult chases, the dog's companionship. Death and transformation were two things I understood. I think I knew instinctively that the tales in my favorite book held an unusually powerful truth in the absence of the usual "happily ever after."

From: "The Most Enchanting Book I Read," in *Remarkable Reads*, ed. J. Peder Zane (New York: W. W. Norton, 2004), 35

A. S. BYATT

Hans Andersen's Snow Queen was not only beautiful but intelligent and powerful; she gave Kay a vision of beauty and order, from which Gerda, with Andersen's blessing, redeemed him for the ordinary and everyday. Andersen makes a standard opposition between cold reason and warm-heartedness and comes down whole-heartedly on the side of warm-heartedness, adding to it his own insistent Christian message. The eternity of the beautiful snow-crystals is a false infinity; only Gerda's invocation of the Infant Jesus allows a glimpse of true eternity. Andersen even cheats by making the beautiful, mathematically perfect snowflakes into nasty gnomes and demons, snakes, hedgehogs, bears. . . . Science and reason are bad, kindness is good. It is a frequent, but not a necessary opposition. And I found in it, and in the dangerous isolation of the girl on her slippery shiny height a figure of what was beginning to bother me, the conflict between a female destiny, the kiss, the marriage, the child-bearing, the death, and the frightening loneliness of cleverness, the cold distance of seeing the world through art, of putting a frame around things.

From: "Ice, Snow, Glass," in *On Histories and Stories: Selected Essays* (Cambridge, MA: Harvard Univ. Press, 2000), 155–56

DEBORAH EISENBERG

No one, I think, has outshone Andersen in depicting perdition. Who could ever forget what happened to that uppity girl who trod on the loaf? Or to vain little Karen, with her pretty red shoes? Who could forget the horrible tortures to which their defects consign these children? But Kay virtually swoons into *his* icy hell, and once he is there, the Snow Queen continues to blaze in all her erotic danger.

"The Snow Queen" shimmers with ambivalence and thwarted or suppressed cravings. The author's stance is impeccable: he recommends to us the rewards of equipoise or eternity, and purity of soul. And yet what the *story* paints with indelible brilliance is the glamour of immobilization and *aesthetic* purity.

From: "In a Trance of Self," in Bernheimer, *Mirror, Mirror on the Wall,* 90–114

MICHAEL BOOTH

There is a ghoulish anarchy to many of his stories—people are garroted, have their brains scattered about and endure other wonderfully arbitrary and brutal deaths, sometimes to the extent that you can't help feeling a good many of these tales are wholly inappropriate for children. In "The Stork," for instance, the eponymous birds plot a grisly revenge on a boy who taunted them: "In the pond there is a little dead baby, it has dreamed itself to death, we will take it to him, and then he will cry because we have brought him a little dead brother." While the moment in "Little Claus and Big Claus," where little Claus dresses up his dead grandmother, verges on the Hitchcockian.

Yet amid all the horror and fantasy, the telling details make it all seem somehow strangely real—like the walls rubbed with witches' fat to make them shine in "The Elf Hill"; or the way the moon sees a Hindu maiden, "the blood coursing in her delicate fingers as she bent them round the flame to form a shelter for it" in "What the Moon Saw."

From: *Just as Well I'm Leaving: To the Orient with Hans Christian Andersen* (London: Jonathan Cape, 2005), 17

CLARISSA PINKOLA ESTÉS

Hans Christian Andersen wrote dozens of stories about the orphan archetype. He was a premier advocate of the lost and neglected child and he strongly supported searching for and finding one's own kind. . . . For the last two centuries "The Ugly Duckling" has been one of the few stories to encourage successive generations of "outsiders" to hold on till they find their own. . . . It is a psychological and spiritual root story. A root story is one that contains a truth so fundamental to human development that without integration of this fact further progression is shaky.

From: Clarissa Pinkola Estés, *Women Who Run with the Wolves: Myths and Stories of the Wild Woman Archetype* (New York: Ballantine, 1992), 167

CLAIRE BLOOM

What I remember most from those early days is the sound of Mother's voice as she read to me from Hans Christian Andersen's "The Little Mermaid" and "The Snow Queen." These emotionally wrenching tales, to which I raptly listened and to which I was powerfully drawn, instilled in me a longing to be overwhelmed by romantic passion and led me in my teens and early twenties to attempt to emulate these self-sacrificing heroines, at least on the stage.

The sound of Mother's voice and the radiance of those long summer afternoons are fused in my childhood memory, creating a pleasurable sensation of warmth and comfort and safety.

From: Claire Bloom, *Leaving a Doll's House* (Boston: Little, Brown, 1996), 9

MAURICE SENDAK

Andersen was that rare anomaly, wise man and innocent child; he shared with children an uncanny poetic power, the power of breathing life into mere dust. It is the intense life—honest, ingratiating—in Andersen's tales that makes them unique. Discarded bits of bottle, sticks, doorknobs, and fading flowers give voice to their love, anguish, vanity, and bitterness. They reflect on their past joys, lost opportunities, and soberly ponder the mystery of death. We listen patiently, sympathetically, to their tiny querulous voices and the miracle is that we believe, as Andersen did, as all children do, that the bit of bottle, the stick, the doorknob are, for one moment, passionately living. The best tales of Andersen have this mixture of worldliness and naïveté that makes them so moving, so honest, so beautiful.

From: "Hans Christian Andersen," in *Caldecott & Co.* (New York: Farrar, Straus & Giroux, 1992), 35

WALTER BENJAMIN

In one of Andersen's tales, there is a picture-book that cost "half a kingdom." In it everything was alive. "The birds sang, and people came out of the book and spoke." But when the princess turned the page, "they leaped back in again so that there should be no disorder." Pretty and unfocused, like so much that Andersen wrote, this little invention misses the crucial point by a hair's breadth. The objects do not come to meet the picturing child from the pages of the book; instead, the gazing child enters into those pages, becoming suffused, like a cloud, with the riotous colors of the world of pictures.

From: "A Glimpse into the World of Children's Books," in Walter Benjamin, *Selected Writings,* ed. Marcus Bullock and Michael W. Jennings (Cambridge MA: Harvard Univ. Press, 1996), I, 435

PART V

Bibliography

Works by Hans Christian Andersen

1. Editions of the Fairy Tales in English

Hans Christian Andersen: The Complete Stories. Trans. Jean Hersholt. London: The British Library, 2005.

Fairy Tales: Hans Christian Andersen. Trans. Tiina Nunnally. Ed. Jackie Wullschlager. London: Penguin, 2004.

The Stories of Hans Christian Andersen. Trans. Diana Crone Frank and Jeffrey Frank. Illus. Vilhelm Pedersen and Lorenz Frølich. Boston: Houghton Mifflin, 2003.

Hans Andersen's Fairy Tales: A Selection. Trans. L. W. Kingsland. Illus. Vilhelm Pedersen and Lorenz Frølich. New York: Oxford Univ. Press, 1984.

Hans Christian Andersen: The Complete Fairy Tales and Stories. Trans. Erik Christian Haugaard. New York: Anchor, 1983.

Hans Christian Andersen: Eighty Fairy Tales. Trans. R. P. Keigwin. Illus. Vilhelm Pedersen and Lorenz Frølich. New York: Pantheon Books, 1982.

The Shadow and Other Tales by Hans Christian Andersen. Ed. Niels Ingwersen. Madison: Univ. of Wisconsin Press, 1982.

Fairytales: H. C. Andersen. Illus. Kay Nielsen. New York: Metropolitan Museum of Art and Viking Press, 1981.

Tales and Stories by Hans Christian Andersen. Trans. Patricia L. Conroy and Sven H. Rossel. Seattle: Univ. of Washington Press, 1980.

Ardizzone's Hans Andersen: Fourteen Classic Tales. Trans. Stephen Corrin. Illus. Edward Ardizzone. New York: Atheneum, 1979.

Fairy Tales and Legends by Hans Andersen. Illus. Rex Whistler. London: Bodley Head, 1978.

New Tales, 1843: Hans Christian Andersen. Trans. Reginald Spink. Copenhagen: Høst, 1973.

Andersen's Fairy Tales. Trans. Pat Shaw Iversen. Illus. Sheila Greenwald. New York: Signet, 1966.

Fairy Tales. Ed. Clifton Fadiman. Illus. Lawrence Beall Smith. New York: Macmillan, 1963.

Forty-two Stories: Hans Andersen. Trans. M. R. James. Illus. Robin Jacques. London: Faber and Faber, 1953.

The Complete Andersen. Trans. Jean Hersholt. Illus. Fritz Kredel. New York: Heritage Press, 1942.

2. Other Works in English

The Andersen-Scudder Letters: Hans Christian Andersen's Correspondence with Horace Elisha Scudder. Trans. Waldemar Westergaard. Ed. Jean Hersholt and Helge Topsöe-Jensen. Berkeley: Univ. of California Press, 1949.

The Diaries of Hans Christian Andersen. Trans. and ed. Patricia L. Conroy and Sven H. Rossel. Seattle: Univ. of Washington Press, 1990.

The Fairy Tale of My Life. Boston: Houghton Mifflin, 1871. Rpt. New York: Paddington Press, 1975.

Pictures of Travel in Sweden among the Hartz Mountains, and in Switzerland, with a Visit at Charles Dickens' House. Boston: Houghton Mifflin, 1871.

A Poet's Bazaar: A Journey to Greece, Turkey & up the Danube. Trans. Grace Thornton. New York: M. Kesend, 1988.

Travels: Hans Christian Andersen. Trans. Anastazia Little. Los Angeles: Green Integer, 1999.

The True Story of My Life: A Sketch. Trans. Mary Howitt. London: Longman, 1847.

A Visit to Germany, Italy, and Malta, 1840–1841. Trans. Grace Thornton. London: Peter Owen, 1985.

A Visit to Portugal, 1866. Trans. Grace Thornton. London: Peter Owen, 1972.

A Visit to Spain and North Africa, 1862: Hans Christian Andersen. Trans. Grace Thornton. London: Peter Owen, 1975.

3. Works in Danish

Almanakker 1833–1873. Ed. Helga Vang Lauridsen and Kirsten Weber. Copenhagen: Gad, 1996.

Breve fra H. C. Andersen. Ed C. St. A. Bille and Nikolaj Bøgh. 2 vols. Copenhagen: Aschehoug, 2000.

Breve til H. C. Andersen. Ed. C. St. A. Bille and Nikolaj Bøgh. Copenhagen: C. A. Reitzel, 1877.

Dagbøger, 1825–1875. Ed. Det Danske Sprog-og Litteraturselskab. Copenhagen: Gad, 1971–1977.

Eventyr. Ed. Erik Dal, Erling Nielsen, and Flemming Hovmann. 7 vols. Copenhagen: C. A. Reitzel, 1963–1990.

H. C. Andersen og Henriette Wulff. En Brevveksling. Ed. H. Topsøe-Jensen. 3 vols. Odense: Flensteds Forlag, 1959.

Mit livs eventyr: H. C. Andersen. Ed. H. Topsøe-Jensen and H. G. Olrik. Copenhagen: Gyldendal, 1996.

Samlede eventyr og historier. Ed. Estrid Dal. Odense: C. A. Reitzel, 1998.

4. Early Illustrated Editions

H. C. Andersens Eventyr. Illus. Vilhelm Pedersen. Copenhagen: C. A. Reitzel, 1850.

Fairy Tales by Hans Christian Andersen. Illus. Eleanor Vere Boyle. London: Sampson Low, Marston, Low, Searle, & Rivington, 1872.

Fairy Stories from Hans Christian Andersen. Illus. Margaret Tarrant. London: Ward, Lock & Co., 1910.

The Big Book of Fairy Tales. Illus. Charles Robinson. London: Blackie and Sons, 1911.

The Snow Queen and Other Stories from Andersen. Illus. Edmund Dulac. London: Hodder & Stoughton, 1911.

Hans Andersen's Fairy Tales. Illus. W. Heath Robinson. London: Constable & Co., 1913.

Hans Andersen's Fairy Tales. Illus. Mabel Lucie Attwell. London: Raphael Tuck & Sons, 1914.

Fairy Tales. Illus. Jennie Harbour. London: George G. Harrap, 1915.

Fairy Tales by Hans Christian Andersen. Illus. Harry Clarke. New York: Brentano's, 1916.

Fairy Tales. Illus. Honor Appleton. London: T. Nelson and Sons, 1922.

Fairy Tales by Hans Andersen. Illus. Kay Nielsen. London: Hodder & Stoughton, 1924.

The Red Shoes. New York: Thomas Nelson & Sons, 1928.

Fairy Tales by Hans Andersen. Illus. Arthur Rackham. London: George G. Harrap, 1932.

The Arthur Rackham pictures are reproduced with the kind permission of his family and the Bridgeman Art Library.

Secondary Literature

Alderson, Brian. "H. C. Andersen: Edging toward the Unmapped Hinterland." *Horn Book Magazine* 81 (2005): 671–76.

———. *Hans Christian Andersen and His Eventyr in England.* Wormley, England: International Board on Books for Young People, 1982.

Allen, Brook. "The Uses of Enchantment." *New York Times*, May 20, 2001.

Alter, Nora M., and Lutz Koepnick. *Sound Matters: Essays on the Acoustics of German Culture.* New York: Berghahn, 2004.

Altmann, Anna E., and Gail de Vos. *Tales, Then and Now: More Folktales as Literary Fictions for Young Adults.* Englewood, CO: Greenwood, 2001.

Andersen, Hans Christian. "Hans Christian Andersen—the Journey of His Life." In Bloom, *Hans Christian Andersen*, 75–91.

Andersen, Jens. *Hans Christian Andersen: A New Life.* Trans. Tiina Nunnally. New York: Overlook Duckworth, 2005.

Andersen, Kim. " 'Genius' and the Problem of 'Livs-Anskuelse': Kierkegaard Reading Andersen." In Sondrup, *H. C. Andersen: Old Problems and New Readings*, 145–60.

Anderseniana. First Series, 1–13 (1933–1946); Second Series, 1–6 (1947–1969); Third Series, 1–4 (1970–1986). Annually since 1987.

Anderson, Celia Catlett. "Andersen's Heroes and Heroines: Relinquishing the Reward." In *Triumphs of the Spirit in Children's Literature*, ed. Francelia Butler and Richard Rotert, 122–26. North Haven, CT: The Shoe String Press, 1986.

Arden, Harvey. "The Magic World of Hans Christian Andersen." *National Geographic* 156 (1979): 824–50.

Atkins, Adelheid M. "The Triumph of Criticism: Levels of Meaning in Hans Christian Andersen's 'The Steadfast Tin Soldier.' " *Scholia Satyrica* 1:1 (1975): 25–28.

Atwood, Margaret. *Lady Oracle.* New York: Simon & Schuster, 1976.

————. "Of Souls as Birds." In Bernheimer, *Mirror, Mirror on the Wall*, 21–36.

Auden, W. H. "Grimm and Andersen." In *W. H. Auden: Forewords and Afterwords*, ed. Edward Mendelson, 198–208. New York: Random House/Vintage, 1989.

Barlby, Finn. "The Euphoria of the Text—on the Market, on Man, and on Melody, i.e.: Poetry." In Mylius et al., *Hans Christian Andersen: A Poet in Time*, 515–25.

Beauvoir, Simone de. *The Second Sex.* New York: Random House/Vintage, 1989.

Bell, Elizabeth, Lynda Haas, and Laura Sells, eds. *From Mouse to Mermaid: The Politics of Film, Gender, and Culture.* Bloomington: Indiana Univ. Press, 1995.

Bendix, Regina. "Seashell Bra and Happy End: Disney's Transformations of 'The Little Mermaid.' " *Fabula* 14 (1993): 280–90.

Bering, Henrik. "A Fairy Tale: The Life and Work of Hans Christian Andersen." *The Weekly Standard*, February 2, 2004, 35–37.

Bernheimer, Kate, ed. *Mirror, Mirror, on the Wall: Women Writers Explore Their Favorite Fairy Tales.* New York: Random House/Anchor, 1998.

Bettelheim, Bruno. *The Uses of Enchantment: The Meaning and Importance of Fairy Tales.* New York: Random House/Vintage, 1977.

Bloom, Claire. *Leaving a Doll's House.* Boston: Little, Brown, 1996.

Bloom, Harold. "Great Dane." *Wall Street Journal,* April 20, 2005.

————, ed. *Hans Christian Andersen.* New York: Chelsea House Publications, 2004.

————. " 'Trust the Tale, Not the Teller': Hans Christian Andersen." *Orbis Litterarum* 60 (2005): 397–413.

Bøggild, Jacob. "Framing the Frame of H. C. Andersen's *Auntie Toothache.*" *Fabula* 46 (2005): 29–42.

————. "Ruinous Reflections: On H. C. Andersen's Ambiguous Position between Romanticism and Modernism." In Sondrup, *H. C. Andersen: Old Problems and New Readings*, 75–96.

Böök, Fredrik. *Hans Christian Andersen: A Biography.* Trans. George C. Schoolfield. Norman: Univ. of Oklahoma Press, 1962.

Booth, Michael. *Just as Well I'm Leaving: To the Orient with Hans Christian Andersen.* London: Jonathan Cape, 2005.

Bottigheimer, Ruth B. *Grimms' Bad Girls & Bold Boys: The Moral & Social Vision of the Tales.* New Haven: Yale Univ. Press, 1987.

Bournonville, Charlotte Helene Frederikke. *Erindringer fra hjemmet og fra scenen.* Copenhagen: Gyldendal, 1903.

Brandes, Georg. "Hans Christian Andersen." In *Eminent Authors of the Nineteenth Century.* Trans. R. B. Anderson. New York: Crowell, 1886.

Brask, Peter. "Andersen's Love." In *The Nordic Mind: Current Trends in Scandinavian Literary Criticism*, ed. Frank Egholm et al., 17–35. Lanham, MD: Univ. Press of America, 1986.

Braude, L. Yu. "Hans Christian Andersen and Russia." *Scandinavica* 14 (1975): 1–15.

Bredsdorff, Elias. "Beginnings in Traditional Folk Tales and in H. C. Andersen's *Eventyr*." *Scandinavica* 21 (1982): 5–15.

———. "A Critical Guide to the Literature on Hans Christian Andersen." *Scandinavica* 6 (1967): 108–25.

———. *Hans Andersen and Charles Dickens: A Friendship and Its Dissolution*. Copenhagen: Rosenkilde and Bagger, 1956.

———. *Hans Christian Andersen: The Story of His Life and Work, 1805–75*. New York: Scribner, 1975.

———. "Intentional and Non-Intentional Topicalities in Andersen's Tales." In Mylius et al., *Hans Christian Andersen: A Poet in Time*, 11–37.

Bredsdorff, Thomas. *Deconstructing Hans Christian Andersen: Some of His Fairy Tales in the Light of Literary Theory and Vice Versa*. Minneapolis: Univ. of Minnesota Press, 1993.

Breslin, Cathy, Judy May Murphy, and Sharon Lechter. *Your Life Only a Gazillion Times Better: A Practical Guide to Creating the Life of Your Dreams*. Deerfield Beach, FL: Health Communications, 2005.

Brown, Charles Armitage. *Life of John Keats*. London: Oxford Univ. Press, 1937.

Brown, Ellen. "In Search of Nancy Drew, the Snow Queen, and Room Nineteen: Cruising for Feminine Discourse." *Frontiers: A Journal of Women Studies* 13 (1993): 1–25.

Brown, Rosellen. "It Is You the Fable Is About." In Bernheimer, *Mirror, Mirror on the Wall*, 47–59.

Brust, Beth Wagner. *The Amazing Paper Cuttings of Hans Christian Andersen*. New York: Houghton Mifflin, 2003.

Burnett, Constance Buel. *The Shoemaker's Son: The Life of Hans Christian Andersen*. London: George G. Harrap, 1943.

Byatt, A. S. "Ice, Snow, Glass." In Bernheimer, *Mirror, Mirror on the Wall*, 64–84.

Cashdan, Sheldon. *The Witch Must Die: How Fairy Tales Shape Our Lives*. New York: Basic Books, 1999.

Cech, John. "Hans Christian Andersen's Fairy Tales and Stories: Secrets, Swans and Shadows." In *Touchstones: Reflections on the Best in Children's Literature II*, ed. Perry Nodelman, 14–23. West Lafayette: Children's Literature Association, 1987.

Celenza, Anna H. Harwell. *Hans Christian Andersen and Music: The Nightingale Revealed*. Aldershot, England: Ashgate, 2005.

Chesterton, G. K. *The Crimes of England*. Whitefish, MT: Kessinger, 2004.

Collins, Emily. "Nabokov's *Lolita* and Andersen's *The Little Mermaid*." *Nabokov Studies* 9 (2005): 77–100.

Dahl, Svend, and H. G. Topsøe-Jensen, eds. *A Book on the Danish Writer Hans Christian Andersen: His Life and Work*. Copenhagen: Det Berlingske Bogtrykkeri, 1955.

Dahlerup, Pil. "Splash! Six Views of 'The Little Mermaid.' " *Scandinavian Studies* 62 (1990): 403–29.

Dal, Erik. "Hans Christian Andersen in Eighty Languages." In Dahl and Topsøe-Jensen, *A Book on the Danish Writer Hans Christian Andersen*, 132–206.

———. "Hans Christian Andersen's Tales and America." *Scandinavian Studies* 40 (1968): 1–25.

———. "Research on Hans Christian Andersen: Trends, Results, and Desiderata." *Orbis Litterarum* 17 (1962): 166–83.

Dante. *The Divine Comedy*. Trans. John Ciardi. New York: New American Library, 2003.

———. *The Inferno of Dante*. Trans. Robert Pinsky. New York: Farrar, Straus and Giroux, 1994.

Davis, Kathryn. *The Girl Who Trod on the Loaf*. Boston: Little, Brown, 1993.

Deleuze, Gilles. *Masochism: Coldness and Cruelty & Venus in Furs*. Trans. Jean McNeil. New York: Zone Books, 1989.

Detering, Heinrich. "The Phoenix Principle: Some Remarks on H. C. Andersen's Poetological Writings." In Mylius et al., *Hans Christian Andersen: A Poet in Time*, 50–65.

Dinnerstein, Dorothy. " 'The Little Mermaid' and the Situation of the Girl." *Contemporary Psychoanalysis* 3 (1967): 104–12.

———. *The Mermaid and the Minotaur: Sexual Arrangements and Human Malaise*. New York: Harper & Row, 1976.

Dollerup, Cay. "Translation as a Creative Force in Literature: The Birth of the European Bourgeois Fairy-Tale." *Modern Language Review* 90 (1995): 94–102.

Doty, Alexander. "The Queer Aesthete, the Diva, and *The Red Shoes*." *Out Takes: Essays on Queer Theory and Film*, ed. Ellis Hanson, 46–71. Durham: Duke Univ. Press, 1999.

Duffy, Maureen. The Erotic World of Faery. New York: Avon, 1972.

Dundes, Alan. "The Trident and the Fork: Disney's 'The Little Mermaid' as a Male Construction of an Electral Fantasy." In *Bloody Mary in the Mirror: Essays in Psychoanalytic Folkloristics*, 55–75. Jackson: Univ. Press of Mississippi, 2002.

Easterlin, Nancy. "Hans Christian Andersen's Fish out of Water." *Philosophy and Literature* 25 (2001): 251–77.

Eisenberg, Deborah. "In a Trance of Self." In Bernheimer, *Mirror, Mirror on the Wall*, 115–32.

Enquist, Per Olov. "The Hans Christian Andersen Saga." Trans. Joan Tate. *Scandinavian Review* 74 (1986): 64–69.

Esrock, Ellen J. " 'The Princess and the Pea': Touch and the Private/Public Domains of Women's Knowledge." *Knowledge and Society* 12 (2000): 17–29.

Estés, Clarissa Pinkola. *Women Who Run with the Wolves: Myths and Stories of the Wild Woman Archetype*. New York: Ballantine, 1992.

Fass, Barbara. "The Little Mermaid and the Artist's Quest for a Soul." *Comparative Literature Studies* 9 (1972): 291–302.

Fell, Christine E. "Symbolic and Satiric Aspects of Hans Andersen's Fairy-Tales." *Leeds Studies in English* 1 (1967): 83–91.

Flook, Maria. "The Rope Bridge to Sex." In Bernheimer, *Mirror, Mirror on the Wall*, 115–32.

Forster, John. *The Life of Charles Dickens.* Ed. A. J. Hoppé. London: Dent, 1969.

Frank, Diana Crone, and Jeffrey Frank. "Hans Christian Andersen's American Dream." *Scandinavian Review* 91 (3): 70–79.

Freud, Sigmund. *The Interpretation of Dreams.* New York: Random House/Modern Library, 1994.

Gambos, Anita L. "The Ugly Duckling, Hans Christian Andersen: A Story of Transformation." *Children's Folklore Newsletter* 26 (2003): 63–76.

Gilbert, Sandra M., and Susan Gubar. *The Madwoman in the Attic: The Woman Writer and the Nineteenth-Century Literary Imagination.* 2nd ed. New Haven: Yale Univ. Press, 2000.

Giroux, Henry A. "Are Disney Movies Good for Your Kids?" In *Kinderculture: The Corporate Construction of Childhood*, ed. Shirley R. Steinberg and Joe L. Kincheloe, 53–67. Boulder, CO: Westview, 1997.

Godden, Rumer. *Hans Christian Andersen: A Great Life in Brief.* New York: Knopf, 1955.

Goodman, Ailene S. "The Extraordinary Being: Death and the Mermaid in Baroque Literature." *Journal of Popular Culture* 17 (1983): 32–48.

Gopnik, Adam. "Magic Kingdoms: What Is a Fairy Tale Anyway?" *The New Yorker*, December 9, 2002, 136–40.

Gornick, Vivian. "Taking a Long Hard Look at 'The Princess and the Pea.'" In Bernheimer, *Mirror, Mirror on the Wall*, 148–57.

Grealy, Lucy. "Girl." In Bernheimer, *Mirror, Mirror on the Wall*, 158–73.

Greenacre, Phyllis. "Hans Christian Andersen and Children." *The Psychoanalytic Study of the Child* 38 (1983): 617–35.

Greenway, John L. "Reason in Imagination in Beauty: Oersted's Acoustics and H. C. Andersen's 'The Bell.'" *Scandinavian Studies* 63 (1991): 318–25.

Griffith, John. "Personal Fantasy in Andersen's Fairy Tales." *Kansas Quarterly* 16 (1984): 81–88.

Grønbech, Bo. *Hans Christian Andersen.* Boston: Twayne/G. K. Hall, 1980.

Guest, Ivor. *The Romantic Ballet in Paris.* Middletown, CT: Wesleyan Univ. Press, 1966.

Haugaard, Erik C. "Hans Christian Andersen: A Twentieth-Century View." *Scandinavian Review* 14 (1975): 1–15.

Hees, Annelies van. "The Little Mermaid." In Sondrup, H. C. Andersen: *Old Problems and New Readings*, 259–70.

———. "Stylistics and Poetics in Some Andersen Tales." In Mylius et al., *Hans Christian Andersen: A Poet in Time*, 67–86.

Heltoft, Kjeld. *Hans Christian Andersen as an Artist*. Trans. Reginald Spink. Copenhagen: Royal Danish Ministry of Foreign Affairs, Rosenkilde and Bagger, 1977.

Hesse, Karen. *The Young Hans Christian Andersen*. Illus. Erik Blegvad. New York: Scholastic, 2005.

Holbek, Bengt. "Hans Christian Andersen's Use of Folktales." In *A Companion to the Fairy Tale*, ed. Hilda Ellis Davidson and Anna Chaudhri, 149–58. Woodbridge, Suffolk, England: D. S. Brewer, 2003.

Holden, Stephen. "The Great, Big Worries of Such a Tiny Girl." *New York Times,* March 30, 1994.

Houe, Poul. "Andersen in Time and Place—Time and Place in Andersen." In Mylius et al., *Hans Christian Andersen: A Poet in Time*, 87–107.

———. "Going Places: Hans Christian Andersen, the Great European Traveler." In Rossel, *Hans Christian Andersen: Danish Writer and Citizen of the World*, 126–75.

———. "Hans Christian Andersen's Andersen and the Andersen of Others." *Orbis Litterarum* 61 (2006): 53–80.

Høyrup, Helene. "Childhood as the Sign of Change: Hans Christian Andersen's Retellings of the Concept of Childhood in the Light of Romanticism, Modernism, and Children's Own Cultures." In *Change and Renewal in Children's Literature*, ed. Thomas van der Walt, 89–100. Westport, CT: Praeger, 2004.

Hugus, Frank. "Hans Christian Andersen: The Storyteller as Social Critic." *Scandinavian Review* 87 (1999): 29–36.

Ingwersen, Niels. "Being Stuck: The Subversive Andersen and His Audience." In *Studies in German and Scandinavian Literature after 1500: A Festschrift for George C. Schoolfield*, ed. James A. Parente Jr. and Richard Erich Schade, 166–80. Columbia, SC: Camden House, 1993.

———. "How Enigmatic Is Hans Christian Andersen? On Three Recent Biographies." *Scandinavian Studies* 76 (2004): 535–48.

———. " 'I Have Come to Despise You': Andersen and His Relationship to His Audience." *Fabula* 46 (2005): 17–28.

Jensen, Inger Lise. "Why Are There So Many Interpretations of H. C. Andersen's 'The Shadow'?" In Sondrup, *H. C. Andersen: Old Problems and New Readings*, 281–94.

Johansen, Jørgen Dines. "The Merciless Tragedy of Desire: An Interpretation of H. C. Andersen's 'Den Lille Havfrue.' " *Scandinavian Studies* 68 (1996): 203–41.

———. "Counteracting the Fall: 'Sneedronningen' and 'Iisjomfruen.' The Problem of Adult Sexuality in Fairytale and Story." *Scandinavian Studies* 74 (2002): 37–48.

Johnson, Kristi Planck. "The Millennium: Vision Leads to Travel." In Sondrup, *H. C. Andersen: Old Problems and New Readings*, 271–80.

Jørgensen, Aage. "Heroes in Hans Christian Andersen's Writings." In Mylius et al., *Hans Christian Andersen: A Poet in Time*, 270–87.

————. "Hidden Sexuality and Suppressed Passion: A Theme in Danish Golden Age Literature." *Neohelicon* 19 (1992): 153–74.

————. " 'What Would the Children Say . . . ?' 'The Marsh King's Daughter' Revisited." In Sondrup, *H. C. Andersen: Old Problems and New Readings*, 235–58.

Kast, Verena. *Folktales as Therapy*. Trans. Douglas Whitcher. New York: Fromm International Publishing, 1995.

Kawan, Christine Shojaei. "*The Princess and the Pea*: Andersen, Grimm, and the Orient." *Fabula* 46 (2005): 89–105.

Kent, Leonard J., and Elizabeth C. Knight. *Tales of E.T.A. Hoffmann*. Chicago: Univ. of Chicago Press, 1969.

Kierkegaard, Søren. "Andersen as a Novelist: With Continual Reference to His Latest Work, *Only a Fiddler*." In *Early Polemical Writings*, ed. Julia Watkin. Princeton: Princeton Univ. Press, 1990.

Klass, Perri. "No Good Deed Goes Unpunished: Or, The Little Match Girl Syndrome." *New York Times Book Review*, December 2, 1990, 7–9.

Kleivan, Inge. "Arctic Elements in the Writings of Hans Christian Andersen." In Mylius et al., *Hans Christian Andersen: A Poet in Time*, 289–300.

Koelb, Clayton. "The Shady Character of Literature: H. C. Andersen's 'The Shadow.' " In *Inventions of Reading: Rhetoric and the Literary Imagination*. Ithaca: Cornell Univ. Press, 1988.

Kofoed, Niels. "Hans Christian Andersen and the European Literary Tradition." In Bloom, *Hans Christian Andersen*, 115–74.

Kramer, Nathaniel. "H. C. Andersen's 'Tante Tandpine' and the Crisis of Representation." In Sondrup, *H. C. Andersen: Old Problems and New Readings*, 7–32.

Kurlansky, Mark. *Cod: A Biography of the Fish That Changed the World*. New York: Penguin, 1997.

Kuznets, Lois Rostow. *When Toys Come Alive: Narratives of Animation, Metamorphosis, and Development*. New Haven: Yale Univ. Press, 1994.

Lederer, Wolfgang. *The Kiss of the Snow Queen: Hans Christian Andersen and Man's Redemption by Women*. Berkeley: Univ. of California Press, 1986.

Le Guin, Ursula K. "The Child and the Shadow." In *The Language of the Night: Essays on Fantasy and Science Fiction*, ed. Susan Wood, 49–60. Revised Edition. London: Women's Press, 1989.

Levy, Michael. "Visions of the Snow Queen." *New York Review of Science Fiction* 16 (2004): 15–18.

Lewis, C. S. "Sometimes Fairy Stories May Say Best What's to Be Said." In *Of Other Worlds: Essays and Stories*. New York: Harcourt, 1994.

Lewis, Naomi. "Introduction." In *Hans Christian Andersen's The Snow Queen*. Illus. Angela Barrett. New York: Henry Holt, 1988.

Lewis, Tess. "A Drop of Bitterness: Andersen's Fairy Tales." *Hudson Review* 54 (2002): 679–86.

Libbrecht, Kenneth. *The Snowflake: Winter's Secret Beauty.* St. Paul, MN: Voyageur, 2003.

Lüthi, Max. *The European Folktale: Form and Nature.* Bloomington: Indiana Univ. Press, 1986.

Mackie, Erin. "Red Shoes and Bloody Stumps." In *Footnotes: On Shoes,* ed. Shari Benstock and Suzanne Ferriss, 233–47. New Brunswick: Rutgers Univ. Press, 2001.

Malmkjær, Kirsten. "Translational Stylistics: Dulcken's Translations of Hans Christian Andersen." *Language and Literature* 13 (2004): 13–24.

Manning-Sanders, Ruth. *Swan of Denmark: The Story of Hans Christian Andersen.* London: Heinemann, 1949.

Mannoni, Maud. "Hans Christian Andersen: A Childhood, a Life." In *Separation and Creativity: Refinding the Lost Language of Childhood,* 143–56. New York: Other Press, 1999.

Massengale, James. "The Miracle and A Miracle in the Life of a Mermaid." In Mylius et al., *Hans Christian Andersen: A Poet in Time,* 555–76.

———. "Ut Poesis (Picturae) Musica." In Sondrup, *H. C. Andersen: Old Problems and New Readings,* 33–73.

Melchior-Bonnet, Sabine. *The Mirror: A History.* New York: Routledge, 2002.

Meltzer, Françoise. *Salome and the Dance of Writing: Portraits of Mimesis in Literature.* Chicago: Univ. of Chicago Press, 1989.

Meyer, Priscilla, and Jeff Hoffman. "Infinite Reflections in Nabokov's Pale Fire: The Danish Connection, Hans Andersen and Isak Dinesen." *Russian, Croatian and Serbian, Czech and Slovak, Polish Literature* 41 (1997): 197–22.

Meynell, Esther. *The Story of Hans Andersen.* New York: H. Schuman, 1950.

Miller, Alice. *For Your Own Good: Hidden Cruelty in Child-Rearing and the Roots of Violence.* New York: Farrar, Straus and Giroux, 1990.

Mishler, William. "H. C. Andersen's 'Tin Soldier' in a Freudian Perspective." *Scandinavian Studies* 50 (1978): 389–95.

Mitchell, David T., and Sharon L. Snyder. *Narrative Prosthesis: Disability and the Dependencies of Discourse.* Ann Arbor: Univ. of Michigan Press, 2001.

Morrison, Toni. *Playing in the Dark: Whiteness and the Literary Imagination.* Cambridge, MA: Harvard Univ. Press, 1992.

Mortensen, Finn Hauberg. "Little Ida's Red Shoes." *Scandinavian Studies* 77 (2005): 423–38.

Mortensen, Klaus P. "The Poetry of Chance." *Fabula* 46 (2005): 55–66.

Mudrick, Marvin. "The Ugly Duck." *Scandinavian Review* 68 (1980): 34–48.

Murphy, Patrick. " 'The Whole Wide World Was Scrubbed Clean': The Androcentric Animation of Denatured Disney." In Bell et al., *From Mouse to Mermaid,* 125–37.

Mylius, Johan de. *H. C. Andersens liv. Dag for Dag.* Copenhagen: Aschehoug, 1998.

————. "Hans Christian Andersen and the Music World." In Rossel, *Hans Christian Andersen: Danish Writer and Citizen of the World*, 176–208.

————. *Hans Christian Andersen and the World.* http://www.andersen.sdu.dk/forskning/konference/verden/titelblad_e.html.

————. "Hans Christian Andersen—on the Wave of Liberalism." In Mylius et al., *Hans Christian Andersen: A Poet in Time*, 109–24.

Mylius, Johan de, Aage Jørgensen, and Viggo Hjørnager Pedersen, eds. *Hans Christian Andersen: A Poet in Time.* Odense: Odense Univ. Press, 1999.

Nassaar, Christopher S. "Andersen's 'The Shadow' and Wilde's 'The Fisherman and His Soul': A Case of Influence." *Nineteenth-Century Literature* 50 (1995): 217–25.

Nielsen, Erling. *Hans Christian Andersen.* Trans. Reginald Spink. Copenhagen: Press and Information Department of the Royal Danish Ministry of Foreign Affairs, 1963.

Nikolajeva, Maria, and Carole Scott. *How Picturebooks Work.* New York, Garland, 2001.

Nissenbaum, Stephen. *The Battle for Christmas: A Cultural History of America's Most Cherished Holiday.* New York: Random House/Vintage, 1996.

Nunnally, Tiina. "Removing the Grime from Scandinavian Classics." *World Literature Today* 80 (2006): 38–42.

Nybo, Gregory. "A Synopsis." *Scandinavian Studies* 62 (1990): 416–18.

Oates, Joyce Carol. *The Faith of a Writer: Life, Craft, Art.* New York: Harper Perennial, 2004.

————. "In Olden Times, When Wishing Was Having: Classic and Contemporary Fairy Tales." In Bernheimer, *Mirror, Mirror on the Wall*, 260–83.

Opie, Iona, and Peter Opie. "Tommelisa." In *The Classic Fairy Tales.* New York: Oxford Univ. Press, 1974.

Orwell, George. "Inside the Whale." In *Inside the Whale and Other Essays.* London: Victor Gollancz, 1940.

Oxfeldt, Elisabeth. *Nordic Orientalism: Paris and the Cosmopolitan Imagination, 1800–1900.* Copenhagen: Tusculanum Press, 2005.

Pedersen, Viggo Hjørnager. "Hans Andersen as an English Writer." In *Proceedings from the Second Nordic Conference for English Studies*, ed.Håken Ringbom, Matti Rissanen, and Graham Caie. Åbo: Åbo Akademi, 1984.

————. "A Mermaid Translated: An Analysis of Some English Versions of Hans Christian Andersen's 'Den lille Havfrue.' " *Dolphin* 18 (1990): 7–20.

————. *Ugly Ducklings? Studies in the English Translations of Hans Christian Andersen's Tales and Stories.* Odense: Univ. Press of Southern Denmark, 2004.

Pickard, P. M. *I Could a Tale Unfold: Violence, Horror & Sensationalism in Stories for Children.* London: Tavistock, 1961.

Pinker, Steven. *How the Mind Works.* New York: W. W. Norton, 1997.

Pinkney, Jerry. Introduction to Hans Christian Andersen, *The Ugly Duckling.* New York: Harper Collins, 1999.

Porsdam, Helle. *Copyright and Other Fairy Tales: Hans Christian Andersen and the Commodification of Creativity*. Cheltenham, England: Edward Elgar, 2006.

Powell, Michael, and Emeric Pressburger. *The Red Shoes*. New York: St. Martin's Press, 1978.

Prince, Alison. *Hans Christian Andersen: The Fan Dancer*. London: Allison & Busby, 1998.

———. "War." In Bloom, *Hans Christian Andersen*, 93–113.

Rasmussen, Inge Lise. "H. C. Andersen: Reminiscences as Image and Echo." In Sondrup, *H. C. Andersen: Old Problems and New Readings*, 199–214.

Reynolds, Kimberley. "Fatal Fantasies: The Death of Children in Victorian and Edwardian Fantasy Writing." In *Representations of Childhood Death*, ed. Gillian Avery and Kimberley Reynolds, 169–88. London: Macmillian, 2000.

Robbins, Hollis. "The Emperor's New Critique." *New Literary History* 34 (2004): 659–75.

Rodes, Sara P. "The Wild Swans." In *Anderseniana* II, 352–67. Copenhagen: Ejnar Munksgaard, 1954.

Rollins, Hyder Edward, ed. *The Keats Circle: Letters and Papers, and More Letters and Poems of the Keats Circle*. 2 vols. 2nd ed. Cambridge, MA: Harvard Univ. Press, 1965.

Rosen, Ruth. "A Physics Prof Drops a Bomb on the Faux Left." *Los Angeles Times*, May 23, 1996.

Rossel, Sven Hakon, ed. *Hans Christian Andersen: Danish Writer and Citizen of the World*. Amsterdam: Rodopi, 1996.

———. "Hans Christian Andersen: The Great European Writer." In *Hans Christian Andersen: Danish Writer and Citizen of the World*, 1–125.

———. "Hans Christian Andersen: Writer for All Ages and Nations." *Scandinavian Review* 74 (1986): 88–97.

Rowland, Herbert. "The Image of H. C. Andersen in American Magazines during the Author's Lifetime." In Sondrup, *H. C. Andersen: Old Problems and New Readings*, 175–98.

———. *More Than Meets the Eye: Hans Christian Andersen and Nineteenth-Century American Criticism*. Madison, NJ: Fairleigh Dickinson Univ. Press, 2006.

Sale, Roger. *Fairy Tales and After: From Snow White to E. B. White*. Cambridge MA: Harvard Univ. Press, 1978.

Sanders, Karin. "Nemesis of Mimesis: The Problem of Representation in H. C. Andersen's *Psychen*." *Scandinavian Studies* 64 (1992): 1–25.

Scarry, Elaine. *The Body in Pain: The Making and Unmaking of the World*. New York: Oxford Univ. Press, 1987.

———. *On Beauty and Being Just*. Princeton: Princeton Univ. Press, 1999.

Schwarcz, Joseph H. "Machine Animism in Modern Children's Literature." *Library Quarterly* 37 (1967): 78–95.

Sells, Laura. " 'Where Do the Mermaids Stand?': Voice and Body in *The Little Mermaid*." In Bell et al., *From Mouse to Mermaid*, 175–92.

Sexton, Anne. *The Complete Poems.* Ed. Maxine Kumin. New York: Mariner Books, 1999.

Sjoholm, Barbara. *Pirate Queen: In Search of Grace O'Malley and Other Legendary Women of the Sea.* Emeryville, CA: Seal Press, 2004.

Sondrup, Steven P., ed. *H. C. Andersen: Old Problems and New Readings.* Odense: Univ. of Southern Denmark Press, 2004.

Spink, Reginald. *Hans Christian Andersen and His World.* London: Thames & Hudson, 1972.

———. *Hans Christian Andersen: The Man and His Work.* 3rd ed. Copenhagen: Høst, 1981.

Spufford, Francis. *I May Be Some Time: Ice and the English Imagination.* New York: Palgrave Macmillan/St. Martin's, 1997.

Stecher-Hansen, Marianne. "H. C. Andersen's 'Historien om en Moder': Allegory and Symbol in the Danish Golden Age." In Sondrup, *H. C. Andersen: Old Problems and New Readings,* 97–116.

Stirling, Monica. *The Wild Swan: The Life and Times of Hans Christian Andersen.* London: Collins, 1965.

Sugarman, Sally. "Whose Woods Are These Anyhow? Children, Fairy Tales and the Media." In *The Antic Art: Enhancing Children's Literary Experiences through Film and Video,* ed. Lucy Rollin, 141–50. New York: Highsmith, 1994.

Sullivan, C. W. "Mother, Daughter, Self: Joan Vinge's *The Snow Queen.*" In *Mother Puzzles: Daughters and Mothers in Contemporary American Literature,* ed. Mickey Pearlman, 101–8. Westport, CT: Greenwood, 1989.

Tatar, Maria, ed. *The Annotated Brothers Grimm.* New York: W. W. Norton, 2004.

Taylor, Archer. "The Emperor's New Clothes." *Modern Philology* 25 (1927/28): 17–27.

Todorov, Tzvetan. *The Fantastic: A Structural Approach to a Literary Genre.* Trans. Richard Howard. Ithaca: Cornell Univ. Press, 1975.

Toksvig, Signe. *The Life of Hans Christian Andersen.* London: Macmillan, 1934.

Travers, P. L. "The Primary World." *Parabola* 4 (1979): 87–94.

Trites, Roberta. "Disney's Sub/version of 'The Little Mermaid.'" *Journal of Popular Television and Film* 18 (1991): 145–59.

Turner, Victor. *The Ritual Process: Structure and Anti-Structure.* New York: de Gruyter, 1969.

Vaget, Hans Rudolf. "The Steadfast Tin Soldier: Thomas Mann in World Wars I and II." In *1914/1939: German Reflections of the Two World Wars,* ed. Reinhold Grimm and Jost Hermand, 3–21. Madison: Univ. of Wisconsin Press, 1992.

Varmer, Hjørdis. *Hans Christian Andersen: His Fairy Tale Life.* Trans. Tiina Nunnally. Illus. Lilian Brøgger. Toronto: Groundwood, 2005.

Villermé, Louis. *Tableau de l'état physique et moral des ouvriers.* Paris, 1840.

Wangerin, Walter, Jr. "Hans Christian Andersen: Shaping the Child's Universe." *In Reality and the Vision,* ed. Philip Yancey, 1–15. Dallas: Word, 1990.

Warner, Marina. *From the Beast to the Blonde: On Fairy Tales and Their Tellers.* London: Chatto & Windus, 1994.

Webb, Jean. "A Postmodern Reflection on the Genre of the Fairy Tale: *The Stinky Cheese Man and Other Fairly Stupid Tales.*" In *Introducing Children's Literature: From Romanticism to Postmodernism*, by Deborah Cogan Thacker and Jean Webb, 156–63. New York: Routledge, 2002.

White, Susan. "Split Skins: Female Agency and Bodily Mutilation in *The Little Mermaid.*" In *Film Theory Goes to the Movies*, ed. Jim Collins, Hilary Radner, and Ava Preacher Collins, 182–95. New York: Routledge, 1993.

Winther, Matthias. *Danish Folk Tales.* Trans. T. Sands and J. Massengale. Madison, WI: Wisconsin Introductions to Scandinavia, 1991.

Wood, Naomi. "(Em)bracing Icy Mothers: Ideology, Identity, and Environment in Children's Fantasy." In *Wild Things: Children's Culture and Ecocriticism*, ed. Sidney I. Dobrin and Kenneth B. Kidd, 198–214. Detroit: Wayne State Univ. Press, 2004.

Woods, Irene E. "Charles Dickens, Hans Christian Andersen, and 'The Shadow.' " *Dickens Quarterly* 2 (1985): 124–29.

Wullschlager, Jackie. *Hans Christian Andersen: The Life of a Storyteller.* New York: Knopf, 2000.

Yolen, Jane. *The Perfect Wizard: Hans Christian Andersen.* Illus. Dennis Nolan. New York: Dutton, 2004.

Ziolkowski, Jan M. "A Medieval 'Little Claus and Big Claus': A Fabliau from before Fabliaux?" In *The World and Its Rival: Essays on Literary Imagination in Honor of Per Nykrog*, ed. Kathryn Karczewska and Tom Conley, 1–37. Amsterdam: Rodopi, 1999.

Ziolkowski, Theodore. *Disenchanted Images: A Literary Iconology.* Princeton: Princeton Univ. Press, 1977.

———. "The Telltale Teeth: Psychodontia to Sociodontia." *PMLA* 91 (1976): 9–22.

Zipes, Jack. *Fairy Tales and the Art of Subversion: The Classical Genre for Children and the Process of Civilization.* New York: Wildman, 1983.

———. *Hans Christian Andersen: The Misunderstood Storyteller.* New York and London: Routledge, 2005.

———. *When Dreams Come True: Classical Fairy Tales and Their Tradition.* New York: Routledge, 1999.

Zuk, Rhoda. "*The Little Mermaid*: Three Political Fables." *Children's Literature Association Quarterly* 22 (1997–98): 166–74.

The Hans Christian Andersen Center at the University of Southern Denmark offers extraordinarily rich resources on its Web site: http://www.andersen.sdu.dk/index_e.html. Included on the Web site are texts (in Danish and English), biographical information about Andersen, bibliographies, Web links, images, and other resources.

ABOUT THE EDITOR
AND TRANSLATORS

Maria Tatar is the author of *The Annotated Classic Fairy Tales*, *The Annotated Brothers Grimm*, and *Secrets beyond the Door: The Story of Bluebeard and His Seven Wives*. She is the John L. Loeb Professor of Germanic Languages and Literatures and served as Dean for the Humanities at Harvard University, where she teaches courses on folklore, German culture, and children's literature.

Julie K. Allen is an assistant professor of Scandinavian Studies at the University of Wisconsin at Madison. She holds a Ph.D. in Germanic Languages and Literatures from Harvard University and has spent several years living and working in Denmark. She enjoys telling Andersen's tales to her three children.